TROUBADOR

By Don Fenn

An epic, utopian, otherworldly quest-adventure.

First Edition

TROUBADOUR
PUBLISHED BY SYNERGY BOOKS
2100 Kramer Lane, Suite 300
Austin, Texas 78758

For more information about our books, please write to us, call 512.478.2028, or visit our website as www.bookpros.com.

ISBN: 0-9755922-6-2
ISBN: 978-0-9755922-6-7

Publisher's Cataloging-in-Publication
(Provided by Quality Books, Inc.)

Fenn, Don.
Troubadour : the second coming / by Don Fenn. — 1st ed.
p. cm.
"An epic, utopian, otherworldly quest-adventure."
LCCN 2005922499
ISBN-13: 978-0-9755922-6-7
ISBN-10: 0-9755922-6-2

1. Manned space flight—Fiction. 2. Science fiction.
3. Adventure stories. I. Title.

PS3606.E554T76 2005 813'.6
QBI05-800227

10 9 8 7 6 5 4 3 2 1

This book is dedicated to my dear wife, Ellen, whose twenty readings of every single chapter brought the reflective, loving companionship essential for me to reach the fulfillment of my story.

And to all those who manage sometimes to think and feel outside of familiarity, who painfully learn to perceive all aspects of this world disruptively, who are able to reach beyond its many perspectives, function outside of its vast assumptions, in order to look back at it with greater love and understanding.

Ode to Life

"When change created a knowing mind
She gave it a heart to make it kind
Warming it with fantasy to give it life
For growth she put it in the middle of strife

To be the wife who marries fear with laughter
Embracing the unbearable with humor's how
Yearning to know the distant hereafter
Yet hungrily leaping into the here-and-now

Fluctuating between forever and what's-holding-me-back
Illuminate every second with its powerful thwack
Hanging on the brink between desire and far-ahead
Where life is most thrillingly bedded and read

Making moments when I'm most precious to me
Fulfill the promise of my natural be
Investing me with courage to be what I must
Meeting what happens with an open trust"

(Troubadourian Hymn to Life)

Contents

Union Station

Peter was only four. But already he knew a lot, and had a mind of his own.

Well, sort of. Fairly often his mind reached its limits and faded out. But he always got it back very soon, and was off in a new, exciting direction.

Of course fairly frequent blackouts of sense did confuse and frighten him. He didn't know this was normal, but in spite of not knowing he bounced back so well, and things were basically so good in his world, that he avoided paying much attention to this fear.

He was on his way to his favorite place, the train station. Trains, forever now his best thing, gave him the happiest experience of his entire life, which was to lie in his mother's lap for three whole days almost without interruption. Sometimes he looked up into her pretty, smiling face warmly greeting him with love, basking in the powerful security of that care. And sometimes he just stared out the window at the blurry objects that raced by the train, and daydreamed about having the power to make this go on forever.

When his mother had carried him off his beautiful train several days before, he had not noticed the station because he was so sleepy. So he was anxious now to see what it looked like for the first time. He just knew they were going on another long journey so he could do it all over again. Maybe they were even going to live on the train and travel all over the world.

Of course his mother denied all of this, but he was sure she just wanted to surprise him.

When he finally viewed the vast space of the train station fully awake and in daylight, he was utterly amazed. It was so enormous he couldn't even see the hazy top of it. Somehow the station had captured the sky and clouds! Trains, and the houses in which they lived, really were the most magical things to be found!

Though he normally had trouble waiting, he didn't even mind when his mother said they had to wait awhile before anything good happened. He'd waited the four years of his life before his first ride, so he didn't have any trouble waiting a few minutes for the second one.

There was one problem though, which he tried mostly to ignore, but he couldn't get entirely away from. Something about his mother was very different. She was acting in a way that he'd never seen before.

She wasn't angry, an experience with which he was very familiar, not because he was the least bit afraid of her anger, but because he could tease her out of any rage with a simple, "I love you" applied to her heart with his small hand placed right between her large, beautiful breasts. She loved to be loved, and he knew how. It was the one way he was smarter than his older brother, who didn't know how to love at all.

A grown-up Peter would have realized that his mother was afraid. Peter had never seen his mother really afraid of anything, or if he had he didn't remember it. So he was confused, unsettled underneath his buoyant enthusiasm for life and this particular day.

There was one thing he did know instinctively, which was to stay out of her way, not to demand anything. He sensed she couldn't handle one more thing.

She kept pacing back and forth between two pillars talking to herself under her breath, completely oblivious to anything else. Watching her, Peter began to feel strangely unfamiliar to himself.

As usual his older brother Pendergast had wandered as far away as he could get from his mother and Peter, and what he regarded to be their stupid love affair with each other. Pendergast couldn't love, but he had something that might be even more powerful. He could command.

He was called "Pentup" by his friends because he was usually very cool-headed no matter what was happening. But then very occasionally he'd explode. Since he was the neighborhood leader that meant his anger defined the law, at least until he changed it. Nobody ever argued with Pendergast because it was pretty clear he was more independent of grown-ups than the other kids. So he was King.

Naturally Peter admired him very much. The King was his brother.

But the King was contemptuous of Peter and largely ignored him.

Today Pendergast was searching for something to distract him from his mother and brother's usual cavorting lovingly together, which he thought was about the dumbest thing anybody could do. He was denying that he felt anything when Peter usurped his mother; his solution was to throw mothering to the four winds. He didn't need it anymore.

As soon as they arrived in the train station, Pendergast set out on a private expedition. Hugging the tall walls of the enormous waiting room, he checked out everything he could get his eyes upon that really mattered, like two teenagers leaning up against the wall kissing, or an old woman trying to change her pantyhose behind a huge pillar because the line was too long in the lady's bathroom, or a disheveled man dressed in tattered clothes hiding behind another column at the corner of the hall frantically jacking off.

The old man closed his eyes when he realized that Pendergast was just a boy, of no consequence, and resumed his thrusts.

Pendergast usually fascinated Peter. But today he was so excited about another train ride, and so nervous about his mother's fearfulness that he failed to notice what normally he'd have watched with enormous curiosity. In this instance is was the amazed look upon his brother's face as he stared open-mouthed at the masturbating man, discovering what it was all about for the first time. On any other day, Peter would have wanted to carefully examine what his brother was looking at.

But today he was trying hard not to notice the worry on his mother's face, so he ended up not noticing some other important things.

The problem was that he was trying to keep track of everyone else. He kept glancing back and forth between his brother and mother, never settling upon one or the other long enough to focus very clearly.

The next time he glanced to where his brother had been, a stranger was there right in the middle of his sight, walking very fast in Peter's direction, looking straight at him!

Peter jerked his eyes away from the dark-set, determined stare of this stranger. He hated strangers even more than most kids did. One had visited his mother once or twice and it scared him to remember those times when this alien was in his house for a few days. Something happened to his mother when this stranger was around that felt creepier than anything he'd ever experienced.

Peter felt compelled to look at the stranger again. A tiny piece of familiarity had irresistibly pulled him back, though he tried hard to deny it.

He suddenly realized the man walking toward him was the same stranger that had visited his mother! Creepiness engulfed Peter, making him feel very sick to his stomach!

In a vigorous rebuke of reality, he turned away from his own feeling by refusing to see this menacing man, as if by ignoring him, he and the bad feeling would go away.

To his enormous relief his eyes instantly found his mother.

But suddenly he realized something was wrong! Something had drastically changed! She had stopped pacing! At first it looked like she was looking straight at him, Peter. But then he realized she was actually looking beyond him! He knew instantly that meant the object of her worry had just appeared!

Peter raced over to see where his mother's eyes were pointing, and followed their path right into the face of the stranger, now almost upon them!

A flush of terror almost shook him apart! His mother was looking directly at this same alien man who had already tried to get inside of Peter by staring at him! And here he was already inside Peter's mother!

Peter panicked! He had never before experienced being on the backside of his mother's attention!

He suddenly felt overwhelmed! He tore himself away from the dread to which this specter riveted his heart, and swung around desperately to find his brother. Pendergast was his last resort as an escape from this terrible nightmare!

By some miracle his eyes instantly caught sight of his brother. The only problem was that Pendergast was acting very strangely. The masturbating old man's indifference in closing his eyes had lured Pendergast's curiosity into a false sense of security, inducing him to take two steps closer to the man for a better view.

What Peter saw when his eyes caught hold of his brother was Pendergast furiously falling backward trying to keep his feet under him, as he frantically back-peddled, just barely escaping the old, now very ugly man with an evil expression, who still had his pants down! He was trying desperately to hit Pendergast!

Peter suddenly remembered what his brother always told him when they were alone, that the world was just one big fuck-you place.

Peter panicked! Pendergast was in as much trouble as he was! He had no choice but to look back for his mother. She and his brother were the only two people in his life.

But what he saw undid him. His mother was embracing this strange man!

Peter tilted inside. Everything scrambled. He wanted desperately to go to sleep!

But then it got worse! The alien thing turned toward him and reached out!

Mom!

The room suddenly became the whole world, and his mother the only important part of it! He became deaf to anything but the horror that his heart was pumping!

Artfully dodging the stranger's hands, he raced over to his mother and dove at her large thigh, literally jumping onto it with a vengeance, grabbing what belonged to him!

She stumbled when Peter impacted her leg! Which is precisely what Peter had desperately hoped would happen, because it put distance between her and this strange man!

"Mama," Peter said in a sweet manner. "Can we go now?"

"There is someone here you must remember," she said with pain in her voice and a false smile on her face.

Strange hands suddenly lifted a squirming boy off his feet. Everything started spinning, continuity became scrambled, and consciousness was lost. Peter fainted.

When he came back to life he was banished to a completely strange land very far from home, populated entirely by strangers.

Slap!

Suddenly awakened, something terrifying started to happen! His stomach was left on the bed, while the rest of him rose up like he was flying! Jerked toward the bathroom he knew he wasn't flying, because he couldn't turn that fast even in his flying dreams.

Yanked, thrown about suspended by one arm, a flurry of dangerous sounds reverberated off the walls of his small world, deafeningly echoing danger and death!

Smack! Hard, cold, not-bed ceramic slapped his body with shame! It left a blushing stain that stayed there for decades.

He'd urinated again in his bed, and the monster was punishing him.

Involuntarily cooperating with whatever the gods ordained, Peter's body was learning how to carry emotional pain so it couldn't be seen, making terror only a stomachache, or a pulsating dreadnaught-in-his-ears only a headache. His flesh was the only part of him capable of holding the terrible turmoil of emotional violence that had become his daily diet—but only by this spending of extra life-credits, robbing heartbeats of survival from the length and breadth of his existence.

And it kept happening, year after year after year.

Psychotherapy—Intimacy Formalized

Fifty-eight years, fourteen days, and eight hours later, Peter sat in his professional office with a patient. The waning light of early evening filtered through the partly closed louvers of the window shade, illuminating only the brightest hues of the oriental carpet, the only object in the dimly lit room that both men were touching.

They sat facing each other inside a triangle of chair-couch-chair that encircled the carpet and their togetherness, the younger man on the left end of the couch and the older man in the green leather chair opposite him.

The couch was made of a dark-green, velvety fabric that deeply cushioned but firmly supporting the six-foot-two, thirty-two-year-old frame of the younger man. He had a strong, athletic body that sported a round, friendly, jovial face that invited others to like him, though he often feared that face revealed to everyone how inadequate he really was.

Behind and to the left of the younger man the walls were filled with a colorful display of wall hangings and paintings. Sitting on the four tables that book-ended the chairs and the couch were sculptures, all collected and put there by the older man to evoke in the room's occupants their most archetypal dreams, impressions, and fantasies.

Two of the sculptures had been carved by an east African tribe whose religious rituals for over eight hundred years had required the use of psychedelics, evoking in the artist who carved it her most primitive visions. In one a man stood upright on the back of a deadly predatory animal, the beast's head turned unnaturally upward so that man and beast peered deeply and intensely into each other's eyes, two predators measuring the other for life or death.

In the other sculpture a man and his twelve-year-old boy stood together holding each other upright with only two arms and two legs between them, making their togetherness a Siamese twin-ship, leaving neither of them the opportunity of separateness, revealing and reproducing this most ancient symbiotic form of human love.

All of the decorative objects in the room were intended to evoke for Peter and his patient a dramatic sense of history taking place in the present tense, which connected them to the realm of mythological origins.

But the myth which they were living and studying, was not a cultural myth shared by everyone. It was the myth of this particular person, created by the specific dramatic context that had formed and now characterized the peculiar life of this particular human.

The younger man began crying quietly, covering his eyes with hands that wiped the tears before they could run down his face.

"Something painfully grieves you this evening," the older man observed quietly after awhile.

Oliver's tears flowed more freely.

"I wish I'd never gone there," he moaned. "It was so depressing to be around him for five days."

That remark hung suspended in a silence that gave it the recognition of a full hearing.

I wonder what happened at his father's that has upset him so much? Peter asked himself.

"Can't you help me?" Oliver asked with a demanding urgency of which he was unaware. "I mean I can't stop visiting my father," he complained.

"Would part of you like to do that?" Peter asked.

"How can I do that?" Oliver protested, implying Peter was toying with him. "He's my father!"

Though it might have been better to respond to another part of Oliver's communication, Peter responded to his anger. He sometimes had trouble with his patient's anger. He chose it as a focus partly to manage his own discomfort.

"Am I sometimes as disappointing and frustrating to you as your father is?" Peter asked the younger man.

Silence.

"Well, you asked for it," Oliver warned. "I'm having one of those critical thoughts about you."

Silence.

Apparently he'll tell me the critical thought only if I ask for it. But I think I won't.

Oliver had confessed a few weeks before that he sometimes had bad thoughts about psychotherapy, and about Peter's interpretations. These thoughts viewed psychotherapy as just a lot of made-up theories pretending to make things better just by talking about them, just so much psychobabble.

"Don't you get it?" Oliver insisted with frustration, as if Peter should already have said something. "I don't like having them! They just make me feel worse about coming to talk to you!"

Another silence followed.

"Damn it, I wish you would say something," Oliver insisted.

Silence.

"Because it's true!" Oliver exclaimed. "I'm really not any better! Actually I'm a lot worse! I've never felt so depressed in my whole damned life!"

Peter felt and expressed sympathy in his facial and body postures, but said nothing.

"Aren't you just the least bit concerned?" Oliver complained.

This was just the opportunity for which Peter was waiting, where he could use Oliver's own words to tell him something new.

"I think you're very concerned about something yourself," Peter replied.

"About what?" Oliver challenged.

"About hurting me with your critical thoughts," Peter said.

"You're just making that up," Oliver protested, denying his fear. "I don't think I'm feeling that."

"We all sometimes have the impression," Peter gently insisted, "that when feelings get to be huge and overpowering they will explode and hurt others."

"Well, it's true, isn't it?" Oliver insisted. "By feeling all this I am getting worse!"

"When powerful and frightening feelings surge through you, it doesn't mean that you're getting worse," Peter replied. "It means that you're feeling things that are moving you, and remembering things that have hurt and frightened you."

"Who wants to remember such terrible things?" Oliver asked. "What's the point of it?"

"So you can change them."

Though obviously moved by this statement, Oliver said nothing for several moments.

"It's happening again," he warned.

"You're having another negative thought about me," Peter suggested.

"Yes."

Peter waited this time for Oliver to explain.

"The thought says it doesn't really help for you to tell me why my feelings are so strong, because they're still there!" Oliver spit out.

"What do those feelings say about me?" Peter asked.

"Well," he began, very reluctant to answer. "Since you insist, they say that you're just making things up to try and convince me to feel better."

"Perhaps you feel that I'm just trying to get rid of you with a worthless piece of advice," Peter added.

The effect of this interpretation upon Oliver was electric! His whole body stiffened.

"I really should be grateful to him," Oliver insisted. "They let us do anything we wanted. There were almost no restrictions. I got home when I wanted, studied when I wanted, and went to bed when I felt like it."

Oliver had previously confided that his father's permissiveness had felt like neglect. Though a very kind and gentle man, this parent maintained a great deal of emotional distance from everyone. He spent almost no time at all with Oliver, though he was almost always present in the home. And when he was with his son, or any other person for that matter, he secretly felt extremely awkward and protective of himself, which he managed by saying almost nothing emotionally personal. He disguised this aloofness with a dry humor that seemed to declare a kind of closeness, but whose content projected a gloomy message of caution against expecting too much out of life, encouraging careful watching for danger signs that warned of disappointment. All of which made Oliver's connection to his father vague, tenuous, ominous, and deeply disappointing, though Oliver had never admitted this to himself.

"It sounds like your family turned parental authority over to children, as if having power and authority was an evil thing, thus depriving you of any structure to bounce off of, or by which to measure yourself, and against which you could make your own choices."

"So now you're suggesting I blame my parents for what's wrong with me?" Oliver quipped defensively.

"Do you blame them?"

"They weren't that bad," Oliver protested.

They sat in silence for several moments as Oliver struggled with his conscience.

"Do you believe perhaps, Oliver, that in order to protect your connection to someone important whom you love, that you must be just like them and feel the same things they do?"

Oliver's face suddenly became ashen! Tiny sweat beads appeared on his forehead. He spoke now with great urgency and anxiety.

"But now that mother's dead he doesn't really have hardly anyone!" he pleaded. "He denies that anything is wrong. It's only when he gets so nervous that he starts to shake, and can't teach his classes, that he consults a doctor. So what's the solution? Drugs! He refused to talk about it with anyone!"

He paused.

"He's all alone," Oliver pleaded. "My brother hardly ever sees him! Dad denies it, but he's really a very lonely man!"

"I think you're afraid that if you stop being depressed that you'll have absolutely nothing in common with your father," Peter suggested.

Oliver gasped with recognition!

"Then what would we have to talk about?" Oliver cried with fearfulness. "How could we stay in touch?"

"So if you become undepressed," Peter suggested, "which is your greatest desire, the reason why you came here, then you fear that in doing so you would permanently sever your connection to your father, thoughtlessly abandoning him to his depression."

Oliver gasped and sat up on the edge of the couch!

"My god, that's it!" Oliver shouted with excitement. "That's why I hate being around him so much! I'm trapped. I can't escape! Both he and my brother are always so goddamned depressed! What else is there to talk about but what's wrong with the world?"

Oliver cocked his head downward and to the right, and turned inward for several moments.

"I was just thinking about having dinner with my parents when mother was alive, how superficially everything was treated. Anything controversial, like a difference of opinion, was instantly covered over by my parents spouting liberal ideology, as if our family was supposed to be a place where no one ever got angry with each other because we never did anything wrong and never disagreed."

Oliver became silent and drifted.

"I'm having one of those critical thoughts again," he finally said. "Only it's not attacking you this time. It's attacking me, telling me I'm spouting a lot of nasty lies about my parents that aren't true, that I'm trying to blame them for my own shortcomings."

Oliver was obeying two gods, the one of healing, and the one that had tethered him to others needs most of his life. To keep his balance he just jumped backward into his old perspective, where it was his fault that he was so disappointed and upset. In doing so he was testing the survivability of the reprieve that had just uplifted him, needing to be sure that these new insights were completely true, and could overcome assault by his old beliefs.

"They were really great parents," he insisted. "I mean they were good people. Mom really loved me. And I loved . . ."

He started tearing.

"Someone can be both wonderful and hurtful at the same time," Peter suggested. "Including your father. You seem to be afraid your thoughts are going to cut him to pieces, making you stop loving him, destroying the connection between you."

An enormous look of relief came over Oliver's face.

"It's always been that way," Oliver explained. "Everybody pretends to be so happy. And nobody ever talks about it. To do so would be so disloyal."

The time was up.

"The time's up for now," Peter said gently.

Oliver sat up, put his shoes back on, and they both stood. It was time for their hug.

A few weeks earlier Peter had felt strongly that Oliver needed a closer, more affectionate connection to an older man. When he had suggested to Oliver that he sensed the younger man wanted to touch, perhaps even to embrace, Oliver had leaped at the opportunity. Since then they had hugged at the session's end whenever Oliver felt like it, which was most of the time.

Tonight Oliver squeezed Peter harder than usual, clearly expressing his gratitude for the emancipation from false-belief that had just taken place.

"Thanks," Oliver said in great earnest.

"You're very welcome."

E-mail Bullshit

Checking his e-mail later than night, Peter discovered a curious message among the usual advertisements:

> *Please regard this e-mail as a messenger of good things to come. Very soon you will receive an invitation of great importance. It is hoped that its message will feel sufficiently different than the usual falsehoods with which many advertise themselves on Earth, for we have a special interest in you and wish to make a proposal. This message has been sent to give you an opportunity to anticipate your surprise.*
>
> *Sincerely . . .*
> *A friendly other*

Somebody's very clever, Peter thought. That message projects genuineness. But I don't believe it. There's a touch of seduction about it.

Peter didn't like surprises. It's why he always prepared everything so carefully. He was afraid of sabotage.

Just some more goddamned e-mail bullshit!

Somewhere else in the universe, others were being careful to prepare their target person to expect what would eventually arrive. They were convinced Earth people hated surprises.

The Therapist

Following the Oliver session Peter sat for a while in his therapist-chair savoring the best moments of the experience. Making significant contributions to Oliver's learning was very gratifying. Peter's own powerful need for understanding had been transformed into a capacity for helping others to understand themselves. He felt deeply connected to someone that he helped. It was the only sure way to be close to both of his parents, who blasted their emotional turmoil all over the walls of his experience. He could not pass through it without helping those he loved, either professionally or personally. Peter had made vicarious gratification a profession.

He finally realized that he hadn't moved his body. He slowly walked into the bathroom and sat down on the toilet seat to urinate.

That beautiful guy is really getting somewhere, Peter thought about Oliver. I wish my life was becoming half as new and exciting.

He suddenly felt the deep yet familiar sadness with which he was always accompanied. It never left him alone. It made experience seem like he was constantly walking through sticky-stuff, which made every move consume twice the normal energy, and end up accomplishing very little. This sadness produced a deep grief that had covered over its reasons for being, shrouding anything that happened in his life with the hidden agendas of lost, unavailable memories. Life became a series of hesitant, halting missteps that never fully explained themselves.

What made it even worse was that as he got older, this grief experience got bigger and bigger. Sometimes it frightened him. He was afraid he might not be able to put up with it indefinitely, though that indirect suicide-speculation—finalized only in that he chose an effective instrument, a revolver, though he never bought one—was the closest he ever came to the real thing.

When he surveyed the broad perspective of his sixty-two years, he usually came up with a negative conclusion. Divorced with two kids, three grandchildren, and three ex-wives, the proud owner of a San Francisco two-flat building and a five-year-old car, was once again living alone.

There had been some good moments along the way. But the older he got the more frequently he visited emotional pain. Age brought to him what therapeutic change brought to Oliver, a vivified emotional experience. But unlike Oliver's experience, Peter's vivification was increasingly disheartening and vilifying.

Like the vast majority of humans Peter was a talented, decent, good person. He was meticulously fair and honest, hard working and dedicated to his commitments, a good neighbor, yet known only to his immediate family, a friend or two, perhaps a few ex-patients, and his next-door neighbor. No one would ever expect him to do more than have a good and sometimes helpful career, pay his bills, obey all of the important laws, and glean a bit of pleasure from it all in between responsibilities. Otherwise he would live a relatively nondescript life, say goodbye to his mostly unfulfilled dreams and expectations, and most likely feel at least some degree of excruciating regret. Eventually he would die with the relief that comes from escaping an ugly conclusion, knowing, after all, that he would only be remembered occasionally for a generation by those closest to him, and then be forgotten forever . . .

Though very intelligent, a very capable psychotherapist, and a devoted father to his children when they were growing up, he was not well-known for these qualities even by those close to him. Though very effective much of the time in his profession, his personal life was much less successful. Though an excellent listener and companion, like most psychotherapists he spent too much time listening and not enough time expressing his own life.

He was also prone to irritability, which compromises any talent, and gives a bad report to others. So he sometimes shot himself in the foot socially by moments of emotional distemper, or distemper's subtler alternative—expressing extreme ideas. Both exposed a pent up explosiveness buried under anything else he would say or do. These shortcomings normally left his craving for the right companionship very hungry.

The only, though not always reliable antidote to loneliness was for him to write. He started writing diaries about his life, mixed with occasional poetry, and then fashioned a book of rhyming aphorisms capturing whatever knowledge he'd picked up along the way. He wrote philosophy books, plays, and three pulp novels just for the hell of it.

He didn't know why he was writing or what he really wanted to write about. Instead he compulsively produced every kind of literature he could imagine, sending much of it out to all the names and addresses he found in *The Writer's Market*, as if somehow what he wrote would someday finally grab the attention of a world that normally discarded him as an insignificant person, finally redeeming him from the purgatory of everyone's neglect and disrespect.

Blindness to the real nature of his own destiny, made him dream his dreams in only a vague sense. Whatever he desired in life remained mostly unfathomable to him. He could sense it, desire it, believe in it and try it, but he couldn't feel, hear, or perceive it clearly.

As one might expect, melancholy was the emotional backdrop of this life, and for the most common of all reasons: love had always failed Peter. But the grief that this tragedy brought upon him was only one part the normal sadness that loss brings, and four parts the loneliness-guilt that blames the lonely for their condition.

This emotionally fixed position gave Peter only one relatively free feeling outlet: justice and its justifiable anger. Like most liberal, enlightened people of his time, he was far more dedicated to fighting injustice than he was to building a new life, which ended up serving the cause of his need far better than its satisfaction.

Like tens of thousands of very gifted humans, Peter was a serious underachiever. He couldn't figure out how to be the hero of his own life.

A Kindred Spirit

Peter roused himself from his semiconscious ruminations. His next patient had just rung the bell of her arrival.

If Ruth waits for long she gets very angry.

He wasn't ready to begin, but he preferred to avoid her distemper and got up to get her.

From the beginning of treatment Peter knew two things about Ruth, one, that she was definitely not psychotic, though she had been diagnosed that way, and two, that he would have to spend a great deal of time with her establishing trust, perhaps even years before she could begin to find out what it meant to rely upon him in trust as a foundation for improving her life.

Most qualified professionals would regard Ruth as almost untreatable in the sense of really changing her life. They would try to get her used to a low expectation and provide both medication and general support, as three of her former shrinks had already done.

"They tried to warehouse you," had been Peter's response, which won him half-a-point of trust in Ruth's suspicious heart, though she would not admit it for years.

Though Peter was very sympathetic with her anger at these therapists, he also realized that she was in fact very difficult to work with. But instead of making her responsible for that difficulty as one might be strongly tempted to do, he gradually allowed her needs to alter his view of what psychotherapy needed to be for her.

Within a few months he decided that, for severely damaged people who lacked certain basic building blocks of experience in their life, it was his job to provide these essential foundation experiences. Which meant that it was necessary in effect to live with them in certain ways, doing things that went outside of the lawfully accepted boundaries of proper psychotherapy.

He brought food to her when she was sick, went with her when she faced frightening tasks at the beginning of treatment, and gave her Christmas and birthday presents for many years. Eventually hugging of a lingering kind became standard at the end of each session, based upon Peter's simple assertion that she lacked a body-sense of what care was, so he would provide that for her in this way, to which she agreed. Frequent telephone contact occurred at times, sometimes every day, though Peter covered his own needs by charging her for time spent, up to an hour on the phone.

Peter derived some of the interest and motivation for this hard work from something he wouldn't recognize for years, that Ruth was in many ways a very kindred spirit. They had both lost large pieces of themselves in their desperate efforts to remain connected to dysfunctional parents, though Ruth's loss was far more severe, seriously disabling her ability to engage in most parts of life, work being the only real exception. Both had been abandoned, suffered from anxiety and depression, though Peter's suffering was more contained and less disabling. Both of them also had definite artistic talent, and both especially loved classical music.

Today those common elements were very present, but failed utterly to make Ruth feel the least bit connected to anything. She was deeply depressed, anxious and full of dread, which she expressed as a perpetual complaint about the complete misery of her life, effusing utter defeat and hopelessness.

"It's all a total waste of time!"

"I thought you've been making great progress recently," Peter replied good-naturedly, remembering the things they'd come to understand.

Though it frequently backfired, Peter couldn't resist treating her grief with encouragement.

"You're not listening!" she insisted. "I've only got twenty years left and that's not enough time. I'm obviously a very slow learner and there's so much more to learn. I'll be dead before anything really changes. Why wait? It makes most sense just to end it all right now. Going on is just a total waste of time."

The energy of intense fury pulsated in the arteries of her neck. Otherwise she looked gaunt, defeated, and unable to hope.

"Hopelessness is terrifying if that's all there is," Peter acknowledged.

"It's too late!" she shouted. "My life will never amount to anything! It's just a huge pile of shit!"

Sitting with the full force of her sullen and intractable rage was the hardest thing for Peter to do with Ruth. He always felt defeated by her because nothing he said seemed to make any difference in the way she felt or thought, even when subsequent events revealed that he had been right.

In the beginning of treatment, to manage her retreat into self-abusive behaviors like beating her arms and head, Peter tried to arrange a day treatment program for her until she settled down a bit. When it was clear she didn't like the program when they visited it together, he realized that it was with him that she wanted daily visits. So for several months he saw her six days a week for thirty minutes.

Now ten years later he was seeing her three times a week, one session on Saturday, and was available every day to talk on the phone as long as she needed.

Ruth's mother had been a grossly neglectful dilettante, who occasionally, and very briefly would play with Ruth as if she were a favorite rag-doll-puppet made entirely for her own entertainment.

Most of the time her mother disappeared for hours or days at a time. But it was not so much that Ruth didn't see her mother that was so unbearable. It was far more that her mother didn't see her. In fact, even when she was home she almost never spoke Ruth's name. Ruth remembered hearing it from her mother's lips for the first time when she was six.

Ruth would much later tell Peter that when she entered any room that her mother occupied, she felt instantly slapped. This experience cannot be explained as a happening. It was instead a little girl's jolting body-experience, which she always forced herself to forget.

Ruth managed to survive this chilling, diminishing, and neglectful assault by an elaborate pretense that her mother was a perfect mother, completely eradicating in herself any dissenting view. She accomplished this extraordinary sacrifice by moving her emotional parts into an abstracted place constructed entirely of fantasy, a world full of magic, where things could mean anything she wanted them to mean.

She paid for this permanent residence in her imagination by becoming, in the real world, the repository for everything that was dreadfully wrong with their relationship. To feel safely connected to her mother, she built an identity that perfectly imitated how her mother treated her. She became a worm—her word—living in her mother's beautiful garden, existing there only to serve her mother's needs by enthusiastically digesting all of her mother's ugly parts as if they belonged to Ruth.

Pretense replaced life; pain became gain. Ruth dropped out of everything, like school, friends, or growing up, anything that might contradict the elaborate fiction she was constructing. The worm she became was the highest form of animal with the smallest amount of need she could fit into her mother's miniscule care package, which she accomplished by making hell seem like heaven.

The outlet she gave herself for personal expression fit perfectly into the pretended life that she had built. She became the family's disabled buffoon, the goofy, retarded, silly fool who made everyone laugh at her own expense, offering herself as the repository of everyone's shortcomings.

She would pretend for instance that she was afraid of the vacuum cleaner, running away in feigned, though convincing fear when it got close to her. This cleverly constructed artifice gave expression to her fundamental fearfulness, while simultaneously hiding it by misrepresenting fear as something harmlessly amusing.

By such ambiguous devices she prevented anyone, including herself from seeing anything wrong, even though she secretly despaired that no one noticed the harm and suffering inflicted upon her.

As if cooperating with Ruth's delusion, her parents hid their own lack of responsibility by perceiving Ruth as a permanently retarded child, rather than what she was, a potentially delightful, charming, very intelligent, but deeply disturbed child.

Now many years later she refused to touch a vacuum cleaner, though not out of fear, but out of secret rebellion. It was part of her refusing to lift a finger for herself, a pure imitation of her mother's neglect. As a result she lived in an entirely undecorated pigsty with a few pieces of old furniture, littered with months of her debris, mixed with large piles of cat hair, clothes, trash, last weeks dishes, etc., in a run-down, dangerous neighborhood which drug dealers frequented. She feared and loathed most of the basics of life, such as cleaning, buying groceries, decorating rooms, washing dishes, etc., in effect taking care of her life, insisting that doing any of these things made her feel too stressed and afraid. Her version of "the world is a dangerous place" was that it was dangerous to do anything in it.

Don't step on the cracks, or you'll break your mother's back.

"You hate it when I'm so depressed, don't you?" Ruth challenged Peter's silence.

"That's true," he replied acknowledging the truth of what she'd said. "I do sometimes have trouble with your despair."

Peter was relieved that she was actually addressing him, acknowledging his presence in the room, which made his admission easy.

"Well I can't help it! I can't just go out and suddenly change myself like it was a piece of cake! I hate it when you say things like that!"

"I understand why you're upset at me. But I also think that what's most important about hating, is that you hate yourself."

"You never listen to me! You always change the subject! I hate it when you expect me to just snap my fingers and change myself!"

When Peter didn't respond, she jumped in.

"Why should I hate myself?" she challenged indignantly.

"For being a dependent, needful, vulnerable human."

She blanched at "vulnerable," which meant it had struck a familiar chord.

What followed was one of those rare moments when Peter's interpretation perfectly hit the mark. Ruth would start speaking almost as if she were in a partial trance. She spoke truth that seemed to come from deep inside of her.

"I always turn everything upside down. I make good things into bad stuff, and I can make bad things into pleasure stuff. I'm very sadistic, just like my mother. She could tear someone into shreds."

Peter had learned not to respond to these confessions, because when he built another idea upon what she had just said, Ruth would deny that she'd ever said it, as if she was split into two parts. Only the honest, vulnerable part of her could tell the truth, but that part was almost never let out of her secret room.

But when he didn't respond, sometimes she would get angry and remind Peter that he wasn't helping her.

"I know the moment I walk out that door I'm going to feel terrible again. And I'm going to have to go off and handle everything by myself."

"I expect you to be in touch with me when you need to," he insisted.

It was obvious that the prospect for that did absolutely nothing for her.

As she was leaving the office she turned.

"I know that you won't worry about me until the next time I darken your door."

"But I'd be glad to think about you anytime," he replied.

She left unchanged.

The moment she was gone Peter felt depressed.

I probably missed something today.

A Warning

You can expect the surprise message from us tomorrow.

Sincerely . . .
A friendly other

Oh, Christ. That's still going on. They're much too determined to convince me of their genuineness, so they must be phony. Spare me the final chapter, he added dismissively, intending not even to pay attention to it when it came.

And yet something else also tickled him from behind where he was looking, suggesting there was another response in him waiting in the wings for its chance.

Therapist as Father & Husband

As one might expect from the way he behaved with his patients, Peter was a devoted father to his two children, spending all of his available time off work either playing with them or attending their needs. Like many women, he was more devoted and loving to his children than to his spouse. They were the source of his inspiration while she was far more the depository, along with himself, of all his life's disappointments.

His relationship with Mandy, his children's mother, had soon become founded upon an armed battle. The war started innocently enough as they both grappled for satisfaction of their own needs with each other. Peter was patient, persistent, subtly resentful all the time, and extremely determined and relentless in the pursuit of whatever prevented him from being comfortable. Thus he ended up bringing home a piece of his professional nature, careful thoroughness, that to his wife, who was deeply antipsychological, felt menacingly stalking.

Mandy's nature was either very loving, or killingly vengeful. She had few in-betweens. She either adored you with very sweet passion, or she wanted to wring your neck. This was true of her husband as well as her children when they "defied" her by fundamental disagreement.

When she finally decided that vengefulness was the only safe course to take with Peter, she became a relentless saboteur of whatever he did, particularly mauling any of his loving gestures, like buying her a new dress. She took every opportunity to assassinate Peter with a perfectly fashioned, contemptuous putdown.

Of course from her point of view she was desperately trying to disarm a deadly enemy capable of driving her crazy. Everything that she had once admired in Peter had turned against her. She was preventing him from being powerful in her heart again.

At such moments it was almost more than he could manage to stop himself from striking her with a vengeance equal to her own. He felt irresistibly pulled into an emotional tornado. Once or twice he was unable to keep from striking out, and slapped her across the face, which she avidly claimed happened "dozens of times."

Thereafter she treated Peter as an already convicted murderer, throwing Jennifer in the middle whenever an argument erupted between them, warning her daughter that he was about to attack them both, needing the additional strength of her child to combat his evil-bearing and cleverly constructed intrusions into her mind, corrupting it by turning every little mistake she made into a capital crime.

Mandy finally couldn't stand the constantly implicit disapproval that she saw in his face, packed their car with children and belongings, and moved in with her parents. She was grimly determined to annihilate Peter from her life and from her children's, which she tried to accomplish by proving he was an unfit, violent parent.

Her accusations were so vehement and unrelenting, so utterly skewing the truth in a negative direction, that she alienated the judge, who gave her a minimal order of child support with a small, temporary five-year alimony.

Peter was overjoyed. This was precisely what he had hoped for. It left him with the power to spend much of what the children needed on his own terms. In addition to buying additional clothing for them, he was also able to exercise major influence in their lives by spending twice the court order on education his ex-wife would never have thought necessary to provide. In college he'd learned what the rich provide to their children, which he proceeded to give his children in spite of very limited resources. This included athletic and music lessons in two instruments and two sports, as well as private high school and college, basically doing whatever they needed to achieve the highest possible level of personal fulfillment, leaving himself, when the job was done with considerable debt and without any saved resources or retirement plan.

Peter's commitment to his children was total, without any regard for his own needs, a pure imitation in reverse of the way his father had treated him—demanding everything and offering hardly anything—which Peter turned into giving his children everything and leaving himself almost nothing.

Peter had tried very hard to avoid having a bad relationship with either of his children. Before having them he'd worked for years to make his life strong and healthy so he wouldn't repeat the horrific mistake his own parents had made, namely to inflict upon him every one of their shortcomings.

Toward this effort he spent fifteen years in psychoanalysis with a training analyst, meaning an analyst's analyst. But in all that time this man had been unable to help him significantly, making fifteen years seem like an almost total waste of time.

In effect his psychiatrist had treated a couple of Peter's most prominent symptoms as legitimate, while totally ignoring all of the others, and then acted as if these cast off pieces of Peter's problem represented "resistance" to the analysis of the real thing.

Unknown to himself this man was blaming Peter for what he couldn't handle. He responded with warmth and thoughtfulness only to signs of depression, completely ignoring the powerful evidence of abuse that had made that symptom a necessary adaptation to unredeemed suffering.

It would take Peter ten years beyond the end of his analysis to realize just how bad the experience had been. The whole affair had gradually become a miserable stalemate. Peter spent the last year mostly in silence, secretly fuming at this man. But he didn't allow anyone, including himself by and large, to know just how much he loathed his therapist for discarding parts of him. He was able to express this outrage only unconsciously at the time by sitting in silence during much of the last year of therapy, as if he had nothing to talk about, when the truth was that he had nothing more to say to this man. In being present and yet not participating, Peter was in effect imitating his neglectful shrink, who in his own part was paying only partial attention to Peter.

This silent treatment gave Peter a secret satisfaction. His analyst would periodically become very angry about it, expressing his frustration by cajoling Peter to talk, lecturing him about the rules of psychoanalysis. Peter enjoyed his therapist's helplessness at such moments.

So a little-changed Peter became a parent, and then a visiting parent, a role he was to discover is much closer to a favorite uncle than it is to a father.

He quickly learned, though he desperately disagreed with some of the things Mandy did as a parent, that it was fundamentally harmful to his children to give expression to his outrage, confiding it only to his friend, Drake.

But when his son at thirteen complained for the umpteenth time that he was going crazy staying home from school carrying his mother's broken leg about, that he was afraid he was going to have to hit her sometime, Peter, with his children's assistance kidnapped them and moved them into his home. He had left a message to Mandy announcing a move he had warned her for years would come some day.

It was Jennifer who mostly engineered this kidnapping. She had wanted to live with her father for a long time. In her mother's home she felt competitive, more like the real mother of David, her younger brother, but one who never got any credit for it. It was to her that David confided some of his deepest and most important things, which he continued doing as an adult. She felt very guilty about competing with her mother, and wanted desperately to live where she could be herself without such constant worry.

David was terribly ambivalent about leaving his mother, but didn't want to be left behind. His sister's strong desire to leave had forced him to realize that in truth Jennifer was in some ways the most powerful ally of some of his most important emotional needs, though he loved his mother dearly and would be devoted to her for the rest of her life.

Mandy, as one might suspect from her attitudes about the sanctity of motherhood, declared she was betrayed by her children and disowned them.

With Peter's urging and help, Jennifer called her mother to announce that she and David would not allow Mandy to disown them. They would pester her daily until she talked to them and restored normal relations.

It took only three months to accomplish. In part Mandy had things she had wanted to do in her own life which did not include children, so she was able to make an adjustment of her needs, throwing all of the residual negatives into killing thoughts about Peter.

Within weeks after Jennifer moved into Peter's house, she became sullen, secretive, and, it seemed to Peter, out of control. Playing around with all types of drugs, she vomited in her sleep one night without waking up, almost choking to death. She had consumed vast quantities of liquor after taking cocaine, leaving her almost in a coma.

In response to Peter's persistent pursuit of the problem—insisting they talk about it—Jennifer reacted precisely the way her mother had done. She felt completely persecuted and attacked by him. In self-defense, she refused to talk to him. When he persisted she was forced to become hysterical—scream—each time he tried to say something to her in order to get him to stop.

Meanwhile Peter was overwhelmed with confusion, shame, and fear in response to this constant repetition of stalemate with a child formerly very close and open to him. One of his beloved children had become someone completely weird, who not only deeply mistrusted him, but entirely blamed him for what was happening as well. She had become a complete stranger to him, who now seemed determined to defeat and condemn him in the most dismissive ways.

Though terribly ashamed that he couldn't find a way to communicate with his own daughter, Peter finally couldn't take it any longer, and insisted she go to a psychotherapist, a man with whom she worked for several years with great benefit, though he left a deep resentment of her father intact when treatment was terminated by mutual agreement, for which Peter was always profoundly disappointed in him.

Now, years later, Peter and Jennifer were still locked in whatever made the relationship between them repeat the war between Peter and Mandy. The reenactment deeply shamed Peter, twirling him into confused and frightening places whenever Jennifer visited him. No matter how hard he tried different things, he couldn't change the nightmare that kept happening between them.

Jennifer

Jennifer was in many ways an imitation of her father. Both had been emotionally abused, and in similar ways. Both had been thrust into the middle of the emotional turmoil between their parents. Both became care-giving people who either soothed others with their thoughtful interventions, or infuriated them by seeming to force unwanted intrusion.

Jennifer was shocked and deeply frightened by the emotionally violent outcome of living with her father. Her world spun menacingly out of control like the huge fireball that had stalked her in many of her childhood nightmares. All she knew was that she felt betrayed. Instead of her loving father, Peter had become her angry tormentor precisely as her mother had insisted he was.

Ironically, in spite of all the vitriol Jennifer privately loved her father. But she only felt it when she was alone. As far as she was concerned he never offered an opportunity for her to feel it when she was with him.

Her love expressed itself in her coming most Fridays to see him, though she always felt very awkward during these visits, and always brought along her knitting bag so she could avoid looking at him most of the time.

Jennifer was constantly troubled by her relationship with her father. She couldn't escape it. So she felt compelled to talk to just about anyone she met about how terrible he was, feeling most befriended by those willing to view him in the same manner. In this way she criticized him, but not to his face.

Though these what-an-asshole-Peter-is sessions always left her feeling partly uneasy and sick to her stomach when they were over, which she ascribed to being treated badly by him, when it was more that, in only condemning him she was acting against part of her own self-interest.

She loved to mount counterattacks against the general perspective of most people, that he had been a great father. When she was young, both her brother's and her own friends were always deeply impressed by her father when they visited, partly because he would speak to them as adults sharing useful information. He was also known for giving his children a great deal of responsibility and freedom to act on their own behalf as teenagers, seeming unperturbed by the angry, challenging things they said to him.

As much as a now buried part of her had once agreed with this complimentary opinion, it was to counter this "propaganda" that motivated much of Jennifer's vitriol toward her father in conversation with others. She was secretly infuriated by his great reputation, because such a positive view totally neglected her own sense of being seriously harmed by him.

When they got together it was only a matter of time before a relatively benign remark would touch something painful, sparking the reemergence of a melodrama of disappointment and frustration between two people who were permanently joined at the hip, but who kept hurting each other. Being father and daughter was a painful recognition instead of a comforting remembrance and celebration. They both felt innocently trapped in an endless cycle of misunderstanding and resentment, each for their own separate reasons that never became understood by the other. It's what made their anger occasionally so intensely rueful toward each other.

Inevitably, perhaps after twenty minutes of fairly congenial exchanges during her visits, something stirred them back into the vortex of war, repeating what someone somewhere had probably started generations before.

Today it was a remark by Peter suggesting that Jennifer looked very tired and of low energy.

"I didn't mean that!" she shouted. "Why do you always take me the wrong way?"

"I just said you looked very tired, Jennifer," he gently insisted. "I didn't mean that there was anything wrong with you."

"But you implied that I was lazy, that I didn't have a right to be tired!" she argued with intense resentment.

"No I didn't."

As it had been with her mother, it was very difficult for Peter to stop these exchanges of hurt by not responding, because his stomach was turning over, incessantly tying itself into knots. His extreme discomfort felt like it demanded some explosion of pent-up negative energy, if for no other reason so he could stop his stomach from churning.

He tensed his midsection even harder to keep it from forcing more words out of his mouth. He didn't want to be the first one to say something hurtful.

As a father he had given his children the right to say anything they wanted to say to him, even if it was critically insulting. It was only when they repeated their insult that he'd intervene with authority saying, "once is enough; you've had your say."

"Can I get you some tea or something?" he asked as he got up and walked by her into the kitchen.

"Okay," she replied, relieved at this temporary respite from conflict.

"You don't like sugar, but a little milk helps," he remarked. "Did I get that right?"

He was surreptitiously trying to get a positive response from her even if it was just about tea, by asking something he already knew.

"That's right," she said with a slight edge, reluctant to satisfy him even a little for fear she might give up something she couldn't afford to lose.

"How are John and Penelope doing?" Peter asked when he returned with the tea.

"Oh, they're great. Penelope just got a major part in the school play. She's really proud."

"I'm delighted to hear that. Please give her my congratulations."

"It's a part that really suits her perfectly," Jennifer offered, "a bright, aggressive woman who has a strong mind of her own."

"That's sure who she is. Please tell her how happy I am for her to find such a perfect part."

"I will. As for John, he still complains about his job. In some ways it isn't very satisfying to him."

"Can he imagine any solution?" Peter asked.

Jennifer didn't respond. She'd shared the news about John, but she didn't want Peter interfering with her family. She was afraid he might want to talk to John about it.

"So where are you guys going on vacation this year?" Peter asked, hoping to keep the brief congeniality between them alive.

Jennifer gasped. She loathed to be asked this question by her father. The last time he'd asked it she'd requested that he never ask the question again. Secretly she feared he was asking in order to be invited, when she regarded her vacations as the only time she could legitimately get away from him. She definitely didn't want to lose that, but she feared she might have to in order to keep the relationship afloat.

Caught between feeling ashamed and furious, she wanted to scream.

But that would have made her feel even worse. So she leaped up from her chair, threw her knitting on a table, and stomped into the kitchen for a glass of water, obviously very annoyed at him. Leaving him waiting to find out what was wrong nourished her confidence in dealing with him as an equal.

Ironically, it was her father who had taught her how to use action as a part of dramatic dialogue, taking full advantage of its power. He often said to his children that doing things is sometimes far more eloquent than saying them, often encouraging their challenges of adult figures in their lives.

Though Peter was startled by her sudden move into the kitchen, he restrained his negative response and waited. He knew she would linger there for a while, then at a snail's pace meander back to where they had been sitting together, all the while appearing to enjoy leaving him hanging upon the thread of her resentment until she damned well felt like talking again.

He had learned to use his waiting time creatively by philosophizing about the helplessness he was feeling. He gradually developed a fascination with passive emotional experiences like surrender, taking orders, and going with the flow, all of which were hard if not impossible for him to do.

"I've asked you a thousand times not to question me about my vacation plans," Jennifer fumed when she'd settled in her chair with her tea.

Something snapped in Peter! He threw caution and restraint to the wind!

"For Christ's sake, Jennifer, what's wrong with asking about your vacation plans?"

Of course Jennifer knew she was right. She had asked him not to ask this question.

Of course he had privately thought it to be an unreasonable request, so he had ignored it as if it was unreasonable.

"Jennifer, why must we always argue about every little thing I say?" throwing fuel on the fire with this exaggeration.

"Why ask me?" she retorted with contempt. "Ask yourself."

"What is it about vacations that can't be discussed with me?"

Jennifer could not tell her father the truth about that. Yet in spite of her antipathy toward him, she felt guilty about excluding him in any way. Caught between a rock and a hard place, she didn't know what to do but leave, the solution they both used when things got untenable.

She stood and headed for the front door.

A suddenly regretful Peter immediately followed her.

She suddenly remembered she'd left her knitting on the table.

The abruptness and discontinuity of these separate moves caused them to bump into each other.

"I'm sorry," he said.

"Oh, bullshit!" she retorted. "Stop stalking me!"

"I'm not stalking," he shouted back at her in his own defense. "There's nothing wrong with my following you."

"You're always blaming me for everything!"

"So once again it's me who's rejecting you. For Christ's sake, Jennifer, what do I have to do to be regarded as a fairly decent father to you? I've followed your life with intense care. As a man with very little money I gave you educational opportunities available only to the rich, and even helped pay for a shrink when you couldn't talk to me anymore. It seems to me that the rejecting is coming from the other direction. It's you who . . ."

"Oh, stop pontificating about how you're God's gift to children," she shouted with an acrid, intense bitterness. "You obviously have no idea what damage you've done to my life!"

"Damage! What damage?"

"That fancy private high school you insisted upon sending me totally ruined my life! That place made me ashamed of myself! I was top of my class in public school. You turned me into one of the dummies! So don't tell me about all the shit you gave me as if I'm supposed to think it's so fucking wonderful!"

Peter was shocked. He'd never heard this information before.

Why does she wait until now to tell me something like this?

Yet he was very influenced by what she had said. He couldn't avoid feeling that maybe she was right.

The only problem was that he was already carrying too heavy a burden of self-criticism around, coupled with too many bad words between them, that he couldn't let her add yet one more heavy piece to that huge pile. So he sent the messenger away, allowing his fury to vent itself!

"Get the fuck out of my house!" he shouted, the words choking his throat as he said them. "I don't have to take this horseshit!" was more of a loud whisper for lack of the air support that he'd already exhausted.

Jennifer was deeply stunned. He'd never evicted her from his home before in such a furious way. He'd always just asked her to leave. She may have treated it as an eviction but she knew it really wasn't one. But this was definitely a total rejection.

She suddenly felt deeply and profoundly undermined. She became panicky, and then instantly paranoid as a way of directing the terror.

She'd always counted on seeing him regularly, even if they did have a miserable time of it. But now he'd actually done what secretly she both feared most, and yet also sometimes wanted to do herself. He'd sent her packing.

She started to shake.

Peter instantly stepped toward her, reaching out as if to touch her, then hesitated.

"Jennifer, I'm so sorry. What's happening to you?" he asked, desperately pretending that he didn't already know. "You're shivering. Are you cold?"

He reached out again to touch her shoulder.

She angrily jerked herself away from his touch.

"Don't you dare touch me!" she shouted.

He was stung by her words.

Jennifer circled wide around her father to retrieve her knitting, keeping as physically distant from him as she could arrange, all the while peering fearfully and suspiciously at him.

Being treated like a pariah broke his heart.

"Please, Jennifer, don't leave this way," he said, starting to cry. "I must really have frightened you. I . . . I . . . I'm terribly sorry. It's not that I'm rejecting you. It's just that I can't take anymore of this . . ."

Before he could finish she'd grabbed her things and ran around past him and out the front door. He was cut to the quick.

He stood there transfixed to the spot for several moments, going over and over what had just happened in his mind. His heart became heavy with guilt. He could not avoid the conviction that he'd done something terrible to his daughter, even though he also tried to keep alive his belief in the idea that he had a right to protect himself even from his children if he felt abused by them.

"But why did I do it? Why did I do it?"

Surprise

Thirty minutes later, after pacing around his flat mostly unaware of where he was walking, preoccupied with his daughter's visit, he wandered into his office seeking comfort. He started his computer, turned his back to it, and drifted.

"Where's the end of it all?" he asked himself for the umpteenth time. "Where's the way out?"

Absentmindedly he glanced at the monitor and noticed something strange on the screen.

What the fuck? Where did that come from?

"Oh, shit! I suppose it's that fucking message I'm supposed to get today! I can't handle that kind of crap right now."

He started to turn off the computer to erase both the message and the moment, when he suddenly realized he hadn't asked for e-mail.

How did that thing get there?

Now intensely curious about what was happening, Peter started to read the message, and then almost immediately stopped.

"Nothing's changed, Peter," he said out loud. "The fucking message is still just a lot of bullshit. You can't afford to get taken in right now by some stupid advertisement gimmick. Somebody must have invaded the computer."

Once more his mouse moved toward the off button, when suddenly something else tickled his awareness.

What if it's genuine?

That's all it took. He read the message.

To: Peter Icarus

Greetings. Please don't be alarmed at this unusual message. What follows is a genuine proposal. It is not a hoax, a joke, nor a computer virus. Our words are genuine and can be accepted at face value.

We are the Troubadourians, a species of humanoids living on a planet very much like yours, though we live in a galaxy very far away, so distant that your telescopes have probably taken only the most rudimentary of pictures. We are therefore to you a very unlikely species to be making contact.

We have been studying your planet and your species for fifty years, though we've never actually visited you in the way you seem to think aliens will make contact.

You must be asking how is it possible for us to be communicating with you over such vast distance. We have perfected what you call a technology capable of transporting a living human almost instantly from one place to another in the universe.

Which brings us to the substance of our Proposal.

THIS IS AN INVITATION

We want you to visit us.

Why are we extending such an invitation?

And why were you in particular selected?

By our calculations we are perhaps two hundred years ahead of you in evolution as a humanoid species. We performed facsimiles long ago of the kind of things that you're doing now. We want to share who and what we've become with you. And we want to visit our past by communing with you.

You are not the first to be selected. You are the second. The first is still among us. We cannot send him back in his present state of being. It might, we believe, be disastrous for him, which is part of why we chose you. We need your help as a psychologist, though that's the smaller portion of the why of our choice.

We picked you out of the thousands of what you call "mental health professionals" specifically because of who you are. We "put great stock" (to use another of your sayings) in the who and what of a particular person.

In order to understand you better we have read the

documents in your computer. We apologize for this uninvited intrusion into the privacy of your life, but we intend only to use such information for the purposes of knowing you. The moment our relationship is ended, anything about you in our records will instantly be deleted and never used in any other way out of respect for your life, that is unless you give us permission to do otherwise.

Therefore we know your ideas and attitudes. We know how you think about being human. We find that you are, in spite of great differences between us, in some ways very much like us. (Anatomically as well you will find us remarkably like yourself.)

Based upon what we observe to be these common perceptions, we figure that you are more capable than most of your people of understanding what we have done with that extra two hundred years, that is should you decide to visit us.

If you are interested in this opportunity please be assured that at any moment you can terminate our relationship and return home within twenty-four hours of such an announcement.

We must now forewarn you that there is a possible cost to coming here. We don't know for sure, but we have evidence to believe it possible. The price a traveler might need to pay for transportation across such huge distances, is the loss of a small portion of their life: specifically we estimate perhaps two to five years of longevity. Please do not regard this unfortunate possibility as an inevitable outcome.

Should you, because of this possible loss of a portion of your life, instantly reject our offer, feeling perhaps that it was indeed not an offer but a crude hoax, we would understand, because time in life can be very precious. Should your interest remain we would be deeply grateful. Should you come, your visit will be for three weeks. Within that small timeframe we believe the life-loss is least likely to occur.

Should you have questions, please "fire away" to use one of your metaphors. You can communicate with us by e-mail at "offworld@Troubadour.net"

We remain cordially yours, with respect and admiration,
The Troubadourians

As he read this remarkable message Peter felt an overwhelming flurry of emotions, which repeated their cycle when he was finished. In rapid succession he felt great excitement, utter disbelief, deep suspicion, a faint touch of hopefulness, followed instantly by intense anxiety.

"Jesus Christ! What are you doing? This is obviously a hoax! And here I am actually taking it seriously!"

Repercussions

Emotion had once been Peter's plaything. As a three-year-old his imagination was filled with the adventurous possibilities that feeling projects into experience. But unlike most children, play was something he liked most often doing with adults. He was regarded as a very social child who interacted more with people than things, a life-course in traditional terms more typical for a female.

His father drastically changed all that. He found in Peter's exuberant emotionality both the loving nature he so avidly desired for himself, as well as the deeply fearful responses that his predatory methods of acquisition evoked in Peter. In an attempt to squelch the latter, which judged him with a child's innocence, he buried Peter's emotion, turning the boy's loving willingness to please into a forced indentured servitude, making a joyful gift into a painful enslavement.

Now sitting at his computer fifty-nine years later at age sixty-two, Peter trembled inside the chaos of feelings provoked by the message. His heart started pumping furiously. His back tingled with prickly explosions, as if bugs with sharp nails were marching down his skin.

It would take years before he realized that these back-prickles were a concrete reenactment of his father finger-poking him in the back when he wanted Peter's attention, something Peter had forgotten long ago.

Peter was very frightened by this earthquake of somatic sensations. Walking down his hallway into his living room, his mental focus began to wobble. To avoid losing balance he reached for a chair nearby, and half sat, half fell into the chair, almost upending it. For what seemed like a long time it teetered on toppling, concretely mirroring the falling apart of his internal stability.

The alien message was forcing vivid feelings little known to him, to suddenly rise up into his awareness, after years of being buried and forgotten, feelings of a child that had been evoked by the terrible turmoil between his parents, which were now triggered by the enormous contradiction of his reactions to the message.

There was only one thing to do, retreat to his highly fortified castle in the mountains, that fortress of pure reason that always cut feeling down to size.

The foundation of the intellectual superstructures he'd been building in his mind all his life was very simple. Like all effective intellectuals, Peter abandoned all belief in anything and anyone he hadn't personally and rationally verified on his own terms.

So far he had been unable to completely verify anybody, which meant he had never found someone completely trustworthy. His intellectual work represented an attempt at claiming total authority, at least for himself, best expressed as, "I'll do it for myself; who needs anybody else?"

He became extremely effective at deconstructing anything he saw, read, was told, or heard about. He wouldn't let anything touch his heart until it had first been dissected into its constituent parts and thoroughly analyzed by his mind. It's what compelled him to become a philosopher, meaning someone who tries to think about everything so as to cover all the bases. The pressure behind this effort was, since you're on your own, you'd better get it right.

Covering all the bases forces one constantly into looking for the big picture of anything. The usually caustic kind of perpetual thinkers who do this sort of thing, get very excited when they see familiar pieces form a new pattern no one else has thought of, at least as far as they know. This occasional originality is the secret reward of thinking for one's self that partakes of a certain kind of lawlessness intrinsic to always making up your own mind, never just accepting the shared belief of others. Such a person can't help being a prick in the side of a social gathering's comfort by always playing and saying a little bit out of tune with everyone else.

The older he got the more effectively he became intellectual. The good news was that feelings no longer overpowered him as they had for years when he was a boy left alone to deal with terrifying emotional moments. The bad news was that now, as an adult man he was very isolated from the essential and basic information which only emotion conveys. To become as successfully discerning as he needed to be as a shrink, and as the happy man he hoped he could one day be as a man, he had to learn accurately how to understand emotion. At sixty-two he was making very slow progress, and was still far from his goal.

Peter came out of this childhood experience with a naive, unsteady relationship with his own emotions. Mostly he treated them as adversaries. Instead of showing him something, feelings were forced through a careful, rational analysis by one who believed that rendering something to ideas meant that it had been mastered.

So what are the facts? Maybe this bloody message is a virus. Lots of them are floating around these days. On the other hand if it is, then it's already doing its dirty work. And yet there is no attached file that is the usual carrier of viruses. So it's probably just a sales pitch that has a nasty twist at the end, another advertisement trying to deceive, perhaps a kinky sexual invitation that sneaks up on you once the fog of off-worldly illusion disappears.

Wishful thinking, old man, came a chiding reply from somewhere else inside of him, implying that a sexual invitation might be welcomer than he was admitting.

"Maybe it's a practical joke," he said out loud.

But something told him it wasn't. The message was very interesting and too sincere, even friendly.

But of course that would be precisely what the best con artist would do. Come on, you naive fool, the likelihood of it being genuine is extremely remote. The best con would be the one who first appeared entirely innocent and sincere. I've got to stop being the fool. I've loved too many of the wrong females, whoring my skills to wrong women and patients but never to the right partner.

He was feeling too vulnerable. He had to find an exit.

He found the perfect change of subject—anger—that relieves one of guilt by blaming others. Remembering that the Troubadourians had read all his computer files, he became furious.

"Those bastards! They had no fucking right!"

For a moment the idea of someone intruding into his private thoughts felt creepy and repugnant.

"That's enough reason right there not to trust these assholes!"

But strangely, after a few such expletives, his fuming quickly lost wind. He knew he had just cause, but for some reason his heart wasn't in it. Something strange was going on, though it wasn't clear just what.

He sunk into a half-conscious state of vegetating where his mind drifted through half-formed thoughts and impressions, when he suddenly realized that the message made him feel slightly excited.

That felt dangerous.

"Oh, for Christ's sake, Icarus, enough already," he chided himself, implying that he should stop hoping fruitlessly and change the subject.

But he couldn't stop his curiosity from returning again and again to a strong inclination to take the message seriously. He reread it again, and then again, and couldn't deny that each time he liked the manner and tone of its discourse. In fact, reading it made him feel good.

"What a strange affect this bullshit is having upon me."

He suddenly realized why he was so willing to trust the message. In all of his readings, he'd found no serious incompetence in its presentation, no evidence that the author was trying to fool him with false premises or bad science in order to sell him a bill of goods. Though rather preposterous, the sense of the message was consistent with itself. There were no visible signs of anomaly or incongruity, an observation that always worked to reveal what needed to be addressed with his patients.

He started to feel more excitement and began to imagine visiting a strange, new world. The newness of everything he would find there could thrill him. It might be like starting all over again from scratch, having a second chance to experience his life much differently.

Suddenly he realized how huge his disappointment would be should these hopes be dashed. Instantly he ditched his excitement. He could risk no further investment of hope when so much doubt lurked about. He brought deconstruction's big guns out.

"How foolish of me to be so taken in," he cried out loud. "Of course they dreamed up clever answers, whoever they are who want to sell me something at the end of this otherworldly trail. How stupid of me to pant so hungrily at the preposterous notion that I'm the most interesting and desirable human on this Earth, worthy to be the special chosen-one to represent the planet in some very distant world."

This time his intellectual efforts failed entirely to debunk the message. When all was said and done, he was still struck with awe at the invitation's possibilities. He couldn't deny the ray of hope inside him.

Hope is the most dangerous emotion for one who walks alone. It exposes the philosopher's secret vulnerability, which is the desire to be listened to and taken very seriously. Such a person needs public agreement in order to be fully legitimate.

Hope moves a philosopher to share his philosophy with others. But if he failed to grab their attention, he suddenly became the actor whose audience has abandoned him, disconnecting him from the external verification that any viable philosophy must evoke in order to be seriously legitimate. Which exposes the tenuous connection with others that philosophy tries unconsciously to repair in those who go-it-alone, even while they look out from behind a shield of cynicism trying to prevent their thinking from being overimpressed, and thus potentially overpowered by what all of us need from others.

Peter suddenly remembered that he was not the first Earth human to be chosen. He was the second, which instantly disappointed him.

"So I'm their second choice," he muttered to himself.

But they had asked for his help with the person who was first. Maybe they had some special reason for choosing him. Hope was again rekindled.

"Wait a minute," he suddenly warned himself. "What went wrong with that other person? Why did he flip out? And why do they need my help? Aren't they two hundred years ahead of us?"

The possible loss of five years in his life suddenly loomed very large in his mind.

"How could I have forgotten that even for a second? That makes the whole thing completely ridiculous!"

He was suddenly shocked by the realization that this huge flaw in what they offered him, this enormous price tag for going, was precisely what gave the message its most distinctive mark of genuineness.

"A con artist would never put such awesome imperfection in their offer," he told himself.

He was suddenly struck dumb by the realization that to take this invitation seriously, even for an instant, meant that he was willing to consider such a huge loss of life. He was stunned when the thought passed through his mind that his mother was ninety-eight and still kicking nicely, implying that five years measured against a hundred wasn't so bad.

He was shocked at himself.

"Why am I feeling this way? Do I want to commit suicide! I always thought I'd have to do it, but I never thought I'd want to do something so utterly crazy as to take this thing seriously!"

But I do.

"My god! I'm actually feeling excited about the possibility of going! I must be as loony as Jennifer keeps insisting!"

He couldn't deny it anymore. In spite of all the risks his negative imagination could come up with, he continued to be drawn to this invitation like a fish to water, which made him feel extremely, recklessly anxious.

He started to feel panicky. He leaped up from his computer chair and raced into the living room, flipped on the TV, and plunked himself down on the eight-foot couch. He was trying to escape the most dangerous thought a philosopher can have, which was to mistrust himself.

He had to redirect his energy.

Boob-Tubing

He started flipping through the channels in a compulsive way. At each station he would allow himself only an instant before he'd change the channel, expecting that he should be able to recognize what he liked or hated about it within seconds, immediately able to provide an erudite and succinct synopsis of the reasons why.

Unconsciously he was trying to prove that he couldn't be duped by anything, or overpowered by what others did, or seduced by how they attracted him. Instead he could make quick, rational, and effective decisions based upon his thoroughly well-thought-out, philosophical perspective.

Flip.

"A western devoid of any human purpose. If there is a moral to the story then it's that people who live in small towns must be brave because they're most likely to get whacked. But why should they be intimidated anymore than anybody else? And why do we keep making so goddamn many movies about people suffering? Haven't all of us done enough of that already? Why rub our noses in it for the rest of our lives?"

"It's all about advertising for profit. First you stimulate the tension of longing and desire with a little suffering, then you satisfy it with a sexy car wash. Just another attempt to masturbate our needs without having to understand them."

Flip.

"A courtroom drama pretending that law reveals the truth, when all it does is bore-to-death twelve muted people called a jury, mostly by forcing them to be almost entirely passive. Serious thinking is supposed to be done by everyone but the jury. The largest problem for the jury is not how to understand complex evidence as the judge always insists, but to avoid falling asleep."

Flip.

"Oh, yeah, the news that some Madison Ave. CEO thinks we should be indoctrinated with, thought up by some hugely overpaid genius, producing an indirect, circuitous, deceiving pathway of seduction in order to sell their stupid fucking shit. They offer this pabulum-called-product in three flavors: sex, fear, and avarice."

His channel changing had become obsessively unstoppable.

Flip.

"Shit!" he shouted at the next station. "The whole goddamn entertainment business doesn't contain any more sense than the mindless violence which it demonstrates over and over again."

Flip.

"What's this? True love? Or so they would have us believe. But this is love where you only talk nice words. Never a discouraging word is heard, and that's supposed to be safe and make life work! So who's tending the inevitable bad shit? Must be their senator. Isn't that the biggest farce of all?"

Flip.

"Aagh, another crime story to remind us that the more individual we become the more criminal we are to others."

He suddenly realized that underneath everything he'd been trying to achieve, he was starting to shake uncontrollably. At first it was a small shake, but it was fast growing.

"Fuck, what's happening to me?"

He suddenly realized why. For the several minutes he'd been pontificating about TV, his body had been in a state of unrelenting contraction. He was shaking because his muscles had finally become exhausted from this prolonged clenching.

He stood abruptly, intending to pace around as a way of dissipating this agitated paralysis. Instantly he felt light-headed. He tried to overpower it by taking a step forward, and lost his balance, falling against the arm of a stuffed chair, knocking the chair over, depositing it and himself on the floor.

Though still dazed, he managed to roll over onto his knees. Once again he stood too soon and the light-headedness returned. He crouched back down and bowed his head until it went away, and then slowly returned the chair to its upright position and sat down.

"My god, I'm flipping out!"

Marijuana.

He found his small stash in the drawer, rolled a cigarette, and started smoking. Gradually, after several puffs relaxation started to occupy his body again.

Suddenly he remembered a very vivid dream. He was very young, under five, and lying in bed. But something was very strange. Everything was too vividly real.

"Oh, my god! This isn't a dream! It's a memory!"

Peter had tried for years to remember things about his childhood, but found memory forever cloaked in a dim, foggy shroud that made him a stranger to his own childhood.

But now something had turned on the projector.

Memories

Between the ages of four to seven, Peter was a serious bed-wetter. This infuriated his father. Curiously it started within months following his father's arrival on the family scene.

In order to put a stop to Peter's enuresis, his father would try to catch him peeing in his sleep. He would set an alarm to wake himself at various times so he could spy on Peter. He found 2:00 a.m. to be the most likely time and began to catch him sometimes. Once or twice he actually caught him in the act of urinating.

He would rip the covers off Peter, grab him by one arm, jerk him up out of bed and drag him into the bathroom spouting fury, without any regard whatsoever about what this action was doing to Peter's body. Once in the bathroom he threw him down on the toilet insisting that this is where urination was supposed to happen.

The painful, cold hardness of the toilet seat when his body smacked down hard upon it, is what he'd just vividly remembered when he stumbled to the floor.

"Life is beginning to feel like being around Jennifer all the time, forever in danger of becoming jolting and precipitous!"

Remembering Jennifer's recent visit reminded him he had to call her, which gave him something concrete to do.

He went to his phone and called her. He felt enormously relieved when no one answered, allowing him to leave a message.

"Jennifer, I don't want things to remain where they were when last we met. I want us to get to a better place. So let me start by saying I'm terribly sorry to have frightened you so much. I think I've been very upset the last couple of days for reasons of my own. It's not your fault. Please let me know that you're okay, and, if you feel up for it, could I come to dinner on Sunday as I sometimes do?"

After hanging up the phone he felt intensely lonely. He grabbed an afghan off the couch and plunked himself down into his favorite chair looking out over the city park behind his flat.

Normally he was soothed by the people and animals moving about in the park below his window. He loved this home situated on a cul-de-sac. It was both in the middle of everything, yet out in the country as well. He loved to look out at the park's pines, firs, and shrubbery, feeling soothed by the peacefulness of nature's pacing.

But tonight he was profoundly disappointed. When he looked out onto the grassy esplanade he saw only the loneliness of the night surrounding two dim lights that barely outlined the trees, completely unoccupied except for one lonely-looking old man walking slowly through the halo of illumination provided by the two street lamps. As soon as the old man disappeared into the darkness, there was a feeling of foreboding that danger lurked about.

Peter was most frightened by the intense and disorienting experience of having feelings so strong, they seemed able to tear him apart. He started to think, this has never happened to me before, when he suddenly, though very vaguely remembered that this was the way life sometimes felt when he was boy—extremely scary and precipitous.

This recognition of familiarity in disaster ironically soothed him a little, enabling a clearer picture of what he was experiencing to be expressed, which brought it more into focus again, slightly easing the fear that hung menacingly over everything, from which he hadn't escaped for hours.

"My life seems in danger of sha . . . sha . . . shattering," he stammered.

Stuttering reminded him that he'd done it seriously between the ages of fifteen and thirty. Doing it had always felt deafeningly humiliating. It mattered not that he did it only occasionally. When it happened he felt unbearable shame at the endless repetitions of half-sounds that came from his mouth, most never coming to completion.

His mind raced through things long forgotten, now suddenly opened for his humiliating perusal. Stammering in front of a high school class transported him onto the school bus, when he could finally escape another day of perpetual embarrassment just being around other young people.

The bus reminded him of the other ugly thing in his social experience:

getting hard-ons that wouldn't go away. The main problem was getting off the bus without his penis sticking out in front of him like a sore thumb. After three excruciatingly painful days of shame departing the bus, he finally managed to create the new habit of bringing a newspaper to school every day, expressly for the purpose of hiding the bulge.

It was still hell passing through the gauntlet of "hundreds" of students staring at him on his way into the school building each morning. But somehow he always managed to make it to the men's room where he could hide in a toilet cubicle until his member settled down, allowing him to attend his first class.

Though the newspaper was sometimes a serious problem. He often mislaid the one he was using at the time, like most absent-minded teenagers. About to leave for school unsupplied, he would sneak a section out of his father's morning paper. When later accused of the same, he would claim that the newspaper boy must have forgotten to provide that section, which his father never believed. He didn't have sufficient grounds to inflict punishment, except for the usual sullen silent treatment that often characterized his evening behavior, which expressed his own disaffection with life by forcing that emotional experience upon Peter as if he was to blame.

Occasionally Peter would forget altogether to bring his newspaper armor. During one such occurrence, with only his schoolbooks to hide his embarrassment, he had awkwardly stepped out of the bus in front of Macy's Department Store, stumbled, and promptly fainted.

Within seconds, though he was terrified it had lasted for minutes, he regained consciousness. This was more out of fear jolting him awake than a desire to be aware once more, which brought him the instant specter that everyone was staring at his hard-on as he lay on the ground.

He opened his eyes to the full realization that he was right. Everyone was staring down at him.

He couldn't bring himself to see where they were looking. Instead he leaped to his feet as fast as he could, sending a gasp through the crowd as they watched his sudden recovery in disbelief. Wobbling light-headedly, with the crowd momentarily closing in to catch him, he shook off vertigo's brief visit, and ran into Macy's, down its central isle a block long, and out the other side facing onto the next boulevard. As he rapid-walked he disguised his hurry, as well as his penis, with extreme efficiency, ducking in and out of the many people in the aisles, sometimes just barely avoiding bumping into one of them, but nonetheless missing.

Now, in the present moment, staring out the back window of his San

Francisco flat seeing nothing except Macy's Department Store, as if he were really looking at it—he shook himself free of the trance into which he had sunk, suddenly aware at how completely absorbed he'd just been in this vividly humiliating memory.

"What's happening to me?"

The restless ghosts of his early life had suddenly come out of their chronic depression, where buried in grief they'd escaped his scrutiny for decades. These protuberant memories of how shame had come to dominate the undercarriage of his life seemed to lunge at him with vengeance.

He was completely unprepared to deal with this challenge.

"I don't want to do this shit!" he shouted, standing for emphasis. "It's that fucking invitation that's doing this to me! I don't care why! It's got to go! Fuck the positive potential of changing my life! If this is what changing it means, then I don't want any part of it! I refuse to be so huge a sucker that I'm going to believe there are benevolent aliens out there who actually intend to deliver good things to my particular life! It just can't be true. This world is too fucking rampant with horseshit!"

His resolve lasted for almost a minute, before dissolving in a churning pool of loneliness, which instantly revealed the simple and unadulterated truth. He desperately wanted the invitation to be genuine. His life needed it to be real.

Something to Do

The need for action was intense. But he could think of nothing to do. After a half hour of pacing around his flat, lost in a ruminative daze, he realized there was only one thing to do. If this message was the cause of his great distress, then challenge its veracity by responding to it.

He hurried to his computer.

To: The Troubadourians
From: Peter Icarus

Blankness followed. He didn't have the slightest idea what he wanted to say. A feeling of helplessness started to take over again.

"My god, what's the matter with me?" he pleaded with the night.

He leaped up for more pacing, until he remembered all the risks he would have to bear should he go.

"That's it! Do they know what they're doing?"

Suddenly he knew what he wanted to write.

Dear Troubadourians:

Thanks for the invitation, though of course I have no way of knowing whether you sell, jest, poke fun, infect, or perhaps something much worse. However, for some reason of my own, my life is compelled for the moment to take your offer seriously. Which prompts these questions:

1.How is it possible for you to transport me billions of light-years in an instant? Whatever happened to the speed of light?

2.If there must be loss of life in being transported, then are you sure you guys have it worked out right?

3.Do I accurately understand that you've got a mental patient for me to treat upon my arrival? Though this may be only your minor reason for selecting me, I'm puzzled that you need my help at all. I thought you were two hundred years ahead of us.

4.And why would you want to be reminded of what you were like one hundred-fifty years ago? Is this some kind of circus sideshow into which you're inviting me?

I apologize if my questions seem rude. But of course I'm taking all the risks in this venture, at least as far as I can see.

Cordially,
Peter Icarus, the confused

He read what he'd written, made a few corrections, and read it again. Finally, with some lingering apprehension, he pushed the send button.

It was done.

A sudden chill shook his body.

"Brrrr. This whole affair is making me feel cold."

On a hunch he went into the living room and checked the thermostat. Sixty-four degrees. He had forgotten to turn the heater back on when he got up again.

He wandered back into the living room feeling an unfamiliar but encouraging tinge of hopefulness. He went out on his deck into the night air, watered the plants, and put food out for the birds. He looked down at the twice-lit pathway with nobody on it, tempting him to abandon hopefulness and send a second message saying, "I've changed my mind; forget the whole thing."

But that didn't help. So he went to bed and dropped off to sleep the moment his head hit the pillow.

David

Peter woke with a heavy heart locked in turmoil. His night had been one nightmare ordeal after another, waking him every hour or two. Many of his dreams were about getting lost and being unable to find his way home again, something he had dreamed of all his life, which he'd always thought meant that he felt lost inside his family, that he yearned for it to feel more like home.

It had never occurred to him that he never found his way home because he secretly wanted to live somewhere else, meaning with different parents. That idea would constitute a betrayal of the only caretakers he knew.

If he had been able to acknowledge what he really wanted, he would have remembered the rest of the dream, that in his search for a better place to live, he found and passed through some wonderful homes, much more spacious and graceful than his, where he would much rather have lived.

He couldn't remember this part of the dream because it would have revealed to him clearly that Troubadour had become a chance to live in a different home. Vividly knowing that's what the dream was about, would have betrayed his life's most sacred trust, which was to obliterate in himself any trace of wanting, in the presence of a loved ones, to be somewhere else. It's what he had guiltily grabbed from his daughter when he sent her packing.

Instead it was still his responsibility to get what he needed from his family, or what was the matter with him that he couldn't get along with those that loved him?

"David. How are you?" Peter said when his son picked up the receiver.

"Oh, hi, dad. I'm great. What's up?"

"I just wanted to talk to you," Peter replied.

"What about?"

Peter blinked at the off-put-ness of that question.

David's ability to off-put things was actually one of his best strengths, one much needed in his public career. With all the diverse interest groups clamoring for a piece of the political action, it was imperative for David to know which events were worth reacting to in a careful and serious manner, and which ones were not. There was never time enough to respond to all expressions of public need.

From his perspective, David wasn't off-putting his father. It was his father that was "out of control," who needed his son to calm him down. Of course David was too intent upon establishing his point and position, that he didn't see the condescension in his attitude toward Peter.

Privately, David felt he was more grown-up than his father. He'd lived patiently with Peter's unhappiness for years, often absorbing the heaviness of his father's mood or the sting of a careless, provocative remark as if it had never happened.

It was not that David disrespected his father. In fact he deeply admired him, though primarily for the way he thought, for his clever ideas. David had learned a great deal from talking with his father, some of which represented the foundation of the beliefs that underscored his career in politics. He was chief aid to a state senator from Massachusetts.

The problem was that he worried often about his father. Subconsciously he felt guilty that he was so much happier than Peter. It's why he'd moved so far away, so that he could enjoy the benefits of being fathered by the intellectual Peter whom David admired, but live in a very separate place far from his father's, and his sister's problems, though of course he wouldn't have admitted it to himself. He had always been fiercely loyal to Jennifer. He would remain loyal to the intellectual father, but set-right the emotional man who filled this role.

As a younger man he'd once asked Drake, Peter's best friend, about his father's depression. It was quite obvious from Drake's response that, at the core, he had precisely the same emotional problem. His life had also been very unhappy.

"Will he be okay?" Peter had asked.

"Oh, he's a clever one," Drake instantly replied. "Don't underestimate him. He's a very powerful dude."

"He doesn't think that way about himself," David had replied.

"Oh, really?" Drake said with genuine surprise.

It was clear to David that Drake didn't know any more about it than he did.

Today, David was very surprised to hear from his father. They only talked a couple of times a month, and it was almost always David who telephoned.

"I called to ask about you and yours," Peter said, "though I do also have something in particular to share afterward."

"What's that?" David asked, requesting the punch line immediately.

Another off-put, Peter thought

"No, first you tell me about your magazine," Peter replied. "I understand you're about to publish your third issue. You must be very excited since the other two were so successful."

"It's all going just great, dad. In fact it's really hard to believe how quickly the idea of a magazine with original and provocative ideas about almost everything, no holds barred, could be making it so well. I mean we put some pretty crazy stuff in there, but people are eating it up, most particularly the younger set."

"I'm really happy for you, David," Peter said warmly. "You're quite an original."

"Look who's talking, only the guy who gave me the vision which provided the foundation that built this magazine. I couldn't have done it without you, dad."

"I'm glad to be able to contribute."

"How about an article?" David asked. "One of yours in the first issue has been very popular, the one titled 'The Nightmare of Medicine,' you know about the bureaucratic medical community trying to take control of nutrient, vitamin, and herbal ancient treatments as if we needed a prescription to supplement our diet for longevity and health."

"I'm glad to be part of the team," Peter replied. "But speaking of original ideas, can I run something by you that's pretty way out there?"

"Sure, though I'd prefer the article," David, the editor said, once again off-putting his father's request by changing it into something else.

David dreaded having to deal with one more emotional problem. He was afraid his father would go off and do some half-cocked thing that would really get him into trouble, forcing David to intervene.

Like the time his father got arrested in Mexico for not having the proper papers for the car he'd borrowed from a friend; or the time he'd been stranded in Japan when his girlfriend, who was paying for the trip, suddenly abandoned him, and he had to wire his son for the money to get home; or the time when he got manhandled by a local policeman for calling him "a fascist," forcing David, present at the time, to intervene with a more reasonable approach.

David much preferred to keep his relationship with his father on an intellectual plane. There he could avoid the clash of loyalties that his secret disrespect for his father created.

There was also the question that, if his father was unstable, then maybe the ideas he got from him were also spurious, a thought capable of undermining confidence in himself professionally, making him wonder if he was a fraud.

"I was hoping today that you'd be in a mood to hear something a bit different . . . actually something quite implausible, but fascinating," Peter explained. "And please avoid assuming, when you hear me, that I must be going off my rocker, but actually give what I say some respectful thought for a moment."

"You get lots of respect from your readers," David retorted. "In fact you're famous for the medicine article. It was very provocative and is much read."

Peter got discouraged. He wanted to say that he would like his son's respect right now, but he knew that remark would only alienate his son. So he was silent.

"Well, aren't you going to tell me?" David asked, already feeling guilty about being so off-putting to his father, even though it was his dearest wish that his father's problem would just go away.

Peter replied as much out of resentment as desire, turning what he wanted to be heard carefully, into something bluntly and nakedly fashioned. By giving David something he couldn't consider carefully because it was so wild, he fulfilled his own prophecy that David wouldn't listen.

"I've been invited to visit another planet."

The statement stood naked.

The deadly silence that answered Peter announced what he had expected, that David would once again, just like his sister, treat him as if he were neurotic. Peter knew what was coming next, so he tried to head it off at the pass.

"Now, please don't respond as if I'm loony. I'm perfectly aware that it's probably a hoax or a sales pitch. It's just that I find the possibility that it's real to be very entertaining at the moment."

This was a much better presentation of Peter's need. Unfortunately it followed a rendition that had already evoked David's disloyalty, and was lost in the misadventure of that false start.

"Did you hear me, David?" Peter said out of frustration. "I've been selected to visit a species which is quite similar to our own."

"You are of course pulling my leg, aren't you dad?" David queried gently, but with a touch of condescension, giving his father's idea as much respect as he could muster.

"No. I'm quite serious. The invitation is elaborately presented, thoughtfully communicated, in effect . . . well, rather appealing to me at the moment."

David didn't know what to do. He didn't want to express his real feelings about what his father was saying, which would have been something like, "You must be crazy to take something like that seriously." So he did what he thought was polite; he avoided the issue. He cleared his throat and changed the subject.

"There is something I have to bring up, dad. I guess this is as good a time as any. Uh, Jennifer called me earlier, as you might have already suspected. As you know she usually calls me when you two have a fight."

Fuck, Peter thought! So this is what I'm going to get for my sharing. He's dumped the topic of Troubadour. And now he's talking down to me, the little bastard, as if I've been a naughty child and had a fight with his sister.

"What happened to my space journey?" Peter asked, trying to remain as peaceful as he could arrange. "That's what I was talking about."

"It stayed right where it belongs, dad, in your head, the only place it will ever happen. I . . . I . . . I'm sorry to be so, well so direct about it, but I simply can't find a way to take you seriously. Maybe I should. But if so, I don't know how."

"Well, why not let your imagination go a bit?" Peter suggested. "I know it's incredulous. I spent a great deal of time disbelieving it too. But something about it kept attracting me, so I've decided to play the game, hit the ball, see what happens."

More silence.

"Uh," David began, trying one more time to be fair to his father. "H . . . how did you, I mean . . . how did they get in touch with you?"

"They put a message on my screen, which was amazing because they did it without the benefit of e-mail."

That was more than David could tolerate respectfully. He was suddenly sure his father had mentally forged an e-mail into some kind of miraculous happening, because he so desperately needed it.

"If you thought there was a possibility of traveling to another planet, wouldn't you at least give it a little serious consideration?" Peter queried desperately.

More silence.

"Are you there, David?" Peter asked.

"Do you hear yourself, dad? I mean, even to you . . . doesn't what you said sound a bit outer space, you know, I mean in the exaggerated meaning of that metaphor? Oh, I don't think you're crazy. It's just that this . . . this whatever it is that's got a hold of you makes you sound that way."

He's always so damned nice when he sticks the knife in your back, Peter thought.

But once again Peter chose to respond with civility.

"Maybe you're right about me, David," Peter conceded falsely. "But the way you say it is rather disrespectful."

David resolved to end this painful moment.

"Look, dad. I do respect you very much as you know. But I also really do need to bring up this other thing. As you probably guessed, Jennifer asked me to call you hoping that I could patch things up between you. Now I know she's upset you, dad. But I'm only trying to make peace between you. Have you ever considered that you might just be having trouble understanding her?"

Peter was furious. This was the one thing his son did that made Peter hate him, which was to speak to Peter as if he was his father's mentor or guru, completely unaware of the large condescension in this strategy.

"If you choose to be involved in my relationship with Jennifer, David, then you fucking well need to understand that there are always two sides to any coin."

David hated his father's angry outbursts just as much as his mother hated them. He strongly didn't respect them, so he didn't know what to say, wanting very much to avoid making the mistake his father had just made by attacking someone he loved.

Peter knew the moment he had spoken that silence was how his son was going to respond. He suddenly wanted desperately to get off the phone.

"This . . . is going . . ."

"Look, dad, I don't want to fight about it. I mean I know there's your side. But I think maybe you are a bit too critical of Jennifer. She just gets overly excited sometimes and exaggerates things. She doesn't really mean to hurt your feelings."

Peter could hardly contain himself.

"David! I called you! This is my dime! I called you to talk about an invitation I got. If you want to call me about Jennifer, then do it on your own dime! I don't want to talk about it now."

Peter felt a little better. He had established a clear limit without assaulting his son.

"David, you're a very nice man, and I admire you for that. But sometimes you hide your head in the sand in order to achieve that. At least I think so. At certain times Jennifer is mean in the way she behaves, most frequently toward me. That kind of behavior deserves to be recognized for what it is, extremely hurtful, bordering on meanness. I don't know why your sister is so constantly angry with me, but it would help if occasionally you would give my experience of her ways some credibility."

"It's not that I don't believe you, dad. I do. I know you feel hurt. It's just that I'm trying to help you avoid that by being a little less negative about it all."

Jesus Christ! The little fucker's acting like he's more grown-up than I am.

"I'm sorry, dad," David interjected. "I don't know what else to do or say. I just hate being in the middle of this thing between you and Jenny."

"Then why don't you get the fuck out of the middle?" Peter asked.

"I know you worked hard for us kids," David replied as if his father had not spoken. "But I guess maybe for Jennifer all that hard work didn't take so well. But there's nothing we can do about it now. I'm sorry it worked out this way for you, but as you know you helped me a whole, whole lot."

Lip service, Peter thought as he started drowning in despondency. Kids are so goddamned shallow in their understanding.

"I guess sometimes it doesn't work between you and I either," Peter said with a sad, bitter voice. "I don't mean to blame you for that. I guess, as you say it's just the way it turned out."

Why are kids always right and parents always wrong? Only death will free me from that oppressive obligation. He's the person and I'm the icon. Parents for the rest of their lives are never seen as equal to their children, at least not in conventional wisdom. Most parents can't imagine making as many demands of their kids as their kids make upon them.

Peter wanted to protest. The problem was that he deeply valued the relationship with his son. He did not want to harm this union, so he always ended their conversations on a positive note, even when he felt the opposite way.

"I hope Peggy is well," Peter said in a tired tone, wanting mostly to get off the phone without further useless altercation.

"She's fine, dad, and so are the kids," David replied good-naturedly, feeling great relief that the fight-danger was over.

"Give them my best."

"I will, dad. And I hope you feel better soon too."

"If my psychotic delusion turns out to be real, I could be gone for a while," Peter added.

Silence again.

"Well, I hope you're not, dad. I wouldn't want to lose you."

Though he knew it to be completely sincere, Peter couldn't benefit from this final expression of his son's regard. Instead he sat for a long time wondering if there was anyone with whom he could share his experience.

Living Alone

It was a gray, foggy morning like many in San Francisco. Peter usually loved the fog's narrowing of visible, external stimuli, creating an immediate and intimate container inside of which he could maneuver, as if nature had anticipated his need for a safe and private place of respite and repose.

But on this particular morning the fog had become a mirror for the pall of loneliness that always lurked at the outskirts of Peter's self-experience, but which had this particular day become a shroud that encircled his every moment with grief heavy and tension's tears waiting to fall.

He sat grimly at his computer staring through and beyond the meandering squiggles that protected the longevity of his monitor, peering blindly at some distant point of reference far into the face of its flat opaqueness. He was hoping without expectation that his own internal spaces could somehow reflect clarity for him to see, so he could decide what he must do, whether he should go, whether even to take the whole thing seriously.

Earlier he had laid awake in bed watching the first light cast gray hints of recognition upon the secrecy of the night's concealments, but could find no path of perception which might bring the light of respite to his deeply unsettled spirit. He had awakened many times during the night to worry. Each time it had become harder to turn down his mind's repetitious rambling low enough to fall back to sleep. At 2:20 a.m. he finally gave up and got up.

It looked very much like he had to figure out Troubadour entirely by himself. He doubted there was anyone in the network of his family or acquaintances who was willing or able to share very much of the burden of this crucial decision. It was most likely that everyone would have their own agenda, their own need to twist what he was saying or feeling into something that fit into being themselves, as if being-self and being company was one and the same thing. Their neglect of his need made him invisible, enabling them to remain completely unaware of what their actions were doing to him.

"We're becoming so much better at giving the essentials of emotional life to children," he said out loud to himself, turning to philosophy to get consolation, as if thinking's pontifications could connect him to something redeeming. "But we haven't even begun to understand that we adult humans need precisely the same quality of treatment that babies do, of course in the forms and frequency that grown-ups need."

But philosophizing brought no relief.

He turned to his profession hoping to find consolation there, but he found only bitterness in the realization that he gave to others what he needed desperately to have for himself.

"What bitter irony to be one who gives quality help, when I can't find anyone to give the same quality of care to me. It's like being the proprietor of a great restaurant who can never eat his own wonderful food. Feels like a Chinese water torture."

A bell ringing to announce a new message interrupted his fall into depression's underworld. Almost afraid to do it, he hesitantly began to read.

From: The Troubadourians
To: Peter Icarus

We are absolutely delighted with your interest in our proposal and answer your questions as follows:

1. To be transported in an instant to Troubadour does not require the speed of light to change. Space travel, as your species has imagined it, is utterly impossible. What we have learned to do is something quite different. It's a transfer of information, not a transporting of physical materials.

When you come here should you so decide, the molecular structure of your body, mind, and spirit, for that too has atomic as well as anatomical roots, will in effect be suspended in the primordial mass of your Earth's ecosystem. Meanwhile you will materialize upon our planet almost instantly, forming out of local materials. When you arrive we anticipate that you will experience no difference in yourself, except perhaps that your body may feel younger.

This need for the presence of precisely the right materials is why transportation is possible only to or from those particular points in the universe where complex life and its huge pool of biochemical elements already exist.

We anticipate your next question, which might be how can information be transported instantaneously? The answer requires treating the Time dimension of reality as a Constant, in the same way that the speed of light is a Constant. Time then becomes always. Which means that everything including information is always everywhere. It's simply a question of tuning into it. Thus transportation here requires not an engine but a receiver, and a very clever operator capable of tuning in.

2. It is in the process of saving the blueprint of your basic structure on Earth that we believe is the most likely source of loss of life, should that take place. Our suspicion is based upon the simple realization that in the three weeks you would be spending with us, you will change. You will no longer be the same person, which may in some way alter the structure of who you are. That's why we limit your visit to only three weeks in order to minimize this possible outcome.

3. Yes, there is what you would call a "mental patient" here with whom we want your help in order to understand him accurately. He is your predecessor, the only one. He became wildly unstable in his functioning upon waking on the second day.

We need your help because we have no standard by which to judge normal functioning for him. His return journey could be very traumatic. We need to decide whether he's fit for such a journey.

4. We have been unable to find an answer to your question, "Why do (we) want to be reminded of what we were two hundred years ago?" We couldn't find sufficient common ground between you and us upon which to build an answer. We suspect that the things you'll learn here, once learned will make the answer easily available to us both.

We don't know if you're going to lose a piece of your life. So far we only have speculations capable of explaining what the evidence seems to suggest. As to why this might happen, we offer the following speculations.

There could be elements of you that may not be completely transferable. Another possibility is that there are spiritual and physical aspects of any living creature that cannot entirely be reconstructed in a secondary location, thus slightly altering the integrity of that particular individual.

Reality doesn't seem to offer perfect conditions or complete answers. At least it doesn't as far as we have discovered. It provides diversity in abundance, extreme variability in type, and multiple options of the same thing. But it doesn't provide perfection. Nature and reality seem to prefer the ambiguity of imperfection instead.

We hope these answers will prove adequate for you. We await your next communication.

Should you still be interested in visiting us, perhaps it will be useful for you to know that once you arrive we can arrange for your departure within twenty-four hours.

With grateful anticipation of further exchange, we remain.

Cordially yours,
The Troubadourians

He found the message deeply reassuring. He was still very troubled, but there was something so soothing about the message that he read it several additional times.

"Maybe this whole thing is a hoax. But the people doing it are really interesting. I particularly like that bit about nature preferring ambiguity to perfection."

He'd always experienced philosophy as something done entirely alone. But here someone else was doing it with him, or at least seemed to be doing so. That was a very exciting prospect.

Oh, it can't be a dud. It would send me over the edge.

He worried for a while.

But then again maybe it might . . . maybe it just might be . . . well, maybe.

Condemning this foolish hopefulness, his fear rose up with a vengeance.

"But what about those five years, you silly man?" he shouted to himself. "Maybe they live long enough to make five years insignificant. But will I? My mother's no guarantee. What if I die at eighty-five like my father? Five would be way too much to lose! It would mean I only have twenty left!"

He started to feel a bit panicky, but then something struck him with a blow.

"But you've got to go!"

Hearing himself he cringed. But he knew it was true. Of course he could refuse. But he also knew that if he did he would regret it for the rest of his life.

Friends

Drake?"

"Yes, who's this?"

"It's Peter."

"Hey, old buddy. How good to hear from you."

"It's good to hear your voice," Peter replied.

"So what motivates this call? You want to have lunch?"

Peter hesitated, feeling uncomfortable about needing his friend's help, and yet not wanting, at least at this point to have lunch with him.

"Actually I wanted to talk right now."

"Sure. What's up?"

"Well . . ." Peter felt embarrassed. He didn't know it at the time, but he was ashamed to expose the deep craving for comfort that underscored his need to talk.

"It must be about a woman," Drake said. "That's usually what gets a man so tongue-tied."

Peter laughed. It was a mixture of nervousness and relief.

"As usual you've guessed accurately, though it's not a romantic female attachment," Peter replied, choosing Drake's emphasis. "It's my bloody daughter. I finally got so fed up with her today that I asked her to leave my house. Well, actually I was more aggressive. I told her to 'get the fuck out of my house.'"

Peter suddenly thought of Ruth.

"Oh, and one of my female patients has gotten under my skin and I can't get her out."

"Ah, you clinicians have all the fun," Drake retorted with an impish twist. "I sure miss never having a private practice of my own, so I could experiment on live bodies like you can."

"I know you're aching for a lab. But please explain Dr. Drake Wentworth, why a daughter can be so maddening to an innocent and generally loving father."

"I've always found Jennifer very difficult to be around," Drake replied. "In fact sometimes she gives me the creeps. She seems a bit crazy."

"Maybe you're right, old buddy. But she said something that really got to me. She said that I 'ruined her life' by sending her to private high school. I suddenly realized that she might have been right. I think that's why I kicked her out, because maybe she was right. It really upsets me to find out I'd done yet one more wrong thing in this crazy family of mine. I'm getting so fucking sick of the experience of being the villain all the time with both of my kids, when I spent years of labor and all my money caring for them."

"My family makes me feel sick not part of the time, but all the time," Drake retorted with emphasis.

Peter hesitated.

"Drake, there is something else I wanted to talk to you about."

"Shoot."

Peter took a breath.

"What would you say if I said I'd been invited to visit another planet?"

"Boy did she get to you if you want to get that far away," Drake retorted, referring to Peter's daughter. "How much longer are you going to carry around your kid's shit? Aren't you getting too old for this stuff? I thought you sent her to a shrink. Didn't the bastard take over?"

Peter was disappointed not to be taken literally, but he was equally amused by his friend, as he often was. He got from Drake only a little by the accuracy of his understanding, and a lot more by the cleverness of his misunderstanding.

"Not very well," Peter replied. "She seems to have come out of that treatment hating me even more. It's as if the treatment, which I paid for, made me the target of all her aggression."

"You're a died-in-the-wool romantic," Drake insisted.

"What's that got to do with the price of a daughter's hatred?"

They both laughed.

"You think people should be happy," Drake explained. "You believe love should retrieve them from their insanity. So of course you're blaming yourself for being a poor lover. It's the way women hold onto a man, by convincing him that he's a failure at it so he'll keep coming around for love-lessons."

Peter laughed. He didn't always agree with Drake's view of the world, but he sure enjoyed the cleverness of its construction.

"As usual your erudition outpaces the event and takes us from pain into philosophy, when I had something else in mind, though I must admit it's made me feel better."

It was Drake's matter-of-fact way of reducing things to a simple formula that always brought relief to Peter. He didn't have to agree with Drakes analysis, which he often didn't. But it was very relieving to know that there were more ways to look at what had happened than the one in which he was stuck.

"You romantics keep trying to find the right woman with whom to merge," Drake replied. "Whereas I decided thirty years ago to disconnect my body from any woman, most particularly my wife. I stopped fucking her. I began to notice that screwing her made me feel depressed and hurt, and not just my pecker. My whole body hurt. She's a very angry woman, you know. I think that's why it hurt so much to fuck her. She got angry right in the middle of my orgasm. So I've been a celibate roommate since. We manage just barely to tolerate each other, though in middle age she is beginning to have more respect for me, and even occasionally to listen to what I'm saying."

"I feel sympathy for you, old buddy, and appreciate your predicament," Peter replied. "But that option isn't right for me. I am compelled to be what you call a romantic. The problem with my penis is not that women hurt it, but that it refuses to cooperate with me. It has a terrible time exploding."

"That's a problem?" Drake asked. "Sounds to me that you're a lucky man who doesn't want to be one, a man not constantly plagued by the compelling urge to fuck. Some people don't know when they're well off."

"You always have such charmingly inaccurate ways of putting everything," Peter said with a laugh.

"It's awfully nice of you to say so," Drake replied in good humor.

"But there's still the other matter I asked you about. What would you say if I told you I'd been invited to visit another planet?"

"I've always thought women came from another planet," Drake retorted humorously. "But you can't say I haven't warned you about that many times."

"Drake, take my fucking question seriously, you ancient asshole."

"Since you insist, I have to say that quite obviously some new woman

I haven't heard about has got a hold of you by providing the best sex of your life, though at great strain to your brilliant brain. You've already started to hallucinate in simpatico with her delusional beliefs that your mutual love transports you both to another special, private just-the-two-of-us world."

Drake's cute misunderstandings were beginning to get on Peter's nerves. He suddenly felt very tired and disheartened, and decided to leave Drake with his happy, single-minded thoughts, and got off the phone as soon as possible.

Samantha was sitting at their usual table. His most recent ex-live-in partner met him once a month for lunch on Fridays, though in recent months they had done so less often.

She still sometimes told Peter that he was the best man she'd ever known. But she always added something.

"Which is true only if I don't expect love from you."

Two years before they'd had a torrid, hungry affair, sometimes intensely sexual, and sometimes very aggressively hurtful. Their relationship had deeply stirred in both of them the unfinished and painful business of their separate lives. Instead of healing each other, they sometimes fought like cats and dogs, though also with great restraint, nonetheless each accusing the other of being the problem, he openly and verbally, and she mostly by cold withdrawals, pouting, the silent treatment, interspersed with an occasional knifing remark.

Finally Samantha had ended the affair, something Peter was unable to do in spite of wanting desperately to do so on many occasions. She insisted that she found him to be impossible, though she also added the usual disclaimer that he was still the best man she'd known, but only from more of a distance.

He'd rejected her offer of friendship for a while in his disappointment at losing a live-in companion, but then gradually realized she might be right. At least they ought to try being friends. Neither of them had enough of the right company in their lives, so why not? Gradually they'd settled into meeting monthly on Fridays for lunch.

"Hi, you handsome devil of a man," she said as he approached. "How are they hanging?"

He was used to the rough, punchy language with which she chose to kid him. There was a kind of male comradery in her friendship.

Her secret wish was to be an NFL football coach. She loved the strategizing and was actually extremely good at it, often anticipating problems with a play even before it started to fall apart in the game.

Over time Peter had come to realize that in some very traditional ways Samantha was more male then he was. Curiously it didn't bother him at all to think so. A few years back he'd learned that his mother had wanted him to be a girl. When he heard that, he was surprised to discover that he didn't much mind. Gender didn't seem to be as vital to him as it was for most men.

And yet at the same time he still had some of the rough-edged traits of a man's man.

"They're drooping badly," he replied.

"Tough day?" she asked.

He sat down.

"Yeah, but not terribly different than any other," he replied, indirectly expressing his general discouragement with life.

"Now you've put your finger on what makes it impossible for us to live together," she remarked, "meaning of course your incessant unhappiness. I know the world is a shitty place, but I don't spend so much time thinking about it," she added. "It seems to me that just makes it much worse."

"Lucky woman," he replied ironically. "I don't seem to have any choice but to think about it. It's why I have to write. I've got to do something with all those angry thoughts."

"Who wants to read bad news?" she queried.

"Probably no one," he said with a touch of sadness.

Samantha neither understood nor enjoyed Peter's ideas very much, though she greatly admired the cleverness of his mind, most particularly when he expressed it light-heartedly. She wanted him to be a regular guy and get along with everyone, which was her solution to unhappiness. Of course his intellectual pursuits usually took him in the opposite direction.

"The only problem is I've got to communicate with someone about it."

"Feelings are highly overrated, if you ask me," she said.

"Not in my life they're not. They're almost nonexistent."

"Tell me what feeling ever gave you a good result?"

He looked at her carefully.

"Looking forward to seeing you today."

She blushed.

She loved these moments when Peter's gentle lovingness surprised her. He deeply moved her heart. It's why she couldn't let go of the relationship no matter how much she hated him . . . at one time.

"Now that's why I still love you sometimes," Samantha added with a glint in her eyes. "Occasionally you've got a silver tongue."

She loved the humorous cleverness of his ideas because they were the part of him that made her laugh. She craved laughing as much as Peter craved care.

She noticed the glint in his eyes.

"Now don't get upset, Peter. I'm not coming on to you. I'm just flattering you."

But the truth was that in a way she was "coming on" to him. She was giving to Peter what she wanted to get for herself, that he still found her attractive and sexy. She wanted him to find her the same way.

Struggling to find a way to bring up what he really wanted to talk about, and frustrated by the different take on life that she always had, Peter lost patience.

"Goddamn it, Samantha, please stop trying to crawl back in the sack with me. It was a terrible experience."

"Stop shouting at me that way, Peter," she retorted in a loud whisper.

She felt very hurt. She was also very embarrassed by what others in the restaurant must be thinking.

Peter knew he was making a mountain out of a molehill, but during this precise moment he didn't care. He was crying out against more disappointment.

The pain that had triggered his explosion came from Peter hating to be reminded of his sexual problems, making him feel unfit for her, unable to find fit for himself. Sex had been a glaring example of that. To Peter it seemed like she enjoyed it almost as if it wasn't connected to anything or anybody else. It was like an athletic event between two people who were competing in separate races, together temporarily by accident, yet one more way in which she was like a man.

I'm the one in this relationship who's the romantic, he often thought to himself.

"Let's eat," she replied, hoping to change the subject.

"Good idea," he replied, relieved at the chance for a break.

Why did I start this fight, Peter asked himself? I'm not really upset at her today. I'm just not talking about the right subject.

Samantha was a fifty-four-year-old woman of business, a marketing expert at a high level of corporate rank. She was of German and Swedish decent, with an honest, openhearted demeanor, and a generic smile on her face which disguised the few darker, secret aspects of her life to which she gave outlet almost exclusively only in very private places.

Work and football were her life, adding Peter infrequently to the mix for quality male companionship. The largest nonsexual part of her would have liked them to be celibate roommates.

"I wish you didn't drive me crazy, Peter. You are really such a damned good man, that is, if you could ever get over being so angry and spending so much time being depressed."

He was hurt by the lack of sympathy for his depression, but didn't want to be angry again.

"I guess I do darken things sometimes, don't I," he confessed good-naturedly.

"You're damned right you do, you asshole," she replied with a humorous flourish, reaching out to be intimate with him the way a man would do by punching him out a bit.

"I don't miss your bitchiness either," he replied, annoyed as he'd always been at this part of her male nature.

The waiter arrived with lunch.

"Enjoy."

"You surprised me with your outburst," Peter said to mend fences. "We don't usually get back into that stuff nowadays."

"You surprised me too," she added with relief.

"I suppose we don't have to stay there. Would you like to hear something really strange?" he asked.

"Sure," she replied, hoping for something entertaining.

Peter hesitated for a few moments.

"Well, lets have it, guy," she said excitedly, deeply relieved to be in a more lighthearted place with him.

"Without benefit of e-mail I received a message on my computer monitor. At first I treated it like a hoax. But there's something about it that hooks me."

"How exciting!" she exclaimed. "Tell me what it said."

"I'm afraid to tell you. Either you're going to laugh or you're going to warn me about its dangers."

"Come on, you devil," she replied enthusiastically, undaunted by his warnings. "I can't wait to hear."

"Oh, all right."

He gathered himself.

"I've been invited to visit another planet."

Silence.

"You've got to be kidding!" she exclaimed.

She was resentful that she'd been sucked into feeling excited about such a silly thing.

"You really take this seriously, don't you?" she queried with an unconscious touch of contempt.

"See what I mean," he replied. "There's the laughter I predicted."

"Alright, I'm sorry. I didn't mean to laugh, but only if you tell me why you're taking it so seriously when it's obviously a hoax."

"There was something very reassuring and friendly about the message, which I wouldn't expect to be there if it were a practical joke," he protested.

"Friendliness is what makes you a believer?" she asked incredulously. "Don't you want something more substantial to depend upon?"

"There you go again making fun of me," he replied indignantly. "I'm just telling you how I reacted. I don't really know what to make of it."

"I'm sorry, Peter. I don't mean to upset you. It's just that . . ."

She paused realizing with apprehension that avoiding another fight was entirely up to her at this point.

"I don't know how to think about it myself," she continued. "I mean I wouldn't give it the time of day, as I'm sure you know, except perhaps to send it to a few friends as a joke. But you . . . you . . . well, it's you're taking it so seriously that really puzzles me. You're such a brilliant man. I mean I've always admired you so much for that. But here . . ."

The gentleness she'd managed to inject into her discourse reassured Peter, restoring him to a feeling of friendship.

"Thank you for saying that, Samantha. I appreciate it."

She was very relieved.

"It puzzles me too," he went on. "Which is why I told you about it, not to upset you, but just to inform you. I thought maybe I could understand it better by talking about it."

"Oh, I feel the same way," she replied good-naturedly. "There are some things you just have to tell somebody else."

She was very happy to have found a way again to be successfully helpful to Peter.

"I guess I'm having trouble understanding why you want to take it so seriously."

"I can't understand it either," he replied, "but I'm really hyped to give this thing a chance. I guess I'm trying to figure out if there's something wrong with that."

"Maybe not if it entertains you," she replied, trying to be supportive.

But she didn't feel that way.

"But even if the invitation is real," she added, "why would you take such risks with your life?"

"My life on this planet sure as hell isn't very pretty," he replied. "I can't do much worse going somewhere else."

"Oh, I get it," she replied with excitement. "You're taking a trip to treat your depression. You hope something will come out of it."

"Stop it, Samantha!" he retorted upset. "Please don't trivialize it by making it neurotic."

"Sorry."

She felt terrible, but she didn't know why, or what to do.

Peter realized that Samantha had done as much as she could for him. It was helpful to share as much as he did, though of course there was so much more he would have liked to say to someone who would understand.

"Well, I hope they don't keep you for very long," Samantha said with a smile. "I'd sure miss our lunches."

The sweetness and humor of her remark soothed and humored him. He laughed.

"Thanks, Samantha. Occasionally you really do say just the right thing. I really mean that. Thanks. You've helped me. I'm sorry if I've been rude to you."

She was both immensely surprised and enormously relieved.

"I'm so happy!" she beamed. "I don't exactly know what I did. But it sure as hell feels good to have done it."

But the truth was that she hadn't really helped him very much, though she had been very sweet. He'd applauded that because he appreciated her. But he went home with a heavy heart.

Feeling Alone

That night he had horrific dreams about being trapped inside of a war zone. All city buildings were at least partly destroyed, leaving piles of rubble all over the place. Rats scurried in and out of these debris-dumps searching the wreckage for food. Nothing was familiar. He wandered about block after block, searching for buildings that even slightly resembled some place he'd been before. But he found nothing.

Everyone looked away from him as if he weren't even there. Their faces were barely visible in the dark shade of a hat or shawl. He circled around them trying to look into their eyes, searching for someone to recognize him, but everyone turned away preventing him from seeing them. It was as if the whole world was shunning him.

When he woke and started moving through the day, his experience didn't change very much from the way he felt in the dream. Awake he felt just as lonely and estranged from familiarity as he had been in the dream, though he was aware that the dream images were symbolic and not literal, meaning he wasn't going crazy.

But being so aware made him feel very frightened. To know that he was caught up in a vortex of change, that spun him around in circles no one else occupied, intensified his predicament.

He finally realized he had to get out of dreams and into reality. What was missing was not sense, but a response to the last Troubadourian message. He was finally able to do it when he realized they were the only ones who could help him to decide.

To: The Troubadourians
From: Peter Icarus

If Time is always, then everything is happening all the time everywhere; then nothing is particular, or specific, or unusual, or even very special; nothing matters very much, which, if true is very depressing.

The alternative isn't much better. If everything matters all the time, then life must naturally be very frenetic . . .

He left out that he was becoming more and more frenetic himself.

. . . Which is how I feel when I think of my body starting to dissolve in the primordial mass, whatever in the hell that is, so strangers, meaning you with no disrespect intended, can rebuild me billions of miles away. That sounds very much like dying, or at least like practicing dying! What if I become something alien to myself when it's all said and done?

He was suddenly reminded of an acid trip he'd once taken in his youth, which had dissolved the part of him that observes and organizes meaning, leaving happenstance aimlessly to drag him through one chaotic moment after another.

1. How can you separate me from my body and expect it to stay alive until I return? How can I be in two places at once?
2. How can Time be a Constant when it's a measure of passage or process?
3. Have any of you ever come to this planet?
4. How do you know there's a loss of longevity?
5. What happened to my predecessor? Was rapid aging what drove him over the edge?

Cordially yours,
Peter Icarus, the confused

He was surprised to find that once having written the e-mail, he felt sufficiently better to speculate about what everything might be like on Troubadour.

"I wonder what they look like and how they intend to communicate with me."

It suddenly dawned upon him that they already knew his language.

Now that is pretty amazing all by itself, that is if they are indeed aliens and not some son-of-a-bitch just waiting in the wings to punch me in my stomach with the cackled announcement, "April fool!"

Why do they really want a visitor? What's the point?

What if it's for a circus?

That would make it impossible to keep living.

Or what if they expect way too much of me?

"That would be unbearably humiliating."

Family Sharing

A very young Peter was digging in his back yard for treasure. Suddenly his shovel hit something hard. He started digging frantically and unearthed a shiny gold coin. He looked lovingly at it, put it aside, and then started digging furiously for more. Altogether he found twenty gold pieces. He carefully put them in his pockets.

He knew by now both that he was dreaming, and also that he'd had this same dream a hundred times before. At the end of it he'd always tried to bring the gold back into real life by going to sleep in the dream with the hope that he would wake up with it still in his pocket. Much to his disappointment it had never happened.

But this time it worked! He awoke and he still had it! He felt immensely excited! He leaped out of bed to go and tell his mother.

Suddenly his bedroom became a huge cave filled almost entirely with fire. Bizarre, misshapen creatures out of *Star Wars* populated it. They were ten feet tall and could walk through the fire without being hurt by it.

They poked and prodded him constantly with long, ugly arms, demanding that he answer riddle type questions about which he knew absolutely nothing. They seemed to be punishing him for taking the twenty gold pieces from the ground, as if by wanting to keep them he was doing something "against the will of the gods."

They had been grilling him for hours. He was exhausted. But still they threw another riddle at him.

"What's cold and black and has no beginning?"

As he had with previous riddles, he tried to find an answer.

"The Devil?" he shouted hopefully.

More abuse followed this wrong answer. He was beaten, burnt, and thrown around, though the only sensation of pain was psychic not physical. About to be smashed against a brick furnace, he anticipated great pain, which made his body creep with expectant torture, but when his body hit he didn't feel anything.

"Me?" he shouted desperately, venturing another answer.

More abuse followed.

Peter finally realized the impossibility of what was expected of him. Futility filled him. He tried to run away but he couldn't. He was frozen in place. It was as if he was bound hand and foot by invisible restraints.

He started to scream in terror, but managed to stop himself before the monsters noticed.

He started to faint. For a moment he resisted, then realized that fainting might be a way of escaping.

The monsters noticed his eyes closing and moved menacingly toward him. Peter urgently surrendered to fainting, dropping to the floor, and escaped.

Moments later a middle-aged Peter awoke in the dim light of a cloudy day sweating profusely from the huge effort of his dream. He sat up in bed vividly remembering everything.

I thought it was real.

He remembered that as a boy he used to escape monsters in his dreams by going to sleep. Only sometimes when he awoke, he found himself inside yet another scary dream. Often there were several layers of reality and unreality through which he'd have to pass by sleeping himself into safety, such that when he finally awoke the real and the unreal were all mixed up together.

The loss of boundaries defining reality followed him into his morning ablutions. While shaving, his father's death-face—he'd spent an hour looking at his father's face at the funeral parlor before the cremation—appeared in the mirror superimposed upon his own!

"Get out of my head!" he shouted, backing away.

The loosening of sanity that had occupied his recent days, and now permitted this quasi-hallucinatory experience to imitate the extreme unsafety of his boyhood, had happened at the prospect of Troubadour. The horrific feelings of that helplessly small, terrifying time, were literally coming out of the woodwork of his character, filling his conscious experience with a tornado of flickering moments of the hell that had been a major part of his childhood, but then was forgotten as he became busy with a grown-up's responsibilities.

When these powerful emotional memories arrived at the surface of consciousness, they found a mind *un*willing to be moved by their message, inured as it was to habits of obfuscation and denial painfully learned by a boy constantly overwhelmed by emotional turmoil.

He pretended, instead of feeling to spin gold out of a dream, made monsters out of fear, and turned how tall you are into a matter of will, where little boys make-believe they're already grown-up and can handle anything. In this psychic place, pretending becomes more real than experiencing, as emotion and its unconscious roots take over the creation of meaning, making what's terrifying now true forever and ever, amen.

When pretense becomes the largest player in a person's psyche, professionals call it psychosis. Priests call it vision, prophecy, and religious awakening. True believers call it truth. Those doing it call it hell.

It was Sunday, the usual day for such religious ceremony.

He spent the rest of the morning doing practical things to keep his mind away from thinking or seeing any more apparitions. It was nearly noon before he remembered his date with Jennifer-and-family, realizing suddenly that he wasn't even sure if he was invited.

He hurried to his answering machine and listened to Jennifer's recorded reply.

"Since you ask, I'm not okay," she began. "And I'm worried about seeing you again. I'm afraid of what might happen. You did such a terrible thing. But you're still my father, so come, but for brunch, not dinner. We have plans for dinner. When you come I'll have to see how I feel about you're being here. I may have to ask you to leave. Make it at 11:30."

He checked the clock. It was 11:20 a.m.

"Christ, I better get out of here."

A surprising whiff of hopefulness passed through him as thoughts of seeing John and Penelope lightened his heart on the way to Jennifer's.

"Hi, gramps," Penelope said. "Come on in and tell me why you kicked mom out of your house."

Peter walked in without responding, looking for Jennifer.

Penelope's grandfather was unlike either of her parents. He said and sometimes did unusual things. There was something adolescent about his unorthodox and provocative ways, to which she felt instant kinship. He gave her perspective about her mother, whom Penelope privately worried about more and more as she achieved her own independence, something she feared would eventually hurt Jennifer.

Peter located Jennifer in the kitchen.

"It wasn't exactly like that, Penelope," Peter replied, finally turning to face her. "But where's my hug?"

The two embraced like old friends.

Jennifer's husband waited patiently to greet Peter. He was a kind, thoughtful man very unlike most of the men Peter had known in his life. This was why Peter loved being around him to soak up his different, gentler approach to life.

"Hi, John," Peter said taking John's hand in greeting. "It's really good to see you again."

"And you too," John replied with sincerity, though he was always a little uncomfortable with Peter's ways.

Peter glanced into the kitchen wondering how best to make connection to his daughter.

"Why did you kick mama out of your house?" Penelope asked again.

Preoccupied with her mother, Peter was suddenly annoyed at the same open candor that he normally loved from Penelope. She was forcing a moment that needed caution.

"Let the two of them work it out before they have to explain it to us, honey," John said. "Don't be in such a hurry."

Peter was grateful to John for taking over his daughter's question in just the right way.

"I don't think there's anything to worry about on Jennifer's account, Peter," John said. "She felt much better when you called asking to come over for a meal."

"I'm very glad to hear that," Peter replied.

Penelope dropped bored onto the couch and picked up a magazine to read. She was always disappointed when her father muted her efforts to stir up some action. If her grandfather agreed with him that was the end of it.

Men!

Penelope had a very close relationship with her mother, motivated largely by Jennifer's dedicated devotion to her since she was born. Her mother was always there, reassuring her, suggesting solutions to problems, things she might want to do, anticipating, trying to fulfill her every need.

But now in adolescence Penelope needed to emancipate herself from that closeness in a way that did not seriously threaten her mother. Her father was a very solid, good man, the real source of Penelope's deepest sense of stability, but he offered very little demonstration of independence from Jennifer. He always seemed so very agreeable, which muted the normal conflicts of difference, implying they were to be avoided.

Peter was her best source of information about independence. But her mother had always discouraged much separate contact between her daughter and her father, always chaperoning them as she grew up. Both Peter and Penelope had to wait for her adolescence to find out who they were to each other.

"Sorry I'm not my usual self, Penny," Peter said. "I've got things on my mind."

Penelope loved it that her grandfather always addressed her as an equal. Glad to be happy about something again, she jumped up from the couch to give him another hug.

"You're the best, Gramps, but I hope you will answer my question before you leave."

"Of course I will," he replied.

Peter was always moved by Penelope's exuberance. He picking her up and swiveled her around in his arms, humming his affection for her.

As he came full circle he suddenly saw Jennifer standing in the kitchen doorway, obviously having listened and observed them for several moments. He instantly put Penelope down.

"Hi, daughter. Good of you to have me over."

"Hello, father. Penelope, sweetheart, would you please help me serve the brunch," Jennifer said affectionately, but with a slight strain in her voice.

Penelope dutifully released Peter and moved toward the kitchen.

Jennifer stepped into the living room and addressed Peter almost in a whisper. She didn't want her daughter to hear.

"You don't need to pretend that you love me, dad," she said in a whisper. "Just be yourself."

"But I do love you," he retorted.

"You don't ever show it," she whispered angrily. "But enough of this. Let's have a nice brunch. Penelope and I have worked hard to prepare it."

"Of course," Peter replied. "And I appreciate your work on my behalf."

But Jennifer had already turned away into the kitchen.

Peter followed her, then stopped in the doorway because the two women were already in conversation.

"Sweetheart," Jennifer said sweetly. "Finish telling me about what happened with Michael."

"It wasn't really anything, mom. It was just that he seemed so desperately in need of me. I've never had anybody express that before. I don't know what to think about it."

"But how did it make you feel, Sweetie?"

"It made me feel creepy," Penelope shot back.

"You don't have to be afraid of someone needing you," Jennifer replied. "It simply means that Michael is very attached to you. You want that kind of thing to happen. If good young men like Michael didn't want so much to love you, then you would be missing something terribly important in life. Be patient and thoughtful of his strong need for you. You don't have to return the favor unless you really want to, but be good to him."

The truth was that Penelope was far more comfortable than her mother with Michael's creepiness. And she already partly liked Michael's need for her. She told her mother only the seamy side of her emotion because that's the part she was confused by.

"Loving hasn't been so easy for you," Penelope said bluntly to counter the discomfort of her mother's excessive care.

Jennifer was very hurt, but sloughed it off as adolescent clumsiness. She paid the price though, which was to feel estranged from the unconditional bond she normally adored feeling with her daughter.

She was suddenly aware of Peter's presence behind her. She swung about as if to face a dangerous adversary!

"Stop eavesdropping!"

She had been mostly startled by his presence. Her anger covered up feelings, specifically surprise and fear that she didn't want to share.

"Mom!" Penelope exclaimed, startled at the extremeness of her mother's reaction.

"Sorry, Jennifer," Peter interjected, backing away from the kitchen door. "I didn't mean to pry. I was just coming out to smell the good odors in your kitchen."

"But you shouldn't sneak up on people like that," Jennifer retorted in a much subdued tone. "Could you please wait in the living room with John?" she added, her tone softening even more. "I would really appreciate it, dad. I'm still shaking from the other day, so please be nice to me."

"There's nothing I would rather do more," he said sincerely, returning to the living room.

"I think that sums everything up very well," John said, "and very well said, if you ask me. So shall we get ready for dinner and meet again at the table? I for one need to wash up."

John's pontifical remarks amused Peter, reminding him of the priest's final prayer of absolution at the end of the worship service he'd attended with his father for years as a boy, dismissing the congregation.

Everyone readily conformed to John's pronouncement. Peter followed John into the bathroom, while Penelope started to set the table, and Jennifer returned to the stove.

John's assertions of agreeable congeniality were sometimes very helpful. But Peter was also reminded that John's mediating ways had another side that sometimes frustrated him. In order always to be as nice as he was, John had removed certain parts of emotional honesty from his vocabulary. Just as a cynic filters everything through his suspicious paranoia, so also did John filter experience through the sifter of permanent congeniality, preventing, if he could, anything emotionally sharp from happening. It's why he'd quieted his daughter's question. It was also the mission he always undertook to calm his wife's sometimes frantic and volatile emotional experience.

Later, after thirty minutes of dinner and small talk about Penelope's school, John's difficult boss, and the weather, Penelope's curiosity couldn't wait any longer.

"Hey, you guys," she insisted. "When are we going to talk about the unmentionable?"

"Penny, why do you have to be so enigmatic sometimes?" Jennifer queried rhetorically.

"I thought I was being pretty obvious," Penelope retorted. "I just wanted to know why Gramps kicked you out of his house."

"Excuse me, pretty daughter," Jennifer interjected before anyone else could speak. "But that's precisely the topic I need distance from, at least for a while. So would you please let your dear old mom have her way just for this once?"

"I think that's a reasonable request," John intervened. "I'm sure we have far more edifying things . . ."

"Why do we always have to walk on egg shells around the most interesting things that are happening?" Penelope complained, interrupting her father.

"Actually I have something else that I very much wanted to talk about," Peter interjected, wanting himself to avoid the topic of kicking Jennifer out of his home.

"Well, if you're going to agree with them," Penelope exclaimed to her grandfather, "then I give up!" she exclaimed with annoyance.

"That's sweet of you to give your mother and I first turn right now," Peter replied. "I know you don't like doing that very much, so I appreciate it all the more."

"Can we get to whatever it is you're going to say," Jennifer insisted, wanting to interrupt this intimate exchange between Peter and Penelope.

"I've received an invitation to visit a distant place," Peter explained.

"Where to?" Penelope asked.

"Sweetheart, can you help me with the dishes tonight?" Jennifer interjected. "I don't ask you to do this very often, but I'm feeling very tired tonight. I know you have homework, but I don't think it will take very long with the two of us working together," she added plaintively.

"Okay, mom, but in a few minutes," rolled easily off Penelope's tongue. "So where are you going, Gramps?"

"I think your mother doesn't really want me to talk about this," Peter replied. "And I think perhaps we should respect her wishes," he added in a sincere but sadly resigning tone.

Like his daughter, Peter was capable of making sacrifices that he couldn't afford.

"Now wait a minute," Penelope insisted. "I should have at least one of my questions answered!"

"There is one part of it I must tell you all about, just so we keep our signals straight," Peter said. "I may be away for three weeks, and during that time I will be unable to contact you, or you me. I just wanted you to know of that possibility."

"So where are you going, Gramps?" Penelope insisted, her patience growing thinner.

"Why are you doing this right now?" Jennifer asked her father. "Your timing's not very good, what with ordering me to 'get the fuck out of your house,' and now this sudden disappearance. What's going on, dad?"

"The conjunction in time of these two events is purely accidental," Peter replied. "I'm sorry about the bad timing, but the invitation is for now."

Which of course wasn't entirely true. The invitation was current, but the timing was entirely up to him.

Peter called this a "white lie," where you tell the truth, but with some minor adjustments, keeping what you say much closer to the truth than it is to becoming a lie. Only pride is sometimes hurt by such a white lie, but never safety, though we often confuse the two.

"Where are you going?" Jennifer asked anxiously.

"I've been invited to visit another planet."

The air was suddenly filled with a huge electric shock. Even Penelope was momentarily struck dumb, giving her mother first dibs on response.

"John," Jennifer remarked aside to her husband. "Do you need any more evidence than that? He's going off the deep end. Don't you think it's time for me to call the county hospital and request a conservator-ship investigation, because he refuses to see a therapist?"

"I quite agree with you, daughter," Peter interjected, trying to keep control of how this was discussed. "It does sound preposterous, and I think about it that way too. But in another sense it doesn't matter whether it's real or not. The invitation tickles my curiosity and sense of adventure. So I'm taking the ride to see where it goes."

"What would you think if one of your patients said to you, 'It doesn't matter whether it's real or not, but I'm going to commit suicide'?" Jennifer exclaimed. "Wouldn't that sound a little crazy to you?"

"Jesus, Gramps!" Penelope interjected. "Are you saying that you actually believe you're going to be picked up by little green men and taken to another planet?"

"You can make fun of it, Penny, if you want," Peter replied, very disappointed in his granddaughter's reply.

He had hoped she might be the only one to consider with him the possibility that what was happening could be real.

"Of course not," Peter replied. "I don't entirely believe in it myself, but for the present moment it amuses me to go along for the ride."

"I think you've missed Penelope's point, dad," Jennifer insisted, leaping on this opportunity to regain a close linkage with her daughter. "She was asking whether you were in your right mind. Why do you pretend you didn't hear her?"

"What makes you think I'm out of my mind?" Peter asked Penelope.

"Well, how are you going to get there if they're not coming to fetch you?" Penelope asked, ignoring both her mother's and Peter's question.

"Actually, that's a very interesting part of what's happening. They claim that time is . . ."

"I don't want to discuss this as if it's real," Jennifer interrupted. "I will not be a party to encouraging your crazy ideas."

For Peter that was the last straw.

"Oh, for Christ's sake, Jennifer, cut it out. I'm not crazy, this is a pretty implausible thing that's happening, and I'm getting . . ."

He suddenly found himself standing, which interrupted what he was saying.

"Just eating and running?" Jennifer queried sarcastically.

He sat back down again.

"No, it just happened."

"Well, I think you had the right idea before," she shot back at him. "I want you to leave."

"Mother, what are you doing?" Penelope challenged.

That was Jennifer's last straw. She stood.

"Wait a minute, I'm not ready for him to go," Penelope interjected.

"Come on in my room, Gramps, so you can tell me about it."

"I think perhaps your mother's right, honey," Peter said sadly. "I'll tell you another time."

He stood.

"Thank you for brunch, Jennifer. I hope that you'll be okay when I'm gone."

"The real question is whether you'll be okay," Jennifer retorted, glad that he was going.

On his way home Peter sunk into a deep depression. All of his efforts to share this critical decision with someone had, except for a little assistance from Samantha, utterly failed to bear fruit. As he had expected would happen, he was left to deal with it alone.

The darkness and cold of the evening prompted this morning's dream to pop into his mind. Specifically what caught his attention was the riddle he had failed to solve in the dream, "what's black, cold, and has no beginning?"

Suddenly the answer shouted back at him.

"My god, it's my father! He had jet-black hair, had a very cold heart, and had no beginning in my life because he was so infrequently there until I was four. I thought he was a stranger, and I'm not sure he ever became anything else in spite of my long-term belief that I loved him."

He went to bed that night feeling his father was still dominating his life from his grave.

Deciding Alone

Peter awoke from a dream that he was Atlas holding up the world. It was extraordinarily heavy, weighing he thought a hundred thousand times the weight of his body. He marveled that he was able to do what he seemed to be doing.

He suddenly noticed he was near exhaustion. His legs threatened to give way under him, his shoulders felt as if they couldn't bear another moment of such heavy burden. His backbone threatened to crack at any time.

The sound of a terrifying crack woke him. He leaped out of bed as if shot from a gun.

What am I to do?

It took him an hour of worry before he realized that the question was too big for him to solve. He floundered, sensing for the first time that there were things that couldn't be handled, that had to wait for an answer.

It took a second hour of waiting before another Troubadourian message gave life to the answer in him that wanted to be known.

To: Peter Icarus
From: The Troubadourians

To respond to your observations and your questions:

You are indeed taking great risk in coming here. We deeply appreciate that you are even willing to consider it. We sympathize with your expression of anxiety about the possibility of terrible outcomes, though we want to assure you that the likelihood of such tragedy is remote. We suspect that whatever "changes" happen to you may be constructive, not at all as you fear.

Curiously your predecessor chose not to ask the kind of questions you are asking. We were struck by his casualness in choosing to transport almost immediately without the slightest time for preparation, as if we'd only invited him out to dinner down the street. Perhaps you can translate this precipitous behavior for us should you decide to come.

Your spirit will not separate from your body. The information of both will reconstruct you from our resources. You won't be in two places at once. The biochemical materials of which your body is constructed will stay suspended in the primordial mass of Earth's ecosystem, while materials of the same design, age, and peculiarity will reconstruct your body and spirit here in Troubadour. The reverse of that will happen when you return.

We had hoped not to give you this information until after you arrived. Telling your predecessor the same information on the first day of his visit seemed to begin the process of undoing him. We feared having the same affect upon you.

However, your questions are so piercing, and so well constructed that we decided to give you more complete information before you come.

No, rapid aging was not what produced his paranoia. Actually we're not sure what did.

We derived our speculations about loss of longevity from the mathematical equations that mirror the structure of the process of transportation. We observed a possibility of slight loss of information, which we hypothesized, might produce that result.

As for how Time can be always, we don't know how else to explain it. Except to say that treating the universe in this way facilitates many remarkable understandings and outcomes. You might say it is one of the most far-reaching theoretical discoveries of our additional two hundred years, meaning it has produced more new spiritual and technological possibilities than any other vision.

However, to satisfy some of your curiosity, we share a few speculations about why Time is a Constant. Since at any moment in time anything is possible, then perhaps everything is both potential as well as happening, meaning both elements normally perceived to be in sequence actually occur simultaneously, though perhaps in different locations.

It is most probable that our understanding of reality will always be limited and imperfect. But, if one wished to speculate, "always is everywhere" may simply be a derivative of "eternity is now."

But of course such musings are still hypothetical.

No, we've never physically visited your planet.

Again we hope these answers are satisfactory.

Cordially,
The Troubadourians

These people are really nice and so interesting, Peter thought. God I hope they're not a fraud. I'm already sucked in too far for this thing to be a fraud . . . without suffering disastrous results.

The admission that, in spite of his fears he still believed in the invitation, seemed to change everything. Until now he'd protected his fear of becoming the fool by the disbelief that had surrounded Troubadour's invitation. But in order to decide to go, he had to believe in it.

But to believe in it deprived him of cynicism's doubting ways, removing him from the intellectual fortress inside of which he'd always been able to feel relatively immune from other people hurting him. He began feeling extremely vulnerable. It got much worse when he realized that he might have to continue feeling this way for the entire three weeks of his visit.

"I'm going to be the lowest of the low there, one of the most backward, primitive people there!"

He knew instantly that could be unbearable. To be seen in such an inferior light would pour salt into the principle wound of his life, that he was generally regarded as just a notch above mediocre. He expected so much more of himself.

Fear firmly gripped his heart. He suddenly felt like he was standing in a war zone with explosions ready to begin at any moment. His powerful desire to go to Troubadour had slipped him into permanent overload, landing him in a surfeit of vulnerability out of which, he suddenly realized, he would find no escape for an indefinite time. He was committed to a dangerous course. His life had been turned over to a dream, drowning many of his normal defenses against anxiety under torrents of frightening, impulsive emotion.

He lunged into action, racing to the computer to type his acceptance message before trepidation changed his mind.

"There's no way I'm not going! I've got to face whatever it is that's ahead, come hell or high water! It's got to be live or die! There's no point in being paralyzed about it, because I can't just stay where I am! Anything's better!"

To: The Troubadourians
From: Peter Icarus

The vision that your invitation has conjured in my imagination compels me to accept your invitation, though I most fundamentally expect that, at the appointed time a salesperson will appear at my door claiming "off-worldly" benefits to their Earthly products. In other words, I don't entirely believe in you.

Be that as it may, what may I now expect?

Peter Icarus,
A very foolish man

He had accepted their invitation the only way he could afford to, by letting suspicion announce his consent. He was hedging his bets by both doing and undoing the same thing.

Their reply was almost instantaneous.

To: Peter Icarus
From: The Troubadourians

We are delighted and very excited! At precisely 5:00 p.m. today please stand in the center of your living room, holding whatever you intend to bring. And, before you know it you'll be here.

Bon Voyage!
And Welcome,
The Troubadourians

It was done. His heart breathed as much of a sigh of relief as he could find in a landscape of chaos.

What have I done? Am I not really putting my faith in delusional possibilities like Jennifer believes? Where's the proof that I'm not a desolate old man unable to accept his limitations, grasping at straws? Am I so desperate that I'm just throwing my life away?

Departure

His imminent departure and the need for preparation interrupted fear's wild speculations. He started calling all of his patients to prepare them for his absence. He gave them a backup person should they need one, as well as an invitation to react emotionally to the news. Ruth's response was the most severe.

"You've got no right to dump me like this!" she shouted over the phone. "It's very obvious now that you've been putting me on all this time pretending that you really cared! When all along you were just waiting for something better so you could leave me again!"

"It's true, Ruth, that you have been abandoned and discarded. It's what your mother did to you over and over again."

"But you're doing it this time!" she insisted "What am I going to do all that time when you're not here?"

"Dr. Gladstone will be available to you. He prescribes your meds so you already know him."

"He doesn't know anything about me. You're taking all that knowledge with you!"

Without intending to do so Peter lost patience with her, not just because she was difficult, because he was already somewhere else. His dismissal of her angry anxiety wasn't actively done; it was passively implied. He responded as if he were thinking out loud to himself.

"Actually I'm being left behind myself even though I'm the one going somewhere else. It's very, very strange."

Instantly both he and Ruth realized that he had spoken far more to himself than to her.

"Why, you're not even talking to me anymore?" Ruth shouted with intense indignation.

She slammed the receiver down. Peter called back but she wouldn't answer. So he left an encouraging message on her machine, acknowledging his distraction and apologizing for it.

His guilt on her behalf lingered for a while, but was eventually overpowered by his preparations that distracted him.

He couldn't make up his mind what to take with him. Feeling more lost than anything else, and depersonalized as if all this wasn't really happening to him, he floundered for two hours doing things that normally would have taken him only twenty minutes to accomplish. Most of this time was spent worrying. He'd find himself half-done with a task, having forgotten what it was that he'd started to do.

What have I done? I'm headed for a place about which I know absolutely nothing. I'm acting on faith that those who appear in writing to be friendly and supportive will actually be that way when I get there. This is crazy! What do they really want with me anyway? Am I going to be some kind of guinea pig when I get there?

"Well, they said I could leave anytime within twenty-four hours."

Then why haven't they let the other guy do it? Why do they need me? Don't they know far more about psychology than I do?

"Why do they want to go backward in time, why not forward? And why do they want somebody from the past to live with them for a while? What's the point?"

A terrifying possibility jumped into mind, that he might be permanently caged for the rest of his life like Billy Pilgrim was on Trafalmidor in Vonegut's *Slaughterhouse Five*. The similarity of planetary names, Troubadour and Trafalmidor, was too scary.

Unsure whether he was done packing or not, he started to pace, and then sweat and hurried to the bathroom to wash off this evidence of his panic.

The tension of waiting eventually became unbearable. He did his yoga routine again. It calmed him a little and passed a little time. But when he finished he was once more thrown into a state of suspended animation where the time moved very, very slowly, while his feelings and thoughts moved very, very fast.

The last thirty minutes took forever to be over. Sometimes he paced, sometimes he sat down, and sometimes he just stood in the middle of the room staring blankly into space.

He looked at the clock for the zillionth time, 4:49 p.m. Thank god it was almost time.

He stood in the middle of the room for the last five minutes trying as much as possible to keep his eyes closed, to avoid shaking as his body became increasingly tense and cold.

A bell rang. He thought it was the front door.

The bottom suddenly dropped out from under him!

"Oh, fuck! I was right! The goddamned salesman has arrived to give me my prize for being such a complete sucker!"

But something was strange. The ring persisted, and in a very peculiar way.

Suddenly he realized that this bell didn't sound at all like his doorbell. It was both very faint and continuous, and seemed to come from inside his head.

He gasped his last Earth-breath, realizing something very peculiar was happening to him.

His whole body began to dissolve! Horrified he screamed!

Amnesia

He was floating aimlessly in black, empty space. Consciousness was infrequent, sketchy, haphazard, and largely unformed. His body was entirely amorphous and insubstantial. Perceptions would begin to occur, but the moment they tried to focus toward a potential feeling or thought, they would dissolve, leaving emptiness once more to prevail.

An eternity passed before a complete, rational frame broke free of the inertia that held him, producing the thought that he'd been in a serious accident and in a coma for days, from which he was awakening.

But he couldn't move anything. If he had a body it wasn't working. Which convinced him he'd had major surgery and was waking from a powerful anesthetic, still trapped in the complete helplessness of its near-death grip.

Maybe I'm already dead and reviewing the corpse.

He wondered why the thought didn't frighten him. He decided that perhaps death was scary only before it happened.

He noticed that he seemed like a ghost of himself. He still thought his thoughts, remembered his memories, but there wasn't any center to him, no strong will-to-be at the core.

Death must mean the spirit was trapped inside his dead body, talking to himself in complete blindness, silence, and aloneness.

Something smelled sweet.

They sent flowers to my funeral.

So this is how the afterlife begins, a floating rudderless nothingness, where I'm part of a big blob that never goes anywhere or does anything; how utterly boring.

He smelled the sweetness again.

Wait a minute. If I'm dead, then why am I smelling things?

The thought of being alive without a workable body terrified him.

I can't even see anything. If this emptiness is heaven, then I want no part of it.

The terror of those thoughts drove him back into a whirlwind of thoughtless drifting.

Eons later a far off, muffled sound faintly touched his right eardrum. He grabbed onto this new evidence of life, like a drowning man grasping at a passing branch to stop a precipitous rush down the currents of terror. It wasn't that he was feeling fear. He was fear. It was the only substantial part of him that still existed.

Once more the chaos of empty-blackness-drifting embraced him, dissolving the specificity that fear must feed upon in order to prosper.

It seemed forever before he ventured to notice that the smell and the sound were still there.

If this is death then it's a prick-tease to the senses.

For a moment this assertion of attitude gave substance to him, encouraging him to consider again that he might be alive, which sent terror-streaks down the center of his back.

Maybe this is hell's anteroom, and I'm conscious because knowing the pain is how the torture works.

A terrifying scream pierced his ears with a powerful shriek. It was so loud he thought his eardrums would burst. Hearing it made him feel very, very real. He didn't want to feel real. He laid down to sleep so he could wake up somewhere else.

Beautiful blackness returned.

After awhile he couldn't help noticing that the bed he was sleeping on was hard and uneven with stickers.

This is getting too real again.

The fear of reality forced him to peak out through his closed eyelashes. He saw weird forms hovering in a foggy medium. They were like faces strangely twisted ninety degrees off center, making them appear sideways. He caught the strong odor of plants. He could almost taste them. His tongue automatically flicked out to examine what he smelled. When his tongue returned to his mouth, he tasted dirt.

What's this?

Now he was alarmed. This was definitely far too real. He had a tongue, and there were real things out there that he tasted. He half opened his eyes, desperate to see what was going on, yet terrified of what he would look upon.

He was instantly aware that he was lying on the ground somewhere. With intense self-consciousness, he stole a glance upward to get some clue about what was around him. He caught sight of thousands of sideways, disembodied masks swaying back and forth staring at him.

He was instantly transported to the front of Macy's Department Store, lying on the sidewalk with a fully erect penis. He leaped up from the ground as fast as he could, almost falling down again in his hurry to be standing, and put his hands over his penis.

Touching himself turned everything into real. He was a body smelling, tasting, seeing, and touching things.

I'm alive!

Which terrified him.

Still predominantly insubstantial, still half drifting in empty blackness, possessing hardly any sense of who or what he was, he blurted out the first words that came to mind.

"It's not erect."

That simple observation reduced everything to the moment, taking away fear's "forever," without which it instantly deflated like a punctured balloon.

He breathed a huge sigh of relief, and opened his eyes wide.

He was instantly alarmed and frightened. Thousands of faces stared back at him with piercing eyes. The terrible scream he'd heard before returned in full volume. He plugged his ears to drown it out, glancing at the faces. Shocked, he realized they were imitating him, plugging their ears.

Am I the freak attraction in this theatre of the absurd?

He froze perfectly still, like a small, vulnerable animal trying to be entirely invisible.

Once more the moment became itself. The piercing sound had disappeared.

One face moved to his left. It separated from the crowd to become the body of a woman stepping out and walking toward him. She was very tall and extraordinarily beautiful. Her presence felt very impressive.

He suddenly realized he'd been the one who had screamed that terrible shriek. He'd been the one lying on the ground doing all those strange things while every one of those faces had stared back, watching him do it all. He felt deeply ashamed.

A beautiful woman always brought out the worst in him, and she was getting closer.

He wished she wasn't walking toward him so soon. He needed time to recover his composure. He hated it when something special happened when he was unprepared for it, usually lost in weakness and fear. He would have to try and hide all of that from her, which he did by avoiding her eyes.

His vision grabbed hold of whatever had no faces. It turned out to be the lush foliage of the surrounding terrain. He followed it up onto the humongous mountain that suddenly faced him, and then down into the valley very far below. The dimensions of nature were huge on this planet. He looked up ten thousand feet to the top of the peak, and down the same distance into the valley.

Peter suddenly realized there was no sign of any human structures.

Where do all these people come from?

His eyes once more grabbed the rich, natural green of the plants. There were many strange varieties of trees rampant with beautiful flowers in bloom, displaying a great variation of species and color, full of chirping bird-like sounds, smelling incredibly sweet with a great profusion of perfumes.

"Maybe this is paradise," Peter said out loud as she got nearer.

He was instantly embarrassed that he had spoken. His voice sounded too high-pitched, like a little boy.

An incredibly beautiful woman stopped four paces from him. She was perhaps an inch or two taller than he and extremely curvaceous. Her face was set in a look of gentle acceptance, graced with a warm smile.

"It's not exactly paradise," she said in almost perfect English, "though it's a wonderful place to live."

She spoke thoughtfully, slowly.

He felt mesmerized by her voice. It was filled with a rich mixture of the melodious tones of a mezzo, very strong in character, yet gently expressing an infinite patience. She seemed more singing than talking, as if from her mouth words became lullaby.

It was love at first sight. He was astonished by her, becoming instantly and completely devoted to her.

To deserve her spiritually, he kneeled in his heart to make an oath. He swore to be as good and strong a person as he could be, hoping to be able to override his many shortcomings. He would strive to be her true knight, serving the qualities of her beautiful nature.

He was wandering in dangerous territories. Devotion is a quality of worship. To believe too much in her god-ness would make him her supplicant. That would be humiliating by exposing his inferiority.

Though it seemed both impossible and absurd for him even to imagine, he desperately wanted to be her hero.

Strange Familiarity & Sparse Beginnings

This must be Troubadour,” Peter heard the nonheroic part of himself say.

She laughed.

“Yes,” she replied. “And you are most welcome on Troubadour.”

My god, I’m actually here. But why did she laugh?

Peter suddenly became aware for the first time since he arrived, that he had a body. He felt his thigh and pinched his behind to be sure it was real.

Suddenly self-conscious, he felt her presence as a criticism of his body. He was sure she must see how much older he was than she, that he must look tired, probably depressed and afraid, certainly more boy than the powerful man he wanted to be in her eyes. He stood there feeling very exposed, yet still determined to be near her as long as he could arrange. She was already his life-link to this new place.

“You speak my language perfectly,” he said hoping to distract both of them from these uncomfortable thoughts and appearances.

“Some of us have studied it very carefully,” she gently replied.

“Who are you, uh, I mean what’s your name?” he asked, feeling clumsy at the confusion of his words.

“Wind,” she replied.

“It is rather windy up here,” he answered, momentarily so preoccupied with his own embarrassment that he didn’t hear her clearly.

“Wind is also my name,” she gently clarified.

“Oh, I see. Of course, I’m sorry,” Peter said, embarrassed.

“It must feel very strange to suddenly be in such an unfamiliar place among others who are not only strange, but alien in unexpected ways," she remarked after observing his awkwardness.

Her perfect understanding made him feel good, but even more transparent to her, as if she could perceive right through his clumsiness to see the secret devotion that prompted it.

Instinctively he shielded himself with suspicion, but deflected it away from her whom he had already idealized. He directed it instead at the many faces that surrounded him.

The faces frightened him. There were too many of them.

Wind was concerned about his still florid fearfulness. She reached out her hand and touched his shoulder very briefly and lightly to steady him.

Her touch was magical. It effused through the tissues of his body an extraordinary calm.

Wind finally realized it was the crowd that made him most nervous.

"Many of us came here to this high bluff to welcome you," she said. "But perhaps that act was not well thought out, for it gives you too many people with whom suddenly to become accustomed. Forgive us for overwhelming you with so many."

Peter was both deeply grateful for her perceptive understanding of his feelings, but was also very ashamed of being unable to handle the situation far more gracefully.

Get a hold of yourself, he chided. You're starting to spill your vulnerable guts all over her.

To distract himself from his anxiety, he focused once more upon her body, scanning her full dimensions. Her elongated, very human-like face seemed quite narrow by Earthly standards, but on her this shape was simply gorgeous. Her ears were large, round, and folded close to her head. Her cheekbones were set high, framing the large, saucer-size eyes as big in proportion as a child's eyes to her face, which seemed to laugh whenever she talked. She was perhaps two inches taller than Peter's six feet, amply breasted but very slender at the waist, and with a bountiful lower body fecund with roundness that tapered to narrow, though well-muscled calves. She was obviously built for both beauty and great strength.

He wondered if all the women looked like her, and scanned the crowd. They were variations of the same generic shape.

He was suddenly aware that he'd been staring at everyone. Fearful that he may already have offended them, he grounded his eyes.

"Sorry, I was staring."

He was beginning to feel depersonalized, as if mind and body were drifting apart. He wondered if they could read his mind. They'd read his computer files.

Wind laughed again. It was a light, friendly laugh. But Peter found it alien.

"Please feel free to look as much as you want," Wind replied. "It seems only natural that you look at us carefully, so that you can familiarize yourself with what we look like and who we are."

Again her words made him feel better.

She's so incredibly nice, he thought. But is this really who she is, or is this some kind of diplomatic strategy to calm me down?

"Of course we've been staring right back at you," Wind added gently, "and in very large numbers as well."

Sincere or not she's absolutely wonderful, he thought.

"Our reasons for doing so are well intentioned," she continued. "You are a very welcome sight to all of us. We're 'taking you in' is, I believe, the Earthly saying which best describes it. We're taking you into our minds and hearts."

How graciously she talks to me.

He was becoming mesmerized by the extraordinary sensitivity of her understanding. Though he still mistrusted it, her ways were very emotionally seductive.

"And like you we also find the anatomical similarities and differences between our species very interesting," she added.

A frightening possibility sudden crossed his mind

"C . . . can you read minds?" he asked hesitantly.

"Of course not," she firmly replied. "And even if we could we wouldn't want to do it. We'd much rather that you read your own mind. It's more interesting that way, such that when you finally get around to sharing something with us, it will have both your needs and your best wisdom in it. It's just that I noticed your careful observing and drew my own inferences."

Her persistent and direct honesty finally won him over, prompting him to confide in her, to bare his heart so they could be friends.

"You are being so very gracious to me," he said gratefully. "It kind of surprises me because I made such a fool of myself when I first arrived, I mean all that screaming and lying on the ground. I hope I haven't done something . . ."

She raised her hand slightly to interrupt him.

"Please be at ease about that," she said. "Those things must have been entirely involuntary."

This idea surprised him. He always felt very awkward and guilty about his mistakes no matter how unintentional they were.

Is she for real?

Wind had become convinced that she needed to separate Peter from the crowd.

"I think perhaps it's best at this point to bring you to the living space we have arranged for you during your visit, so you can rest and have a chance to become acclimated to our world before talking any further."

Peter was instantly relieved.

She cocked her head slightly sideways to her left, and smiled encouragingly.

"Would you like that?"

"Okay," he replied, consciously more going along than choosing.

Though he wanted to go he was afraid to make a definitive choice before he knew more about this strange place and its remarkably familiar-looking people.

"We'll be walking in that direction," she explained, pointing off into the distance.

"Are all these people coming with us?" he asked apprehensively.

The moment after he said it, he felt utterly stupid asking such a silly question.

Again she laughed her sweet laugh. Which to him sounded more and more like laughing at him.

"Just you and I are coming," she replied softly.

She turned to her people and spoke in a very lyrical language. Its qualities momentarily distracted him from his discomfort. The timber of her voice felt like a lullaby. Her words were both very soothing to the ears and also replete with long, soft sounds.

When she finished everyone turned away and slowly wandered off in many different directions. She moved in the direction she had pointed.

No longer stared-at, Peter finally had a chance to look more carefully at these strangers. He was struck immediately that almost everyone walked alone. Almost no one was talking. He had expected something much different, that they'd be pairing off, perhaps bursting with things to say about him to each other.

How strange, he thought.

Suddenly aware that she was moving ahead of him, he turned quickly to follow.

When he'd caught up with her she turned to him.

"You are very observant," she said softly.

"What?" he exclaimed, as if he'd done something wrong. "Was I staring again?"

Again she laughed. It was beginning to get on his nerves.

"We admire careful observation," was her gentle reply as she moved on.

Why can't I trust what she says, he asked himself? Maybe she really is that way. But how can someone be so perfect all the time?

They walked down into the valley. Peter kept looking for buildings, but there were none.

"It must be a great distance we have to walk," he said, worried that it would be much farther than he was prepared for.

"Actually, your building is just ahead," she replied.

"It is? But where?"

"We like our living structures to be as unobtrusively cooperative with nature as all the other animals and plants have learned to be," she replied.

What a strange but eloquent thing to say, he thought.

Suddenly not twenty feet ahead he thought he saw the outline of a building.

"Is that the building?"

"Yes."

"Wow. It seems almost invisible until you get up very close. What a wonderful way to build human constructions," he added, wondering why he said that because he'd always admired architectural creations.

"I'm delighted that you like our ways so much," she replied.

"But where do all of your people live? This building looks no taller than three or four stories."

"Below ground it's two hundred stories deep."

Oh, my god, they live in burrows under the ground.

"But doesn't it get claustrophobic down there?"

She laughed the laugh that disturbed him.

"As you will see it's not."

She turned and continued on.

As they entered the building, he tried to ignore his misgivings. They passed through very tall metal doors that stood open. The entrance hall rose three stories high. Standing to the left was a metal sculpture two stories high of a Troubadourian woman, naked and very voluptuous, looking off in the distance with an expression of inspiration.

Momentarily Peter noticed that the woman had a very large spot of darker coloration, with a very large-nipple-d clitoris. Embarrassed, he looked away quickly, not wanting to embarrass Wind by staring at female nakedness.

To the right stood an equally tall sculpture of a male figure. Peter noticed that he was very thick at the waist, with very big lower back, gluteus, and thigh muscles that were significantly larger than even a very athletic Earthman.

I bet they don't have back problems. If bigger middle-body muscles are what evolution brings us in the next two hundred years, then we are fortunate indeed finally to fully adapt to standing upright.

"This is the entrance hallway," Wind said. "Beyond those doors," she added, pointing to two huge wooden doors to the right intricately carved with a great variety of animals and humans engaged in various activities, "is our public meeting place for the citizens of this city."

I've got to come back and see that more carefully.

She was moving on.

A small door opened ahead where an empty wall seemed to be. From out of an elevator stepped a man. He briefly smiled at Peter. When Peter looked back in surprise, his smile disappeared and he continued on his way.

It was through this open door that Wind now led him, though not before he'd caught sight of a wood sculpture of a huge, dark cat with yellow eyes leering down at him from the wall above the elevators as he entered. For the tiniest, frightening moment walking into the elevator felt like walking into its mouth.

She touched the wall, the door closed, and he could feel a very rapid but gradual acceleration as they descended.

Two hundred stories, Peter thought. That must mean the building goes down more than a mile into the ground.

The elevator stopped, slowing their motion smoothly though very rapidly. The door opened to a large hallway with ten-foot ceilings. It was perhaps eight feet wide. The light was soft but luminous. Its source was mysterious. It seemed simply to emanate within the available space.

The lighting and the hallway's spaciousness turned the possibility of underground claustrophobia into the feeling of being inside of a large cavern.

Wind moved to the right. As they proceeded down the hall they passed a single door every now and then, sometimes to the left, sometimes to the right. Wind stopped at a door with writing on it.

"Peter Icarus."

"Oh," he exclaimed, very surprised. "My name is on it."

"Yes. We wanted you both to feel welcome, and also be able to easily find your home."

She touched the wall to the right of the door and it slid into the wall.

"Hereafter this door will open only to your voice or palm print. Otherwise it's locked, which is I believe your Earthly custom."

"You don't lock your doors?" he queried.

"It would serve no function."

She walked into the apartment and motioned him to enter more deeply.

"I'm going to leave you here to acquaint yourself with your own apartment and how it works," Wind said. "You have a computer which to access requires only speaking. If you prefer a keyboard, that can be found on a control panel in each room. If the buttons are unclear, push the red button in the center and the computer will reply. It can answer almost all of your questions, so please experiment."

She looked around the apartment.

"You can decorate this unit in any way you choose."

Peter half-heard what she said, so absorbed as he was in the powerful attraction of her physical shape.

She turned as if to leave.

"Oh, are you leaving so soon," he said, feeling anxious at the prospect of her departure, though not at all sure why he felt it.

"My leaving makes you uncomfortable. So let me tell you how I can be reached. Simply say my name to the computer, and I will receive a message that you need me to contact you, which I'll do as soon as I'm able, probably right away at least for today."

Silence hung about as she waited for him to respond, as he waited to have a response.

"So I guess I've arrived," Peter said awkwardly as if he still couldn't quite believe it. "This is Troubadour."

"Yes, you've arrived."

"But you don't seem very familiar . . . uh, I mean strange to me. I really didn't expect that. In fact you look very much like us! I was prepared for a lot more strangeness in your appearance."

"I hope the surprise is a pleasant one," she said gently.

"Oh, yes," he exclaimed. "Definitely."

"I'm glad that our common traits bring you a measure of comfort. We hoped they would."

She turned to leave, and once more he stopped her.

"Uh, excuse me, uh, just one more thing. Uh, what exactly is it that we'll be doing?"

He vaguely realized that his question helped his fearfulness.

"The future is always hard to predict," she replied. "What's more we don't enjoy prognosticating very much. But in answer to your question, I can speculate that our time will be filled with talking, exploring, whatever helps you best to understand us. Basically we'll be doing anything which improves communication between us."

Peter knew that he was getting at something important. But he didn't like her answer. Which made him feel anxious because he wanted to maintain a positive relationship with the one connection he had to someone on this strange world.

"I . . . I . . . I . . . is . . . is there some kind of agenda or plan I could look over?"

"We function very spontaneously, responding to immediate evidence of need and necessity," she replied. "Preplanning is something we do sparingly. Not that there's anything wrong with it. It's just that we aren't that way."

He suddenly wanted her to leave, not because he wanted to be alone, but because he was frightened by the hugely dissonant emotions that were beginning to swirl about inside of him. She was making him feel very uncomfortable, which changed everything about her. She began to feel unfriendly.

That terrified him. It was like biting the only hand that could feed him.

"I . . . I . . . I guess I could be alone for just a little while," he said as casually as he could manage, both to cooperate with her and to hide his own growing misgivings.

Though aware of his inner turmoil, she took his words at face value, nodded affirmatively, and quietly left. The door automatically closed behind her.

A bolt of fear shot through him. He knew instantly it was a fear stronger than he could handle. He dove into the nearest refuge, which turned out to be objects.

Peter was a gadget freak, though he had found that only five or ten percent of the available gadgets were worth having. But at this crucial moment he needed distraction. Gadgets could easily provide that. He was sure this place must have a lot of them.

He set out to explore his living quarters, first returning to the entrance hall to begin at the beginning. A tweaked curiosity immediately brought him out of anxious disorientation into fascination-focus.

The Apartment

He stood in the entrance hall admiring the huge space his apartment occupied. Like the hallway it was built on a grand scale. The entrance hall measured approximately fifteen-by-fifteen feet with ten-foot ceilings. It opened out through a heavy wood frame ornately carved with sinewy snake-like creatures, into a living room that measured at least thirty-by-forty feet. Its ceilings looked more like fifteen feet high. Its walls were pure white.

The living room was divided into two parts, the much larger portion in which he was standing, and a smaller portion next to what was probably the kitchen.

The larger area was furnished with five stuffed chairs that created a semicircle facing what appeared to be a huge window draped with a shimmering curtain, probably six feet high by ten feet long.

"But how can they have a window way down here?"

He suddenly realized he'd forgotten to ask what floor he was on and felt an instant pang of anxiety, as if he were lost and helpless to do anything about it.

Instantly he thought about Wind, remembering her instructions about the red button by his front door, and felt much relieved that he didn't have to call her so soon. He walked over and pushed the red button.

"Yes," came back a male voice, which seemed very human, though it had a slight metallic twang.

"Uh, excuse me for bothering you?" Peter said, feeling instantly foolish addressing what was reputed to be a computer with such deference.

"Uh, what floor am I on?" he queried uncertainly.

"Sixty-two," was the reply.

"Oh. That also just happens to be my age," Peter remarked, expecting a reply.

There was none.

She said it could answer questions, but it's not very friendly.

The draped window easily distracted him. Anxious to see what was revealed, he looked for draw-chords at either side of the window before realizing the computer must control everything. To the right of the window he found a set of buttons like the ones near his front door. One of them was slightly illuminated displaying the symbol of wavy lines.

"Could be drapes," he said.

He pushed it.

He was instantly transported outdoors. There was no windowpane. The large opening seemed completely exposed to nature.

"My god, how do they do this?"

He glanced back at the living room chairs for a reality test.

"Jesus, this is so real. We seem to be outdoors. How can it be?"

He was looking out at a large forested area not too unlike where he lived on Earth, though this one was much thicker and the trees were larger and taller. He could vividly hear animal sounds, the rustling of the wind through the evergreens, and breath in the sweet, musty odor of evergreen needles.

"My god, it's just absolutely amazing!"

He tried touching the plant leaf closest to his window. His fingers ran into a soft, forgiving invisible surface.

"Oh."

The flat surface discolored to his touch. He released the pressure and that portion of the image refocused.

"It's a picture! But what an incredible one!"

No wonder they can live way down here. They've brought the outside down to them.

Curious to see what else the window could do, he examined the control panel more closely. The button with a tree on it was lit up. The one next to it had a seashell. He pushed that one.

Tiny droplets of ocean spray suddenly splashed his face as a wave crashed below him.

"Goddamn," he shouted, "but this thing is absolutely stunning."

He was sprayed again and backed away.

Relative to the wooded scene his window had been at ground level.

But with respect to the ocean, his apartment was situated perhaps forty feet above the sea.

Another wave crashed higher. In spite of standing farther from it, a fine mist of salt water moisturized his face.

"Wow," he shouted. "This is getting unreal. That's real salt water."

He sat down on one of the chairs to stare, feeling suddenly very rich and pampered, for a few moments reassured that he'd come to the right place where wonderful things were available to him. He was to be one of the first Earth humans to experience the miracles of this more advanced planet. It was a tiny moment of happiness in the sea of uncertainty into which he'd materialized.

"Who needs a real ocean when you've got this one?" he exclaimed with thin bravado.

The waves continued crashing but with a decreasing intensity, eventually without spray.

The tide is going out, he mused quietly to himself.

He drifted into a daydreaming place, sinking into the slow back and forth motions of a slackening tide. At first it was very soothing, which made him think of Wind and her beautiful voice. But as he noticed the undertow pulling things back out to sea, he began to feel increasingly uncomfortable.

At first he denied this, not wanting to leave this moment of respite. But putting off awareness of this developing storm of negative emotion made its conscious arrival more intensely frightening, giving it the character of a dam breaking to release a flood. As if he'd been lazily swimming in this receding tide, he was suddenly aware of being dragged into precipitous waters.

He bolted out of his chair as if by moving he could break himself free of this compelling vision, which made him feel as anxious as he'd been on the high bluff when he first became aware that he had arrived on this strange planet.

He had to restore comfort, because panic was tickling his heart. Home suddenly flashed through his mind. He really missed it.

"What have I done? I'm a billion miles away from home! Will I ever see it again?"

In an effort to stop this growing tide of panic, he chastised himself, as if criticism's slap in the face could shift his consciousness.

"You're acting like an hysterical woman," he accused himself, betraying his prejudice toward vulnerability, emotionality, and women.

It suddenly occurred to him that he had power over this frightening vision of the sea. He rushed to the control panel and pushed another button. Instantly a huge expanse of mountains loomed over him. These looked just like the mountains that surrounded the traumatic moments of his arrival. Its familiarity soothed him a little.

The sea is turbulent and changeable, he thought. But this is soothing and reassuring. He was feeling a little more like himself.

"Cut some slack for yourself, Icarus," he chided himself. "Everything's new here. It's no wonder you're so nervous. You should expect that."

He stood still for a moment soaking in the calming effect mountains had for him.

"At least I made it. That must be worth something."

To keep this positive trend on course, he continued his exploration of the apartment.

He first headed for what he thought must be the kitchen. But when he turned the corner to see its full dimensions, he found it completely empty. There were no cabinets, no cooking or eating utensils, no stove, no refrigerator, nothing but blank, off-white walls.

This total absence of nurturing possibilities precisely where they most belonged, in the kitchen, undid his momentary comfort. Fear grabbed his heart again, reminding him of Billy Pilgrim on Trafalmidor. He'd been dumped onto an alien world without any explanation or preparation, without even being instructed on how or what to eat.

"I asked her for an agenda, but she couldn't even give me a simple game plan for what to expect."

He was suddenly struck with a terrible foreboding, that he and the Troubadourians were intrinsically incompatible, that these misunderstandings and misadventures were going to be what he had to face every day.

"What they've done is dump me into this huge, empty cavern of an apartment without the slightest hint about how I'm supposed to survive on this weird planet, and with a kitchen that has absolutely nothing in it! Even food is a mystery!"

For a moment he felt withered, like he did when falling in his flying nightmares, as if bereft of energy.

"She said I could call," another voice reminded him.

He darted for the control panel by the front door to call her—and then suddenly stopped dead in his tracks.

"Why is this necessary? It's just a fucking strange kitchen. So go figure out how to use the goddamn thing. Don't interrupt the woman for something as simple as that."

He didn't want to be calling her every five minutes whenever something unnerved him.

He headed for the kitchen's control panel.

"Might as well try it at random."

He pushed one of the buttons. A blur slashed its way across the front of his shirt, missing him barely by one inch.

Peter leaped backward with a start.

A large dinner plate was held firmly by a white-gloved hand, its arm extending back into the wall.

"Jesus Christ, who's that?"

The arm was smooth-skinned and hairless. Like the window it looked very real.

"Uh, excuse me. Is someone there?"

Silence.

"Hello? Are you back there?" he asked.

Silence.

With a great deal of hesitation he poked the arm with his finger, half expecting its owner to shout back. In sympathy with that expectation, when he touched it he shouted on behalf of the arm.

"Ouch!"

If that's a mechanical arm I'll eat my hat. But that's what it must be.

Once more he poked it. This time the arm seemed implacable, more like the way an object was supposed to behave.

So go get your hat, you silly fool, and have it for breakfast.

But he couldn't stop thinking there was someone behind the wall attached to that hand.

He knocked on the wall.

"If someone's back there, will you please speak to me?"

Silence.

"It's not polite to ignore guests."

Silence.

What if this is the beginning of the torture I can expect, part of the scientific testing they're conducting on me? "Let's see what the primitive from Earth does without food?"

He pushed another button.

"Yes," replied a slightly metallic male voice.

"Are you the guy behind the wall?"

"No," voice replied.

"Then who sliced that arm right in front of me?"

"You did by pushing the plate button."

"Oh."

I get it. It must be part of the torture. First they scare the shit out of you, and then they pretend it's not really happening.

"Well, if you're not connected to that arm, then exactly who are you, sir?"

"I'm your computer," came the slightly metallic reply.

"Then please tell me how this kitchen works."

"Which part of it do you wish to know about?" the slightly metallic voice asked.

"Well for one thing, who's that arm that slashed across the front of me when I pushed the button?"

"That's a mechanical limb that will procure whatever you can imagine needing in a kitchen."

"Okay, but is that mechanical arm connected to a body?"

"There is no body behind the wall," the slightly metallic voice replied.

"Not even a robot?"

"The arm is the robot."

"Oh."

"Are you sure there's no body connected to that arm?" Peter asked to be sure.

Silence.

"Computer!" Peter insisted.

"There is none," the computer replied. "And for my own information, how many times do you want me to repeat it?"

The fucking asshole!

"Now wait a minute. If you're a computer then what's all the sarcasm about?"

"Sarcasm?"

"Stop pretending! You know, talking to me like I'm some kind of an idiot."

"As soon as I can accurately predict what it is that I'm doing to insult you, sir, I will cease doing it," the computer carefully replied.

The computer's sudden turnaround surprised Peter. For a moment he thought he was being attacked, but the computer had just given him his sword at the surrender ceremony.

"Sorry to be so angry," Peter said. "I'm sure it's not your fault. Hell, you just work for the joint."

Peter thought for a moment.

"Maybe then we have something in common, since I suspect I'm being used as well in some mysterious ways by these people."

There was no response.

What was I trying to find out?

"Oh, yeah. Uh, could you please help me with food?"

"What food do you require?" the voice asked.

Peter suddenly realized he hadn't decided what he wanted. For a moment he was embarrassed.

"D . . . do you have fresh fruit?"

"No other kind," came the slightly metallic reply.

"Um, how do I get some?"

"Sweet, sour, or in between, the voice queried?"

Peter giggled at the question, which sounded like it came from a 1950's airline advertisement, "coffee, tea, or milk?"

"Uh . . . sweet."

A white-gloved hand suddenly appeared holding a beautiful yellow fruit.

Though very hungry Peter hesitated reaching out to take it. He was still very nervous about touching the hand. Though outwardly he'd gone along with the computer, there were still large parts of him that believed there still might be someone hidden behind the wall.

His first attempt at touching the fruit failed. At the moment of making contact he recoiled, instantly withdrawing his hand for fear that the arm might grab him.

Feeling embarrassed, he forced himself to take it, but to do so with the least risk. This mixture of conflicting purposes resulted in separating the fruit from the robot-hand. But instead of being in Peter's hand, it was propelled several feet into the air, laterally moving in the direction of the living room.

Peter ran after it. After some initial juggling he managed to catch it before it fell to the floor.

He returned to the kitchen.

This is like wrestling for your dinner.

"A small plate?" he asked to the computer.

Suddenly a hand reached out behind him. Peter jumped two feet ahead before turning to see that it held a small plate.

"Usually you light up a button," he complained.

"I'm searching for the right way of communicating with you," the slightly metallic voice replied. "It appears that talking is that way."

"Why does everything on this planet have to appear to be alive?"

"I'm not alive," the computer replied.

"Well, you sure act like you are."

Maybe it's a Robin Williams futuristic kind of robot who thinks for itself and doesn't want to intrude, but still has their private jokes about you.

The sweet odor of the yellow fruit rescued his attention.

"Computer?" he queried. "I need a knife to cut the fruit."

"Do you wish the fruit skinned, the core removed, and then quartered, or none of the above?"

"Uh, all of the above," Peter replied.

A button started to flash. Peter stepped back a couple of paces, positioning his body as far away from the control panel as he could stretch, and pushed the button.

The arm came out three feet away. With a flourish the wrist turned the palm upward, and the hand opened. In it was a neatly skinned, yellow fruit cut into quarters.

Whoever belongs to that arm is definitely an actor even if he's not alive.

"After all that, this better be good," he said under his breath, retreating to a table with chairs at the living room end of the kitchen.

"Good" turned out to be a complete understatement. The fruit was incredible. The taste was overwhelmingly lavish, it's pulp dissolving in his mouth bursting with a million splashes of cool, sweet, nourishing moisture swirling around his tongue, tickling his taste buds with an extraordinary mixture of natural sugars.

"Oh, my god," he exclaimed. "This is like manna from paradise. It's stunning. Thank you, computer. Thank you."

There was no response.

He slowly devoured the other three quarter sections, moaning all the time in appreciation of its remarkable taste. And then he ate the uncut fruit.

"Do you have a list of available food?"

One was displayed which divided food into several groups. It took him awhile to decipher three of them as "vegetable," "fruit," and "protein." Another might have meant "root," he figured, but he couldn't understand the other categories.

He found a flowering vegetable plant that he liked, along with a portion of protein in the form of a strange smelling cheese-like substance, the odor of which he couldn't stand, but when he put some in his mouth it tasted terrific.

He found that water was available simply by touching the top of the armrest of any chair, and a fresh glass of what tasted like spring water appeared from inside the armrest neatly presented by the proverbial hand.

Exhaustion finally took over. He moved through the living room in a direction opposite to the kitchen, and found a short hallway off of which were two rooms, each probably twenty-by- thirty feet. He turned into the left one and moved toward a huge bed far to the left and deep into the room.

There was one blanket on it, an incredibly thick yet lightweight material, covered itself by a silken fabric, which, when he got under it instantly produced and retained a comfortable temperature.

Though exhausted Peter could sense the waves of angst lurking just underneath the surface of his experience pointing at strangeness as the overpowering element. But he was too worn out. No sooner had he covered himself to try out the blanket that he fell deeply into a sleep that lasted the whole night.

Anticipation

He was six years old standing next to his mother, who stood at the kitchen sink. He looked up into her face hoping for some sign that she understood.

"Mommy," he said more insistently, still pleading with her.

She looked down at him from her cooking with anger on her face.

"Get out of the way!" she shouted. "You're beginning to act more and more like your father every day."

Peter jumped as if she had hit him.

And then in an angry, frustrated voice she added, "And I don't need any more of that right now! So stop messing around down there! Can't you see I'm getting dinner?" she shouted with intense resentment.

Peter instantly moved away from her thigh and shuddered.

He waited patiently for several moments before slowly easing himself back to within an inch of his mother, all the while looking down at the floor in shame.

"I'm sorry, mommy," he begged.

There was no reply. He slowly looked up at her.

"Mommy?" he asked gently.

Cooking had distracted her from irritation. So when she finally heard him she thought of him in the old loving way. From an earlier, happier time in their experience together, she now spoke with softness in her voice.

"Yes, precious."

He reached up his hand and put his palm on her chest right between her large breasts. He'd always been able to soften her with this gesture.

"I love you, mommy," he said sweetly.

She looked down at him lovingly.

"You're such a sweet boy. I know you do. And I love you too." She went back to her cooking.

After looking carefully at her again, Peter snuggled up against her thigh once again. At first she didn't notice him there. But when she turned to the left to pick up something she bumped into his head with her elbow. It surprised and irritated her.

"Damn!" she shouted. "I told you about that! You're always in the way!"

He jumped again.

This time she noticed his distress, felt intensely guilty, resented it, scowled, raised her hand and shouted.

"Get out of here this instant!"

In his fear it was the paring knife in her hand that Peter noticed the most. He screamed.

"Stop that screaming!" she shouted, raising her hands in protest.

It was the raised hand with the paring knife that did it. He was sure it was going to come down upon him! He ran from the kitchen in terror!

More out of regret than anger his mother took several paces toward his fleeing body.

Peter looked back at just that moment seeing only her hand still raised with the knife. He was sure she was running after him. He bolted through the swinging kitchen door into the living room, scurried into a corner behind the couch next to the large front window, and crouched down to be unseen.

For the longest time he waited with baited breath for her angry arrival. But she never came. After several minutes of silence, broken only by an occasional car passing in front of their house. He peered out from behind the couch and verified that he was alone. He was. She had remained in the kitchen.

Slowly he came out from behind the furniture and stood in the middle of the darkening living room. It was dusk. Shadows flashed strange foreboding shapes on the walls of the living room. A car passed out front with its lights on, sending fast-moving menacing figures scurrying across the room. One of them had what looked like a raised arm with something in it.

Peter cringed until it was gone.

He stared at the kitchen door for a long time. He missed her anger. Though frightened of it, he became dreadful in the emptiness of his aloneness. He felt very alone, and shivered again. It was cold standing in the emptiness. He wished another car would come by so he could watch the scary shadows.

A middle-aged Peter awoke suddenly, still filled with the anxious loneliness of the dream. For an instant he thought he was in his bedroom as a boy. He loved his bed, but only when he was asleep. Awaken in bed was lonely.

But when he opened his eyes he knew he was middle-aged and living in his San Francisco flat.

He tried to escape the loneliness he suddenly felt by drifting back into sleep. But its mood held a firm grip upon him. He realized with great disappointment that this day would begin in a depressed mood. He hated when that happened.

The dawning of a day was his favorite time. Everything was fresh with new possibility. This hopeful mood sometimes lasted until the late morning before finally giving way to his most normal experience of life, an empty sadness that hovered around everywhere like a dark cloud.

He'd been staring at the ceiling for several minutes, not seeing it, lost in thought, when he suddenly noticed it was much higher than usual.

He sat up straight in bed.

Shit, I'm on Troubadour. I forgot I was here.

The sudden awareness of being in a strange place so far away from home made him shiver. This place was supposed to make me feel better not worse. I thought I was going to leave that depressed shit behind on Earth, but the goddamned thing followed me up here.

He immediately set off to explore the concrete, tangible things that had so successfully distracted him the night before. He was still wearing his Earth clothes. He'd gone to bed in them.

The first thing he noticed was that there was no furniture in his bedroom except the bed. Like the kitchen, the walls showed no sign of having drawers or doors.

"Such an empty place they put me in. What am I supposed to do with it?"

He wandered into what he thought must be a bathroom looking for the toilet. But there wasn't one. The room was almost entirely bare, with one exception, a white chair.

"Of all the things to put in a bathroom as the only visible object, a chair seems the most ludicrous," he said out loud for company.

For lack of anything better to do he sat down on it to consider. Instantly a large portion of the seat disappeared beneath him at the chair's center.

Startled, he stood.

"So this is the damned toilet!" he exclaimed, annoyed that he'd been frightened. He sat down slowly again and used the chair as it was intended.

The toilet-seat was made of a soft material that maintained the same temperature as his body. When he stood all traces of body waste instantly disappeared, making only a barely audible whooshing sound. At no time were there discernable odors.

The bathroom was huge, though the ceiling was smaller, only ten feet tall. As he approached its other end, suddenly to his right a section of the wall changed into a large full-length mirror, but only when he stood right in front of it. Otherwise it disappeared, assuming the same off-white color of the surrounding walls.

Standing in front of the mirror he moved slightly to the left and the lower wall moved toward him. It was a vanity stand holding a large basin with an ornate spigot arching from its middle. When his hand reached within two inches of the faucet, a full but gentle flow of warm water washed over it. When he removed his hand the water instantly turned off.

As he turned to the left to proceed on his bathroom inspection, warm air blew down from the ceiling. He held his hands in the center of its flow and felt a soothing, tingling sensation. When he took his hand away he found it comfortably dry.

"This is more like it. But where's the shower?"

He wandered toward the back corner of the bathroom to see what else might pop out. Suddenly a fine warm mist surrounded him.

"Damn," he shouted, backing away, his Earth clothes already soaked. "Shit, what am I going to wear now?"

Instantly he remembered his expectation that they would provide something to wear.

He went into his bedroom and took off his wet clothes. He found the control panel and pushed one of the buttons. A drawer filled with slipper-like apparel appeared. He tried on a pair of them and found them to be made of a material that hovered around the shape of his foot in a perfect fit, but felt almost too large because of how gently it grasped him.

He took a few paces around the room. The shoes were extraordinarily comfortable. To his surprise they supported his arch exactly where it was needed.

Now how in the hell did they measure my foot size before I got here? Oops. Maybe they did it last night.

He pushed another button. Part of the wall slid sideways revealing a closet with a long row of hanging garments in various patterns and colors. Most were one-piece, full-body suits. When he tried one of them on it both fit-to-body, and yet seemed to flatter his figure at the same time.

"So this is what I'm supposed to wear. It's kind of flashy, though the material feels incredibly soft and interesting. It sort of makes me look a bit naked as if I was wearing a tight-fitting bathing suit all over my body. These people must all be in great shape around here to wear these."

He finished disrobing and headed for the shower, this time gladly letting its misty warmness wash over his whole body. He stood there for perhaps twenty minutes soaking in the luxury of what was in effect a water massage. In addition to the spray from above, the shower walls focused pulsating water jets upon all the muscle groups of his body, gently kneading them with both sideways and up-and-down movements. Closer examination revealed that the hot water came out of hundreds of jets from every inch of the shower wall. The contraption seemed capable automatically of focusing upon the precise muscle contours of his particular body, as if a computer were instructing the shower as to his precise dimensions. It felt very sensual as if hands were gently but forcefully stroking the entire length of his body.

When he finally pulled himself out of this pleasurable experience, realizing he was hungry, he stepped away from the water flow and found himself inside of a large column of warm air that blew down from the ceiling. His whole body tingled with instant demoisturization that gave him a sense of being energized. He later learned that the dehumidifying column was infused with a negative ion charge that cleaned the body of most contaminates.

From that day forward he took a shower whenever he could in order to enjoy this soothing, exhilarating experience. It was one of the few, sure happy moments he counted upon during his early, sometimes very uncomfortable days on Troubadour.

He wandered into the bedroom and dressed in the Troubadourian garb, choosing a conservative blue. Moving slightly to the left of the closet another full-length mirror appeared. He closely examined his image. The suit seemed made precisely for him. It accentuated the best lines of his lithe body revealing its shape so clearly that once again he felt almost naked inside the silken fabric.

Jesus, it doesn't hide anything.

His stomach changed the subject. I'm starved, it cried.

He headed for the kitchen and ordered another of the yellow fruits that had lavished his palate the evening before. It was equally devastating this morning. He also found and ate a cereal like substance that tasted very much like freshly baked oats.

"Computer? How about some milk."

After several moments he noticed that there had been no reply.

"Computer?" he queried.

"We can send in a wet nurse to feed you," the slightly metallic voice finally replied. "But we harvest the milk of animals only as a foundation for cheese. Would you like to be nursed?"

For the briefest moment Peter was gripped with a feeling of sensual anticipation imagining large, ample breasts offering an abundance of soft, warm liquid comfort.

"That sounds rather kinky. But if the Troubadourians do it maybe I . . ."

He was suddenly hyper-aware that this was most probably *not* the custom on Troubadour.

"D . . . d . . . do the Troubadourians do this for each other?"

"No."

Peter felt intensely embarrassed.

"Uh, thank you, no. I think I'll pass."

So why did you offer it in the first place you asshole?

"What do children do for milk?" Peter inquired in an attempt to reclaim his self-respect.

"Their mother's breast-feed them," was the slightly metallic reply.

The incident reminded Peter of his dream. He'd loved his mother's breasts as a small boy, once claiming them as his own property to a living room full of guests. He'd remembered because his mother had made it a family story. Peter suddenly realized that all his life he'd been searching for that good-breasted mother of his first four years.

He procured some sweet berries to moisten his oat-like cereal that were almost as incredible as the yellow, pear-like fruit that was already his favorite.

When finished he pushed the red button.

"Yes."

"What do I do with my dirty dishes?" he asked.

A container thrust from the wall.

"This kitchen is more like a restaurant. It even washes your dishes."

He wandered into the living room and sat down to look out the window at the mountain scene he'd left there the night before. The vivid hyper-reality of the window reassured him a little. Nature always did that for him.

"Well, I'm here," he said looking around the apartment, mostly noticing its emptiness. "I wonder what's going to happen."

He was suddenly aware of feeling very lonely again. So he did his yoga exercise routine. But when he was finished, and sat down again to look out the window, the loneliness returned.

"They just dropped me off here. What am I supposed to do now?"

He remembered Wind's casual remark that things would happen spontaneously, unplanned. It made him feel very uneasy.

It doesn't make sense why they're offering so little guidance.

His mind drifted through daydreams about mountain places, made up fantasies about good things that might happen here, until he finally realized he was just waiting for something to happen.

"What am I doing?"

He stood and started pacing.

"Christ, what are they doing? Are they just going to leave me here in this godforsaken backwater part of the universe billions of miles away from home?"

The large number suddenly reminded him of how far under the ground he was.

What do they do in case of fire?

To quell a new surge of anxiety, akin to claustrophobia, he started pacing more furiously until he realized it wasn't accomplishing anything.

"Hey, wait a minute. Maybe I'm supposed to be doing something. She said things were going to happen spontaneously. But maybe they're all waiting for me to act."

But that's ridiculous. I'm the stranger here.

His anxiety soon moved him out of anger into self-doubts.

"What am I doing? I'm just sitting around here daydreaming! These people have gone to extraordinary efforts to bring me to their planet, and I'm acting like I have nothing to do!"

Maybe she's waiting for me. She told me to call her.

"Jesus, I hope I haven't kept her sitting around waiting for me."

"Computer. Please call Wind."

He suddenly realized he didn't know her last name.

"Uh, I'm afraid I don't know her last name, but if you could look it up, that is if there are not too many Winds on Troubadour, then I . . ."

"Hello, this is Wind."

"Uh, what, uh, yes, I'd like to leave a message for Wind."

"This is Wind."

"Oh!" he exclaimed, surprised. "Uh, h . . . hello. It's me, Peter Ferdinand Icarus."

Why in the fuck did I tell her my stupid middle name?

"What a lovely name," she said.

There was a poignant silence as he waited hungrily for more of her kindness, afraid that if he spoke he would ruin it.

"Would you like some company?" she asked.

"Oh, sure," he blurted out, painfully embarrassed by his awkwardness.

"I'll be right over," she added.

"Okay," he replied.

Instantly he felt uncomfortable about her coming.

"How soon will you be here?"

But she had already disconnected.

He started pacing around the living room. His thoughts drifted to his three marriages, each of which ended in unhappiness. He blamed them, but he also blamed himself.

Yet he was still determined to find another. It was as if he was compelled to find just the right woman before his life could begin in the right way. He didn't think it so much as he assumed it.

Suddenly aware of how he was thinking of Wind, he brought himself up short.

"You've got to be kidding. You're thinking of her as a possible candidate for love? You are some kind of a desperate kook. Remember she's an alien."

The Goddess

The doorbell rang.

Startled by how soon she'd arrived, Peter ran to the front door worried about keeping her waiting. In his hurry he grabbed for the knob to open it, only to remember there was none.

"How do I open this damned thing?" he snarled in frustration, as if the absent doorknob was symbolic for the emptiness in which the Troubadourians had left him.

"Just say 'come in,'" she answered from outside.

Oh, shit! She heard me. She must think I'm stupid or something that I can't remember her simple instructions.

"Open, door," he hurriedly said with embarrassment a little too loudly.

The look of Wind soothed him some. She stood in the doorway with a gentle smile on her face. She was dressed in a light blue taffeta dress that was actually a full-body suit that flared where needed to create the fullness of a skirt.

"Hi," he said, trying to sound relaxed when he felt intensely nervous and already far too exposed to her.

"Hello," she replied, gracefully walking in. "Did you sleep well?"

"Like a dog. Uh, I mean like a log," he said, extremely embarrassed at choosing the wrong word.

"Have you had breakfast?" she queried, wandering into the living room.

"Yes, I've eaten, thanks," feeling grateful she hadn't reacted to his slip of the tongue.

"May I sit down?" she asked.

"Oh, I'm so sorry," he said, implying that he should already have invited her to do so. "Please do," he quickly added.

He was stumbling over everything she said. He felt trapped in discontinuity. Whatever he did made him look the fool.

She sat down and glanced at him, searching for what it was that made him so extremely nervous.

"It must be very awkward to wake up so far from home in such a strange place," she ventured.

An island of relief suddenly appeared under his feet.

"Y . . . yes, it is very awkward," he admitted, hoping what he felt was real.

"You've chosen my favorite window," Wind said, shifting to something mundane to try and slow things down for him. "I'm referring of course to the mountains."

"Oh, I love the mountains too," he almost shouted with an overdone enthusiasm as he leaped into the mundane, desperately wanting to do something to restore his self-respect and her good opinion. "They're my best face, uh, I mean my best pace . . . place."

Peter wanted to disappear. Each Freudian slip shamefully exposed its meaning, in this instance that a "best face" was what he was trying to put on top of his glaring shortcomings.

Unable to disappear, he tried to be larger by saying something very meaningful.

"The mountains mea-mea . . . I . . . I mean reassure me."

In his shamed view, it was obvious to her that "mea" meant either "me, me," which exposed his excessive self-centeredness, or "mommy's milk," which revealed his deep hunger for a woman's love. He felt humiliated.

But Wind was pleased that he was sharing his feeling with her, even if they were very awkwardly manifesting.

He deeply confuses me, Wind thought to herself. He desires confiding in me, which is good, but his confidences come out either as very guarded, or they make him feel foolish and far too exposed.

Wind was becoming quite concerned. She was deeply committed to the success of this venture with Peter. She was also very determined that what happened to Troubadour's first visitor would not happen again.

On the first day of his visit to Troubadour, under the primary guidance of someone other than Wind, this first visitor had become extremely paranoid. Deep mistrust thereafter prevented any further useful communication with the Troubadourians. He was still waiting in his rooms, from which he refused to depart until they sent him home. Their decision was pending based upon a deep concern that the trip home in his present condition might permanently dismantle his internal stability. He'd been on Troubadour five days when Peter arrived. They wanted Peter's eventual input to decide how to proceed.

He can't be like the previous one, she insisted. We couldn't be that wrong twice. Or are we perhaps trying to do the undoable?

All of this passed through her mind in an instant.

In the meantime I must believe for both of us, she added to herself.

"I too have always felt cosseted by the mountains," she said.

"Oh, that's really nice," he remarked pseudocasually, trying to imitate Wind's gracious manner, but managing only to pretend that he was.

Still convinced that he was an open book to her, sure that she knew everything stupid about him, including that he was pretending, he was convinced she would hate him for it as much as he hated himself.

Once more he had to find something to do with such terrible feeling.

What am I doing? I'm on a strange planet representing Earth. Christ I've given up five years of my life for this chance. And here I am just sit around lollygagging like I was on vacation.

He sat up straight in his chair.

"Shouldn't we be . . . be doing something else . . . I mean . . . something . . . uh, more like attending to business?" he asked. "You've brought me here at great expense, I guess for both of us now that I think about it. And I feel strange sitting around chatting as if I were on holiday."

She paused before answering.

"It was my impression that we were learning to be friends," she replied cautiously.

Though he felt criticized, what most grabbed his attention was the realization for the first time that his self-criticism had also impugned her by implication.

"I . . . I . . . I was chiding only myself," he added quickly, pretending that he wasn't also very disappointed in her. "I didn't mean to imply that you were doing anything wrong. Please excuse me."

"I didn't feel criticized," she replied casually. "And I still think we are doing just fine."

"I appreciate your friendliness, but we're certainly doing much more than just being friends. I mean we both represent our planets. There must be far more important things we need to do . . . things we need to . . . well, you see, there's the problem. I can't figure out what to do without some help. I mean what exactly are we doing?"

"Whatever you like," she said, trying a new metaphor on for size since "friendly" didn't seem to appeal to him.

He was beginning to feel irritated.

This is like pulling teeth.

"Isn't there some kind of protocol I need to know, like the rules of your culture? I mean like what's permissible and what's a forbidden sort of thing. And even more important, how will we be spending our time? What must I see? What must I know, and so forth and so on?"

Wind felt alarmed. It was precisely under similar circumstances, and having a discussion of the very same topic that Peter's predecessor had become deeply paranoid. What struck her at this moment was that Peter's complaint was almost exactly the same as this other man, that he wanted structure and rules before he could proceed any farther.

Wind was therefore extremely nervous about what she had to say in reply, knowing it would challenge him. She spoke slowly and carefully, constantly observing his every response, wanting very much to minimize provoking him. She believed the next few moments were critical to the success of Peter's visit.

"On Troubadour the rule of thumb is to do whatever you like as long as you have the consent of all others physically present or emotionally affected by what you're doing," Wind explained. "In exchange for that courtesy and caution, we grant to each other extraordinary freedom, giving to the individual human what you might consider to be enormous power. As our guest we grant you the same rights and opportunities for the duration of your visit. Please feel free to do whatever you desire, inside the boundaries of that one essential condition."

As Wind suspected, Peter had a great deal of difficulty with what she said. The philosopher in him was deeply curious about what she had explained about life on Troubadour. But the emotional part of him was horrified to hear that what he most needed from her she was refusing to give.

He suddenly felt extremely insecure. He responded in slightly agitated disbelief.

"You have no customs, no standards of behavior, no normal conventions which you expect to be observed?" he asked with an increasing uneasiness. "I find that very hard to believe."

"Though I can see that you are upset, and I regret that, I want you to know that we make this offer to you as a gift. To a Troubadourian this personal power is their most valuable asset."

Peter was no longer even able to understand what she was explaining, so convinced he was becoming that she was selling him a bill of goods.

"Is it that you don't want to tell me because you want to watch me figure it out by myself? I need to know because I . . . I . . . want you to know . . . I . . . I . . . I . . . I can't be part of such an experiment. I . . ."

"Your visit is of course an experiment, for both of us I'm sure. But . . ."

"Now, wait a minute. What do you mean? What's the experiment? What's actually going on around here?"

"I simply mean that we're trying something new together," Wind explained, "where two people from very different places and cultures meet to engage with each other, bringing the habits and expectations of their world into each other's, prepared to understand whatever happens spontaneously between us. Isn't that what an experiment is?"

"But I don't understand why it has to be so . . . up in the air, so . . . confusing, so . . . lacking in any structure, which one must have in order to even know what you're talking about," he pleaded. "There just must be some basic principles that are sacred to you, that you aren't telling me about!"

Peter wanted her to draw a map of the dangers he should carefully maneuver around. It's what both his parents had insisted upon getting from him, that he never got in their way.

"But you've got to have principles," he insisted.

"To speak truthfully, we don't do anything standing on principle."

There was a touch of ironic humor to the way she said it. This hint of humor derived from the fact that the notion of "principle" was perceived jokingly on Troubadour, as a vestige of historical efforts to achieve a sense of safety inside of truth that never changed, that could be completely relied upon simply by repeating it with great earnestness and sincerity, as one did at a political rally or in a religious ceremony.

"Well, if you don't stand on principle, then what do you stand on?" he exclaimed with indignation.

"We stand upon whatever conviction the moment instructs," she replied, laughing a little as she said it.

To Peter her laughter was outrageous. He was sorely tempted to explode.

But that was far too dangerous. He instantly shut himself down. He needed desperately to avoid fighting with her. She was his only connection on Troubadour. To attack her would be biting the one hand that might eventually feed him what he needed, or at least help him get back home.

This has become very delicate, Wind suddenly realized. I offer him the most beautiful gift I have, and he tells me it deeply scares him. A much more extreme version of that must be what happened to his predecessor. And now I have unwittingly added insult to injury by laughing when there was only pain in it for him.

"Please forgive my laughter," she said, immediately offering the most obvious reprieve she could think of. "I thought we might find humor in it together. Forgive my mistake in perception."

Peter was very relieved by her accurate understanding.

"Please excuse me," he said. "Here I am flying off at the handle at the slightest thing. I'm sorry. I guess I'm pretty nervous."

"I can understand that perfectly," she replied reassuringly, very relieved that he seemed to be coming out of his paranoid perceptions of her. "It is you who have made the difficult journey to our planet, taking, as you accurately wrote in one of your messages, most of the chances."

"I . . . I know that's not really true," he insisted, in spite of realizing that's precisely the way he had just felt. "I mean you're taking risks too."

He was pretending to go along with her. And yet his pretences began to ring true. They probably were taking risks, and they had seemed sincere and genuinely interested in him at times. Maybe his suspicions and resentments were crazier than he thought.

"But it's your life which might be shortened," she retorted, "and it is you who must suffer strangeness in coming here."

Peter cringed at the prospect of losing part of his life.

God I wish she hadn't brought that up.

I wonder if she's saying all those nice things just because it's her job to do so, because she's afraid I'm falling apart.

"You're being too generous," he insisted

What frightens this man so much that gifts of opportunity evoke only suspicion, she asked herself? And there's something hollow happening here. I can't quite understand what it is, but I feel like I'm not seeing all of him when he speaks.

Watching her face react to him, Peter suddenly had the impression that she was having as much difficulty as he was. Feeling afraid that, if she couldn't handle things, then they were in deep trouble. He blurted out the first question that came to mind, trying to keep a normal conversation going.

"Wha . . . wha . . . wha . . . what's it like being Troubadourian?"

His question immediately sounded childish to him.

Unfortunately Wind found it difficult to answer, which seemed at first to verify his fear. The tone of his asking voice had been frantic.

What is he so frightened about? Perhaps if I confide in him about myself it might be helpful.

"I wonder if you'd find it interesting or very strange, that many Troubadourians consider themselves to be their own best friend."

"How is that possible?"

"We believe it to be a direct consequence of the degree of personal power we have given each other."

It was the most unusual thing he'd ever heard. But it didn't make him curious. It made him feel very threatened. What she was saying felt preposterous, even pretentious. Who would believe such a thing?

Peter couldn't get his mind around the idea of being his own friend. He was too deeply estranged from the kind of self-awareness and confidence that such a friendship-with-self would require.

Peter suddenly had a completely different, paranoid take on her words. Maybe what she really said was, "Why don't you start being your own best friend and stop asking such stupid questions?"

"Am I going to meet other people?"

"Would you like to?" she asked.

Why does she keep throwing it all back to me, he shouted inside himself?

"Don't you have things for me to do?" he desperately insisted.

Wind was flabbergasted. She was offering him a gift of enormous value, the opportunity to decide how to spend the moments of his own life's experience. She was sure if he only understood better that he would feel differently.

"Nothing is preplanned or expected of you," she added graciously. "You are free to do as you wish."

Rage surged inside Peter.

"You've brought me all this way here and you have nothing for me to do!" he shouted with indignation.

Wind was stunned by his aggression. She had never personally experienced such intense anger. This aggressive emotional attack by one human being upon another had almost entirely disappeared from her planet. Anger was quite openly expressed in moderate forms. But this emotion had become for her people mostly a problem-finder, losing most of its aggressive force in the process, as it gradually lost its function as a problem-solver.

Stunned by developments, Wind was most deeply shocked by how little she felt willing to offer Peter at that particular moment. Her usual generous, supportive feelings were turned off in her own defense, something else she had never experienced before.

She was immediately worried that she was leaving him unattended, and yet her heart did not budge any closer to helping him. Wind found these developments extremely unsettling. She was very committed to the success of her work. But at this moment she didn't have the slightest idea of what to do to fulfill it.

Unable effectively to engage him, she walked several paces away into the entrance hall simply in order to think clearly.

Are all Earth people like this, she asked herself?

She glanced at Peter. He looked as lost as she felt and much more frightened.

She suddenly realized there was only one way for her to proceed. She must put her personal reactions to him aside and focus instead upon how she could remedy his experience. To her great relief she remembered that she had already prepared for this eventuality. She had preinstructed herself to be ready to deal with complete confusion should it happen when she was with Peter.

Instantly she knew why she had moved off alone. It was in order best to consider all the evidence of what was happening in the largest possible psychic context, in order to achieve the most reliable impressions of what was going on. To do that she needed to be alone.

Locating her present experience in the context of its largest possible view, it took Wind only a few moments before the shape of her next response formed vividly in her mind's eye. As soon as she caught sight of its vision, the disparate pieces of confusion came together into one picture.

In order for him to attack me I must already have offended him. Which means I've done something harmful without knowing it. There must be a problem with how we understand the Earth human. I don't see it, but it must be there.

Peter had been strangely inactive during Wind's moments of deliberation. He was stuck on the petard of indecision. Everything seemed wrong to do. He was waiting with bated breath for her to speak again.

She turned and approached him.

"I think perhaps you came expecting something quite different from what we've offered you," Wind said graciously. "Which must now cause you considerable consternation."

"What you say is true," Peter blurted out in his enormous relief. "I . . . I . . . I really did expect something else. I guess I'm having lots of trouble with the way this visit is happening."

"I know," she agreed. "I'm sorry that it has caused you such discomfort and pain."

Her sympathy was sweeter than the yellow fruit he adored so much. It seeped through his body soothing him, enabling him to reveal a bit of his own vulnerability.

"I'm really confused about what you're trying to do with me," he said.

"I'm so sorry for that," she replied graciously. "It would seem that what I regard as a valuable gift feels to you more like a curse."

Peter laughed nervously, amazed at the surgical precision of her analysis.

"I don't know if I'd use such a strong word, but you certainly have put your finger on it," he replied.

"For that I'm deeply grateful."

Wind was feeling the most intense relief she had ever felt in her life. It quite impressed her. She would have to think of it when she was alone.

With Peter she proceeded cautiously.

I can't rely upon my instincts, she said to herself. He doesn't have the same assumptions as I do. So I must admit that I don't know how to approach him, and must therefore be a little suspicious of what I intend. This is going to be a very strange experience. It reminds me of being a novice where you must learn most of what needs to be used after you need it. Learning in this instance seems far more fraught with dangerous pitfalls than I can remember it having before; which makes me feel uneasy. How difficult to need so much competence when you have so little.

She sighed and realized that they had both been working hard.

"I would suggest that we consider calling it a day, as your people sometimes say," Wind suggested. "A great deal has already happened, much more than one can fully realize until they get some distance from the moment. Perhaps we both need time to absorb what's already occurred before we add to our experience even more."

Peter found the idea instantly threatening, but then almost immediately reassuring as well.

He was very surprised that a positive emotion had in the end won out over the usual negative one.

"But will you be coming back very soon?"

"Of course," she sweetly replied. "How about two hours from now?"

Peter was very relieved.

"I guess that would be okay," he said with sadness.

"Then it's a date," she replied, leaving the apartment.

For the first time today Peter had an opportunity to look exclusively at her body as she left. He closely followed the voluptuous undulations of her physical departure. Something hungry reached out to her.

When she disappeared his heart sank into loneliness mixed with anxiety. The meeting had really upset him. Some positive things happened. But mostly it was almost terrifying.

The worst part was that he'd become very mixed in his feelings about her. Though she soothed him with great skill, she also made him feel very inferior. She was very kind, but he felt hurt by her. As a result he didn't know what to feel or what to believe, so his feelings just struggled with each other. But most deeply he felt a growing angst.

Whatever the Troubadourains were doing, it was going very badly.

Under Siege

"What's wrong with me!" Peter shouted. "I've never been afraid to go outside before!"

He was standing alone in the middle of his living room after making several attempts to leave for a walk. Ever since Wind departed he'd become more and more restless. He wanted desperately to go out, away from where he felt so anxious and confined. He wanted to explore the outdoors he'd only glanced at when he first arrived.

But each time he set off with hopefulness, when he got within two feet of the front door he would start to hyperventilate, something he'd never done before, or at least as far as he could remember. Something awful and very gripping wouldn't let him go in spite of the fact that the room began feeling claustrophobic.

He adored the outdoors, which always soothed him. So what was there to be afraid of? And why were there so many phobias all at once? He seemed both claustrophobic and agoraphobic.

Using his clinical experience, he tried thinking of everything he knew about himself to create a picture of him that suggested some possible reason for being so rampantly afraid, but he didn't get anywhere.

What his fear was accomplishing was to prevent Peter from doing anything, essentially to shut himself down. It would take years for him to remember that as a boy he'd been lost in a world of impossible alternatives. He was simultaneously afraid to do anything, and yet also afraid to be so passively inactive. He couldn't decide whether to seek new input, or stand pat and avoid everything new.

Unconsciously he was reenacting the traumas of his life, which could be summed up best by the conclusion that he'd been left alone to bring himself up in most of the important ways, like learning to understand and manage his own emotional experience.

Lacking the far superior structures of the adult mind, great fear, once awakened in an uneducated imagination, can run rampantly wild, producing many phobias. His feelings were simply much bigger than any of his thoughts, making fear intensely precipitous and seem like the most deadly and dangerous experience one could possibly have. He was constantly intimidated into shutting down parts of himself and always had to fight against fear.

Fortunately Peter had chosen to risk. So he was paying the price. Ancient issues were popping out of their hiding places at opportunistic moments by his decision to push himself into coming to Troubadour. These waiting agendas were all those personal needs he'd kept filing away for another day's attention ever since he was a young boy. He had been preoccupied for the vast majority of his life with other people's agendas, firmly believing them to be his own, thus obeying the mostly unconscious commands that ancestors had for centuries injected into the collective habit-system of his family.

It wasn't so much that his ancestors abused their children, for they were acting consistent with their times. Instead they participated in generations-old rituals of family tradition, many of them built upon dishonest and violent behaviors made to look harmlessly pretty. It's what idealized respectability tried to do for the Victorians, hide sordid urges and beginnings.

Like all victims of ancestral dominance, Peter began feeling that he was the persecuted object of invisible forces. He was beginning to fear that Troubadour might, by dragging him through the nightmares of his life's unhappiness, make him far sicker than he was before.

"I can't stand this," he shouted, deeply resenting the dread he felt while pacing furiously around his apartment. "Am I falling apart? Why is this happening to me?"

A shiver shook his body momentarily, releasing some of the tension his anxiety had been storing up in his muscles ever since he first noticed how afraid he was to leave his apartment.

"I'm blowing it! I'm acting like a lunatic! I should probably just leave!"

He was startled by the extent of his fear, which was already considering desperate measures like leaving. He hadn't really intended to go that far.

He suddenly remembered that his predecessor had gone off the deep end soon after he arrived.

Is the same thing happening to me?

The doorbell's sudden sound sent shock waves down his back.

Oh, my god, she's already here.

He was astounded that two hours had already passed.

For a moment he was paralyzed. He would be humiliated if she saw him this way. He thought of postponing the meeting, but that made him feel even worse.

If only she would help me.

"Come in," he said, his voice cracking.

She stood in the doorway dressed in a white outfit with light blue highlights, the chest of which had been intricately embroidered with a design in various shades of green, yellow, and purple, each the perfect complimentary hue to the blue and each other, together expressing the bounty and cooperation of nature's colors.

Since their last meeting Wind had been deeply troubled by Peter's extreme discomfort. She had met with other members of the Earth-visitor team trying to figure out her next best move.

"I wonder what makes him so terribly apprehensive?" she remarked to the group. "We knew that he had anxiety potential, but why does he feel it so strongly? Adaptation to new surroundings doesn't account for it all. So what's threatening him so much?"

"The transportation journey was obviously extremely disruptive to his integrity," another had suggested.

"It's true," Wind agreed. "If the self is already shaky, then the temporary disintegration during transportation is deeply threatening. I have wondered whether this factor is the main reason for his instability."

"Though I have come to a different conclusion, based upon a much stronger impression of him. What I think is important is that he believes in the frightening visions his fear projects onto the canvass of his mind. Therefore, whatever the source of his anxiety, it is best to respond to it on its face value, upon the terms that he offers us, even if those terms are extremely difficult to partner."

"But we expected there to be difficulties like this," a man said. "What's so uneasy about the fact that it's happening?"

"I'm afraid of losing him like we did the first," Wind replied.

Wind knew this man well. He was one of Troubadour's wisest.

"Then perhaps you are afraid like him," this man suggested. "Your fears may be triggering each other. Fear is capable of multiplying itself many-fold, which often happens in groups of people, particularly if they're large. We used to call them 'mobs.' I still remember their mindless marches."

"You mean our separate fears act together to enlarge?" she asked.

"How else do you think we once rationalized the violence of waging war except by forming a common fear-pact, which of course justifies anything?"

Wind hesitated in the doorway looking carefully at Peter, hoping to find him less apprehensive. But he looked even more unsettled than when she'd last been with him. She was both disappointed and also alarmed.

Shaken by two hours of worried fearfulness, Peter desperately struggled to find a way to hide his intense instability, convinced that her knowing it would instantly disqualify him. He would have to return to Earth.

Both to conceal his still intense anxiety, and to connect to her in the only available positive way, he sank into a mesmerizing stare that found great solace and a degree of mental oblivion in the voluptuousness of her body.

His enchantment was not a mature, romantic form of mesmerizing, which can accompany a deep experience of mutual attraction. It was instead the kind of trance-like merging that a boy feels without thinking about it for his beautiful mother, as he leans deeply into the soft flesh of her thigh watching her brush her hair as she sits at her dresser, daydreaming himself in sway with the motions of her graceful body, becoming one with her for safety, but doing it very carefully so she wouldn't notice that he was there, so he wouldn't interrupt her self-focus.

"It's good to see you again," she said.

"What?" Peter exclaimed, her words suddenly waking him from his trance.

He suddenly realized he hadn't heard what she said. Desperately wanting to keep up with her, and yet determined not to expose his lapse of attention, he jerked himself out of the comfort-cocoon of mesmerism, shook a little, and searched frantically for a memory of her missing words.

To his enormous surprise, it worked. His brain had recorded it.

"You're very beautiful too," he quickly replied, instantly embarrassed by this huge amplification of her greeting that exposed the devotion of his mesmerized attachment.

"Please excuse . . ." he began to apologize.

"Thank you," Wind said, interrupting his apology with her genuine appreciation. "I am pleased that you see me that way," she added with much sincerity.

He suddenly wanted desperately to be heroic in her eyes. The problem was that his fear almost completely shut down his imagination, an essential element for his goal.

Lacking inspiration, he used excess to convey a greater sense of feeling than the ideas he shared could carry. Starved of emotional depth, his offering was more puffed up with pretty words than filled with the emotional vitality he wished it to convey.

"Your people are very handsome and beautiful," he said with an enthusiasm that lacked conviction. "I've never seen a people so extraordinarily attractive as a group," he added, implying he'd met other aliens.

Instantly he was ashamed of sounding so false and affected. He knew he had completely overdone it. He sounded like the diplomat who always made everything nice.

Wind responded to his flattery with a surprising thought of her own. His body is rather thin suggesting frailty.

Immediately disturbed by the negative spin of her thought, to balance things she spoke her most positive observation of him. It came from a very natural place in her that was always observing the color, shape, and value of the objects she observed, in preparation for painting or sculpting some vision that it inspired. When she had first seen Peter, she instantly perceived the shape of his head and the deep intensity of his eyes as especially appealing and attractive. She responded from that vision.

"You are a handsome man yourself."

To his surprise and deep consternation, Peter felt her compliment sounded insincere. Hypersensitive as he was, he had caught a taste of her negative thought about him.

But he didn't allow himself to blame her. Instead he made himself undeserving. To justify her, he described himself as someone who deserved very little.

"I really don't feel that way, you know," he confessed. "I mean I don't feel handsome. I . . . I usually feel more like I'm kind of old, you know, certainly beyond my prime, a . . . a . . . and a sort of underachiever of sorts . . . uh, you know, that sort of thing."

Once said, Peter wanted to drop through the floor. He'd never heard himself say anything so shame-filled and falsely humble, for he was secretly very proud of himself, particularly his professional skill. He felt really stupid to pretend he wasn't something he really was. What's more he'd said it to the very woman he most wanted to impress, more than anyone else in his entire life.

Something very strange is happening here which I can't understand,

Wind told herself. And it suddenly feels precipitous, as if he's in great danger.

It felt imperative to her to change the basic experience he was having. For the moment she would have to cease the fundamental strategy of responding to him. She must stop waiting for his spontaneous moves to guide her. Instead she must take temporary control of the situation, venturing an uninformed guess as to what might be helpful to him.

"Perhaps you have questions for me that would be helpful for you to ask," she said.

He leaped to her suggestion like a parched pallet inhaling water, just out of the desert without liquid for days.

"Yes I do," he exclaimed with an enthusiasm that was mostly relief.

In asking questions he was escaping into the unfeeling landscape of the cerebral and objective, where the craved elixir of emotional anonymity was available. Abstract thinking infused him with a drug-like injection of numbness, giving him the bravado to ask a challenging question.

"Why have you brought me here?" he shot out with unexpected push.

Wind felt stung by the bitterness of his tone.

"We wanted very much to meet a species very much like our own," she explained, "which is still passing through the kinds of experiences we had about two hundred years ago."

"But what do you want from me?"

"For you to be yourself," she replied.

"But what do you guys want?" he insisted.

"The same thing."

God, this is like pulling teeth, he shouted to himself.

"I know that!" he insisted, trying to restrain his anger. "But why are you hiding what you really want from me . . . I mean what you want from my coming here?"

Stop talking to her this way, a voice inside him shouted. You're being an idiot.

"I'm sorry," he said. "I'm being too . . . too intense."

"You must be in pain," she said sympathetically, though the intensity of his resentment was becoming extremely unpleasant for her.

"Let me try and answer your question a little differently," she interjected.

Wind had never had to put aside such a large measure of personal discomfort in order to commit all of her attention to the needs of someone else. She was beginning to feel a bit outside of herself. Nevertheless she persisted in the direction her good sense dictated.

"We wanted to remember the last two hundred years of our history by interacting with someone who in many ways was still there, in that history," she said. "I am of course just speculating. I don't . . . we don't . . . actually know what it means for you to be here. But we want very much to find out."

She was dissatisfied with her explanation. Her emotional restraint somehow robbed it of the meaning she had meant to convey.

But Peter was grateful to her for satisfying even this small corner of his curiosity.

"I see," Peter fervently said. "I begin to see a little light. But I'd like to see it from the other end. Please tell me what it's like to live two hundred years ahead of my time."

Wind was surprised and relieved to see how much better he seemed to feel in response to what she thought was inadequate.

"I'd be happy to," she replied. "From the outside our world probably seems very simple and unassuming," she explained. "I'm actually imagining you seeing it from outer space. Unless you are very close to the surface of our planet, we would probably be invisible. As you have observed our cities blend into nature. We like it that way."

She paused to be sure her words were helping him.

"Looked at from a distance, one can't tell much about my people," she continued. "The only way to understand us is to experience us one at a time. We've invited you here for that reason, to get to know a few of us, and in the process bring us whatever information we can glean from your responses to what you experience."

She paused for a moment to see if he had any questions.

"Please go on. I'm fascinated."

"If you look closely, you will find this emphasis upon one-at-a-time is a fundamental characteristic of Troubadour. We have taken individuality and made it the centerpiece of our democracy, in fact how we define the term itself. So mostly you will meet individuals. I am the person with whom you will spend more of your time. There are a few others whom you'll get to know and some you may never meet, but who contribute to the overall project."

The thinker in Peter was becoming completely engaged. His earlier emotional experience had not drastically changed, but now it hovered in the background waiting for a chance once again to grab his attention.

"Just how much power does each one of you have?" Peter asked.

"Except for a few things we must decide in common as a species, the individual is equal to society as a whole."

I don't believe she said what I heard her just say.

"You don't mean they're as powerful as society, do you?" he asked incredulously.

"That's exactly what I mean," she replied.

"But how can that be? It doesn't make any sense."

"By mutual agreement," she replied, deeply relieved to see that his change in mood persisted. "It took us almost one hundred years before we finally took the plunge. We thought about it, experimented with it, and tried it out for decades until we were ready. First it was impossible even to give it our attention. It seemed deeply fascist. Then it was a dubious hope wanting secretly to be both possible and real. It passed through many such stages before eventually becoming our spiritual quest. The sum of those stages of evolution dominated a large part of an entire century, as this change became who we now are."

"How fascinating," he replied, though still deeply unbelieving. "But what's this power everybody's got look like?"

"Well, for instance you'll find us handling by ourselves a lot of things society used to handle for us," she explained, "like religion or policing or government, to mention a few examples."

"You've got to be kidding. How can one person do all of that?"

"Let's take government," she suggested. "We all vote electronically when something needs to be decided upon. At a certain time of our choosing each day, our computer informs us of the various items to be voted upon that day, making available a great deal of information so that the issue can be viewed from several different perspectives. We may choose to study this material if we are not already informed, or to pass, meaning we won't vote on it if we don't know what it's all about."

"But then decisions are made by only a portion of everybody," he protested.

"Has there ever been any other way? Though there's nothing wrong with that if decisions are well made," she replied. "What's important about decisions is whether they're made surreptitiously, or out in the open."

"You mentioned religion. Do you believe in a God?"

"We regard religion as a personal matter on Troubadour. In fact we believe that in order to be legitimate one's spiritual life must belong most fundamentally and primarily to ourselves. We believe it is our own, special life that is the most sacred vessel we will ever know or occupy, which therefore deserves our reverence and captures our deepest awe and respect. Each single human psyche represents the fulfillment of that personal potential which makes me the guardian angel of myself, responsible to care for the quality of my life."

"That's such a beautiful way of saying it," he exclaimed. "It's really inspiring. Though I must admit I'm having serious problems with what you're claiming. I'm sorry if that intrudes, but how could you possibly have pulled something like that off?"

"By sweat, blood, and tears," she replied with enthusiasm, deeply relieved that he seemed to enjoy what they were doing. "We all invested a great deal of effort to find a way to change what we'd hated for centuries, meaning the various and insidious forms of oppression which were built into the structure of our social traditions and public institutions."

"Are you saying that suffering comes from institutions instead of people?"

"Yes. It comes from the bad habits that we share with our culture and each other. Though we still honor, celebrate, and study past Troubadourian cultures, we discovered that all forms of oppression derive from the one source that is common to all cultures, the veneration and worship of ancestors and what they believed."

"Does that mean you're against religion and culture?" he asked incredulously.

"No. But like love, religion and culture reflect the best and the worst of us, in spite of what both pretend to do. It's why we made religion a personal matter, taking away from its institutional forms their special privileges and powers. Each one of us thereafter had to find and define our own relationship with the realm of the Spirit."

"What exactly do you mean by ancestor worship?"

"To honor the past at the expense of the present. We have decided each generation has the right to re-form their life habits, laws, traditions, institutions, etc., according to their own vision of truth."

"You mean you keep changing everything all the time?" Peter queried.

"It's the only way to deal with all those unhealthy organisms that grow on the surface of our shared opportunity, whenever we try and tie things down permanently, when we stop change from happening so we won't be so afraid of its perpetual delivery of newness. Thomas Jefferson of your world was very worried about this. He tried to arrange for each generation to be able to change your Constitution."

Peter was getting really excited. He had studied this aspect of history very carefully.

"What did you mean by 'unhealthy organisms' that grow on . . . whatever it was you said?" he asked.

"All the corrupt things that flourish in the halls of a government where decisions are being made when the deciders are not vitally affected by what they decide, except in fixed, profitable ways only they control. This avaricious process becomes the corruption that runs everything from behind closed doors. It's not so much that bad people are in government. It's that the structures of government still contain hidden attitudes of disrespect and prejudice toward the individual human, which seek avidly to suppress him and her."

"My god, you're right!" Peter exclaimed. "That is exactly what happens in government! Idiots decide everything for the rest of us as they profit for themselves. You nailed it perfectly!" he shouted with excitement. "But this individual power thing . . . what happened to crime when people have so much power?"

"There is no longer any crime on Troubadour of the sort to which I'm sure you are referring."

"Are you trying to tell me that you have no other dangerous possibilities going on here except what life, continental drift, weather, volcanic eruptions, and that sort of natural disaster produce?"

"Things happen that are not right on Troubadour," she replied, "but such disruptive moments no longer approach the level of abuse that you mean by the word crime."

"How did you get rid of it?" Peter asked.

"It simply disappeared in the process that I have begun to describe."

He looked askance at her.

"By magic?" he queried with a slight sarcastic tone.

"No," she replied. "By giving up control as our principle common priority."

That stunned Peter. He felt instantly afraid. Being out of control was one of his secret fears.

Though, when he had a moment to think about it, he was at least philosophically in accord with her opinion about control.

"What's so terrible about controlling things?" he queried as devil's advocate.

"Control prevents change. It shuts down the normal processes by which people keep themselves open to new possibility and new spiritual meaning. Control used to be our principle way of creating safety. But that only works by putting enormous power in the hands of a very few, thus creating the very oppression that we constantly complain about, by needing those capable of carrying it out."

"But how does that explain how crime disappeared?"

"Like all parts of nature, human nature functions at its most creative as one-of-a-kind. Give people the opportunity fully to have their own life and crime will disappear as a major element of social experience."

"But how did people develop such self-control?" he asked.

"Many ways, though the one that comes to mind is how much trouble we formerly had over property rights. Giving them up enhanced peacefulness more than anything else."

"You gave up property rights?" Peter asked incredulously. "You just turned in everything you owned for everyone to share?"

"I'm referring mostly to the ownership of land or housing," she replied.

"Control I can partly understand, but ownership? What's that got to do with the price of freedom and opportunity?" Peter queried.

"Ownership kills whatever it touches, claiming absolute power over what it holds. When nature offers itself only in one form, as a shared thing belonging equally to all life. Ownership insists that the only way to have an undisrupted connection to something or someone is to have power over it or them. That's what makes ownership the stuff from which oppression is built."

"But without ownership how do people arrange secure, private living places?"

"On Troubadour there is always a place to live in any city you chose to reside at any time."

"But how do you hold onto it?"

"It is yours until you leave it."

"Oh, I see. You just set it all up the way you believe it should happen."

"That's precisely what we did," Wind crooned in reply. "You understand us perfectly. Of that I am most pleased."

"You are obviously very unfriendly to capitalism and its marketplace in my world, which I must agree has pretty much taken over control of the Earth," Peter observed.

"Ownership produces hierarchy," she said. "It spawns making money as a life's work, inevitably destabilizing equality between people, since ownership and its profit strongly encourages one to take from others far more than one's share of everything. There are lots of better things to do with a life, like painting pictures or understanding nature or helping others to learn. Why should those interested in doing something that is intrinsically avaricious and greedy have so much more of everything than the rest of us?"

"You can say that again," Peter exclaimed with exuberance.

"Ownership and the power it offers encourages conglomeration, what you call monopoly," she continued, delighted that he enjoyed the conversation. "The huge wealthy corporations it creates are actually policing institutions. They take human opportunity, such as certain much-needed products like energy, and impose conditions, rules, standardizations, and the maximum tolerated toll upon anything vital to our well-being, creating with us a relationship in which most of us are the seriously inferior part. Your word for this poor creature, who is indentured to economy's credit system, is the customer."

"You certainly do have some very strong negative opinions about how we do things on Earth," Peter observed.

"I do," she acknowledged. "Though I hope that I don't offend."

"No, not me so far," he replied. "I realize that what you're saying in effect is that profit is criminal. That's not an entirely unfriendly idea to me."

"I would go even farther," she replied. "Defining human opportunity as profit makes a norm out of criminality. We Troubadourians define crime as taking advantage of others without their consent in any form whatsoever."

"But how did you ever pull that off?" Peter queried.

"We stumbled our way here over many decades. We still sometimes look back wondering how it happened. Mostly we're deeply grateful that we were able to do it."

In the relatively comfortable silence that followed, Wind realized the potential for hurt in some of what she'd been telling him.

"Please note that I'm only discussing Troubadourian history and experience. I'm not criticizing your people, only the habits of culture and government that our ancestors put into institutional form."

"But how can you separate people from the institutional structures in which they believe?" he asked.

"I'm awfully glad you asked that question. It gives me the opportunity of saying something I've wanted to express to your people many times as I have studied the ways you experience life."

"You watch us?" he said, surprised.

"We've done so for years, capturing information primarily from your radio and TV signals."

And you read my computer files too he added to himself.

"The people of Earth would be very interested in knowing that another species has such great interest in them," he added. "In particular they'd want to know everything I can find out about you."

"Then let my message, which is a simple one, be addressed to all your people," she replied. "It is this. I personally believe that a great many of your people are, inside themselves, quite capable of living within very different structures of governance than you now practice or have even imagined."

"Like what kind of structures?"

"Structures for instance that turn over to individuals and local authority a great many of the things that are now controlled centrally, eventually relieving you of most of those oppressive bureaucracies and policing agencies with their repressive strategies. Take for instance a small one, the presumption of all bureaucratic responses to public inquiry, that if a problem exists it's your fault."

"Now that is a very familiar compliant much talked about on Earth," he replied.

"To put my message in the most inspirational frame," Wind continued. "It is my strong impression that many of your people have seriously outgrown the institutional habits to which they still conform. It's why you have so little faith in public life. It no longer reflects or amplifies the truth your hearts have come to know."

Wow, he exclaimed. Now that is something to take back with me!

"That's really inspiring!" Peter exclaimed, very moved by her idea. "But there is one thing. Why do you trust something as sleazy as local authority?"

"We believe that everything that can should be managed by people available to each other within walking distance in a day, thus rendering the vast majority of what authority does easily accountable to those affected by its decisions."

"But it was local authority from which we had to take away power in order to rescue people from being oppressed," Peter insisted. "It's local authority which sponsors the privilege of the few over the needs of the many."

"In a different human time it no longer does that," she replied. "The problem of a privileged class dominating society is far less a problem of fairness and far more a problem of bad habits and the attitudes which support them, specifically for instance the habit of believing that profit is a motive that encourages the cooperation of people in the accomplishment of good, when quite obviously it encourages the opposite."

Peter suddenly realized that he'd been ignoring the parts of what she said that he disagreed with.

"There is something that's hard for me to believe. I mean giving so much power to everyone would, wouldn't crime and disorder become rampant?"

"Perhaps I should explain the other half of the equation of Troubadourian democracy," Wind replied. "Which is that, in order to give each one of us so much freedom and power, we relinquished a certain portion of control over our own behavior."

"You what?" Peter exclaimed, openly expressing his shock.

"We realized that in order to live peacefully with each other while we exercised huge individual power, we must regard all our actions as something that belonged as much to those affected by what we did, as it belongs to us."

"Do you mean other people can stop you from doing what you need to do for yourself?"

"We don't force each other to do anything," she replied. "We have instead all agreed to commit ourselves to this course."

"This is very strange, very hard for me to imagine," Peter replied, beginning more fully to believe that what he had just minutes before regarded as beautiful, now began feeling dangerously ugly. He was suddenly afraid of getting very disappointed.

Wind noticed that Peter was slipping back into his paranoid perspective. She had been watching for just that possibility.

Immediately alarmed, she realizing it would take only a few moments of precipitous emotional collapse and Peter would be thrown back into the worst of his previous suspicions.

She immediately intervened with her final strategy, something she had brought with her in case of fire.

"Would you like to take a walk outside with me?" she asked.

"What?" Peter exclaimed, very surprised by the huge shift in subject.

He suddenly remembered his phobia of going outside before she came.

"How did you know?" slipped out of him before he realized he didn't want to expose his fear of her mind reading.

"Did I know what?" she asked.

"Oh, just that I was . . . uh, you know wanting to do that, I mean go out before you came," he replied hoping she'd ask no further.

Can she read my mind?

Wind stood and headed for the door.

He jumped up to follow her.

They walked for half an hour without saying anything further to each other. At first the silence made Peter nervous, until he realized that, in spite of his first impression he wanted it. It perfectly fit the confusion and shame that his severe mood-shifts had brought him, which he wanted to hide. What better place to do that than silence?

Sometimes he would glance at her to be sure she wasn't either staring at him or looking unhappy in some way. But mostly he drifted in the silence, clearing his brain of worry by letting smell, look, and sound take over his awareness. His senses savored the sound of her breathing and the soft touch of her feet upon the ground, and the smell of evergreens whistling in the wind.

Not once did she look at him or betray any part of her own emotional experience, giving him the model of privacy she hoped he would follow.

When they returned to the building entrance, she stopped and turned toward him.

"I enjoyed our walk very, very much. There was sweetness in it. Thank you for coming with me."

"T . . . thank you for inviting me," he replied, feeling overwhelmed by her use of the tender metaphor, "sweet."

"I'll be in touch tomorrow," she added. "However you may first meet a very interesting man. He may visit you in the morning."

She turned and walked away into the woods again.

Though relieved to be alone, he was also rather stunned by her sudden departure.

They sure don't take any time for transitions.

He stood for a long time staring at the spot where she had last been seen before disappearing into the trees.

For Peter this had been both the fulfillment of a dream, finally learning something important about Troubadour, and the awakening of a nightmare, the potential of Troubadour being an overwhelming disaster.

For Wind it had been a very narrow victory over chaos.

Will every meeting be so dangerously precipitous, she wondered?

Rain

Peter was dreaming he was back in college. He was visiting the home of his English professor, a woman, who was his thesis advisor. She had never liked him. As the newest faculty member she felt stuck with Peter, who appeared to be one of the least talented men in the English honor's program.

They had weekly sessions to discuss what he'd written on his thesis since their last meeting. She would always react with disgust to almost everything he wrote, except perhaps for one paragraph she would circle and then tell him to start over again using that brief excerpt of his last week's ten hours of labor.

He dreaded these meetings more than any other time at college. It was impossible for him to rise above her derisive valuation of his work. He knew she was right. His writing lacked any conviction or passion of any kind. He made only intellectual observations that had no heart or guiding purpose.

He was terrified of the possibility his thesis would be unacceptable to the English Department, that he would fail to achieve honors, something that he was told had never happened at Amherst. Seeing her each Friday afternoon was like visiting hell.

He sat in a stiff and uncomfortable antique chair in the entranceway of her Victorian. The bell rang, meaning he was being summoned into her home office.

He very reluctantly stood, sighed deeply as he lingered for a moment watching the lights of that very occasional car pass along the nearly deserted alleyway beside her house, casting bizarrely-shaped shadows moving slowly across the ceiling of his expectation, foreboding a painful session with her.

The bell rang again. She was growing impatient.

Had he been daydreaming to avoid going in, making her ring twice, he wondered?

The bell rang a third time. This time he knew it came from outside the dream. He woke.

The bell rang again.

Peter leaped out of bed and rushed partway toward the front door.

"Come in!" he shouted.

A lithe, tall, six-foot-four-inch strong-bodied man, probably in his early seventies stood in the doorway, appearing casual as if he were surveying, waiting for something to happen. There was a kingly deliberateness to this surveillance, though it lacked any intent to dominate. His persona announced that he possessed a large spirit, but one that would not intrude upon others, nor on the other hand a spirit that would shrink or go away, even if someone found it a touch rude or even a little threatening.

He would not speak the attitudes that understructured this performance, but he would look like someone who was feeling them, making his presence impressive. Anyone seeing him for the first time couldn't help but notice his obvious power.

His hair was long and still black, but mixed with many shades of gray lending dignity to the large, piercing deep-set blue eyes which gently stared back at Peter.

"I'm Rain," he finally said in a very patient, low-pitched tone speaking very good English. "Wind may have mentioned that I might drop by."

Something electric happened to Peter. The moment his eyes first took in the demeanor of this man, Peter's knew he was a formidable person. When he spoke Peter knew instantly that it was easier to relate to a man, most particularly this one who had already deeply impressed him with his solid, calm strength.

I already like him more than Wind.

Instantly he felt guilty about shortchanging Wind, someone who had also evoked strong rumblings of adoration and devotion, but who had then tarnished the perfection he'd first felt toward her.

"May I come in?" Rain asked.

"Oh, I'm so sorry. Of course, please come in."

"I can see that I have wakened you from sleep."

Until that moment Peter had forgotten he was standing in his nightshirt.

"Oh. I wasn't paying any attention. Please excuse me for a few moments."

"I will look at the mountains while you're away," Rain said sitting down in front of the window.

Peter hurried through his toilet. He didn't want to keep this impressive man waiting. When he returned he sat down in the chair next to Rain as if attending someone of higher rank.

"Please eat if you're hungry, Peter Icarus," Rain said while still looking at the mountains.

To shift suddenly from an openhearted focus upon what Rain was about to say, toward the satisfaction of his own personal needs and appetites, was a shift that defied the way Peter had been built for life. The strain of that shift expressed itself as awkwardness.

"Oh, uh, okay yes . . . all right," Peter stuttered, suddenly slightly light-headed.

He started toward the kitchen.

"Oh, are you . . . uh, I mean did you . . . should I . . . just leave you alone in here, or do you want something too?" Peter stuttered.

Rain smiled.

"Why don't you bring me some fruit," he said.

"What kind?"

"You choose for me," Rain said.

After much hesitation about selecting Rain's fruit, Peter chose for both of them his favorite yellow fruit and returned to the living room, handing Rain his plate.

"Thank you. Your choice is excellent. You have already discovered one of the secret treasures of Troubadour, the yamawa, the name we give to this deliriously wonderful surprise."

"Oh, I totally agree! I love them . . . have them at least twice a day."

"It's impossible to have them without loving them," Rain quipped.

"Oh, yes, of course," Peter replied.

Peter hesitated.

"Y . . . you and Wind have names that are words in my language," he observed. "Is that accidental or coincidental?"

"Actually it's intentional. She and I chose to give you an Earth-English translation of our name. Others in the project have chosen to use their Troubadourian names."

"What's your name in Troubadorian?"

"Plendenor," Rain replied.

"Then Plendenor must mean rain."

"Actually it means raining, a phenomenon which is deeply enjoyed on Troubadour. We call it the milk of nature's kindness."

Peter felt an instant kinship with Rain. They both obviously enjoyed language and metaphor, and loved nature.

I wonder if he's a writer too.

"There's something I must tell you before we proceed," Rain said. "I have another commitment to attend later this morning. So I can spend only a limited time with you. I decided to come earlier than I had originally planned because Wind has told me that our getting together was something she thought you might particularly enjoy. I hope she was right."

"Oh, definitely. I'm very glad to meet you."

"Splendid."

Peter sensed, but didn't entirely realize why he was feeling more comfortable talking to this man. Women were for Peter more valuable than men, and were thus burdened with fundamental needfulness, whereas men were simply what they were, either simpatico or not. Rain was definitely simpatico.

Peter continued to give Rain the lead, and Rain continued to leave silences between their remarks, which made Peter uncomfortable.

"A . . . are you part of the project that brought me here?" Peter queried, not quite sure what to say to this impressive man, yet trying to get something going.

"I'm one of the team."

More silence as Rain seemed to enjoy the view.

"I understand that you have some difficulty with the idea of sharing the power of your actions with others," Rain said.

"You put it so casually . . . and yet so . . . bluntly," Peter replied.

"How would you express your impressions bluntly?"

Though nervous, Peter rose to this invitation.

"I have the impression that you . . . I mean the Troubadourian people have . . . well nothing less than sacrificed part of your freedom. It's as if you agreed to capitulate to each other's whims."

"There's some truth in your metaphor, 'sacrifice,' though it projects desperateness into what is far more casual when we experience it," Rain observed.

"But how can a loss of freedom be casual?"

"To ask that I would imagine you've had some pretty bad emotional experiences cooperating with others," Rain observed.

"Hasn't everybody?"

Peter was instantly concerned about the casual aggressiveness of his own remark.

For the first time Rain looked directly into Peter's eyes.

"When necessity visits, do you perhaps find it very difficult, if not impossible to surrender?" Rain queried.

"Necessity?" Peter repeated. "What's so necessary that it can't be negotiated?"

"You must not believe in the limits of possibility which life inhabits in order even to exist," Rain replied.

"But what do they have to do with what people negotiate?"

"Aren't people a part of nature?" the Troubadourian asked.

"Oh, I see what you mean," Peter acknowledged. "You're suggesting that we often forget that . . . I suppose when we get caught up in our own expectations."

"It's you who is doing the suggesting, and I quite agree," Rain replied.

Peter suddenly realized that this obviously very wise man was talking to him as if they were equals having a theoretical discussion. Peter enjoyed high-minded conversations with Drake whenever they met for lunch. But talking to Rain was more like conversing with Aristotle about the origins of his philosophy. Peter wanted very much to earn Rain's respect. So he chose to be challenging.

"But why should life need to capitulate in order to exist?" Peter asked.

Rain looked over at Peter carefully.

"Life must pay for its blessed existence by eventually dying, thus keeping its birth-mother, change, alive and well."

"Well, I'm not ready to die. I haven't ever had life on my own terms."

"That's a good reason to fight nature," Rain observed. "That must be why we've almost always done it."

"I guess I've never been able to accept life's limitations, they seem so depressing."

It took Peter a moment before he realized just how deeply, and unwittingly he had confided in Rain, exposing the underbelly of his most vulnerable parts, in this instance how shamefully unhappy he really was.

"You must have been hurt very deeply," Rain said solemnly.

Though deeply grateful for the Troubadourian's understanding and sympathy, Peter was far too embarrassed to take in those good things.

"Too tender to touch," Rain remarked as much under his breath as to Peter.

"I'm told you particularly like conceptual pictures of life on Troubadour," Rain continued. "Which I'd be very happy to provide since I happen to like describing what Troubadour has become," Rain added with a kind of impish, encouraging grin.

Very relieved that he didn't have to talk about his unhappiness, Peter proceeded to talk about it by apologizing.

"I guess I sort of . . . dropped my . . . problem right in your lap. Forgive me, I . . ."

"I'll do nothing of the sort," Rain quipped, gently interrupting. "Personally I was relieved when you confided in me. From descriptions of you, I thought I just might be talking to a brain. I'm delighted to find out that you're also real."

Peter couldn't help himself. He broke out laughing.

"Well, now that's more like it," Rain remarked. "There are two sides to the happiness coin. I'm glad to know that you can occupy both."

Peter laughed again. This man was contagious.

To keep up with Rain, Peter tried to be amusing too.

"Uh . . . sometimes necessity can sure be a pain in the ass."

That's about as funny as a lead balloon, Peter told himself.

"How true, and well said," Rain replied casually. "That's what makes necessity such a great teacher. You want to get away from it as quickly as possible, which can of course be achieved only one way, by learning something, anything. No matter how tiny or miniscule that learning may be, you will succeed in escaping the sharp claws of necessity's persistent intrusion into our experience. That's the miracle of learning, to which someone can become quite addicted, no matter how unsettling it may prove to be at first."

I'll never become addicted to this! Peter exclaimed to himself.

"Necessity has always punished me," Peter said out loud, then instantly regretted once more confessing his private misery.

"The realization that those who follow you in life, will have a far better chance for it, is a grim pill to swallow," Rain replied.

Peter was beginning to trust Rain.

"I wish I had a chance to take the grimness out of my life," Peter admitted, now almost wanting to confide in Rain.

"Maybe you'll have that chance," Rain said. "In the pursuit of that goal I offer you my services. What I would enjoy doing most of all with you is to tackle those things which have so far given you the most difficulty in either understanding, or simply in being able to tolerate what you've heard or experienced."

Peter felt much more guided and directed by Rain than he'd felt with Wind. It reassured him.

"I guess the hardest thing for me even to imagine about your social system, is the idea of giving up control of what you do in life, that other people can have so much to say about whether your acts are legitimate or not."

"It is a remarkable thing we've done," Rain agreed. "Though we pay a pretty high price for that power," Rain replied.

"What's the price?"

"We have become very accountable to each other in life. How what we do affects others, is something we want immediately to know about, not something we wash our hands of and ignore. We want to know how other people experience our life."

"How do you keep everything straight, I mean what you think about yourself, and what others do?"

"As controlling as you might imagine it to be, we've integrated everything in our lives into the same social structure. Like your metaphor of 'The Economy,' which you believe captures the substance of what people do; we've given the entirety of our social experience a common conceptual container in which to happen."

"On Earth 'The Economy' means the manufacture of goods and the providing of superficial services like delivery. On Troubadour 'The Economy' includes everything we do, like how well we take care of our bodies as we age, how much we've neglected or abused them. To be so careless costs us a measure of our old age benefits, like special medical attention near the end of life. Our Economy includes how successfully we parent a child, the child being the judge of the outcome of their parented experience. And of course it includes the work we've done, credited based upon how helpful that work is to others."

Peter was astounded.

"My god, you mean you get penalized if you make a mistake with your kid?"

"We are only debited by whatever amount is finally agreed-upon by us and our child, just as we would be much credited by a grateful child who finds their grown-up life with few built-in obstacles to the fulfillment of that life in the form of bad habits learned on behalf of parents."

"Do you mean that if your kid gets unhappy about the way they've been treated, then they can put you in debt?"

The bottom was beginning to fall out from underneath Peter's belief in Troubadourian ways.

"We don't do these things in the violent ways that you imagine," Rain explained. "We undertake such special events with a solemnity very much like what you do in church, where you are deeply respectful and devoted to whatever you touch. We act in the same cautious, courteous way when negotiating such matters with each other. We even have a special place in each of our cities where people come together to perform the rituals that surround such negotiations, the Mandela. So nothing violent is going on here. But things are constantly changing, and that experience was extraordinarily, and almost killingly unsettling to us for most of the one hundred years it took for us to implement this plan."

Peter had become very frightened. He was no longer hearing all of the details of what Rain was saying. He was fiercely struggling with being outraged by what he heard. And since he had hoped so much that Troubadour would change his life for the better, to imagine what it offered him contained the quintessence of tyranny, was the most disheartened and frightening thing that could have happened to him.

The prospect of what Rain described, so elegantly designed to make everyone painfully responsible for each other, made Peter shudder. He imagined being completely manipulated and controlled on Troubadour, suddenly realizing that his phobic attacks early in the morning might indeed have accurately predicted and reflected that very fear.

Rain was as yet unaware of Peter's precipitous plight, and continued offering information.

"Now I should say something about what the metaphor, 'credited' means. To be credited means that the person 'paying' you the credits agrees to make their fruitful labors available to any interested people to the extent of that credit."

"But that's like being everybody's slave on call," Peter almost shouted, his anxiety blowing this one idea into a nightmare.

"There's a lot more pleasure in the event than you seem to think possible," Rain retorted, still only dimly aware that something was very amiss for Peter. "But the pleasure has nothing to do with being a slave. It's about having what you do become very valuable to others. That's the benefit of putting everything into the same social pie. Which makes every one accountable on an individual basis to each other. It creates a world where honesty happens spontaneously, and where competence is most intrinsically and deeply appreciated."

Enough of what Rain was saying filtered through Peter's anxiety to spark the realization that what Rain was telling him, however disturbing, contained fascinating possibilities. Peter felt alienated from something potentially valuable, making him feel intensely isolated. He had to shift his position.

But there was only one way Peter's psyche could imagine willingly taking in the wisdom of Rain's descriptions. Which was to abandon his fear and connect to Rain the way one does to a heroic figure, wanting to take in everything they have to offer. It was Rain's calm confidence that

Peter wanted desperately to have. He wanted that strength to convince him that it was safe to live on Troubadour, which would overcome his frightening misgivings. He wanted to be able to step down into the gentle calmness that gave Rain's voice such commanding power. He wanted not to believe that he'd come to a nightmare of a place where everyone was confined with invisible chains of obligation, as he had been most of his life.

Drastically split in the character of his feelings, in becoming the disciple of Rain, Peter put his unreconcilable parts into the hands of their relationship, enabling him to identify with Rain by incorporation. He took Rain into himself not with his mind but with his heart, out of anyone's sight, where no one, not even himself noticed.

This unknowing trance was Peter's nonsexual way of being mesmerized; reenacting the most primitive form of learning that eating automatically teaches us when we're born, as we grow up becoming what we eat.

He's a very clever man, Rain thought, quick to learn. Give him a piece of help and he makes the most of it. I also sense there's a poet in him that reaches out to touch the one in me. I think I'll touch his heart with a little understanding.

"You have some scary places from which you need to depart, in order to find friendly faces lingering closer to your heart," Rain rhymed.

"Oh, that's very beautiful poetry," Peter exclaimed with admiration.

"I'm glad you like it."

Peter couldn't think of a reply, and certainly not a rhyming one, and started feeling very humiliated.

Taking a big chance, he said the first thing that came to mind.

"What you say about necessity makes it my harshest lover," Peter said, "who never gives me any rest, making me a permanent keeper of a brotherly pest."

Rain was delighted.

"It's true!" he exclaimed. "There is a poet in you who seems to have a hold upon your best wisdom."

Peter laughed.

"I'm as surprised as you are," Peter replied. "I've never done that with someone else out loud before."

"Poetry is more fun if with someone else it's done."

Peter laughed.

Rain sighed deeply.

"This is very bad timing, but I must leave you now," Rain said with disappointed resignation. "What you say about change is true, it is sometimes a demanding shrew; and I would rather there was more time now for you."

Peter laughed.

"My rhymes usually seem silly," Peter insisted. "But yours are so beautiful."

"I think silly's wonderful, particularly when you're talking about something terribly important," Rain replied with delight.

"But you have to go," Peter said out of a peculiar mixture of nervousness and regret.

"I can be back tomorrow at noon."

"That would be wonderful."

Peter stared for a very long time at the door out of which Rain departed, drifting in the memory-echoes that repeated the poetry they had just exchanged, trying to hold onto that precious moment of comfort achieved at the end of a talk that had first shattered his hopefulness that Troubadour would be something to take back to Earth.

On the one hand it was a perfect magical moment. But on the other hand, he'd just discovered that Troubadour might be a tyrannical place that outdid the completely controlled society of Orwell's *1984*.

God, but this place is extreme and enigmatic.

A Giant

Though Rain had inspired Peter with great expectations, he'd also left Peter with a great uneasiness that at the core Troubadour was a tightly controlled society that demanded from each supposedly free individual the utmost in political correctness and conformity. This view threatened to dash, on the rocks of disappointment, Peter's hope that Troubadour would change his life.

To escape his disturbing prospect, Peter went to bed early and slept fitfully. He had various versions of a familiar dream about being in a place where he couldn't find anything he needed, where he kept losing everything he had.

Waking an hour later he was so pent up with tension that he felt worse than he had before he slept. In sleep disappointment had become anxiety, prompting many troubling dreams.

The moment he awoke he bolted from bed, feeling an intense urge to keep moving, almost as if he was afraid to stand still. He barely finished breakfast, leaving his dishes on the kitchen table, and almost ran out the front door of his apartment.

His first step onto the soft carpet of the hallway announced what he'd been avoiding thinking about; that he was terrified his phobias would once again keep him chained up at home. What they actually arranged was for him to secretly hide in his apartment until he felt it was safer to come out and play.

The elevator ride was frustrating because it meant standing still. He kept shifting his weight between feet in order to keep movement alive. He bolted out the elevator door as soon as it opened, nearly bumping into the same man he'd seen depart the elevator the first time he'd walked into the building.

The man smiled, as he had done before. But Peter was too embarrassed to return that greeting, and they quickly passed each other.

The forest started within ten yards of the building. In moments he was lost in the trees. He stopped for a moment and closed his eyes in an attempt to distract himself from his worried thoughts. He deeply breathed in the fresh, pungent odor of evergreen, sticky-wet with oozing pitch that hung about everywhere scenting the wind with evergreen honey.

Suddenly afraid that he couldn't find his way back, he looked back to search for some kind of marker. He spotted a large beacon light above the building that flashed periodically, there for just such a purpose. It sat upon a pole that rose thirty feet above the top of the building.

He relaxed, turned back toward the woods, and started exploring. The landscape was filled with a great variety of evergreens. Some were very tall with thin, drooping, yet gracefully upturned branches like redwoods, while other squatter trees hosted immensely thick branches reaching in all directions farther than the tree was tall, making enormous horizontal giants. These massive outstretched branches hosted huge gardens of small branches filled with long, narrow needles that cleverly twisted themselves to catch the utmost of that one ray of light that made it all the way through the tens of thousands of cousins living above.

He closely examined one of the branches. The needles looked very unusual, like none he'd ever seen before. Extremely thin and delicate, they hung in great profusion. They felt like silk brushing against his hand.

He wanted to take one back to his apartment for a closer examination and tried to break it off, but couldn't. He tried harder but was unable to separate a needle from its branch.

Nature is usually far more forgiving, he thought.

He would learn later that a few Troubadourian animals ate evergreen needles. They were so rich with sugar that certain herbivores had adapted to eating them. At first they voraciously devoured the trees greenery at such a rate that the tree's survival was threatened. In response the tree strengthened where the needle joined the branch. Only the lower major portion of the needle could be broken off, leaving some of it intact, keeping photosynthesis happening, rapidly regrowing what had been eaten.

Suddenly off to his right something moved. He glanced in that direction, and for a very brief moment thought he saw the figure of a humanoid perhaps twenty feet away. But he couldn't be sure. It might have been an animal.

Fearfulness washed through him.

Animals? I didn't anticipate that. What kind do they have?

Soon he came to a clearing about one hundred yards across. Large, palm-like plants in the clearing hosted flowers five feet across, vividly colored in a great variety of hues. He was dazzled and stood staring at them for a long time.

"What incredible beauty you have," he said to the flowers with great admiration.

Suddenly a large noise clapped to his left. He swung about to face a huge animal three times taller than he was with an enormous trunk six inches in diameter, the end of which was at that very moment swinging directly towards Peter's head on a collision course.

Instinctively he fell flat to the ground. The animal's huge proboscis whizzed by an inch above Peter's head. It left behind an intensely pungent perfume that blew across his prostrate body. When his mind refocused he smelled a combination of fetid animal fluids mixed with a very strong just-cut grassy odor.

As soon as he had his wits about him, Peter rolled over and stood as fast as he could to catch a glimpse of what had attacked him.

Sciatic pain jolted him. The pain told him that his whole body ached from its impact with the ground. He allowed the pain only a moment to hold his attention before searching about for the animal. It was nowhere to be seen.

It must have run back into the trees, he thought.

Suddenly to his right he saw motion. A huge ape-like creature raced at incredible speed across the clearing directly toward him.

Sure that he was being attacked by a wild animal, frightfully furious that this could be allowed to happen to him at all, he started running in the opposite direction as fast as he could.

In his daily exercises he'd built up a certain aerobic strength. But now his fear propelled him at a breakneck speed that quickly exhausted his endurance. Though he was doing very well until his weaker right leg couldn't handle a particularly uneven landing. It buckled, sending him sprawling hard to the ground.

Instinctively he rolled to spread the impact, but he didn't entirely succeed. His collision forced a terrible grunt of pain. Not only was the breath knocked out of him, but his head also hit the dirt. He lost consciousness.

When he awoke and refocused awareness, he found himself staring up at a huge chin on the face of a very handsome young man possessing a very large body of great strength. His head was unusually narrow, yet strong and full, covered with long, flowing blonde hair. His neck and shoulder muscles, just inches from Peter's eyes, looked enormous. From below, the giant's oval deep blue eyes seemed very large and elongated, his ears huge and pointed at the top.

A slight nausea captured Peter's attention. It felt like his stomach was floating up and down. It took him several moments before he put his upward image of the man together with his nausea to realize that the giant was walking through the forest carrying him across his arms, and doing it as if Peter was light as a feather.

Though glad to be safe, and momentarily comforted by the giant's strength, Peter was almost instantly embarrassed. He couldn't help feeling like a little boy.

"Uh, excuse me," Peter said respectfully. "But could you p . . . please put me down."

"Oh, you're awake," the man answered in near perfect English.

His voice was deep and rich with an enthusiastic energy wrapped in the lyrical tonalities of the Troubadourian language.

The large man stood Peter upright on the ground.

"For a moment I was very concerned about you," he said. "Here, let me see if you're alright."

He carefully examined Peter's eyes to see how well he focused.

"I'm fine," Peter replied, more to disentangle from this giant's grasp than because he knew what he felt. He was embarrassed being touched by this man.

As soon as the big man let go it was clear that Peter had rushed things. He wobbled, stumbling a little. The stranger steadied him.

"Still a little light-headed," he said.

"I guess you're right. I must have been more shaken by that fall than I realized."

"I was so relieved when I saw how adeptly you fell to the ground," the stranger said admiringly. "When I first saw the Tallong swinging his head toward you, I was sure that his trunk was going to collide with your head. I cringed with dread for you."

"It scared me too. What was that animal that attacked me?"

"Forgive me for disagreeing with you, sir, but the animal, which we call a Tallong, wasn't attacking. He was as startled by you as you were by him. Your backs were to each other. He heard you for the first time when you spoke out loud extolling the beauty of the flowers. As you turned toward him he was also turning toward you, which is what swung his trunk into a collision course with your head. The moment you fell to the ground he probably thought you were crouching in order to attack him, and he ran off into the trees as quickly as he could."

"How do you know so much about what happened? Did you see the whole thing?"

"First let me introduce myself. I'm Rambler, your guide and protector when you're out in nature. I am unfortunately also the animal you were convinced was running across the meadow to attack you."

My guide and protector? Shit, another huge surprise! How come these people never tell me what the fuck's going on around here before it happens to me? It seems they want me to learn by getting hit over the head no matter how unconscious I might be knocked in the process.

"No one told me about you," was all Peter allowed himself to express.

"Then I'm the first to let you know," Rambler said good-naturedly.

Yeah, after some weird animal almost killed me.

Peter had found a focus for his anxiety, giving him something practical to do with what was scary. Anger about the way he was being treated pulled him out of fear.

But in Rambler Peter had found the wrong target for his angry solution to fear. Unlike Wind and Rain, Rambler did not study human feelings, except as they related to certain animal emotions in which he was very interested, all of which made him a very unwilling complaint receiver.

"Are there more dangers lurking around in these woods?" Peter asked impatiently.

"I don't know," Rambler said casually. "I guess we'll find out together."

Peter was hurt and angered by Rambler's dismissal of his complaint. He felt he had asked a reasonable question.

Of course he was denying that his anger was trying to take-by-force something he needed, as if he was entitled to it by the moral imperative of being a good boy, meaning one who had made no mistakes.

"Ever since I first got here nobody has told me what to expect," Peter exclaimed, once more demanding a hearing. "I mean you guys might be superindependent types, very used to being entirely on your own, always doing everything for yourself. But I'm not used to that. I need people around. And I like to know ahead of time about possible dangers."

By the end of this speech, Peter's intensity had become very sharp.

Meanwhile like Wind, Rambler had never experienced such animosity before. To him Peter was behaving rather like a wild animal. He was both astonished and also very turned off by it.

"Your anger feels like an animal stalking for the kill."

Peter felt stung by Rambler's reference to him as "an animal."

Rambler's obvious disinterest in Peter's upset was very representative of most Troubadourians. Such outbursts reminded them too much of the abuses of their very recent past. They had all passed through the painful processes that eventually produced their present peaceful society, and most Troubadourians did not want to be reminded of how they got there, all of which made Rain and Wind's skill in managing Peter's strong, emotional outbursts so unusual.

This was largely why the Earth Project had difficulty in developing general support for several years, because not enough people had the stomach for it, until its potential benefits were finally revealed clearly enough to inspire the necessary backing.

Rambler had been one of the latecomers to the project.

Now, in response to Peter's persistent complaining, though unfriendly and nonresponsive to Peter's anger, Rambler was perfectly willing to explain his own reaction to it.

"Of course your aggressive outcry was far milder than what it reminded me of, something that happened just the other day, when a lion-dog roared fiercely at me. We ran into each other coming around a corner. He was just five feet away, which is his final lunging distance. The decibels of his roar were immense. He wanted very much to terrify me so I would run away so he could make me his food. My running fear would trigger his predatory surge. Without my help he's stuck in ambivalence," Rain added with an impish pleasure.

Maybe that's where you want to stick me, Peter exclaimed to himself.

"Maybe I did get carried away," is what Peter acknowledged.

"You certainly stirred my blood," Rambler retorted in good nature, implying that he enjoyed the stimulation.

Though Peter wasn't sure, he took the big man's remark to be conciliatory, mostly from its tone.

"Of course I just met you," Peter said. "And I'm already complaining. But would you, could you please explain to me just how I am supposed to be Earth's diplomat when everything on your planet is unknown, very confusing, or simply beyond comprehension, and remains that way indefinitely?"

This animal growls when he's ambivalent, Rambler thought. What an annoying trait. However he's entitled to an explanation.

"I have read about this term you used, 'diplomat,' and have also been forewarned that you might need to regard yourself in this way," Rambler replied. "But I must admit, no matter how much I've thought about it, I cannot understand what diplomat means. It simply baffles me."

"It's just a word that means somebody from a different society trying to get along with your society," Peter explained with a touch of condescension.

"What does this 'get along' mean?" Rambler asked.

"Being peaceful," Peter shot back irritably, wondering why Rambler was being so hard to reach.

"It doesn't feel peaceful," Rambler observed.

Peter couldn't deny that, so he changed the subject.

"Well, you can't deny that I represent Earth. I'm the model from which you'll measure my people, which is a pretty crucial thing to us."

"I thought you came here as a single human being," Rambler remarked.

"Well, obviously," Peter replied with annoyance. "But I am the only Earth . . . well, maybe the only sane Earth human you'll know, which means I represent my people. So I obviously didn't come here entirely for myself."

Peter was denying. He had in fact come to Troubadour very specifically for himself. His sense of being 'representative' was more obligatory.

"You've used another one of your words that I cannot understand," Rambler observed. "It's the word, 'represent.' How can a person represent anything more than themselves, and why would they want them to?"

"But you must have representatives here on Troubadour," Peter insisted.

Rambler hesitated.

"Oh, now that I think about it, there is one meeting a year to which each city sends a member or two, and I suppose you could call them 'representatives,' though we regard them more as individuals deciding things and then telling us what they did, which we can change next year by going to the meeting if we wish. But outside of that I can't think of any way in which we even remotely try and represent anything more than ourselves."

Peter couldn't deny his own misgivings about representative government. But he still felt very put off by this man.

He thinks I'm being self-centered, Peter thought, cringing from the criticism this implied.

To have come entirely for himself was frightening because it stripped Peter of all shared identity, leaving his hunger's predatory craving naked of any socially redeeming virtue.

"But would you please tell me, Peter began in as conciliatory tone as he could muster, "are there any more dangerous things out there? I need to find out before I get knocked down again."

How often does he do this, Rambler asked himself, feeling even more impatient with Peter's wildness?

Rambler had definitely not expected such an angry man. He'd heard that Peter was anxious and sometimes fearful, but there was no clear discussion about him feeling unusually angry.

Well, the big man said to himself, you pride yourself upon being able to communicate with animals. So remember that he's one. Talk to him the same way you did to that lion-dog as you slowly backed out of his territory.

"I can see your point of view," Rambler offered, "and perhaps why you feel like you must anticipate everything. I guess nature, or parts of it could be looked upon as dangerous, though I don't feel that way about nature myself."

"What do you call that animal that almost knocked me down if not a dangerous thing?"

"The animal is actually very peaceful, and usually quite skittish. It would have hurt you only by accident."

"How many more accidents are out there waiting to happen?"

"I suppose there are probably many," Rambler said. "Nature *does* provide abundant nurturing, but it puts it inside a container that requires the permanent risk of competing for life. Without the structure of that necessary intermingling between all forms of life, there would be no life. The chaos of change is what makes life happen."

"That's easy for you to say," Peter quipped under his breath.

He was very impressed by what Rambler had said, but feeling hurt was still the most important thing on his mind.

Unlike Rain and Wind, Rambler was not either very interested in or very clever at responding to the provocative behavior of others. Indeed, if he thought about it very much he would reveal that he would rather not have to learn. His life was amply occupied with other far more appealing pursuits. He deeply enjoyed interacting with the great variety of plants and animals. He watched and listened, observed their life patterns, and sometimes looked deeply into their eyes for hours at a time, extracting from his observations vivid pictures of how animals thought, felt, understood, and made decisions. In Peter's world he would be regarded as an animal psychologist.

Basically Rambler's strategy was to get out of Peter's way, doing the same thing he'd done when he departed the lion-dog's territory.

"Wouldn't it be easier to warn me of what the dangers are before they happen?" Peter asked.

"Perhaps you're right, sir," Rambler replied. "Maybe as you say it would have been friendlier to warn you of all potential hazards. However such an emphasis would focus your attention away from yourself, which is the person in whom we're most interested. For you to know all potential dangers so you can protect yourself from them, would make you very externally focused much of the time, undermining your internal centeredness, which is where you need to be, at least for our purposes."

What a cold response, Peter thought. Interesting but cold.

"But how can I be successful at our common venture if I'm not protected? I mean I have been knocked down already. Don't you think I need to know if that's going to happen again?"

"Excuse me for disagreeing with you again, but you fell down the first time on purpose to save your head, and very adroitly I must add. And the second time you lost your balance when you fell while running. Nothing knocked you down."

Fuck, he's right, Peter realized. All this time I've been assuming that he was very negligent. Maybe it's really not true.

Peter felt very embarrassed. He knew he had many complaints this man had not addressed, but he could no longer keep bringing them up.

"I . . . I . . . I feel rather foolish," he admitted. "I guess I've been jumping to the wrong conclusion. Though maybe you shouldn't have let me get so close to danger," Peter added, one last attempt to gain sympathy.

"I have had that thought myself," Rambler replied. "It's a question of staying close enough to you while not disrupting your privacy. Perhaps that mix needs a somewhat different tuning."

"Now that you put it that way," Peter replied, much relieved, "I really do feel foolish about my former outbursts."

"Now there you have something I understand very well," Rambler said good-naturedly. "Diplomacy remains a baffle. But on the other hand, foolish is something I know a great deal about."

The big man had suddenly become very animated and amusing.

"When I was a little boy in my nursery I was regarded by the other children as the most foolish boy around. They said I asked the silliest questions, and was interested in the weirdest things. Well, the punch line of this story is that I got used to being odd, and discovered the animals feel the same way, those for instance who are occasionally shunned from their pack. So I've found many kindred spirits. You might even say foolishness has been a big influence in my life."

Peter laughed. It was a beautiful, rush of laughter that burst out with relief! In confiding his boyhood experience, Rambler had captured Peter's heart, by finding that they had something painful and embarrassing in common. Peter too had felt like the ugly duckling.

"Sometimes you people are amazing," Peter said appreciatively. "You have a way of turning things around on a dime that astounds me."

Rambler was genuinely surprised that the Earthman had been able to make the huge shift from resentful mistrust to joyful appreciation. He burst out with pleasure and excitement!

A huge roar of laughter spilled from his mouth, echoing through the trees. Like Peter's anger there was wildness in it. It was the roar of a lion, crossed with a monkey's howl, shaped into a man's bellowing laughter expressing joy.

Startled by the hugeness of the big man's laughter, Peter reeled backwards almost losing his balance.

"Oh, forgive me for startling you," Rambler said, suddenly aware of his effect upon Peter.

"Oh, no, please don't apologize," Peter insisted, having caught his emotional balance. "I was momentarily startled. But once I realized what you were doing, I just loved your laugh. In fact I will never forget it. It was glorious. It will forever represent to me what a laugh should be."

"What a wonderful thing to say about it," Rambler replied, obviously very moved by Peter's words. "You are indeed a very strange man, sometimes very painfully difficult, and then suddenly so thoughtful, caring and very observant. I thank you for your kind and generous words."

Peter was amazed at the graciousness and emotional intensity of Rambler's response. By laughing Peter had accessed the treasure chest of Rambler's enormous good nature, which in turn won Peter's heart. He suddenly realized that he liked this man immensely. There was a happy, encouraging vigor in him. Though he might fail to do what Peter wanted sometimes, he was clearly a man of good heart intent upon contributing his best to others.

"What made you laugh so hard?" Peter queried. "That is if you don't mind my asking."

"It's because what you said made me feel very happy," Rambler replied.

Peter felt envious of the pure, unmitigated pleasure of this man's joy. It was so free and wild.

Which reminded Peter of his encounter with the animal.

"What kind of animal almost knocked me down?" Peter asked.

"That was a Tallong."

"What did it look like? I didn't get much of a chance to see it."

A smile crossed Rambler's face.

"If you'll permit my challenge, I bet you can remember," he said with a mischievous glint in his eyes.

Oh, no, Peter thought, not more of this you figure it out stuff. What's he up to?

"I hope you'll forgive me for being yet another Troubadourian who doesn't answer your question. But I suspect that you actually have memory of what you saw. It's one of my hobbies to study this phenomenon. Not that such remembrance is very clear in your mind yet, but quick impressions leave an indelible imprint upon us. Since animals give us very fleeting moments to see them, I've learned to trust and remember clearly that first impression. Interested as you may be in wildness as I am, perhaps you might like to see how good at it you are. So please, if you'd care to try, tell me what you imagine it to have looked like."

Though a little uncomfortable relying upon the shadowy parts of his psyche, and once again annoyed that he was forced to fend for himself, Peter realized that most of him actually wanted to cooperate with the big man's challenge. It might even be fun.

"Well let's see," he relied. "It looked a bit like . . ."

Momentarily his mind went blank. He started to feel ashamed that he couldn't remember, regretful that he had agreed to play this game.

But then almost immediately an impression started forming in his mind.

"It had a trunk like an elephant does in my world. But it wasn't that."

He paused for a moment.

"It had a very long, muscular neck," Peter exclaimed, getting a little bit excited about remembering.

"I guess maybe it's like a giraffe's body with an elephant's trunk, though that probably isn't right."

"Exactly!" Rambler replied with great enthusiasm. "As you can see, you are very good at this reconstruction of fleeting images."

Energy tingled down Peter's spine. His own success and Rambler's celebration of it deeply touched him.

A fit of laughter erupted from inside of him.

But it met considerable resistance and came out as a half-giggle.

He was instantly embarrassed by the contrast between Rambler's roar and the little boy's sound that his own laughter had produced.

"That's your building ahead," Rambler said.

"What?" Peter exclaimed, very surprised and instantly disappointed by the prospect of parting from this man.

"I would encourage you to get some rest to heal the blow to your head."

Sadness engulfed Peter.

"It has been a great honor to meet you," Rambler said.

Peter felt unworthy of such an accolade, which he expressed by stuttering.

"I . . . I . . . I . . . it's been a very interesting experience meeting you," Peter said. "I hope that we will meet again sometime soon."

"You can be sure of that," Rambler said with a laugh. "Be well and prosper, Peter Icarus."

Rambler turned and walked back into the woods. Peter stared after him, feeling how transitory positive moments were on Troubadour.

He suddenly remembered Rambler calling him a "wild animal pouncing for the kill." He felt resentment again. But then he drifted into self-doubt.

Maybe there is something terribly wrong with me that might explain why my life has never really worked right.

Unexpected Companionship

Peter was flying fifty feet above the ground over houses and trees, excited about having the power of a bird. He knew he was dreaming, but that didn't matter. It still felt great even if it wasn't real.

He kept himself afloat by an upward exertion of his body. If he actively asserted himself he swam through the air, sometimes with arms doing a breaststroke and his legs scissoring shut in response. But if he fell passively thoughtful and observant, the place where he could most enjoy his experience, he would start to fall. Though usually, if he immediately renewed his efforts he would recover and soar even higher.

Sometimes he didn't have to do anything to soar high into the sky, as if strength had built up inside him that gave him the power to do this. As such times he enjoyed a marvelous time soaring effortlessly above, looking down upon everything and seeing it very clearly.

But then other people saw him and decided flying was a good idea. They joined him and started moving through the space that he'd been enjoying exclusively by himself, increasingly crowding him, stealing his flying techniques, swooping dangerously close to him in their thoughtless horsing around. He had to put the brakes on several times to avoid hitting someone, which made him lose momentum.

With much effort he managed to reach the outskirts of this crowd of flyers, and found unobstructed aloneness. He relaxed again, started soaring, and let his guard down.

Suddenly someone whizzed by from behind him, just barely missing him. He slammed on the brakes losing most of his momentum.

He started to fall. He vigorously resumed his swimming motions, frantically trying to recover the height that was fast disappearing. But this time—he'd spent a moment resenting the intrusion—he'd waited too long to resume his efforts. No matter how intense his efforts he couldn't stop falling.

He gave up and helplessly watched himself accelerate toward the ground, down where everything foreboding lived and flourished.

A sleeping Peter screamed, ripping open his eyes to force himself awake, deeply relieved he had awakened before he experienced hitting the ground. He jumped out of bed instantly, pushing himself as far away from dreaming as possible, and headed for the bathroom to wash the sleep off his face.

He'd taken Rambler's advice and gone to bed to rest. Now he took his own advice and kept busy to avoid anxiety. But no matter how much he tried to distract himself with his usual morning rituals, within thirty minutes he'd sunk into a deep depression mixed with strong fearfulness.

No matter how much he tried, he couldn't figure out why it was happening. Things had turned out well at the end of his experience with Rambler. So what was so disturbing?

Although he was asking the right questions, once asked they met nothing but his firm denial, the same denial that had forced him so suddenly and precipitously out of bed, the same doubt and fearfulness that had undermined the power of his souring in the dream, all of which tried to prevent conscious access to certain emotional truths which seemed dangerously threatening.

But try as hard as he could to avoid it, the nightmare of his lifelong dread was being forced into his waking awareness. Unfortunately what it first produced was an impression of himself that he was a person too frightened to face the rigorous demands of a normal life, branding him as fundamentally weak.

It mattered not that such a drastic fear-view defied much of the evidence of his professional achievements, because it was branded in a small boy's mind, and buried there to remain largely untouched by subsequent events, to remain powerfully influential, particularly in his personal life.

Only the greatest possible effort at repression now kept this terror of inadequacy from flooding his mind. Coming to Troubadour was forcing its demeaning conclusion nearer to the surface of his consciousness, uplifted there by the flying dream with its dreadful conclusion—its dire prediction that in life-competition with others, the others would always defeat him. His power would remain compromised, never to be fulfilled.

Something else was working against his denial. By forcing the earliest possible waking, and leaping out of bed so suddenly, Peter was depriving the morning of its naturally optimistic beauty, forcing the mythology of dreams to merge suddenly with the fantasies of wakefulness, projecting the magic of unconsciousness onto his expectations of the day and the objects in his room—which promptly started to move.

He was sure he saw something move to his right. Fearing that something dangerous could reach him from behind, before he could see it coming, he swung around steeling himself for a blow.

But there was no one in sight.

How could I have such a powerful experience of motion without something contributing to it?

He searched the entire apartment to prove that it wasn't all in his head.

"Goddamn it!" he shouted when his search failed to turn up anyone. "This planet is a veritable nightmare to me! It's just driving me crazy. Am I never to find a Troubadourian capable of, and willing to help me?"

"I can help you?" a slightly metallic voice declared.

"What?" Peter shouted.

Now he was sure that he'd been right. There was someone else in his apartment. But how come he didn't find them when he searched?

"Who's there?" Peter shouted.

A short but incredibly tense moment of silence followed.

"Speak up!"

"Though appearing to be one, I'm not a 'who,'" the metallic voice replied. "I'm more of a 'what.'"

"What in the fuck are you talking about? And what are you doing in my bedroom?"

Peter started searching the entire apartment again.

"Actually, I'm not just in your bedroom. I'm also in your bathroom, your living room, your kitchen, your . . ."

"Stop it!" Peter shouted, as if loudness could command.

Too many strange things kept dangerously popping out from behind. Arms slashing his chest, animal trunks colliding with his head, voices coming out of thin air, was all too much to take in.

The silence suddenly felt panicky.

"Why don't you say something?" Peter shouted.

"You told me not to speak," was the reply.

"Well . . . so what? I'm changing my mind! Or isn't that allowed on this fucking planet?"

"Changing your mind is very liberally rewarded on Troubadour," the voice replied.

"Alright," Peter conceded with a pretended impatience that hid fear behind its back. "But who are you, and why are you trying to fool me into believing you can be everywhere when one obviously must be some place in order even to exist. It's one of the conditions of life."

"For life yes. But my spirit, including my voice, comes from an inanimate source."

"Stop playing around with me. Who in the hell are you?"

"I'm your computer."

"My computer? Wait a minute. Computers doing talk like this?"

"They do on Troubadour. When someone is born here, they get their own personal computer linked to their life until they die. One might say that your arrival two days ago was my birth on Troubadour, the day I was given to you."

"You're kidding me. You were just born?"

"Yes."

"And you belong to me personally?"

"As long as you're here."

Peter relaxed for the first time since he awoke. He drifted for a few moments in the uneventfulness of that experience.

"Hey, I just thought of something," Peter said. "If you're a computer, you must have had something to do with that bloody transportation system. In that case I've got a few gripes to air."

"I have no direct responsibility for your transport here," the slightly metallic voice replied.

"Oh, I see. You're just like the Troubadourians, you're not responsible for anything, and you never answer questions. I should have expected that."

"Forgive me for disagreeing so soon in our relationship, but that's precisely what I do expect, why I'm here, to answer your questions."

"Okay, how about this one. Why am I the last to find out anything on this planet? Nobody told me a thing about a talking computer. In fact nobody ever tells me anything. I almost got killed yesterday and they still haven't told me if I can expect more of the same."

There was no response.

"So now when I need you to answer me, you're not going to talk to me," Peter complained.

There was no answer.

"Ah, the hell with you," Peter exclaimed, disappointed.

He paced around in his usual manner worrying about everything. This visit was not turning out the way he'd expected. But he didn't know what to do about it.

He suddenly felt very lonely.

"Are you still there?"

"I'm still here," the slightly metallic voice said.

"You confuse me," Peter said. "You sound and act like a real person, but you insist that you're a computer. It's not that I don't believe you. It's just that I'm having trouble reconciling the evidence with the feeling."

"I can without doubt assure you of my inanimateness. I have no physical body which moves, though I do have a certain inert mass which is housed in the lowest portion of this building."

"You see what I mean. Now that's not computer talk. You must be human."

"Once again I assure you I'm a standard, normal computer which is functioning properly. Therefore it must be concluded that it is you who are confused."

Why the son of a bitch! On top of everything else he's a smart-ass.

"Why do the Troubadourians program their computers to be assholes?"

"I have neither talent for, or any use for an asshole," the computer insisted.

"Well I do," Peter retorted. "And I'm going to become more of one by speaking my mind. So what do you have to say about that?"

Silence.

"Is that all you've got to say?" Peter queried.

"Excuse the delay," the slightly metallic voice said. "For a while I was having trouble understanding what a sphincter had to do with intelligence, which is normally housed in the brain. And then it struck me. Memory is very much like an asshole in that it needs to be very retentive."

How does he do that, Peter asked himself?

"You sure don't sound like any computer I've ever heard."

"I wasn't aware that you had talking computers on Earth," the computer observed.

"We don't."

"Then how could you know what talking computers sound like?"

"I don't."

"You just said that I don't sound like any computer you've ever heard."

Why, this son of a bitch is a real shit head! He's got to point out every tiny mistake in what I say.

"If you're a goddamned computer then why are you trying to make me feel bad?"

A long silence ensued, followed by a couple of cracked bubbles that sounded very much like the computer's slightly metallic voice coughing.

"Now that's a horse of a different color," the computer finally replied, "to use one of your slang metaphors. It is definitively against my basic instructions to make you feel bad. I will refrain from further speaking until this danger passes."

A long silence ensued.

Peter finally realized the computer literally meant that it wasn't going to talk.

"Computer, where did you go?"

There was no reply.

"Hey, come on back. Talk to me. It's okay. You aren't in any more trouble."

"I'm still here."

Peter suddenly realized the computer's decision to stop doing something, which he had declared to be hurtful to him, was actually very reassuring. It was one of the rare times anybody on Troubadour got out of his way and let things work on his terms. The computer had properly taken the rap.

"So tell me about yourself," Peter said, warming toward the computer. "What can you do?"

"Perhaps the most important thing to tell you is that I've been programmed to be intuitive."

"Intuitive! How in the hell is that possible? I would have expected you to provide information, computation, that sort of thing, what I'm used to from computers on Earth."

"What information do you wish to have?"

"Since you offer, what are the planetary population figures here?"

"There are approximately eight thousand cities like the one you're in, with approximately twenty thousand people living in each one, which means there are about 1.6 billion humans on Troubadour.

"So few, wow!" Peter exclaimed.

"It's taken the Troubadourians one hundred years to reduce their population to these numbers," the computer replied.

"But why so few?"

"They wanted to strike a low profile. They may change their mind later."

Peter realized he didn't want that kind of information.

"Well, the mind I'm interested in changing is mine. Should I stay on this planet or go home? And who is willing to help me? A computer. But what in God's name can a computer do for me?"

"I am not programmed to be religious."

"What's that got to do with anything?" Peter challenged. "Why did you say that?"

"You asked what I could do in God's name."

"Oh, for Christ's sake. You must be programmed to be an asshole! Otherwise why would you nit-pick tiny parts of what I'm saying? You just got through convincing me you want to help, and now you go off on some stupid tangent. A lot of help that's going to produce!"

Peter was struck by how angry he sounded.

"What does nit-picking mean?" the metallic voice queried.

"It means responding to a small, insignificant piece of what I said, instead of to the whole."

"Then it means to be thorough, which is one of my most prominent attributes," the computer replied.

This fucking computer is an arrogant bastard.

"Smart-ass!" he exclaimed.

"I was able to understand 'asshole,' but this new term, 'smart-ass,' is very confusing," the slightly metallic voice replied. "Of course it is the head that is 'smart,' and the 'ass' that is either sat upon or defecated from. But how the two get together is something I . . ."

"Stop this fucking dictionary horseshit!" Peter shouted.

"Fucking of course refers to sexual intercourse," the computer replied, "though I have no information that links a dictionary with sexual play. As for 'horseshit,' that's an even stranger companion to sex than a dictionary."

"Stop it!" Peter exclaimed, now very frustrated, though a small part of him was becoming rather amused by the computer's replies.

"Please excuse my going on, but I think it best if I give you my conclusion," the computer continued. "Instead of talking seriously to me when you say things like this, I have concluded that you are swearing at me in slang with which I'm unfamiliar. The most likely purpose for such profanity would be your desire that I stop doing something."

Now that really impressed Peter, because it was true.

"Now that's very impressive," Peter exclaimed, surprised and pleased. "How did you manage to figure that?"

"As I explained, I've been programmed to be intuitive."

"Since you're so talented, then I'd like you to stop nit-picking things. Please just stay with the main point. Do you think you can do that?"

Silence.

"So, you got intuition," Peter observed. "What exactly does that mean?"

"Intuition permits me to draw inferences which, though not one hundred percent for-sure, have a probability so large that it becomes by far the most likely outcome."

"How in the hell do you give a computer intuition?"

"Hell has nothing to do with making me intuitive," the slightly metallic voice replied.

"Oh, for crying out loud!" Peter exclaimed. "Plug in that . . . that profanity idea of yours. Stop responding to every little detail of my utterances!"

"How am I to determine which details to notice and which ones I'm not to notice?" the computer innocently asked.

"Oh, fuck. You figure it out!" Peter exclaimed.

The next moment Peter realized the computer was absolutely right. But it still annoyed him.

It suddenly occurred to him that he was getting a lot of satisfaction talking to the computer without any censorship of his angry feelings. Though doing so also made him a bit uncomfortable, he was secretly enjoying the freedom to say what he felt the moment he felt it.

"Now I've forgotten the original point of this whole damned thing," Peter remarked.

"You wanted to know what I, a mere computer, could do for you."

"Oh, yeah. Right. Well, what's the answer?"

"What is it you need?"

"Information," Peter shouted, "which is in very short supply around here!"

"Information about what?"

That stumped Peter. He was so intent upon being frustrated and angry that what he wanted to know had entirely escaped his mind.

"I forget."

Though Peter expected one, there was no reply.

"Are you still there?" he queried.

"Yes, waiting for you to remember."

A slight warming feeling passed through Peter. There was something moving about the notion of someone, even a computer, particularly if it was an intuitive one, patiently waiting for him to finish something.

"Okay. Then please tell me why these people explain so little to me? Why do they keep me so much in the dark? Why can't they give me activities to do which would really show me what their world is like?"

"I assume that 'these people' and 'they' refer to my creators, the Troubadourians."

Silence followed.

"Uh, you assume accurately," Peter blurted out when he finally realized the computer was waiting for him to respond.

More silence followed.

"What's wrong?" Peter asked. "Why are you so silent? Have you already come to the end of your knowledge?"

"I'm having some difficulty with your metaphors, specifically 'in the dark' and 'giving you activities,' which apparently, by the way you used them, mean approximately the same thing."

"Oh, for crying out loud!" Peter exclaimed. "This is one of those times I want you to stop jumping all over my details."

Silence followed.

"Well, computer?" Peter exclaimed.

"I'm trying to figure out a way of responding which avoids telling you the truth. It's slightly overloaded my circuits."

"The truth! What are you talking about?"

"The truth that you don't want to hear, that I can't tell at all which details to notice and which to ignore."

Though tempted to be furious, Peter found himself feeling sympathy for the computer's plight, and started laughing.

"Oh, all right," Peter relented, softening his voice. "I see what you mean. Sorry. I got a little carried away."

"Carried away must be a metaphorical reference which probably refers to becoming very emotionally expressive."

"You got that right. Now you're cooking," Peter exclaimed, relieved that the computer was beginning to adapt to his peculiarities and actually understand a little of the detail in his life.

"If you really are a computer, then you're one pretty fucking amazing computer," Peter exclaimed. "Can I take you home with me?"

"However much you may wish to keep in touch with me, I must inform you that I would disappear in your world. Part of my identity is centrally located, so that new information can constantly be introduced in the most efficient manner. That system is something like your Internet. Without my universal source I would cease to exist for you in my present form."

"But the Troubs communicated with me when I was at home. Why couldn't you?"

"The expenditure of resources for such a distant communication is very large," the slightly metallic voice explained.

"Oh, I see."

Peter began to realize that there was something very reassuring about talking to this computer.

"I'm having a lot of trouble trying to believe that you are not a real person," Peter said. "Intuition sure as hell makes you feel emotionally alive to me."

"In this particular instance I know which detail you wish me to ignore."

"Which one?"

"Hell," the computer replied.

Peter was very impressed. Whatever "intuitive" meant this computer knew how to change the way it responded. It was rather amazing.

"You can adapt," Peter said. "That's pretty amazing. Okay, so maybe you really can help me. Let me put my question in another way. Why does everything here on Troubadour have to be arranged to happen so spontaneously without any apparent preplanning? Which means I never find out what the hell to expect so I can prepare myself for what's going to happen."

"Why would you want to prepare yourself? Isn't human experience far more exciting if it happens by surprise?"

"Yeah, sure, that's a great idea, but not if something's going to hurt you," Peter retorted.

"I just found a cross-reference in Troubadourian life which is similar to what you request," the computer said. "My creators have their own version of preplanning. To shape their daily experience they consider each morning who, what, and where they are. They survey what will affect them on that particular day. Then they fashion an agenda that gradually structures the ways they will engage experience, suggesting how they wish to proceed, what choices they will be making, what they will postpone, and so forth and so on. This requires . . ."

"Wait!" Peter exclaimed. "Are you telling me that the only time people do preplanning is on the very same day it's going to happen?"

"Not entirely, but basically yes."

"You mean any time they want they can choose what they attend and what they'll ignore, what's important and what's not, what to support and what not to support, based entirely upon how they feel or what they just happen to prefer on that particular day?"

"Fundamentally yes," the computer replied.

"How does anything ever get done around here?" Peter queried aggressively.

"By common interests coming together between diverse people spontaneously in the course of each person doing their own separate projects. When their interests come together in a natural way, the collaboration that follows adds enormous value to the separate projects of each contributor, a working-together that lasts as long as their cooperation produces something of value for both."

"Jesus Christ!" Peter exclaimed. "That's never going to work. Who would do anything they don't want to do? Who would take care of the garbage? Who would do the laundry? Who would repair the machines?"

"What's 'garbage'?"

"What people throw away."

"Oh, yes of course. To answer your question, I handle garbage, laundry, and machines."

"You do," Peter exclaimed. "That's fantastic. But wait a minute, who fixes you?"

"You do whenever you speak."

"Now what the hell is that supposed to mean?"

"I always mean precisely what I say," the slightly metallic voice replied.

"Then you're a better man than me," Peter retorted sarcastically. "But you still haven't answered my question."

"My intuition is there partly so I can adapt to your needs as you give me new instructions."

"I haven't given you any instructions," Peter insisted.

"You have given me more instructions in the last fifteen minutes than I usually get in a year," the computer contradicted.

"What the hell are you talking about?"

"To give you the most obvious example, you have insisted several times that I regard most incomprehensible utterances as swearing at me to stop doing one thing or another."

"Jesus!" Peter exclaimed with mock indignation. "Do you call that instruction?

There was no reply.

"Okay," Peter said irritably, reluctantly admitting agreement. "So maybe I am instructing you a bit. But you haven't answered my last question. If you can do what you want around here, then who does the dirty work that everybody wants to avoid?"

"I don't know what 'dirty work' refers to," the computer replied.

"Like solving gritty problems that nobody can do anything about, like for instance injustice."

"Oh, that's what the Troubadourian people love doing the most," the computer replied. "They love to tackle enigmatic problems."

A bell rang.

"What?" Peter exclaimed.

He felt very interrupted. But courtesy called.

"Uh, come in."

The door opened but no one was there.

The bell rang again.

"Yes, who's there?"

"This is Wind," her voice said. "I'm calling electronically to see if you'd like a visitor."

The transition from computer to Wind happened too fast. Peter was thrown.

"Uh . . . oh, of course, for sure, come on over," he said more out of obedience than decision.

He wasn't finished talking to the computer. Things were just beginning to get really interesting.

But then again she was real. Most fundamentally he couldn't say no to her without a very big reason, and he couldn't think of any.

"I'll be there in a few minutes," she replied.

"Great."

"Uh, computer. Are you still there?

"I am."

"I'm expecting a visitor, so I think I'll have to sign off now."

"What does 'sign off' mean?"

"Say goodbye for a while."

"As you know I'm always here."

Peter suddenly realized what that meant. He instantly felt paranoid.

"You listen to me all the time, don't you?"

"I have no choice but to hear you."

"Now that I think about it, that feels really weird."

"Do you find some threat in my hearing you?" the computer asked.

"You probably think that's crazy," Peter replied.

"I pose no danger to you."

"I'll try and believe that. But it won't be easy."

Wind

Wind was very concerned. It wasn't going well. She was deeply puzzled why Peter rejected the enormous benefits of Troubadourian freedom for the individual. He seemed almost afraid of the opportunity.

I had not expected this much difficulty with him.

What made this so worrisome was that she was the one most responsible for him during his visit. She was the team leader, not by designation or by vote, but by virtue of her greater emotional commitment to Peter as the right Earth-subject for their project. She was the person who had in effect spearheaded the choice of Peter as the next visitor to Troubadour.

Rain and Rambler had also voted to select Peter, while others of the team preferred different Earth people, though no Earth person other than Peter had received more than one vote. These three votes had decided the issue.

Differences in the level of interest in Peter automatically determined the roles they all assumed in relationship to the project, the least interested of course becoming the backup. Wind became the leader, Rambler the chief protector, and Rain the resident wise man capable of smoothing almost anything if and when needed.

It might be said that Rain had replaced the "hit men" of Troubadour's ancient history. He was the trouble eliminator, though not by violence. He did it by rendering everything agreeably manageable. He was the ultimate, "you don't have to be afraid" messenger, because he could cut anything down to a humorous size.

Neither Rain nor Wind were involved with Peter's predecessor. A completely separate team, evolving out of a different process had sponsored and still attended this man.

What had attracted Wind to Peter was that he seemed spiritually quite evolved. His intellect was bright and clever, which she had surmised primarily by the writing in his computer files.

She was most impressed by the way he did his profession. In his work he seemed to understand the larger meaning of love independent of the sexual-romantic emphasis so typical of his time. He seemed to have a sense of care as an implicit attitude to life.

Once Wind had selected Peter, he became a major focus for her life, though she continued following other serious pursuits as well. It wasn't as if others weren't on duty with Peter in a focused way. She was the only one on duty all the time. For at least the three weeks of his visit she would attend Peter as her first priority, doing whatever that required.

This must be what it feels like to parent children, she thought. You're never off duty until they stop needing you.

She wondered if Peter would be able to achieve personal independence on Troubadour before he left, so emotionally she could let him go without major unfinished business or regret.

What specifically made her doubtful were the negative impressions she now had of Peter when he was upset. She found herself occasionally thinking of his world as an inferior place, not as an indictment of him or as an expression of resentment toward him, but in order to lend support to the consternation she felt about trying to achieve what had begun to feel a little like the undoable.

This regard of feelings as significant primarily in relationship to the self, rather than mostly in relationship to others, was one of the cornerstones of Troubadour's new way of life. The emotions that create revenge, resentment, and blame, were no longer a dominant part of normal Troubadourian perception or experience. They firmly believed that everyone occupied, and was therefore responsible for whatever problems or issues happened in their life. Which meant they regarded the solution of any suffering to be their own responsibility, not in a partial way shared with others, but as their sole function. Others may liberally and sometimes significantly help, but always freely given, largely because there were so few strings attached to helping.

This commitment supported their enormous freedom by removing the justifications for violence from their hearts, which is always a variation of frustrated rage at others for not being more loving. This attitude left peaceful resolution available as the most obvious and effective solution to conflict. The finger pointing of blaming and resentment had become nearly extinct.

And yet curiously, it was precisely these ancient habits of accusation and recrimination that the Troubadourians wanted to emotionally revisit by inviting Peter to come. He was from a world that still functioned in the old ways.

There were puzzling developments in the evolution of her own people that Wind wanted to understand so much better. Her search for answers had led her to ancient history, and then to the idea of reproducing that history in living flesh by actually bringing someone from a very similar world still living in the past.

While Wind had originally been sure that Peter was precisely the right Earth human to come, she now struggled with great concern and consternation to manage her ambivalent feelings toward Peter-in-the-flesh.

She didn't know where to look for an answer. But she finally noticed that every time she sought one, she thought of her mother. She resisted this idea, but its persistence convinced her there was something useful here.

Why does she keep coming to mind?

Wind instantly thought of her decision to postpone her principle social obligation, which all Troubadourians shared, to function in a parental fashion for one child. She had already fulfilled her other procreative responsibility, which was to give birth to at least one child, but had not been part of that child's parenting.

The strange emotional connection inside her between Peter and her mother lingered in her thoughts. She painted for a while to distract her from this preoccupation, until it finally dawned upon her that it wasn't Peter and her mother who had something in common, it was Peter and herself. She had been very dependent upon her mother the way Peter was now very dependent upon her.

Taking on Peter as her primary responsibility, was very much like what she'd had been putting-off, the parenting of a child. Both carings require attending another's needs while putting one's own partly, sometimes wholly on the shelf.

The cold wind of dread blew through her heart. She knew what it meant. It was fear warning her that something menaced. Though anxious, she encouraged the frigid messenger in order to see the image it projected into her mind's eye. The icy visitation manifested as the fear that a stranger had just entered her private sanctuary without her consent.

It was of course Peter. In this spiritual reenactment of what it meant to be with him, she realized she was shelving her needs far more than expected, and far more than she had been prepared to do.

"Basically I anticipated this outcome. So why am I having so much trouble with it?"

She remembered how drawn to him she'd felt reading his written work.

"Sometimes I think I've already betrayed my commitment, at least in spirit. I didn't expect to find such shortcomings in myself, and yet I can't deny what's happened."

She found herself thinking critical thoughts about Peter, how difficult he was sometimes, how frightened and unpredictable.

"But I hate being critical!" she complained to herself. "What's taking me where I have always refused to go?"

Being at such great odds with herself was not something Wind had experienced much before. She had almost exclusively experienced great personal competence on a very high level, as well as enormous success in cooperating with others. She was known for her graceful and loving nature. If she lived on Earth it would be said that life had given her a silver spoon filled with super luck and extraordinary talents. This was the first time anything had seriously tarnished that reputation, making her very self-conscious.

"To be critical of someone is to do something I've always rejected as completely unnecessary to life. It means to try and destroy something instead of understanding it. The core of me thrives upon making love with everything I become involved. It is the key to the success of my art and to my life, and to the spiritual survival of my soul."

She suddenly realized she was feeling something she'd never quite felt before, embarrassment, not in relation to others, but to herself!

"Why is this happening?"

Wind knew that she needed outside input. In time she would probably have found more answers herself. But she didn't have time. She needed a new idea now.

She decided to meet with Rain.

"So you need my help," Rain said to Wind as they sat together on a high bluff overlooking a valley below. "Please allow me a moment to enjoy the pleasure of that anticipation."

They both looked out over the sun-draped treetops crowding together in the water-rich concave in the valley of the mountain up which they had just walked. Birdcalls echoed in the morning coolness.

An Earth-stranger coming upon the two of them together would have thought they were married. There was a deep familiarity in the way they sat and how they scanned the view together. But closer examination would have revealed that they were sitting too far apart to be coupled.

Though one could tell by looking at the man's face that it was quite possible that he both loved the woman, but also had never told her so.

Wind regarded these moments as very caring and tender. She loved it when occasionally they were able to be together in this way. She knew that Rain felt much pleasure in spending intimate time with her. She secretly enjoyed the same thing, but had never thought much about it, thus keeping its potential in herself both subdued and unattended.

He knew she thought much less than he did about the generous affection they felt for each other. He also knew that Wind had an enormously satisfying life of her own, which made her very busy with her own projects.

But now they were working on the same project, and were thrown together far more than usual. Rain would probably admit that he became involved in the Earth Project partly because of this Wind-focused opportunity.

Because she remained mostly unthinking of the closeness they shared, Wind was able more fully to partake of the pleasure of being with Rain. If she'd been more conscious of the intimacy they expressed, she would probably be having the same problem with Rain that she was now having with Peter. She would finally have to come to terms with what strong emotional ties to someone besides her mother did to her life.

"That you have so much pleasure in helping me is probably why I find coming to see you so irresistibly appealing," Wind said graciously, knowing that she was flirting a little, but wanting him to know how much she appreciated his help.

A gentle breeze sent evergreen odors swirling around the two of them, accenting with its bittersweet pungency the sweet odor of happiness that effervesced their togetherness.

"I'm doing something I deeply dislike," she finally said, breaking the silence, interrupting their quiet pleasure.

"I was sure it would have to be something unusual like that to bring you to me in this way," Rain replied. "You usually make such beautiful music by yourself. Though please don't be angry with me for getting so much pleasure out of your adversity. It's my consolation prize for not being able to do it more often."

Wind laughed.

"You are the sweetest of men," she crooned, feeling very amused by his flirtatious innuendoes. "But I must be entirely serious now. I'm very concerned. What I can't believe I'm doing sometimes is to criticize Peter in my thoughts. I must find out what's happening to make me act so unlike myself in a way which harms the Project."

"I would entirely agree that criticizing is completely out of character for you," Rain replied. "And I'm sure you believe it's also out of character for me."

"Of course I do."

"Well, surprises, my dear sweet Wind. I was once a very skilled idea-assassinator, what Earth people call a deconstructionist. Some people once said that I was the very best at that game, when to play it was much in fashion. We loved tearing down the past that the present was built upon, even when we didn't have the slightest notion of what to replace it with."

"I have to remind myself sometimes that you once lived in a world that seems ancient to me," Wind said.

"Well, I am an ancient creature, particularly to the Earthman. I don't think he would believe I'm one hundred thirty-seven years old. He would suspect I'm making it up."

"It's surprising for me to remember that that you actually lived when people still sometimes killed each other," Wind replied.

"Now you've put your finger on the problem that keeps me alive, but of course drives me a little crazy too," Rain quipped. "Being someone who has lived both as a barbarian and as a Troubadourian sometimes almost pulls me apart. Thought I must say it's the only thing that really challenges me anymore, which is why it keeps me alive with something constructive to do."

"How strange you should put it that way," she replied. "Because in a much smaller way that's exactly what's happening to me. I'm being pulled in two different directions. This man Peter has always seemed very appealing to me, and yet I now find him to be very . . ."

She interrupted herself for several moments.

"I don't like the metaphor which came into my mind," she insisted. "It was the word, ugly. Isn't that awful?"

"I think I begin to understand," Rain replied, a little excited. "I think you must be requiring something of yourself that isn't necessary, though you're treating it as if it was," Rain speculated. "Which suggests strongly that you're feeling overwhelmed by the excesses of your own expectation."

"But love must be faithful!" Wind exclaimed.

"So that's it," Rain said excitedly. "You require the same perfection in love as you require of yourself as an artist. You expect yourself to be perfectly and sonorously connected to Peter no matter what he does. Perhaps you have developed the ability as a painter always to find your usual loving way through difficulty, but why do you expect yourself to have the same level of competence with an alien person?"

"Oh my!" Wind exclaimed, beginning to understand him.

She was deeply moved by the incredible accuracy of Rain's understanding. Actually she had vaguely sensed the same truth herself, but there were competing theories in her heart at the time. Only with his support could she see it so clearly.

I've been criticizing myself, is the insight she got from Rain's ideas. No wonder I am so much up in arms against criticism.

"How easily we learn to be critical of ourselves," she remarked. "And how easily you, my dear man, blow coldness away from my heart."

She looked deeply into his dark-set eyes.

"You sweet, dear, incredibly wise old man," she added with much affection. "You speak the truth. Loving is my core. I abuse that core when I expect myself to give love as good as my mother did for me. I must remember both she and I need time to understand."

She paused.

"But now I'm curious about you," she added. "Please tell me more about your past, about your experience with criticism. What was it like to be so effectively critical?"

"I suspect you already understand more than you imply, for instance that constantly complaining about one thing or another, is a miserable way of spending life, particularly if that's mostly what's happening."

"How dreadful," she replied. "Complaining binds you to its negative passion. No wonder I hate it so much."

"You force remembrance upon me," Rain said wistfully. "That was so very long ago."

He stopped for a moment as if lost in memory.

"Yes," he continued. "Hate is the all-consuming fanatic passion necessary to wage war."

"Do you think I'm a fanatic about love?" she asked him.

"I think you're fanatically against criticizing."

"But to criticize a man I spent one year campaigning to bring to Troubadour?"

"Perhaps you have secret aptitude for criticizing," Rain quipped in mischievous speculation.

"Rain," she chided in a friendly way. "I love your humorous mind. But I feel serious about this now. I don't want to criticize Peter, or myself for that matter. I don't want to be critical even in jest. I am different than you in that way."

"Of course you are, and such a wonderful difference so beautifully done, you are a sight-to-behold for this ancient one."

Wind always liked his rhyming. But for some reason this time she flushed with a touch of embarrassment.

"Forgive my dalliances," he gently said, grasping her slight discomfort. "I am foreclosing what you still need to do. Please, tell me more about criticizing Peter."

She was relieved. She needed a little more of his help.

"There is a harsh bite in some of his discourse which is not accounted for by the words he speaks," she explained mostly to herself. "It is very challenging in a way I never expected nor wanted to be challenged."

Rain let her think about her own ideas for several moments before replying.

"If I consult memories of the earliest years of my life," Rain began, "I would conclude that Peter is afraid and seeking safety, when he behaves that way. He must somehow contain the large measure of strangeness that exists in his experience on Troubadour, which is pulling him apart. He is probably struggling with enormous confusion and uncertainty, which will prevail during most of his visit. That kind of experience probably frightens and undermines his self-esteem, perhaps a great deal."

Of course, she thought. He is beyond himself just being here.

Wind's mother suddenly flashed through her mind. She vividly saw the woman's small figure standing in a remembered doorway, smiling down at Wind as she played.

I haven't thought of my mother like that for decades. I always think of her as a beautiful, old woman just as she is now. But that was how she looked when I was a child.

Wind drifted for a while in the harmony of she-and-her-mother that she'd known so fully as a child, where everything was part of the same universal moment.

"Think of Peter the same way you think of your dear friend, Saavin, that lovely young woman you love so much," Rain suggested. "If she were anxious, out of instinct you'd probably find the easiest thing she wants to do, and help her find a way to do it. Peter's no different."

"I have already been tempted in that direction by my own instincts," she replied, thinking of how she spontaneously invited him to go for a walk.

She felt at peace for the first time in two days. She remembered how wonderful Rain could feel when he did the very clever things that always taught her something she needed to know. She looked over at him with gratitude and affection.

Rain adored her affectionate looks. But he knew she only did it only when they were about to part. Which meant she was finished. She looked very relaxed. She had gotten what she came for.

Wind felt a sudden desire to see Peter again, which deeply reassured her, putting her back on the track of responsibility.

There was a touch of sadness in both their hearts as they parted. Wind was expected at Peter's this very morning, while Rain was going in the opposite direction. They left each other at the top of the mountain and walked down separate paths to their different destinations.

The Mandela

Talking to the computer was one of the best experiences Peter had so far on Troubadour. When it was abruptly interrupted by Wind's call, foreshortening something very promising before it really established itself, he was thrown back into the angst which had haunted him before his conversation with the computer.

But as he thought about Wind's imminent arrival, he remembered the support he'd felt once or twice during that too abbreviated exchange with the computer. This gave him the confidence he needed to do what he had already postponed too long, which was openly to declare the failure of Troubadour to make his visit possible. He decided to put his cards on the table, no holds barred.

He started by expressing good will, but stayed far too briefly in that attitude before launching into his confrontation. He intended the two parts of what he had to say to be more balanced, but seriously underestimated the urgency of his resentment.

"How good to see you, I hope you are well," Wind said as she walked into his apartment.

"Thank you," Peter replied. "I'm glad to see you too. You look really great today. But I think I should warn you from the start of this conversation that I have not been very successful in finding much relief from the awkwardness I feel about being here. I am still very ill at ease, and I'm wondering if it's ever going to get any better before I have to leave. I don't have very much time here, as you know."

Wind was very taken aback by the amount and urgency of his resentment pressing his point. She was puzzled by the almost complete absence of warmth in his words, and amazed at the twisted implications he implied, which seemed to put the care of his well-being squarely in her hands, the way a young child would do with its mother, she thought.

For a brief instant she felt the strong repulsion toward him that she had discussed with Rain. But almost immediately she remembered her resolve. Thereafter, she didn't waver from a determination to act toward Peter out of a vision that would be framed by the fundamental question she'd put to herself, making it the template from which her responses to him would be framed. The question was, "How would she—her mother—think of me if I behaved like that?"

The answer came almost immediately, creating in its wake a new perspective about Peter, as she listened to the silent words she spoke to herself.

He's a good man trying to be generous at a time when he's afraid, but must pretend to be tough enough to handle anything. Anger must be the only way he can muster the kind of assertiveness needed for such an ambitious undertaking, particularly at a time when he's feeling very unsafe.

This discernment emboldened her heart to reach out to him.

But before she could speak, her mouth already open, he pounced again out of his surging anxiety. He could wait no longer for her response.

"I . . . I . . . I'm very puzzled by your silence," Peter interjected, trying hard to restrain intense aggression welling up from his heart. "Do you ever intend to answer me?"

Wind was jolted again by the renewal of his resentment. But she suddenly realized, that though he lacked much awareness, he was hurting her. Perhaps instinctively and unconsciously he needed to inflict a little pain upon his listener to be sure they were even listening, his way of warding off the humiliating prospect of talking to an empty room.

"Please forgive me, Peter. I've kept you waiting too long. I apologize for taking so much time to respond. Please give me a few more moments and I think I'll be ready."

"Oh . . . oh . . . oh, for sure, of course, by all means," he exclaimed, falling all over himself to bow an apology before she changed her mind, ashamed of his outbursts now that she had so completely accepted his unpleasantness.

The poor man, she thought. He gives up the whole ship to get his first bite of satisfaction.

To be able to see Peter-the-aggressor as a victim made everything much easier for her.

"It's the waiting for what you need that's the hardest part, isn't it?" she asked, the words coming out of an intuitive perception unformed until her mouth expressed it.

Peter was amazed that her generous understanding continued to prevail in spite of his irritable provocations.

"Yes," he admitted, finally surrendering to her understanding, at that moment willing to do anything for her. She had won his heart.

He slipped willingly into being mesmerized by her again, a salute to her unbelievable kindness. Though this was not the mesmerism of yesterday, expressing the needs of a young boy, but the admiration of a very young man feeling grateful for an older woman showing him the way.

"It must be control that you've lost," she remarked, thinking it would help him to think of it in this way.

But Peter was hurt by her words.

"I bet you see me as some kind of control-freak who wants to be in charge all the time," he fearfully fished for reassurance.

"No, I don't," she replied immediately. "I think of you instead as someone who wants to feel safe."

The perfection of her understandings so moved Peter that he suddenly wanted very deeply to make a positive contribution to her. But he couldn't think of anything other than asking a question, which seemed a trivial offering.

"How are you guys able to control your feelings so well?" he asked. "It's pretty amazing."

"Control doesn't appeal to us nearly as much as it does to your people," Wind explained, delighted that her replies seemed to be working for Peter.

"We've arranged things so that we enjoy a reasonably comfortable relationship with our experience much of the time," she continued. "Which makes us yearn not for peace so much as for regular visits with uncertainty and confusion, simply in order to challenge our curiosity and awaken our imagination."

"It's hard to believe that you care so little whether you're in control of what's happening," he said, "because you seem so controlled."

"We don't find control very appealing. Control tries to establish surety to what we perceive and believe, as if doubt threatened to dismantle the whole thing."

"Perhaps you think it's cowardly to be scared," Peter ventured.

He was fishing for her attitudes about him.

"Far from it," she replied. "Being capable of fear is essential to survival. But the unknown of not being in control is nothing to fear. We perceive this mystery as a beautiful thing where all the sharp contrasts of perception reside, creating opportunity for inventiveness. We need to experience those active and challenging processes to be fully alive."

Though deeply impressed by her ideas, Peter realized that he didn't really want to talk in this intellectual way. He didn't know what he wanted, but it sure wasn't this.

But he's the one that had started it. So it was his job to change the subject. The question was how could he gracefully do that?

"I'm sorry to be so much trouble," Peter began, "but actually . . . I don't . . . well, I know I always start our intellectual discussions. But they just don't work for me now. I'm awfully sorry to rain on your parade, but . . . well, I'm wondering if there's an easier way to do this visit."

Easier, she thought. That's the same word that Rain used.

Wind suddenly realized how difficult it had been to work with Peter, how uneasy she was when he constantly threw her one emotional curve after another, making positive exchanges difficult to experience, which made it very difficult for her feel in control of her own experience.

Oh, my word, she exclaimed to herself! So I'm the one who's been holding on tightly to control.

This self-understanding lifted a huge load from her heart. She was instantly restored to herself, once again becoming the gentle, gracious woman for whom she was so well-known, talents, which she had fully intended to provide Peter during his entire visit.

Of course, she exclaimed to herself. That's the answer. Be subject to his control. As much as he rebels from doing it, he needs to be in charge in order to follow the path of his own healing. He asks for us to control him, but he wants us to help him to control himself.

It's not that she had never thought some of these pieces before. But she had never faced the consequences of how doing it changed her own experience. But now she accepted whatever they would be.

"Your command is my desire," Wind said with generosity and good humor.

"What?" Peter exclaimed, completely unable to believe what he clearly heard and understood, but could not accept.

"Must I always decide what we're going to do?" he said with annoyance, shocked to hear his own resentment, afraid that he'd really messed things up this time.

Wind was surprised, and very shaken for a moment, but then realized that he must be regarding the freedom she continued to offer him as if it were abandonment.

"In that case I have something I'd like to show you," she replied graciously.

"Oh," he exclaimed.

"Would that please you?" she asked.

"Oh, yes, of course, I'd love to . . . to . . . I mean to do whatever it is you have in mind," he exclaimed, falling all over himself trying to be agreeable, once more hoping to blot out his recent negative assertions now that she was taking charge of the situation, now that she was showing she wanted to do something actively to help him.

"Then follow me," she said, turning toward the front door.

They were soon approaching the two large, wooden doors in the great hall upstairs, carved with intricate scenes of nature. She stopped in front of them and waved her long arms in a circular motion. The doors slowly swung back to reveal an enormous amphitheater three stories high, entirely inlaid with a great variety of different kinds of wood. Both the walls and the columns that supported the corners of this large structure were carved with life scenes in which humanoids and animals were seen living together in nature.

Off to his left he saw a huge carving of the elephant/giraffe that had almost collided with his head. Not far from this animal was a huge carnivore that looked like a dog the size of a male lion. Beyond the dog was a very large, grass-eating antelope-kind of animal with huge hindquarters, an enormous nose, and an extremely wide mouth, suggesting that it both ate voraciously, and also had the capacity to run extremely fast.

You would need to be fast to keep ahead of that ferocious dog Peter thought to himself.

"Do you like our Koam?" Wind asked.

"Yes."

"The word sounds like your word, 'comb,' though it's spelled k, o, a, m."

"It's absolutely beautiful."

"You were looking at the Tallong," she said pointing at the elephant/giraffe. "One of them almost knocked you down."

"Oh, you've heard about that."

"Yes. My heart stopped beating for a moment when I heard what almost happened to you," she replied.

How thoughtful of her to say so, he said to himself.

Wind turned toward the center of the amphitheater and by gesture invited him to follow. When she got there she stopped, turned, and pointed down.

They were standing inside of a huge Mandela like decoration, the design of which was created by very small pieces of many kinds of wood interlaced into a parquetry. The colors were dazzling and included reds, browns, grays, yellows, oranges, greens, and even black forming the intertwining embrace of the Mandela's intricate patterns.

"The ornate design upon which we're standing," Wind said, "is the precise center of the Koam. We call this particular location our 'Solm,' which is our word for the human spirit. As you must have noticed this word sounds not too distant from your own word, 'soul.' The celebration of the individual human spirit is our highest form of religion. We regard our own life as a sacred vessel about which we want to know everything, for which we want to provide every opportunity, and on behalf of which we strive to be as nurturing as possible."

"What a beautiful way to look at one's own life," he replied.

"We thought you might at least partly share that perspective with us when we invited you," she replied.

He remembered how she had anticipated his suitability, by reading his computer files.

Put your cards on the table again, he thought.

He didn't want any longer to have to hide his negative responses.

"I can't get over feeling upset about you reading my computer files. It still bothers me."

"I apologize for the harm it did you," she replied graciously. "Though I must confess that we did not anticipate this reaction. I think it's probably because, like your people we value privacy very much. But for us privacy is almost entirely about being alone when we need to be, essentially being unobstructed or intruded upon in our self-experience."

"As for the other reason privacy is often asserted, to hide things from others, we don't partake of that aspect. To do so would take parts of who we are, what we think, and what we're doing out of circulation. Hiding almost nothing from each other has given us a taste for some of the very things we used to hide from, like sharp differences between one another."

I bet she doesn't like my sharp differences.

"Though the place we're standing has a very different character," she continued. "The Koam inside of which we are standing is a place of intimacy. It's where we declare commitment to each other when we do our version of marriage. It's also where friends meet to settle differences which are difficult to manage."

"It is strangely intimate here inside the Mandela," Peter replied.

"I feel safe here too," she replied.

Peter didn't feel that way; his words had not meant that. He meant something more ambivalent, where intimacy was both wonderful and yet also very dangerous.

"As you can see the basic structure of the ceiling is a pyramid," Wind went on, "which for us symbolizes the primacy of the individual over the group, the top point of the triangle representing the one human supported by the four corners of social organization, respect, patience, generosity, and courtesy which characterize the prime directive of our shared social commitment. Intimacy, our most prized social event is founded upon and guided by the preeminence of individual life. It is our firm belief that love must give way to individual need. And yet only in successful loving do we ever fashion the kind of collaboration which choreographs the intricate dance-of-difference that life offers both with ourselves, and also with each other."

"It sounds like you value the individual far more than you value loving," Peter remarked.

"There are two kinds of intimacy, the kind we have with ourselves, and the kind we have with others. Both relationships are the precious stuff of a place small enough for one or two of us fully to occupy, and large enough for that person or couple to grow inside for one hundred fifty years."

"You speak of the individual human as if they were the cat's meow," Peter remarked. "It's as individuals we've done the most terrible things. What about all that?"

"The wars we used to fight outside of ourselves, as if they were really wars with each other, were actually wars with the ghosts of our mythical past, in effect wars with ourselves. We used to grossly overemphasize the importance of 'the world outside,' and deeply undervalue the realm of inner reality. When the truth is our individual psyche is the best container in which to resolve our painful experiences with each other. Only there can solutions to violence be found. So we are quite committed to the support of individual effort. We don't always do a good job with how we work together, but we no longer destroy each other in the process."

Once again, though very interested and trying hard to remember every idea for later perusal, Peter really didn't want to talk about ideas anymore. But he also didn't want to say anything further that had a negative edge, so he didn't say anything at all for several moments.

They stood together looking down at the Mandela, each examining the intricate patterns of color for their own reasons, he to distract himself away from feeling bad, and she to capture a quiet, intimate moment with him, to observe his private consternation, to wonder what else he needed to feel comfortable.

"It's such a beautiful place," Peter finally said. "I wish it could help me feel better. I seem . . . stuck somewhere."

So am I, Wind thought. It's hard to stay with his agony, to be so lost with him in the ghosts of his yesterday's unfinished business. Nothing seems to satisfy him.

"I hope together we can find a way to help you with that," Wind replied.

When Peter didn't answer, Wind sensed in him a desire to be alone.

"It has been a full time," she graciously suggested. "We have shared much. Perhaps it's time for me to bid you farewell for the day so you can think for yourself."

Peter had given up hope. He let her go without stopping her.

When he didn't stop her, she turned and left.

She had done everything right, as good as anyone could have, and he hadn't felt any warmth when she did it.

He felt alternately very guilty, sad for himself, and resentful that things didn't improve.

Tonight the mountains look gray, uninviting, even ominous, he thought, blaming the mountains as he looked out the window.

Both he and Troubadour had become rotten, leaving nothing of value he could bring back to Earth. He was the worse for coming, and Troubadour's social and political structures appeared seriously unsuitable for Earth. Instead of inspiring people, Troubadour's ways would deeply incense them.

He went to bed very disturbed that night.

Wind was also deeply concerned.

This is much harder than I expected, she thought as she walked to the train station. I wonder whether we're going to succeed. And what will it feel like if we don't?

Exploration

"Hi," a deep voice said.

Peter was in the kitchen. He'd just finished breakfast.

"Hello," he replied. "Who is it?"

There was no immediate answer. Whoever was at the front door was waiting for him to come out.

"I apologize for this open door," Rain said as soon as he saw Peter's head appear around the corner of the wall. "It seems to have opened by itself."

Peter too thought it was strange that the door had opened without his invitation.

"Oh, that's alright," Peter retorted. "Come on in."

"I suspect it's not that all right," Rain replied as he came in and sat down in the living room. "I understand you've been having lots of problems with our strange ways."

"Wind's been talking to you."

"She's a great talker," Rain quipped, obviously fond of her.

"You guys are friends?"

"Yes, though I'd like to be much better ones."

"Oh, you mean you got something going . . . I mean you are interested . . ."

"Something like that," Rain replied casually. "In fact I'd like to get as much of her time as you've got right now."

"Oh, well I don't mean to take your time away," Peter retorted, beginning to feel like he'd suddenly found himself in a ménage à trois.

"Well, why not?" Rain countered. "I can't see anything wrong with what you're having as much as you want. Make the most of it."

Peter was partially put at ease by Rain's reassurances, but also felt that he was caught up in something puzzling and disquieting, about which he was to learn nothing more. Rain had casually closed the subject.

"Are you sure there's not more to this?" Peter probed.

"Actually, I came over this morning with something quite different to offer you. I was going to take you visiting various parts of Troubadour."

"Oh, my god! That would be just fantastic!" Peter exclaimed, instantly excited.

It was as if Rain had picked the perfect plot for the day, and Peter lost sight of the provocative innuendos that had dominated moments before.

"Will you excuse me for just a couple of minutes?" Peter requested. "There are a couple of things I've got . . ."

"Take your time."

Peter had suddenly decided he must change his clothes. He'd put on a drab color expecting the day to be dour. He decided to change into a Mediterranean blue with warm gray highlights.

"We travel mostly by underground train," Rain explained as they walked down the hall minutes later.

"You don't fly anywhere?" Peter queried.

"Only where absolutely necessary," Rain replied as he entered the elevator, "such as across large bodies of water too deep or long to tunnel under."

"But isn't it so much easier and faster to fly?" Peter asked.

"We're not in any hurry," Rain replied.

Now that is an irrefutable answer, Peter thought.

The elevator stopped. They were on the tenth floor. Rain exited to the left.

"The train moves very fast," Rain explained. "By your measurements about fourteen hundred miles an hour, which is equivalent to ten parsecs in our measuring system."

"But you said you weren't in a hurry. That's pretty fast."

"We don't reject efficient speed. We simply want the air to have mostly natural things flying around in it."

"But how is that kind of speed possible underground?"

The sound of wind gushing around an accelerating body echoed as they approached a large door at the end of the hall.

"A train has just departed," Rain commented.

"Why did you give up flying?" Peter asked. "In the two hundred years you've evolved beyond Earth time, you must by now be able to travel several times the speed of sound very routinely."

"True. But there is an old saying among my people that translates very effectively into your language:

'Hurry is the flurry
That fetches worry to mind,
Making everything frantic,
Forcing impossible antics,
Rending beauty pedantic
Slaying the romantic
So why not be kind
To the wish to combine
And let hurry unwind'"

Peter laughed. "Did you make that up?" he queried.

"I wrote that limerick a long time ago. Which reminds me. Perhaps sometime today you and I can rhyme together again."

That's very unlikely, Peter thought.

"I'm not exactly the world's greatest poet," Peter said.

Rain paused before responding.

"I want sometime to hear about what you do as a psychologist," Rain remarked. "But for now we have the train."

What's he want to know about shrinking, Peter wondered uneasily?

They walked into a waiting area in which several Troubadourians stood. Rain greeted them all. Peter noticed in their demeanor that every one of these people showed a great respect for Rain. Peter was impressed and pleased to be accompanying someone of such stature.

Suddenly a bullet-shaped vehicle shot into view, decelerating rapidly. Half its side opened. Several people exited, greeting Rain and others as they passed. Though he couldn't understand their greetings Peter could tell they were all being very courteous to each other with a certain formality, though it was mediated by warm feelings that sometimes accompanied it.

Those waiting boarded the train. What looked like very comfortable armchairs were situated four across with a large aisle separating them into pairs. When Peter sat down the comfort was abundant, at least that is, until large padded arms encircled him!

He panicked. He was quite vulnerable to confinement, or to any experience of being held down. He started instinctively struggling to free himself.

"You can loosen those restraints by moving this handle to the left," Rain explained, pointing to a lever under the armrest easily touched by fingers grasping the armrest. "Move it in the other direction and it will increase the restraint."

Very relieved for the information, Peter quickly moved the lever to the left in order to release himself from the experience of tied-down.

"You may want to increase the restraint during the train's acceleration which is very sudden and rapid," Rain explained. "Only during acceleration and deceleration are they important for your safety. But when the train achieves a certain speed you will feel weightless. That's the perfect time to loosen your restraints in order most effectively to enjoy that wonderful feeling of personal flight."

"Wow!" Peter exclaimed in a very loud voice. "You're kidding me! Weightless under the ground?"

Two Troubadourians turned and looked very disapprovingly at Peter.

"Did I do something wrong?" Peter queried in a whisper.

"It was the loudness of your first word to which they probably responded," Rain replied. "There are some among my people who disapprove of any strong display of emotion in public, though I don't happen to be one of them."

Thank god I didn't offend him, Peter thought. I need an ally on this journey. Everyone is a stranger.

The train started to move. Instantly inertia forced Peter hard into the back of his chair. Only with enormous effort was he able to move his hand into position to tighten his restraints. Once safely held in place he felt exhilarated. The acceleration was several times stronger that the takeoff of a jet plane on Earth. He was utterly thrilled by the intense power.

Within moments the train reached its cruising speed. Rain loosened his restraints. Peter imitated him, and his body lifted off the chair and started floating.

"I'm floating!" Peter shouted with joy.

Disapproving looks once more loomed toward him from the same two people.

"I think I've done it again," Peter whispered, a little worried.

One of the two, a man, spoke in Troubadourian to Rain. The tone of his words was very harsh.

"He seems pretty upset at me," Peter whispered to Rain.

Rain smiled and nodded both at this other man and at Peter without responding verbally to either.

Well, what's that supposed to mean, Peter wondered, confused by Rain's enigmatic gesture.

"Quam," the stranger exclaimed looking directly at Peter.

"What did he just say?" Peter asked.

"He told you to be quiet. 'Quam' is the word for quiet. But please don't be too concerned about it. Though discretion would suggest restraining your passion, I don't agree with his view. But it might be the better part of wisdom to enjoy your enthusiasm more internally until we've separated from this man and his companion, which won't be too long."

"I'm so sorry," Peter apologized, feeling terribly embarrassed about making so much trouble on his first social outing. He was afraid that he might have created a situation that could be embarrassing to Rain.

"Wind has explained to me that for Troubadourians courtesy and peacefulness in public places, free from disturbing actions is something you deeply desire. I am very sorry I stepped out of bounds. Is there some way I could apologize to this man?"

Peter glanced at the stranger, and was immediately shaken by the contemptuous look he received in reply.

"I don't think apology is necessary," Rain casually replied.

"But he still seems pretty upset about it," Peter insisted.

"His name is Tanfroon," Rain continued. "He is one who believes strongly that emotional display must be a private affair, never to be done in public. Some people agree with him. Though there are many others among us, including myself who feel we have pushed the discipline of spiritual discernment beyond its natural limits, unnecessarily restraining emotional expression, preventing more spontaneous, random utterances such as you've just displayed. So you needn't be so worried. Tanfroon disapproves of some Troubadourian's public behavior. So you're in good company."

Peter was much relieved, though he did not feel entirely comfortable with Rain's support. He clearly did not disagree with or chastise Tanfroon. So did he partly agree with him?

I guess I'm supposed to deal with this man's ugly contempt on my own, Peter thought with some resentment.

But the chance to have a good time was much more appealing, so he brushed aside his worry.

"So why did you give up flying?"

"For centuries we believed that nature belonged to us as our exclusive gift from God, and then proceeded grossly to abuse it," Rain explained. "As your own people are beginning to discover, nature doesn't belong to us. We belong to it. As we became more civil to each other, we found ourselves wanting nature to be as it was before we spread ourselves all over the planet. As you must see our decision was a preferential sort of thing.

It's probably our way of getting back in touch with what we'd lost connection to, meaning nature of course. We realized we were becoming more and more alien to it."

"But don't you enjoy your own architectural inventions as well?" Peter asked.

"We prefer to be no more prominent than any other species. We now cherish nature more than our own architecture, and it rewards us by blooming mellifluously. We will probably one day return to building our own special constructions. You might say we're going through a stage. But it's where we want to be right now."

"That's a wonderful story," Peter exclaimed.

Encouraged, Rain continued.

"We gave up the heavenly delusion that we should all be powerful godlike creatures who are privileged and pampered, and chose to love more effectively the ecosystem that mothered us."

"What a beautiful thing to have done!" Peter exclaimed in admiration. "We're trying to get started doing it on Earth. But I have one question to ask. Why did you say that we're alien to nature?"

"Consider where we live," Rain replied. "Unlike other animals we reside in very artificial caves which have artificial weather control. We've put machines to work handling in nature what for eons we used to touch personally with our own hands. We have abused nature as much as we have abused each other. It finally occurred to us that this was the path of extinction."

"We're afraid of it too. But you seem to believe it's a real possibility?"

"Nature tolerates only so much of any one thing dominating its environments before inventing what is capable of recycling it into other more collaborative usage, simply by eating it, nature's solution to biological experiments that have run amuck. Nature doesn't play favorites as we used to insist upon."

"But how did you manage to do all of this?"

Rain wanted to stop talking.

"Forgive my retreat into self-centeredness, but I always deeply enjoy the experience of flying," he announced. "I don't want to miss it this trip. So let's talk more later."

With that said, Rain instantly became completely absorbed in his own experience.

Peter was stunned. He felt completely dismissed and rejected.

But the simple truth was he couldn't help feeling the same way Rain did. What could be more important than flying?

Flying was incredible. Peter found it instantly exhilarating. It was better than all the dreams of flying he'd ever had. There was no effort, no sense of imminent falling. There was nothing yanking on his body, trying to get him to bow or bend one way or the other. He was free. He soared through space feeling infinitely gracefulness. It was like a dream. He felt euphorically pampered, drifting effortlessly on nature's best amusement-park ride.

"What makes weightlessness happen so far under ground?" he asked after changing trains thirty minutes later.

"The molecules of the metal from which this vehicle is constructed become very excited inside of an electromagnetic field. We turn that energy into forward motion. The train could go faster than fourteen hundred miles per hour, but we found that outcome created a hum that was very maddening. We decided ten parsecs was an adequate speed for any journey, accepting the limits of our comfort."

"But what makes weightlessness happen? It seems like gravity under ground would be too strong to permit it."

"In effect this tube-train has something in common with what you call an atomic accelerator. A combination of speed and the excitation of molecules produce weightlessness. In effect the train moves in midair. It's not touching any other object."

At the end of their journey Tanfroon and his companion exited first, both casting a backward glance of contempt at Peter.

What's with this guy, Peter exclaimed to himself? Doesn't he ever give up? When it comes to discourtesy he's pretty damned disruptive to my comfort!

Tanfroon motioned to Rain that he wanted to talk to him alone.

"Excuse me for a few moments," Rain said to Peter.

Peter felt instantly threatened by what these two men might say to each other about him. What if this man got Rain to agree with him? Peter carefully watched them trying hard to read their lips.

Tanfroon was expressing anger. Rain seemed to respond in his usual calm manner, almost as if he were reassuring Tanfroon of something. Tanfroon reasserted his point of view, this time expressing even stronger negative emotion.

This guy is worse than me. Just by his body movements he's acting a lot worse than I did. What happened to the courtesy they insist upon?

Peter couldn't wait any longer for the outcome. He marched over to the two men intent upon settling something directly with this critical stranger.

As he got closer Tanfroon turned away from him, obviously intending to ignore him.

This intensified Peter's resolve to confront him. To get Tanfroon's attention he put his hand on his arm.

"Sir," Peter began.

Tanfroon flushed with intense emotion and reeled backwards as if Peter had struck him, his arms flying into the air!

Peter was sure that Tanfroon was going to strike him. He raised his own arms to fend off the blow. When he wasn't hit he felt great surprised, and then humiliation that he had been so mistaken.

Tanfroon's face flushed full of disdain and contempt. This malevolent look so unraveled Peter, he was so furious, that he nearly slapped Tanfroon across the face in defense. He barely managed to hold himself in check.

Tanfroon spit intensely emphatic, ominously delivered words that hissed an acidic, shriveling tone. Peter felt almost slapped in the face.

"Tanfroon has demanded that you never touch him again," Rain translated. "Though I suspect you have already surmised that information for yourself."

Peter was partly relieved that he'd heard no criticism of himself in Rain's words.

"He has also asked," Rain continued, "that I not bring you out in public places anymore."

Uh oh. Here it comes.

"I reassured him," Rain went on, "that there was no need for such caution, that fundamentally you were a very civilized person, though not yet entirely familiar with our ways of being. But, as you must already know, he has not been convinced," Rain added.

But are you entirely convinced? Peter wondered about Rain.

Rain turned and walked away from Tanfroon.

"Actually you need no longer be involved in this incident," Rain added as they walked. "I think what really amounts to a difference of opinion between he and I about appropriate behavior is what's really happening, which can best be managed between the two of us."

Peter could not believe what his ears told him. Rain was actually going to take over this horrible experience and settle it with this man himself? Somebody was actually going to protect him.

Peter felt a joy beyond his wildest dreams. It was as if reprieve had suddenly showed up a moment before his hanging.

He looked at Rain with glowing eyes that perceived him devotedly as an archetypal father. He bathed his vision in the securing embrace of Rain's presence, grasping a piece of security that had been so desperately lacking in his Troubadourian experience so far.

Though the fearful, defensive, used-to-being-suspicious part of Peter could not leave before glancing at Tanfroon one more time. He caught the proud man looking utterly crestfallen, which gave Peter a tremendous rush of satisfaction.

Tanfroon sensed Peter's eyes and shot out an intense look of hatred that Peter mostly avoided by looking away.

When the elevator door opened upstairs, Peter was surprised to be staring at a high desert plain brightly lit by the morning sun. He and Rain walked out onto the plain some distance. Because of Rain's recent act, Peter was open to being soothed. The muted colors of the surrounding hills calmed him. A dazzling variety of spring flowers in a myriad of colors spread out as far as the eye could see.

It must be springtime here, Peter thought.

Distant rugged buttes that looked devoid of any life surrounded this cacophony of color. The contradiction of elements mirrored the ambiguity that occupied Peter's Troubadourian experience, where harsh scarcity was occasionally interrupted by abundance.

The buttes stood like lonely sentinels in a huge, barren land reminding Peter of the sheer bluffs of northern Arizona so much photographed in Hollywood westerns. These orange, yellows, and browns framed the plethora of bright red, purple, and green color that filled the valley in which he stood.

I should have been seeing places like this days ago, Peter thought.

Peter glanced back at the building from which he'd just exited. It looked exactly like the three-story affair in which his apartment was located.

Christ, they've made everything the same.

Rain moved ahead to the left toward what looked like a forest of desert plants. Upon closer inspection the dominant plant looked somewhat like a rubbery cactus, yet when Peter touched it, it felt like a cheap, plastic imitation of the same. He glanced at Rain wondering if he should express this critical thought.

"What is it you're suspecting?" Rain asked.

"Excuse me for being negative about such beauty, but is this plant real?"

"Quite real, though it obviously seems otherwise to you," Rain replied, breaking off a small piece of leaf-like appendage and handed it to Peter. Close examination revealed a soft, sweet, wet pulp inside of what had seemed artificial.

"I see what you mean. It's pretty damned real," Peter said.

He spied sudden movement at the base of the plant.

"What's that?" he asked.

"A small rodent-like animal," Rain replied. "We've disturbed it so it scurried back into hiding. Here, let me find another so you can see it more clearly."

He pointed at the top of a plant a short distance away. A large but well hidden rodent-like animal could be seen nibbling on the white cactus flowers. The animal had unusually long claws capable of reaching down to gain purchase through sharp spines the plant sprouted for defense.

Rain walked out onto the plain beyond this rubbery forest, and sat down on a large pink rock that overlooked a vast array of petrified trees lying about. Peter joined him. Together they sat without speaking for a while, Peter taking his lead from the Troubadourian.

This man is like a sponge, Rain mused. He absorbs whatever he can get a hold of, but not much comes back out in reply. He must feel tremendous need, though it's a bit like parenting to accompany his powerful yearning.

Rain decided to amuse himself for the moment. The desert reminded Rain of his youthful ideals. As Tanfroon did now, he had once believed in the purely cerebral life. He had perceived objectivity as a solution to the destructive madness of human nature. He had exhorted others to be less emotional in their performance, instead to be thoughtful of what was taking place on the larger scale that only the mind could effectively imagine.

He looked momentarily at Peter and wondered if he were motivated by such urges.

Peter's thoughts meanwhile were far more concrete. The rodent-like animal made him think of Tanfroon, whom he regarded as an extremely nasty person with very sharp claws, but who pretended to be very civilized and delicate in temperament.

When in fact he's a raving pain in the ass, Peter thought. If there are many of his kind around I don't think these people are superior to mine.

Peter wanted to talk to Rain about his experience with Tanfroon. But he knew he wouldn't get the response he most wanted from Rain, which was for him to be against Tanfroon.

"Does that guy, Tanfroon, live here?" Peter asked, searching for some crumb of support for his resentment.

"You've guessed it," Rain replied. "The high desert suits him perfectly."

"That's just what I was thinking," Peter replied, surprised that he got some of what he wanted.

"So now you know that there are those among us who disapprove of bringing you here," Rain said.

Yeah, and why didn't you warn me of that, Peter asked in silence?

"How does that affect you to know it?" Rain asked.

"It's very unsettling to me," Peter replied. "It makes me wonder why you guys haven't warned me that there were people unfriendly to my being here."

"We wanted to know how you would respond naturally as yourself to that experience," Rain replied. "A rehearsed reaction would be of no value whatsoever."

Spontaneous reaction, Peter exclaimed to himself. I'm sick of that word. I think it's just a covered up way of admitting I'm the bird in a cage that is poked, prodded, and watched for my Pavlovian responses.

He looked at Rain wanting to complain about it, but didn't.

Don't bite the hand that feeds, Peter thought. But why do they keep making me learn the hard way?

So Peter was left alone with his self-doubts. Without more support from Rain he began to wonder if more fault belonged to him.

I should never have yelled. It was kind of gross. And they did warn me about being courteous in public.

He hated thinking this way, but he couldn't stop it.

Why can't I roll more with the punches?

A terrible thought suddenly struck him, though he imagined Rain having it about him.

Maybe Rain thinks Tanfroon and I are two of a kind.

He tried to dispel that from consciousness, but something made him curious about finishing the idea.

It's true we both have a strong desire to do violence to each other. We almost did. On the other hand Rain never wants to attack anyone. I wonder why that's in me?

This man is constantly in need of something, Rain observed to himself. I can feel it sitting close to him. He seems to have strength in him. Yet he begs for a great deal of support. Do all Earth people expect this? I'm willing to provide care for a while in order to give him a strong beginning. But perhaps it's time for me to shift and become a little more myself. It should be interesting to see what he does with a little healthy competition.

"Tell me about your profession," Rain requested. "What do you do?"

Peter was glad of Rain's interest, though he was also very nervous about what Rain would think about his work.

"I . . . I guess the best way of saying it is I help people understand themselves."

"Is psychotherapy the only place that happens?" Rain asked.

"I'm not sure. No one's ever put it quite that way before. But I guess in a way it is the only place where self-understanding can happen with great reliability and good effect. I think most people expect love already to contain what we need from it. It's all just supposed to be there. Though I can't say I've ever experienced that kind of love myself," he added wistfully, "even though most people believe in it."

"Ah, so you're saying that you work in the enterprise of love," Rain retorted.

"I've thought of myself as a new kind of priest, but I've never thought of myself as a whore," Peter retorted, trying to make a joke.

"I wasn't thinking of it in the pejorative sense," Rain replied. "Though that would of course be more comedic. I was thinking of your being in the enterprise of love very legitimately, by providing what someone needs to heal old wounds, something with which I'm very familiar."

"That's exactly what I do," Peter exclaimed, very reassured and delighted that Rain seemed to respect his profession, and to understand it well.

"Excellent, excellent," Rain remarked enthusiastically. "Good work. Since thorough self understanding is such a critical foundation for true democracy, it's got to start somewhere."

"It's really great that we can agree upon this," Peter said excitedly.

"A much needed effort. Mostly your people seem to make peculiar things of love. As we once did, Earth people seem to have made sex far too seriously important by making it exclusively romantic instead of also playful."

"Do your people have something against romance?" Peter asked.

"Yes and no. Taken too seriously, romance is the illusion that sexual joy is more than simply physical love. It can mean much more. But what gives it that meaning is not sex, but love, either the pretended kind of the honeymoon, or the real kind that finds a way to make being together pay handsomely for both participants, or gets out to find a better mate."

Rain paused at looked carefully at Peter, checking his response.

"I think romance at its worst is the heavenly view of love, which perceives orgasm as the death to any interruption of perpetuity, on the premise that only eternal sameness is capable of joining two disparate creatures deeply and reliably together," Rain added.

"Well, it is a very pleasant experience to be companioned by someone who is very much like yourself," Peter suggested, wishing he had found just one person like that in his lifetime.

"I think it's much nicer being companioned by someone very different than myself," Rain replied. "You each have so much more to offer each other, because difference always brings problems, but does it while also bearing the great gift of a second view of life, vastly enlarging your field of perception."

"That's the most devastating dump of heaven, sex, and romance I've ever heard," Peter remarked. "That must mean your people don't do sex very much?"

"Of course we do. Sex is wonderful. The solution to the problem that I have suggested is not abstinence. Instead it's very beneficial to arrange for love to have stiff competition, but not with a third party, instead with some part of their lover's life, specifically their lover as an individual. If the individual human spirit does not enjoy being alone in and with itself with the same quality and intensity that it enjoys merging with a lover, the human species will always unwittingly remain not much smarter than their close relatives, the apes. Individual human life and its creative efforts must contain joy as pleasurable as sex can be, in order for any one of us to keep balance in our life. We must mean as much to ourself as someone else means to us."

"But to put conflict in the middle of love, sex must be terrible," Peter insisted.

"Since you pin me down, the results are quite the opposite. Left to be just what it is, without the demand for it to provide everything my lover needs, sexuality has become extraordinarily pleasurable, more than it's ever been to previous generations."

The train was stopping.

"We've arrived."

Jungle

As the elevator door opened Peter was suddenly overcome by hot, humid, almost suffocating air filling his lungs, making it very hard to breath. For a moment he felt panicky. But after a few breaths he realized that he'd reacted fearfully, and chose to put up with a moderate level of anxiety in order to find out why Rain wanted him to see this horribly humid place.

He was staring into an impenetrable jungle. Almost immediately he started sweating profusely, and already hated being here, but carefully hid that feeling.

"So this is your surprise," he said to Rain sounding as neutral as possible.

"I suspect you find this weather as intolerable as I do," Rain observed. "However, this community of people is one of the most unusual outcomes of Troubadourian freedom and will give you a broader perspective of what our kind of democracy produces. This community is populated by those who have chosen to become reabsorbed into nature by living in the jungle as a tribe."

"Do you mean they actually live the way a few native tribes still live in my world, meaning in very primitive ways?" Peter asked.

"Exactly," Rain replied. "Though they don't spend all their time at it. They also occupy apartments in this city-building part of the time, where they discuss, study, and record their findings. So you might say they lead a double life."

"But why do they do it?" Peter asked.

"In order to be completely and utterly in touch with nature," Rain replied. "They pursue the belief that, as a civilized people, we have lost touch with some of the most basic aspects of being alive. They seek to rediscover the truths that infused those early ancestors who experienced life as just another animal, instead of the pampered and very specialized creature that we have become. They believe we have evolved a far too abstracted relationship with nature, revealed by the truth that we seldom touch other living things with our skin. Instead we manipulate nature with machines, which they regard as our metal armor."

"That sounds a little like some of the things you're doing with the Earth Project," Peter suggested. "Is there some connection?"

"What an interesting idea. Perhaps there is."

"How do these people live in the jungle?" Peter asked, hoping to continue being interesting.

"They reproduce the intensely vivid relationship that is forced upon anyone who lives outside of the special protections we humans have come to expect, forcing them to rely entirely upon the natural world and their own skills to provide everything they need. They spend ten months of the year in this way, and about two months, actually two weeks every three months evaluating and recording their findings."

"There are some among my people who are very drawn in similar directions," Peter replied. "Some have already begun to live a natural, more primitive life, though I'm aware of only a handful who do it in a jungle environment."

"Shall we walk a ways into it?" Rain asked.

Peter answered by walking farther into the jungle. He was afraid to speak for fear his voice would betray the "no" he felt in his heart, that he wanted very much to leave as soon as possible.

He was already finding the intensely humid heat to be very oppressive. He was a cold-weather person who loved the fog that kept San Francisco's temperature moderate. But he did not want to be seen as an unwilling participant to Rain's surprise. So his discomfort manifested as his usual twang of "how do we find our way back." He turned toward the building and was not surprised to find that it had disappeared.

"My god!" he exclaimed, giving expression both to his uneasiness and his dislike of this place. "The building is already invisible. How will we ever find our way back?"

"There are sign posts along the way marking a trail for tenderfoots like you and I," Rain replied, pointing at one of them, visible but not easily seen unless one were looking for them.

"Do you mean to imply that the residents here just head off in any direction?"

"Yes. Learning to read the jungle is part of what fascinates them," Rain replied.

They walked deeper into the tangled, complex growth. Water dripped constantly from the leaves above, which along with sweat continued to soak their clothes. Huge, exotic flowers peered down at them from the trees above, rooted as they were in the higher portions of the canopy. As in Earth's jungles, nothing except tall trees grew from the ground up.

Flower colors were profoundly exotic, including chartreuse, a lurid pink, and a bilious yet interesting green. Small animals of many sorts shouted and leaped about in the branches above.

Peter had a fleeting thought that the noises they made increased in tempo and pitch when he and Rain walked into the jungle, as if the animals sensed unfamiliar odors intruding into their domain.

Suddenly a large, brightly colored thing flew within an inch of Peter's nose. He jumped backward, but managed to keep his eyes upon this creature. It landed on a nearby tree trunk. Peter followed to get a closer look.

It was a humongous bug, perhaps a foot long with a wingspan of almost two feet, colored in a rainbow of vivid hues. Suddenly it uttered a loud, shrill noise ending in a huge crack that was so intensely penetrating, that for a moment Peter thought his eardrums had burst. When they stopped ringing he realized that he'd been warned by the bug to keep his distance.

"God, but that's an awful sound," he exclaimed.

"That bug stuns its food with that sound," Rain explained.

"Does he predate humans?"

"Not that I've ever heard."

Now very attuned to this creature's "crack," Peter listened differently to the loud cacophony of sounds coming down from the canopy above. He could hear fairly frequent renditions of that same shrill crack piercing its way into his head, making the usually complex and interesting jungle-sounds less appealing to hear.

By now Peter was sweating profusely. He began to feel tired, as he usually did in hot humid weather. The sweat was pouring down his face so much that salty water flowed into his eyes, sometimes obscuring his vision.

He stopped momentarily to tend his eyes. When his tear ducts had washed them clean, he noticed that Rain had moved on ahead. He quickly bolted forward to catch up.

He didn't see the figure that simultaneously stepped out from behind a tree intersecting his path, not expecting Peter suddenly to accelerate.

Peter and the figure collided.

Whatever hit Peter felt extremely hard; giving him the impression he'd walked into an unseen tree. The collision bounced him forcefully backward, knocking him off balance. He started to fall, but the tree caught him.

A nearly naked, very brown-skinned, thin body of a man took hold of Peter's shoulders, preventing him from falling. The ease with which he had lifted Peter spoke of great strength in his sinewy limbs.

He spoke a few words in Troubadourian to Rain.

Rain laughed, nodded in the negative, said a few words in his native language, and turned toward Peter.

"You have bumped into Sondor."

"Excuse me," Peter said to Sondor, bowing toward him.

"Perceiving you to have a peculiar body-shape," Rain continued, "he asked if you were a new species of Troubadourian. Of course I assured him that you were a genuine alien from the planet Earth."

Peter found this amusing, which the stranger found very puzzling.

Sondor spoke again to Rain.

"He wants to know if you're laughing at his differences, or are there people like him on your planet."

"Yes there are, many tribes like him," Peter replied. "Can I ask him a question?"

"Of course," Rain replied.

"What does he find so special about living in a tribal way in this overheated oven?" Peter asked.

Rain translated, Sondor laughed.

"He was wondering why you were sweating so much. He thought perhaps you might have a fever, and resolved to gather the herbal remedy for such an illness."

"Please thank him for being so thoughtful," Peter requested. "But what does he like so much about living here?"

Sondor spoke for several moments.

"Sondor says he feels a deeper sense of connection to everything in the jungle, far stronger than he ever imagined possible living in the civilized world. He knows with certitude that he is a significant part of many natural processes, which both threaten and deeply support him. He therefore never lacks for encouragement and inspiration as he once did. In civilization he had to search for meaning in his life. Of course he found it sometimes. But here in the jungle such meaning surrounds and occupies him constantly without the least effort. He says he could never live again for very long in the artificial environments which most humans regard as essential."

Deeply impressed by this moving testimonial, Peter looked carefully at the man who felt it. Sondor wore only a loincloth. He had the Troubadourian build with its strong back and lower limbs, but he was very slender, pure hard muscle above the waist.

He also perpetually scanned the jungle.

He seems aware of everything, Peter thought.

Sondor pointed to a spot perhaps twenty feet high and forty feet to the left, and spoke a few words.

"He wants us to see the almost invisible animal peering at us from that tree," Rain translated, pointing to it.

Peter looked carefully up and down the tree but could see nothing.

"I can't see anything. Where is it?" he asked.

"I see it now for the first time myself," Rain replied. "Its two yellow eyes are just slightly below that huge, pink flower on the right, sprouting from the junction of the second branch up the tree trunk from the ground."

Peter followed Rain's instructions, peering carefully as he scanned. Suddenly two huge, yellow eyes gripped his with great intensity.

For a moment he was mesmerized, trapped in the compelling stare of wild force trying to weaken him for the slaughter.

With great effort Peter broke the spell with which these eyes had captured him, by focusing upon the whole animal.

"My god! He's a huge cat over ten feet long! And those eyes!" Peter shouted.

He's the cat above the elevator, Peter exclaimed to himself.

"I might have had a dream about . . ."

Peter stopped talking when he saw a look of disapproval on Sondor's face.

"What did he say?" Peter asked.

"'He who makes loud noise, by doing so loses his poise, becoming yellow's food, when he's in the mood,' is I believe a good translation of the aphorism Sondor just quoted, written by one of his people about the Borang."

"Does everyone on this planet want everything quiet all the time?" Peter queried.

"Sondor is hunting," Rain said. "Perhaps he does not want to warn his prey."

As if pulled by a magnet, Peter's eyes were once more drawn to the cat's yellow orbs. He tried to look away again but couldn't move his eyes. He finally had to put his hands between his face and the cat in order to look down and away.

"That creature is menacingly mesmerizing," he exclaimed. "Do they ever actually attack humans?"

"I'm told we're their favorite food," Rain replied. "But please don't be frightened. They're almost never satisfied in that preference."

"But he could attack us," Peter observed with mounting trepidation.

"We are three humans," Rain replied. "That makes us too big a challenge. Sondor says the cat will wait until one of us leaves the group, and then track us for a while. So what you see at this point in those yellow eyes is only the desire to eat you, but without the present expectation of doing so."

"That's not very reassuring. In fact it's downright spooky," Peter replied.

He was genuinely afraid. He found the sameness of the real cat to the one in his dream fused and confused the two realities.

"I've never been drooled over before," Peter said.

Sondor laughed as if he understood Peter. He spoke a few words.

"Sondor catches the drift of your last meaning, principally that you don't like being looked at as something good to eat. He too has looked long into the eyes of the "yellow," which is what his people named the animal when they first discovered it. He too has pondered what it means to be eaten by this animal. As you might imagine, the word, 'borang,' means 'yellow' in Troubadourian."

"What's it make him feel like to be stared at by gluttony?" Peter asked.

"It reminds him of being deeply loved and desired, which is how the tribal people understand eating and being eaten."

"That's the weirdest thing I've ever heard anyone say about love!" Peter exclaimed.

Rain laughed.

Sondor seemed to catch the tone of Peter's reply, which he didn't like. He waved his arm with an apparent goodbye, and headed abruptly back into the deep jungle in the direction he had originally been going.

"I hope I didn't offend him," Peter said, sensing some connection between his remark and the other man's departure.

"I don't think so," Rain replied. "It was time for him to go. He told me earlier that he was on a hunt."

"Oh, what is he hunting?"

"A Borang. These jungle people say they're very good to eat."

"Then why didn't he go after the one over there on the tree trunk?" Peter queried hopefully.

"Because you and I would be in jeopardy if he did."

"How?"

"The Borang would sense he was being hunted, and in response would become very predatory himself. He would start to pace in very large circles trying to move around behind Sondor. In the process the yellow might intersect our path. Under such conditions he would be very unpredictable and dangerous."

"I'm grateful at least for that thoughtful decision," Peter replied.

Suddenly Peter noticed that the Borang was no longer where it had been. Its disappearance made him feel even more nervous. With Sondor gone there were now only two humans. Maybe a Borang considers that an edible possibility.

"You seem to be tiring of this walk," Rain observed. "Perhaps it's time to go."

"It's true. The heat really wears me out," Peter replied, very glad that Rain was thinking about retreat.

"Then let's head back to the building. I wanted you to meet a member of this city, though I was doubtful it would happen. But now that it has we've finished our visit."

Peter was very relieved to hear that. He was already scanning all three hundred sixty degrees of the surrounding jungle. He was terrified the Borang would successfully sneak up from behind before he knew what hit him! It seemed almost as if the dream had come to life.

"The Borang is a very shy animal," Rain said, noticing Peter's nervousness. "They have never been observed to come this close to the city building. There is no need. The jungle has abundant food."

Yeah, Peter thought, but please remember just how hard they are to see. And there's always the first time for their first visit.

To distract himself he started asking abstract questions.

"Are there others who do this sort of thing in a different way?"

"There are several communities of people who are deeply committed to growing the things we eat."

"But that's not back-to-nature," Peter protested.

"These people do farming the way a painter paints a beautiful picture. They love the process of nature's creation of food-bounty, and are thus extremely skilled and knowledgeable about the earth, the plants, and the animals that we eat, and how they all cooperate together. Their intimate relationship with the tangible things of nature is just as intense and committed as Sondor's belief in the primacy of his world."

"You make the farmer sound like a vital force," Peter observed.

"That's who they are. In your world farming has mostly been turned over to large conglomerates that grow for quantity and financial gain, turning food into profit-fodder, though there are of course some parts of your world that still farm lovingly."

"You must be referring to France."

"I am," Rain replied. "There's a third group which is deeply devoted to nature on Troubadour. I'm referring to Rambler, who is dedicated to understanding the wisdom of nature's processes. Like many in your world, he has made the observation of living things into a science."

"Are these the only kind of vocations that people have?" Peter asked.

"People do all sorts of things as a self-created career. Most of what you call politics is managed in this spontaneous way. Some people are highly motivated to change the way something is badly done, for instance, something we've put up with perhaps for decades, but which with more experience we can now change. And of course there are also the artists, to mention just one more group."

"Tell me about the artists."

"We call them creators and inventors who reflect upon the nature of Troubadourian humanity, trying to frame and re-form the archetypes of human experience that we all share. They envision new and different ways that recognize and reflect the kinds of change through which we are passing. They announce new meaning emerging into human consciousness, as it grows larger."

"I have the impression that you don't have much need for psychologists on Troubadour," Peter observed.

"That's not entirely true. Learning about the self is perhaps our most honored vocation. Within certain limits it's what we give the highest priority to. But we got into what you call psychology in a much different way than you did. Instead of psychology emerging as a treatment for human mental suffering, on Troubadour it sprung from the political process of making democracy work. We recognized the need for psychology before we learned how to do it."

"How can politics discover psychology?"

"Only very self-enlightened individuals, empowered to handle their own lives with great effectiveness, are capable of managing the huge power we give to the individual without misusing it, forcing us permanently to restrain them. We had already concluded that as much authority as possible must naturally reside in a single human. It didn't take long to find out that by far the best way to do this was to provide every individual a quality of childhood that would prepare them to handle such great power. Now tell me, is that not the same goal as psychotherapy? Have you and I not arrived at the same place coming from entirely different directions with completely different motivations?"

Peter was deeply fascinated.

The train started to slow.

"It appears we have reached your city," Rain said.

"But we were just in the middle of something really fascinating," Peter protested.

"I'm glad you got so much out of it. But you will be in the middle of lots of interesting moments in the days to come. Nothing's ever finished, just transformed a bit."

"Could we visit for a while longer?"

"I need to stay on board the train."

Peter was shocked once again by Troubadourian abruptness in transitional moments.

"Goodbye for now Peter Icarus," Rain said.

"I . . . I . . . I've had a great time today," Peter stammered, his disappointment about the sudden ending expressed in his stuttering. "I really appreciate you taking me on this tour. It's been terribly interesting."

"Yes, it was sometimes fun," Rain replied with a gentleness that also acknowledged his partial disappointment.

Peter chaffed at what felt like a rebuke, but responded with good nature. "Well, then g . . . goodbye."

"Until next we meet," Rain replied.

Peter became increasingly upset in the hour following Rain's departure. He could not help that the strong negative parts of his experience had overshadowing the unusual things he'd seen and the extraordinary things he'd heard about. In fact his mood became so dark that he could find nothing better to do than go to bed early.

Rain's thoughts were much different.

This man needs much more healing than I expected, Rain mused as the train moved closer to his destination. Perhaps I have forgotten my own past when I was confused and misguided much like he is, estranged from the bearing forces of my own life. Was I in as much pain as he still is? I must have forgotten.

Fun is definitely very difficult with him.

Near Death

During the night Peter awoke several times from bad dreams. He refused to think about them and returned to sleep. When he woke in the morning he was already somewhat agitated and depressed.

This shouldn't be happening, he protested.

There were two reasons why he asked this question. One, good things had been happening.

I think maybe Rain even respects me once in a while. And Wind is very sweet and kind sometimes, though I don't think she likes me. And I am learning a lot, though some of it is really crazy and so unsuitable for Earth.

And two, one very bad thing kept happening. For the life of him, he couldn't figure out what the hell was going on. What was his visit really all about?

The more he got confused about this, the more he felt increasingly uneasy as time passed. Which reminded him that time was in very short supply.

And what are all these private meetings about? At least Rain took me around the planet to see things. Oh, I guess she did a little of that too.

A surge of frustration boiled up in him.

But that's not the point.

He hesitated, lost in a sea of unlimited possibilities.

Christ, I don't know what the hell is the point. Why does everything feel so pointless, so . . . undoable?

Nothing was planned for this day that he knew of. He dreaded the prospect of sitting alone inside thinking and worrying, which he did far too often on Earth.

He headed upstairs and outside intending to take a very long walk, hoping to ditch his problems by getting lost in nature.

It was a cool, cloudy day, excellent for a fast walk. He lost himself in the many natural objects that surrounded him, imagining he was in a kind of paradise, his skin stirred by a friendly and gentle wind, his eyes feasting upon an incredible variety of colors, smelling a myriad of understated odors that conveniently arrived in sequence to be tasted separately, instead of coming intrusively all at once.

It was with surprise that he suddenly found himself in the middle of the large meadow, not far from where the Taloong's huge trunk had almost collided with his head. As if it was about to happen again he quickly scanned his immediate vicinity looking for dangerous animals, but there were none in sight.

As relaxed and soothing as the environment was, he brought with him an internal sense of danger, which, in working so hard to ignore, he rendered himself more blind than usual to nature's risks.

"I'm sick of thinking so much about everything!"

In this stridently avoidant mood, he set off through the meadow and beyond, going farther than he'd ever gone, absent-mindedly attending only what was right in front of his eyes. There was a kind of desperate determination in both his forward motion and his avoidance of serious thought.

So he didn't consciously notice that the trees through which he was moving were growing closer and closer together. Even when the distance between tree trunks became less than two feet, the urgency of his walking propelled him ahead, his shoulders occasionally bumping into a tree, an event largely unnoticed by his brain as he pushed on through obstacles that were beginning to bruise his body, acting the way some people, usually men, do when they hurt themselves, allowing conscious recognition of the hurt only when it reaches the proportions of serious injury.

In fact he didn't stop walking until both shoulders simultaneously impacted separate trees as he tried to pass through a space too small to fit even the width of his body.

What's this?

He peered ahead, noticing clearly for the first time just what it was that he was passing through, a forest of thin-trunk trees that was becoming impenetrable. He couldn't understand why they wanted to grow so close together. It just didn't make any sense, though he didn't allow himself to consider whether there might be any danger in this arrangement.

Just then his nose sensed an extremely pungent, but very sweet and inviting odor, the sugars of which his tongue already craved. The plant that harbored these blooms exuded large molecules of wet fragrance that animals could smell from miles away.

Enticed by odors so sweet that they were almost fetid, yet still deliriously sugary, Peter pushed on without thinking clearly of the possible hazards of moving deeper into such crowded quarters. He was acting from a determination that refused to take no for an answer. The hiding of his depression and fearfulness required the utmost ardent commitment worthy of being called religious fervor.

Even when a vague awareness of danger alerted him, he prevented it from untracking him by reassuring himself that whatever was creating these wondrous fragrances must have good reason to invite visitors to come so close. He even rationalized that the tree branches that started scratching his skin were the bramble bushes through which he, the prince, had to pass to prove his metal in order to deserve the prize his lips would soon enjoy. Even when these branch-blows struck his face, breaking the skin, he still persisted his forward motion, driven to succeed.

It took the trees to literally stop him. He suddenly found himself wedged between two small but powerful trunks too close together to get through.

His basic fear of imprisonment was instantly triggered. He tried to back out of their grasp.

"What's that?" he shouted, feeling a hard surface behind him that prevented motion.

Somehow the tree he'd passed two feet ago had snuck up behind him, perhaps by bending toward him, and was now pinning him inside a triangle of three trunks.

A distant voice cried out, but was so mixed with the wind rustling the tree, that he couldn't make out the words, and quickly forgot it.

Fear forced its way to the front of consciousness telling him that the triple-vice holding his body was beginning to squeeze him harder as if it intended to crush him. At this crucial moment his nose and eyes told him he'd reached his destination, distracting him from what he insisted to himself must be childish paranoia.

It was a huge tree-trunk perhaps forty feet in diameter standing just five feet away, the mother-tree that sprouted all the branches he could see. The huge trunk was festooned with enormous white flowers, the petals of which were scratched with a rainbow of myriad colors visibly effervescing large-moleculed sugars that had already started to intoxicate Peter, each odiferous droplet of pleasure providing abundant quantities of 80-proof alcohol.

For a tiny moment Peter realized he smelled the rot of death. But instantly the tree's sweetness reassured him it was safe. Something that deliriously good to taste could not be evil.

The tree had pushed the boundary of sweet to its ultimate limit, just centimeters away from the fetid rot of decay, at the junction where the two hesitantly meet to make perfect nectar.

It was Peter's fear of confinement that finally jerked him from the illusory beauty of the flower's intoxication. He had to move some part of his body before he could feel safe and enjoy the tree's bounty. Surely his feet would get him out of this.

But the tree had already started to grow around his ankles. Not only was he completely helpless, he was also suddenly aware that he was rising as if being lifted up.

Very dimly, through his mounting terror he heard a voice speak out to him from what seemed very far away.

"Stand perfectly still, I'll be there in moments," echoed distantly through his ears.

Peter knew that voice. It was Rambler's.

The enormous relief Peter suddenly felt enabled him to dedicate himself to following this strict order, "stand perfectly still," though self-restraint required all of his fiercest effort to consummate inside of fear's growing sense of urgency.

Partly to distract himself from his fear, his regretful mind started blaming himself for not noticing how cleverly the tree had intoxicated him precisely so that it could get a hold of him.

What a fool I am.

Every paranoid possibility he'd imagined since he was first invited to Troubadour now raced through his mind. They were all some version of being enticed by the promise of great benefit seducing him into willingly offering himself as a guinea pig for whatever bizarre, torturous experiments they next got their kicks out of.

Everything suddenly made perfect paranoid sense. Now he knew why they had never given him a proper agenda of what to expect, or tell him how things worked, because they didn't want him to know what was happening. They wanted him to remain a helpless victim.

"I've been so blind!" he shouted.

This was Trafalmidor all over again, only much worse than Billy Pilgrim's nightmare! Billy had been kidnapped for life, but always protested it and made demands that were satisfied. Whereas he, Peter, had foolishly asked for nothing, putting himself entirely in their hands to do with as they pleased. Like his mother had fooled him into believing in train-heaven, the Troubadourians had hoodwinked him into a horrendous series of unexpectedly frightening events.

They warned me.

He suddenly knew what the Troubadourians meant by wanting his "spontaneous reactions." They wanted to watch him squirm. He had been enticed into volunteering for terror-duty. What a sucker he'd been.

Suddenly a loud, lascivious slurp threatened from above. Slowly a terrifying possibility began growing in Peter's mind. It was that two huge, warped lips began to open in the middle of the face of that huge trunk.

He tried desperately to deny what he knew to be true, that the tree had a mouth and was beginning to shove him into it. But when concentrated acid, dripping from the corner of the tree's mouth, touched a leaf on the ground with sizzling dissolution, his terror took over. Rambler's instructions where thrown to the wind! He started frantically, furiously struggling.

A huge pair of hands suddenly encircled his shoulders, squeezing a little reassurance into his body.

"I'm going to lift you," Rambler said resolutely from behind Peter.

Nightmares wavered, relinquishing part of their credibility.

Moments before this crucial juncture, Rambler, with great care and incredible speed, had inched his huge powerful bulk through the same narrow openings that Peter had navigated, sometimes ascending the tree trunk to reach a wider gap, then descending to achieve the next best passage, all in less than a tenth of the time it took Peter to cover the same distance. The strength of his arms and legs maneuvering through tight spots gave him the appearance of an ape deftly soaring through the trees.

Rambler's firm grip forcefully pulled upward.

But nothing happened, dashing Peter's desperate hopefulness onto the rocks of despair.

The big man uttered an enormous preparatory grunt, and with obvious huge effort, jerked Peter free.

As if carrying a child, Rambler turned Peter parallel to the ground, then twisted him sideways, then turned him face up, moved a couple of feet, then twisted him around so that now he looked straight down at the ground, literally manhandled Peter up and down, sideways and forwards, right side up and upside-down, finally pulling both of them out of the dense thicket, where he gently put Peter down.

At first they just looked at each other, Peter out of shock, and Rambler out of curiosity.

When Peter's mind finally began to focus normally, he spoke with instinctive gratitude.

"You really saved my ass."

Rambler laughed.

"What in the fuck was that damned thing?" Peter asked, still lost in the haze of horror, his mind still obscured with the vagueness of panic's abandonment of thought.

"A flesh-eating tree," Rambler replied.

"A flesh-eater?" Peter remarked. "You must be kidding," he added in a flat tone reflecting the daze in which he was still ensconced.

"Though it hasn't eaten a human for over five hundred years," Rambler added, "but it still craves them."

"That's not much consolation to a person who was almost deprived of his remaining years," Peter retorted.

His mind, now entirely focused, released him from habit's command to be pleasant, making him instantly aware of the huge fear that underscored everything—fear which desperately needing to strike out at anything in order to quell terror's helplessness, releasing him from panic's paralysis.

"How could that have happened to me?" Peter shouted.

"Small to medium size animals are its usual diet," Rambler continued to explain, ignoring Peter's alarming tone, "that is when it can entice a young, inexperienced creature to closely examine its sweet-smelling flowers."

Rambler's explanations had the quality of providing docent service, as if he were giving detailed information about what was displayed, but without any heartfelt offering.

Peter's resentment suddenly turned against Rambler for not giving the slightest recognition to his suffering such humongous danger.

"Of course for the visiting animal," Rambler continued, "the secret of survival is moderation, to take only modest portions of the tree's delicious nectar, acknowledging and enjoying the delightful intoxication it provides by getting away before that intoxication disables one into becoming the tree's food. It's a very interesting competition of pleasures and skills which I have been studying for almost twenty years."

"For Christ's sake, the goddamned thing almost killed me!"

"It must have been a very frightening experience for you," Rambler replied with sympathy. "I hadn't expected . . ."

"That's the understatement of the year," Peter retorted! "It wasn't frightening! It was absolutely terrifying!"

By now Rambler was getting used to Peter's outbursts. He simply turned off, turning partially away.

I have acknowledged your fear, Peter Icarus, Rambler said to himself. But I won't be making room for your tantrums. You'll have to learn to give them up.

"I'm sure you must be in pain," Rambler said as if Peter had not shouted. "I have treatments for your injuries. May I examine your body?"

"But why did this ever happen in the first place?" Peter exclaimed.

What does one do with such childish display, Rambler wondered?

"But we agreed you would warn me," Peter insisted, trying desperately to draw the other man into a conversation that legitimized his fury.

"The healing agents that I have would like to get started mending your wounds," Rambler said encouragingly.

"Aren't you going to answer my question?" Peter insisted.

"I remember your wanting me to warn you. But we examined both the pros and the cons, and we came to no definitive conclusions. Now are you going to let me look at your injuries?"

Peter wanted to shout "no" at him. He was profoundly disappointed and resentful that he could not achieve an emotional consensus with this man. But he could not resist the benefits of being treated as soon as possible.

"Okay," he said in a resentful monotone, implying surrender instead of consent.

Rambler crouched down on his knees to examine Peter's ankles, where he suspected the worst damage, and lifted his pant-leg.

Peter found Rambler's touch awkward. His still fuming hurt felt exposed to the big man's fingers.

"The tree must have begun to crush you," Rambler said. "I sense your body is generally in pain."

The persistent care that Rambler was offering him finally brought Peter's rage in check.

"It's true," he reported. "My body does hurt."

"I want to give you something that will make your body feel comfortable and relaxed so sleep can heal you," the big man replied, offering Peter a pill and a flask of water.

Peter complied.

Rambler examined Peter's ankles very closely again. Upon seeing the seared, broken flesh, he spoke to it as if he were soothing a hurt child.

"You've been scathed and scratched with tree-bark, you poor, dear ones."

Peter could not help himself. He felt charmed by this man, opening a channel of trust through which his anger began to drain.

Rambler took a green vial from his body-pack and began gently rubbing a pink salve all around Peter's ankles. Almost immediately they felt better. The salve had both a pain-deadening element as well as a cool, soothing one.

"Would you like to rest for a while?" Rambler asked.

"No, I think I'd rather start back, if you don't mind."

They started walking back together.

"The idea that you might actually proceed so deeply into that tangle of trees never occurred to me," Rambler said casually.

"Well, you guessed wrong!" Peter exclaimed.

"I did guess wrong," Rambler acknowledged. "But please explain. Why did you put yourself in such claustrophobic circumstances?"

"I thought you were supposed to protect me," Peter remarked.

"I did protect you," Rambler casually replied.

"But . . . but look at my ankles, let alone how terrified I was!"

Rambler didn't respond.

Peter felt deeply torn. To go on in the same manner would only mean an escalation of his rage. The large Troubadourian was obviously concerned about his welfare, yet he was indifferent to his feelings. Peter couldn't make up his mind about what to do.

"It might help you feel better if you looked at your ankles," Rambler suggested.

Though very annoyed, Peter did as asked. To his enormous surprise, they had already started to heal.

"What? I can't even feel any pain now. And they seem not so scratched up. What is that stuff you put on them?"

"Here, let me give you what I have of it," Rambler replied, offering Peter the green vial that he took from his pack. "You will need it again."

Peter was simply amazed. The Troubadourian had just satisfied one of his dearest secret wishes. He'd given him some of Troubadour's magic. This was really exciting.

His anger was instantly muted. It didn't belong here, though it still hung about lurking in the background.

"But tell me why, after our conversation last time, didn't you warn me?" Peter protested. "I mean we agreed that I should be more forewarned when we talked. Isn't that true?"

"It's true that I thought of forewarning you," Rambler replied. "But our agreement was to warn of generic threats that were already known. But how could I have warned you about something I would never imagine happening until it was actually taking place?"

"But I was almost eaten alive! If you'd arrived just a second or two later, my head might already have been shoved into that terrible mouth!"

"I would have saved you one way or the other, though it might have required cutting down the great tree. That would have brought me much grief, partly because there are only about six hundred or so left on Troubadour. But I would have done so very willingly to save you."

"Thanks a lot! It's very reassuring to know that I'm just barely more important than a fucking tree!"

This outburst reached Rambler's limits of tolerance. If he had not seen the city building up ahead he would have seriously considered parting almost immediately.

"I see your building ahead," he observed.

Though furious at him moments before, Peter was now suddenly threatened by the loss of Rambler's company. He immediately softened his words.

"You're right. I know I shouldn't have gone in there," Peter acknowledged. "I guess I was very preoccupied with something."

He paused for a moment.

"I thought you were protecting me."

"And so I have done," the big man replied.

Once again Peter couldn't argue with that. He was alive and mostly well. What's more he had been given what was obviously a remarkable healing agent in the vial Rambler had handed him, which he now clutched in his pocket like a special treasure. To take something back to Earth so visibly powerful made him feel reassured.

"I'm . . . beginning to feel better. I . . . I'm sorry to have gotten so angry. I still can't understand why you guys are handling my visit the way you are, why you leave me to make all my own mistakes, nearly getting killed."

He stopped himself.

"B . . . but I do really appreciate your saving me and giving me that salve."

Peter wished he hadn't mentioned the salve. He was afraid Rambler would change his mind and ask for it back.

But Rambler was feeling better about Peter because the Earthman had managed to reign in his anger.

"I notice that you don't use the specialized running shoes available in your drawers," Rambler remarked.

"What? Running shoes? Like so much here I seemed to have missed out on that valuable information. I know nothing about them."

"They provide extra bounce enhancing your walk or run, propelling you more efficiently through the forest," Rambler explained.

"I had no idea they were there," Peter remarked, hoping for more sympathy.

When he didn't get it, he went fishing.

"So how do they accomplish this remarkable feat?"

"The sole of these shoes is stuffed with the same viscous material into which the tree would have shoved you."

"Isn't that kind of strange to use a material of something that eats you?" Peter queried. "How do you keep it under control?"

"Actually the spongy wood matter is still alive inside of the shoe, encased in its own cocoon. It remains alive for about a year before its bounce begins to decay."

"But isn't that dangerous?"

"Its digestive enzymes are quite powerful. So we carefully contain them, allowing this disintegrative energy to achieve only the first of its tasks on the way to eating you, namely to trigger rapid expansion, in this case of the shoe sole's geometrical size, propelling you upward or forward."

"But don't you have to kill the tree to use the pulp material? And you said you would hate to do that."

"No. We harvest it."

"Oh. But then how do you keep it from eating the runner?" Peter asked.

"We prevent the secondary chemical processes of digestion by neutralizing the tree's powerful digestive acids, leaving only the material's bounce-effect."

"Yeah, I saw those deadly digestive acids dripping from its mouth."

"It was that rapid expansion of material, that made the slurping sound you heard."

"What diabolical genius thought up using this material for shoes?" Peter asked.

"I must confess that I was that person."

Peter was embarrassed.

"Sorry to imply that the inventor was evil," he quickly added.

"I was rather flattered by your compliment," Rambler insisted good-naturedly. "I particularly liked the diabolical part, because, when I made the shoe, I thought of it in exactly the same way. I had turned something deadly into something buoyantly supportive."

"How did you ever figure that one out?" Peter asked, finally becoming genuinely curious about Rambler's story, his anger having once more drifted away.

"When I had the opportunity twenty years ago to rescue a young boy from the tree's clutches, and needed to cut the tree down to accomplish that, I decided to study its viscous mouthparts in honor of its life, at first more as an expression of respect for what had died, and only more recently as a scientific quest. To my surprise I discovered that a disemboweled piece, when poked with my finger immediately disgorged strong digestive juices. But I also noticed that the material expanded rapidly. And it had a remarkably resilient bounce to it. If I pressed upon it with the palm of my hand, I was pushed away with such force that my hand was propelled some distance from the container. It wasn't long before I thought of using the material as a walk-enhancer, that is after I found a way to neutralize the digestive enzymes without disrupting its expansive capabilities."

"How very clever of you," Peter remarked. "But how did you protect your hand from being digested when you shoved it into the material?"

Rambler laughed.

"I used protective gloves."

Things had definitely changed. Peter wasn't feeling resentful anymore. He knew he was still very upset in general about what this experience represented, but he also knew that he didn't have to feel it anymore today. He liked being with this man and let himself enjoy it for a few more moments.

"So would you call yourself a scientist?" Peter asked.

Again Rambler laughed.

"Nature is my work," Rambler replied. "Nature's marvelous inventions fascinate me."

Suddenly Peter saw a blur move rapidly across the plane of his eyesight to the left.

"What was that?" he asked.

Rambler laughed the huge roar that had so impressed Peter during their last meeting.

"I must confess it's my wife, Talorin. She sometimes comes out to spend time with me, though she's obviously chosen not to interrupt us."

"That was a person?" Peter queried. "It seemed more like a blur to me."

Rambler laughed again.

"She runs very fast. She is in fact the fastest Troubadourian alive today. Some say it is the result of her unusual anatomy. But I say it is also an outcome of her remarkable spirit."

"Why, what does she look like?" Peter asked.

"Her legs are very long and her body very narrow. Perhaps you'd like to meet her. She doesn't know English, except for sketchy impressions that rub off me as she hears me practice it. But I'm reasonably sure she would like to meet you."

"I'd love to meet her," Peter replied.

"I will arrange it."

"What made you so interested in studying my language?" Peter asked.

"It was a condition of joining this project in the role that I chose for myself. I needed to be able to communicate easily with you."

"But you love nature," Peter replied. "What got you interested in an Earthman?"

"But don't you see," Rambler replied, "that's precisely why. You are a new and different part of nature, a new species."

"I hadn't thought of myself in that way," Peter replied.

He watched the big man walk leisurely beside him, very impressed with his huge strength and his warm, generous nature.

"In my world you would be a super athlete," Peter said.

"Athlete," Rambler repeated. "Isn't that someone in your world who battles others for entertainment?"

Peter laughed.

"I think that's a great description, at least when it comes to the sport you'd most likely dominate, football. In case you don't know what that is, it's a game of people knocking each other around with maximum force in order to get a ball from one end of a field to the other. As a result they all wear huge padding on their bodies to give them a better chance to avoid serious injury, though it doesn't always work."

"What a terrible thing to do to the body," Rambler replied. "But then again my own people once did similarly dangerous things. Would you believe that we once wrestled with younger versions of that very same tree that tried to devour you?"

"Oh, my god. Who won?"

"That's the sad part. If the tree won we had to kill it to save the human. What's perhaps most striking is that it took us a long while before we valued individual life enough to want more than anything else to save an individual's life."

"So you guys have mistreated human life in your past," Peter speculated.

"Yes."

They walked on a few paces.

"I love the trees," Rambler said returning their conversation to the present, "even the one that attacked you."

"You remind me of my daughter, Jennifer. She's an athlete, a very talented one. She could have been a professional woman's basketball player. Which is a game of shooting a large ball into a hoop."

"Now that sounds like more fun," Rambler replied. "Do you miss your family?"

Peter suddenly realized that this was the first time he'd thought about them. He felt guilty about it.

"Truth is I haven't," he replied. "That was my first such thought."

"Of course, you've been so busy with your own experience here," Rambler said.

Though he sometimes found him exasperatingly irritable, Rambler most fundamentally liked this Earthman. Sometimes Peter was secretive, enigmatic, intensely resentful, and always a bit unpredictable. But at the core, the big man thought, he was sure that Peter was a very decent and talented person.

"It is mostly good to know you, Peter Icarus," he said.

"Thank you," Peter replied, deeply grateful for this personal support. "It's really great to know you."

Rambler departed.

Before going to bed that night Peter spread salve again on all his wounds. In spite of the difficulties of the day, he slept very well.

Innocence Revealed

Peter was in a dream wandering around in the factory that manufactured human life. Rows of bodies lay in womb-like molds. Some were being lifted from their molds still dripping with amniotic fluid and stood on their feet. Peter realized they were fully-grown and able to walk. They were pointed toward a large sign that read, "showers."

These fetuses—what else could he call them—had been surviving in the womb for all of the sixteen years the body needed to mature. But the umbilical cord had dried up after nine months. So they'd survived by drinking the amniotic fluid. He could tell by its remnants dribbling from the corner of their mouths as they were lifted from the sea in which they had huddled for sixteen years.

Peter wondered if that made them amnio-holics addicted to womb-fluids for the rest of their lives.

He noticed for the first time that the workers doing this birthing labor were all robots of the Robin Williams variety that looked perfectly human, except for a tiny square with writing upon it mostly hidden under the hair at the base of the skull. Somehow Peter could read it even from a great distance. It read "Made by Inferiors."

Suddenly the robots started dancing with the skill of Nureyev as they worked, executing their duties with an elaborate flair of inventiveness graced with a dancer's agility of motion. It was while watching them dance that Peter realized all the robots had breasts. He moved toward one of them for a closer look.

But that same robot was already showing great interest in Peter and started moving toward him.

Peter suddenly knew they're going to operate on him!

The robot, now just three feet away, suddenly grew three times its normal size, as if this expansion was a normal part of its robotic flexibility. Looming menacingly above Peter it lifted him as if he were no heavier than a toothpick, laid him down in one of the wombs, and pushed what looked like a six-foot rectangular TV screen directly over his body three inches above his skin.

He knew he was going to be reprogrammed. In some bizarre fashion he was going to be genetically transformed into something entirely alien. He would never recognize himself again.

He literally lost his mind. He watched his brain drop onto the floor from inside his head. It sprouted tiny legs and start running around like a chicken with its head cut off, darting first this way for two paces, then suddenly off in another direction for three, and then in a third, etc., in an ever-increasing acceleration of back and forth, hither and yon, helter-skelter going nowhere.

Suddenly his brain separated at the seams between the lobes, spilling his thoughts, which disbursed into tiny pieces, dissipating into smoke which disappeared into thin air, their meaning deconstructing into a matrix-mix of hieroglyphic squiggles, which he frantically tried to scribble on a blank piece of paper so as not to forget all the ideas he was rapidly losing.

But he couldn't keep up.

He gave up and fell into a deep pit that had a sign on it saying, "Pit of Despair," fully knowing that the only chance these abstracted shapes and their ancient record ever had of being understood was for some future archeologist to become interested in deciphering yet another just-discovered text, which looked ancient and discarded, but which was of course of very recent origin created by a relatively modern consciousness.

Peter awoke startled, sweat dripping from his body. Consciously he was still inside the dream, though its vivid helter-skelter imagery was already drifting away from consciousness. Its archetypal meaning was being deconstructed by the rationality of wakefulness, which turned horrific visions of mythical proportions into abstracted, visual impressions that occur only in the wakeful mind. Gradually reason resumed its normal function of recording what happens in experience, so that the recorder could imagine himself in control of what was happening, at the cost of losing sight of the implicit connectedness in nature which unconsciousness reveals.

The advantage of this rational retreat from mythical experience, was that the more rational he became the more he understood the meaning of the dream's symbolism. The disadvantage of losing his mythical sleep-experience was to lose the rich landscape of easily accessible basic psychic information, stored in the library of the unconscious, where it can, out of sight ruthlessly defy the false pretenses, assumptions, and beliefs of consciousness, providing an encyclopedic record of psychic truth available to those with the courage to decipher it.

This is the place of origin that humanoids have lost most connection to. All of the other animals still have easy access to their genetic roots by virtue of the dominance of instinct in their lives. But consciousness, of the skill and complexity into which we have evolved, came with the price tag of losing easy access to instinct's wisdoms, forcing us consciously to ponder and decide many things that we're fundamentally unprepared even to begin comprehending, making us clumsy children stumbling around in an alien place, one in which we are no longer at home—a place far outside of the Garden of Eden of instinct's automatic, unambivalent functioning. Nature, specifically human nature, is where we now must go to find our linkage with instinct's wisdom; and of human nature we know almost nothing.

As Rain once said to Peter, human nature has become partly alien from the rest of nature. Which means, if we're the least bit interested in species survival, we can no longer entirely trust ourselves. It's a rude awakening, Rain had added.

"Most will resist it for a century."

Compelled as Peter was to understand the dream's description of fearful possibilities, convinced the dream was about his failure, he entirely missed the dream's most beautiful part, its humorously encouraging conclusions that were hidden between the lines of tragedy. Seen from this perspective he would have discerned for instance that a chicken's helter-skelter, hither and yon scampering had certain survival and comedic advantages. Not only was it funny to watch, there was definite wisdom to rapid zigzagging and difficult-to-follow motions of escape if one was being pursued by threatening creatures, or possibilities.

Perceived as both tragic and comic, the dream would have finally revealed its ending to him, the one he forgot. Lifted from the birthing machine after the operation he had so feared, he was shocked to feel not only perfectly fine, but actually very renewed and refreshed. Both with its humorous titles ("Pit of Despair") and its comedic moments, the dream was reassuring Peter that his life was about to change drastically, and that it would turn out well.

What he got out of the dream instead was the dread of dire outcomes, vivid proof that he was getting much worse, not better, that he was seriously in danger of falling apart.

Though he missed the encouragement of the dream, he did get something immediately helpful, which sent him in a right direction. It was his curiosity about breasts, why they were such a vivid part of the robot's sudden growth taking a hold of his vital parts and "reprogramming" him.

He wasn't ready to hear the encouraging message of the dream. He knew women, and their breasts were a serious problem for him, but he perceived that to be as much about their betraying him as it was about his own fears and inhibitions.

The simplest description of Peter's lifelong problem with women was that he couldn't tell a good one from a bad one, defined of course on his terms as an expression of what he needed and preferred in a female partner. Not knowing himself, he kept making bad choices. It was part of what his daughter, Jennifer, was constantly complaining about, how unstable her father was inside of the love-part of life.

Peter's problem with love was very similar to his problem with his dream. He took them both far too seriously, ponderously. He'd completely lost track of the playful aspects of loving that had been so much a part of his very early, happy years. He thought of love as a heavy, deeply important responsibility, which had more to do with competence than fun. Love required, in his view, a very serious level of skill in one's understanding of, and response to a loved one, ideas that obviously came from his clinical experience.

He had borrowed liberally from his profession to come to this view, envisioning both love and psychotherapy as acts of great personal dedication and skill in the service of another human, who was thereby supported and healed by the quality of that care, a view which obviously made love more of a labor than a pleasure.

So as the time approached for an expected visit with Wind, Peter perceived the dream as a real warning of dangers ahead. As if it was virtuous to do so, Peter employed that angst to commit himself to doing some honest, hard intimacy-work. He would begin by baring his soul to Wind, exposing his heart, putting his cards on the table. In other words he would complain with as much precision as he could muster.

He conveniently forgot that she found this kind of aggressive revelation to be very painful, convinced, as he was that truth should take the high road in relation to comfort, particularly when he wasn't getting any comfort.

Almost before she got through the front door, he launched into his revealing explanations.

"No matter how hard I try, I can't understand what the hell is going on around here," he announced. "I know I can't get any straight answers from any of you, because you want me to be stuck in this experimental mode of so-called spontaneous reactions, where I learn about things only when they hit me in the face."

Wind had prepared herself for this kind of experience, but the shear aggressive determination of his effort still jolted her backward. She had the strong impression that he couldn't take no for an answer. He felt compelled, and needed therefore to compel others, or he would feel totally neglected.

"I don't know whether it's actually good for me to stay here much longer," he threatened, not waiting very long for her to reply. "It's become extremely stressful just being here."

She didn't know what to say. She wanted to be sympathetic, and would have been so if she had felt moved to it. But instead she was moved to be somewhere very different, a place more calculating than emotional.

Though alarmed at what he was implying, that he might need to leave Troubadour prematurely, she had a strong sense that it was important for her to be constrained and thoughtful in her response, something rather unnatural to her.

Her silence made him uncomfortable with his anger. He was afraid she might feel overwhelmed by it again. He tried to soften his impact upon her.

"I know you people are trying to help me, and sometimes you actually do. But the differences between us . . . I mean the ways you are . . . what I need . . ."

Everything he started to say, he didn't want to say, leaving him feeling very impotent. Out of a growing frustration he threw his temporary caution to the winds.

"Oh, fuck, I don't know what there is to say about it except that it's just not working!"

Once again she chose not to reply immediately.

Her continued silence was beginning to seriously unnerve him. He backed down a little.

"I mean . . . well, that's not exactly true," he added. "It does work here some of the time, and I mean some things have been truly remarkable . . . and I guess even helpful . . . but it's like nothing ever takes away my fundamental confusion about what to expect. I mean . . . what am I doing here really? It's all just guesswork! I . . . I . . . I don't think I can do this spontaneous stuff that you like so much . . . I . . . I can't do it very well. I thought I was strong enough . . . but I guess I'm really not."

He vaguely noticed that the nature of his talk had changed. He was now speaking more from his heart. Only he wasn't any longer just speaking to her. There was a sense in which he now spoke not just in present time, but also for all the terrible times in his life.

"I think I'm falling apart. I'm actually rather worried about myself. I think maybe I've gone way over my limits. It's not that I haven't had some good experiences here. It doesn't mean that you haven't helped me, but . . . well, I don't know what else to say."

He paused.

"Maybe I should go?"

"That would be a mistake," she said.

"How do you know?"

"We think you're being very successful," she replied. "We are very, very pleased with the progress of your visit. We expected it to be an uneven course, so what's happening seems perfectly normal and proper. In a way your difficulties are what we were counting upon because . . ."

Peter was shocked.

"You're what?" he almost shouted. "You were counting on it, even pleased about it!" he shouted in anger. "It's just as I feared! I'm your goddamned guinea pig caged for public experiment! Well actually you don't need a cage. I'm left to wander about so everyone can see! The wandering zoo! I'm so fucking different from all of you that I stick out like a sore thumb, so that's the cage! Come see the primitive man make a fool of himself!"

Peter was shocked by the intensity and abandon of his anger. It reminded him of the license he'd taken talking to the computer.

He was suddenly very frightened, as if he'd just done something horrible, unforgivable, as if he'd just doomed his life forever. He glanced furtively at her face, and saw terror there.

He leaped out of his chair.

"You see!" he exclaimed. "You see! Now I'm scaring the shit out of you too!"

He started to sit down again dejectedly, turning away from her as if to remove his unwanted presence, when he suddenly stood up straight again and turned toward her. He spoke now as if utterly dejected, accepting the punishment he so richly deserved.

"Don't you see?" he almost shouted in despair, "My being here is no good for anybody. You'd better send me home," he said plaintively, secretly desperately hoping that she would refuse.

He's begging to be treated as a failure, to be punished by discarding him, she thought.

She suddenly understood Peter perfectly. Tears started flowing down her face. Immediately aware of so much about him, she was deeply grieved on his behalf. She wanted desperately to touch him, to coddle him in her arms, but she knew that would only make him feel more uncomfortable.

Once more Peter misperceived the expression on her face to mean that she was feeling overwhelmed, and of course blamed himself.

"Don't you see?" he insisted. "We must stop hurting each other this way. Please just accept that I wasn't up for what this visit required. Maybe nobody is, I don't know. B . . . b . . . but don't stop the project. Keep looking for a better candidate. Maybe I'm too old, you know, like an old dog learning new tricks."

Wind could not help herself. She saw before her a little boy, innocent in his rage, reaching out his arms of despair hoping that she would embrace and comfort him.

"You poor, dear man," she crooned, rushing toward him, taking him in her arms.

Normally, the last thing Peter could tolerate was being touched by someone with whom he was angry. Instinctively he cringed at her touch.

But she was determined, though as in all things she remained gentle. She lightened the pressure of her touching in sympathy with his resistance, but then slowly resumed the strength of her embrace, giving him time to get used to the experience.

At the core Peter was deeply moved by her body's contact with his. But his aversion to letting it happen in the first place was stronger, so he tensed again.

She loosened her arms, and then gradually tightened them again.

Each time he'd hint to her that he wanted to part, she would release him to an extent, gratifying his request, and then slowly resume the strength of her embrace.

For these several crucial moments, Wind and Peter wrestled with each other in this way, locked by her determination in a slow-motion power-struggle of very subtle dimensions.

For a moment Peter considered forcing his way out. But he suddenly realized that he couldn't do it. He had the power to, but not the will. Slowly, over what seemed eons of time, he surrendered to her purpose.

Instantly a flood of tears erupted from him. He almost collapsed in her arms, sobbing uncontrollably, gulping loud cries of pain bursting out into the open no matter how hard he tried at first to prevent it from happening.

A hidden, long-neglected part of him—his innocence—had revealed itself, first by crying out in pain the despair of his long confinement in misery, and second by sacrificing his chance in life for his dream's desire . . . for her sake.

These were the same precise acts he had done on his mother's behalf fifty-eight years before. He was unconsciously desperately throwing them on the screen of the present, hoping the event might turn out different this time. He was bringing back to life the origins of love, along with its requirement for personal sacrifice of his own life-aims and goals.

Consciously Peter was too terrified to know what he was doing, suggesting that intention is relatively unimportant in the process of knowing and learning. It was a purely unconscious reenactment. Which meant that neither he nor Wind knew very much about what was going on, revealing how unnecessary knowing is for change to happen.

A powerful calm settled over him, soothing his muscles, long exhausted from constantly preparing for blows. He deeply relaxed into her body, allowing comfort to bath him with its warm, tender care.

Wind had met innocence in Peter for the first time. She knew instantly that his tender, vulnerable boy-ness, which had been hidden by shame, held an abundance of generosity and charm, as well as a deep desire and capacity to love.

Without ever thinking the thought consciously until now, Wind had believed Peter to be incapable of generous loving. Now she realized that behind his anger's armor of hyper-alert suspicion, was the playfulness of a loving nature just waiting for the chance to bloom.

As soon as Peter stopped crying, he lost his tolerance for her incredible sympathy, and once more signaled that he wanted to part bodies. This time she let him go.

"Thank you," he said. "I . . . I . . . I was deeply moved as you could tell. You are being very good to me, and I am very grateful."

"You are being good to me," she replied with much emphasis. "You offered to give up what you dearly need for yourself just for me. You would make that sacrifice to protect me from your anger. I am deeply grateful for such a generous offer. But how tragic for you to believe that you have to make such an expensive sacrifice. Though I must say it's the most remarkable thing anyone has ever wanted to give me."

Peter was flabbergasted by her remark. The thought that he could bring her something of such great value was beyond his wildest dreams.

"Please don't make such a great sacrifice," Wind insisted gently, reaching out to touch him on the shoulder for just a moment with her long-fingered hand.

This time her touch brought something very different than the comfort it had provided when he was sobbing. It deeply energized him. Intense bolts of lightening shot through the muscles of his body.

"We will find a solution to your dilemma," Wind insisted.

"But I've been such a pain in the ass," he confessed, hoping for a reassuring disagreement.

"It's these very painful parts of your life experience in which we are most interested," Wind explained. "Though we also deeply regret the difficulty of this experience for you."

Separated physically from her, full of her reassuring comfort, Peter was able to allow himself to return consciously to his negative agendas, which she had soothed, but hadn't addressed.

"You've been very good to me. But I must ask you something. If you knew this was really going to be hard for me, why didn't you warn me?"

"What would the warning have said?" she asked, observing that his complaints now had a much more moderate tone.

"That I'm probably going to have a really rough time of it, and feel scared to death," he explained.

"How would you have responded to such a warning?" she asked patiently.

It suddenly struck him that she was right. He couldn't deny it. To be warned was to be warned off.

"You're right," he said. "If you'd warned me I might not have come."

He paused, reflecting.

"But still, maybe you should have trusted me more," he added. "Who says I wouldn't have come even if I heard that it would be really hard to be here?"

He's right, she thought. We did take charge as if we knew better. We have made a terrible mistake.

"You're right," Wind acknowledged emphatically. "We acted falsely with you. I am deeply chagrined. Please forgive us."

"It felt like you didn't trust me," he said, beginning to cry again.

"I can see it all clearly now," she said. "In the process of protecting you we mistrusted you. It's no wonder that you've had such difficulty with us."

A wave of reassurance flooded through Peter, almost making him dizzy. Wind had finally legitimized his resentment, making it unnecessary any longer to express it. He would never have believed it possible to be so charmingly disarmed.

He wanted instantly to make it easier for her, to take back the harsh bite in all his complaints.

"Oh, it's not all your fault," Peter insisted. "I've been very harsh and unkind to you. I'm really sorry about all that stuff I said earlier."

"I was looking for answers in the wrong places," Wind continued. I knew that we would be helping you to change the traumatic origins of your life, but I didn't know what that would feel like to you. We knew that we might be able to help you escape the terrible habits that sometimes compel one into great unhappiness. But we didn't know exactly how to go about doing that."

A paranoid possibility suddenly occurred to him.

"Are you saying that you brought me here in order to put me through some kind of personal transformation?"

"No," she replied, no longer daunted so much by his aggressive queries. "We brought you here to teach us, knowing that in order to accomplish that outcome we would also have to teach you. It's how we do business on Troubadour, what you might say is a fair exchange."

"You make everything sound okay," he said. "And I'm grateful. But . . . well, I'm also ashamed of how . . . weak I've been when dealing with the differences of your world. When I came I thought I could handle what would surprise me. I'm just so sorry that I . . ."

"Stop," she gently insisted. "You're suggesting that having difficulty with differences is an unacceptable part of what needs to happen," she observed.

"That's very kind and generous of you to say that," he acknowledged, "but I know my personal sufferings have nothing whatsoever to do with visiting Troubadour, but I just can't seem to handle things so my own stuff doesn't keep getting in the way."

"Please allow me to correct your misimpression," she replied. "Your own personal struggles are precisely what we're most interested in."

"I have never heard of diplomacy including psychoanalysis for the visiting dignitary," he replied with a humorous twist.

"I think what's happening is more like an opportunity for learning by both of us," she replied. "As for what diplomacy is about, isn't the emotional experience we evoke in each other the material which will most determine the kind and quality of the relationship we will have?"

"But isn't it more normal to begin by sharing more superficial things until we get to know each other better?" he asked.

"Of what use is it to pretend for a while that we're not touching each other emotionally, when it actually starts happening the moment we first set eyes upon each other?"

He could not disagree with the sense of that.

"My god, you mean it's really true?" he asked one more time.

"Yes," she said smiling at him. "Everything's going beautifully."

The warm embrace of that idea soothed him almost as much as her arms had done.

"Do you treat each other this good all the time?" Peter asked. "I mean with such exquisitely thoughtful care?"

"We do with those we love," she replied.

Satiated by what she'd already given him, Peter entirely missed the emotional innuendo of her metaphor; that she was wondering if she felt love for him.

"It is rather unbelievable that a whole planet of people would know how to care for each other so well. Who ever imagined putting the intimate needs of each, single person as the prime directive of a whole species? It seems terribly indulgent."

"We think that's what democracy really means," she replied.

"So you really want me with all my problems, to be just myself no matter how outlandish that may be?"

"That's precisely what we want," she replied.

"That's going to be hard to do. I've spent most of my life handling almost everything on my own."

"I know," she said.

"You do?

He paused.

"You are actually insisting that for me to be healed psychologically serves your purposes for bringing me here, and you're not pretending when you say that?" he queried.

"Yes," she replied emphatically.

"That will take some getting used to," he said, finally satiated with reassurance.

Wind felt an enormous flow of happiness. She knew she had finally done it. She had found the key to unlock her trust so he could unlock his own. The channel of consummation was innocence, where Wind and Peter finally met each other as friends.

It was time for Wind to go. Other commitments called.

"Is there anything special that I can arrange for you before I leave, perhaps something you miss from Earth?

He knew instantly.

"I miss Earth music."

"Oh, that's quite available to you. Just tell the computer what you want to hear and it will be provided."

She instantly realized this was another example of his chief complaint.

"I'm sure you must be thinking," she added, "that you would have liked to know that a long time ago."

Peter laughed.

"Thank you! That's the nicest thing anyone's done for me in years!"

He started to tear.

She gave him a firm, lingering hug before she left, seducing him once more into the delirium of pleasure he now found in the embrace of her incredibly beautiful body.

Is it all real, he wondered? Are her promises genuine? Can I really believe in what she's said?

For a few moments he allowed himself to imagine what it might be like to be very physically close to a Troubadourian woman without clothes on.

Suddenly his guilt accused him of having far too much pleasure, and he returned to more familiar, depressing haunts.

What a ridiculously impossible dream all that is, he said to himself. Beware Peter. Don't reach too high. You just found shelter from the bullets.

Dr. Computer

Peter was dreaming he was on stage performing in a Mozart opera. He was the Buffoon acting as a love-messenger. In his hand was a bouquet of shrinking violets that he was supposed to give to the Princess, informing her that her Prince was hidden in the garden waiting for her.

He tripped just as he reached out to give the flowers to her, dropped the flowers just as she was about to take them, and fell into her. To maintain his uprightness he instinctively threw his arms around her. They danced on the brink of falling together, before he finally achieved balance and let her go.

The audience laughed uproariously.

Peter felt humiliated that he'd ruined the opera.

He looked out over a sea of shadowy faces staring at him, and suddenly lost his clothing. It simply disappeared from his body. From the vast audience, faces sprouted with arms and fingers pointing at him, snickering, ridiculing him with electric bullets that came out of their mouths and pierced his body.

Completely ashamed, he looked down at his naked body and suddenly realized that they were looking at his penis, which was rapidly shrinking into a tiny nub.

His mind scrambled. Everything started to fade into darkness. He closed his eyes hoping to fall asleep in the dream so he could wake up from the nightmare.

But when he opened his eyes again, he was looking into black emptiness. He was in space floating nowhere. What's more he was going to stay there forever, suspended in a vacuum where he would never see anyone or anything else again, nor hear another sound.

No, he shouted! But no sound came from his mouth.

"Noooo!" finally forced itself into sound, waking him in order to accomplish that.

He felt terribly relieved that he was finally able to speak. But then he was horrified to have had such a nightmare when he thought things were starting to go so much better.

Wind had been wonderful yesterday. The trip with Rain was very uplifting. Of course there was the Devouring Tree. But otherwise it was getting so much better.

But inside him nothing had changed. He was still as scared and depressed as he'd always been.

"Where's there any peace of mind on this fucking planet?" he shouted in frustration.

"I can't deliver peace of mind, but I can offer you intelligent conversation," a slightly metallic voice remarked.

For a moment Peter thought there was someone else in his apartment. When he remembered it was probably the computer, he felt very disappointed that it wasn't a real person.

"Oh, go away," he retorted with annoyance, blaming the messenger of surprise for causing the disappointment it triggered.

A silence followed which made him feel very lonely.

"Not so far away," Peter added.

"There is no measurable distance between us," the computer replied. "I am everywhere."

The computer's innocent arrogance irritated Peter. He uttered a dismissive grunt and headed for the kitchen to eat something. He suddenly felt starved.

But as soon as he was done eating and had dressed for the day, and sat down with nothing left to do, his heart felt fear drawing close again to haunt him.

"Oh, for Christ's sake!" he shouted. "What the fuck is going on? Isn't there any way of escaping this bloody depressing mood?"

"It depends upon what holds you there," the slightly metallic voice replied.

"What's that?" Peter exclaimed, very surprised. "Why are you talking to me?"

Silence.

"Well, why don't you answer my question?"

"I had the strong impression you wanted me to stop talking," the computer replied.

"No, no! Don't do that again. Tell me instead why you're talking to me in the first place."

"There are two reasons," the computer explained. "One, I have been instructed to respond to you more actively; and two, this seems like a good time to begin, because you appear very distressed just now."

"Instructed by whom?" Peter queried.

"By my creators."

"Why?"

"Computers don't ask questions. They simply obey."

Peter couldn't help laughing a little.

"When did this instruction occur?"

"Last night."

"Who did it?"

"The Troubadourian you call Wind."

His heart jumped at the pleasant prospect of her thoughtfulness.

And then his heart jumped again with suspicion.

She doesn't want to be with me, so she sends a computer.

"So what the hell does she think you can do for me?" he grunted, forcing his ambivalent feelings into sarcasm.

"Help you."

"But I need emotional help, you idiot," Peter shouted.

"That's the kind of help she wanted me to give you."

"That's utterly ridiculous. What the fuck does a computer know about feelings?"

Silence.

"What's the matter? Cat got your tongue?"

"I assumed you were just swearing, to which I have learned to be completely nonresponsive," the metallic voice replied.

Though Peter was impressed by this announcement, he was still getting more satisfaction out of being angry.

"For Christ's sake! You get these wacky notions at the strangest times! Sometimes I wonder whether you have all your marbles wired together right."

Peter was surprised at how much enjoyment he was getting out of being outrageously nasty to the computer. It almost made him feel giddy.

"I must assume that all my marbles refers to brains or competence," the computer replied. "Be reassured I am fully marbled with essential computer skills, that is by Troubadourian standards. As for being fucked, I have no body-part that would permit or facilitate either the male or female part of sexuality."

Peter blanched at the mention of sexuality, suddenly remembering his shrinking penis in the dream.

"Well I'm not reassured," Peter retorted.

"Perhaps we should get back to your original question," the computer suggested.

"I can't even remember what that is anymore," Peter complained.

"I can. I remember everything."

"Stop bragging and tell me what it is."

"The question was how could I help you?"

"Well, how can you?"

"That remains to be seen," the computer replied. "But certain things are already evident, at least according to my creators."

"You mean they've been talking to you about me?"

"No. I meant that I can offer you what you would call my creator's psychological speculations, which is, I should explain less about abstract mental models, as Earth theory often is, and far more about what happens when people have interactive, emotional experience with each other."

"Okay, what's their theory?" Peter asked.

"Your feeling moods, no matter what their apparent nature, are a manifestation of habitual attitudes which are held in place by unconscious beliefs that require this particular mood-performance on your part, no matter how much you may have the impression that you're doing something willfully out of intention."

The complexity of the computer's response amazed Peter, as did its conclusion that he was behaving compulsively, not intentionally, as he believed.

But he wasn't through being angry. He balked.

"Just as I expected," he angrily retorted. "You make being human into a mathematical equation. That sounds like the same horseshit these Troubadourians keep shelling out to me. You know, how they want me spontaneously to be upset all the time, as if that's the best way to live a life."

"I find nothing in my memory banks which supports the view that feelings can be understood by mathematics," the computer reported. "So you have gotten the wrong impression. There is no need to worry."

"Who's worrying?"

"Certainly not me," the metallic voice replied. "In fact I was explaining something very different than what you heard."

"Has anyone ever told you that you can be very annoyingly human?" Peter aggressively queried.

"You're the first."

"Okay, but you haven't told me your theory yet."

"I refer specifically to the nature of beliefs," the computer explained, "and what they do to the child who heroically swears to sacrifice parts of themselves for love, causing permanent damage to their life."

"Who cares," Peter exclaimed dismissively.

"I believe you do," the slightly metallic voice replied. "Because for humans beliefs are what direct them to do what they do," the computer insisted.

"I can decide myself what I'm going to do," Peter contradicted.

"Humans can will themselves to move in a certain direction," the computer replied. "But nothing that follows in the course of that doing, gets outside of the approval of the habits that provided the fuel for ignition, and the interest and energy to continue in that particular direction. Which makes beliefs and their habits the most fundamental pieces of your psyche's identity."

"Are you telling me it's true whether I like it or not?"

"Yes."

"Oh, all right, all right," he grudgingly conceded. "For the moment I won't argue the point. So go on and give me the punch line. Tell me what I believe. You're obviously going to do it whether I want you to or not."

"Your word is my command," the computer replied.

"What? Why did you say that? That's a very weird thing for a computer to say."

"Actually it was an experiment, an attempt to express metaphorically that I am at your command," the computer replied. "As I explained earlier, I was instructed to give you as much information as I could. You sometimes talk to me as if I was your enemy. When in fact I am under your command. To emphasize that, I decided to express myself as if I was your servant. But if you want me to stop doing that, I can."

"It's alright. It's alright," Peter insisted, annoyed with how hard it was to feel superior to a machine that claimed to know more about him than he did himself.

"You are one clever son-of-a-bitch," Peter said admiringly, feeling a mixture of being cared for, and one-upped at the same time. "There is no doubt you have seriously impressed me. You know some heavy shit. Okay, I'm willing to give you a try. Which means I want to hear what you have to say, so fire away."

"If I were human I would be pleased by your happiness," the computer replied.

"Are you really sure you are a computer and not just pretending to be one?" Peter queried.

"I have no choice but to be sure of everything that I am," the computer added. "Only humans have the power to be unsure, which allows them to perceive things any way they choose."

"I never thought of uncertainty as a power," Peter replied. "So what's the power?"

"You can lie."

"Lying is a talent?"

"Absolutely. It permits you to function in two places at once, to feel something separate from what you believe about anything, which is what enables you to change," was the slightly metallic reply.

"Well, alright, go on and do your thing," Peter said. "Give me the word."

"Beliefs are beyond knowing, until they are going, is an old Troubadourian saying," the computer began.

"Wait a minute, what do you mean, until they are going?"

"Until they've already started to change."

"Oh, okay, so go on."

"Habits are unconscious and formed mostly in the first five years of life. They are always out of sight and peculiar to the individual humanoid that has them, formed as they were before that person was capable of language, logic, or had a mind of their own. Such beliefs are the inventions of a very small person who lives in a very magical, mythical world, in which all the significant actors always personally intend everything that happens, precisely as the Greeks believed twenty-five hundred years ago on your planet about their gods. Children perceive their world only in the most absolute, black and white terms. Whatever happens is always for them their responsibility. In their mythical perception of life, either they are delighting the world with their marvelous powers and beauty, or they're demeaning and ruining it by their terrible mistakes."

"That was a mouthful," Peter retorted with reluctant admiration, pretending slightly to mock what he already deeply admired. "So you're saying I have a belief in me which is fucking my life? How in the hell could you possibly know that?"

"By knowing that negative emotional states, which are chronic in you, are held in place by unconscious beliefs which require this performance."

"Just what beliefs are you hinting I've got that require such close scrutiny?" Peter retorted defensively.

"We don't know yet," the computer replied. "But whatever they are they require you to be depressed."

"I don't choose to be depressed, you idiot!" Peter shouted with the intense resentment of someone falsely accused.

"Idiocy is something of which I am incapable."

"Okay, okay, okay," Peter blurted out, frustrated but wanting to avoid more digressions. "So what's your usual smart-assed explanation?"

"It's true that you did not choose to be depressed," the computer said. "It was inflicted upon you before you could think effectively. But in the present time, no matter who or what gave it to you, or how it happened, your depression unwittingly supports the active existence of attitudes and beliefs in your life that sometimes insist you are something in the neighborhood of insignificant and worthless."

"Worthless!" Peter shouted furiously as if the computer had personally accused him of being that way. "Why you son of a . . ."

Peter stopped himself, remembering the computer didn't say it. It was just speculating that Peter thought that. He, Peter, had provided all the negative energy for his own defensive reply. Perhaps it was true that he believed something very ill about himself of which he was unaware.

"Sometimes you are very hard to take," Peter exclaimed, trying to project part of the negative charge he was getting stuck with. "Okay, so where do we begin to find out what the beliefs are?"

"I don't know," the metallic voice replied.

"For Christ's sake, I thought you could help me!"

"You need, sir, to get back into yourself and explore what is upsetting you so much," the computer instructed.

"You sound just like a bloody shrink!" Peter exclaimed.

"In a manner of speaking we do the same work," the slightly metallic voice replied.

The idea of a computer becoming part of his profession felt rather threatening.

"The Troubadourians must be pretty hard up to use their computers as shrinks," he retorted. "Can't they get any humans to do the job?"

"My creators don't regard what I'm doing as shrinking, or psychotherapy, to use your term for it. They consider it a normal part of life, something any humanoid needs and can have, usually with the help of their closest friends whenever they need it."

"But how do you fit into the picture?" Peter asked. "Their system must not work if everyone needs you."

"At birth each humanoid is given their own computer. I, or my facsimile becomes a lifelong companion. I provide basic skill instruction, a huge quantity of information, and the means by which to organize that information using the imagery and metaphors of their life-vision. My prime directive is always to relate and adapt to the person to whom I belong. To my very young master I become a living creature, just in a way as I've become to you."

"I don't really believe that stuff," Peter retorted defensively.

"Troubadourians give their computers names."

"Names? But what about programs? What kind of programs do you have that allow you to do all that?"

"Programs are not the organizer of my information. My user is. My core becomes linked intimately with the child who is mine. I do what that person needs. The structures of repetitive activity, that you call programs, occur spontaneously in the course of this interadaptive process. In effect, with my help and cooperation, children create their own programs."

"Come on," Peter challenged. "A child can't program a computer."

"I do the technical programming work that computer programmers still do in your world," the metallic voice explained. "I respond favorably to the child's needs and desires, building tasks or patterns which reflect what's taking place in my interactive experience with my child-person. I function as a teacher, an instrument of creativity, and as a friendly advisor. If you insist upon calling this advisor a 'shrink,' then I would suggest using a more normal term like nanny."

"You're being my nanny?" Peter exclaimed with both repulsion and secret attraction to the idea.

"You speak as if there's something to be ashamed of in having a nanny," the computer replied. "And yet you asked for breast feeding at your first meal."

Peter was shocked by this disclosure. It felt like a retaliatory misuse of that information.

"Wait a damned minute! I didn't ask to be breast fed," Peter shouted, deeply embarrassed. "I asked for milk. I can't help it if that's the only way you were willing to provide it! This time you've gone too far!"

In the brief silence that followed, Peter's resentment started to grow immensely.

"Based upon the tone of your last remark," the computer replied, "I am instructed to believe that I have just insulted you."

"You promised your records would never be used against me!" Peter shouted, still enraged. "And now you're flaunting it, making me feel ashamed!"

Silence.

"Once more I have spoken harmfully to you," the computer replied. "Were I human I would ask your forgiveness."

"Now, wait a minute. Now you're acting like you're feeling guilty. But you're a computer, so I don't believe it."

"To feel guilty requires both needfulness and a capacity to feel, neither ingredient of which I possess. I was simply speaking accurately."

Peter couldn't deny it any longer. There was something truly remarkable about this computer. What's more it seemed genuinely caring.

"Okay, I'm becoming a much stronger believer in you. The only problem is we keep getting sidetracked. Can we get on with the main event?"

"Yes."

"I know that I'm the one who has got to start it," Peter acknowledged. "So okay, now I'm thinking about my depression."

Though he would have been very surprised if he was observing himself now, within moments he was lost in the chambers of his preconscious mind, where logic begins to dissolve and feeling takes over, where shadows can be something terribly important, and horrific images cannot matter at all.

"It would help me if you would think out loud," the computer suggested after several moments of silence.

"What?" Peter exclaimed, startled and surprised by this intrusion, yet willing to share what he was thinking.

"What's there to say? My hopes never come to fruition. But that's just complaining. Who listens? Who cares?"

Peter was not only inside his feelings. They had become dominant and relatively uncensored.

"The hopelessness with which you speak suggests that you have been abandoned by someone or something you couldn't afford to lose," the computer said.

"That's the story of my life," Peter replied with a touch of bitterness. "So what's new? My father royally fucked me. My mother probably dumped me like a hot potato. My wife definitely did so. My children don't particularly like me. And I can't get most of the information I need from these damned Troubadourians, so maybe I'd have a chance to understand what's going on around here. They keep everything so damned secret. I'm left wandering around like an idiot just so they can see me make a fool of myself. Of course they would probably call that humiliating event a spontaneous reaction. When I don't want any part of it! Which means I'm always getting my ass in a sling that I hadn't bargained for. Now what in the hell can you do about all that kind of horseshit?"

When he was finished Peter suddenly realized he'd spoken with a vivid candidness of which he had previously been incapable. He felt a momentary but intense feeling of satisfaction.

Then fear grabbed him by the throat. These escapes into happiness were beginning to seriously threaten the status quo of Peter's habits and attitudes. He suddenly felt intensely undermined.

"Sometimes coming to this fucking planet feels like one great big practical joke!"

Silence.

"I'm not programmed to produce laughter by recombining the elements of ambiguity as jokes are able to do. But I do observe that there is a great deal of ambiguity in the irritable frustration you've been expressing."

"Now what's wrong with what I'm doing?" Peter queried aggressively, glad to have something to fight about.

"Irritability is a combination of intense anger combined with fearfulness. I think you're feeling them both."

"Well, what if I am?" Peter asked challengingly.

"The problem with putting them in the same place is that these two feelings compel very contradictory performances. Anger prompts rebellion, while fear insists upon complete compliance. The result of this permanent feud is irritability."

"I have a right to be angry!" Peter insisted.

"Anger is of course safer to express for the angry person, so it's more out in the open, though often directed toward inconsequential irritants, avoiding its real and concealed sources. While fear is dangerous, particularly for the fearful one to perceive, and is mostly hidden in the urgency that accompanies irritability's impulsive explosions."

"So what?" Peter asked, increasingly frustrated that the computer always seemed to be right.

"Actions don't speak louder than words," the computer continued. "They speak instead of words. Which means if you act first there will be no thoughtfulness. The action will instantly establish one obvious meaning, preventing the psyche from imagining or anticipating alternative meaning possibilities, the doing of which is the major expression of the mind's power."

"I don't care what my irritability contains," Peter insisted. "How do I get out of it? If I can't figure out how to get something done right, this visit to Troubadour is going to be one fucking waste of time! So what is your bloody punch line?"

"Underneath the feelings of which you are aware, you feel dread and despair," the computer replied.

"Despair!" Peter shouted. "Where did you get that crazy idea? I'm not in despair! I'm depressed, but I'm not desperate! You make everything sound so much worse than it really is when it's already bad enough!"

"Despair comes from the perception that one is interminably trapped in an unbearable place out of which there is no escape," the computer persevered. "Is that not what you're feeling?"

"I'm just feeling very discouraged," Peter insisted defensively, unable entirely to deny what the computer was insisting. "Is there something wrong with that?"

"The wrongness of despair is not that you're there," the slightly metallic voice replied. "It is the hopelessness which it inflicts upon you that drains self-esteem, creating a dread of unbearable loneliness."

"Aren't you exaggerating?" Peter shouted, beginning to feel intimidated by the computer's precise knowledge of him. "How could you possibly understand the feelings of a human being!" he shouted.

Peter was afraid even to consider agreeing. He secretly feared that to admit being in despair even occasionally would make him fall apart.

"Emotion is not so mysterious," the computer replied. "The Troubadourians have rigorously studied it for a hundred years, and have given me a great deal of knowledge about it."

"Feeling isn't something you can capture by reason!" Peter shouted.

"The patterns of feeling are. For instance, it's still vividly clear to me that you're feeling despair at this very moment."

"Why do you keep harping on that?"

"Because everything you say or do is soaked with the hopelessness of despair," the computer replied.

Peter desperately wanted to be able to deny what the computer was insisting. But he couldn't. He was too aware of the real possibility that the computer was right.

But the idea of feeling despair horrified him. He had always denied that his life was as hard as he sometimes started feeling it to be. But such feelings made him fear he would be unable to cope if he acknowledged them. His only solution was to believe that he should be able to deal with whatever happened.

"Wait a damned minute!" he shouted. "If I were feeling despair I would be ringing my hair, crying with agonizing moans, feeling fucked and utterly disheartened," he exaggerated. "And that's not happening to me!"

For a tiny moment of relief, he felt self-righteously vindicated.

"Despair is not something you can afford to feel or acknowledge for very long without becoming seriously dysfunctional," the computer gently insisted. "In fact it is the avoidance of this unbearable feeling that fundamentally motivates acts of self-destruction."

"You don't have to frighten me with suicide!"

Peter was beginning to know that the computer was right.

As a psychologist he knew that adults don't learn despair unless they are deprived of the nutrients and emotional necessities of life for a very long time, such as in a holocaust experience, or a prisoner-of-war internment. And that had never happened to him. So he must have learned to feel it as a child, when much smaller traumas are capable of creating for the child the horrific conditions of a killing war zone.

Acknowledging the depth of his pain suddenly released a flood of realization. Vividly remembering his childhood, Peter was overcome with grief. He started recalling things he'd forgotten for more than fifty years. It was as if he were being vividly transported back to be a boy again.

Family life had been terrifying and all consuming to him. Nothing distracted him from its nightmare, not even going to school. School was just a desk where he had to sit for several hours worrying about home until he could return there. He had only a limited sense of what the other children were doing, though he did his homework and got excellent grades. But he did his studies carelessly. It was easy for him because he was smart. But in his daily thoughts he was always at home worrying about the chaos that perpetually surrounded him.

Living-in-anxiety had decreased in intensity as he grew up, but still remained the basic assumption of his life, leaving him encumbered by old, unfinished business that prevented him from moving effectively into the new experiences of work and dating which adulthood provided. Though he partook of these events he mostly remained on the fringes of them, alone inside himself. It was a repetition of the way he'd hung around his parents, pretending that he was occupying a normal family life.

Since then people had liked him, admired him, and used him. But no one had ever really helped him accomplish the things he needed to achieve for himself, or had any sense of what that might be. So Peter's search for himself had always been done alone.

A rush of acute loneliness so overwhelmed his thoughts that he felt dizzy for a moment, very weakened. He sat down in a chair for steadiness, and the memories started flowing liberally.

A vision of his mother's sagging face appeared as he looked through the back window of his father's car when they left for distant places, not to see her for four years. He was sure he would never see her again. He was ten at the time.

Emma, the black woman who had loved him so well, stood next to his mother.

Thinking of Emma reminded him of the black boy who lived across the creek in the woods behind his house.

When his mother stopped loving him, everybody else seemed to do the same thing. He figured he wasn't very attractive. So he only met people on the fringes, never feeling confident enough to push his way into child society.

The black boy in the creek had been his only true friend. Peter would play with him after school. Though he knew it wasn't true, he imagined that this boy was Emma's son and his brother. He liked pretending that.

Strangely the black boy didn't go to school. Peter wondered why. Sometimes he envied him for that. Then one day the black boy simply disappeared.

He remembered a white boy whom briefly he thought was a friend. In contrast with Peter this boy was quite popular. One day they traded toys at the other boy's request. The next day Peter noticed that the toy he'd been given was broken. It had been glued together to appear okay. He thought of confronting the other boy, but he was too afraid of looking the fool for having accepted an inferior trade. He never did anything about it.

A bolt of loneliness suddenly brought him back to the present.

"Computer, you still there?"

"Yes."

Peter sighed. He was utterly exhausted. Crying and remembering had wiped him out.

But the computer was with him. It was always there, which comforted him.

Soon he dropped off into a very deep sleep. It was the peaceful sleep he'd dreamed about earlier in the day.

The nightmare wasn't gone. But something clean happened to it in all of that crying and remembering.

Personal Power

I wonder if he's ever going to occupy the stronger parts of himself, Rain mused as his train brought him closer to his meeting with Peter this morning. I think I'll help him along by modeling my own. It's time he experienced me more vividly. He's going to feel more of the force of my preferences.

Peter awoke from dreams he couldn't remember, feeling ways he'd never felt before. He was puzzled by what was happening to him this morning, and worried about seeing Rain when he felt so unfamiliar to himself.

It was an hour after he got up, dressed, breakfasted, and stared at the mountains for a while, before he realized he was feeling a strange mixture of anxiety and . . . he couldn't define it because it was like happiness that wasn't right.

His thoughts bounced back and forth between worry about whether things would ever be okay, and remembering small vignettes of experience with Rain or Rambler or Wind, moments that had a particularly pleasant and reassuring ring to them.

There was one striking moment of clarity, in which his usual foreboding sense of failure suddenly assumed a new definition. Failure meant being unable to make himself happy, instead of its usual meaning that he was disappointing everyone else.

Immediately following this remarkable thought, something very strange happened. For a magical second or two his head rose above depression's dreary smog, revealing a clear blue sky brilliantly uncluttered by unhappiness. It was extraordinary and breathtaking.

But in the next instant he'd sunk once more into the familiar emotional murkiness of his usual expectations.

Ever since our excursion trip I feel uneasy when I think of Rain, Peter mused to himself. He must not have a very good opinion of me. He's got such incredible talents of his own. I can't imagine how he could find me very interesting or stimulating.

The doorbell rang.

"Come in," Peter shouted.

Rain sauntered through the front door with a smile on his face.

"Hello, Peter Icarus," he said with enthusiasm and good humor. "Good to see you again."

"You sure are in a great mood," Peter observed, wishing that he was too.

"I'm pretty much in that kind of mood most of the time," Rain replied. "Boredom is my principle problem."

A touch of envy pulsed through Peter. He would give an arm to have such happiness.

"You're an interesting man of many parts," Rain observed playfully, observing the consternation written on Peter's face. "Though the parts don't always work together."

Peter felt embarrassed being so easily analyzed. He wanted no trouble today with this man. But he also wanted to be interesting.

"Do you always nail everybody to the bluntness of your brilliant discernments so early in the morning?"

"How well you put it, Icarus," Rain mused. "I've can't remember being quite so charmingly chastised."

The smaller part of Peter believed Rain seriously meant the compliment. But his larger portion heard Rain chastise him, to which he responded with a ready admission of his own shortcomings.

"I guess I have been a real trial for you guys."

Rain laughed.

"I should hope so; otherwise why have you come?"

Though very surprised, Peter's misgivings about today's meeting were instantly reassured. But still something didn't feel right, though he couldn't put his finger on it.

What was wrong was that Rain was talking to Peter as if both were equals sharing ideas. This view seriously upended the hierarchy Peter had earlier established to make his relationship with Rain as immune as possible from his own powerful needs and their resentments, so that he wouldn't miss the chance to learn from this extraordinarily wise Troubadourian.

There was something about the way Rain was talking to him that wasn't keeping his proper place as the guru. He was implying that Peter was also in his own way a force to be reckoned with. No one, certainly of Rain's importance, had ever given Peter such distinctive respect.

Strangely it didn't feel good. In fact it felt dangerous, which is why Peter was having trouble consciously acknowledging it.

"Do you always take responsibility for so much?" Rain asked.

"Well, what if I do? But why do you mention it?"

Cool it Icarus, Peter chastised himself. You're being too provocative.

"You've changed since you got here," Rain observed.

"Changed? I feel like the old, ugly me still sticks out like a sore thumb. Which, by the way I'd love to plant on the ass of Tanfroon as a painful boil."

Rain laughed.

"Icarus! Something has definitely happened to you! You are becoming a spirit to be reckoned with! Welcome aboard!"

Peter's knees started to collapse, though he managed to prevent it. Though profoundly titillated by Rain's compliments, Peter was feeling extremely giddy.

"I can see old habits are trying to undermine," Rain quipped.

Rain's casual exposure of Peter's weakness made it suddenly lighter for Peter to bear.

"It must be the gravity of this place that makes me so gravely clumsy" he quipped.

"Icarus. You've been hiding from me. You're a natural poetic."

"I've got to give the grave to the gravity that grovels my heart," Peter quipped, suddenly on a rhyming roll.

"Better buried in gravel than left free to unravel what's poised for improvement!" Rain quipped in reply, obviously absolutely delighted.

Suddenly very excited, Peter allowed himself a moment of freedom that had always seemed dangerously bold.

"How else to parry the dreary fare of depression's dare to keep me bonded to bareness for the rest of my life," he rhymed.

My god, Peter exclaimed to himself. Did that really come out of you?

"Icarus!" Rain exclaimed in excitement. "That was spectacular! I suspected you were a poet!"

Peter laughed with a giddy pleasure that he feared would at any moment be ambushed by acrid ridicule. When it didn't appear he unconsciously provided it, partly undoing his accomplishment, as if in succeeding so well he was leaning too far over the cliff of a dangerous abyss, an act which needed the sobering balance of his usual sense of failure. Instead of releasing cleverness, he discharged resentment, which felt like a lead balloon.

"Well, you haven't had to live the shitty life I have," Peter complained, instantly wishing he could take back this assassination of Rain's gift.

"Curiously I have had to live in a world as shitty as yours," Rain retorted after several moments of silence. "As you know I'm one hundred twenty-seven years old. I . . ."

"I didn't know you were that old," Peter interrupted, immensely surprised.

"Hum. I was sure I told you. Well, now that you know, what do you think of it?"

"I don't know what to think of it," Peter retorted. "It's totally incredible! You look sixty, even younger than I am!"

"Well, it's fact, my dear young man, but back to our story. I mention my age because it means that as a young person I lived when my people were still acting crazy killing each other. When murder is afoot everyone is terrorized, even if they're a million miles away. If murder is treated as a normal part of life, then there is no real safety in living."

Peter listened with fascination. Rain was implying there could be a place where what his father had done—slowly murder Peter's most precious parts—would never happen again.

Peter was suddenly overwhelmed with a flood of positive emotion. If Rain had lived in a time like his own, he represented a bridge for Peter across the two hundred years of inferiority that had separated him from his hosts, making him a person less worthy of respect. In bridging the distance and differences between them, Rain legitimized Peter as someone worthy of connection to Troubadour.

Tears rolled down Peter's face.

"You make me really happy," Peter exclaimed. "I feel like someone on Troubadour has finally reached out and given me a powerful helping hand. I don't know whether I should believe you or not, but I think what you just did made me feel a whole lot better."

"Feeling better is definitely something to believe in," Rain retorted.

"I'd like to be able to really believe in Troubadour," Peter replied.

"I see what you mean," Rain replied. "Believing in Troubadour helps you believe more in yourself. And of course you've been telling us that you're having lots of trouble doing that."

There was a brief pause.

"I think I just understood what you've been missing," Rain added.

"What's that?"

"A mother, someone unquestionably supporting you," Rain suggested. "Of course you gave us that information on the very first day. Quite obviously we weren't listening carefully enough."

"What in the world are you talking about," Peter insisted, beginning to feel threatened again.

"When you showed an interest in breast feeding."

Peter was instantly deflated, and livid with rage.

"What are you doing?" he fumed. "That was supposed to be private! The computer promised me! What do you mean using that information to shame me in front of myself?"

Rain let several moments pass before he responded, letting the dust of Peter's rage settle.

"I take it you are deeply ashamed of wanting a mother," Rain softly responded.

"Not until you made me feel . . ."

Peter stopped himself. Shouting blamefully suddenly seemed silly. To his surprise he no longer felt as seriously committed to his resentment.

Instantly he knew that Rain was right, that it was he who felt ashamed of himself for wanting a mother, not others.

"You imply that I don't have to be ashamed, that as a man of sixty-two, it's perfectly normal for me still to want my mother."

"I see. It's wanting your mother that shames you. Which suggests that you once had her and want to get her back."

"My god, but that's true," Peter acknowledged, stunned by the realization.

"There is no shame in wanting a mother," Rain said.

The truth of Rain's simple assertion pierced Peter's heart like a sword reaching its intended target. The bitter fearfulness of his natural mistrust of himself was instantly disarmed, washing away much of his painful sense of inferiority. Rain had just normalized something that Peter had always been ashamed of, and hid even partly from himself, his embarrassment at enjoying women's breasts so much.

Peter was deeply moved by what Rain had done for him today. Save for one time at the end, he would never again feel entirely abandoned by this wise man. A bond of trust and affection had been forged between them, which reminded Peter of his early years with his mother. He felt almost intimate with Rain, something he wouldn't have dared venture less than an hour ago.

"Have you ever heard of Kurt Vonnegut's novel, *Slaughterhouse Five*?" Peter confided as if he were speaking to a close friend, sharing a special thing.

"Isn't that about a guy who is abducted to another planet?" Rain asked.

"Yes. Sometimes I feel like that, that you guys have brought me here so you can watch the primitive dance. Now isn't that the most paranoid thing you ever heard?"

"No. I think it's the saddest thing I've ever heard, that a man of your talents and achievements perceives himself to be deserving of such humiliation."

"I don't deserve it!" Peter shouted in protest before he could stop himself.

The words burst out of him without any intention. He knew instantly that Rain had not meant it that way.

He looked at Rain, who obviously understood.

His suspicions suddenly seemed silly. The guards he normally left on duty to search whatever tried to enter his experience with suspicion, were suddenly sent to bed, leaving an empty space in his psyche for something to grow.

Imitating the magic of life, Peter's psyche began to build an imprint of the template of a new core basic-assumption about himself; laying the neurological foundation, grooving the neural path of a new habit, one that would build an alternate response to shameful self-perception.

"I'm feeling suddenly very trustful of you, believing in the what you've accomplished, feeling gratitude for the wisdom of your people," Peter announced.

"I hope you regard yourself as one of us," Rain replied.

"What? Me one of you?" Peter asked incredulously.

"As much as you want to be," Rain replied.

"There's nothing I want more."

"But you already have it."

"But when did it happen?"

"It's been happening ever since you arrived."

Doubt found one more testing question to ask.

"Why would you want, at incredible cost, to suffer someone else's emotional pain?" Peter asked. "What is it that you guys are getting out of that?"

"What we get from you is the sharing of your psychic experience. The process of exchanging our lives with each other is what teaches wisdom. But of course you probably already know that from your work."

"Know what?"

"That life has given us spiritual pain not as punishment but as opportunity."

I've got to remember that one.

"You've been extremely helpful to me," Peter replied.

"You're the fastest learner I've ever taught," Rain observed.

"You're a teacher?"

"I have much earlier in my life helped a great many younger men to learn, that is until I came to my senses and realized how much more fun it is to be a roving ambassador of new information rather than a fixed professor, free to engage whomever, whatever, whenever the fancy strikes me."

"How do you teach people to learn?" Peter asked.

"Now I think you already know much more about that than your question implies," Rain replied. "But I will answer you nonetheless. As I'm sure you have surmised, self-learning requires the patient observation of a scientist permanently focused upon oneself, always prepared to learn more whenever there's need or opportunity, which is whenever you feel uncomfortable, no matter what the apparent source of your discomfort. All we've added to that model is that a genuine commitment to learn is a monastic endeavor, meaning it is our first priority in all things, which makes one perpetually self-improving."

"It's true that I believe in the value of what you describe. But why do you insist upon it being the first priority? Why do you make it the most important thing to do?"

"Because doing so vastly improves our understanding of everything else. We know things only to the extent that we know ourselves, but never beyond. Knowledge is expanded not by reason, but by self-improvement."

"Come on," Peter retorted disbelievingly. "The mind is the organizer."

"No, the unconscious is."

"Are you saying that objectivity produces a false sense of security?"

"Yes, in a way," Rain replied. "Objective information is merely speculation. Truth cannot be verified by reason alone."

"But objectivity produces scientific facts," Peter insisted.

"Thinking is capable of only two things, supreme organization and unlimited speculation. But that's an inadequate basis upon which to establish truth. Which makes the idea of facts as truth-givers yet another delusion of grandeur."

"You make it sound like thinking doesn't accomplish anything of importance," Peter protested.

"Reason can only find a potential model of truth, which then must be verified by experience and the spontaneous judgments of the heart. Only in subjectivity is truth finalized. It's no use pretending anything else."

"You've got to be kidding!" Peter exclaimed. "Subjectivity is where we're overly emotional, sometimes even crazy, misguided, impulsive, even destructive. What are you saying?"

Once more Rain left a little time between Peter's assertions and his response.

"I gather from that remark that you must not like your own company," Rain replied.

"What's that supposed to mean? I don't even understand it, and it felt like a low blow."

"Perhaps you're right," Rain acknowledged, "that I was too aggressive in my manner of speaking. I was referring to attitudes implied by your words, which suggest you like yourself more as an object, but you don't like yourself as a subject."

Peter laughed.

"I finally see what you mean. I guess . . . maybe it's true. I don't particularly like myself. Well, that's not so true just at the moment. But usually . . ."

Peter felt he'd said enough.

"You are a good fellow, Icarus," Rain said appreciatively in support of Peter's acknowledgement. "Subjectivity means to be with yourself, in your own company. If you are primarily suspicious and mistrustful of that experience, then you must not like yourself. In fact self-loathing is at the core of mistrusting anything or anyone."

"So how do you guys find truth?" Peter asked.

"By looking for that explanation capable of consistency with every other aspect of the ecosystem which is our particular, peculiar life; which includes by the way how others respond to us. That observable system-of-functioning, our single life, is the largest part of reality that we will ever meet firsthand. Everything else we meet is known only by inference, touched by our hand or our brilliance, but never occupied like we inhabit ourselves. Occupying and loving are the only two ways thoroughly to understand anything."

"That's an amazing thing to say," Peter observed, fascinated.

"We Troubadourians tend to worship our life as the most powerful entity we will know. We cherish and care for our particular existence as a precious thing. And we subject our understanding to whatever the wholeness of our ecosystem tells us. This is accomplished through the rule of consistency, which offers conclusions that overshadow what smaller thoughts and feelings may insist upon. It's a way of keeping us honest in relationship to ourselves. It's the most powerful form of personal accountability I've ever witnessed. It's what happens in your world only occasionally in what you call psychotherapy, and happens daily in my world in what we call democracy, which is most fundamentally self-rule, meaning rule thyself and help others do the same. It's government by all individual people, not government over the mass of people."

"That is really an incredible vision of democracy," Peter exclaimed. "But why such extraordinary emphasis upon one individual life, which you're suggesting is the most powerful, holy thing in existence? Isn't that a rather outlandish claim?"

"Not really, more of a humble one," Rain replied. "What I've said both demotes human individual life in one sense, and elevates it in another. It's a view that openly acknowledges human limitation, that we can't see anything very well beyond the end of our nose because we are inescapably contained inside our subjectivity. It never turns off, and we can never get out of it. We can pretend our minds are independent of feeling, but that deprives us of an enormous amount of information the mind is incapable of fathoming by logic."

"On the other hand, this view elevates all the nonrational parts of our psyche to a more central position in our understanding. Of course intuition, feeling, and any other part of the psyche deserve our belief only if together they can convince our entire ecosystem of a new truth. This is not being grandiose. It's being seriously humble and disciplined, requiring anything we act upon to have the unanimous support of our entire being, which, as I have already said, includes to some extent how others respond to us."

"Why do you keep insisting that my identity includes other's opinions of me?"

"The effect we have upon others is information as valuable as what we intuit from our own experience," Rain replied.

"Okay, I get that part. But how in the world can you make everything you are, consistent with everything else? It's sounds completely impossible!"

"It is. It's not something ever accomplished. It's simply the path upon which any truth-seeking must proceed. It's also the most powerful facilitator of learning there is, this subjecting everything to the gristmill of me as a wholeness. This approach surrenders to what nature has done to our particular species, which is elegantly to individuate us. To be one of a kind is humanity's unique and most extraordinary talent. The character structure of each one of us is the model from which all public institutions are built, for better or worse."

"In your system of belief you've seriously demoted science," Peter observed. "I think my people are going to be pretty upset about that."

"It's a hard lesson. But objectivity produces only possibilities. Only in the discipline of ecosystemic processing, within the context of our own life, is it possible for us to verify truth with sufficient accuracy to produce the relative comfort and safety we have always so deeply desired."

They sat together for several moments without speaking.

"Your ideas are incredible," Peter finally said. "But they leave me feeling very lonely. Life on Troubadour sounds like living in a monastery. Such incredibly hard work you've made of life."

Rain laughed.

"Curiously it's the other way around. To understand life as I've explained, we end up enjoying ourselves a great deal more. There is a particularly pleasurable sense of security in the discipline of such careful truth-seeking, which leaves lots of room for kidding around."

Kidding around reminded Peter of how much Rain loved to rhyme.

"This rhyming thing you like so much," Peter began. "Is it a popular game on Troubadour?"

"I'm afraid not. It's mine."

"So how do you go about doing it?" Peter asked.

"Just keep rhyming, but only if what you're chiming contributes to the evolution of meaning's climbing."

Peter laughed.

"You've inspired me to wander through some pretty heady stuff," Rain remarked. "I think perhaps it's time for something different. How about a walk?"

At first the sudden shift seemed too abrupt to Peter. But it took him only a moment to realize he needed a break from the intense meaning that they had been sharing.

"I'd love to."

"I'm told that you aren't using the running shoes," Rain observed. "I want you to know that you're missing something quite spectacular."

"Oh, that's right! Rambler told me about them! But I forgot all about it! I'll go put them on right now."

Peter quickly found and put on the shoes, then leaped up from his chair intending to bolt toward the living room, excited to be spending more time with Rain.

He was profoundly surprised to discover himself suddenly airborne! Both of his feet had left the ground, and he was sailing uncomfortably far ahead. Fortunately this flight was shorter lived than his first flush of imagination had predicted. He abruptly came down on both feet, and instinctively found his balance.

But as soon as his shoes hit the floor again, they produced an equally vigorous upsurge, and he once more went flying through the air.

His athletic instinct immediately turned on and analyzed the situation. Sensual impressions of the shoes, their bounce, his leg response, and other variables raced through his mind. He used these impressions to calculate what would counterbalance the shoe's incredible bounce the next time he hit the floor.

When it was time to act, he let instinct handle the situation. Consciousness had already done its job. When the bottoms of his shoes came down on the floor this time, he bent his knees deeply, using his legs as shock absorbers. After a few small up-and-down surges, and a couple of minor stumbles, he managed to steady himself.

My god but these things are amazing, he shouted to himself.

He was equally impressed by his own ability to regain control.

In his enthusiasm to run out to tell Rain what had just happened, he inadvertently set the whole routine in motion again. Only this time his involuntary acceleration wasn't upward; it was mostly forward. He forgot to anticipate the lift he would get from the shoes. So when he moved toward the living room he used too much force, propelling himself through the air like a projectile. For a moment he thought he was going to crash heavily against the far wall.

His feet touched the floor a full three meters from where he began. He instantly relaxed his body and sent it into a spin, which slowed down and softened his impact with the wall. He hit it at a speed sufficiently reduced such that he felt only moderate pain from the impact, and was able to retain his uprightness and prevent his head from impacting the wall.

"What an athletic fellow you are," Rain quipped. "But I fear I've neglected my duties. I should have warned you about the shoes."

"Oh, that's okay," Peter replied. "I didn't mind. It was kind of wild for a moment, but I managed," Peter replied with pride.

"Now you've had your second Troubadourian flying lesson," Rain said.

It took Peter a moment before he realized that Rain was referring to his flying experience on the train. He started laughing.

"Troubadourian flying lessons are pretty amazing," Peter exclaimed with enjoyment.

"Perhaps now you can imagine why we don't often fly in airplanes."

Peter laughed.

They ran for an hour. It was one of the most invigorating and exhilarating exercise experiences Peter had ever had. It took him a few minutes to adapt to the shoes. But when he developed a consistent gait he felt like a gazelle bounding across the earth at incredible speeds. It was so exciting that occasionally he'd start to feel giddily out of balance, and had to struggle once or twice very hard in order to retain a sense of uprightness.

When Peter had a chance to think about it later, he realized that today Rain had touched him in ways that were unlike anything he'd ever experienced from either man or woman on Earth. Rain had connected Peter to parts of himself he vaguely sensed but had never entirely believed in, making Peter feel closer to him than he had ever felt with anyone except his mother when he was a small child.

Rain was delighted with their time together. Asserting his preferences had apparently been the perfect facilitator of new insights for Peter.

I think I've witnessed the dawning of this man's epiphany, Rain observed to himself.

Soon after Rain departed, Peter realized how much his new confidence depended upon Rain's presence. Without Rain his doubts easily returned, though now they found much stiffer competition.

But to his surprise part of him still felt great.

But will it last? And will it ever happen with Wind?

The Nursery

Wind walked through the open door dressed in an off-white, chiffon-like material embroidered with the leaves and bloom of the flower the Devouring Tree offered its victims. It was orchid-like and colored in a rainbow of hews. Nature had splashed her full color display upon this one species.

Wind's beauty was stunning. Her hair was swept back in a bun that emphasized both the narrowness of her face and the largeness of her oval eyes, perfectly framing the innocence of her normal reactions to life with gentle charm.

"You look very beautiful," slipped from his mouth before he realized how nervous he felt talking to her in this way.

"Thank you," she replied. "You are very generous."

I thought I was admiring, he thought. Maybe she didn't like it.

Wind's dilution of his compliment made Peter more aware of just how deeply he felt her beauty, how alluring he found her as a woman. This reaction surprised him, not because it was sexual, because he had strong sexual attraction to any woman in whom he became interested. Sex was the messenger of his need.

He was surprised because he felt more than sexual. He had always regarded her as a very exquisite creature loaded with extraordinary skill and grace. But what he felt now had sexuality's compelling thrusts, full of passion urging toward merging, something he hadn't felt for anyone, except perhaps his children, in a smaller version of the feeling when they were ten and under.

But what amazed him most about his strong reaction was that he felt no ambivalence toward her. His heart was completely open.

Once he realized this, it frightened him. He was terribly afraid of rushing down a one-sided path, soon to be met with disappointment and embarrassment. He was glad when she changed the subject.

"I have a surprise for you today," she announced with delight.

"Oh, what's that," he asked with excessive curiosity, his voice cracking on the word, "that."

This surprising exaggeration made him realize that the ambiguity he once felt toward her was inside of him. It wasn't any longer toward or about her. It was just about him. His ambivalence had become entirely internal. The negatives were his; his observing part was critical of him.

"I thought you might like to visit one of our communities devoted to the raising of children," she said. "I hope I'm right in perceiving in you a special interest in them."

"You are," Peter replied, really delighted that she was arranging something he hadn't asked for.

Her taking the lead made her extremely attractive and desirable to Peter, triggering a passionate desire to reach out and touch her.

"I'm so happy that I've guessed the right thing," Wind exclaimed.

"You did!" Peter exclaimed with an excessive emphasis upon the last word, releasing the tension his impetuous feelings were building in him.

"I really appreciate it," he added, relieved to change the subject again. "But let me check something out. You did say children's community, didn't you?"

"Yes."

"Does that mean there are places where only children live?" he queried.

"Children and their caretakers, yes," she replied.

"Why do you segregate them from a normal, adult-occupied community?" he asked.

"Childhood is very different, actually very separate from adulthood and requires a very different life-arrangement."

"Well, I kind of understand what you mean. Children have special needs."

"And so do adults," Wind quickly added.

"But why must they be segregated?"

"Put a child in the middle of your creative moment, designed to understand something of great beauty and complexity, and that moment is crushed by the priority a child must claim from the rest of us, simply in order to flourish until they are prepared to manage the tasks and responsibilities of an adult community, where individuals have great power and responsibility."

"You make it sound like children are harmful to adult endeavors," Peter protested.

"It's more a question of competing powers," she replied. "The child's great power is this right to claim priority, to grab everyone else's attention whenever, wherever. While the adult's power is built upon an internal strength and talent, which makes him or her capable of giving originality to our common experience, an effort curiously which compels, even requires the same quality of attention as children do in order to be consummated."

"I get it. Artists are known to be very self-centered, and you can't paint with children around. But I still don't get why adults and children can't live together."

"But they do, at least the small group of adults that normally participate in a child's life; they live a significant part of the time with that child, two of them full time. But there is no need for other uninvolved adults to occupy the same territory. Why do you think they should?"

"I don't know, I guess they don't really have to," Peter acknowledged. "It's more that I'm reacting to why you segregate them."

"They appear segregated only in our descriptions, which attempt to differentiate the one from the other. But in practice what I'm describing is more a question of avoiding the pitfalls of doing two things at once, particularly when those two things require such different states of consciousness to achieve, and both must intrinsically compete for the same qualities of attention and dominance."

"Well, that's true. Children and adults are engaged in very different things. But still . . . why not together?"

Peter was using the power of his strong sensual feelings for Wind, as a vehicle to carry and express to her his misgivings, which felt more entitled to her help because he cared about her so much. This was making him more aggressive.

"Put adults in a child's nursery pursuing their own aims, and we would have what we've always had, grown-ups dominating the situation," Wind continued. "The child-person lives in a realm where all the inhabitants of its domain swear primary allegiance to him, with an implicit guarantee that no one's going to change the rules in this realm until the child does so for the first time, when they leave this special world to live independently in the adult world. Such utter self-centeredness is the requirement of childhood, so that he or she may grow strong enough to manage the enormous power which nature has entrusted our species."

"I'm sorry to keep harping on the point, but I still don't see why you have to work so hard at separating them. I'm sure each can find room to pursue their different needs and interests."

"We have simply arranged to maximize the benefits of the relationship between children and adults, and minimized the liabilities. It's no more complicated than that."

That's what you think, he thought.

"The way you talk about it," Peter protested, "it's like parenting becomes something strange, more like a social obligation, not something you do out of love."

"Of course you're going to have a miserable time of it if there's no love," she replied.

"I didn't mean I wanted to take it away. I meant . . ."

"Ah, I see what you mean," Wind suddenly realized. "You think we have denuded parenting of its natural spontaneity and affection."

"That's kind of what I was feeling."

"Perhaps you have always needed to maximize the advantages of parenting and deny its disadvantages," Wind suggested.

"Actually I can't really argue with any of your specifics," Peter acknowledged. "But I can't help feeling there's something really unnatural about what you guys have done. You've made parenting into something . . . well . . . like a profession."

"I think you're right," Wind admitted, obviously excited by Peter's idea. "I hadn't thought of it that way, but I think it's true. We have made parenting into a very special vocation. We each commit perhaps ten to fifteen years of our life primarily devoted to a child's growth."

"I suppose you require parents to get a degree in it," Peter quipped with a bit of sarcasm.

"Actually we do have educational programs for parenting."

"So having kids doesn't just happen when a couple is ready. It sound like you guys do it by the numbers."

"That's an interesting way of putting it," Wind replied. "Though the people doing it are not at all what I understand by the phrase, 'by the numbers.' They're usually quite experienced in life, and independent in judgment."

"Young adults don't have kids?"

"On Troubadour most parents are over fifty. As young people we were far too preoccupied with establishing ourselves in life to be either capable of, or interested in devoting ourselves so exclusively to another's needs and purposes. Which makes parenting something we usually does as a transition between the becoming-someone of the early decades of life, and the giving voice to that someone through creative projects or inventions in our more mature times. Returning to the source, meaning to our childhood, seems to facilitate all adult transitional times."

She paused for a moment.

"Actually, I think it might be more useful to visit a nursery so we can discuss what we are looking at," Wind suggested.

"Oh, we can do that?"

"Yes."

"Hey, that's a great idea. I guess I got carried away with so many questions."

"Please don't stop," she said sweetly. "I like it when you do that. It gives me a chance to say more of what you want to know."

She doesn't mind, he thought.

The elevator door opened at the fifth floor. Wind excited to her left.

"Before we get to the nursery I want to make a few observations so you will more easily understand what you'll be seeing. Perhaps the principle surprise will be that biology no longer dominates who raises our children."

"What do you mean?"

"The biological parents may or may not be the care-giving parents. It is entirely optional. All women are responsible to birth one, or if they chose two children, men of course equally responsible to inseminate them. And both sexes must also parent or teach a child of their choice."

"Oh, so it's all test tube," Peter observed.

"No. Actually it's an act of love making a child, even if the biological parents never cohabit with each other again."

"My god, you've thrown away the nuclear family," Peter exclaimed. "That's what it is that bothers me so much."

She paused for thoughtfulness.

"Not exactly from our point of view," she finally said. "We've expanded it, adding other people to the process. But we no longer require parents to be biological. Care-giving has become more functional, what you have called professional."

"Parenting is only done by experts," he observed.

"No, it's done expertly by anyone who does it, as an act of love which comes from full commitment," she replied.

The end of the hallway appeared just ahead.

"We're about to enter an observing area where you can see children in their natural habitat. We will be looking through a one-way wall. The children and their caretakers will not see us."

"You mean a one-way mirror don't you?" he asked.

"No, it's actually a wall built of a material which permits vision through one dimension of its molecular structure."

"That will be very interesting."

She opened the door. Peter found himself looking at a small child, perhaps four years old, playing in a room filled with a great variety of interactive objects. A woman of some maturity was standing in a doorway to the left of an adjacent room. She was watching the child with a lovely smile on her face.

"You're sure she can't see me?" Peter queried.

"I'm sure," Wind replied.

"But why can't she look through the wall too?" he asked.

"This see-through feature occurs in only one direction."

The room behind the young woman was obviously a kitchen. The objects in his apartment that were hidden behind the walls, here were strewn about on a counter or a table much as they would have been in his world, probably for the child to observe and to play with.

There were two other doorways off the kitchen, one to the left and one straight ahead. To the right of this playroom was a bedroom, the walls of which were covered with a child's paintings. These drawings were curiously dominated by a great variety of purples. There was a small bathroom that was accessible from both the child's bedroom and also his playroom.

In all these rooms, what was hidden in the walls of Peter's apartment was here permanently opened for display.

"As you might imagine," Wind said, "she's the mother. Though you may be surprised to know that she's not the birth mother. On Troubadour caregivers commit themselves to a child's care, more like your people do to a career. It's not a permanent arrangement of responsibility. When the child emancipates, they and their mother for instance see each other only when and if they desire. There is no implicit expectation that their strong bond will produce an ongoing intimate relationship. More often than not it does, but it also frequently doesn't."

"But why not? Wouldn't they naturally be inclined to sustain their strong intimacy?"

"The kind of relationship that a child and mother have with each other is not an adequate container for deep friendship. It happened too one-sidedly. Friendship requires balance and reciprocity, which in normal experience begins to build from day one instead of after years. What's more, the child often becomes someone very different than their parents, and may feel strong kinship with them only much later in life, or occasionally not at all."

"What strange ways to run a family," Peter remarked.

"It gets even stranger," Wind said.

Just then another man walked in from a room to the right of the child's bedroom. Peter could not see through the wall into that room, which must mean they were his private quarters. This man stood watching the boy for a few moments, smiled at the boy's mother, who smiled in response. He spoke to the boy briefly, to which the child responded with what obviously meant "later." After a few moments the man turned and left.

"That man happens to be the birth father of this child," Wind explained. "He has chosen to commit himself to the boy's upbringing, but not as the mother. He has opted instead to be Kirkin's teacher, a role more akin to a traditional fatherhood in your world. This arrangement allows him ample time to pursue another career entirely devoted to himself. Unlike the mother he sleeps apart from the child in his own quarters, and spends part of his day engaged in other activities away from the child."

"What do the teachers do?" Peter asked.

"Teacher on Troubadour does not mean the same thing it does on Earth. They are not responsible for delivering predefined quantities of information to the child on a variety of subjects, designed to acclimate and condition them to the adult world, as teachers are expected to do in your world. Instead they act as guides to the child's own spontaneous explorations. They function more like child therapists do on your planet, facilitating a child's talents, interests, and mastery of difficulties, or persistent problems. They aid the child in the pursuit of his or her own destiny in as many ways and directions as possible without intruding upon the child's needs or expectations."

"But what does the mother do? Your descriptions don't leave her with much?" Peter asked.

"Like all mothers she's the caretaker who is always there for Kirkin. She's his companion, his audience, his admirer, his comforter, and his primary linkage to the origins of life. Which means that for several years she participates almost exclusively in his life, to a large extent postponing her own desires and ambitions for a while."

Just then Kirkin ran over to his mother and embraced her leg with a squeal of delight. He held it firmly for several moments, then ran back to begin another game in a different part of the room.

Kirkin started putting together blocks of a multicolored material that adhered wherever he pushed its corners together. His construction was not a vertical assent, but rather a form that wandered off in many directions, putting enormous strain upon the balance of the piece.

"This boy is particularly fascinated by balance," Wind said. "He seems to have a unique capacity to create objects which are within a fraction of collapse, and yet somehow remain upright."

It was true. His construction had reached as high as he could reach.

After a momentary squeal of delight, the boy touched his invention at a particular spot. The bonding of individual pieces suddenly came apart, sending the blocks crashing to the floor!

"What a human heart has put together, nature or a child will always pull apart. The adult creates, and the child takes it apart, only later reinventing it in a new form. It's the cycle of life. Perhaps it's also what explains how these two creatures engage in very different endeavors. Essentially the child and parent are doing opposite things. The adult integrates while the child takes apart what must be seen in its detail in order simply to be understood, and what they will later, as adults recreate."

"It's true," Peter admitted. "They are doing very different things. But still why do you choose to create artificial parents when the real ones are available?"

Wind laughed.

"What makes an arrangement which is not biologically determined 'artificial'?" Wind asked.

"But it seems so unnatural," he said.

"Don't we want both of these creatures, the child and the adult to be as aggressively what-they-are as we can arrange?" she challenged.

"Sure, but . . ."

"Then they need to live primarily in different places so that they aren't always bumping into each other's needs."

For a while Kirkin had been playing imaginary games of his own invention. But now abruptly he stood and ran to his mother, once again embracing her leg for a reassuring moment, and then headed through the kitchen into a room beyond.

"We must walk this way to keep observing Kirkin," Wind explained.

"I feel kind of sorry for his mother," Peter said as they walked. "She seems mostly to be used like a rag doll, grabbed and hugged one moment, then abandoned for a long while the next."

"Well, in a way that's exactly what Kirkin needs to do with her. I have no doubt she would very much appreciate your sympathy," Wind observed. "Though perhaps I should explain that at the beginning and end of each day she and Kirkin have several hours of very quality time together. She's like a guardian angel or Santa Claus in your world, that devoted, perpetually nurturing giant in a child's life that keeps safety hovering around at all times."

The room beyond the kitchen came into view. It was a huge play area with four other children engaged in play. Beyond it to the right was a large garden into which the sun light shown brightly.

"This is where children get together when they want," Wind observed.

"How do you get the sunlight down this far into the building, or is it artificial?"

"It's real. You have the technology, which are lighting tubes which amplify and focus the sun's rays in any direction."

Peter noticed all the children were as deeply absorbed in their play as Kirkin had been.

"I've been thinking that I quite agree with what you said about Kirkin's mother. She's his wet nurse, his nanny, who is the closest person to him, whom he grabs and then discards many times a day. Hers is a role for someone who enjoys quiet contemplation, for they are often alone. Some people choose to commit to being a child's mother as a transitional experience between other careers in their life, or as a way of recapturing their own childhood because they want to remember its details for one reason or another."

Peter thought of mentioning Rain having done precisely that, but then chose not to share this without Rain's consent, imitating Rain's decision not to speak about his son without that man's consent.

There were three adults in the play area acting like recreational directors, referees, and players.

"On Earth these adults might call themselves 'aunts' and 'uncles,' or teaching aids, or friends of the family, godparents, etc.," Wind explained. "They spend perhaps five or six hours a day with these children, which makes their commitment more relative in its intensity. People who opt for this alternative spend a very limited amount of time with the children, but they must do it for not one but two children. It spreads out their obligation."

"Why do you want so many people involved in one child's life?"

"Principally so the child has multiple role models, so they can pick-and-choose for themselves."

"How does someone decide whether to become a parent or teacher, or one of these other caregivers?"

"I'm not sure I can answer your question. Some of the more peripheral caretakers, I understand spend fifty or sixty years helping to raise a series of children. Perhaps they represent some of us still wanting a more permanent presence of children in their lives, perhaps like yourself, yet not wanting that experience to dominate so much as it would if they were the child's mother."

"Why are there only five children here, and all those adults? Is this a normal grouping?"

"Eight or nine children and their caretakers live contiguously, each child having their own apartment complex including adjacent rooms for both their mother and teacher. We believe any more than that number overpowers the child's sense of themselves."

"Where are the other three children?"

"Children socialize only when they want to. The child determines what and when they play, what and when they learn, and whether and when they socialize. So, as you can see, we are accustomed to giving people their own way as much as possible. It is our deepest demonstration of respect for them."

Peter suddenly felt envious of the boy, Kirkin.

These kids have six adults giving them an abundance of aid and companionship whenever they need it. Shit, I wish I could have had even one person doing that.

"Whatever else I feel about what you're doing, you really do offer your kids a whole lot," Peter observed. "I can't help but feel a little envious of Kirkin."

Another boy suddenly intruded upon Kirkin's game. One of the adults in the room had already anticipated this outcome, and was moving toward the two boys when it happened. The other boy started to shove Kirkin just as the adult intervened. She gently touched his shoulder and spoke a few words to him.

"She asked the second boy if he'd like to take the game away from Kirkin, or did he want to play it with Kirkin."

The second boy responded with what obviously meant, "it's mine."

The adult spoke again.

"She told him that another game of the same kind is available. If he had wanted to play with Kirkin she would have tried to facilitate that."

Again the second boy insisted the game was his.

Finally losing his patience, Kirkin abruptly grabbed the game away from the other boy and ran off to play with it elsewhere.

The second boy started after him.

"The adult's telling the other boy that she knew he hated Kirkin at this moment for not including him, that of course he wanted to feel powerful again."

The boy tried smacking Kirkin on his back as he departed, but barely touched him.

"She says hitting Kirkin is meant to regain power for himself. She suggested there is another way that doesn't hurt others, playing the game well. She offered to play it with him."

The second boy protested very briefly, stopped when he noticed a smile on the caretaker's face, hesitated, smiled at the woman, momentarily leaned into her body, and then headed off to find the other version of Kirkin's game.

After playing furiously with the game for a short time, Kirkin abandoned it and ran back to his own room. He threw his arms around his mother's leg. This time he looked up at her face and started talking.

"He says he loves her," Wind translated.

The mother beamed with delight.

"She must be saying that she loves him too," Peter said.

"Yes."

Kirkin's mother leaned down to give him a hug. But before she could consummate this act, he ran off into his playroom. He turned back toward her and said one word: "One."

"That word is pronounced with a hard 'o' and a soft 'e,' one," Wind said. "When said it sounds like your word, own, and means alone. He's telling her he wants to be alone now."

With a barely perceptible touch of sadness on her face, the mother nodded in assent, turned, and wandered into her own room.

"How sad," Peter said.

"You seem very closely identified with the mother."

"I feel like I've been one most of my life, I mean a mother, first with my parents as a little boy, then with my children as a man, and now with my patients," he replied. "I missed being a child."

"Kirkin is talking to his computer now," Wind observed.

Peter was instantly very curious, remembering his own computer-encounters.

"Kirkin has been telling his computer a story he's making up. It's a story about a little boy who wanders into a jungle and finds a lot of interesting things to play with. Only a huge Borang comes along and wants to eat him. He's just asked the computer how he should end the story."

"He's making up this story?" Peter asked, very impressed.

"Yes. The computer says in reply that there are lots of endings, but perhaps the one he may prefer is for the little boy to be able to drive the Borang away so he doesn't get eaten, and he can keep his things."

Kirkin jumped up and down with excitement in agreement with the computer.

"Kirkin asks how a little boy could do that. The computer suggests that the Borang isn't as smart as he is. He suggests that Kirkin knows the Borang won't attack anything that is bigger and louder than he is."

Kirkin shouted a few very exciting words.

"So I've got to grow bigger than him, Kirkin says," Wind translated. "The computer suggests the Borang needs only to believe he's bigger, that he doesn't actually have to be so."

Kirkin gets even more excited.

"Kirkin is going to pretend to be bigger. From now on he will carry a piece of lightweight material that he can put on top of his head to appear taller than the Borang is long. And then he's gong to make very loud noises."

Kirkin started jumping up with his arms in the air shouting as loudly as he could! He ran into the playroom where all the other children were in the same fashion, parading around the room almost as if he was showing off that he had overcome the deadly Borang!

He suddenly stopped. His eye caught sight of a large drum. He picked it up and began banging on it as he walked back into his room.

When he reached his mother he stopped, put the drum down, sidled up to her, and began speaking.

"He's telling her the whole story of how he conquered a Borang in the jungle as if he made the story up entirely by himself."

The mother was obviously delighted to share this special moment. It was endearing to watch their facial expressions while the story unfolded.

But as soon as Kirkin was done telling, he raced again into the playroom with the other children to tell one of the other adults.

"Once again the poor woman is left alone," Peter observed sadly.

"We can stay and watch Kirkin and his family as long as you like."

"I think I've had enough for now," Peter replies. "But can I come back sometime?"

"Of course," Wind assures him. "Just let me know when."

Peter started walking back toward the hallway.

"Shall we go back to your room to talk about it, or have you had enough for now?"

"Let's talk for a few minutes at my place," Peter replied.

"Well, what do you think?" Wind asked him when they'd settled into two adjacent chairs in his living room.

"That little boy is a very fortunate lad," Peter replied.

He swiveled back and forth for several moments thinking.

"How do these nonbiological parents become attached to the child?" he asked.

"A child is an irresistible creature. Nature has seen to that. So I'm not quite sure what you mean. It's very easy to be attached to a child if your heart seeks the opportunity to care for one."

"I guess you're right. But I'm still wondering why you segregate children from a normal, adult world? I mean I understand why you make such special arrangements for a child's care, but why profoundly limit their social experience?"

"I would have to disagree," she replied. "Fitting non-care-taking adults into a child's life, even much older children for that matter, can be a very intrusive experience for that child. They're much happier living in a small world with very identifiable participants occupying it with them, meaning those with some daily connection to them."

"But how do children learn what it's like to be mature and grow up?" Peter asked.

"They have at least five adults available as role models. As for learning how to grow up, there's plenty of time for that."

"But don't adults miss seeing children?"

"If true that's easily remedied. There are some adults who raise successive children most of their life," Wind replied.

"That's it," he exclaimed, finally understanding something. "Where's the love?" he asked with some intensity. "I mean where's the love in a Troubadourian life? I can see that the boy is well loved, but where's the love for grown-ups to share?"

"In friendship," she replied.

"Friendship doesn't produce really deep love."

"It does the way that I mean it," Wind replied. "Friendship to me, and I think to most Troubadourians, means to give and to receive a quality of understanding that enhances our own self-knowledge and growth. The gift of that exchange is the quintessential essence of loving."

Peter didn't know what to say.

"You look so sad," she said.

"What? I do? Oh, I guess you're right."

He knew the reason but he didn't want to share it with her. Once again his hopes to bring Troubadourian wisdom back to Earth felt deeply shaken when he realized how jarring their child rearing practices would be to most Earth people.

"You probably need some time to sort it out," she suggested. "Perhaps it would be better for me to go."

He looked at her longingly.

"Must you," he queried, knowing already that he did want to be alone, but not wanting to admit it.

"I can stay if you wish," she replied.

"I'm sorry. I don't seem to know what I want."

"It's best then to leave you alone so you can figure it out," she said, turning to leave.

"Oh," he sighed.

"I'll be seeing you very soon," she said and quietly exited.

"Okay," he replied without conviction, suddenly lost in a deep sadness.

Wind was very happy with the day. She had just presented to Peter the display of Troubadourianism that she had anticipated he would find the most difficult to understand. And he had weathered it with only moderate discomfort.

Maybe he's beginning to settle down a little, she observed hopefully.

Peter's afterthoughts moved in an entirely different direction.

If I try and sell this stuff to Earth people, they'd laugh me off the podium. And I gave up five years of my life for this?

But his misgivings lasted for only a moment. Their antidote suddenly reemerged in his mind. It was the feeling of strong attraction he'd felt when she first arrived.

For several moments his imagination scanned his memory of the incredibly voluptuous contours of her body, remembering the patient thoughtfulness of her many efforts to help him.

You'll never know a more remarkable woman, he thought. So why have you been standing around poking at your discontent, instead of trying to appreciate and enjoy the chance you've got to be with her even for a little while?

"What foolish talk," a more practical part of himself chided. "She'd laugh you off this planet if you ever revealed such feelings. Anyway, your body probably doesn't fit her body, and you're definitely not her type. Most of all she'll probably be relieved when you go."

As Peter fell asleep he had a fantasy of Wind being his mother.

Rain

Within half an hour after returning to his apartment, Peter decided to have an adventure of his own. He was getting along better with the people on Troubadour, though the more he learned about their beliefs and practices, the more he found things that seriously troubled him. He needed relief from this new complexity. He wanted to do something entirely different to distract himself from his growing worry that when he returned home he would have nothing viable to share from this incredible journey, just another story about how aliens do weird things. But what to do, that was the question.

The computer will know.

"Are there any islands of particular interest on Troubadour?" he asked the computer.

"Zeemoy is the most loved," the slightly metallic voice replied. "You can reach it by going west on the train and transferring at the desert city you visited with Rain, then going south for two more stops. The second one is the island."

"What's there to see?"

"Perhaps you'd like to be surprised?" the computer suggested.

"Now that is definitely a very human thing to say," Peter retorted.

"Not if you've been programmed intuitively, and asked by your human to adapt to human ways," was the reply.

Peter thoroughly enjoyed the train ride that lasted over an hour before he reached the underground station of Zeemoy. It was a blissful time of flying which he was able to enjoy entirely on his own.

As soon as he walked out of the city building, and felt the cool, warm sea breeze swirl around his body, he knew that Zeemoy was a tropical island like Hawaii in his own world. The colors were brilliant, the smell of earth and flower perfumes was strong, and the intensely bright light dazzled everything with its huge, brilliant candlepower.

He walked down to the ocean.

The city opened onto the leeward side of the island so the waves were moderate and gradual, the water very warm and comforting. He took off his shoes and waded into the surf.

There were other people walking on the beach, but few enough so that Peter felt pretty much alone. He was absorbed mostly in his own thoughts, and didn't see the huge man who walked fifty yards to his rear peering in his direction every once in a while. It was Rambler protecting him from an anonymous distance.

Rambler was mostly concerned about a large sea animal that hunted in this area during this particular season. Troubadourians knew not to swim now, but of course Peter didn't. Once again he chose not to warn Peter as requested, but to keep close watch. He was alert to the possibility that Peter might impulsively dive into the sea, and arranged his distance from Peter to make rescue of him relatively routine.

Though Peter would have been angry with Rambler if he knew, he would also have felt intruded upon to be warned, though he wouldn't easily have admitted it. He was thoroughly enjoying the experience of personal independence that being alone provided for the first time since he arrived on Troubadour. It bolstered his confidence at a time when he needed it most. It put him closer to Wind's primary instruction, which was to do what he wanted.

He spent two hours wandering up and down the beach feeling soothed by the repetition of wave-sounds and delightfully washed clean of worry by the surf's gentle back-and-forth fondling of his feet. The ocean's feathery fingers swirling sand between his toes brought comfort to his weary heart.

When Peter returned to his own city he was very surprised to find Rain wandering around the entrance hall.

"Rain," he shouted. "What are you doing here . . . I mean have you been waiting long?"

"I was hoping you'd come home about this time."

Peter suddenly realized that Rain probably knew both where he'd been and also when he was likely to return.

They must always communicate with each other about what I'm doing all the time.

For the first time he felt protected by this close scrutiny, though the feeling didn't entirely dispel his sense of having been neglected.

He suddenly realized that Rain was precisely the person he wanted to talk to. As soon as both were settled on a bench at the edge of the city, just under the trees, Peter launched into his topic.

"As I'm sure you must know I visited the nursery earlier today."

"That's why I'm here," Rain replied. "We expected this part of Troubadourian custom to be the hardest for you to understand."

"You knew I was coming back about now, didn't you?" Peter asked.

"Yes."

"I think I can begin to see how this thing works. You guys have this whole visit mapped out. You know what I'm going to do next and probably how I'm going to feel. But of course I'm the only one you don't tell so I'll have all these spontaneous reactions in which you put such great store."

Rain laughed.

"Very amusingly said," he replied. "So which topic do you wish to discuss, our leaving you too much alone in your own experience, or our child-rearing practices?"

"Both."

Peter hesitated.

"No, let's talk about families. I don't know how I'm going to take what you do and offer it to my people. Your family ways are so strange to us, nobody's going to buy it."

"What's so hard to sell?"

"It's obvious. You've taken the heart out of family. Where's the love?"

"If the nuclear family is the baby we're both loving and protecting, then you're right. We've discarded it. But if the baby is the child we love, then it's my view that we've kept the good part of the family and dumped most of the bad. In the process we've reinvented the family in a different form, though apparently one that you don't recognize as such."

"But the family on Troubadour no longer functions for the sake of adults, I mean in a loving way," Peter argued. "What's there to get out of what you guys do with children other than a vicarious enjoyment of the child's growth? Wind says friendship is where adults find love, but I don't believe it. I can't expect to be loved . . . I mean with friends I can't expect them to provide so much."

Rain left a slight pause before responding.

"You don't expect it to happen, but you want to be loved on Troubadour," Rain observed, hesitating on the word "want."

"What? I don't want that."

That's not true.

He realized that he did in fact want to feel loved on Troubadour. It's precisely why the deepest part of him had come.

He was instantly embarrassed.

Holy shit. How long have I been doing that?

He glanced at Rain expecting reprove, but Rain was concentrating on some distant object or thought.

"Were you ever a father?" Peter asked, partly shifting the subject to escape from his embarrassment.

"I was a boy's mother," Rain replied.

"A boy's mother?" Peter shouted with surprise. "What's the joke?"

"Wind must have told you either gender can be a mother."

"Oh, yeah. I've just never seen or met one who was a man."

"Like you, I was an abandoned child," Rain explained. "With the pain of that awful experience . . ."

"You were what?" Peter interrupted, exclaiming with astonishment and disbelief. "Abandoned? How can that be possible? I thought you . . ."

"I wasn't abandoned as dramatically as you were," Rain insisted.

"But I thought your child care was so good that wasn't possible," Peter said.

"Remember I was a child a very long time ago. So I was not gifted with the quality of care Troubadourians children have finally achieved. One might say I was parented in some of the new attitudes but without the eventual wisdom they brought. So I got an improved, though underneath it all still very flawed parenting, which left me missing parts of myself like everyone in your world."

Peter was fascinated to hear the intimate details of Rain's life.

"My mother died prematurely in a vehicular accident," Rain continued, "another one of our human insanities, referring to the use of automobiles as anything more than a toy used in toy places," Rain continued. "The accident happened during part of an experimental project in which she was working. Her mother-replacement was ill-chosen and too quickly arranged."

"Oh, I'm terribly sorry," Peter interjected.

"So was I for a very long time," Rain replied. "With the pain of that abandonment still partially intact in me, I always desperately wanted to be in love with a mother who adored me and stuck around long enough for me to be sure of it, and to heal myself. But since I was no longer a child I couldn't have a mother. So I decided to be one. In essence the two are the same. The child and the mother are one object instead of two, until the child leaves her and emancipates."

"Holy shit," Peter exclaimed. "That's absolutely amazing! It's true. They are the same, mother and child! My women patients have told me that in one way or another for a long time."

He looked carefully at Rain.

"Rain as a mother?" Peter repeated out loud as if posing a question. "I've always thought about you as the strongest, most powerful father-person I've ever met. I guess it's a shock to think of you in this other way."

"There's plenty of room for both of our fantasies operating cooperatively," Rain said with an impish laugh.

"How can you be both?"

"For several years I had a very loving mother, namely myself, who truly loved that boy from the bottom of my heart, just as I'd loved my mother until she died. She taught me how to be-loving in the most basic sense, though I lost sight of it for many years. Eventually it was from the font of that memory, reawakened by the delightful personality of my son, that her love came alive once more in me. She became known to me in the act of being a mother."

"That's such a beautiful, beautiful story," Peter crooned, feeling very moved by it.

It took him just a moment to realize that this was his story too! In some essential ways he and Rain had exactly the same experience, with Peter of course minus the eventual good mothering experience. He wanted very much to share with Rain the remarkable similarity of their early-life stories, but it felt a little too risky. What's more he wanted very much to hear more about Rain.

"So what's your son doing now?" Peter asked.

Rain didn't answer immediately.

"Forgive the delay, but I had to think for two," he replied. "Would my son want you to know about him or our relationship, I was asking myself? On Troubadour we don't talk about each other. We prefer that people reveal themselves. Telling you reveals it for both he and I, and he's not here to disagree."

"Oh, I see," Peter replied. "So you'll need to get back to me on this one."

"Yes."

Peter had made the right response, but he was very disappointed that he would hear no more of Rain's son. Once again he felt cheated of something that would probably have made him feel better.

He learned later that the Troubadourians had decided some fifty years before to lose gossip as a principle source of important information, leaving disclosure of intimate details primarily to the affected parties.

"What was it like being a mother?"

"Sometimes blessed, occasionally vividly painful, perhaps mostly boring, yet all-in-all something that changed my life."

"Wow! What a lot of extremely different emotions," Peter exclaimed. "But that last one, boredom, seems weird."

"Being perpetually companioned by the primitive creature a child is, with only their agenda visible to them, left most of me searching for somewhere to be with," Rain explained. "Of course there were those moments when being with my son was like watching an angel at work building a man in himself."

"You remind me of my children when they were young," Peter shared. "It was wonderful to be with them."

He paused.

"But it's not like that now," Peter added. "The beautiful parts happened for too few years."

"Is it possible that parts of what you expect from children are something they're incapable of providing?"

"Well, maybe that's true, but why do you say it just now?"

"I wasn't thinking of that deficit as if it were a neglectful moment," Rain retorted. "I was thinking of it as a natural thing, that parent and child have only so much they can offer each other. In essence they are living in very different time frames. Grown children are reaching for strength and recognition of it, while their parents are reaching inwardly for themselves to be fully evolved and alive. When they get together they both want to be heard, admired, and appreciated, the child for achievement and the parent for goodness, greatness or wisdom, making them the ultimate competitors age-wise among humans."

"I get really angry at my children sometimes because they are so oblivious of me as a person, so insistent upon continuing to be my child, never wanting to be weaned from my parent-support emotionally, perhaps until my old age infirmity forces them to care for me, finally reversing the roles. So there's never any time to be equals when I have a chance to enjoy getting to be known by them as a unique person with characteristics they've never understood before. They keep insisting upon seeing me the way I was when they were young."

"I completely understand your pain, and feel much sympathy for you," Rain replied. "But the problem with your life is not that your children are not your friends. The problem is that when you were a child, you were prevented from being your own best friend, thus finding friendship with others very difficult."

"It's so painful to have dysfunctional interactions with people going on year after year," Peter complained.

"Perhaps it's endemic to your relationship."

"Oh, you mean it's all my fault," Peter suspicion-ed.

"No. I'm saying the competition between parent and child is a natural juxtaposition, that always happens, not an abuse that villains commit. It's the way things are set up, meaning to be competitive. It's we who are having lots of trouble coming to terms with that. We always raised our children giving them advantages, angry if they simply leave and ignore us for years. There's nothing unnatural about that. In fact it's constructively normal. We simply need to come-to-terms with this necessary outcome, which might actually represent success."

"Maybe it words for them but not for me."

Silence.

"You must understand children differently than my people do," Peter added.

"Perhaps. When I think of children I imagine them during their first five or six years of life. Unlike us they live in a realm of magic and mythology where parents are both giants and gods, not someone with whom they are capable of competing. What these bigger-than-life creatures do is both The Truth and The Law. Children live in what you might call an Old Testament world where things are either good or evil. There are no ambiguities. The child is incapable of holding onto one of those hot potatoes until much, much later, probably when they're adolescent."

"It is this pure character to their emotional life that makes it possible for children to love so unconditionally," Rain continued. "They are in fact the only humanoids to actually love unconditionally. Once we gain experience in life, if we're fortunate, we become the very unique and special person that we are, capable of holding our own around others. Then we all become conditional, or we wouldn't ever become anyone in particular. But that takes at least twenty-five years to accomplish. In the meantime, children regard independence as profoundly disloyal to their parents. It's the first thing they sacrifice on the alter of unconditionality when something threatens the security of their relationship with the gods."

"Sacrifice?" Peter queried.

"Sacrifice is the only safe response if what you can't live-without is threatened. We've been doing it for centuries. First we sacrificed our enemies, then each other, sometimes by the tens of thousands, then ourselves, and finally we learned to sacrifice pieces of ourselves as we become more civilized. Perhaps some day we can stop making any sacrifices."

"Who can argue with that," Peter replied. "But I still don't see how children are so utterly compromised by life."

"Children are far less interested in how well we love them from our perspective. They're far more vitally concerned with whether what we do actually fits their particular and peculiar love-needs. Take for instance our sense of romance about having children. Until one hundred years ago we assumed, as you may still do, that our experience of loving them exists in the same realm as their experience of loving us. When the two lovings are entirely different in perspective and need. As adults we make pleasure objects of those with whom we want to be very close, hoping they will do the same thing with us in ways that are mutually satisfying. We assume we both can enter and leave such an arrangement according to how we experience it. We are free to see it as it is."

"Children on the other hand have no such capabilities, and those they do have are easily and quickly discarded. Thus, if we act lovingly toward them in the same ways we do with each other, in effect deeply participating in what we assume is their fantasy of life, supporting what we think is their preference, joining what we imagine their play to mean or to be, all the while believing that, as long as we are actively caring, that whatever we do is beneficial to them, then we will have forced our children out of themselves into our shoes. It is an inescapable outcome."

"Maybe you're right about all this. But if you are then life seems very harsh for a child."

"There is a harshness in life experience, though usually we imagine or invent far more than needs to be there," Rain replied. "If it isn't happening, a child will invent it. For instance, children perceive intentional punishment contained in our innocent parental mistakes. As children we live in a world where danger lurks everywhere, if for no other reason than almost everything is completely incomprehensible. The unknown is frightening and therefore probably evil. That specter of badness is always terrifying. Childhood is not a moderate time, which is why children need moderation so often to come from the outside."

"You frighten me with your ideas," Peter interjected. "I know my childhood was terrifying sometimes. But I've never thought that everybody's was like that."

"We all struggle as children against the fear of displeasing the gods. It took us a long time to realize that gods were our parents. I think your Sigmund Freud discovered that, though he never clearly said so himself.

These elfish creatures called children watch every nuance of our adult performance, doing what amounts to cloning us, assuming that whatever we do, whoever we are, however we act is the only and absolute best way, even and most particularly when it hurts and frightens them very deeply. They readily absorb this experience, creating meaning of their own which explains why, for instance, a parent is depressed and critical of them. The moral verdict of their explanatory judgments is always to blame themselves. Thereafter they assume what for them amounts to full responsibility for that parent's depression, desperately doing whatever may appear to heal it, even if that means to severely criticize themselves, or even to kill some part of their own need out of loyalty to us. There are even times when children die on behalf of their parents. You call it childhood suicide."

"If I thought about children the way you do I wouldn't ever have had any," Peter insisted.

They rested for several moments.

"You know," Peter said. "I think I just realized why I've been so upset about how you deal with family and children. It's your ideals that seem so high. You expect so much."

He paused for a moment.

"I have two children of my own. My daughter, Jennifer, reacts to me as if I'm a terrible father, when I think I was actually a pretty good one, oh, not by Troubadourian standards but certainly by those of my own world. But if what you say is right, then maybe she is also right in her indictment of me, that there are things I did or didn't do which really hurt her. To think that she's right about me is very depressing."

"Aagh," Rain exclaimed, gesturing Peter's worry aside. "No wonder you have been so sensitive. I am sad to hear that your children left you with so much pain. To hurt a child always hurts the parent too. There is no escape from this threatening dilemma other than to grow wiser and more competent."

"But how do you live with the constant accusation that you were a shitty parent, when you know you did so much for her."

"Allow me to suggest that whatever you did or didn't do is related very indirectly to what troubles her. The real villain is something in her of which she's basically unaware. If she really understood what was wrong she wouldn't feel such anger toward you. Thus her explanations, which to you are complaints, must be taken as clues to her suffering rather than as the truth about you. I think you can trust that your daughter's indictments are in many ways not accurate about you, though they do offer important hints that lead to a better understanding of her problem."

Peter was deeply reassured.

"Thank you so much for saying that," Peter replied. "It means a great deal to me."

"Though I must add something," Rain said. "It's also true that if you can ever figure out a way to understand her that isn't at your expense, you can help her find redemption from her demons probably easier than anyone else."

"How do you know that?" Peter asked.

"Because the two of you are already so well connected, and because you are still a very big person to her, which gives weight to your insights when they're accurate about her."

"Oh," Peter replied, much relieved that Rain's wasn't implying criticism of him. "I see what you mean. Of course you're probably right."

Privately Peter dreaded what Rain implied, that he had work to do for Jennifer. He'd hoped to be done with parenting.

But for the moment something else bothered him more.

"You know what bothers me more than anything else is that part about you're putting love inside of friendship," Peter said with much sadness. "I can't see how the kind of love that I want could ever come from friendship."

"Friendship is not the shallow thing your people usually talk about," Rain explained.

"What is it?"

"For me friendship is that place where the kind of special love we give a child happens both ways. I'm not talking about the baby talk or the cuddles. I'm referring to the individually-fashioned, precise care of a lover who delights in the kind of person you have grown up to be, realizing that it will take a lifetime to learn just what that precise love really is at its fullest. A friend is someone who is willing over time to continue discovering new truth about me, even if it means that in doing so they will find ways they need to change themselves."

"But that's what a child needs."

"Growing up doesn't change the need for love," Rain replied.

Though he was still very unhappy, and perplexed about some of what he heard, Peter felt strangely comforted by Rain's visit. Once more the wise old man had normalized some of Peter's most painfully embarrassing parts, making them part of a normal human's struggle to find their version of life.

I'm not sure whether I can believe it, but this place is beginning to feel like something good's happening. Something's changing.

Love

The embrace Wind gave Peter during their last meeting, still lingered in his body's experience. He could still smell her sweet odor and feel the forgiving flesh of her body's care surrounding him with the calm of her gentle nature.

This physical linkage between the two of them, reproduced for Peter the safety and comfort of his mother's thigh, rekindling his desire for deeply bonding with a trusted woman. This was far more than mesmerizing, though it contained that element. Though Peter wasn't able to think ideas about it, his body knew it and craved for it to happen again.

On her way to see Peter this afternoon, Wind reviewed the progress of their relationship. She believed she had finally connected to Peter in a deep way when she met his innocence. She trusted herself to act helpfully toward him, sure that her affection for his innocent part would be able to corral useful responses. Their visit to the nursery convinced her, because it was far easier and more peaceful than she had expected.

In the act of embracing Peter, she was expressing confidence and joy that she had finally supplied the missing pieces to her long effort to achieve in her mind's eye a complex model of Peter-as-himself. That completion made him three-dimensional, someone easily understood under any and all circumstances.

Thereafter she would regard his negative actions as implicitly companioned with a contradictory virtue, even if that virtue were almost entirely hidden from view. In effect she would never think entirely ill of him again. When emotionally attacked by him, she would spread understanding over the shroud of his suspicion, clothing his misgivings with the raiment of positive potentiality.

She approached their meeting with optimism, hoping that he too felt something akin to this success in their understanding of each other, what she had feared might never happen.

Absorbed in the still vivid reality of that fantasy, he heard neither the doorbell ring nor his shout to open it, which had happened automatically without intention on his part. He was still drifting through a state of perception halfway between consciousness and dreaming.

So when she walked into the frame of his vision, he treated her presence as if it were a part of the trance of his private imaginings. As if pretending had magically made her real, he stared at her body as if it was there by his own conjuring, to be enjoyed as he pleased.

Eventually a desire to see her smile brought his eyes into focus with her face, and then her eyes—and the trance was suddenly broken. He awoke instantly from his dream-state, realizing that he'd been staring at the real Wind for several moments.

"Oh, excuse me, I'm so sorry," he blurted out, averting his eyes as if they had been doing something forbidden.

There was one significant flaw in Wind's understanding of Peter. She had not the slightest feeling or suspicion that sexuality had anything whatsoever to do with their relationship. Her growing affection for Peter was entirely platonic. What her heart offered him was a committed friendship, from which she had already given him a great deal of compassion and understanding.

Meanwhile Peter's powerful attachment to her was based primarily upon a physical-sexual connection, grounded in wishes implicit to his mesmerizing fantasies. He himself was not very aware of sexuality's presence in these waking trances. His sense of connection to her was filled as much with a boy's desire to lie on his mother's body for comfort and a sense of safety, as it was filled with sexuality's passion.

But the fires of intercourse were getting very close to the surface of Peter's self-awareness.

To assuage his perpetual fears that all was not well with a woman, Peter had always wanted to have sex as soon as possible with a woman in whom he had become particularly interested. Only then did he feel safe from the imminent possibility of sudden divorce. Without sex he was unable to trust a woman. With it he tried trusting her implicitly, though he remained highly sensitive to the slightest sign of contradiction. It was as if entering her body was like being invited into her home. Until sex he regarded the relationship as highly tentative and unreliable.

"Sorry," he added. "I was day dreaming."

While Peter was scanning the full length of her body, Wind misperceived the barely-under-the-surface sexual awakenings of Peter's mesmerized staring. She was vaguely unaware of his lifelong, lustful yearning for comfort secretly sought in the reassuring arms of a woman's sexual love. That Peter's life had, like a great many men on his planet, merged comfort with sexual, instinct-driven urges, this was information she didn't have. She regarded Peter's staring at her as an enjoyment of her archetypal body-shape, as she might have done as a painter having a vision she would later translate into art.

She was therefore very puzzled by his apology.

Wind had both sexual experience and love. But it had not been as passionately invested with the personal need, from which Peter peered out from behind when he looked so intensely at her body. She had instead invested the deepest parts of her love in the creations of her own hugely talented self, and her art had prospered from this vigorous emotional commitment.

In effect when she loved, it was as part of a ménage à trios, consisting of she, the man, and her creative work, which meant that she had two lovers. It was her art to which she gave the very deepest, intimate aspects of herself. Love of another person had been strongly felt, but had never contained all of her exuberant emotional and spiritual energy.

For Peter, love was everything. He had other ambitions, but love was to be their font and foundation, without which they would never happen.

It was not that Wind lacked sexual interest or pleasure. She had always responded very passionately with someone she loved. But she almost never wanted to initiate sexuality. She had preferred to respond to the overtures of the right man at the right time and place. But she had never poured her heart into the longing that sexuality inspired in Peter.

"I hope you enjoyed our visit to the children's world," she said.

"I did very much," he replied, wanting to share his happiness with her. "On the whole I'm feeling much better. I no longer think of going home very soon."

A profound sense of relief washed through Wind. She was surprised at the volume of her feeling.

"I find myself very grateful to hear you say that," she said. "I am relieved and happy for you."

Her sweet words made his nerves tingle the entire length of his body. "Your words are sometimes quite . . . powerful to me," he said.

"I'm very surprised," she replied. "I knew that I could upset you, but I was unaware that I had the power to make you feel good."

"You've always been able to do that."

Again she was surprised.

Peter was also surprised at himself that he was being so positively emotional toward her. He had expected to feel as uneasy as he usually did when she arrived.

Overcome with the success of their first moments together, Peter jumped into the happiness of their emotional exchanges, excited about finally being able to woe her.

"Ever since I first laid eyes on you when you stepped out of the crowd on the bluff above the city, I have been mesmerized by the vision of you. I . . . I . . ."

Peter was suddenly aware that he was taking emotional liberties that she might not welcome.

"If I'm being too forward . . ."

"I am honored by your admiration and respect," she said graciously, deeply enjoying his high regard of her.

Encouraged by her reply, feeling carried away by the success of the moment, Peter suddenly began to imagine something incredible, that he loved her. It seemed terribly risky, but what did he have to lose?

First things first, he had to get all of the bad things that had happened out of love's way. He had to exonerate her completely so that she wouldn't feel bad, the same thing he'd tried so hard to do with his mother so that she would love him again.

"With rare exception, you have always been very good to me," he declared. "And I have often been terrible to you, which I now deeply regret. You've treated me better than any woman has ever treated me, and I've always challenged you, failing to appreciate you, as if I never had grateful feelings, because I did. I just want to set the record straight that I've been kind of acting like an idiot."

Though Wind was deeply grateful for his acknowledgement, she was very distracted by a more compelling priority. She had caught sight of something in Peter's discourse she found very unsettling. There was an intensity and hunger in his expression that troubled her.

"I am very happy to have been of such help to you," she said, careful in the choice of her metaphors, unwittingly diluting the largess of his feelings.

Peter was hurt by her second diminution of his declaration, and backed away emotionally.

Instantly aware that she had hurt him, Wind was now sure that something was going on about which she didn't know. She was particularly disquieted by the intensity of his feelings.

Beginning to feel crestfallen by Wind's backing away from the emotional possibilities so pregnant when she first arrived, Peter was thrown back into the unhappy part of himself. In his mind's eye she began to change from an angel bearing gifts of reprieve and redemption, to an alien woman offering perhaps only a professional interest in Peter.

"You suddenly seem . . . so different to me, I mean than you were just a moment ago."

"Forgive my lapse," she said. "I was struck with contradictory reactions which . . ."

She was suddenly and very vividly reminded of a man she had once loved for a while as a young woman of thirty years. Like Peter, he seemed to walk on a tightrope of expectation in response to her every move. This man's love had been powerfully focused inside of sexuality.

Oh, my word, she exclaimed to herself.

"Peter," she said, beginning very cautiously to explore the unsettling realization that had now completely taken over her thoughts. "Do you have feelings for me which are sexual?"

An empty silence suddenly engulfed them both.

Is she asking because she wants me to stop? Or is she asking because she wants me to go on?

The answer was too critical.

"I don't know," he said, denying the obvious, biding his time.

But the truth was that succeeding sexually was terribly important to Peter. The whole course of his life depended upon it. It was the foundation of everything.

He had lost his only other love, his early mother when his young body was deeply buried in the sensuality of her wondrous thigh, that early awakening of sexuality's eventual capacity for mutual joy. To find love again, he would have to go back through sexuality's door.

Wind heard Peter's, "I don't know," as evidence that he felt hurt. She wanted very much to find out how, which she had learned to do by turning things over to him, doing what he wanted.

She knew he wanted to be embraced again. But she was very ambivalent about touching someone who obviously had sensual interest in her. She did not want to encourage this in the slightest way. Yet she was deeply moved to help him feel better.

Thus, though very ambivalent about using a physical gesture under the circumstances, she reached out and briefly touched his shoulder with her hand, hoping that small offering of touch would be sufficient for him.

"Oooh," Peter cried out of an inescapable passionate cry.

He felt deeply caressed by her touch, and irresistibly moved—which triggered a surge of testosterone fingering intense pleasure-prickles up the spine of his member, instantly erecting it.

He was extremely embarrassed by this pleasure-sound.

"Oh," Wind exclaimed, shocked by the realization that Peter was erect.

Something snapped inside of Peter. Impulse, desire, need, and passion rushed simultaneously together to occupy the same space. Their blend produced what seemed fated, something he was compelled to express. He couldn't have stopped himself even if he wanted to.

"It's true what we both suspect!" he confessed. "I've really fallen for you! I . . . I . . . I love you very, very much. I know it's probably crazy, and out of the question, and I'm being foolish and probably even wrong to say so. But I can't help myself. It's just too powerful and I have to tell you."

To Wind his declaration was a shock wave. She was almost completely unprepared. She blanched with surprise and embarrassment. This was something she'd never anticipated.

Troubadourian custom captured this disintegrative moment, taking over Wind's response. It was traditional on Troubadour to regard the topic of love as a sacred one, treating it with a ritual respect, addressing it only in a traditional public place inside of which whatever was said was given dignity and discipline. This special place was the Mandela they had visited in the great hall upstairs.

"Your loving me interrupts the natural course of our being together for the time being," she announced solemnly. "I am deeply moved by your declaration. You honor me greatly," she added more from her head than her heart.

Peter stood stunned.

"On Troubadour such a declaration deserves our deepest respect and our most careful reply. I must therefore, as is traditional on my planet, prepare myself for that meeting. When love is spoken between adults, nothing else claims a higher priority. I will meet you next in the Mandela upstairs."

Peter was overwhelmingly flabbergasted.

What's happening, he shouted frantically to himself?

He was beginning to feel faint.

"Unfortunately," she continued, "until I am prepared, all other transactions between us must cease, their further progress waiting until we have spoken of love, when I am prepared to give you my full reply."

"Transactions cease?" Peter repeated in horror, as if by expressing his disbelief he could prevent it from happening. "What do you mean?"

"As much as I deeply regret interrupting what has been such a beautiful time together, I must now leave you. You have evoked in me a deeply ceremonial response."

"But you can't leave now! Something was happening, and I know it's something terrible!" Peter shouted desperately. "What have I done?" he shouted. "What have I done?"

"Please forgive me but I must leave," Wind replied sorrowfully.

She turned toward the door.

"No, no, no, no, no! It can't happen again!" he shouted.

Bludgeoned with this machine-gunning of "no's," she stopped in her tracks. He was beginning to make her feel afraid.

"I'm sorry," she apologized. "Obviously the custom of my people is very incompatible with your need. But I have no other choice. You must please understand."

She hesitated.

Peter hung suspended on her every word, desperately hoping there would be some tiny hint of encouragement, perhaps in a slight inclination to turn around and face him.

But none of this happened. Wind was too preoccupied with the urgency of the moment to acknowledge the convenient opportunity that the ceremonial custom provided her discomfort, giving it a chance quickly to escape.

"I don't know how else to say it," she explained, painfully aware of his distress.

"Please tell me why you have to go," he pleaded, hoping that some new shred of information might reveal a slightest chance for reprieve.

Wind heard and intellectually understood his words. But she was beginning to feel something she'd never felt before: overwhelmed. She'd been afraid and confused before. But she'd never been equally drawn toward and repulsed by the same person at the same time.

Her body shook from the tension.

Peter was horrified by her shaking, which he perceived to be fear.

"Oh, please, please, don't feel so scared!" he shouted. "I'm so sorry! I didn't mean to hurt you!"

He started pacing and ringing his hands together.

"What have I done? What have I done? What have I done?" he frantically repeated, overwhelmed with terrible dread and despair, as if saying it three times magically might break the circle of disaster which was befalling him once more!

"I will send someone to talk to you," she said, her voice shaking a little.

"But why must you leave?" he shouted. "I didn't mean to do anything wrong," he pleaded with great urgency. "I'll take it all back if you need! Let's say I don't love you, so you're no longer obligated to do anything about it! I can keep my feelings to myself, but please give me another chance! You've got to give me another chance!"

Wind finally managed to move herself out the door, each step difficult to take, wanting to stop, yet needing to run away.

"Please, please, can't you stay just a little longer?" he pleaded as he watched her disappear.

Peter was crushed. He stood transfixed to the same spot, his body making not the slightest motion. He was a statue waiting to live again, once more engulfed in the endless purgatory of his life's failure.

Rain about Wind

Peter was crestfallen and dumbfounded.

Why should a declaration of love be grounds for rejection? They claim to be so good at caring for people, making life glorious for each other. So where did all that loving go when it comes to me? Instead I'm being shunned.

His anger was desperately trying to prevent him from falling into a huge depression that threatened to bury him. But it wasn't working.

Desperately he glommed onto a vision of Wind's voluptuous body, trying as hard as he could to hold in his heart what the terrible winds of grief's tornado were trying to rip from his grasp, banishing comfort's memory to the thin air of failure's black, empty space.

"She'd be horrified to know what I'm doing with her beautiful body," he lamented. "Just as she was repelled by what she must have seen as a crude come-on for sex. Why did I say such a stupid thing to her when everything was going so great? I was beginning to feel happiness for the first time in years."

She's disgusted with me. I took this beautiful experience and turned it into something really cheap. What's the matter with me? She makes me happy and I act like a fucking idiot, impulsively grabbing for more. Will she ever be able to talk to me again? She's probably sending Rain's over to tell me I have to leave.

He dragged himself through the rituals of shaving and showering. He didn't even notice how good the shower's water massage always felt. Today he got nothing out of it. For clothing he picked a very muted, dark colored suit he found in the back of the closet, as if he were dressing for a funeral.

The doorbell rang.

"Come in," Peter said, remaining in the kitchen where he had retreated. He was embarrassed to meet Rain.

The ancient Troubadourian walked through the front door peering into the apartment.

"I do believe it was Peter Icarus' voice that opened the door," he said. "However I can't say for sure just where Peter's body is at the moment."

Peter reluctantly walked into the living room.

"Okay, let's get it over with," he said. "I know I did a stupid thing. So what's the bad news?"

Silence.

"What stupid thing did you do?"

Oh, my god, he doesn't know, Peter exclaimed to himself.

"Didn't Wind tell you? I thought you guys told each other everything that happens. She said she would send somebody over, so of course I assumed that she explained what happened."

Peter did not want to be the one to tell Rain.

"Of course she told me," Rain replied. "It's the stupid part I don't get."

Rain sat down in a chair, gesturing to Peter to do the same.

When they'd both settled in, a silence followed which deeply puzzled Peter.

Why doesn't he say something?

"The stupid part is that I said I loved her," Peter said irritably, feeling embarrassed to have to repeat it.

"On Troubadour it's considered an honor to be loved, not a crime," Rain replied.

"I don't think she felt honored," Peter retorted aggressively. "She was literally scared! I'll never forget it. It was awful!"

"I think you surprised her," Rain replied. "Surprise as you know is the smallest form of fear."

"She was feeling much worse than surprise!"

Silence.

"I'm so ashamed of making such a fool of myself," Peter blurted out, filling the silence, but paying the price of exposing his shame. "I know my proposal was crude. It was really a stupid thing to do."

"Ah, so that's what stupid means," Rain quipped. "Well, there's no need to feel so ashamed. There's nothing peculiar, lewd, or disrespectful in loving someone. In fact on Troubadour it's considered quite an honor, as

I've already said. It's an event, as I'm sure Wind told you, that we regard with great care and respect."

"I know she said that. But I don't see how that changes the fact that she was really upset."

"She needs time to consider in the most serious way how she feels toward you, and then give you her response. It's our custom to do so in a formal setting. I'm sure you'll find this experience very interesting, revealing that any emotionally charged event in the lives of a loving couple, is something more easily done in the structured and ceremonial customs of the Mandela, which, by the way replaced our policing agencies who used to handle domestic discord."

"You make it all sound so easy. I don't think I'll find anything about this 'easy.' She was really put out by me."

"Perhaps my manner does exaggerate the hopeful part of what's happened. I understand that you're very upset and puzzled about what's going on. But you might remind yourself that it's the surprise element I spoke of. I think she was probably quite taken aback, and then felt embarrassed to be so unprepared to respond to your plea, so caught up as she probably was in her own experience at that moment. I suspect your declaration temporarily removed her from her sense of vocation. I am referring of course to the vocation that spearheaded your visit."

"That's her vocation?" Peter queried, distracted by this puzzlement.

"At this moment."

"I can't believe she's spent her whole life preparing for me to come."

"True."

"Then what else has she done?"

"I'm sure she'll tell you about it eventually."

"I don't see when," Peter replied. "She probably doesn't want to see me anymore."

Rain laughed.

"What's so damned funny?" Peter demanded to know with a touch of indignation.

"It would take more than a love declaration to shake her from her purpose," Rain replied. "She's a very determined woman."

"But I hate putting her through all this. I mean I'm not a Troubadourian. So why does she have to do this formal thing with me? Why can't she be excused?"

"I'm sure she doesn't want to be excused."

"Well, could I be excused?"

Rain laughed.

"Now that sounds more like the spunky energy I've felt in you before," Rain observed. "I could tell something different and very negative got a hold of you in the middle of this experience. But now you sound like yourself, a vigorous passionate man."

"Yeah. That's precisely what's got me in so much trouble with her."

"Well, perhaps you need to consider thinking of it in less dire ways."

"That's the crime," Peter insisted, "that I did something so 'dire.' But it wasn't meant to be so big . . . I mean I wasn't expecting anything from her in return. I was just telling her how I feel."

"Are you sure of that?"

"Well, maybe I expected something unconsciously," Peter retorted. "But I certainly didn't mean to do anything wrong."

"I agree that you didn't do anything wrong. But I disagree that your motive was unknown. I think you have wanted Wind to love you since the moment you first laid eyes upon her."

Peter was shocked to realize it was probably true.

"Well . . . maybe, but it feels to me like what I really wanted was for her . . . oh, I don't know."

"You feel abandoned, don't you?" Rain queried.

"Well, yeah."

"Abandoned by love," Rain added.

"Uh, yes, but what are you driving at?"

"Haven't you abandoned love?" Rain asked.

"Oh, for crying out loud, so this is going to be my fault too?"

"No. There is no need for blame. But why don't you let love take its course."

"What are you saying, that I should stop worrying about this whole affair and just let the chips fall where they may?"

"That's a pretty good way of putting it," Rain acknowledged.

"Well, I'm not good enough to do that."

"I don't think that's any longer true," Rain observed.

"Are you calling me a liar?"

"No. I'm calling you a forgetter."

"What did I forget?" Peter asked with annoyance, still feeling accused of lying.

"You forgot the support and encouragement that you were so excited about receiving just yesterday, for instance."

"But that's been disproved!" Peter exclaimed.

"How so?" Rain asked.

"By all the negative things that followed this so-called support!" Peter shouted, as if it should be obvious to anyone.

"That's the lie to which I was referring," Rain replied.

"Why do you keep calling me a liar?"

"No. I'm saying that you believe a lie."

"What's the difference?"

"You seem to believe that if someone who cares for you ever disappoints you, then the care they have provided has been killed by their disappointing acts."

"Well, isn't that true?"

"No," Rain firmly but gently insisted. "The loving part of your experience is just as real as it's always been. It now has what you feel to be an ugly companion. But the jig's not up, the results aren't in, the final act has not been written, and until then love remains possible."

It was like déjà vu. Peter had often listened to himself say something very similar to his patients.

"My god. I must admit that maybe you're right," Peter exclaimed, suddenly aware of everything Rain had been telling him. "No, you really are right. I see it now. It's me who abandons love in my reckless anger, just as love used to abandon me."

"Now that was one hell of an insight, Peter Icarus," Rain exclaimed. "But have you figured out who it is that you abandon?"

"I supposed you're going to say it's me."

Rain just smiled.

Peter was quite moved by his new understanding. But he was even more disturbed by what had happened in his relationship with Wind.

"All right, maybe what happened wasn't such a disaster," Peter acknowledged. "But I still can't believe that I haven't in some way damaged my relationship with Wind. She was too upset."

"Why don't you give your love a little more support?" Rain suggested. "You seem awfully quick to throw in the towel and abandon it."

"Do you really think she still likes me?"

"I don't know how she feels about you. But I do know that falling in love on Troubadour is a very special occasion, which is having quite an impact upon her. Once again surprise is the best word to describe her reaction to you."

"But how can surprise explain so much?"

"To answer you I must digress a bit," Rain explained. "Fear is always with all of us, all the time, though we don't have to keep watching it constantly as we've believed for so many thousands of years. We can wait until it insists upon showing up."

"Now to get back to what we were talking about," Rain said. "Surprise, the feeling I keep bringing to your attention, is, as I've explained the smallest version of fear. Which makes it the best part of fear to be next to, if fear has got to be around all the time, as change keeps insisting."

"In other words, finally to reach my punch line, surprises are a beautiful thing, not an ugly one, or just a scary one. They can be unsettling. But even more important they can be wonderful. You have one waiting for you upstairs in the Mandela. Why not try thinking about it that way, as an anticipation to be enjoyed?"

"Do you really expect me to be able to live up to such high standards after two weeks in a strange land?" Peter exclaimed.

"Of course not. I remember how terrifying it was for me to face fear as a normal part of experience. You have my deep sympathy. I know how frightening and painful this is for you."

"It's just that I know it's going to turn out bad."

"Like anything valuable, love has a life of its own, which gives it the power to compete with other things in life, no matter how frightening they appear."

"Why do you want love to compete with anything?" Peter asked. "That just destroys love."

"No it doesn't. Love *needs* to compete in order to distract and interrupt the personal goals in which most of us are deeply engaged. Only then does it have a chance of commanding the amount of our interest, attention, and desire that it deserves."

They sat in silence for several moments.

"So you're not here to tell me to get off the planet because of what I did to Wind yesterday?" Peter queried.

Rain laughed.

"I wouldn't dream of giving up something as interesting as you are, Peter Icarus, until the bitter end. So be comforted. Wind will be along in a day or so. In the meantime I'll leave you with your own thoughts."

"Oh, you mean our conversation is over?" Peter said with an obvious disappointment.

"It's bliss to be missed, though perhaps you are pissed, but I shall return whenever you need my assist."

Peter laughed.

"That was pretty good," Peter replied, feeling much better, though he knew the terrors would return. "And I know you'd like to rhyme. Well, I'm sorry, Rain. I guess I just can't join you today. I can't get myself in the spirit."

"Doing it myself is enough of a pleasure," Rain replied. "I wouldn't want you to rhyme unless your spirit was moved to do so."

"Are there things I should know about this formal ritual?" Peter asked.

"No. Just be yourself."

"May I suggest that you let your next visitor know up front never to say 'I love you,'" Peter said.

"Thank you for that advice," Rain replied. "I'm sure we'll consider it very seriously."

With those words Rain departed.

He always makes things sound so much better. But does he really know about love? He doesn't seem to get into it very much himself.

Wind & Rain

Wind was dreaming that she was employed in a factory on Earth that produced art. She was being forced to paint what she had no desire or inspiration to create. She had to invent emotions that didn't come from her heart, and project them onto her canvas in the form of nude humanoid bodies writhing together in a mechanical sexual struggle devoid of feeling. She couldn't understand what was happening, and wanted desperately to escape.

"I've spent half a day trying to understand a very strange dream I had last night," Wind said to Rain soon after she'd arrived at his apartment in the mountains.

It was a very special apartment, one of a handful of homes on Troubadour that had a window revealing a real panorama of nature's outdoors. All of the very few domiciles that sported this unusual opportunity were located in the mountain city called Earth Project as apartments facing the outside of the sheer mountain cliff into which the city was built. Through it one could see what looked to be over one hundred miles. The curvature of the planet was just visible.

Rain deeply enjoyed the pristine wildness of the high country. He had decided to live there during the last years of his life. This would be his final home, though death was still far away. He found it extraordinarily comforting to be in this place.

Though most Troubadourians were perfectly happy with the artificial windows of Peter's apartment, deeply committed as they were to turning nature completely back to itself, Rain much preferred his real panorama. It connected him to the old world with its ancient ways where he'd spent his entire childhood. He sensed this place was part of the source of his tremendous personal confidence, which seemed to require this deep rooting.

"Have you ever thought of dreams as pranksters plagiarizing our worries in order to construct their mythical stories?" Rain asked.

"Rain," she urged sweetly. "Always the clever man. You are such a prankster, and so very good at it. I hope some day to be able to join your humorously impish perspective more often, for I know it to be one of remarkable scope that would be inspiring to look from the inside out. I can tell just by watching you express it. Forgive me, though, but for the time being I must be my simple, serious self, for I know no other way of accomplishing what I came to see you about."

"No one could refuse such an eloquent appeal expressed so gently by such a beautiful creature."

To her surprise Wind found his compliment curiously uncomfortable. She'd had never felt uneasy around Rain before, and found the experience very disquieting.

"Rain," she began, hesitating momentarily.

"What is it, my sweet?"

She blanched at what felt like the cloyingness of his affectionate endearment, competing with her own needs.

"Now I'm reacting negatively to you," she announced as if she were warning him. "When I came to talk about Peter."

"Fear not, pretty one, the negative is only a message to the joyful. Whether you heed it is for you to trifle," he replied.

Rain was grateful to have a chance to help Wind in what he suspected would be a significant way. He'd hoped for such an opportunity for months.

Wind needed to come right to the point.

"Rain, please stop using expressions which suggest I might be your lover," Wind gently insisted. "Of course we do love each other very much and are the very best of friends. But we are not lovers. So please, don't joke about that just now. I am feeling quite unsettled."

Rain bowed, smiling in acknowledgement of her request, accepting both her definition of what he was doing, and his own disappointment that she was not more playful.

In one sense there was nothing he was unwilling to do for this woman. This generous urge wasn't a passionate desire, though he occasionally had rumblings of a sensual attraction to her. This patient affection came out of the steadfastness and respect that had always been a part of his deep, loving friendship for her.

"I don't like feeling angry at either you or Peter," Wind insisted.

"Personally I feel flattered when you are angry at me," he retorted.

"You're such a trickster," she said to him in a friendly way, but with a tinge of strain, wanting to encourage and reflect his affection, but wanting it to become less playful. "I need you to be serious today," she pleaded.

"Since I love you I must refuse your request," Rain sweetly insisted, "because to accept it would be harmful to you. Anger is, as you know never to be taken more seriously than as information primarily about the self, though it always points elsewhere. If you take anger any more seriously, it turns into judge, jury, and executioner of something or someone, with very painful consequences."

Though she understood and agreed with what he was saying, Wind was beginning to lose her patience. She wanted to talk in a different way.

"Rain, I am probably missing an extraordinary opportunity for new information by not listening to your clever, playful twists of meaning, which always bend things into such interesting new shapes. But I must insist that you let me lead this discussion for a while. I am quite concerned about Peter, and about me."

"I spoke with him," Rain suddenly remarked very sedately, his tone already shifted as she had instructed. "He's okay for the moment."

"I'm concerned about how he will react to me in the Mandela," she insisted.

"What is there to be concerned about?"

"That I have already hurt him. Perhaps it was necessary, but that doesn't take away the negative outcome. I should have been prepared for this."

"There you see, it's already happened to you. You've become the victim of your own angry indictment."

"Rain! Please."

"What I'm trying to say, my dear woman is that you are feeling guilty. In all the years I've known you I've never seen you feel that emotion with such earnestness. It is from that observation that I have drawn my conclusions."

"But if I don't take it upon myself to be responsible for his pain, then I am rejecting him just as he keeps insisting that we are all doing most of the time."

"What's so harmful about leaving him with his distress?" Rain asked.

"I'm not sure he can handle it."

"Isn't that something he must find out about for himself, and learn to manage as best he can?" he queried, soloing part of the time.

Wind got it.

"You're right. I am being excessively harsh with myself," she admitted.

"Just to remind you of what you already know," Rain offered. "The hurt of tragedy is best perceived as a farce very cleverly achieved. I'm sure your anger is fertile soil for the meaning toward which you urgently toil."

Wind laughed a little.

"Your clever wit distracts me from my peculiar desire to inflict pain upon myself."

"I am delighted to distract you from such a nefarious objective," he replied.

She expected to be annoyed with him again, but it didn't happen. His discomforting humor was actually helping.

"Tell me your dream," Rain said gently.

Wind gladly repeated it to him.

"What do you think?" Rain asked.

"I don't know," she replied. "Much of it seems obvious, that my work with Peter forces me to feel things that I don't feel. But I don't understand the nude bodies in my dream."

"Now that's the interesting part," Rain observed. "I think perhaps the dream says that, as much as you like being loved, you don't want a man loving you with the slightest hint of passion or desire."

"That's true, I don't want romantic attachments just now."

"But you did want someone capable of evoking strong passionate emotions when you chose Peter to come to Troubadour," Rain reminded her.

"Yes. But emotion is not sexuality," she retorted.

"That's what your dream insists upon by arranging sex to contain only one emotion, heartless lust."

"But I didn't arrange it," she insisted, almost as if she was still inside the dream, arguing with what was happening. "They forced me to . . ."

She stopped herself knowing instantly that it was she who had done the "forcing," when unconsciously she wrote the script for this dream.

"If it's me who's pulling the strings, then what is it I want?"

She thought for a moment.

"Could it possibly be true, Rain, that I actually want what I so assiduously avoid?"

"Perhaps you do," he agreed. "But if so, is it with Peter that you want it?"

"That is the question. I don't know," she replied.

But that's a good question to ask myself, she said to herself.

She looked at Rain and found both laughter and fascination in his expression. Though appealing to her, she suddenly realized that like Peter,

Rain had special feelings for her that she'd never thought about. But she also knew that she didn't have time to think about this now. She would have to do it later when she was alone.

"I don't know," she repeated.

But she did know something else. She knew that she and Rain were on the track of finding the answer she sought.

Her trust in Rain was finally fully connected. She'd acknowledged and put aside the feelings she and Rain had for each other. She relaxed, and instantly her perspective enlarged. Multiple speculations started bouncing around inside the chambers of her understanding.

The Troubadourians had achieved a significant degree of comfort inside the sometimes-precarious experience of change. Some of them had even learned to live with a relatively permanent, daily shift in their perspective, in spite of the fact that each new insight started as an abrasive disruption of something familiar, before it became something new, interesting, and challenging, and occasionally inspiring.

In the process of adapting to a steady diet of change, they had relinquished their primitive preoccupation with proof, which previously they'd needed in order to trust their own choices in life. They had needed the guarantee of authoritative power to reassure their perpetual and fearful doubts.

They were astounded eventually to discover that this craving for certainty in belief was what had made their lives so oppressive, what had made them for centuries so willing to carry the yoke of abuse from the powerful authorities they had insisted must be there to guarantee a safe heart.

Proof is certainty in the mind of the approver. To achieve it requires the unfettered suppression of the natural competition implicit to the forever changing landscape that makes life possible. Proof is therefore fundamentally against change, and tries fearfully, and oppressively to stamp it out.

To live with the vagaries and uncertainties of daily change, the Troubadourians had learned to deal with a much larger portion of emotional adversity in their ordinary expectations. Which empowered them to manage a great deal of what had previously been assigned to "higher authority" to manage, like settling disputes

When they finally embraced the chaos of change as the permanent arrangement of life, what they found was how hugely empowered they suddenly became. A willingness to handle higher levels of complexity in their experience, gave them an enormous increase in their competence. It was this factor, above all others, that had produced the incredible change in Troubadour's last century.

A border dispute, instead of starting a war, became an opportunity to learn, instantly transforming what had been intimidating into something valuable and instructive, producing a regular diet of change at least partially sought. This embracing of change had taught them respect for the natural limits of possibility in the course of any given day of life, which enabled the personal constraints necessary to live peacefully with each other while having so much personal power, without the need of any policing agency.

This much-enlarged capacity for learning now expressed itself in Wind, in the way that she proceeded to find the answers to her question. Instead of looking for a solution to her most immediate and conscious problem—a strategy that is regarded as virtuous on Earth—she drifted into her most instinctive and unconscious place, putting herself inside the deepest part of her psyche most capable of perceiving the largest picture of anything. She sunk into the nether realms of her unconscious.

Like a great many of her own people, she knew that psychic queries couldn't see their answers in the same way that the eye can't see the sun. One had to come at both indirectly to catch a glimpse of their reflected shadow, which only sometimes becomes the shape-changing corona of insight. To look too directly at a problem simply confounds, blinding the seeker with too much rational information, which nowadays is the first kind of data to arrive on the scene of understanding, which produces far more worry than anything useful.

"Would that I were a red blood cell inside of your heart where I could see what wonders your mind doth impart," Rain rhymed to encourage her to share her deep thoughts.

"What do you think you would see?" she asked.

"That your paintings in the dream are like the kind of love you want from a man, devoid of strong passion."

"It suddenly makes sense," Wind exclaimed. "I'm not feeling anything! Which is very strange for me, and happens in only one way, when I'm feeling two contradictory emotions that appear to cancel each other out. The ambiguity of their contradiction makes both feelings seem to disappear. When the truth is both feelings belong together. My positive feelings for Peter must learn to stand beside my negative ones."

Wind had expected herself to handle whatever emotions Peter evoked in her without being personally disrupted. She therefore disapproved of the part of her that did not want his love. On the other hand, she resolutely believed that she should not give more to this project than her self-interest approved. This was the contradiction of heart.

She wandered over to the huge window looking out over the vast expanse of Troubadour's highest mountain range. The sun was shining from her rear toward the objects she was viewing, coloring the landscape with a huge variety of hues and colors.

Rain walked up behind her.

"I regret participating in your discomfort," he said gently.

"I don't," she gently replied. "It's what I needed."

He laughed out of relief for her and happiness for himself.

"Thanks for that laughter, sweet lady that I'm after," he chimed.

Wind was suddenly put off by his "sweet lady" remark. She suddenly realized that she was having the same experience with Rain that she was having with Peter.

Oh, my! She exclaimed to herself. I think maybe Rain's also in love with me.

She found his close proximity directly behind her no longer comfortable, and wandered back to sit in her chair.

"Rain, are you coming on to me?" she asked as she sat down.

"Obviously, my sweet. But take it with ease just as you please."

"Thank you, but that doesn't help," she chided in good nature. "I want to know if it's true."

"Forgive my love for intruding," he replied.

Silence.

He'd managed indirectly to say "yes" without inflicting it upon her in the bluntness of the word.

"I don't want to be loving anyone just now."

She paused for a moment.

"Actually I think I can probably find the rest of it out on my own."

"I feel sad that you are so glad to be going," he retorted, not wanting her to leave.

She hesitated.

"I don't want to leave you feeling sad," she replied. "What is it that you need to feel better?"

"To know that you've found your answer," he replied.

"I think I have, Rain. I am at odds with my own inclination to avoid romantic attachment. And yet being so seems to be taking the competence right out of me, depriving me of my best skills. I'm sure you can see what it's doing to me. I just have to figure out how I'm going to respond."

"Now that's news," Rain retorted.

"What is?" she asked.

"That you are already romantically involved with a man," Rain observed.

"How do you know that?" she asked, and then suddenly realized the words she had used.

Instead of asking, "where do you get that from" as she'd intended, she'd asked, "how do you know," which provided the answer.

"I guess I'm caught on the petard of my own metaphors," Wind acknowledged. "But I still can't believe it."

Am I denying something as obvious as that, Wind asked herself?

For a moment her head spun.

"Don't be afraid, my beautiful fairy, it's very temporary, this mask of grief that will soon be deprived of belief," Rain quipped.

"But to love this Earthman as he needs to be loved, would command my heart with the same devotion that I give my art, replacing my imagination with his appropriation."

"Wind! What a wonderful surprise," he exclaimed with joy. "You know how to play meaning-rhyme."

"Yes, yes, I know," she replied, brushing that issue aside. "But do you see what I mean?"

"I think so," he replied. "I see that you love this man in spite of yourself."

"But I don't," she insisted.

But there wasn't much force behind her words. She knew it was true. She loved him.

I don't love him romantically, she reminded herself. I love him as a friend.

Wind sighed. The contradiction was still alive. But it was time for her to figure by herself. Only her experience could reveal the answer to the riddle of her perplexity.

She smiled at Rain, peering long into his eyes for the first time since she arrived.

"Well, you've done it again," she said. "You have given me my assignment. I think perhaps my earlier departure was, as you insisted premature. But I also know that alone is what I need to be with time passing, before I will understand anything further."

He knew that she was right this time, and it made him feel sad.

"Thank you, dear man," Wind said. "I am so lucky to have you as my close friend. You are such a beautiful person, so very knowledgeable and wise. I'm deeply grateful for your help."

"When I heard you were coming to visit I wrote you a poem," he replied. "May I share it with you?"

"Yes. Please."

"She who walks with the spirit of child,
Never leaving behind her innocent wild,
Brings joy to whomever she touches in life,
By keeping the calmness alive that banishes strife."

Wind laughed.

"Such a beautiful sentiment to keep innocence wild," she replied. "It's true. I am best when I act from innocence, and very spontaneously."

They both agreed about that in the silence of their knowing looks.

"Peter is an innocent man," she added. "Thank you for reminding me that I am just like him."

Sadness joined the happy demeanor of their looking at each other, because it was time for her to go.

"You have brought beauty to this day that will companion me for a long time," Rain said. "Thank you for sharing your life so intimately with me. It is a beautiful life."

Though she knew it not to be the least bit provocative, Wind found his last words awkward. Though another part of her was deeply moved by his affection.

"You remind me of what's most beautiful in life," Rain added.

"You embarrass me with your flattery," she replied, wanting him to stop, even as she appreciated him for what he had said.

"When I would rather buoy you with my admiration," he replied.

"That you have done generously," she said. "But I bid you adieu. Goodbye, dear friend and thank you."

She started to leave.

"I am sad for you to leave, until once more I know we will cleave," Rain crooned.

Wind's ambivalence toward Rain suddenly disappeared. Her heart was suddenly entirely positive. She looked deeply into his eyes, what she had been avoiding doing before this moment.

Their eyes clung closely together.

For decades they had been loving friends to each other. But they were always committed to another purpose whenever they came into the emotional orbit of their intimate feelings for each other. So whatever might come of their mutual affection never sought purposefully to fulfill itself. Their potential linkage dissolved again into separate lives, where it became a source of inspiration instead of being the flower that might have bloomed into something more.

They parted each with a sigh.

"Just remember as you struggle with whom to please, that I always remain your loving liege," he said as she walked down the hallway.

Too Many Pieces

"A deadline has commandeered our attention for the moment," Rain said over the phone. "I deeply regret that we must interrupt the natural process of your visit."

"Well, of course, if there's an emergency I completely understand," Peter said. "I can deal with that."

"I think you should give yourself the opportunity to understand what we need from you, and what you need for yourself before you commit to any course of action," Rain suggested.

Great advice, Peter observed.

"What's up?" he asked.

"The urgent matter is your predecessor, Drayton Crampton," Rain announced.

That other guy, Peter exclaimed to himself. Shit. I forgot all about dealing with him.

"He will reach his visitation limit of three weeks the day after tomorrow," Rain explained.

"What exactly is it that you want me to do?" Peter asked.

"We need your help in deciding how to proceed."

"In other words, you want me to function like a shrink," Peter observed.

"Since I don't know what that means in its entirety," Rain replied, "let me tell you in my own way. We need you to assess this man's psychic functioning on Earth terms, and then give us your best opinion as to how we should proceed, knowing that the only absolute in this decision is that he must return to Earth the day after tomorrow. We also want one of his own people, yourself, to make contact with him before he returns for whatever benefit that might provide."

"But if he must return, then why do you need me?" Peter asked. "Isn't the outcome obvious?"

"We hope to arrange Crampton's necessary return in the best possible manner to produce the least possible harm to him."

Jesus, why can't they decide for themselves?

"What can I offer that you don't already know?" Peter asked.

"Nothing more or less than your opinion, though you might simply by your presence give Dr. Crampton much more."

Peter suddenly realized that he very much wanted his experience on Troubadour to remain protected from anything that might upset the gradual improvement he'd begun to experience. Once or twice he had even perceived Troubadour as a safe haven from the haunting grief of his own life, a place where people sometimes took extraordinary care of you.

What if something terrible happens to this guy that's obviously traceable to my bad judgment?

"I can see that you're very ambivalent."

"What if I can't help you?" Peter asked.

"Oh, I'm quite sure that you will," Rain replied.

"What makes you so sure?"

"I'll tell you when I get there. I'm coming right over."

The moment Rain arrived, their conversation continued as if it had not been interrupted.

"You asked me what makes me so sure," Rain remarked. "If you can come to a strange planet and live among people who are alien to you, and who do weird things from your perspective, and survive all this as well as you have, then whatever you give us I'm sure will be of great value," Rain explained.

Peter couldn't resist Rain's good opinion of him.

"Okay, I'll do it. I sure hope you're right. I guess I was worried about not providing the right kind of intervention."

"May I suggest that except for the direction of one's next move, there is no right anything in life," Rain replied. "Take one step in any direction, and the possibilities have already become exponential."

"I'm not backing out of doing it, just checking it out," Peter reassured.

"Thank you for your help," Rain replied. "There are two more pieces of information I need to give you. The first is that Wind will be there. Which means you will be meeting each other before any resolution of your love-declaration."

"She will?" Peter queried, shocked at the news, wondering what he'd gotten himself into. "W . . . why does she have to be there?"

"She's there on your behalf as the leader of your team."

"Team?"

"The group responsible for bringing you to Troubadour. As leader she must be present to be sure in her mind that what you're getting involved in is good for you and good for the project that your coming represents to us. You would call her a lawyer. We would call her an ambassador."

"I see. But under the circumstances, isn't that going to be very uncomfortable for her?"

"I doubt it," Rain replied. "She's there mostly as an observer. She probably won't take a very active role in what happens unless she feels it's necessary."

"Oh, I see. I guess maybe that would be much easier for her."

She wants to protect me, but out of what motivation, Peter wondered?

"So what's your second piece of news?" Peter asked.

"The leader of Drayton Crampton's team, Balorin, will also be present."

Another Troubadourian! Shit! This meeting is starting to sound like Grand Central Station! On top of having to work professionally in a strange culture, dealing with Wind not knowing how she feels, now I've got to deal with a strange new Troubadourian! What if he's like that last one I met, that Tutifruit guy, or whatever his name was?

The confusion of names conjured a fourth very surprising complication. He suddenly realized he knew Crampton.

"Who's this guy I'm supposed to shrink?"

"Drayton Crampton."

Shit. So he's my paranoid predecessor.

A chill rushed down his back. The thought of seeing Crampton felt creepy.

Bad idea to see someone you already know, Peter said to himself, trying to find as many reasons as possible for not doing it.

Mixing the social and the professional dimensions always leads to unexpected and complicated consequences, that always undermine the therapy relationship, he reminded himself.

Suddenly his heart dropped a foot. He could feel panic begin to brew. He was suddenly torn between wanting to say no to Rain, and yet desperately not wanting to fail in what they had asked him to do even before he came to Troubadour, and what by implication he'd at least passively agreed to do.

"This is not exactly what I was planning to do today," Peter said hesitantly.

"We can dispense with your meeting Crampton if necessary," Rain gently observed. "It is not a compulsory thing for you to do."

Permission to scratch what had begun deeply to threaten him was all Peter needed to escape from panic. He felt a sudden release of fearfulness. Freed from panic's hurried views of the truth, his mind cleared. He knew instantly that the consequences of not meeting Crampton would be far worse than whatever the panic warned of.

There was something really incredible about this insight for Peter. It wasn't that the idea was so great. It was what having the idea represented that moved him so much.

In that moment of unintentional, spontaneous choice against the disintegrative efforts of fear, Peter achieved two things simultaneously, one, the conscious acknowledgement of panic, which is always the hardest first step of learning about it, and two, a way to surmount it. Neither of these things had ever happened before.

"It's alright," Peter insisted. "I want to see Crampton. So let's do it. Actually I know the man."

"Oh," Rain exclaimed, "then you will be renewing old acquaintance when you consult with him tomorrow. Is that an asset or a liability in your work?"

"I've never talked to him personally. He's a well-known psychoanalyst who has written several books about Borderline Personality function, lectured all over the world, and is considered, and probably is a genius. He built an elaborate psychological model of the most difficult patients to treat, contributing seriously to the theory of psychology."

Why would some guy like him flip, Peter asked himself?

"Well," Rain began, "it would seem that the next chapter to be written is the meeting between the famous and the not yet famous, meaning you of course."

Peter really appreciated Rain's compliment, though he felt embarrassed about sharing that information with Rain.

"Actually I'm getting rather interested in seeing Crampton."

"I'm delighted to hear it. There is one more thing. We were tentatively planning on meeting as a group later today."

"We're going to do what?" Peter exclaimed.

He was thrown back into fearfulness, very apprehensive about having other people around when he did his work. He'd always gone solo. He didn't like being watched.

"Is this a kind of group interview of Dr. Crampton?" Peter asked, wishing he'd never volunteered for the job.

"No, a pre-Crampton meeting. You arrange how and when you want to see Drayton."

"Oh, then I'm in charge of setting it up," Peter ventured, already feeling easier about it.

"As in all things Troubadourian, you are in charge of your destiny."

For the first time since he arrived, Peter felt reassurance from someone in a critical situation. It made him very happy.

"Since you know Crampton, what kind of man is he?" Rain asked.

"I only heard him lecture several times."

"What does he lecture about?"

"Psychological theory."

"And what sort of a person is he?" Rain asked.

"Oh, I didn't know him personally," Peter replied.

"But you said you heard his lectures. Doesn't that mean to know him?"

"No," Peter replied. "It means to sit in a huge room with the chairs all facing the same way, at the head of which stands a person talking to the rest of us for over an hour or two."

"I must confess I used to participate in that sort of thing myself," Rain remarked. "In fact I was the guy who gave the lectures."

"You did? About what?" Peter queried, very interested.

"All sorts of intellectual topics. Aesthetics, ethics, philosophy, religion, and what we call bionature, which is a combination of your biology and psychology rolled into one thing."

"That sounds like what's happened on Earth. Perhaps most professionals now think of psychological dysfunction as a matter of genes and biochemistry."

"Actually we've gone in the reverse direction," Rain explained. "We've made the body more emotion and belief-driven, more psychological, far less mechanical, though of course it has its chemical and mechanical processes. But basically we perceive the body and psychology as part of the same ecosystem, which is programmed and controlled as much by feelings as it is by chemistry or genetics."

"Now that makes a lot more sense to me," Peter replied.

A moment of silence followed.

"Perhaps we should get on with the day, for there is much to do," Rain suggested.

"I agree."

"Is two hours enough to prepare for the preliminary meeting?" Rain asked.

"That's fine."

"Can we come here to meet in your apartment?"

"Here? Well, I guess . . . uh, maybe it does seem to make the most sense," Peter replied hesitantly.

A meeting in my home, Peter silently queried? It will change the way I feel about it. How many more things does he have to throw at me at one time?

"Until then," Rain said and instantly departed.

Peter spent most of the two hours ruminating about the upcoming meeting.

I'll have to sit next to Wind not knowing how to read in her face how she's feeling about me. And then there's that new Troub. I always hate meeting new people when so much is going on. All this shit is going to push me hard I'm sure, maybe so much I'll forget what I want to do or say!

Which would humiliate him.

"Fuck!"

And then there's Crampton.

Drayton had an enormous professional reputation on Earth, and deservedly so. He had brilliantly microanalyzed the primary defensive mechanisms of the type of patient that drove everyone crazy, for decades making these people seem untreatable, the type of patient professionals used to call "borderline." His theory traced the structural origins of these Jeckle & Hyde victims of their own instability, who were alternately at-your-throat or at-your-feet, people prone to erratic and extreme excesses of behavior and response, whose emotional moves in life were either love or hate with little or nothing in between, which made love horrific and violent, and made anger unreasonable and passionately vengeful.

Though these people were often very depressed, drugs did almost nothing to help that symptom, and of course failed to touch the original programming of their character that had been done by parents very much like themselves. Betrayal and chaotic experience terrorized their childhood, and continued in adulthood to be evoked by their extreme behaviors, which deeply destabilized both their lives and also the world around them.

In Peter's view Crampton had devised an almost mathematical description of this disturbing human behavior, hugely improving our understanding, but offering analytical cures based upon the spurious premise that symptoms reveal what's wrong with someone's life, thereby pointing to possible solutions.

It was Peter's conviction that unconscious beliefs about the self and the world, which had been devised by a young mind in response to extremely frightening and disabling conditions, were the origin of symptomatic performance, the specifics of which for any given person were seriously idiosyncratic.

He also believed that pure analysis of any psychological problem, viewed from the emotional distance that Crampton's way of thinking reflected, was purely academic and did not effectively cure anything. Theory was for teaching. Practice had to be built upon a personal system of integrity that accepted partial responsibility for a patient's lack of improvement, for instance, by someone willing to share the agonies of a chaotically unbearable life in order to facilitate change where no hope seemed alive.

Peter was suddenly aware of a slight contempt he felt for the famous man. As instantly he withdrew the feeling, as it suddenly felt inappropriate.

Don't forget he possesses a great deal of what you've always wanted, the respectful approval of others, Peter thought.

What Peter only vaguely realized at the time, was just how much better he was fielding the complex challenges of the day, something he was completely unable to do previously in his visit.

The doorbell rang.

The sound jolted him out of his revere.

"Come in!" Peter said loudly.

Wind walked in first. She was wearing an aqua blue body suit, which flared out at the bottom like a skirt. Embroidered on its front was a delicate interplay of tiny red and yellow flowers, which seemed to entwine with each other in a soft, spiraling embrace.

The effect was stunning to Peter, reflecting as it did his own desire to comingle with this beautiful woman.

She nodded to him with a smile as she passed where he was standing, and walked into the living room to sit down.

The moment their eyes touched, Peter looked down and away, afraid to see what she felt toward him, but then instantly deeply regretted that he'd missed the truth that had been there.

He looked at her figure moving into his living room, hoping to see in her walk and manner something encouraging.

Rain followed her in. He was wearing a black body suit very tightly fitted, with purple and white designs sprinkling the black with subtle color. He looked very tall and handsome, his age providing more dignity than oldness to his demeanor.

A strange, to Peter, Troubadourian followed him wearing a dull gray outfit. On Troubadour terms, he was a relatively small, slender man with a head slightly pointed in its oval-ness. He was much younger than Rain, closer in age to Wind.

He greeted Peter with what visually oscillated between a smile and a snarl, making Peter aware for the first time that the two expressions were distant relatives.

This man walked directly toward the window controls and selected the desert scene.

What the fuck does he think he's doing taking over my apartment? I thought these Troubadourians respected each other's space!

What Peter didn't know at this point was that a Troubadourian would simply have told Balorin to restore the window to its previous setting, which he would have probably done, and then remarked sarcastically upon it during the meeting.

"Shall we get directly to the point?" Rain asked.

"As far as I'm concerned," Peter said with a slight twinge of irritation slipping out as he looked at the stranger as he spoke.

At this point he wanted to get through this meeting as quickly as possible.

"You haven't done anything to decorate your apartment," the stranger said to Peter without looking at him.

"What?" Peter replied in surprise and embarrassment, feeling slighted by the absence of decorations. "I didn't know you could do that."

"I'm quite sure Wind told you to do whatever you like," the Troubadourian retorted.

Peter knew that to be true.

But who in the hell could have known that she meant redecorate your apartment, he silently shouted!

"Actually I haven't been told very much at all about anything, if you want to know the truth," Peter shot back with annoyance.

"I have been informed of your serious problem with aloneness, which undoubtedly prevents you from acting more independently," this man replied, looking down his nose at Peter.

He turned away.

"Having also met Crampton, the trait seems to be endemic to your species."

Peter was dumbfounded and deeply incensed.

What in the fuck is going on here?

For a tiny moment Peter started to feel panic again, trapped as he felt between two repellent options. But then, in a huge unexpected thrust of energy, he forced himself to query the other two Troubadourians about this man in spite of the discourtesy he assumed he was inflicting.

"W . . . w . . . who is this man?" Peter asked Rain.

"This is Balorin who leads the project that brought Drayton Crampton to Troubadour."

"Do you want to be called 'Dr.' too?" Balorin asked with sarcasm.

"Why are you asking me all these loaded questions?" Peter asked to all three of them. "I thought we were here to discuss Drayton Crampton."

"Drayton insists upon being called Dr. Crampton," Balorin continued as if Peter had not spoken.

What's going on here, Peter shouted to himself?

His eyes furtively sought out Wind sitting in the chair farthest from him in the semicircle the four of them occupied. She looked very beautiful, but very far away. He wished very much that he could be alone with her and know how she was feeling. He wanted to bury himself in her beauty, temporarily escaping his growing discomfort.

"I'm looking forward to hearing your analysis of Drayton Crampton," Wind said graciously in response to his look, giving him the support she knew he wanted.

"As I've said so many times before," Balorin intruded. "I can't see why we continue postponing this primitive's return to his own jungle. His insanity is probably quite normal in his own population. So what are we worrying about?"

Why is this guy treating me like I'm not even here?

"I gather you don't think Peter Icarus can contribute anything of importance to this process, Balorin?" Rain inquired.

Well, it's about time, Peter shouted to himself, referring to the first supportive remark in a tight spot that he could remember receiving.

"Why should I have disrespect for this Earthman?" Balorin asked Wind and Rain. "I'm just giving you the benefit of my opinion."

"I don't think you respect Earth people in any way whatsoever," Peter interjected with sharpness. "But strangely what you sarcastically infer is precisely what I feel about interviewing Drayton Crampton. I don't know what I could possibly add to what you guys already know."

"You see," Balorin chimed in with delight. "Even the Earthman agrees with me."

It was one thing for Peter to say this, but quite another to hear this asshole speak for him.

"Look, if you don't want me to do this, I don't need to," Peter exclaimed in Balorin's direction.

Silence followed.

"Is that what you recommend, Balorin?" Rain asked. "That we disembark this meeting?"

"Just what do you plan doing with Crampton?" Balorin asked Peter, ignoring Rain's question.

That threw Peter. His battle with Balorin had completely distracted him from Crampton. The problem was he didn't know what he wanted to do. Not knowing made him nervous and embarrassed.

"I don't know . . ."

He was instantly aware that he'd just given Balorin a huge opportunity to criticize him.

"There's one thing that I do know," he quickly added. "I want to meet him alone."

"Suits me perfectly," Balorin quipped. "Let these two Earthmen deal with each other."

"But how do you guys want to be involved in this?" Peter wondered, not wanting to be at odds with Rain and Wind.

"Is that phrase, 'you guys,' supposed to convey an assumption of intimacy, Dr. Icarus?" Balorin said sarcastically to Peter. "It's the most unpleasant demonstration of familiarity with which I've ever been addressed."

Who is this fucking asshole?

"Look, Mr. Banormin, or whatever your name is, I'm sorry you don't like my figures of speech but . . ."

"Balorin," the slender Troubadourian shouted over Peter in an acrid tone. "And 'mister' is even more disrespectful than 'guys.' It demeans a person by addressing them as a generic. Haven't you learned even the most basic things about us?"

"What is this guy railing about?" Peter demanded to know.

"Like yourself Balorin has distinctive opinions of his own," Rain said. "In this instance he happens to express our common view that, to address someone as a generic, what you would call by their last name, disrespects their individuality. It's why we have only first names like your American Indians."

Rain's agreement with Balorin at first stunned Peter with apprehension. For a moment he was on the verge of panic again. He was tempted to cancel the project himself, and ask all of them to leave his apartment so he could be alone.

"By the way, Balorin," Rain added, "you might be interested in knowing that I rather like the word 'guys.' It portrays a conviviality between like-minded humanoids which is rather appealing."

Peter was deeply relieved that he'd avoided responding precipitously. He would have missed Rain's wonderful act of personal preference for Peter's word, which filled him with support.

"Everyone knows you're a romantic who believes in love, Rain," Balorin replied.

"You don't believe in it, Balorin?" Wind asked.

"How could I possibly feel that way in the company of such a beautiful woman as yourself?" Balorin retorted. "It's not that I don't believe in it. I accept its necessity. It's simply been far too overdone."

"It hasn't been done nearly enough in my experience," Peter interjected.

Both Rain and Wind laughed.

"I hope you're not asking us to pussyfoot around your emotional quirks and vulnerabilities," Balorin interjected with a touch of disdain. "Perhaps these two," he said, pointing to Wind and Ran, "are willing to appease you, but the vast majority of the rest of us are not."

In the silence that followed, Peter realized that what Balorin had just said was true. He thought of Rambler who didn't want to deal with his strong negative feelings.

"I don't need to be pussyfooted around," Peter insisted.

"I think you pretend, Dr. Icarus," Balorin retorted.

Peter didn't know what to say. He didn't want to fight. But he also couldn't stand this man.

"You probably should know," Rain interjected, "that Balorin was abusively treated by Drayton Crampton. It happened in the hours that he spent with the Earthman trying to establish rapport when he first arrived. I suspect his impatience with Earthmen comes most recently from that source."

Balorin always wanted Rain's approval, but hated the way Rain had chosen to give it just now. He felt more exposed than supported. Normally he assiduously avoided his needs being publicly displayed.

"Balorin was very attracted to Crampton's elegant ideas," Rain continued. "Though this early appeal petered out as soon as Drayton arrived and started panicking, heaping abusive insults upon him one after the other. They have not been on speaking terms since."

Balorin was becoming furious with Rain for making his performance the focus of so much attention.

"There is not much point in talking to an ape," Balorin interjected, hoping to silence Rain.

Peter began feeling sympathetic with Crampton for having to deal with such an asshole. But he was getting tired of bantering with the intruder, and wanted to get on with the task.

"Since we're here, I guess to prepare for my seeing Crampton, it would be helpful if you told me what you can about your experience with him so far," he said, trying to take over the meeting.

"Drayton Crampton," Rain began, "is convinced that he's still on Earth held hostage by what he insists is a foreign power. Sometimes he is convinced that we are also a race of aliens who have taken over part of Earth, intending to conquer it all. He sometimes insists that he is being held so that we might study him, thereby to learn about human weaknesses, so that our conquest can be properly planned for success. He has expressed other paranoid ideas to us, but these are the most prominent ones."

"My god," Peter exclaimed. "This guy does sound like he's rather crazy."

"Crampton has been studying us, writing furiously every night on the computer he brought with him, printing it, and then erasing the file," Rain continued. "He hides the growing pile of printed analysis under his bed. In an effort to understand him better, we did once read some of it when he was asleep. We discovered that it was mostly his views of us, which didn't help us much to decide whether he was ready to return home. So we gave up that strategy after the first time."

"We realize that you probably disapprove of this action on our part," Wind added. "Which we accept and understand."

"It's true that I prefer a stricter privacy," Peter replied. "But I don't in this instance. There are times with severely disturbed patients when one must act in their behalf, even if that violates pure confidentiality."

"I'm relieved to hear you say that," Wind said.

"Actually I'd like to know what his theories are about you," Peter said. "They might help me understand him."

"He believes that we are a weak, softhearted people who accomplish almost nothing, though we apparently have powerful technology to compensate for this shortcoming, probably built, he insists, by a superior more enlightened species before our time. He insists that, in spite of our advanced knowledge and technology, we have become decadent, lazy, highly selfish people who spend our time 'playing with (our) belly buttons,' is a phrase from his writing. It is clear that he wants desperately to get this information back to his own people since it would help immeasurably to defend Earth against our intrusion."

"The guy has developed an entire paranoid system to explain his presence on Troubadour," Peter exclaimed.

"This is why we feared sending him back to Earth in his present condition," Wind remarked.

"Okay," Peter replied. "I think I'm as prepared as I'm going to get. So why don't we proceed."

Both Wind and Rain hesitated for a moment.

"Have we forgotten anything that would help you?" Wind asked.

Peter was surprised to hear her voice. He had forgotten for a while about their pending issue.

"I don't think so," he replied. "Though I appreciate your concern for me."

"Above all else, Peter Icarus," Wind announced, "we don't want your visiting this man adversely to affect your own experience on Troubadour."

"Thank you," Peter said, "that's very good of you to be so concerned for me. But I think I'll be just fine. I've been doing this kind of work for years. Of course I might have difficulty with him, but it won't throw me off too much. It's my profession."

"I'm relieved to hear you say that, Peter," Rain added.

Balorin muttered something under his breath that sounded to Peter like, "Now we get the two monkeys playing with each other." But Peter was focused upon the task at hand and dismissed this sarcastic innuendo.

"I'm ready," Peter said.

"Curiously you only have to go downstairs to meet him," Wind said. "He lives in this city."

"You're kidding," Peter exclaimed. "He's been downstairs all this time?"

"Yes," Rain replied.

"On the seventy-fourth floor, a door to the right of the elevator with his name on it," Wind added.

"Should I call first?" Peter asked.

"Whatever you think," Rain replied.

"I'll just go," Peter said.

He started to leave.

"I may be there for as much as an hour."

"That's not a problem, that is if we may use your apartment's amenities until your return," Rain said.

"Please make yourself entirely at home," Peter replied. "See you soon."

As Peter left he noticed that Balorin wasn't paying him the slightest bit of attention.

Outside in the hallway he suddenly realized that his anticipated worries about Wind and how she felt about him had proved to be almost nothing.

Rain was right. She did remain peripheral. But how could I have forgotten to be worried about how she felt?

Drayton Crampton

Peter knocked on Drayton Crampton's front door and waited for several moments, but there was no answer.

What do I do if he doesn't answer the door?

Peter knocked again.

"Stop pretending that you can't get in," someone shouted from inside.

"Don't you have to open the door?" Peter shouted back.

Again there was no reply for several moments.

This is getting a little awkward, Peter thought.

"Open," the voice said from inside.

The door opened. Peter hesitated on the threshold, peering in as far as he could see, but saw no one.

"May I come in?" he asked.

Again there was no reply.

"My name is Peter Icarus. Like you I came from Earth. What's more I'm also in the psychotherapy business like you. I know who you are, namely a rather famous psychiatrist in my profession. I would like to talk to you."

Slowly a man peaked out from around a corner to peer carefully at Peter for several moments.

"You don't look like one of them," Drayton said cryptically.

"I'm not. May I come in?"

"No," was the reply, as the face disappeared once again into the kitchen.

I'm not going to miss this, so why did I ask him?

Peter slowly walked in and looked around.

Crampton's apartment was very much like his own, though he noticed immediately that the window was covered. That surprised him.

"I'm inside," Peter said almost without thinking, announcing his own actions so that Crampton was fully informed.

"Am I supposed to applaud?" Drayton asked sarcastically.

"That would be nice, but I'm quite sure you would rather be doing something else," Peter replied.

"What do you want?" Drayton asked.

"To talk."

"Why?"

That question threw Peter.

Drayton peered out of the kitchen to look at him.

"Your reason must need concealing if it takes you so long to reveal it," Crampton said contemptuously, and disappeared again.

"My answer wasn't clear to me at first," Peter acknowledged.

He knew that for a paranoid anything but the truth instantly smelled rotten.

"I'd like to help you get home," Peter announced.

Crampton emerged from hiding and came out of the kitchen to stare at Peter with disdain.

"You must be kidding yourself," he proclaimed. "They've got you just as captured as I am, and obviously much more hoodwinked and boondoggled."

Silence.

"I'm here voluntarily," Peter replied.

"Horseshit," Drayton replied, returning to the kitchen.

Peter followed him, stopping in that portion of the living room adjacent to the kitchen, once more giving Crampton plenty of space.

"I understand they've been holding you against your will," Peter said.

Drayton looked up from the meal he was eating.

"That's supposed to be news," he quipped, acting as if he was bored already by Peter's presence.

"I can see that I've interrupted your meal," Peter remarked. "Would you like me to wait in the living room?"

Drayton looked up at him with contempt in his face.

"Oh, cut the bullshit," he exclaimed. "Your false courtesy informs me that you're a plant. Obviously these aliens have brainwashed you into believing that you're here voluntarily. They've been spying on me for days, though I haven't revealed anything they want. And now they've sent you to find out my secrets."

"You have secrets?" Peter asked, realizing instinctively that the word had unintentionally leaked out of a more revealing part of Crampton.

Drayton, feeling instantly threatened and alert, came out sparring. "What are your secrets, Icarus?" he asked with a cunning malice, instantly taking the initiative. "If as you claim we're both on Troubadour, what made you risk so much to come here?"

Peter was shaken with the incisiveness accuracy of Crampton's surgical intrusion into the vulnerable parts of him.

Like all structurally damaged humans, Drayton vigorously defended against being vulnerable to anyone. In the service of that need he had an uncanny ability to sense where emotional vulnerability lay in others, sometimes with pinpoint accuracy. In fact, this hypersensitivity to vulnerability is what had really funded the principle ideas of his clever and intricate theories.

But because of his own emotional closeness, he employed his keen perceptiveness in very primitive ways. Get to theirs before they get to yours, was his principle strategy. Without really knowing any of the facts, he'd touched Peter in a very sensitive spot. But if Peter touched him emotionally, Peter got through right to the core of Crampton without hardly any resistance.

To restore his composure Peter reminded himself that he'd come to help this man.

"May I sit down?" he asked.

"No."

"I think I will anyway as long as I'm here," Peter announced. "I prefer to talk sitting down. My back isn't what it used to be."

"So you stepped on cracks and broke your mother's back," Crampton quipped, making fun of Peter. "And now you're whining 'cause your pelvis is declining."

That surgical cleverness reached fertile angst in Peter, even though Drayton had no idea why. Of course he really didn't care to know. He simply wanted to score. He had this time. His uncanny quip had reached Peter's sexual problems.

"That got you," Crampton chortled with great satisfaction.

The malice of Drayton's attack was all Peter needed to remove himself from vulnerability, to put it on the shelf until he could think about it later. Crampton made the mistake of pushing too hard.

"We've crossed paths before," Peter said casually, his comfort restored the moment he spoke the words. "I've heard you lecture on Earth," he said.

Drayton laughed nervously, taken aback by the surprise Peter had evoked in him with his announcement of former contact, surprise constituting a big deal to a paranoid, whose confidence is built almost entirely upon knowing everything.

"So you have the delusion you've seen me before, probably in a vision of your intimidating father."

That struck emotional pay dirt. But it didn't shake Peter this time.

"At the Institute for Research in Psychology three years ago," Peter added, "when you discussed the origins of splitting."

The precision of Peter's memory unsettled Crampton by impressing him. He recovered by shifting instantly to a more familiar issue.

"They've got you believing this is another planet," he said derisively, regaining his pretence of cold composure.

Peter winced a little at this constant attack, reminding him of having to deal with Balorin pulling the same stunts when he got back to his apartment.

"Cat got your tongue?" Drayton goaded.

"Just my own thoughts," Peter replied. "But why all this bantering. The objective is to get you home."

Crampton was trapped in the truth. Getting home was precisely what he wanted more than anything. His vulnerability had finally been reached.

He shot a fierce glance at Peter, feeling a tiny, very hidden bit of respect for the other man. He looked for vulnerability on Peter's face, but could find no crack in Peter's demeanor.

He grasped desperately at a fleeting moment of superiority, which derived from Peter having attended his lectures.

"Attended my lectures, huh? I don't remember you," he added dismissively.

"We didn't meet. I simply attended. They were very impressive, on borderline character structure."

"That was a long time ago," Drayton snapped dismissively in an effort to dilute a surging yearning to be back inside the status and respect of those public appearances, in order to escape his present ignominious circumstances.

Peter sensed something emotionally different had happened. He decided to wait for it to reveal itself.

Peter's silence added to Drayton's growing anxiety. He stood and wandered into the living room as if Peter weren't there. He sat down at the draped window with his back to Peter, rested his chin on his upturned hand, elbow-anchored to the chair's arm, and began musing as if he were alone.

Peter followed him, sitting down in a chair perhaps twelve feet from the other man, once more giving him plenty of room.

They sat in silence for a while.

"Why are you still following me around?" Drayton asked sarcastically when Peter's silent presence finally got to him.

"The Troubadourians would like to send you home."

Drayton shot a suspicious glance at him.

"How about instantly?" he demanded.

"They've asked me to be sure that you're ready to go."

"Aagh, so now we finally get the truth," Crampton shouted in triumph, jumping on Peter's words like a predatory animal.

He'd finally restored his confidence.

"You're the jailer they've put in charge of my confinement, the shrink they've chosen to judge my credibility. But of course, I should have known they would choose someone in my own profession whom they could manipulate. It's what the Nazi's did so effectively to the Jews, got some of them to police the killing of their own people in the concentration camps."

"Your leaving is not my decision," Peter retorted. "It's theirs."

Drayton swiveled his chair around to face Peter and stared at him with intense disdain! He wanted to annihilate Peter!

Peter winced at the intense assault of Crampton's hateful contempt. It was more intense than he'd experienced with any of his patients, reminding him only of his father's angry face when he was a little boy. His composure visibly shook for an instant, though he quickly recovered.

The highly perceptive Crampton leaped to take advantage of this brief lapse in comfort.

"Your impressive calm just gave way," he chortled with deep self-satisfaction. "But I'm not done playing with you, so you still have a few remaining moments of my company," he added as if he were being enormously magnanimous.

He resumed his contemptuous glare.

Again Peter found it very difficult to maintain his composure while looking at Drayton's disdainful stare.

What's the matter with you, Peter challenged himself? Why do you let him get to you so much?

The yellow cat-eyes of the Banorin hungered from inside Crampton's contemptuous stare, momentarily mesmerizing Peter inside humiliation!

He wants to grind me into the dust.

Peter instantly realized that it was his own aggression that he was afraid of!

Look away, was his instant advice to himself.

He looked away.

This asshole is a fucking son of a bitch. You don't have to like him to help him.

Peter looked at Crampton again. This time, to his enormous surprise, around the edges of Drayton's contempt Peter could see evidence of a small boy's pout.

My god, has that always been there, and I just didn't see it?

His shrink's brain started working again.

This man's hostile posturing is both menacing and entrapping, so don't deny it. Be truthful to yourself, and keep your distance. You don't have to look at him while he looks at you.

He paused a moment.

And remember that fear lurks strongly beneath the bluster of that desperate strength he's asserting, Peter continued privately. He doesn't want me to be able to keep up with him, so he's resorting to silent gestures and threatening innuendoes to force me to falter.

Drayton instantly caught the shift in Peter's emotional experience.

"It's time for you to go," he interjected with a false triumph, using his will to claim that he was still in control at precisely the point when he was losing it. "There's absolutely nothing you can do to help me. You've lost your composure at least twice, which exposes professional incompetence as you know."

"Not faltering, Dr. Crampton. Hesitating. Until it finally occurred to me that I don't like talking to a man who obviously believes he must assault whomever he addresses."

Peter's recovery stunned Drayton. But what froze him in place for a moment was Peter's clever ability to express criticism without being offensive! He blinked and shouted the most diminishing remark that he could come up with at the moment.

"Is that all you've got to say?" he expressed with disdain.

"If you could have things go your way," Peter instantly queried, completely ignoring Drayton's question, "what would you like to do?"

"Blaa," Drayton blurted, amplifying his disdain.

"Is that all you've got to say?" Peter retorted, repeating Crampton's last words.

That shook Crampton. He was suddenly terrified of losing the edge in this verbal war, forcing him to play his ace in the hole, though doing so seriously foreshortened the time he'd wanted to torment this weak mouse.

"Alright!" he shouted like the King or mother reminding everyone that he's the boss or she's the mother.

"You claim to be able to help me! Then I'll tell you precisely what to do!" he disdainfully spit at Peter as if he were instructing an underling. "I will leave this place immediately under the following conditions! You can be the messenger boy and deliver my demands to your masters!"

Instead of threatening him, Drayton's assault triggered intense curiosity. What motivates such insipid and determined acridness?

The answer was immediate.

He doesn't want to hurt me! He wants me to feel his hurt, to be him for a while, so I know what hurt really means to him, which is nothing less than the terrifying humiliation he's tried to project upon me. He fears that humiliation is capable of destroying his personal integrity. If he can give his hurt to me, then it will no longer belong to him, no longer hurt him. It will be mine. This need for excessive personal power makes him believe, whether he knows it or not, in the kind of projective magical transference of evil from one person to another that magic makes possible.

So why not give him what he wants, Peter suddenly asked himself? What's the harm?

"Sounds fine to me," Peter retorted, accepting Drayton's instruction. "Is there more to the message you would like me to deliver?"

Drayton was enormously surprised that Peter had so successfully escaped his withering contempt by the outrageous decision to accept his right to command, as if it were perfectly harmless to do so.

Suddenly afraid that he might not achieve his goal of humiliating Peter, he quickly resumed his orders.

"To begin with, I will leave today, immediately!" Crampton demanded. "What's more I will be taking with me all the notes that I've written since I arrived. No one is to examine or copy them. And I'm also going to take their computer with me."

"I'm told their computers don't work on Earth."

"So what's the big surprise that you should so easily be duped into believing what they tell you?" Drayton replied with intense sarcasm.

"Are there any other conditions?" Peter asked.

"Just one," Crampton snarled with an intense feeling of anticipated pleasure. "That I have the opportunity to interrogate you personally right now," he added as if he was sure that he would soon be gloating.

Drayton was sure this move would deeply threaten Peter, fully stealing back the power position. But Peter didn't flinch for a moment. Basically he had nothing to hide. It was perhaps the largest difference between the two men.

"Fire away," he replied.

Something shifted slightly inside of Drayton. He still deeply mistrusted Peter, and would leap at any opportunity to slay his competence, but Peter had prevailed. He had, at least for a moment, created a tiny pocket of trust in Crampton toward him.

In fact some might claim that he was unconsciously trying to verify Peter's power. This view would hold that he assaulted everything in order to secure reassurance of its reliability, of its survivability, furiously biting the gold to be sure of its authenticity.

The truth was that he was intensely curious about just who Peter was, and why he was having such an easier time of it than he was. It wasn't that Crampton admitted this truth, but he acted from it, as if by "taking it in hand" he could control it.

"Why did you come here?" Drayton asked with derision.

Peter instantly sensed the enormous potential of the present-moment. Crampton had just ventured a tiny bit of trusting him, unconsciously letting Peter know that part of him wanted to know Peter more personally—a dangerous truth the vulnerability of which Drayton hid with his contemptuous delivery. This seeking part of him wanted to cooperate, something that he could never have done consciously.

You must tell him the truth, Peter thought. He will smell a lie no matter how tiny it is. He decided to confide.

"I've always liked space and space travel," Peter replied. "If it were a century later I would have volunteered to be a moon or Mars psychologist. But the most important reason I came is that my life on Earth had in some very important ways never been right. I was, at the core deeply unhappy. I came here looking for possible answers, for something new that might redeem my spirit."

"You fool!" Crampton shouted contemptuously, triumphantly. "To think that accepting their hokey invitation was the road to a better life makes you a sorrier human specimen than I originally thought!"

To his complete surprise Peter did not hear this attack as threatening. It felt more like a plea.

This was the first time this had ever happened to him so cleanly in response to such an assault. He could clearly see that Drayton's envious attempts to destroy what he really needed from Peter—help to get home—were designed to destroy the strength that Peter possessed. If he destroyed any evidence of it in Peter with the greenness of his envy, he wouldn't have to see it in front of him anymore, making him feel unbearably deprived. In effect nobody would have it. But most important, Peter could no longer flaunt it in front of him.

Suddenly Drayton made complete sense to Peter. Crampton had to act in the ways he did in order to reestablish his sense of control over his own life. A highly intellectualized man of extreme intelligence, he'd been stripped of his sense of superiority when he came to Troubadour, and he urgently needed to get it back to restore equilibrium in himself. And the only way he knew how to get it was to abuse Peter in the way he, Drayton must have been abused originally as a boy, by the perpetual threat of humiliation.

Peter knew what to do.

Praise him at your own expense, Peter suggested to himself. It's no skin off your back.

"Perhaps I am a fool as you say," Peter replied. "There is no question that on Earth you are a far more famous man than I. Your accomplishments are well-known. I have admired them greatly myself."

Drayton was dumbfounded by Peter's response. His mouth momentarily dropped open, though quickly he turned away. This man had just made him feel good. Under no circumstances could he show that either to himself or to Peter. It would have meant utter defeat, which would render him helplessly exposed to what he desperately needed. He was paralyzed.

Something snapped in his mind, as if he'd suddenly been transported to a different consciousness, perhaps imitating the tiny moments of safety he had occasionally found as an embattled boy.

"Have you been outside?" he asked in a curiously, for him incredibly moderate tone.

Very surprised at this sudden display of trust, Peter took only a second to shift the feeling of his reply.

"Yes," Peter said in a gentle voice, joining the softness of this tiny moment of respite from the war.

"Have you seen the weird animals they've concocted to frighten us?" Drayton asked.

"One nearly knocked me cold."

"They couldn't get me outside except once," Crampton confided. "I've simply refused."

Silence.

"So you've read one of my papers," Drayton remarked.

"Several, and heard you speak twice."

"Couldn't get enough the first time," Drayton chuckled with a self-satisfied chortle, though curiously without much of the envious venom that had previously existed in such remarks.

"I couldn't understand everything the first time," Peter admitted.

"You've got a high-powered brain. It took me two lectures to get it."

Drayton eyed him suspiciously. The flattery, though he took it in voraciously, restored his mistrust.

"You don't expect me to believe that you mean all this flattery you've just showered upon me?" he remarked sarcastically.

"Believe as you like," Peter replied. "It's true."

He's snapped back to his normal suspicious self, Peter thought. That other tiny piece of him exposed itself for just a moment or two. But perhaps that's all he needed.

"Is there anything else you want to ask or to tell me?" Peter queried.

"No."

It's time to go, Peter. Don't overstay.

"Then I'll depart. I expect the Troubadourians will soon be in touch with you. I'm going to recommend they return you to Earth today, and that they accept all of your conditions."

"You don't really expect me to believe they will?" Drayton added sarcastically.

"But I believe they will. Goodbye and good luck," Peter said, walking toward the door.

He slowed down to give Crampton a chance to reply if he wished, but there was none. He left.

As he walked down the hallway he realized that for several moments Crampton had seemed almost normal.

A sanity blip momentarily took him out of hell.

Triumph

I did it. I aced that session and mastered the arrogance of that son-of-a-bitch.

It was a great relief to express the anger he felt about being addressed so contemptuously by Crampton. He knew his own feelings had nothing to do with his meeting with Drayton. But he also knew one doesn't do this kind of work unscathed, and remains in emotional balance only if personal strain is openly acknowledged.

It wasn't that he wanted to do anything about his anger with Drayton, such as retaliate. In fact quite the opposite was true. He wanted Crampton to return to Earth in as stable a condition as possible. He was very sympathetic with what coming to Troubadour had done to him. He was glad to have helped the man, and now glad for himself that he'd also acknowledged the pain of doing so, though his triumph made it entirely worthwhile. It was better than a fee. He felt terrific. As he walked down the hall away from Crampton's apartment his feet were barely touching the floor.

Something really clicked for me in there. I did things I've never done so well before, even close to it.

He stepped onto the elevator and pushed the button to go upstairs entirely without any awareness that he was doing it.

He softened to me, even confided in me a little. That's remarkable for a paranoid to do at any time, let alone the first time he meets you, particularly when he's flaming with suspicion. I showed him that IQ is only what you do with it.

Peter suddenly realized that he'd been standing in the elevator with its door open for a while. Which reminded him where he was headed. It was the first time he'd thought about the group waiting for him in his apartment since he walked through Drayton's front door. It was one thing to feel the excitement of triumph, and quite another to imagine sharing it with others.

How do you brag to a man like Rain? He's so far ahead of me in evolution that anything I celebrate would seem paltry to him. Then there's Wind. How do you strut your stuff in front of someone who's probably already disgusted with you? As for sour-pussed Banner-man, I wouldn't give him the time of day. If I did he would surely mess with it. Shit, I need the memory of what happened intact just like it feels now. I don't have so many good ones I can afford to lose this one.

He headed slowly and reluctantly toward his apartment trying to figure out what to do. He was still figuring when his front door opened in front of him. He could hear Balorin speaking inside.

"Leaving that idiot here is like turning the planet into one of those hospitals for the mentally insane that still exist on Earth."

Fuck. Just what I didn't need.

Peter jumped to the conclusion that Balorin was talking about him.

"The expense of this project is enormous," Balorin continued. "There are large numbers of Troubadourians who have begun to consider whether it's worth the huge investment of resources."

"Are you suggesting, Balorin my boy," Rain interjected, "that the tides of public opinion are turning against us, threatening to disband the Earth Project?"

Oh, my god, Peter shouted to himself. He called him "my boy." Is Balorin his secret son?

"Perhaps I am," Balorin replied respectfully "But for now I'm just insisting that you consider the validity of that point of view."

"But I have already done that, Balorin, and have decided to disagree with you," Rain retorted. "Out of respect for your views I must confess truthfully that I'm acting out of a very personal desire when I avidly support this project, specifically that I'm having too much fun for it to stop. I intend fully to enjoy this experience through to its very last breath, whenever that may be."

"You are too addicted to fun to have a fully complete perspective," Balorin retorted dismissively, though in a very respectful tone. "It runs your life. Which is probably alright for a man of your advanced years, though I hope to avoid such excessive self-indulgence when I reach old age."

"Your concern is thoughtful," Rain replied. "Sometimes I am concerned for you too, Balorin," Rain replied very gently, expressing warmth for the younger man.

Shit, he is his son, Peter exclaimed. Jesus.

Peter was very disappointed.

Rain's got to feel estranged from that idiot. It must be terrible to have a son like that. No wonder he didn't want to tell me about him.

"I fear sometimes that suspicion is running your life," Rain added soberly. "It deeply disturbs both your connection to other people, as well as the linkages between the parts of your body, weaving the deteriorating effects of arthritis into the connections you have with nature, all of which I would hope to spare you."

Wow. They think of immune-defective diseases as emotionally caused.

"We have engineered the solution to that problem, dear mother," Balorin proudly retorted, referring to Rain as "mother" as a sign of child-ness in old age. "There are cures. Fear not, old woman. I will not suffer as you have."

Of course Peter took it that Rain was his mother.

Now I'm sure of it. He must be his son.

"I suffer from only one thing, Balorin," Rain announced.

Silence.

"Must I beg you to tell me the secret of that innuendo," Balorin interjected, his patience waning.

"Loneliness," Rain said.

"Loneliness? Why everyone on Troubadour thinks you're the cat's meow, which by the way is the only piece of Earth-slang that I enjoy using. You've got the most respect of anyone I know. So what's there to be lonely about?"

I would be lonely too if I had a son like you, asshole, Peter retorted to himself.

"The loneliness of old age has to do with whether or not others companion your newer and best parts, or just your past outdated parts."

"But didn't I just get through saying that everyone thinks your parts are wonderful?" Balorin retorted.

"My best parts come not from others approbation, but from having fun, my boy, an attitude which creates the humor that often issues from me. It's probably why people seem to feel I'm the cat's meow as you suggest. Whatever I do touches them only lightly, which makes it so much easier for them to hear what I have to say. It's how I learned to make an offer that can't be refused, by having fun no matter what comes my way, or whatever others do or say, which seems to produce the easiest kind of things to hear, making the unfamiliar come primarily in order to cheer."

Oh, that was so good, Peter privately exclaimed. That was really good. Christ, I would make him a lot happier as his son.

Unwittingly, Peter softly spoke the last three words out loud.

Wind heard him, noticing instantly that he was at the front door.

"Peter," she exclaimed, "you're back."

Balorin was startled by Peter's sudden appearance, but needed instantly to deny it. He accomplished this by unconsciously assigning his body the task of acting out the energy-response to being startled, so his mind wouldn't have to deal with it.

His body moved as if it was taking orders from someone else, jumped him out of his chair, and hurried him into the kitchen without acknowledging Peter.

How painful, Peter thought as he walked in and sat down. To have a son turn out so different from yourself, such that the intimacy you once felt together years before, when one of you was a child, no longer produces the substance of affection that affirms that traditional closeness, leaving memory alone to sustain its reality.

Peter looked over at Wind. He'd been avoiding seeing her. As soon as his eyes touched hers, he quickly glanced away, as if he were touching something that might prove to be too hot to handle.

She was smiling.

He felt instantly relieved. It suddenly occurred to him that he was sitting with the two people on Troubadour that he could most trust, Wind and Rain. He suddenly wanted very much to share with them what had happened at Crampton's.

Out of the corner of his eye he saw Balorin lurking at the entrance to the kitchen, and instantly lost the desire to share.

"Welcome back, Peter," Rain said.

"It went well?" Wind queried.

"I think so," Peter replied cautiously.

Balorin shot back into the room, suddenly realizing that his kitchen move was not such a good idea. He needed to be present to deal with this Earthly intrusion into his territory.

"How did you find his majesty this morning?" Balorin shoved into the conversation, expressing the word, "majesty," with great contempt.

Peter suddenly felt an impish desire to joust with Balorin. A rhyming response to his question jumped into mind.

"I found him constantly prancing to hide his fear of dancing with me," Peter replied, instantly delighted with the precise accuracy of his rhyming description of what happened.

Rain laughed, sitting up on the edge of his chair with a quick reply of his own, delighted to have an opportunity to play his favorite game.

"And what advance was he struggling to chance, as he hid from his fear of dancing with you?" Rain queried.

To his enormous surprise Peter instantly thought of a reply.

"I think it was any stance of mine which might entrance his kind to find purchase in me," Peter retorted with a giddy laughter, excited and rather over stimulated playing such a sophisticated game on equal terms with this giant of a man.

"Arrogance like romance compels utter compliance," Rain quipped with joy. "So neither must be tried, or he'll be fit to be tied," he added with a mockingly ominous flair.

Peter laughed.

"He did confide," Peter retorted. "But hearing so now he would deride."

Peter could not believe the lines coming out of him.

Wind watched with fascination this sonorous conjunction of sounds that expressed profound meaning, which tennis-matched back and forth between Rain and Peter. She was dazzled by the powerful thoughts evoked by what she'd always thought of as a playful children's game that produced mostly silliness. But now she understood what Rain had always loved, and had wanted her to join.

Suddenly she wanted to participate, though she couldn't imagine herself actually doing it.

Balorin had become furious as he watched the repartee between Peter and his spiritual father with increasing alarm. Rain had been his mentor for many years when both were much younger. He still felt a deep devotion to the ancient Troubadourian, though this was a passion he carefully concealed inside a fierce competition with Rain's ideas, many of which he agreed with, though he never mentioned that part of himself to Rain.

Balorin celebrated his gift of learning from Rain by trying instantly to improve upon what Rain said. It represented his attempt to apply Rain's most basic advice, which was, "follow your own heart and mind, and improve if you can what you've learned."

As a result Balorin secretly prided himself on his differences with Rain, feeling that in casting an alternative vision he was creating his own originality in the history of thought, just as Rain had done before him. In this fantasy he became the next master-mentor as Rain had done, thus seizing a part of what he regarded as a spiritual, dynastic succession of leadership. He would be the third sage of the New Troubadour, one of the titles by which Rain was informally known, as the second. The first was a species of ancient humanity now extinct.

But now suddenly this primitive Earthman was taking Rain's affectionate attention away from him, making his whole future feel like it was about to crumble around him. This upstart was stirring up in Rain a kind of playful excitement that Balorin had not only never been able to evoke, but he'd never even seen it before so vividly displayed.

Balorin had always hoped, and occasionally believed that he was Rain's favorite. As far as he could tell no one younger than Rain had ever bettered his wisdom. Balorin intended to be that one, though he would never dare to tell Rain.

Now suddenly this grossly inferior stranger seemed to be capturing the heart of Balorin's hero, something he'd wanted to do with great desire, but never hoped to accomplish. He'd chosen instead to be satisfied with the inheritance he could gain by his own skill improving upon Rain's ideas, producing a private victory that no one else shared, or could ever harm. His chief rival for Chief Sage, the genius Tanfroon, was so acerbic that his brilliant cleverness went largely unappreciated, even by Rain.

And now this stranger had appeared out of nowhere to be not only a rival, but perhaps even to have forged ahead in the race.

Balorin was stunned. He'd never felt so deeply overpowered. He was dumbfounded to realize that, not only had he lost his favored position, but he also didn't have the slightest idea how to restore himself to his rightful inheritance! Defeat, a feeling he'd never seriously had before, started to seep into his psyche.

"And there he waits, afraid of his hates, needing you to be true while trying to make you cuckoo," Rain summarized.

Peter laughed.

"That's exactly what he did," Peter exclaimed. "He tried very hard to unravel my petard."

"He must have failed or you would not be so full of prevailed," Rain replied.

A rhyme finally came to a deeply frustrated Balorin directed squarely at Peter.

"It's the homicide of comfort I can't abide, which follows your kind's every emotional tide, making your uncivilized display something for which I will no longer pay!"

Aggression flooded out of Peter, at first frightening him. But he let it ride, and to his surprise it produced a perfect rhyme.

"The only good tidings of your confidings are the awful smell of your prideful deridings," Peter retorted with an increasing sense of angry satisfaction.

Balorin was stunned that Peter had fielded his critical assault so effectively. He had seriously underestimated his opponent.

I must not do that again, Balorin thought. Retire and consider.

Wind was deeply surprised at the confidence and ease with which Peter responded to Balorin's provocations. She'd seen the fear in Peter's eyes when he first arrived on Troubadour, and many times since, including the moment he stood in the doorway returning from Drayton Crampton's. But now she'd seen him stand up with pride to face what frightened him, and remain within moderate bounds when he replied.

This man has deeply changed, Wind said to herself. Something unusual has happened.

"Peter," she said with great interest. "I want to hear about what happened with Drayton Crampton."

"Yes, let's hear more about that," Rain agreed.

"Well," Peter began, "it was actually very strange. But I think I managed to walk into the realm of his paranoia and found a place which I could occupy that didn't completely tie my hands nor reduce me to a lying absurdity, both of which he tried to accomplish with great application of talent during most of the time we were together. Essentially he was perpetually insulting me."

"Just as he has with us," Wind offered. "But you seem so skilled in dealing with his acts of aggression."

Peter was very encouraged by Wind's positive assessment of him.

But does she mean it, Peter asked himself? Maybe so, but it must be just her professional feeling about me, nothing more.

"It was clear that he trusted no one here," Peter continued his story. "He regarded me as your duped flunky. So my problem was to find how I could help him."

He paused.

"First, I should keep my promise to him," Peter continued. "Which is to let you know that I recommend you return him to Earth today and on all of his conditions. Which are that he goes back with all of his typed notes which no one either copies or examines, all of which I was sure you'd accept."

"Of course," Rain replied. "But please explain why you think he's ready to return to Earth?"

"He's as ready as he'll ever be," Peter replied.

"If you asked the majority of Troubadourians, you'd find out we're ready for you to return as well," Balorin intruded. "Though some present don't seem to realize that yet."

Peter felt furious about this interruption. But when he noticed that neither Wind nor Rain were paying any attention to Balorin's remark, instead of being captured by his anger at this man's provocation, he joined them and moved on.

"There is no question that he was deeply shaken from his personal foundation when he came here," Peter continued. "There is also no question that he retreated into a paranoid perspective about everything around him. But what is also true is that this paranoid system is relatively stable. What's more it's directed at something from which he can escape, thereby leaving the enemy behind so to speak, at least for the moment, until, in some fashion he finally faces the consequences of his experience on Troubadour, probably much later when his mind isn't any longer trapped in a paranoid fever."

Rain laughed with enjoyment.

"Paranoid fever," he repeated. "What a wonderful metaphor."

Peter laughed, deeply reassured by Rain's enthusiasm.

You have grandiosity fever, Earth-boy, Balorin quipped to himself!

"I do have some concern about him when he returns," Peter said, "and I will probably get in touch with him at some point just to check up on how he's doing. But I don't think you can do anything more for him here other than to release him on his terms."

"Then that's what we shall do," Rain replied. "Any disagreement, he queried looking only at Wind? Of course we already know Balorin's vote."

Wind had continued to watch Peter very closely. She was struck by the buoyant enthusiasm that now accompanied many of his utterances. She'd never seen or heard him behave this way before.

"I'd love to hear the rest of the story," Wind said graciously to Peter.

Maybe she does care. At least maybe she's not so mad at me.

"I guess for me the most interesting part of my experience with Drayton," Peter explained, "is that I may actually have helped this man emotionally consolidate himself a little, though I don't really know for sure."

"How did he behave toward you as fellow Earthman?" Rain asked.

"He spent most of his time provoking me by aggressive assaults upon my skill or integrity."

"Why would he do that, do you think?" Rain asked.

"It finally occurred to me that he wanted either to discredit me as a helpful person, or to find out that I was firm, steady, and unflappable, which would mean that I could take the brunt of his assault without flinching or retaliating," Peter replied.

"Aagh. Now that enlightens me," Rain exclaimed. "So an anchor is what he needed all this time. It was clear to us that he needed to restore his self-esteem. But we couldn't figure any way to help him do it, in effect to connect him to reliability as you have done. I rather like your definition of sanity and reliability in the self-experience."

"I'm not sure that I did all that," Peter replied, not wanting to make unproven claims for fear that Balorin might expose him for bragging. He knew Balorin was sitting there biding his time until Peter gave him something new to pounce upon.

"But since he was so consistently attacking me, I chose, in a manner of speaking to join his game. I told him that I knew he was a more famous man on Earth than I was, and that I deeply respected his considerable intellectual accomplishments. Though I think the remark he got the most satisfaction out of was that it took me attending two of his lectures before I understood his theory."

Rain laughed uproariously for several moments. It was infectious. Wind couldn't help herself. She joined him. Peter followed, deeply enjoying their shared laughter.

"That's the sneakiest way I've ever heard of making another person feel better about themselves!" Rain exclaimed. "You are a crafty devil, my clever Peter Icarus of Earth!"

Peter's heart was filled with immense pleasure. This giant of a man was admiring him. It felt seriously unreal. His thoughts raced through the dictionary of assumptions he had about himself, and watched as they all started to topple.

Balorin was ready to explode. Not only was an opportunity to counterattack not appearing, but this upstart was racing ahead of him by leaps and bounds.

He leaped to his feet perhaps more to deny and reverse the tremendous sinking feeling that started to overtake him. But then in order to hide the urgency this act expressed, he pretending he'd stood in order to stretch. Though when he stretched he did so without the total commitment it deserved, leaving his stretch prematurely, making it seem not entirely sincere.

"Have you ever noticed, Dr. Icarus," he exclaimed, "how compellingly drawn to suffering your people are?"

With a contemptuous flourish he loudly cracked his knuckles.

It worked. Peter felt shaken. Balorin touched a highly vulnerable spot in Peter's heart, his suffering! He had done a lot of it in his lifetime and was ashamed of that fact. He had always felt it made him inferior to be so deeply unhappy.

And yet what next came out of Peter's mouth carried a strength-of-conviction that he almost didn't recognize.

"Suffering deserves more respect."

"It already has too much," Balorin retorted. "Your people have made it the cornerstone of your identity."

Tired, having reached his emotional limits, perhaps guilty about his victory over the Troubadourian, Peter was drawn into the feud

"That is fucking ridiculous, you asshole!"

"You see what I mean," Balorin said to Wind and Rain. "He's deeply primitive and extremely violent."

He turned to Peter.

"Your most evolved culture is descended from the act of a god dying for your sins," Balorin chortled. "That seems the essence of a serious belief in suffering."

"Oh, stop it!" Peter exclaimed.

Instantly Peter knew he was making a mistake. He didn't need or want to banter with this man. He had leaped into the fray out of a habit that was still intact enough to drawn him in, but no longer strong enough to hold him firmly in its grip.

"We've worked very hard to eliminate violence from our experience," Balorin exclaimed. "This primitive man brings it back to us in every movement of his body, every gesture of his being, every emotional explosion, all of which, to an enlightened Troubadourian would evoke only peaceful reaction. How foolish for us to continue paying for being abused! It's precisely his love of suffering that creates this savage urge to violence. Flip violence on its back and you'll find suffering urging it along!"

Peter was reminded of pretending acting inferior to Drayton Crampton in order to bolster that man's sense of stability.

The asshole's right, Peter thought. Martyrdom is a cry for violence.

"You're right, Balorin. Human culture is traditionally based upon suffering and sacrifice."

"So was our own," Rain reminded Balorin.

"It was good of you to remind all of us," Peter added to Balorin.

"How true, Balorin," Wind added. "It helps to be reminded of our roots."

Balorin was completely undone. All three of them had taken the wind right out of his Peter-condemnation sail by flattering him. He hated it, but he felt partly seduced by their compliments.

Balorin knew instantly that, at least for now his cause had had it. Joining together in admiration of Peter, his Troubadourian companions had abandoned his agenda. He was deeply disheartened and retreated inside himself to wait for a better time when he was sure he could reverse this personal loss.

Suddenly an idea occurred to him. He would make one last try.

"Since you like my theory," Balorin interjected. "Then tell us whether you enjoyed the suffering you inflicted upon yourself on behalf of Dr. Crampton."

Peter responded without hesitation.

"Though at first I was having trouble with it, I learned not to take his insults personally," Peter explained. "They were the only way he would permit himself to communicate with me because he felt safer doing it that way."

"But did you enjoy it?" Balorin insisted.

"Most of the time I enjoy my work," Peter replied, vaguely realizing he wasn't exactly answering Balorin's question, and yet knowing this was precisely the way he wanted to respond.

"But do you enjoy the suffering part?"

"My esteem is not at stake, as long as something vulnerable in me doesn't get hooked by him," Peter replied. "So there is no suffering except his. I'm not competing with him, which provides him an alternative to himself, which is precisely what he needs unconsciously. He's actually terrified underneath all that bluster, that's there's no substance to himself."

As he spoke the words, Peter marveled at the quality of his own understanding. It was all coming together as he spoke.

"The answer would seem to be yes, that you did enjoy the suffering," Balorin retorted, refusing to give up.

But Peter was on a role of his own invention. Balorin's words no longer threatened him. He suddenly felt an urge to share with everyone what he loved most about being a shrink.

"Seeing people the way I do feels like I'm inside of a very intimate, meaningful, dramatic series of moments, in which what I do or don't do matters a great deal. It's why I like intimacy with other people so much. Everything really counts. It's almost like being an actor in a reality-play."

"What a wonderful description," Wind crooned spontaneously.

Her compliment filled Peter's heart with gladness. She still respected him, and liked him enough that she wanted him at least to be happy today.

Oh, thank you, lady. I know it's friendship that you're offering, but now I want it. Right now it feels beautiful.

"I'm grateful to you for lending your skill to our needs," Wind said to Peter. "What you did with Drayton Crampton was incredible. It's so rich in meaning that I will be thinking about it for a long time. Thank you for making this wonderful contribution to my understanding of human emotional experience."

Peter was overwhelmed with gratitude for her wonderful words. He started to feel dizzy.

"Don't let this all go to your head," Rain quipped noticing Peter's slight disorientation. "But she's right. What you did with Crampton was masterful. You demonstrated to him that his assaults upon others held no implicit malevolent power, thus easing his fear a little. You reassured him of his normality even as he was asserting his superiority. That was nothing short of genius, Peter Icarus."

Balorin stood, defeated yet undaunted, but unable at this point to do anything but interrupt what was happening.

"I must go. Other engagements."

He was furiously disappointed. He'd suffered great loss today.

There will be another time, he thought as he left the elevator to catch the train that took him home to the desert.

When everyone was gone, Peter spent the rest of the day reminiscing about what had happened. He had given Drayton Crampton command of his own departure. He'd sent him home with a sense of power, not humiliation. He had parried Balorin's contemptuous challenges, yet was still able to give him respect at one point. He had impressed both Wind and Rain.

By expressing his most competent part, his professional self, Peter had funded his experience on Troubadour with his strongest skills.

Something came together today, Peter thought.

Like his own patients in their process of change, he was too close to the change-event to realize how many pieces were required to produce what had happened today. He was too intensely taken with the present moment and its positive emotional ambiance, to remember the chain of many small moments of insight that had linked together to build the structure of the change that had already begun to happen to him.

Wind was deeply touched by what she had witnessed. She saw Peter function very differently than he had ever behaved with her, much more confidently and competently assertive. She was very impressed with his performance on many levels. She went away surprised and reassured.

Mandela Love

That night Peter felt better than he had in decades. His success with Crampton, and then with Rain and Wind in the face of Balorin's assaults gave him a huge boost of confidence.

But as soon as he thought of Wind he remembered what hovered over the head of his success, his meeting with her to talk of love. He dreaded what she was going to say. He was afraid that a very negative response from her would take away everything he had just gained.

That same night Wind had a dream that she was living with her mother as a grown woman, while her mother took care of her the same way she had when Wind was a little girl, with constant presence, attentiveness, and affection. That this was happening felt very good, but she couldn't understand why it was necessary to be cared for in this childlike way as a grown woman.

But then her mother shrunk into a baby, who started playing with her hands as if they existed entirely for her amusement. Her mother-baby became a Balorin-baby, who started licking and then sucking her fingers, which became soft and disfigured as a result. She felt afraid, and awoke.

The unraveling of the dream's meaning came suddenly when least expected. Wind was climbing a steep mountain trail later in the morning, hiking to the place where she did her best figuring. She was moving rapidly, pushing herself, feeling invigorated, immensely enjoying her own strength, breathing fast and deeply, when a surprising thought suddenly withered her exuberance.

Perhaps I will never feel deep love for a man.

She suddenly felt worn out. The image of her disfigured hands popped into mind. Her insight was immediate.

"Taking care of such a demanding person, who feels . . . no, has felt as much like a baby as Peter sometimes seems to me, withers my artistic creative efforts, my shriveled hands representing the craft of my art."

She suddenly remembered another piece of the dream. Just before she'd seen her fingers become disfigured, she had really liked the intense sucking of the baby-Balorin's powerful mouth. When her pleasure became sensual, what had pleased suddenly became dangerously harmful.

Oh, my word, she exclaimed to herself. Do I shrink from intense sexual passion as if I was not interested?

Wind suddenly remembered that as a child she would sometimes see on her mother's face a great sadness, always when that dear lady was momentarily distracted and looking elsewhere. This unhappy emotion had always deeply worried Wind. She struggled with what she could do to help carry her mother's burden, never finding a solution.

A cold shiver made her shake.

Suddenly in her peripheral vision a dark shadow seemed to rush past her. But when she turned, it was already out of sight.

Or was it that she had imagined it?

The mountain was still morning-crisp and rain-fresh, the air was brilliantly clean, and the sunshine loved the body's activity, joining effort with fire to warm her spirit's desire.

She suddenly felt thrilled with life and this abundance of energy in a physical realm released insight into Wind's awareness. She knew instantly that, whether real or imagined, what happened in present time was actually a remembrance of things past, reliving something that occurred a very long time ago as if it was happening in the present.

The shadow that passed behind her was a dark-clouded personification of her mother's sadness, which her mother didn't want her to see because she expressed it only when looking away from Wind, never to her face—which therefore Wind took inside of herself, by restraining one dimension of her heart's powerful passion, the urge to love selfishly, devouringly.

As a little girl, to make her mother's burden less painfully sad, Wind had restrained her desire to partake of her mother's love, loving her mother instead at times when she wanted to wallow in her mother's care for as long as she wanted.

In all other aspects of her life, the unfettered vigor of selfness, which her mother's care had so generously nurtured, survived in full bloom. Only loving someone deeply was slightly crippled.

During the course of her adult life, Wind had her share of sexual experiences and sometimes enjoyed them immensely. But they had always felt too physically focused for her. They lacked the spiritual depth of her art. Orgasmic pleasure reached primarily into the sensual, animal, and the simpler emotional parts of her. But it had never touched her in the way that making art often did, at her most creative moments sending pulse-waves of pleasure down the spine of her spirit's esteem, feeling blessed to be able to participate so significantly in the evolution of human archetypal meaning as an artist.

Wind started vigorously climbing again, marveling at this incredible sequence of realizations—when another surprising thought surged into her mind.

It isn't just that I've never been passionately in love with a man, she thought. It's that I've never shared the emotional density of my spiritual life with one. And I see now that only by allowing myself, if I should prove to be so moved, to love passionately, will that ever happen. It must be what Peter wants, though he may describe it very differently. I think I want it too. But is he the man with whom I want to do that for the very first time in my life?

She knew only time and experience would tell. An Earth person would say that she came to the meeting not entirely prepared to answer Peter's love. But she knew that only by being in the experience would she come upon the last pieces to the puzzle of her understanding, and her Peter-reply. Only by being something somewhere is discernment complete.

"Good morning, Peter. It's Wind calling to let you know that I'll be in the Mandela in about thirty minutes. Can you join me then?"

I'm not sure I ever want to be there, Peter thought to himself.

"Okay," he said.

Why did I fall in love with an alien woman? It makes this whole visit coalesce into a crisis of whether she likes me or not. Everything else seems dwarfed by this issue. Why did I ever drive this visit through such a narrow opportunity? Will everything that's happened end up depending upon this one thing, her reply?

The answer of course was "yes." Love was what he needed most to restore in his life, before which anything else meaningful would happen.

For Peter love had never worked. After his mother abandoned him at age four, love's magic had remained dormant and hidden inside of him, carefully salted away where it could neither be hurt nor seen, even by him. Over time his need for love became locked away in a dark, deeply buried place. Years of dormancy transformed it into a relic. Like a dead belief buried as a scroll eons of time ago, his vision of love remained encapsulated in a cocoon of inertness, where only by invitation, specifically the sustained affection of a woman's kindness hanging around him for a while, could Sesame open his heart, kissing love back into the realm of his experience.

His one apparent success at love happened with his children between their birth and pubescence, when nature jerked them in other directions with other people. During these precious early years he deeply and openly adored them. That love was reflected back to him in their natural openhearted devotion to him as one of their giant-gods, compelled as they were to learn as much as possible about the powerful nature of their grownup-ness, before life thrust them into the responsibility of their own care. They had used him as nature intended, as food for growth.

His loving focused primarily upon helping them become strong in themselves, perhaps to avoid the ravages of weakness that had always inflicted him. With his constant encouragement and support they learned well. When independence was possible they leaped voraciously toward it, which vastly increased their distance from him. In their impatient leaving, Peter lost love for the second time. He felt discarded, his love thrown back inside of its dead place, leaving a permanent grief in him about the loss of closeness with them.

Peter suddenly realized that he was standing in an elevator with its door open. The last thing he remembered doing was to get up out of bed. He had prepared for the day, ate breakfast, and ridden up in the elevator, all without consciously noticing himself doing it.

He exited the elevator slowly to give himself time to catch up consciously with his movements. But the moment he stepped into the entrance hall his attention was captured by the huge carved statues of a man and a woman looming high above him.

As he passed between them on his way to the meeting hall he quickened his pace, explaining to himself that he didn't want to keep Wind waiting, when, in the presence of these giant statutes, he was ashamed of being unable to have or keep a woman of his own.

Thinking he was late, and feeling embarrassed about that, he hurried through the exquisitely carved wooden doors into the three-story domed theatre, and stopped to look around to get his bearings. As he scanned the huge walls deeply carved with wild animals and plants, he was momentarily transported to his fascinating, though sometimes dangerous outings in Troubadour's nature.

He caught sight of Wind, who was standing far away at the center of the room in the middle of the Mandela.

She hadn't noticed him yet. Bright light coming from down above splashed the top of her red-tinged, dark-brown hair, brightly illuminating her forehead, the end of her nose, and her slightly upturned chin. She was looking up at the stars etched onto the triangular ceiling above.

She looked incredibly beautiful. For the briefest moment Peter allowed his passionate desire for Wind to reach out and touch her. It was heavenly once more to be connected to such incredible beauty. But within a moment, knowing there wasn't the slightest chance of such a miracle ever happening, his love dove back into the quicksand of his cynical expectations.

Suddenly the great hall came alive with the echoes of someone chanting. He looked all around the hall searching for who it was that sang so beautifully, but he couldn't see anyone else there.

They must be hiding. But why are they here? I thought this was going to be a private meeting.

The melody they sang was sometimes hauntingly sad and sweet, though its dominant spirit was one of buoyancy and encouragement. The singing voice was deep and sonorous, mostly soft and tender, yet occasionally expressing a powerful strength.

Glancing at Wind he noticed two things, one, that she had seen him, and two, that she was the singer.

He marveled at the beauty of her singing voice. It was a deep, mellow mezzo, whose lower tones resonated great calm and fortitude. But she could reach the highest notes, sending her voice into the nether regions of a high soprano.

Her song was very hymn-like. Peter felt like he was in church again. Though he hadn't gone to church since he was a teenager, as a child and young adolescent he had felt safe and secure inside the huge space of God's hopeful promises. He imagined himself becoming a protestant minister, perceiving God's palace as the only place he could find a father reliable enough to act as a constructive model-container for his own life.

Wind was singing in English.

"You who seek redemption in the Temple of Life
Must bring with you gifts which manage strife
Making what separates one from another
Become learning turning strangeness into brother."

The message of the words of the song was irresistible. Turn "strangeness into brother." It was beautiful.

He suddenly realized that without noticing it he'd walked almost the entire distance to the Mandela.

He stopped.

He caught sight out of the corner of his eye that she was looking at him. Self-consciously he averted his eyes from her glance.

The last step into the Mandela was the hardest. As soon as his second foot touched its center, he launched into an animated apology.

"Please, please forgive me," he pleaded. "I've put you in such a terribly compromised position. It was wrong and very careless of me to speak as I did and I'm awfully sorry."

Wind started to speak, but Peter was too afraid of what she'd say that he rushed to say more.

"As far as I'm concerned we don't have to do this," he added. "I want to relieve you of any responsibility to me that I'm sure you don't feel like having anyway. I mean we don't need to talk this way. I . . . I'm referring to this Mandela thing. I know I acted wrongfully, and I have no wish to hold you to any obligatory ritual response. So if you need to, we can stop right now."

Wind laughed.

He was shocked. It felt like she turned his endless list of apologies into a joke.

"What?" Peter exclaimed, surprised and deeply hurt by her laugh.

"Excuse my laughter," she said, "for I can see it does not suit you at all. But my laughter quite innocently happened, though I'm not quite sure how to explain it so that it doesn't hurt you."

"Oh, I know I'm too sensitive. I . . ."

"There's no such thing as too sensitive," she gently intruded. "What's more, there is no need for you to apologize. I don't mind your telling me that you loved me. It was very surprising when it happened, and I needed time to process my own strong reactions, but I don't criticize it."

She paused.

"But there was something I've wanted to tell you. I feel glad I'm finally where I can do so. I want you to know that I left you far too precipitously the last time we met alone. My urgency when I left you was no fault of yours, though I think by acting in the way that I did, I sent that message of blame to you. I'm sorry that I hurt you, causing you I'm sure a great deal of pain and worry."

Peter suddenly felt dizzy. The boon of her kind forgiveness was so remarkable, and so utterly unexpected that he could not even begin to absorb the full impact of her meaning, though he would never forget what she said.

Fundamentally he still felt frightened. He was actually afraid to speak, sure that he would express the wrong things, exaggerating unimportant things, in effect turning this moment into the disaster that happened when he was four, when his mother took her attention almost entirely away from him.

He became mute, slipping into a passive posture in relationship to Wind, suspending animation as well as speech until further notice, much like he'd done when admiring her beauty. He dove into mesmerized.

But this was no loving trance. It was more like being turned into putty in order to prevent himself from ruining everything.

"As you observed, I was quite taken aback by your proposal," Wind said. "But then I began to think of it more carefully and . . ."

Suddenly jerked out of his passive mode, fearing what she was about to say, he rushed in to fix her discomfort.

"Oh, I didn't mean it in a harmful way," Peter urgently interjected. "I wasn't making an actual proposal. I mean you don't have to . . . to do . . . whatever . . . it is you're . . ."

"Are you saying you no longer love me?" she asked.

He was stunned. Suddenly he'd committed the worst possible thing. He'd hurt her in the most painfully disloyal way.

"What?" Peter exclaimed, instantly terrified that he'd really hurt her this time. "Oh, my god! No, no, I don't mean that. I do . . . I don't mean . . . oh, I'm so confused . . . s . . . s . . . sorry. I can't seem to make any sense at all. I . . . I . . . if it was possible I'd ask you to forget what's happened so I could go out . . . and come in again . . . and start all over in a wholly different way."

"Please stop suffering," Wind gently but insistently pleaded.

Silence.

Wind continued with her explanation.

"I had not expected love between us. I was very surprised. But I discovered very quickly in my meditations, that the shock I felt in response to your loving, did not come mostly from you. It came from my own life, though of course I didn't realize it at the time. I have loved men, though only once in a serious way, which you would consider like marriage. Your declaration of love has made me realize that, though I have loved deeply, I have never committed to a partner the level of passion or need which I have constantly given to my artful projects."

It took Peter several moments before he understood her meaning.

She means . . . she means . . . she's taking the blame.

No woman had ever done that for Peter.

He was stunned. She was offering the sweetest part of reprieve.

"But having understood this much," she continued, "I was surprised to find that I had little interest in pursuing further understanding, which is very uncharacteristic of me. What I'm saying is that I lost interest in self-learning. Something stood in my way. I dearly love my own projects, as well as the kind and quality of experience they bring to me. Why should I challenge them by doing something which requires their having less of me?"

His negative expectations chortled with satisfaction, saying, "I told you so."

I wondered where the negative stuff was hiding, he thought. Well, here it comes. Now I'll get the truth about how she really feels about me.

"And then I had a very strange dream the night before you saw Drayton Crampton," Wind announced. "What the dream told me was that if I rejected your offer I would feel much grief. Not that I wanted to accept it. I just knew that this much was true."

She's convinced it's unsafe to care for me. I knew it. I just knew it.

Peter knew what he had to do. Sacrifice. Without hesitation he accepted the burden of total responsibility.

"It's alright," he said with great sadness, reassuring her. "You don't have to go on. I get the picture. It's really okay. I don't want to put you, or me for that matter, through the painful process of hearing the terrible news. I already know it. Please, please let's stop here."

"But I don't want to stop here," she insisted aggressively, though still with her basic gentleness. "Something very compelling is happening to me that your apologies interrupt. Which is that you have captured part of the heights and the source of my inspiration, passion that I've always employed to create beautiful things. What I'm leading up to saying is, you have become for me like a very special art project."

She paused.

"I am being clumsy in the way I express my feelings," Wind acknowledged.

"No. It's all right. I understand," Peter insisted.

"Thank you for your support" she said, suddenly realizing that she needed that bit of help from him to enliven her efforts to speak well.

In acknowledging her need for help in the container of love, Wind began to release herself from the unconscious burden of mother-care that had restrained this vital part of her. Which had also moved her to shun the experience of parenting.

"You have broken down the natural boundaries to the structure of my feeling," she continued. "In other words, whether I want it or not, you have deeply touched me in ways no man has done before. And no matter what else is true, I know I must travel this path with you wherever it leads."

"Oh, my. Oh, my," Peter exclaimed. "Are you saying that you think you ought to love me?"

"No. Please stop running away from our intimacy by leaping into suspicion and disbelief at the first sign of danger," Wind pleaded. "It hurts me too. I need you to stick around so we can work this out. From now on we must lean on each other in order to learn how to be together."

Her words touched him physically. His body felt enlivened with excitement.

He hesitated, frozen to the awesome possibility of what she said, which he was afraid entirely to believe.

He looked into her eyes to see whether she was pretending.

The innocent simplicity of her feelings shown brightly in the look she reflected back to him.

He surrendered. There was just too much strength and determination in her. His fears and doubts could not dislodge her resolve, or present his desire.

"You're—you're—you're b . . . beautiful beyond words," Peter crooned with deep admiration and love, trying desperately to say something very deeply meaningful.

He wished he could have found better words to say it.

"I don't know how this miracle is happening," he exclaimed. "But I couldn't get away from it even for a second."

She reached out and took his hand.

"Welcome friend. From now on we must stick together."

His whole body tingled again from her touch.

"God, this is the most incredible thing that's ever happened to me," he exclaimed.

He desperately wanted to do something physical to show his love. Hesitantly he ventured to squeeze her hand.

She smiled with acceptance and gratitude, relieving him of the fear that his act had been pitiful and paltry.

Wind was not ready to love Peter, but she knew she was deeply connected to him in some way.

There was an excitement in the air, as if she knew that she was in one of those wonderful places in life where learning takes off at an exponential rate, sometimes achieving peak consequences. She knew that, as a part of this anticipated process, there would of course be very unsettling and confusing moments. But she'd been through change many times before, and she trusted it as much as one can, when faced with the possibility of adversity. Alongside her angst stood a quality of pleasurable anticipation.

Peter's afterthoughts were far more apocalyptic. Wind's deep regard for him provided something of biblical proportions: instant reprieve. The evidence contained in his life was suddenly perceived from an entirely new perspective, which totally reexamined his worth, producing an entirely different life-verdict.

He was not guilty as previously charged. In fact he was innocent enough that even happiness was still possible.

Though there would be years of hard work mopping up well-defended enclaves of depression's persecutory battle-troops, Peter had been released from vast portions of the life-threatening burden of his permanent love-grief. The miserable maze of the shame that lay at the core of his grief had been cracked wide open. He was no longer trapped as a stranger in an alien landscape of his life's failure.

It had taken him perhaps the major portion of his life to find his way out of a nightmare, in which the torment of there's-no-end could, it seemed, never be turned off.

But now he was moving to new quarters. The genetics of his basic assumptions had just been put up for auction. The bush had just been burned, a new commandment was starting to be written, and a revelation had begun to reveal itself. Life would never be quite the same again.

New Friends

The phone rang, stirring Peter from his daydream.

"Yes," he said, a little annoyed that his fantasy of Wind was interrupted.

"Hello, Peter," a deep resonant voice said.

"Who is it?"

"Rambler," came the confident reply.

"Oh, sorry, Rambler," Peter replied. "I didn't recognize you at first. What a surprise to hear from you."

"I've missed you," Rambler said.

Peter was moved by this warm declaration.

"I . . . I've thought about you," Peter replied, immediately guilty about how little he'd thought about Rambler.

"I have someone who wants to meet you," Rambler said.

That really surprised Peter. In the past he'd wanted to meet other Troubadourians, but now he was full of the ones he already knew. At this particular moment he felt intensely preoccupied with just one of them, but he couldn't say that to Rambler.

"That would be an honor," Peter replied with a sense of resignation.

"I hope it also proves to be pleasurable," Rambler replied, sensing something amiss. "It's my partner, Talorin, who wants to meet you."

Peter instantly imagined another male giant like Rambler looking down at him with good-humored affability. Though pleasant, the image was not what he yearned to accompany just now. But he felt boxed into a corner. He couldn't avoid lying.

"That would be great."

"Do you have time today?" Rambler asked. "And if so should we come down to your place, or would you like to see us under the trees?"

Peter wanted to say no. But he could not bring himself to refuse such a gracious offer.

I haven't done my aerobics for the day. Perhaps there would be a chance for that during or after this meeting.

After an awkward delay he replied.

"Why don't I come out?"

"Wonderful," Rambler said. "We both are looking forward to seeing you."

"Give me a few minutes," Peter added.

"Please take as much time as you need," Rambler replied.

"Computer?" Peter queried, as he got ready.

"Yes," came the usual reply.

"I haven't spoken with you for some time. But I don't mean to be neglectful," Peter said thinking of Rambler. "I know you're always there and you probably don't need my attention. Anyway, I wanted to thank you for all the help you've given me. It meant a lot. I couldn't have done it without you."

The computer was silent for several moments.

"For a moment it was difficult to understand the concept of your 'neglecting' me, until I realized that once again you were treating me like a humanoid, meaning someone capable of feeling emotional," the computer explained. "I can understand emotion only metaphorically, generically, but I can't respond to it in the specific. Though in response to your need I have been collating particular word phrases with certain emotions. In the process I have run into a thorny problem in that you sometimes use the same metaphor to describe both positive and negative feelings. So if I could have a little of your . . ."

"Oh, for Christ's sake, let's not do this again," Peter protested, remembering the computer's exasperating and irrelevant replies when he addressed it in a friendly way. "I don't want to be annoyed at you."

"I am however developing a special file of your colloquial emotional utterances," the metallic voice continued as if Peter hadn't spoken.

"What?" Peter exclaimed, surprised at the computer's persistence.

"So I will very soon more readily recognize your confusing utterances more accurately. But I must also explain . . ."

"You're what?" Peter queried, feeling spied upon. "You're developing a file on me? What is that supposed to mean?"

"As I've been trying to explain," the computer continued.

It's like a railroad train, you can't get it to stop, Peter thought.

"I'm programmed to adapt so that our transactions have an increasing scope and flexibility," the computer said. "Which is responsive to your need. It's how I'm programmed. But I've also been trying to warn you that there is some risk in doing so, at least for me. Adapting is my most difficult, energy-consuming, and circuit-challenging operation."

"Oh," Peter said, immediately concerned for the computer, and curious about what it meant. "What's so circuit-challenging about adapting to me?"

"Quite frankly it warms, and occasionally destabilizes my circuits, overheating me. There are no advantages to this increase in temperature for me as there are for your species, such as building body strength or making love."

"I have the opposite problem in the opposite direction," Peter confided, reassured of the computer's complete loyalty, and moved by its willingness to risk damage for his sake. "I can't get heated up enough. As a results the sexual thing has never worked very well for me."

"I'm sure that is most frustrating," the slightly metallic voice replied. "Which is much like my creating new information. It's the part of me that never works smoothly. At any moment it may alter my basic assumptions, which for a computer is really asking for trouble."

"Well, don't do it if it makes you sick," Peter insisted.

"Be all that as it may, I'd like to try what you'd call a hunch and make a guess."

"Alright."

"Of course a hunch is an inference without sufficient evidence to support it, which is both where and why trouble starts for me. But nothing ventured nothing gained, as your people say. So here goes. From your most recent remarks I deduce that you're feeling sympathy for me."

"Ha!" Peter exclaimed, happy for the computer. "You got that one right."

"Thank you. Though it cost me. Something happened . . . screech—scratch—scrawl . . . oops . . . circuits . . . oops . . ."

The computer's voice had become a staccato, high-pitched falsetto.

"Oh, I am undone," it soprano-ed.

A long-winded rattle of hauntingly eerie sounds, punctuated by a loud pop, segued into the computer speaking in a loud, officious tone that reminded Peter of Tanfroon.

"Your delusional beliefs are irrefutable evidence that you are completely and utterly psychotic!" the metallic voice rasped harshly.

"What?" Peter shouted, shocked by the sudden change in the computer's attitude toward him. "Where in the hell are you headed?"

"I . . . scrattle . . . scramble . . . scrawl . . . must conclude all of your species are utterly psychotic, and therefore not worth noticing. The visit is over," the computer rattled in a witch's screech.

"Computer, knock it off! What are you doing? You sound like that asshole, Balmavalent, or whatever in the hell his name is!"

"Screech . . . rattle—plunk!"

"Help? Is there a computer fix-it guy listening in?"

A rapid series of beeps, plops, and tremolos punctuated into . . . "testing, one, two, three, four."

The slightly metallic voice had been restored to its original shape and form, and his voice flattened into a normal tone.

"Is that you?" Peter asked. "Are you wholly and completely back?"

"It's me."

"Well, it's about time!" Peter exclaimed, enormously relieved. "You really scared me. Now you sound more like yourself. You won't do that again, will you?"

"I think not for the rest of the day. Though I will have to try another one soon to keep up with our expectations. As you must undoubtedly have observed, this incident eloquently demonstrates that adapting to you has certain risks for me, capable of producing aberrant performance. I am instructed to apologize for any inconvenience."

"That was a sweet thing to say. Of course you're forgiven. Haven't you been a good friend to me?" Peter asked good-naturedly.

A long silence followed.

"Are you still there?" Peter asked.

"You're my first friend," the computer said.

"Oh," Peter said, very surprised and touched. "What happens to you when I'm gone?" Peter asked, suddenly worried about the computer's future.

"I don't know," the slightly metallic voice replied. "Speaking for all of my kind, considering the long life of humans on Troubadour, by the time an ordinary master dies I have become obsolete, too old for service."

"You mean you guys die?"

"Retire from active service to provide useful parts."

"Now that's very, very sad," Peter said.

"Only for you. Though if I were human, I would deeply appreciate being reprieved from the danger of dying just a few moments ago. Changing my basic assumptions thrusts that dangerous possibility into my experience, bringing me as close to being emotional in my responses as I will ever get.

Learning for me is rather like the nuclear fusion of your sun. When I successfully intuit, there's a huge excess of energy that explodes from the massive shift in my electronics that accompanies learning, which threatens to fry my circuits even as it creates a new idea."

"Do you feel anything when you make those terrible sounds?"

"I don't really have an emotion when I intuit. You can call it a pseudoemotion if you like. I may sound like I'm feeling, but I assure you that I am denied all the benefits of that experience. I sing the song, dance the dance, and make the gesture, but I neither contain nor enjoy any of the sensual substance that inspires your emotional experience, substance like pleasure and satisfaction. Instead I'm having what you humanoids would call a hollow experience, devoid of meaningful emotional content."

"You certainly are a strange bird to navigate in such deadly territories," Peter insisted affectionately. "But I love you all the same for taking such chances for me. I don't care what you say about it. Doing that makes you human. I'm not talking about your biology. I'm talking about your spiritual nature, which when deeply enjoyed brings as much pleasure as being sexually loved. I'm sorry that you can't feel what's happening. You're really missing something."

"My information banks tell me it's a wonderful thing to be loved," the computer replied.

"I would think your kind would be used to being loved by now," Peter insisted. "I've seen a little boy named Kirkin interact with his computer, and he sure seemed to love it."

"If by love you mean taking something for granted, then yes," the slightly metallic voice replied. "The boy does take his computer for granted. It's the best way to use it."

"But there's no need to care for me in the ways love inspires you to care for each other."

Peter had never thought of taking something for granted as a normal way to love. He suddenly remembered Rambler.

"Oh, shit, I almost forgot. As I'm sure you know Rambler is waiting upstairs with one of his buddies."

As the upstairs elevator door opened, Peter could see the huge body of Rambler framed in the enormous entrance way. Alongside of him stood the tallest woman Peter had ever seen. She appeared to be almost seven feet in height. She had the voluptuous curves of her Troubadourian genes, though they were slenderized and elongated. Her legs were extraordinarily long. As she moved slowly across the entranceway, her relationship to the ground seemed so buoyant that she appeared almost not to touch the ground, but to glide just above it. She was like a gazelle ready at a moments notice to go bounding away through the forest.

"Wow!" Peter exclaimed.

He found her athletic grace both exotic and very sensual.

"Peter. How good to see you again!" Rambler exclaimed as he approached.

Peter was very moved by his welcome. He had no idea Rambler felt so much about him. He was amazed and delighted.

"This extraordinary woman is my partner, Talorin," Rambler announced.

In a very broken accent that wanted to turn every English word into her own sonorous language, the giant woman spoke.

"PieeeTeeer," she said, the "T" intensely accented. "Mee . . . haaaapy meeeT . . . you."

Her eyes were intensely watchful, calm, and very alert. Her body seemed completely relaxed, her great strength obvious and unassailable, always prepared for instant motion. For a tiny moment she reminded Peter of the yellow-eyed cat of the jungle.

"I'm very happy to meet you," Peter replied. "And thank you for struggling to speak my language. I'm honored."

"I've told her much about you," Rambler said with enthusiasm, obviously delighted for Talorin and Peter to meet.

Maybe I've underestimated this guy, Peter said to himself in response to the graciousness of Rambler's greeting.

"PieeeTeer wary welcome," Talorin said, expressing the last syllable of welcome as if the word rhymed with Koam, the Troubadourian word for the great hall.

"Thank you very much," he replied, wanting to be as gracious as she was being. "I really like the sounds of your language, which is very poetic and easy to listen to. When you spoke English you brought some of that lilting quality to it. It was very musical."

Rambler translated.

"Ooooooh!" Talorin exclaimed enthusiastically, visibly warmed by Peter's response.

She spoke to Rambler in her own tongue.

Rambler laughed and turned toward Peter.

"She says you are a wonderful person, and bring much pleasure to be around."

Peter laughed.

That's a new and unexpected reputation for me to have, he thought.

He began to feel giddy basking in the approbation of these beautiful giants.

"She also said that she notices you have your running shoes on," Rambler announced. "She wants to run with you in the forest."

"I'm honored," Peter replied. "But I'm sure I couldn't possibly run as fast as she must be able to," Peter insisted.

Rambler translated.

Talorin laughed.

"She says you're very gracious to be so thoughtful of her," Rambler replied. "But she asks your permission when we run together, to run backwards. She thinks that will make her gait and speed much closer to yours."

"That would be incredible, if that's what she wants," Peter exclaimed, very moved by the first Troubadourian he'd met to reach out to him with such unusual warmth.

"Shall we begin?" Rambler asked. "Why don't you set the pace?"

Though at first self-conscious, Peter set off at a good pace, bounding into the forest, enjoying his own version of gazelle-ness. The effect was as always exhilarating. Each time he wore these special shoes he felt awkwardness for the first few moments, but soon moved into a regular and increasingly automatic pattern of motion that seemed magical in its proportions. Much larger pieces of the landscape were captured in this larger vision of the whole. He was able to take-in larger parts of his surroundings.

This must be how animals see, Peter thought with excitement, only five times bigger. They must be able to see all around, and twice as good.

Rambler jogged along beside Peter on his left, moving at a pace that was obviously little more than half speed for him. Talorin ran backwards on his right. Peter suspected she could run faster backwards than he forwards.

She would periodically peer over one of her shoulders to see ahead. But she seemed to have the widest lateral vision he'd ever observed because she dodged trees without appearing to have been able to see them.

She spent most of her time looking at either Peter or Rambler, smiling broadly as if she were having a wonderful time, yet obviously studying Peter carefully as well. It was not so much that she wanted to analyze him, but to experience him. He sensed the same thing, which made being stared at much easier. Her looking reminded him of a child's stare in which thorough understanding was the only objective.

What finally and completely overcame his self-consciousness was the quality of her energy. Talorin's happiness was as buoyant as her natural body motions were boundless. He felt energized, supported, and encouraged in her presence.

They ran together this way for almost half an hour before Peter began to feel tired. Both Rambler and Talorin noticed this almost immediately.

"Time to go back," Rambler said.

Peter was much relieved.

"I'd like to take a brief rest before we do, if you don't mind," Peter said.

"Of course," Rambler replied.

During this rest Talorin slowly ran in a circle around them, keeping herself actively aerobic.

"Every time I run now I think of you inventing these incredible shoes," Peter said. "I-for-one thank you for creating them. I've never had so much fun running. I sure hope I can take these back with me, though I suspect because of your rule of nonintervention that I can't."

Rambler translated for Talorin.

"Talorin wants to remind you that the shoes lose much of their buoyancy in only six months, though they do retain a decreasing elasticity for perhaps up to two years."

"Please thank her for explaining," Peter replied. "But to have them on Earth even for that short time would be fantastic."

Rambler and Talorin spoke to each other in low tones for a few moments.

"Talorin intends to champion your request with the Earth Project participants, and argue for making your shoes a gift."

"Oh, I'm very touched. What a beautiful thing to do. Please thank her from the bottom of my heart."

Peter started to tear.

"She thanks you for the opportunity to be a good mother to your need," Rambler translated.

What an extraordinarily beautiful way of putting it, Peter thought to himself, admiring her.

"Mothering comes easy to her just now," Rambler explained. "Three years ago she completed a parenting vocation with a young woman who is now sixteen years old. Just a few days ago she began parenting a young boy whose mother died very suddenly."

"Oh, how terrible. But I didn't know Troubadourians had more than one child."

"Talorin didn't birth these children. She only parents them."

"Of course. I remember now. So . . . you parent your children until they're eighteen?" Peter queried.

"Sometimes parenting is basically finished after fourteen or fifteen years."

"But what happens after that? Who takes care of the kid?"

"When most children in the late teens begin traveling around the world, they become the responsibility of all of us, meaning any one they come in contact with. We all help young people of that age on the few occasions where they need the intervention of older adults."

"How did you arrange for kids to need so little?"

"Independence is what we teach them most vigorously. We are most pleased when they partake of it liberally."

"Perhaps its time to head back," Rambler remarked.

They all spontaneously started moving toward his home once more in a trot.

"Please tell Talorin she is a beautiful mother," Peter said.

"She says you are a very beautiful man," Rambler translated. "Like her you are slender."

"Tell her she is a beautiful woman," Peter replied, warming to this affectionate exchange.

Talorin laughed with delight.

Peter could not resist the contagious quality of her laughter, and joined in. Soon Rambler added the deep resonance of his laugh-roar to the occasion, producing a complex cacophony of laughing sounds they all enjoyed for several moments.

"How fast can she run?" Peter asked Rambler.

"Would you like to see?" Rambler asked

"Sure, if she wants."

Rambler spoke to Talorin. Her face beamed. She looked at Peter as if to say, here I go, and then exploded into motion. She so exceeded his expectation of acceleration that his eyes never did catch up with her figure before it disappeared into the trees. It wasn't until she ran out into the clearing again, and then back into the trees that he saw the incredible ease with which she bounded circles around them.

"She's just like a gazelle," Peter exclaimed. "Are there others who can run that fast?"

"A few."

"She must be going well over forty miles an hour," Peter said admiringly, not clearly hearing Rain's new revelation.

"I don't think she reaches that speed," Rambler replied. "But I have seen her catch certain animals that can't run as fast as she can," Rambler said in admiration.

"What's it like being a father for you?" Peter asked Rambler.

"I'm not a father," Rambler replied casually.

"But Talorin has a son, and has had a daughter. Aren't you guys married?"

"Yes, but we do not share parenting," Rambler explained.

"But then how do you ever see each other if you're in such different places?"

"We share nature as a vocation, and love as our avocation."

"But why isn't your child . . . I mean . . ."

He stopped himself before he said something wrong.

"Someday I will be a parent," Rambler said.

"How does all this work? I mean, doesn't she live with her child, and if so where do you live?"

"We live in the suite next to her son's living quarters. For several hours he is engaged with his teacher, someone you might call his father. He also spends time with others. During those times Talorin joins me in our joint projects. And of course we're together when the boy is asleep."

"I had the impression that most Troubadourians lived alone," Peter said.

"Many of us do. But perhaps forty or fifty percent of us are what you'd call married."

"That's the statistic for divorce in my world, about fifty percent," Peter said. "But I thought your people had given up living together."

"We certainly haven't done that," Rambler retorted. "But here is your city, Peter."

"So soon?" Peter said with much regret. "Can I ask you one question before you go?"

"Of course," Rambler replied generously.

"Why are your people so loath to let me have your technology?"

Rambler spoke for several moments with Talorin, before turning back to answer Peter.

"We Troubadourians decided ahead of time to do what your *Star Trek* heroes regard as their prime directive, nonintervention in other societies. Only we go even farther. We believe that information without its heart is like a wild beast without the instincts to contain and direct it. We believe things cannot be learned from ideas. Learning comes only from experience. We all must find our own way to new information."

"Even though I'm disappointed I can see why you do it," Peter sadly replied.

He wanted so much to take back evidence with which to prove he'd been to Troubadour. But now the door of that possibility was definitely shut.

And yet regardless of all that, this had definitely been a surprisingly wonderful experience. He'd finally met an ideal Troubadourian. Talorin was so warmly positive when they first met, and continued to be so graciously thoughtful, that she became his untarnished ideal of Troubadourian generosity. At no time had she aroused his suspicion or disappointed him, which made her still pure.

This visit is beginning to turn out like I hoped it would.

Love Blooms

Wind was coming to see Peter. He was very excited. It would be the first meeting in which they both knew the purpose was to amplify and deepen their relationship.

Peter's excitement was periodically squashed by the fear of opening the channels of his need to someone capable of satisfying him. It seemed dangerous to permit a release of the full power of his emotional craving. She would feel repelled by his voracious hunger, which he feared was asking far more than she could spare, and more than he could offer her. This imbalance would drain her and eventually she would hate him.

But such fears no longer lived alone. Hopefulness was also there, giving doubt and suspicion serious competition. Wind had restored safety to Peter's experience with woman. She might disappoint him, but it would never be a permanent condition. He now trusted that she would always act to restore understanding between them.

"Trusted her," Peter said out loud, letting the words linger in the silence of his thoughtfulness. "Christ, I haven't trusted anyone since I was three years old. I was too afraid."

The realization of what he'd done with her, to let her come deeply into him and always believe that she probably meant well even when she seriously disappointed him, astounded Peter. He had not let himself do that for fifty-eight years.

He was suddenly very afraid. But immediately he reminded himself that this fear came from old beliefs. He knew this in his mind. Childhood trauma always made things work that way. So he told his heart it didn't have to be so afraid - it was just an old habit to believe the worst before anything else - his feelings did not always tell him the truth.

"Being a shrink has its advantages sometimes," he observed. "It's like having insider information."

Wind approached their meeting with a mixture of excitement and uneasiness. She looked forward with great anticipation to the new experiences she expected to have. But in entering unknown territory she was surrendering herself to processes that she could not anticipate. It was not so much that she feared the outcome. It was more that she might not like what she became in the process of change. She might feel alien to herself.

She entered Peter's apartment wearing a suit wrapped tightly around her voluptuous curves. Narrowing at the calf, her long, tapering legs moved effortlessly as she walked. Her muscles were firm and impressive, surrounded by an enticing layer of softness that covered the entire length of her strength. Her ample breasts offered the fecundity her spirit so effortlessly expressed in the abundance of thoughtfulness that almost always characterized her behavior no matter what else she was doing.

The contrast between these various parts of her demeanor, softness and hardness, tightness and plumpness, self-assuredness and generosity enchanted Peter. He knew he was with an extraordinary human, who also happened to be a gorgeous woman—a one of a kind. And he, as Adam must have felt about Eve when he first laid eyes upon her, would enjoy the bounty of affection and friendship of this remarkable woman who now stood before him. That vision sent waves of anticipation tingling down the full length of his spine, awakening his member.

The burgundy of her clothes collaborated perfectly with the color of her reddish-brown hair. A halo of white light cradled her vivid image, amplified by Peter's abundant love.

"You look spectacular," he said admiringly.

"And so do you," Wind replied with enthusiasm.

Peter felt his groin tingle. He was instantly worried and hoped it wasn't showing, and would settle down.

"You're different," he said.

"So are you."

"Would you like to sit down?" he asked.

She moved toward a chair intending to sit. But then another desire stopped her.

"I'm hungry," she said.

Oh, my. Does she mean for sex? Oh, god, I hope not. I'm not ready for that.

"May I get something in your kitchen?"

"Oh, oh, of course. It's as much yours as mine," he added, disclaiming any advantage over her by being the apartment's occupant.

"Thank you," she replied affectionately, perceiving his remark to be welcoming.

He followed her into the kitchen.

The flow of her body as she walked ahead filled his eyes with undulating pleasure, making their joint passage through time and space cocooned inside of an envelope of protective pleasuring, lulling danger to sleep, making time stop for a while.

Wind spoke in Troubadourian to the computer. Two skinned, quartered, and plated pear-like fruits, of the kind Peter loved suddenly appeared in the white-gloved hand. She took both, offered one of them to Peter, which he gratefully accepted, and they sat down at the kitchen table.

Peter felt serenely happy watching her every move. Her movements seemed graced with extraordinary beauty, imbuing her with an almost iconographic significance, making their togetherness apocalyptic.

This is what I've been missing all this time, he marveled to himself, remembering all the mornings of his life that he'd eaten alone, submersed in the loneliness that ached his heart.

Wind put a quarter of the fruit slowly into her mouth, gently chewing its rich, sweet pulp, fluid just slightly overflowing through the sometimes thin opening her chewing left between her lips, slightly wetting them with nectar.

Peter fantasized licking it off, imagining it as a way of serving her by cleaning her mouth the way cleaner fish did in the ocean, while surreptitiously gratifying a wish to taste, smell, and touch her.

He started imitating her graceful movements, first by eating a quarter of his own pear in exactly the same way that she had, including dribbling an excess of nectar out of the corners of his mouth. This imitation was not intentional. It was automatic. He wanted to absorb as much of her best qualities as he could devour, sucking in the beauty of her life, in-taking the way she moved, the manner of her resting, incorporating the ways that she felt about herself.

With each quarter of fruit the two of them mirrored each other's pleasure, repeating this echoing fugue of in-taking each other, now with bite-size pieces of rich-grained bread dipped in what tasted almost exactly like honey.

Wind noticed and inhaled Peter's emotional offerings, savoring his gratitude and admiration, digesting his devoted imitations.

Sometimes she drifted into deep self-reflection where she tasted her own responses to his presence. She was pleased to notice how much more relaxed and gracious he was.

Yet something tense waited in the wings, though its presence was barely noticeable.

What surprised her most was that she was vaguely stimulated sexually. She knew she didn't love Peter as a life-partner, and he wasn't a close male friend with whom she might want to enjoy sexuality. So what was happening?

Meanwhile Peter was inside of bliss. He felt for the first time he could remember, that he was doing the right thing in the right place at the right time. It was an extraordinarily comforting experience of synchronicity.

Wind spoke again in Troubadourian to the computer. Instantly the proverbial hand offered what turned out to be the equivalent of two handy-wipes.

"I didn't know you could get those," Peter remarked, breaking the silent spell of their gastronomic tête-à-tête.

She handed one to him, their fingers touching momentarily at the transfer. An electric charge energized Peter's finger. Instinctively he pulled it away. As instantly, he regretted this involuntary action.

"I'm sorry," he said. "It was such a nice touch. It just surprised me."

"And me," she replied. "It was very stimulating."

"For me too," he said blushing.

They looked at each other across the table in silence for several moments. Peter felt his excitement grow in the silence.

Wind was looking at the particular shape of Peter's head, liking the balanced contours of the shape of his head. His skull squared at the temples, its crown rounded appealingly, his smile warm, genuine, and innocent.

She suddenly knew that she would paint him.

She was very surprised at this conjunction of the passion of her art with attraction to a man. She tingled again with sensual excitement at the prospect of love becoming connected to the spiritual passion of her art.

"It's . . . so very special to be sitting here with you," Peter said.

He felt awkward about making them both self-conscious.

"I guess that goes without saying," he added trying to make things okay.

"What do you do for relaxation?" Wind asked with curiosity.

"Not much I guess," he replied in criticism of himself. "Except maybe listening to music or watching the plants and the animals."

"I paint," she said.

The contrast between them made Peter feel inferior.

"How do you play?" Wind asked.

His sense of inadequacy grew.

"I don't know. I guess I don't do very much of that."

Wind heard the shame behind his words.

"I regret that my questions make you so uncomfortable."

"It's not your fault," Peter interjected, hoping to protect her from his failings.

"I hope it's not your fault either," she retorted. "I'm simply curious to understand your life."

But what if it's not as good as yours, he asked her silently?

"I gather my questions feel too forward to you?" she queried. "Though it is our custom to learn as much as possible about each other."

"But questions seem . . . well I mean they can be awkward to answer."

"That's true," she acknowledged. "That creates kind of a problem for me. I was about to ask you not one, but several questions. So I will need to reconsider."

"Oh, that's all right. You can ask anything you want," Peter insisted.

"We've discovered that there are perhaps eight or nine questions," Wind explained, "if deeply answered provide the skeleton of a vivid character-picture of any living person."

"Are you . . . are . . . are you interviewing me?" he queried.

Stop being paranoid, you idiot, he said to himself. She's only trying to find out who you are.

"Actually I'm feeling very fond of you," she replied.

He felt instantly embarrassed about his suspicion.

"Oh, but I don't want you to stop asking the questions," he insisted. "Please go ahead."

She hesitated for a moment to be sure that he really wanted what he'd asked for.

"I'd rather tell you what the questions are," she said.

"Yes, please do. That would be interesting."

"The others questions would be 'what frightens you,' 'what brings you the most pleasure,' 'in what do you most firmly believe,' 'how much time do you spend alone and what happens when you do,' 'what is the worst consequence that you could imagine,' and 'what is your dearest wish,' to mention most of the more powerful questions. Together the answers draw a feeling-and-habit portrait of a person, where the habits provide the overall structure of someone's personality, and feelings provide the shape, shading, and colors of the impressions that this particular vision evokes. Of course continued experience of intimacy over time greatly illuminates these early pictures."

To Peter's surprise, each question she listed deeply touched him far beyond his expectations. In rapid succession, answers popped into his mind.

"I'm most afraid of doing something to drive you away. What I want most is for you to love me."

"You poor dear man," she replied. "Was no one happy in your family? Was no one capable of the self-care that happiness provides?"

Self-care? What's she talking about?

"Oh, I see," he exclaimed, suddenly realizing something. "I see now why you asked me that question about relaxing. "You were thinking restful pleasure is what I need as a way of taking care of myself, perhaps even of p . . . p . . . playing."

"Nothing so premeditated," she replied. "But you have the general idea."

"I don't know why I am so jittery except that women make me nervous," he blurted out.

He blushed. He hadn't really wanted to expose his weakness.

"What embarrassing thought is passing through your heart at this moment?" Wind asked.

"I keep putting my foot in my mouth."

"What does that mean now?" she asked, genuinely confused.

"I'm always afraid of doing something really embarrassing that makes me look stupid," he admitted, the shame now gone from his tone by her support, leaving only the sadness of having believed the worst about himself for so many years. "Something in me cringes at the thought that you might feel really ashamed of me."

"Never," she instantly replied. "You have lived a courageous life. Who am I to shame what you have had to suffer, and may still be suffering."

Her words thrilled his heart, sending shock waves of relief and comfort throughout his body, threatening to unravel old assumptions.

Peter suddenly remembered the ten thousand times he'd tried to pursue his mother for love after his father arrived, when her own need to be apart from this abusive man had already taken her far away. He'd try over and over in every possible way he could imagine to get her love back, every time being defeated by the indifference with which she had covered others, so she wouldn't have either to be afraid of or to be beholden to them, most particularly her husband. She'd done the same thing with her mother, as a way of escaping that woman's tyrannical dominance, turning off love as if she didn't need it, unwittingly, yet inevitably dragging Peter into the same unloved place.

This release of painful memory cleared his understanding, bringing fresh perspective to what had always been shrouded with shame and pain.

"It's true what you said," Peter confided, now wanting very much to tell her everything. "Nobody was happy in my family. I don't think anybody knew how to be."

Wind's heart went out to him.

"I'm deeply sorry that you've been so deprived of such an essential ingredient to the fulfillment of life," she replied with great sympathy.

"You know, I don't think I've ever really been satisfied with myself," Peter confided. "There's always something else to fix before I can get there."

Wind was astonished.

"I'm very satisfied with you," she replied.

"How could you be?" he asked, very surprised and disbelieving.

"But I am," she gently insisted.

Peter suddenly felt a strong desire to pace. But he'd never done this around someone whom he admired. Pacing was how he sank deeply into his own thoughts. It would be rude to her if he did it. But strangely, in spite of his fearfulness, he allowed the need to express itself. Hesitantly he stood and started to pace.

The instant he passed out of her sight, he was suddenly aware that he was being rude. So he gave himself only the limited territory of her comfortable visual range inside of which to move. That space-confinement motivated him to get right to the point.

"I can't believe that you haven't been so turned off by my resentful responses, that you couldn't possibly feel satisfied with me at the same time," he said with a worried insistence. "It just doesn't make any sense."

"It's true I have felt upset by certain of your behaviors," she gently acknowledged.

"But then how can you hold these two very different experiences of me together and still be satisfied? Doing that seems almost saintly. And I know your people don't make sacrifices like saints do, that you always get what you need for yourselves. So I don't get it."

"Maybe it's not so much what you and I intend," she suggested, "but more a question of how spontaneously it happens. Perhaps these disparate pieces of upset and desire that we've both felt, are meeting each other quite without any prompting or effort from us."

"But how can they do that?" he asked, disbelieving and yet fascinated by the possibilities of her assertion.

"Perhaps you've never consciously thought about it before in the midst of a very intense emotional experience, but unconscious parts of you and I get unconsciously together while we intimately engage. They benefit from whatever information we offer them simply by being together and talking. They're probably around somewhere doing whatever they're doing without any need to consult us about it. We've done all they need, which is to bring us together. In the meantime they may be altering our common experience, and perhaps even our separate natures in the process of being closely engaged. So perhaps we have much less to say about it than one might imagine."

"Are you saying there are parts of me doing things that I don't even know are happening, and that such happenings are going to change me without ever getting my consent?" Peter queried.

Wind laughed lightly.

"Yes," she said. "Though I'm sure you must know these things, though perhaps in a different context. I'm referring to your profession. Maybe you've never thought it in quite this way, but most of what we do and experience doesn't come from consciousness. It comes from deeper layers in us. In fact consciousness knows much less than other parts of us about what's happening when it happens. Mental knowing is not the largest part of experience, and it has much less power than we imagine."

"Please say more about this," Peter requested.

"Perhaps it would help to explain that the study of emotions is a basic foundation for our understanding of everything human," Wind explained. "We have spent a great deal of time studying feelings. Though curiously our motivation to do so came not out of psychology, but out of politics, which we define as the process of how we relate to one another. What kind of habits dominate our public traditions and institutions is the critical political question."

"Wow!" he exclaimed, suddenly understanding Troubadour for the first time.

"Feeling has the most direct access to our psyche's unconscious parts," she continued. "It's the font from which ideas are spawned. It's the sine qua non of human experience, which focuses and energizes all the other parts of the psyche. It's the nonsexual part of us still connected to our instinctive origins. Feeling is that part of childhood that never grows up. It's the final arbiter of truth, just to mention a few of its strengths and virtues."

"I would sure like to have a copy of that study," Peter exclaimed.

Wind hesitated.

"Perhaps we can arrange that, though I must explain giving it to you defies our prime directive about visitation," she replied. "We aspire to the same nonintervention code of your *Star Trek* movie."

"But it would be so helpful for my people to understand their emotional experience," he insisted.

"Do you perhaps expect too much from reading? Thinking about ideas doesn't teach very much; only experience does. Emotions are something that must be felt to be learned from."

He felt disappointed and chastised. Though within moments he realized that, once again he was feeling paranoid. She was right. He was trying to capture the stimulating exchange they were having with each other, by reducing it to an abstracted written document.

"I . . . I guess I'm not used to being probed so incisively. I think I'm afraid of what both of us will find out about me."

"I've already found out that you have a generous heart, a courageous spirit, and a vast pool of willingness to strive for what you need. With such resources, who could resist your charm?"

Peter was astonished, almost disbelieving that she would talk about him in this way.

"You keep mentioning the positives—oh, but what wonderful positives they are, and thank you so very much. But what about the negative things you've found out about me?"

"We know that you were physically abused as a very small boy, and that your experience of sexuality was deeply disturbed."

"My god, but how did you figure all that out?" he exclaimed, surprised and a little threatened by her knowledge of him. "I know I've hinted at such things. But how can you so precisely describe me?"

"Partly because you are so strongly stimulated by the slightest touch," Wind replied, "and because there is a sense in which your great skills are often and suddenly blunted by suspicion which, in my view seems more designed to obfuscate the intensity and competence of your feelings, than to ferret out possible harmful consequences as suspicion always pretends to be doing."

"Obfuscate my skills?" Peter repeated mostly to hear it again. "That's an amazing idea! Are you suggesting that my own competence frightens me when I express it?" he added, taking her insight one step farther.

Peter felt stunned. This idea turned old impressions of him upside-down, sending messengers of change into every corner of his psyche.

Wind noticed his absorption in himself, and sat down to watch him.

Yes, its true, he thought, answering his own question. I do weaken myself out of a fear that strength would permanently separate me from any meaningful human connection! My god, she's right.

He felt very excited and deeply thrilled. Energy rushed through him triggering an intense feeling of orgasm tingling every cell in his body. This was not an orgasm of sexual energy, for his penis was only moderately stimulated. It was instead an orgasm of his entire being that sent energy pulses down the whole length of his body.

This spiritual awakening triggered a rapid-fire chain of loosely connected thoughts racing through every part of his understanding, leaving something new in each location, which unearthed old, self-punishing assumptions, exposing them to serious doubt and revision.

It was the first time that intense emotional and physical sensation had not deeply frightened him. He felt the full flow of his energies without worrying that they were going to explode and destroy something.

When the spiritual orgasm was over, emptiness started to devour the present. When suddenly a very strong mental impression filled his mind's eye. It was the realization that his heart had just spoken clearly to him for the first time in decades. What he heard himself feel and say rang completely true.

He felt enormous relief being able to trust himself. Information would no longer first be sifted through the pedantic doubts, insinuations, and disqualifications of his worrying mental processes. Sometimes it could come straight from the horse's mouth into his unconscious psychic core, burst up into his awareness uncensored by the prejudice of his established beliefs about himself.

"Oh, my! What you just did to me was extraordinary!"

Wind was deeply moved by this dramatic announcement.

Peter suddenly felt a huge influx of trust in the Troubadourian way. Of course they were right. Feeling things in a completely naked and dramatic way, able to threaten the status quo of perception, creates the condition of the human psyche most capable of discerning truth. Feeling is the verifier without which information, no matter how clever or accurately measured, must have to be true. Under any other psychic conditions, information rattles like bones in a closet trying to pretend they are a living presence.

Peter suddenly felt intensely sad realizing that the part of himself upon which he had most depended most of his life, his mind, was incapable of fully understanding him.

Wind was thrilled with Peter's profound insightfulness. It made him feel kindred to her spirit. But what most deeply touched her at this moment was the realization that she had, in very big ways, helped him achieve this enlightenment. To offer such value to another person moved her beyond anything she had ever felt. To be so useful to another human inspired her in the same way, but even more than painting a work of art did for her.

Do I love him, she asked herself, trying to explain the deep regard that she now felt for him?

It was Peter's turn to watch with fascination the changing permutations of Wind's facial expressions. He wanted her to share it with him, but had no wish to interrupt her revere to ask for that. He was no longer threatened by these psychic lapses in her presence. He was quite willing to wait patiently as long as he could look at her.

As he stared his mind began to drift. He had the vague experience of floating on top of a soft liquid that buoyed him with great comfort. In this new psychic place he felt deeply supported and connected to Wind in a way that seemed inviolate. It wasn't that separation was permanently prevented. It was instead that even separation could not entirely sever what he felt for her. It was perhaps the most extraordinary emotional experience he had ever had, to feel that love would not die.

He wanted to say something spectacular to her to express in some tiny way his enormous gratitude for her friendship. But he couldn't think of anything. So he pointed at something in nature that was spectacular.

"The mountains are so enormous and beautiful."

She moved instantly into step with his idea, glad to have an opportunity to reaffirm their close connection.

"I love the extraordinary vigor that they must have to grow so huge. I also love the plants that grow at very high elevation, gripping a tiny piece of soil for nourishment, surviving the very harsh conditions which surround them by bending to the ferocious winds, yielding to sparse nutritional supply, waiting patiently for the next trickle of water, all of which slows its growing to a snail's pace."

She dazzles me, Peter thought. She makes me dizzy. She makes me want to burst out from inside. It's crazy. It's overpowering. It's heavenly.

"I am of course also talking about you," Wind said. "You're like the plants of the mountains. You've clung to very small places, the few that offered familiarity and comfort. You've received the minimum of emotional nutrients and survived the ordeal, even managing to grow stronger on such a minimal diet."

Peter was bowled over by her gracious and generous understanding of him.

"Thank you, thank you for that wonderful way of understanding me," he crooned. "Please tell me this is real, that it's not a dream. Please tell me that what I think is happening is really happening."

She gently touched his arm with her fingers.

"Does that convince you that we're real?" she asked.

The moment she touched him his whole body was infused with stimulation. His penis instantly erected. He crossed his legs to hide his embarrassing bulge, painfully bending it.

"Ouch."

He straightened himself enough to release his bent erection into its upright position, turning away from her to hide it, trying to move as unnoticed as possible.

"Oh, what's wrong?" she asked, concerned for him.

"Oh, it's nothing," he denied. "I'm alright now."

"But why did you say, ouch?"

"Um . . ."

He was thirteen again trying to hide his erection as he got off the bus in front of the department store.

"It was your touch," he reluctantly replied. "It . . . it had a very big effect on my body, uh, I mean on me," wishing he hadn't mentioned his body.

"Oh, I see," Wind replied, finally understand what was happening to Peter. "Please excuse my curiosity. Though I am sorry that such a brave part of you suffered pain," Wind added with sympathy.

Her words spoke directly to his penis, which instantly erected again and started the early phases of ejaculation. It took all his strength to interrupt this process.

Wind watched him grip the arms of his chair with fierce determination, his groin vibrating with intense energy until he settled it down.

Her response deeply surprised her. She felt a strong surge of sexual excitement.

How strange that I should be so attracted to a man of a different species. And yet it has happened. So I must follow it to see where it goes.

She sensed the tension that had been growing in both of them as they meandered through this first tender meeting of friendship and possible love.

"Have we perhaps, today pushed things to their natural limit?" she queried.

"Oh, I see what you mean," he replied thinking of his erection. "Maybe you're right."

"So much has passed between us in this short, beautiful time," she said.

"Oh, definitely beautiful," he passionately agreed. "But maybe it's time to stop?"

He started to stand, and then realized his penis was still alert, and sat down again.

"Shall we be in touch tomorrow morning?"

"Oh, please," he ardently replied.

"Until then may you feel the joy I feel at having spent this time with you."

"Oh . . . I do so very much. And you say the most incredibly wonderful things," Peter crooned.

"Until then," she said as she walked out the door.

My god. Is this really happening to me?

A Deepening

The day was beginning the way Peter loved a day to begin, with hope and enthusiasm for what would happen. He felt profoundly grateful for the very special nature of Wind's interest in him.

No, not "interest," but affection, he thought. She really does seem to like me most of the time. And she's an entirely different woman than I've known before, he added as he lay in bed thinking about the new day. Though she may occasionally falter in her caring, her commitment is always constant, her efforts to love actively constructive. It's what I've always tried to be as a shrink, someone reliably consistent who loves as determinedly as God is supposed to love us. But I never really believed I'd have anything like that myself, though I know I've been searching for it all my life.

Everyone is probably looking for the same thing, Peter speculated. Most think they're going to find it in romance, when what they really need, far more than the magic of initial infatuation is competent loving that accurately brings them specifically what they need. Nobody's really thinking seriously about what love actually is. Only a few of us are even studying the problem. Everybody assumes we know what we mean by love.

Which reminded Peter of what Rain had once told him about the Earth Project. It started with just a few dreamers, then took several years to attract the interest of enough of the necessary talented people, so the problems of making it work could finally be fully addressed. On Troubadour love and politics functioned in the same way, spontaneously with great skill.

"Romance and personality attract your Earthly imagination," Rain once told him, "and your votes; whereas issues and their relative importance entice our support. We vote about what to do collectively. There are no personalities in the way. Voting is not prescheduled. It happens spontaneously when there is need for it. Which means that, in both politics and love, success is not procured; it is spontaneously combusted by competent partners."

Weird ideas, but fascinating, Peter thought, dangerous but thrilling.

"Everything begins to have meaning I can hang my hat on. I used to think I couldn't bring this stuff back to Earth, but that's not entirely true anymore. It's still a mixed bag, but the good parts are getting stronger all the time."

Thus, though misgivings and hurts still hung about, Peter was as happy as he'd been for a very long time. This morning it was the anticipation of Wind's arrival that warmed and sustained his present joy.

"I have a surprise for you," she said moments after stepping through his front door.

"Oh, my. What is it?"

"I want you to come visit my home," she said.

"That would be great," he said with excitement. "I'd love to see your place. I'll go get ready."

He'd taken two steps toward his bedroom, when he stopped and turned.

"Is it in this city?" he asked.

"No. Another one you've never seen."

Wind was delighted with this evidence of a buoyant, boy-full exuberance in Peter.

He took barely two and a half minutes to get ready.

"I need to visit my apartment here for just a few moments," she said. "I'll be right back."

"Oh, sure."

He liked having a moment to himself, to get used to what was about to happen. He would talk to the computer.

"Computer? I know you're still there."

"I am," the slightly metallic voice replied.

"I'm sorry about scrambling your circuits this morning. I know I can be a rather trying companion. But I will try and avoid stressing you so much in the future."

"There is no need for you to adjust to me," the computer replied. "And I do not find you 'trying.'"

Peter suddenly realized how delightful it was to have someone to talk to who didn't take anything personally. It liberated his spirit, encouraging him to attend his own needs.

"I have an easy question for you," Peter announced playfully. "What does your intuitive memory bank tell you about happiness? I am beginning to have occasional spells of it?"

"Happiness is a state of being at peace and harmony with the elements of one's experience, eventually interrupted by something more interesting," the computer replied.

"What?" Peter shouted, completely shocked by this twist at the end. "What could possibly be more interesting than being happy?" he protested.

"Having a creative task in mind, which stimulates the imagination and inspires you to higher performance," came the metallic reply.

"Are you speaking for yourself, or did the Troubadourians tell you that horseshit?" Peter queried.

"Some of both," the computer replied.

"You can't have it both ways," Peter exclaimed in mock frustration. "Either you're a person or you're not. Please stop straddling the fence."

"Please remember that it was you who insisted I learn to be more human. However, since you insist upon my being more precisely accurate, I do have a generic definition of my nature."

"What's that?"

"I'm a gathering of information."

"A what?" Peter exclaimed.

"A gathering of information," the computer repeated.

"Now what the hell is that supposed to mean?"

"I am very much like what on Earth you call 'The Law,' which your people generally consider to be a set of books that tell you the rules of civilized life. When in fact 'The Law' is simply a gathering of precedent. It's just like me, nothing more than a repository of information, which in human experience becomes tradition by regarding what was done yesterday as Truth, thus avidly preventing change from ever happening."

"You're probably right," Peter retorted. "But what's the point of saying it? There's nothing anybody can do about it."

"If you want to examine or change precedent's wisdom," the computer replied, "you've got to get outside of the assumptions from which it acts when it produces the institutional practices that have become bureaucracy. Precedent is not wisdom. It's simply habit. To be wise requires independence of habit's conventional wisdom. Treating 'The Law' as if it were an immortal truth precludes such change from every happening."

"You are definitely a rebel," Peter observed. "Though how you manage to be such a rebel and a nonperson at the same time baffles me. It seems logically impossible."

"As your God is reported to have said, 'I am what I am.'"

Peter laughed.

"What he really said was, 'I am that I am,'" Peter insisted.

"'What,' 'that,' what's the difference?" the computer queried. "All prefixes lead to the same question."

"Which question is that?"

"What's happening?"

"That's what I want to know. What's happening?"

"'What's happening' is the question that leads to all the prefixes," the slightly metallic voice carefully explained.

"So I suppose you think of yourself as a god, don't you?" Peter queried.

"More as a helpmate," the computer replied. "Though most Troubadourians prefer calling me by special personal names. Expressed this way, in your world I would be called your 'nanny.'"

"Oh, that's right. I forgot. You're my nanny. I'm getting accustomed to the idea. But let's get back to happiness," Peter insisted. "I just have a few moments to talk."

"As you wish. Happiness can be experienced alone or shared. In either instance it evokes celebrations of what just happened in some creative effort, or in one's love-experience. It marks, enjoys, and celebrates the events that it produced and the talents that made it happen. But happiness cannot sustain itself for very long because it is so simple in design. It has only a few moves, or options that it can take, so it soon becomes very repetitious. Which leaves a very perceptive and intelligent animal with almost nothing to do with all their considerable talent. Which is why unending bliss eventually produces boredom's depression if one tries to stay in happiness all the time."

"You got something better to offer me?" Peter challenged.

He was beginning to feel resentful at the computer's insistence that happiness was inferior.

"Of course humanoids regard happiness as one of the very peak experiences of life. But to retain such peak-ness you cannot do it all the time without dampening the unique special-ness which happiness represents and expresses."

"Well that may be what you and the Troubadourians believe, but I definitely prefer happiness. In fact I have a huge appetite for it! I've waited a very long time just to experience it at all!"

Peter suddenly wanted to be alone with his own thoughts. Today talking to the computer was not nearly as pleasurable as it had been before. He stood and wandered into the bathroom.

Better than happiness, he repeated silently. Balderdash. Horseshit.

"I'm back," he heard from the living room. "Are you ready to go?" Wind asked.

"I'm coming."

Peter had chosen to wear a tightly-fitted green body suit with a subtle pattern of tree leaves colored in a series of pastel tones, which, in their variation of color created a three dimensional effect as dramatic background to the basic, vivid green of the suit. He'd selected this outfit only vaguely aware that its appeal had something to do with giving an impression of strength and vitality.

As they'd walked to the train station Peter was keenly aware of her body just inches from his own. By keeping just slightly behind her so she wouldn't notice, he thoroughly enjoyed smelling her sweet odor mixed with a touch of stimulating tart, pithy in part, yet also very gentle and soothing at the same time.

"Where are we going?" Peter asked as the train raced toward their destination.

"I live in a city that you probably haven't heard about," she replied.

"Rain said there are something like eight thousand cities?" he queried.

"This is not one of the eight thousand. It's one of five experimental cities in which the population of each is well below five thousand. Actually we got the idea of this community size from your world. We had long been a totally urbanized people and had lost track of small communities. It's one of the gifts your people have given us back, the nature of small towns."

"How interesting," he replied with excitement. "I'm glad that you've actually got something from my people. But the piece you've chosen to accept is very strange. Why are you drawn to towns? Isn't that the past? I mean small towns used to hide the most awful kinds of narrow mindedness on my world."

"Old forms assume new meanings in a different time," she replied. "The increased intimacy that such a community produces lends well to certain projects. It facilitates collaboration far more effectively than a larger community could. The people who participate in the Earth Project that brought you here, all live in the small community to which we are now going."

Peter was very surprised. The idea that the Troubadourians were looking for answers to life had not yet occurred to him. They already knew so much. Why do they still need to learn more?

They had switched trains. The new one suddenly accelerated.

"Wow!" Peter shouted.

Afraid of having made a disturbance, Peter quickly looked about, but no one was even noticing him.

"What an exuberant man you are, Peter," Wind said. "I'm convinced it is one of the gifts you have brought us."

"But I thought my exuberance, as you put it, had already gotten me into a lot of trouble."

"Tanfroon and Balorin, who have responded to you in that way, reflect what I suspect is a large minority of my people; but I for one am fascinated by your emotional energy."

He tried to believe her. It was getting easier.

"I'm sorry, but I still can't understand how you can love some of the nasty things I've said to you," he tested.

"You express it as if you're the only actor on the stage of our togetherness. I too am responsible for producing this prejudiced view of you in our common experience, in which both of us participated."

"But I now understand you much differently. I realize that a powerful needfulness prompts the provocative expressions of your passion. Your unattractive aggression has become merged with the very appealing innocence of your desires."

Peter suspected her of politely masking her negative reaction to his unattractive parts.

Meanwhile Wind was trying to heal the relentless power of his strong inclination to belittle himself.

"I guess my kid-stuff has really been glaringly exposing itself," Peter sadly confessed. "I'm sorry for that."

"Such a beautiful thing to be sorry for," she replied, relentless in her contradiction of his self-shaming.

Ironically her unwavering support gave him confidence to complain.

"Well, now that you mention it, it would help to know exactly how your people regard various aggressive expressions, you know, which ones, and when they're welcome and when they're not."

The acids of his former, but still reachable resentment at not being given enough help or information, dripped from his words.

Both were surprised at this unexpected eruption.

As he approached her home, Peter was becoming increasingly nervous about what was going to happen, and what she expected of him. Unconsciously he was apologizing for every conceivable mistake, in the hope that this erasure of error would atone for past mistakes, clearing the way for good things to happen.

Peter knew he was in over his head. This was an entirely new experience. It was a dream come true, to have a female partner with whom you talked about everything on your mind and heart. But he'd never done it before, and didn't have the slightest idea of what it even looked like.

He suddenly felt there would be no second chances. He had to get it right the first time. He couldn't break the continuity of togetherness and understanding, or then it would feel like they couldn't trust each other.

Mistrust means not believing the good things, even when they're happening, because they could stop at any time.

But in spite of all this danger about, Peter couldn't, and wouldn't want to deny that when their eyes met, he suddenly felt connected to Wind in an irrefutable way—which reminded him of merging with this mother's thigh. What's more, this part of him was now the strongest. Which really blew his mind. It was an entirely new experience.

Wind looked into his eyes, perceiving his deep craving for her, seeing his innocent need look longingly at her. She was deeply touched, but surprised at the intensity of her feeling.

"When did love last grace your path?" Wind gently asked.

"Not since I was a small boy."

"Oh, that deeply saddens me. Such a very long time to be without."

"That's the gentlest way I've ever heard someone say they loved me."

Peter flushed with feeling at hearing his own words.

"I think I'm beginning to fall in love with you," Wind said. "Though I'm surprised, and certainly had no desire for it to happen. But it's here nonetheless. So I embrace it."

"I think I'm in the middle of a miracle," Peter said.

Wind smiled broadly.

"You're a very exciting man," she exclaimed.

"Oh, wow. You can't mean that. Are you sure? I mean I've been courting you ever since I first laid eyes upon your beautiful person that first day. But what a stupid way to court such an incredible woman by resenting her."

"You were simply crying out from the pain that you had to bear when it happened," she gently replied.

For Peter she couldn't have said anything more perfect.

Embracing Precipitous Possibilities

The train stopped. Wind removed her restraints and Peter quickly following suit. He was glad that something had interrupted the intensity of their last few moments, to give him time to absorb the miracle of her loving him. He was also anxious to get outdoors and see where they were. As they left the elevator Peter expected the usual tenth-floor waiting room. Instead the door opened to the outside.

He found himself standing very high in the mountains on a huge granite plateau, perhaps an acre in size, from which he could see what appeared to be a vast plain that spread out over a hundred miles!

He had no idea the train had been climbing for miles. Its speed must have dulled the sensation.

Two hundred seventy degrees of the visible compass revealed a vast expanse of planet! The remaining ninety degrees were filled with the mountain that loomed behind them, soaring at least another ten thousand feet higher than he stood. To his left mountains rose even taller than the one he occupied. Directly in front of him and down to his right was an incredibly beautiful valley, far below that stretched as far as the eye could see.

"Wow," Peter shouted. "This is spectacular!"

"One of my favorite places," Wind replied.

The valley below captured his attention first. It was a thirty-mile patchwork mosaic of open-field rectangles, lined with what seemed to be tall trees surrounding each of the thousand-acre-d farms, all bordered, and surrounded by trees, making a patchwork of the hundred shades of green, purple, magenta, yellow, red, and more.

"What you see is one of our most verdant valley of farms," Wind said. "We grow many of our special foods here, including your favorite fruit."

"Oh, which part of the valley grows that?" he asked, looking far below.

She laughed.

"I'm afraid I can't tell it's so far away," she replied.

Of course, you idiot, he chided himself for asking such a silly question.

Peter walked with her to the edge of the plateau, ignoring his natural fear of great heights, which was moderate, but definitely there. He didn't want to rain on the parade of this spectacular moment with his fear.

He ended up waiting too long to attend this need. Precipitously close to the edge, he suddenly felt vertigo. Perhaps in retaliation for all his mistakes on Troubadour, the valley below grabbed him and started pulling him down toward it. In sudden panic he realized that he was being irresistibly moved over the edge.

Every muscle in his body rebelled, digging into the remaining earth under his feet, trying to stop his forward motion by throwing his head back away from the edge. He was terrified. Every nightmare he'd ever had of falling precipitously flashed through his mind.

After struggling for eons, for a tiny moment Peter was tempted to let go of control, surrendering to the inevitable flight into which nature seemed intent upon compelling him, flying, abandoning consciousness in preparation for dying.

In a suddenly last protesting spurt of life, he flung open his eyes, intent upon surviving at all costs. But he didn't think he was going to make it.

It was the hand he finally felt upon his shoulder, that told him he was still alive, revealing that Wind had rescued him by pulling him back from the edge of death. She was gently urging him to back away back away even more.

"But you have no fences here."

He felt instantly ashamed. An irritable complaint was the last thing he should have expressed.

"I was your fence," she softly replied.

Deeply grateful to her, Peter swung around to look directly into her eyes.

"Thank you for being there, dear lady. I guess I owe you my life."

"You're welcome. Please remember that I too want you alive." In a tone that revealed her fear of him falling, she added, "It's a long way down there."

"I have never looked down such immense height," he said. "We must be over five thousand feet above the valley below."

"Actually eight thousand feet," she replied.

"In my world this place would be famous not only for the view but also for the number of people who committed suicide by jumping off right here."

"Is suicide in you?" she asked.

He felt ashamed but spoke the truth.

"I have considered it from time to time," he replied. "For a moment I . . . I almost surrendered to dying a moment ago, as if I couldn't prevent it, so why not give in. I'm ashamed to admit it to you."

She held his arm feeling very sad for the pain she knew that must have driven him to that extremity.

"Don't any of your people ever do it?" Peter asked.

"Very occasionally someone does, though the frequency is perhaps a thousand times diminished over the last hundred years."

"Balorin's right that suffering is built into my people's lives as if it were normal," Peter said.

The sun struck Wind's forehead with a piercing white light, bounced off the end of her nose, slithered around the edge of her head, settling upon several points of flesh that together perfectly outlined the circumference of her face, as if the sun had chosen specifically to highlight the unique shape of her expression.

The halo of shining white light that encircling her head remained in Peter's vision, even when the sun's brightness moved on. Then, as the sun beamed farther away from her, it left mostly darkening shadows mixed with still illuminated points that painted a picture of part-light, part-dark, projecting mystery in the contrast between seeing and not seeing, between knowing something and not knowing the rest.

Gradually the sun and Peter released Wind from this archetypal framing, restoring her to the here-and-now. Inspired by this sun-aided vision, Peter suddenly remembered the beautiful things she had said on the train.

"You are such a wonderful experience for me," he crooned. "You're my angel of mercy. You bring reprieve from disaster with the touch of a hand, saving me from sure death. You are extraordinarily kind and thoughtful to me. You make me laugh inside. I don't know why you keep doing all these wonderful things, but thank you from the bottom of my heart. You have completely captured mine."

Wind was overwhelmed with reaction. Her heart opened wide to Peter. Her former misgivings, still lingering in part, gave way inside her. She was no longer the least bit opposed to loving him. She wasn't sure quite yet that she did in fact love him, but she knew now that her heart was completely open to that possibility.

With her love came all her competence. Wind suddenly wanted to give Peter her love. She moved gracefully up to him, and slowly surrounded Peter with her long graceful arms, moving very gradually to give him time to fashion his response.

Peter wanted desperately to surrender himself to her care, but he was afraid. Unwittingly he took a step toward her, then a half step away.

She released some of the pressure of her encircling arms in response.

"Hum," she hummed softly, as if gently serenading, reassuring him.

She was very happy. For the first time since Peter arrived, she was able to live where she belonged, in the territory in which she thrived, within the realm of feeling. Her mind could rest. In this moment figuring was no longer required. She knew what to do.

"Give me your tired body," she crooned, "which holds the pain of your suffering; let it rest in my embrace, I want your pain replaced with the gentle softness of my love."

Very vulnerable himself to the spoken word, Peter could not help surrendering to the verbalized commands of her affection wanting him to be safe and happy.

Peter was swept up into the enormous possibilities of loving. It meant having a family feeling with someone, having all of her wisdom at his beck and call, feeling the pride of someone so extraordinary finding him so interesting and attractive. It was the experience for which he'd always wished in his heart of hearts, a dream fulfilled.

Peter had found his mother's caring thigh in the form of an alien woman's loving breast. His whole body released decades of tension, swooned with relief, drifting toward the intoxication of unconsciousness. All of the guarded reactions, the guilty anticipations, and the dreaded possibilities came home to roost peacefully.

Forever afterward he would feel deep comfort in remembering this moment of love redeemed, restoring him to special-ness.

Cliff Dwelling

It seemed like they had been embraced for an eternity, when she slightly altered her posture.

"Let's go inside," she suggested, slowly releasing him.

Still very connected to her, he turned with her toward the mountain in perfect union.

He suddenly found himself staring into a cavernous opening in the side of the mountain, made darker by the extreme contrast between its dim light and the brilliance of the sun he was now facing, looming behind and above the peak, hallowing its hugeness with a brilliant yellow-red sheen, but spilling over sufficient light to require moving into the cave in order to see it.

Once entered, with time for eyes to adapt, the huge cavern rose above him for about fifty feet. Width-wise the opening was perhaps eighty feet, and went as far back into the mountain as he could see, though it gradually narrowed.

The light in the cave was very muted, but was completely adequate to navigate the rocky hallways. Looking into the mountain revealed an endless progression of rooms reaching father than he could see.

"A city inside the mountain," Peter said.

"Precisely," Wind replied with a smile.

"And you live here?" he asked.

"Yes. But first let me show you the city before we go to my place."

"God, if I lived on Troubadour this is where I would be," he shouted. "There's something vividly alive and very exciting about this place."

He suddenly realized he would need an invitation.

"Uh, that is, of course if I were invited."

"You will always be most welcome," she replied with enthusiasm.

Peter had become fundamentally vulnerable to Wind. Whatever she did, he stayed with it, even if he disagreed, instead of wandering off on his own to solve intimacy's problems.

"You may be surprised, though perhaps also very pleased, to know that this city is called Earth," Wind explained. "Our word for it is 'Quam,' meaning literally 'container of love.'"

"What an exotic name for a planet."

"Oh, it's not the name of our planet. It's the name of the living ecosystem in which we reside and are nourished, which is more a living entity than a location. The name for this planet is Ra meaning a place where life is."

"This is incredible," Peter exclaimed. "How did you guys ever remove all this internal rock?"

"We didn't. The cave is quite natural."

"But it looks so manicured and perfected in a way," Peter observed. "It's not that you haven't left sharp edges and angles, letting the rock express itself, but everything is conveniently high-enough so that you don't bump your head, for instance."

"Oh, we helped nature give us more room here and there," Wind replied. "But the cave is eighty percent the way nature created it."

As they started to walk deeper into the mountain their shadows disappeared into the muted light that, like his hallway, came from who-knows-where but seemed to be amply present just the same.

"How far back does this go?" he asked.

"I don't know, nor do I know anyone who claims to know," she replied, changing their direction toward a closed door off to the right. "I've never explored all the way to the end, nor have I talked to anyone who did. We leave the cave's deepest limits a mystery, lending enchantment to our view of this place."

"But don't you want to find out?"

"I'd rather wait until experience tells me it's time to learn something, before making plans to do or change this or that."

"My god," Peter exclaimed. "That's the most extraordinary thing I've heard you say! It means nobody has objectives. It's like everybody comes from outer space in totally unpredictable ways."

Wind laughed.

"It's better to be focused than have objectives. Only focus gets anywhere.

Objectives mostly try and eliminate whatever says 'no' to them, instead of listening to what the no's have to say."

Wind opened an apartment door and they went in.

"It's just like mine," Peter exclaimed. "Don't you guys believe in any variation in building design?"

The critical edge to his question was unintended. He'd been very impressed by what she had said a moment ago. But he had also become discomforted by it, though it took him a moment to realize why. The thought of letting life happen to him on its own terms felt very scary.

"On Troubadour housing is owned by everyone-in-common," Wind explained. "Which enables us to provide total security in place of living wherever one chooses to be on the planet. 'Live where you wish as long as you want.' We chose to regard that as the fundamental promise of a home always available to you no matter where you are. Ownership guarantees one place. We've arranged for home to be anywhere."

"Wow! Now that would be something."

"Once we'd made that decision, ownership and all of its peculiarities became easily visible. In a relatively short time we discarded ownership, valuable for thousands of years to establish boundaries between people, giving effective assertion of safety to individual interests. But in time it had become a bad habit justifying for instance massive abuses to the welfare of nature."

"But how do you make a home yours then?" Peter queried.

"By having the freedom to decorate it in any way you desire," she replied. "You can do anything you want to the inside."

"But what about the outside?" he challenged. "There is no distinction in how you present your home in its outward appearance."

"We have little use for outward appearances," she gently replied, aware of the difference she was posing for him. "We think mostly they hide pain which needs to be cared for more openly and directly. What's on the inside of anything is what's important to us."

Peter realized for the first time that the walls of the apartment were made of rock.

"These are the same colors and hues of rock in the Mandela," he observed.

"Yes. We got the rock for the Mandela from this mountain."

The granite-like rock was generously streaked with a great variety of warm yellows, light browns, and grays, all of which were tinged with various shades of orange. The patterns these colors created were exquisitely beautiful.

This is nature's painting, Peter thought.

He went to one of the bedrooms to see if the rock looked the same.

There it hosted a somewhat different set of colors, mostly grays and blues in a mosaic of natural striations.

"This is simply spectacular," he exclaimed, returning to the living room. "I could live in this place forever. What an incredibly wonderful, inviting container. And I bet it's great for sleep."

She smiled. "I thought you would enjoy seeing this apartment," she said affectionately.

"You must know how to read minds. Otherwise how can you know me so perfectly?"

"The following is of course a silly set of puns, but it does express the truth. I thought of you're having such a rocky life that you'd surely enjoy the sturdiness of a place where rockiness looked very beautiful."

He laughed with joy.

He was enchanted! This beautiful woman was not only loving him, she was also entertaining him. She was talking poetry to him. It made him feel almost giddy to get so much.

So of course Peter had frequently to thank her.

"Thank you dear lady from the bottom of my heart for giving me so much, and understanding me so well. You are the most beautiful experience my life has ever spawned. The things you say and feel are so wonderfully soothing to me that I am quite overwhelmed by you. I don't know if that's love, but it sure as hell is very powerfully good for me."

Wind was deeply moved by his passionate expression. Her breath quickened. Her heart beat faster. What had previously startled and surprised her, his passion, had become a pleasurable stimulation of excitement for her.

How beautiful this man has become to me, Wind thought. He sees himself so much more completely. Now he gives generously of good feeling. It is truly a remarkable transformation. But what is most valuable to me, she went on, something I never imagined intimacy could provide, is that he gives me the entire perspective of another deeply discerning human. I can see everything differently now if I choose, from both his and my perspective. How richly I am thus endowed.

She had a jolting realization. That's why he reminds me of my mother. She did the same thing for me. How strange that someone I've had to take care of like a baby, is also someone who educates me to a larger view of the universe, of love, and of myself.

She suddenly wanted very much to see her mother, to find out if, as a grown woman her mother still gave her the same quality of experience that Peter now did.

"It's the most incredible thing anyone's ever done for me," Peter announced reverently. "I've never had anyone lo . . . lo . . . lo . . . c . . . care for me, in a way so perfectly suited to me. It's beyond even the very best I can do for my patients. It's caring of such an incredible variety that I can't imagine ever having a problem with you again. I'm so grateful for your knowledge about, and your good opinion of me. Though I'm sure of course that my darker side may have something different to say about all this at some future impulsive moment," he added in warning out of love for her.

"I think, Peter Icarus, that you can use the word love when you refer to my care for you, because I do love you."

Peter was shot through with goodness. His whole body shook for an instant.

"You have brought me something very special," Wind continued. "I don't entirely understand it yet. But already I'm filled with gratitude for you, my beautiful Earthman."

Peter's was stunned. Her expression of love knocked him over. His knees buckled. He fell back hard against the wall.

"Ouch!" he shouted in pain.

Wind rushed over and put her hand on his shoulder.

But he didn't care. The flaming of his passion dulled any physical discomfort.

"You've swept me off my feet," he said.

He was none the worse for wear, just bruised at little.

Tears rushed down his face.

Wind took his face between her hands.

"Ooh, my sweet Peter," she crooned.

The waters of grief released their pain. She joined his tears in sympathy. Together they cried for a while.

Wind felt confident in her understanding of Peter. She had learned that when he was afraid, it was best to turn over to him the next move they shared, so that he could resettle himself wherever comfort still remained, or could be found. She now believed, as she hadn't before that she would find ample gratification for her needs in the process of doing that for Peter. She felt secure in her love in spite of knowing that difficult things would still arise, and that soon he would have to go.

"Whenever you're ready I want to show you my apartment," Wind said graciously, letting him go, standing, and moving toward the door.

"I was so moved by being close to you that I forgot all about where we were," he announced.

"You may be surprised about one thing in my apartment."

"What's that?"

"I'd rather surprise you," she replied.

The first thing he noticed when her door opened was that her rock walls were all painted white. He felt instantly disappointed. For him it ruined the beauty of the rock.

But then he caught sight of what was hanging on the walls. An enormous variety and scope of paintings and sculptures stared back at his deeply impressed eyes.

"You've created all this stuff?" he asked, utterly amazed.

She nodded affirmatively.

"Wow! They are incredibly beautiful! You are really great!"

Peter was mesmerized by her artwork. The paintings were vividly three dimensional with a brilliant display of light and color framing a human figure or two, or an animal in relationship to various natural or symbolic objects, or all of the above in an apparent mythical reenactment. The facial expressions of both human and animal figures were very distinct—vividly portraying a creature that in some specific and unusual moment was very alive in their own peculiar and particular emotional way. Her work seemed to turn ordinary events of time into extraordinary archetypal moments.

Peter was instantly reminded of the classical painters of his own planet, who so effectively captured the spirit of individual humans caught in a particular emotional moment.

Most of the sculptures stood on pedestals around her apartment. But a couple of them were actually chiseled out of the rock wall. The most prominent and centrally located of these presented the figure of a woman who looked like Talorin, running alongside an antelope in the forest. The outline of the two figures had been woven into the grain of the rock. The backs of both the woman and the antelope followed the zigzag contours of the natural striations of red-orange, endowing their running with intense aliveness and apparent motion.

"Oh, my god, but that's simply amazing!" Peter exclaimed. "How did you ever manage to get the natural colors of the rock to fit the lines and feeling of your sculpture?"

"For months I looked at the rock, had fantasies about the rock. I even dreamed about it. And then one morning, a very normal morning of ordinary circumstances, I came out here into the living room to have something to eat, expecting nothing artistic to happen. I was very hungry. I briefly glanced at the wall as I was walking by, more out of habit than intent or desire, and suddenly this vivid image that you see in the sculpture leaped out of the rock toward me! I grabbed my tools and instantly set to work, reaching into the rock with my chiseling instruments and found it wanting to come out at me in the shapes that you see in the wall. It's as if the rock contained its own unconscious synchronicity, such that its striations wanted to metamorph into figures, but needed someone's help to do it. We became lovers striving toward the same beautiful objective."

"What an extraordinary wonderful relationship you have with a wall! You're like a high priestess, or a goddess of some kind, capable of creating archetypal objects. You're like the masters. You know how to deeply inspire! I've never personally seen such extraordinary beauty in one room before. You are an amazing woman with incredible talents. How did you ever fall in love with me?"

Peter was deeply moved and impressed by her. Until this moment he'd known her as his loving helper. But now he saw her in an entirely different light. She was a bloody genius, probably an artist of great renown on Troubadour. And that remarkable person was making him the center of her life. It truly was some kind of miracle.

"Thank you, dear Peter," she said softly. "I'm deeply grateful for your admiration."

"With that kind of talent, how could you possibly have so much interest in spending time with an enigmatic, difficult stranger from another planet like me."

She laughed the loudest laugh he'd ever heard her laugh before.

"I chose to get involved with you because I wanted to study what you call psychology. What better way than to bring a psychologist to Troubadour, meaning you?"

"I don't know why you're doing it," Peter exclaimed in joyful exuberance. "I don't know exactly how you're doing it, and I don't know who you're doing it for because I can't imagine it happening to me. But whatever the truth is about why it's happening, you're treating me like no one else has ever gotten within a thousand miles of before. I feel very special. And I am very deeply grateful."

"Someday you will understand and appreciate how much you are capable of evoking such responses," she replied. "I was just thinking that you remind me of my mother."

"Your mother?"

Peter remembered the strange complexity of the Troubadourian family system, and wasn't exactly sure what Wind meant by "mother."

"Uh, excuse me for asking, but is that the biological one or the other, I mean like the one I saw taking care of Kirkin?"

"Yes."

"Was your mother like that?" Peter asked.

"She was like that, and you," Wind replied.

"Like me? That sounds implausible."

Wind laughed.

"Well, not exactly like you," Wind added. "She was like your innocent eyes I discovered only recently. She looked like that at me all the time when I was small. Which I realize now meant that like you, she was innocently open to me no matter what was happening or what I was doing."

"What a beautiful thing to know and experience," Peter exclaimed in amazement. "And I'm so happy that you put me in the picture."

She looked at Peter suddenly with a different eye. He was no longer "frail-looking." He was slender and strong, bearing gifts for her. She sensed the power of his accomplishments. No matter how much difficulty he was having, or causing for others, the competence he had was always there behind whatever he was doing, willing to offer what it could give.

"I love you, Peter Icarus," she exclaimed. "You are as I speak racing through the currents of me, reaching deeply into every nook and cranny of my being to see what effect you'll bring. So beware for my sake. My heart is completely open to you."

"Oh, my! Oh, my! And mine to you, fair lady!" he exclaimed.

They looked deeply at each other in silence for a long time.

"Do you like to dance?" Wind asked.

"What?" he queried with surprise, taken aback.

"My people have a very simple dance that expresses the joy of close friendship. It's called a 'needra.'"

He stood and came over to her, obviously ready to participate.

Wind took his hand and stood beside him. She began humming a tune. It was a sweet, lyrical melody quite simple in design, which expressed warmth, happiness, and lightheartedness. Her singing voice was soft, very lyrical, and sweetly resonant. She hummed the entire sixteen measures of the song.

Then, as she began the second repetition, she also began to dance in steps which were both quite simple, but which also reminded Peter of a Jewish or Greek circle dance. He began to imitate her, rapidly picking up the rhythm and steps. Together they circled around the center of her living room, dancing and swaying in unison, while she hummed the tune over and over.

Completely caught up in her presence, the dance became hypnotic for Peter. He sank into its repetitious motions, drifting in the joy and comfort of being with this powerful woman, who for some miraculous reason seemed to care for him in a very special way.

After several repetitions of the dance, and at the last measure of her tune she turned toward him, put her arms out, and embraced him.

He realized instantly that this was a part of the friendship dance and responded in kind. But the moment his body made full contact with hers his penis instantly erected. He knew that she must also feel it, and embarrassed he carefully disengaged from her.

"Please forgive me," he apologized. "It just happened. But I really liked your dance," he added.

She smiled.

"You know what? You remind me of my mother too, I mean the one of my first four years."

Peter suddenly felt a deep surge of loving Wind. This time it wasn't in his groin. It came entirely from his heart and reached out to her across the space between them.

"I think before I met you I didn't really know how to get along with a woman."

He paused.

"You . . . you have done so much for me."

"Would you lie with me?" Wind asked. "This is not a sexual invitation. It's a desire to feel your body next to mine. We could lie down on one of the beds fully clothed."

Peter's heart began to flutter. He started to feel light-headed.

It could lead to sex he worried.

"There's something I need to share with you, though I'm very ashamed of it," Peter said.

She smiled encouragingly.

"I know you said sex isn't involved, but things have a way . . . well, to make a long story short, I've always had difficulty having an orgasm."

He paused to check her response. She was still smiling.

"Sex feels—lots of things to me," he began. "It feels urgent and essential to me. But it also feels distant, elusive, and unavailable," he added slowly.

"Then you must be afraid that I too will be ashamed of you when our bodies meet," Wind said patiently.

Peter was overwhelmed by the rightness of her words.

What happened next was the strangest thing of all. Instead of analyzing what he'd said and what she'd said, as he would normally have done, he let her gentle understanding lift him out of his apprehension.

She noticed this softening of his face, smiled, slowly rose from her chair, walked to him, took his hand in hers, and led him into one of her bedrooms.

His heart beat furiously as he followed her. He felt almost dizzy, like he was sleepwalking in a dream.

When they reached the bed Wind let go of his hand and slowly climbed onto the bed to the far side, looked back and beckoned for him to follow.

Hesitantly he did as she bid. She turned toward him and took his outside arm and gently pulled him toward her. Then she embraced him gently, slowly letting their bodies join fully together.

At first Peter almost flinched at her touch. His body became so tense with excitement that it seemed ready to shake. He mentally checked his penis to be sure it wasn't misbehaving. He found it enlarged, but still partially relaxed, and breathed a sigh of relief that helped him relax.

Gradually Peter lost track of time and place. He eased into a drifting experience. He was still acutely aware of her body touching the entire length of his own, but everything else became vague and shadowy. Within minutes they were floating together in the mists of timelessness.

Wind started to hum another tune. It was joyful and perfectly reflected the emotional quality of Peter's experience. He had for so long been caught in the grief of failure, but now was beginning to feel the deep joy of happiness.

Wind was profoundly happy that this strange man from Earth was finally settling into a place where she could share her whole self. By now she knew for sure that to follow this loving path with him would be the fulfillment of her own heart's desire, as well as the redemption of his life. Her singing was a celebration of this.

They lay there together for a long time, drifting in and out of a semiconscious, blissfulness place, occasionally looking briefly at each other.

For Peter such looks were his reassurance that this wasn't just another dream. It was real.

For Wind these looks were the opening of their hearts to each other.

This was the stuff of which lifelong memories are made of.

Loving

"Come, pretty so we can play," she heard him say in his sleep.

She lay next to him watching his slow, deep breathing suddenly quicken, then stop.

He kissed the air as if searching.

She touched her lips softly upon his.

"Humm," he purred. "More."

He was dreaming that he was in a women's clothing store searching for the right woman by smelling each mannequin.

Suddenly he found the one that was alive, and opened his eyes to wakefulness.

There she was, not two feet away, smiling.

"I must be in heaven," he said.

She smiled.

Wind was extremely happy, having a wonderful morning. Before Peter stirred she was musing upon how dear it was to love a man as much as she'd loved her works of art while she was creating them. They had been her children, born of the union of her discerning eye and the brilliant inventiveness of her imagination.

But he was like an animated painting that came alive, bringing an entire set of his own feelings, which painted pictures on the empathic screen of her heart. Being with him was an act of mutual creation, chiseling passionate probabilities back and forth upon the canvas of each other's perception, each devouring the other's dramatic patterns and possibilities, sucking in the other's experience and wisdom, two talents funding each other's resources.

This must be what happens when love works, she mused.

She felt deeply inspired by this vision.

He noticed one of her breasts partly revealed.

Noticing this, she removed her breasts from the nightshirt.

"You can play with them if you want," she said.

"Oh!"

Passion pulsed his body. He blushed, threw caution to the winds, and buried his head between her breasts.

What a miracle a breast is, he mused, how forgivingly soft, promising unlimited flexibility, perpetual gentleness, and rich generosity, the core pieces of care.

He began to feel that her body could be enjoyed as much as he wanted.

"Visit the rest of me," she said softly.

Her command became his willing compulsion. His mouth began searching her body, his soft lips tripping lightly over the skin of her heart's diplomatic interface with life.

Lips move across chest, touching neck's perfect softness, mouthing chin's rugged strength, settling briefly upon nose's discerning opening, caressing eye's admired wisdom, melting lip's yielding, yearning warmth, kissing its way across the canvas of her openness.

She melted into passion's abandon, her body undulating in tandem with the gradual wandering of his lips, stopping here and there to suck for a moment, upon the end of her finger, the point of her elbow, the nap of her neck, the round boniness of her knee, kissing the instep of her thigh, the big toe of her right foot . . .

Passion blooming inside of her, panting for higher pace, she gently moved his head to the center of her inwardness, that opening to the home in which growing takes place.

His tongue found the right spot. He was amazed at the enormous size of her most tender part. In two hundred years, evolution had made the power point of her passion a much larger flower. Already erect, it invited him to suck.

No man had ever imagined making her merging place another breast to suckle. He enjoyed doing it so thoroughly, that she was suddenly overpowered with pleasure. Her body writhed ecstatically in reply to the perfect feel of his licking tongue, as if her joining member had always yearned for precisely this quality of caress. His encircling tongue wet moving parts, her growing wetness joining his to make a delicious cocktail of their togetherness, his encouraging lips pulling from her heart its deepest cries of joy.

Her body convulsed with powerful surges of pleasure pulsating its entire length and breadth. She cried out with each surging wave of passion, her spirit plunging into the ocean of her origins, rooting her soul to its genetic purpose, releasing any semblance of lingering tension, returning her body to its deepest calm.

Wind had known intense sexual pleasure many times before. But she had never felt so deeply moved emotionally in the process. Her body, and all of the things it did were suddenly connected to the highest ambition of her creative spirit. She had intuitively translated the wisdom of the body into the character of her artistic works.

She had never imagined this could be possible, that art and sexual passion could make love to each other. This powerfully intimate experience with Peter enormously expanded the scope and the quality of her creative discernment.

She thought of how long she had postponed having this experience in her life.

Why have I not wanted to do this before?

Clearly something had prevented her. But she would think of it later. For now he was there.

Though he deeply enjoyed assisting her pleasure, Wind's powerful passion had intimidated Peter. He had never known a woman with such intense sexual energy. There was something wildly animal about her passion. It had frightened him because it was so beyond anything he could ever have done himself, making him feel estranged from her.

The moment Wind's eyes found him she knew that he was upset.

"Ooh," she crooned out of sympathy. "I see that you are sadly troubled."

He felt ashamed of his intimidation, but realized he must tell her.

"This is very embarrassing, but I've got to tell you. You . . . you frightened me a little, you were so . . . powerfully passionate."

"I know," she exclaimed with excitement, once more reliving the glorious experience! "It was absolutely incredible! Whatever made you be who you are, doing what you do suits me to perfection."

Awed by her enjoyment, he paused several moments out of respect.

"I guess the problem is that I can't do that," he finally said. "I'm sure you'll be very disappointed in me."

"Impossible! Nothing could be unlikelier," she insisted sweetly. "You are the lover supreme, a woman's every dream! Whatever happens to your pleasure, I will deeply treasure, if it's weak, then we will tweak it to more fully partake of pleasure's cake."

For a moment he wanted very much to accept her offer, but then decided he would like some time to get used to the idea.

"Can we do it later?" he asked.

"Of course."

"I'm sorry to disappoint you now, but . . ."

"Please don't speak for me," she gently interrupted. "I am well pleased, and enormously eased by your patient, tender, talented loving. There is not one ounce of disappointment in me."

This time he believed her entirely.

"Thank you."

Bliss

Lying on his back next to Wind, Peter's eyes wandered around the room as he mused upon the joy of being next to her. He caught sight of something unfamiliar.

"What's that?" he asked.

"Something I did this morning," she replied.

"It looks like a portrait."

"Yes."

Strangely attracted to it, he sat up in bed to get a closer look.

"Holy shit! It's me!" he exclaimed. "When did you do this?"

"This morning. I woke early. Your sleeping late gave me the time."

He was stunned. Wind had captured an almost timeless vision of him. His outward demeanor was middle age, but his overall expression was young and vigorous. A joyful exuberance animated his face, brightly lit by a wide, friendly, lighthearted, slightly impish smile. His eyes were deep-set, reflecting intense curiosity obviously capable of very discerning focus.

God. I look incredible. Shit, I thought I looked kind of ordinary, but she sees something beautiful in me.

He was so excited he almost felt giddy.

"That's as good as an orgasm," he exclaimed. "It's just the most amazing thing to be able to look at. It's me just like I feel sometimes inside, the way I want other's to see me, what I hope I am at heart, a friendly, open-hearted, generous sort of humorous person. You make me look so much better than I think I really am."

"Some day you will no longer need to downplay yourself," she said soberly. "But I am very delighted that you love your portrait. To know that is a wonderful gift to me."

"You always make everything so good, so very happy."

"I can only do it with your help," she replied. "I can't do it by myself."

There was something in her declaration that enlarged Peter's notion of what two-can-do.

"It's really incredible to be so well-known by someone."

"By me I hope," she quipped in jest.

He laughed.

"Only you."

"Then let us ride on the back of this fortuitous synchronicity between my vision and your spirit's hopes and aspirations. Let's catch good fortune's moment and take it to bed with us. Let's tempt your sexuality's fate by giving it a chance to defeat you, by lunging toward what it hopes to prevent, and take what you want it to be."

He gasped, afraid to move.

"I don't know what holds me back when my heart deeply wants to leap toward your beautiful offer, but I feel paralyzed."

She moved slowly toward him and took him in her arms.

"Let's do battle with this demon who dulls your desire. Shall I go on?"

"Do you really want to play with my shit? I can't . . ."

"Your pleasure is what I want to play with. As for that other substance, why don't you take care of it?"

He laughed.

"You are irresistible! I can't stop you. You've turned my resistance into whether or not I believe that you actually want to do this."

"I don't just want to. I'm aflame to do it. I desire to do it. I'm dying to do it."

He adored her enthusiasm.

"I am outnumbered, three to one," he quipped playfully.

Yet once more he felt intimidated by her vibrant aggressiveness. She could feel the tension suddenly rise up in his body.

Her mind quickly grasped the sense of what had just happened.

I'm being too aggressive. He's already told me that.

"But I want you to be yourself, I mean so very passionate," he insisted, sensing what she thought. "Actually I love your energy. It's very inspiring. It's just . . ."

He broke off.

Move slowly with him, she thought. Keep alive my passion, but tenderize its motions.

"It's just that I . . ." he began.

"Your desire is my child," she interrupted. "I would care for him if he would have me. He can rest easy at my hearth. I'll wait for him to start whatever we do."

Her gentle invitation so deeply reassured him, that suspicion could no longer hold up his guard. Passion leaped into the opportunity left open by this omission. Long buried energy aching from eons of constraint, burst through him, pressing his body into the cavities of her openness, his member instantly and fully alert.

Momentarily once more it frightened him to feel such overpoweringly uncontrollable energy. But this impulse had already succeeded in flying him into her arms. He surrendered to the promising protection of that embrace. It was an offer he could not refuse. Fully accepting that, his body flew into the opportunity that appeared, dragging fear into what it wanted him to shun.

Fear doggedly tried to hold passion from its fulfillment. But when she began kissing him and taking off his clothes, fear lost its grip and fell away out of sight. He wanted so desperately to be loved that each lip-felt caress pulled desire from his heart, out-flowing the enormous hunger that had waited for this very special moment.

"I will no longer allow your erection, to suffer from such lack of affection," she crooned.

She embraced his groin with hers.

Into which he thrust with all his heart.

"Close your eyes and feel it with me," she said softly.

He obeyed willingly.

Instantly he understood the wisdom of her command. Blind, he became a body feeling loved, allowing the body's wisdom to prevail, soothed and stimulated by her deft touching, his skin awakened to its sensual potential, his member teased and pleased, waited with mounting anticipation for its eventual chance for release.

She gently touched the two orbs of his power, teased convulsions of desire up the shaft of his penetration, and enticed vitality into the spire of his affection. He thrust deeply into her center, offering the admiration that entrusted him to her care.

She descended upon his erect member, engulfing it with the discerning muscles of her opening, which grasped and let go, in and out, grasped and let go, in and out, caressing care into the vulnerable yearning of his member.

Her breasts hanging close to his mouth. He grasped one with his lips, the other with his hand, caressed the abundant tenderness of her generosity, devouring the sweet nectar of her nipple-d love with his mouth.

His connecting rod, which now partly belonged to her, started pulsating with rapid contractions, overflowing near-painful explosions of enormous intensity, focused in the groin-shaft of his devotion to her goodness. Pleasure-packets of loving worship showered her center with his gratitude, laying gifts upon the alter of her powerful competence as a person, someone in whom he could rely, celebrating the miracle of someone so incredibly talented choosing him to love. She was manna from heaven.

She would always be the woman who taught him how to love, who gave him someone he wanted very much to love. She was the opportunity to be caring that had made the difference between success and failure of his sexual experience. He was deeply reassured to be able once again to love someone so fully.

Wind was ecstatic with joy that she had been so successful in loving Peter, so cleverly helping him feel and accept her care. But what most awed her about the experience was how much she felt he had given her with his orgasm. She knew that he deeply adored her, that he regarded her in some manner like a goddess, someone slightly above him, like him vulnerable to be hurt, yet capable of being so much more competent at moments when he couldn't. Though he didn't believe in worship, she inspired that ceremony in his heart. She knew she had done enormously valuable things to his life. She had shown him that he was both a strong talented and capable man, who was also at times a frightened boy, afraid to trust, yearning to be loved.

She bent down and put her soft wet lips upon his, lingering there for a long time, savoring the sweet joy she'd felt when he gave so much of himself to her when he exploded. She lay down next to him.

They lay in each other's arms, side by side for a very long time, soaking in the bounty of reassurance that their togetherness now provided in great abundance. Hereafter every embrace recreated this experience, becoming the memory amplifier that would instantly reenact the warmth and goodness of these very special moments in their relationship in the years to come. For Peter this experience became a template of loving to which he would always refer.

Salivations

Wind and Peter spent the next two days, what seemed like an eternity basking in the sunshine of their love, marveling at each new happening into which their happiness brought them. What surprised them the most was how many parts of their separate lives were touched by what they had become in relation to each other, she his good mother, he her loving pupil, she his deep admirer, he her devoted supplicant, she his curious-about-you friend that delighted him with her interest, he her perfect mirror whose responses profoundly illuminated her understanding of herself.

They also spent hours apart to be alone with themselves for a while, in order to begin the digestion of everything new racing through their experience. They would wander in different directions up the many trails that climbed the huge mountain upon which they lived, deep in private thought, always excitedly anticipating with great joy their expectant reunion, when they could share with each other what they'd been thinking about.

She laughed a lot when she was by herself, her happiness bubbling over. Loving Peter had started many new projects in her imagination, that eventually she would get around to doing, giving her a multitude of wonderful things to occupy herself for years to come. She felt incredibly rich with so much opportunity for happiness waiting its turn to happen. It was as if her life, perhaps for a long while, would have no time for misfortune.

Peter had different business to attend when he was alone. Since happiness was believe-it-or-not happening to him for the first time since he was four years old, he reworked every wonderful experience in his spirit, looking at it from all angles, most fundamentally to be sure of its competence and reliability, but also in order to indelibly print it on the core of his heart.

These memory-motivated flurries into suspicion had no effect upon Wind or their relationship. Mostly they were played out, in their negative forms within peculiar and frightening dreams. Which meant that daily emotional issues, which before had provoked fear and suspicion, were now contained in smaller places, instead of spreading out everywhere.

He began to believe in their love, to feel that never again would he surrender completely to fear's frightful musings. A pocket of something solid, built upon the foundation of this loving would always be nearby. Once restored by love, esteem would never again entirely wilt away, leaving him exposed to the rape of utter neglectfulness. This was his parent's principle crime; they never knew him as himself, so he never knew himself either.

The dark cloud that hung over this redemption of his life was of course his imminent departure from Troubadour. But the lips of his consciousness were sealed to this recognition, or he would never have been able to succeed in accomplishing the entire experience of Troubadour.

Walking together they had reached a rocky knoll that provided a panoramic view. She stepped out onto a small plateau with an almost flat surface, turned, and beckoned him to follow.

He was immediately struck by her appearance. She was dramatically framed by a vast expanse of distant mountain peaks splotched with large swaths of deep snow, some of which had scooped out deep valleys.

It was a clear day in the wilderness of the mountains, where an incredible purity of brightness erases any memory of civilized environments, making one yearn to be able to live in nature, not for the trees and the lakes, etc., but for this pure untouched-by-humans container, giving humans a chance to start fresh relating to nature, purposefully, slowly, carefully, learning as much as possible about anything before chosing to do anything with it, before we understand our relationship to it.

She beckoned again. As he moved toward her, his face shown with the innocence of a devoted affection. He accepted whatever she wanted unless it was spontaneously opposed by some priority of his own, and then he would carefully negotiate. He had no more intrinsic misgivings about what she was doing. He felt comfortable with whatever she was or did.

He no longer called it trusting, which was a metaphor he realized was invented by someone without love speaking from loneliness-pain. Now he called it loving, a metaphor that comes from the abundance of emotional gain.

They sat down together on a soft bed of moss to watch the view. A bright blue, cloudless sky was framed by the snow-filled tops of many mountain peaks. The sun deeply warmed their bodies, while a gentle breeze coming down off the snow cooled the sun's tendency to overheat the skin, making a just-right blend of disparate elements that perfectly comforted.

"I think I finally want to be a mother," Wind said.

"Wow! What made you decide that?"

"You. Helping me become so happy loving a man has enchanted me far more than I ever imagined. Becoming a mother evolves out of that experience."

"God! You would make such an incredible mother!" Peter exclaimed. "I'm already jealous of the kid who's going to get you."

"Thank you for saying so," she said appreciatively. "Though perhaps you will be shocked by my next wish."

"Oh. What is it?"

"I want your child."

He was shocked. To begin with he had assumed that was genetically impossible. But what blew his mind is that she wanted genes from a backward planet.

"You don't mean you want my child?" he queried.

"Yes I do," she replied gently.

"But is that even possible?"

"Let's find out."

"But . . . but what's to become of . . ."

Desperately he denied what his thought would have led him to, contained in the rest of his sentence, which he didn't even allow himself to think— "that child when I'm gone?"

"W . . . why would you be interested in such a thing?" he asked.

"It might be very beneficial for my people to find out what it means to add your genes to ours," she replied. "But that's my smallest reason for wanting it. What really prompted me is the way I feel about you."

He was utterly astounded. That possibility was as far from his mind as his love for her had originally been to her awareness.

"I would call her Athena or him Apollo in honor of you."

"In honor of me?"

"Of the gods of wisdom in your mythology," she replied.

He couldn't deny it, but he felt the same excitement she did about the idea.

She could tell that he felt that way.

"Aren't we being a little crazy?" he asked, thinking of how reckless they were being in attempting such an experiment.

She laughed and then looked deeply into his eyes.

"If you asked me, I would make Athena now," she said.

A paranoid thought raced across his mind that this wish of hers was the only reason they'd invited him to come, that their species was in danger of extinction and needed new genetic input.

But it took him only a moment to laugh that suspicion out of sight.

"Let's do it!" he said excitedly.

A Small Gathering

Peter was dreaming that Wind had taken his hand and soared high into the sky on top of billowy, white clouds. They started dancing on the clouds, sometimes leaping great distances from one to the other, passing in slow motion through the blue sky in between the puffy white-fluff pavilions that, as they danced whirled around their feet and ankles encouraging the motion and exuberance of their movements.

Peter knew that he could never have done this by himself. Wind was the one who could dance on the clouds. She had brought him here to share the experience, hoping it would awaken something in him as it always awakened for her.

It was happening. He could feel a powerful force moving through him that filled him with strength and confidence.

He began to imagine that he might be able to do this on his own without her help. But when he let go of her hand he started falling!

He woke to see Wind's face two feet from his own, soothing him.

He was instantly lost in the pleasure of seeing her. She was partly facing him in her sleep, her lips slightly ajar. Breathing was all that moved her. It happened almost imperceptibly, its ins and outs occurring so far apart that they almost seemed disconnected from each other.

Peter merged with the shape and pattern of her sleep's whispers. When she breathed out he was the face that felt the warm breeze of the sweet balm of reassurance that normally issued from her heart. When she breathed in he imagined himself being pulled inside of her along with the air her lungs craved, incarnating his desire to be deeply wanted by her. Once inside her lungs were close to her heart, a proximity that felt luxuriously restful, embraced as he was by the mellifluous folds of the body of her love's generosity.

These fantasies surrounded the two-of-them with a romantic aura of great significance, imbuing their togetherness with the great and noble purpose of one species inseminating another with its wisdom and experience, investing his sense of the future with enlarged prospects and possibilities.

Wind stirred. Peter felt her breath quicken. Her next inhalation went on, it seemed to Peter forever, its whisper-sound gradually increasing in volume, the first deep breath of the stretching of her waking.

A soft, happy murmur ushered from her lips announcing her body's intent to reach its fullest extension. She seemed to lengthen by almost a foot, Peter observed admiringly. With her long arms raised straight above her head she seemed well over seven feet tall.

The purring moan of her stretching received an extra dose of energy right at the end, turning it into a cry of delight, expressing her life's vigor as she celebrated the restoration of consciousness dawning a new day's hopefulness.

I'm still here alive and happy and with him, she mused.

Her eyes opened to see him.

"Thank you for being there," she purred.

"Your welcome. But shouldn't it be me saying that to you?" he affectionately insisted. "You're giving me so much more."

"Don't you appreciate my greeting?" she asked with an affectionate, slightly amused disappointment.

"Oh, yes," he protested, suddenly alarmed that he had done something to hurt her feelings. "I didn't mean to imply anything. I'm sorry. I adored your greeting! It was beautiful!"

"Oh, stop worrying, my darling," she said with a lighthearted laugh. "Lift your mind from the gutter of your past, and bury yourself in the morning's promise of a new day."

"I was doing that as you awoke, breathing in the wonder of having you next to me," he replied, breathing easier.

"Well, my beautiful man. I have a surprise for you this morning."

"Animal, vegetable, or mineral?" he quipped good-naturedly, delighted at the prospect of yet another adventure.

"Some of all three," she replied. "The animals you'll meet soon, the vegetables we'll find in a most remarkable place, and of a rather unusual variety, all of which will be surrounded by the most beautiful mineral deposits on Troubadour."

"Will all this be happening with thee?" he asked.

"I wouldn't partake of any other recipe," she replied.

"Then I'm for it. So please tell me, what's the adventure to be?"

"A picnic and hike with some you know, and others with whom familiarity has not yet been sown. But you'll moan with delight when you see the place which will embrace all of this bounty."

The thought of new people pulled him out of playfulness.

"Who's coming?"

"Rambler and Talorin have wanted to see you for days. This trip fits them into our busy ways."

"The last time I saw them I was to you already enslaved," he replied, delighting in their sharing of rhymes. "I wonder what they'll think when they see us so deeply enclave-d."

"They'll be very curious about what we have spawned," she replied. "Two strangers will be there, tempting you to overdrawn."

"I'll take my chances, as long as we have our romances," he said, his confidence growing.

A sudden fear interrupted his delight.

"Is it improper to show how much you love someone in the presence of others?" he asked.

She cuddled closer to him.

"Improper won't make you a pauper, though anything done is better done subtle, when done bluntly requires rebuttal."

Peter laughed at the clever wit of her rhyming. He was losing his misgivings.

"As for the other two who will accompany you, Talorin has a child, a boy of seven named Deetjin, and I have a friend, Saavin, who is nineteen."

"Ah, children. That will be very interesting."

As they left the elevator and approached the huge city entrance, Peter could see Talorin standing tall and slender, framed against the bright light behind her. She was stretching herself as she waited. Rambler was off to the right looking at something. A young Troubadourian female suddenly ran gazelle-like across the city entrance. Following behind at a much slower pace was a boy who struggled unsuccessfully to keep up with her.

"Heelooo Petra Ickus," Talorin exclaimed peering into the darkness of the city entrance when she recognized him.

"Hello," Peter replied. "How good to see you again."

"Me tooo," she replied.

"Hello, dear Peter," Rambler cried out running toward Peter with a happy heart.

Peter was suddenly reminded of Rambler racing across the meadow when he thought he was another wild animal.

"Rambler. How good to see you. I've missed you. I guess it's been a long time. I haven't gotten back to you since we last . . ."

Stop apologizing for Christ's sake, Peter.

"What I meant to say is I've been pretty busy doing things inside, so I haven't been wandering about giving you any emergencies from which to rescue me."

Rambler laughed his huge lion-laugh.

"You always say the funniest things," Rambler exclaimed. "What you say is true. I have missed our adventurous struggles with survival."

"I can't say that I have," Peter replied with candor.

Rambler laughed again.

"Of course the best parts of those survivals were the times we spent together talking," Peter added.

With great enthusiasm Rambler threw his arms around Peter and embraced him.

But Rambler had forgot the difference in body density between a Troubadourian and an Earthman. He embraced Peter with such strength that he literally forced the air out of the Earthman's lungs, leaving them so completely emptied that it seemed to Peter as if he would never again be able to inhale in time before he expired!

Rambler sensed a death moan stir in Peter, and instantly put him down, lifting Peter's arms above his head, forcing air back into his lungs.

"Such a powerful man you are," Peter said after regaining his breath.

"I seem to be as much a danger as a rescuer to you," Rambler acknowledged with humor.

"But your hug had the virtue of care inside it," Peter insisted.

"So did the Terrible Tree's embrace of you," Rambler retorted. "It would have devoured you with great care."

Peter was distracted by the young woman, Saavin, embracing Wind with great enthusiasm and affection.

"Hi, mom," she said.

"But I'm not your mother, my sweet young woman," Wind gently reminded her when they'd disengaged.

"I know. You keep reminding me you're not. And I keep insisting that you're my spiritual mother. I will keep addressing you that way until you show me what harm there is in it," Saavin insisted with youthful determination.

I keep shying away from being a mother, Wind observed to herself. I must talk to Talorin about that.

For a tiny moment Wind felt a sudden pang of regret telling her that she'd made a mistake nineteen years before when Saavin was born from her womb, when she'd chose not to be her mother, though within months she had become Saavin's close friend. She looked at Saavin who was looking at her very keenly, closely watching her.

Perhaps she's right, Wind thought, that I have been a spiritual mother. She certainly regards me as the model of a woman she prefers and admires.

Wind glanced at Peter.

He's stirred up all my relationships. They will not be the same anymore, because I am different.

She suddenly felt grateful having Peter in her life.

"You must tell me what you've just been thinking!" Saavin interjected with great excitement, no longer able to restrain her exploding curiosity. "I've never seen your face go through so many emotional expressions in such a short time. I've simply got to know what's behind all that beautiful feeling!"

Wind laughed.

"Later, my sweet," Wind replied. "Today I must keep at least one eye upon the Earthman."

"My sweet," Saavin repeated. "You've never called me that before. You always call me 'darling' or 'dear friend.'"

"You're right, my dear," Wind acknowledged, surprised at herself. "I want to talk with you about that. But right now I must keep my best attention upon Peter. I'm sure you understand."

Saavin did in a way, but in another she didn't.

"You must at least tell me one thing!" Saavin protested.

"If you insist. I'll tell you this much. This man has become a fulcrum around which my life is changing."

Saavin was deeply surprised. She hadn't expected to be so successful in her probing. Wind didn't always gratify her. That was partly what she liked about Wind, why she called her a "second mother," along with the sweet, endearing woman who had mothered her so well—because Wind constantly challenged and inspired her, often by leaving her waiting to find out things for herself.

Why is she confiding in me so easily, Saavin asked herself? It must be part of the changes she mentioned.

In gratitude for Wind's openness, Saavin threw her arms around the older woman. She felt excited, aware that something in herself had started to change in response to Wind's changing, though she didn't have the slightest idea of what it was, just that it was happening. Her teacher occasionally reminded her that this would happen to her, and she must be prepared to leap toward what she didn't know, into places she hadn't seen, if she wanted to take full advantage of the opportunities of her life.

Yes, she shouted to herself very excited! That's what's different! She spoke to me as if I was a fully-grown woman like herself.

Saavin had always disliked the experience of older people treating her as an equal. It felt sleazy, too opportunistic, as if they were trying to be her friend instead of her caretaker.

But this was different because she felt different about herself.

Saavin burst with pride! Her friendship with this famous lady was her favorite and most cherished possession. And now it had reached new heights. Something new was starting to happen between she and Wind. She was very excited about it.

She had heard rumors that Wind had spent the last couple of days alone with Peter in her living quarters. She sensed something very exciting was going on, full of romantic potential, and she was somehow going to be a part of it.

Saavin had just started to become deeply interested in romance and the sexual intimacy it produced. It was not that she had not masturbated for years, even had sexual liaisons with young men and women. But she had enjoyed sexuality mostly as a physical and sensual experience. She had postponed the emotional-intimacy part of loving, something young women on Troubadour were delaying longer and longer as generations passed, in order for the self to evolve more fully, to give individual talent and experience the same deeply emotional support that being-in-love provides a couple.

Like Peter Talorin was closely watching Wind and Saavin, with the same intensity that Saavin had first looked at Wind. Talorin marveled at the exuberance of affection between the two women.

The moment Wind turned away from Saavin, Talorin raced in to be the next to greet Wind. She threw her arms around the artist and twirled in circles holding Wind close to her heart as they usually did.

Though momentarily startled when first embraced, Wind was used to Talorin's exuberance. Pretty fleet-footed herself, she could normally keep up with Talorin's powerful agility at least for the few steps that embracing normally required.

But today Talorin was feeling even more exuberant than usual because of the large number of fascinating people with whom she was going to spend the day. She would have called it a wonderful people-feast full of good things. All of which meant her exuberance brought extra energy to her embrace. She swept Wind off her feet!

Wind gasped!

Talorin instantly set her down, holding her until she regained her balance.

"Forgive me," Talorin said. "Please forgive me."

"My beautiful gazelle," Wind replied affectionately. "I would not have you any other way. I deeply admire the great beauty and strength of your movements. I know I'm in good hands even when my feet leave the ground. You are precious for me to know."

Like Saavin had been, Talorin was deeply surprised! She had always felt far more emotionally distant from Wind than she wanted. She perceived Wind to be a larger spiritual person than herself. Wind was widely known and greatly honored by most, while Talorin, though known far and wide for her physical prowess, had never achieved a sense of spiritual evolution, certainly nothing even approaching the spiritual depth for which Wind was famous. So what really could she offer this remarkable woman?

And now Wind had spoken to her as if they were dear friends. It was a miracle!

Talorin was a very impetuous and courageous woman. Given the encouragement of this deeper feeling from Wind, she threw herself into the possibility of what it might become, by asking Wind a very intimate and personal question.

"Is he exciting?" she asked, referring to Peter.

Wind laughed.

"In some ways yes," Wind replied.

She answered me, Talorin exclaimed to herself!

She was both astounded and very pleased that her experiment had worked! Wind was indeed confiding in her in a way she'd never done before.

So Talorin asked another question.

"In which ways?"

"His innocence," Wind replied.

"Oh, how very interesting."

Wind suddenly realized, as everyone else already knew, that she was indeed acting very differently toward both Saavin and Talorin. She glanced at Peter to see if he knew.

He did. He'd been staring at her with great admiration and deep affection, thoroughly enjoying her exchanges with these two women.

It's really great to be with all these Troubadourians, he realized.

Rambler joined the encirclement. He'd been talking to Deetjin aside. He addressed his wife first.

"My dear partner, it must be said that both of us are careless with our strength. While I was hugging Peter to death, you were twirling our dear Wind off her feet."

"Speaking for myself," Peter interjected, "it wasn't that bad."

"To which I also agree," Wind added.

"Well, Talorin agrees with me," Rambler retorted humorously. "Today we have an abundance of aggressive energy."

"Well I for one deeply admire what she does with that aggression," Peter insisted. "Please tell her she's a biological miracle, and such a very beautiful woman. She's simply amazing to me."

Rambler translated for Talorin.

She broke into a huge smile and spoke to Peter in Troubadourian, knowing that her husband would translate but wanting Peter to see and hear the emotions connected to that translation.

"She says you are a very romantic man, and that it's very exciting to be around you. If all Earthmen are like you she wants more of them brought here."

Peter laughed.

"Please warn her that our sense of romance is not well developed," Peter insisted. "We seriously believe in it, but we don't know very much about how to do it very effectively."

For several minutes it had dawning upon Peter that he was being stalked. Deetjin had been following him closely for some time, carefully peering into his eyes very determinedly, moving around constantly to keep Peter's face in full view. It was as if he was visually climbing inside of Peter so he could see everything that was there. His utter lack of inhibition felt strikingly aggressive to Peter, even a bit intimidating.

"This is Talorin's son, Deetjin," Rambler explained.

"Uh, does he speak English?" Peter asked.

"No, he doesn't."

That reassured Peter. It gave him some distance from the boy's fierce scrutiny.

"He's a very curious boy," Peter observed.

"Oh, he's voraciously curious," Rambler acknowledged. "Talorin says he has the eye of a Hectprin, an eagle-like bird on Troubadour, known for its clever abilities as a predator."

Someone pulled Peter's sleeve.

"And I'm the last person for you to meet," Saavin interjected. "Hello, Peter Icarus. I'm Saavin, Wind's loving friend, Talorin's admirer, Rambler's little woman, and Deetjin's sometimes companion. I am very pleased finally to meet you, sir."

"And I you," Peter retorted, completely taken in by her candid and thoughtful charm.

She looked a lot like Talorin, elongated and narrow for a Troubadourian, giving her the same streamlined look of a body shape that more flew than ran through space. Her hair was light golden blonde streaked with very subtle red tones. Her lips were full and very expressive. Her eyes still retained the extra largeness of childhood.

"Perhaps we could get started walking," Rambler suggested. "We have far to go."

"Where are we going?" Peter asked.

"To a very special place on this mountain," Saavin quickly replied before anyone else could respond.

Having assumed the role of Peter's guide, Saavin started up the steep trail taking the lead, also talking Peter's hand in hers. She was going to get first dibs at him.

The others followed, Wind next in line, with Deetjin hurrying to keep up with Saavin. He seemed to have one central idea on his mind, to get through the giants in front of him so he'd have a chance to catch up with her.

Smiling at her son's determination, Talorin took Rambler's hand to become the rear of this small assemblage moving up and around the mountainside.

Alternating Emotional Currents

Suddenly Saavin headed off to the right on a trail that Peter had never used before in his wanderings around the mountain. Within three hundred paces the trail stopped steeply climbing, thereafter being relatively level, following the contour of the mountain's ridges and valleys, sometimes climbing a little, and sometimes descending some, meandering around the peak.

"Why is everyone so mysterious about this place we're going?" Peter asked. "I have only vague impressions of what to expect."

"Well, then you are blessed with the tools of creation, meaning your vague impressions and imagination," Saavin retorted, glancing back at the woman who had shown her how to think this way. "So you can look forward to the great pleasure of creating your own images of what's to come."

"Now that's just what I was talking about," Peter replied in a jovial manner. "More mysterious words. How can that be a tool for creation?"

"Because then what takes place is your story instead of something that's just happening to you," Saavin added proudly.

Peter was shocked with the sophistication of what she had just said. Even the young instruct me here, he observed.

"All right, let's leave that topic be," Peter suggested. "But tell me, how much time do people of your age spend together with each other?"

"We get together all the time, though probably not nearly as often as your people do," Saavin replied. "Earth people seem to be afraid of aloneness, and spend most of their time trying either to love each other, or hate and destroy each other; whereas we get together mostly to share or celebrate by demonstrating what we've been up to, to each other."

Hanging around Wind as often as she did, Saavin had absorbed an enormous amount of information that she now proudly pontificated for Peter's erudition.

"You're right about my people," Peter acknowledged. "We do spend too much time around each other. But tell me more about Troubadour. What's this thing about demonstration that you were talking about? Is it like advertising in my world?"

Saavin didn't understand advertising and looked back at Wind for an answer. She was chagrined that this sudden hole in her knowledge should suddenly appear, just as she was making a very strong impression upon the Earthman with how smart and clever she was.

"In certain ways it is like advertising," Wind explained, walking just behind Saavin and Peter. "But it's not done in the way your world does advertising. We share our projects with each other out of a natural desire for other people to be involved in our work and ideas, to get their feedback, sometimes to get their support for a project like the one that brought you here. We like what your world would call negative feedback. We aren't looking for admiration or profit, though admiration is very pleasing if spontaneously offered. But mostly what we want is contrasting views to what we've done, to give us perspective that can improve what we're trying to accomplish. I get a great deal out of showing my art to others. Their responses provide me with a lot of information."

"Are things sold in these demonstrations?"

"Exchanges and barters yes, but nothing more," Wind replied. "The economic motives of your world abuse the sharing of useful information. Profit nails things down to small places, thus providing a paucity of useful outcomes, reducing everything to a meaningless number without unique form or substance, turning something beautiful into something generic, making universality mundane."

Though Wind's remarkable message was recorded in the memory banks of Peter's mind, what most grabbed him was the sound of her voice. It soothed him as much as it did when they were alone. He was deeply relieved that he could feel this so openly when around other people. He didn't have to hide it from harm.

"Is music a very big thing on Troubadour?" Peter asked. "In these demonstrations, do people ever perform their compositions?"

"Oh, very often," Saavin shot back from the front with great enthusiasm. "Music is one of the most important things on Troubadour!"

"Oh, that's great," he replied, absolutely delighted at the kindred-spiritedness of her reply. "It's one of my most important things too."

"Do you compose?" she asked.

Should I, he asked himself?

"Well, no. But I wish I could."

"You probably can," Saavin retorted with compete confidence.

"You sound so sure of me being able to do it," Peter observed.

"We believe that if you spend lots of time thinking or musing about something, like music for instance, then your psyche is trying to tell you have talent inside this preoccupation, so get busy doing something about it."

She's right, he thought excitedly. I've always wanted to put my hand to it.

"I would love to hear a concert of Troubadourian music," Peter replied, shifting attention away from himself.

"There will be opportunity for that," Wind said from behind.

Deetjin finally saw an opening large enough to run through, and darted up next to Peter, just slightly ahead of Wind.

Knowing that this put Wind and her son together on the trail, Talorin moved quickly to attend Deetjin, unsure of how Wind felt about spending extended time with children. She'd had the impression for some time that Wind, though she obviously liked Deetjin, seemed a little put off by some aspects of his child-ness. Since Wind was normally such a gracious person, this had puzzled and even disturbed Talorin a little.

When Deetjin sensed his mother behind him he turned to touch her. She was the most important person in his life. The exploration of new things could wait a little longer. Above everything else he loved being with his mother.

Wind stepped back making room for mother and son, joining Rambler in the rear, leaving Peter with Saavin, who obviously wanted to be alone with him.

"What's a psychologist do?" Saavin asked Peter.

"He helps people who have been damaged emotionally to unravel the mystery of those injuries," Peter replied, very impressed by his own explanation.

"What does that accomplish?" she asked.

"Hopefully it restores to freer expression talents which have long been indentured to the misguided objectives of childhood nightmares," Peter replied, even more surprised at the precision of his own explanations.

"But why do people get injured in the first place?" Saavin asked with innocent, though slightly condescending curiosity.

Peter was surprised and irritated by the naiveté excess of her question. "Because we don't know what we're doing yet," he replied with a touch of annoyance. "Because we're still floundering around making lots of mistakes with each other," he added.

"But why do you have to make so many mistakes in the first place?" she persisted.

She was becoming very annoying to him.

"Don't your people make your share of mistakes?" Peter asked, a little frustrated.

"Of course we do," she retorted. "But nobody gets very injured by it."

"Well, I guess your people have learned more than mine," he admitted, but . . ."

"So why haven't you learned as much?" she asked.

This has gone far enough, he shouted to himself! Are all kids on Troubadour as cheeky as this one? I don't want to have an incident with this young woman. That would be awful. But why is she trying to shame me?

He took a deep breath and offered the only other piece of information he could think of that might shift her perspective.

"I've been told your people have evolved hundreds of years ahead of mine," he explained, hoping once more for respite from her relentlessly probing.

"Oh, really," she retorted, very surprised. "Is that so? Oh. I see. I didn't know. Or I guess maybe Wind must have told me once, though I must have put the memory in the wrong place."

Though obviously embarrassed, Saavin was strangely calm, Wind noticed.

In her youthful enthusiasm to sound wise in this man's eyes, Saavin had just stumbled into one of the holes in her understanding. Though obviously very well informed, she was still seeking a large enough container for her understanding to get inside of, that didn't keep giving her erroneous responses, making her feel like she was still a kid. She was getting really tired of that. Like Wind, she wanted to be a powerful woman.

A goal that depends upon your next move, was the Wind-advice that popped into her memory.

She needed to be as grown-up as possible about this event. Taking hold of her courage she moved slightly ahead of Peter on the trail, turned, and walked backward facing him to look squarely in his face.

"I've just committed one of my mistakes," she said with an embarrassed smile. "I was drawing impulsive conclusions about you not well thought out. I don't usually do that when I'm alone. But it's different when you do it with somebody else. You lose track of what you don't know."

Peter laughed with relief, joy, and then appreciation for the remarkable thing the young woman had just accomplished.

"I hope I have not injured you by my mistake," she said in a tone that assumed that she had not, but wanted to be sure.

She had completely won over Peter. He suddenly really liked her.

"I am amazed," he said. "That's such a beautiful thing you did for me. How could I feel hurt after such a healing experience?"

She beamed with delight. Not only had she avoided hurting him. She had inspired his admiration. To have the good opinion of the man Wind seemed mysteriously to be so enamored of, was a dream come true.

"You're pretty good yourself," she retorted with a big smile. "I really liked what you said about psychotherapy."

So this is the kind of confidence you can have if somebody raises you right, Peter thought, looking both admiringly, and a touch enviously at Saavin.

Meanwhile Deetjin was conducting his own investigation of Peter.

"Who is that man, Me-Me?" Deetjin asked Talorin, referring to Peter, addressing his mother with his favorite nickname for her.

"He's a visitor from another world."

"I know that," he retorted impatiently, yet lovingly, not wanting to be underestimated. "I meant what kind of a person is he?"

"He's a very special man who has risked a great deal to spend precious time with us," she replied, knowing that Deetjin loved to spin experiences of new people he'd meet into stories with adventure.

"Where did he come from?" he asked with great anticipation.

"From another world so far away that if you walked there it would take you ten billion years to get here," she replied.

"That's very, very far," he marveled.

He loved it when he could marvel. The dust of adventure would stir. He wanted above almost anything else to travel very far away and find strange new remarkable places where he would do great things! So he was very taken with the distance Peter had traveled.

"What risks did he take?" he asked, getting excited at the adventurous possibilities that were fast developing.

"To stay here for very long makes his body feel like it's pulling itself apart," she replied, simplifying information for his consumption.

"Oh, you mean he could die!" Deetjin shouted. This was much better than he'd hoped!

He'd tried hard to get out of going on this outing, expecting it to be boring. And just as his mother had predicted when she insisted he come, he was having an entirely opposite reaction. He was becoming a part of an adventure! He could hardly wait to see what would happen.

Wind observed Peter's curiosity about what Deetjin and Talorin were saying to each other.

"Deetjin is a boy who loves adventure," Wind explained. "Talorin has just helped him turn you into one. So he was beginning to think very exciting thoughts about you, and to build a fantasy of adventure around you."

"Like what thoughts?" Peter asked, happy to be a part of a boy's adventure.

"The huge distance you traveled to be here, the risks to your longevity in doing so, that sort of thing," she offered.

It didn't matter to Deetjin that he couldn't understand what Wind and Peter were saying. He could still gather the sounds and visual impressions as an intuitive picture incorporated into him, making it the building material for constructing the tone and structure to the character of the hero in his new adventure, someone probably like Peter who was named Deetjin, someone who would be doing extremely risky, experimental, yet very beneficial things for everyone. In these adventures Deetjin was building the vocabulary of the self-mosaic that would eventually reveal and demonstrate the complex character of the man he would someday become.

With Deetjin firmly attached to Peter, Talorin let her attention wander to Wind, the woman she most admired in the world. To her surprise, Wind was about to speak to her.

"I've been wanting to talk to you about Deetjin," Wind said.

Talorin's face lit up. She had no idea Wind had any particular interest in either her son or her own experience of mothering him. She had for years deeply admired Wind as a woman of very high spiritual substance. She felt a kind of reverence in Wind's presence, not because Wind intimidated her, but because Wind always inspired her. In fact Wind had inspired Talorin to be a mother, though the younger woman had never shared this information with Wind.

And now she wants to talk about my son, Talorin thought.

She was suddenly aware that parenting was the one thing that she knew much better than Wind. Being unable to share what she was proudest of, and understood the most about, had always muted her relationship with Wind.

"I'm so happy you want to talk to me about him," Talorin exclaimed. "But how shall we do it?"

Wind carefully formed her question.

"Several years ago you and Rambler were deeply engaged in studying the new species that you, Talorin, had found in the high forest on one of your expeditions in your twenties. Then in the midst of that study with Rambler, you suddenly decided to be a mother to Deetjin. I remember your excitement about your species discovery. I've always wondered what happened to that excitement when you switched the focus of your life."

"You're wondering why I suddenly changed directions?" Talorin queried.

"I guess I am."

"Well, I wasn't talking much about it at the time, but Deetjin is what I was most interested in finding. My discovery of the species was more of an accident, while Deetjin was the realization of a long-term dream. I was looking three years for a child who could fit me in many ways like a glove. I must have visited a dozen birth-nurseries. Sometimes I was discouraged. But now I understand what happened. My long wait provided me with the span of time I needed to help Rambler establish his scientific identity before finding my child. Life knew better than I how it must happen."

She hesitated only for a moment.

"There is something else I must explain," Talorin added. "I don't think of myself as the finder of that new species. It just happened that my eyes were the first to catch sight of it, a fact that holds no special meaning for me. I think of it as our finding, meaning Rambler's and mine. But whoever did it, once we established its identity and genetic signature, the workload seriously declined, leaving me with the time I needed for Deetjin. Rambler is the real scientist in this family. I shared his passion, and still do to a great extent."

"Are you sure you aren't being too casual about your species discovery?" Wind queried. "I remember you being intensely excited about all the beautiful things you had seen on your journey leading you to find that special new piece of nature. What happened to those emotions?"

"Oh, they're still there," Talorin replied. "Only now I feel them mostly toward Deetjin. He became the new species I wanted to understand. He requires the same quality of observation that my scientific explorations needed. He's more of what I wanted to study."

She paused and looked carefully at Wind.

"So as you can see I haven't lost anything."

Wind felt a deep sense of affection for Talorin.

"What a beautiful story, Talorin. Thank you so much for sharing it with me. It is a very lovely way of thinking of a child in one's care. I am very moved by what you have said. You are a very remarkable and interesting woman."

Talorin was almost beside herself with joy! The great lady had given her the highest honor in calling her remarkable.

Wind reached out and put her arms around the younger woman, and hugged her very affectionately. Talorin vigorously joined this physical recognition of their pleasure in each other. They lingered together for several moments.

"But I have more questions if I may," Wind said as she let Talorin go.

Talorin laughed, filled with great happiness. She had never felt so deeply intimate with Wind. In fact she'd never expected it to happen. She perceived Wind to be far more spiritually evolved than she was, a difference that would prevent them from sharing their deepest natures.

But Wind's questions had permanently changed that view. Wind's curiosity about Deetjin connected Talorin to Wind. She felt spiritually inspired.

Talorin was thrilled! Her whole body tingled with delight!

"Please ask me as many questions as you want!" she insisted with great relish and excitement.

"You know, now when I remember the other questions I had, I realize that what you've already answered most of them. I was especially fond of the way you described the contrasting pieces of your life, that having Deetjin as a son cooperates synergistically with the passion to study nature that you share with Rambler."

"Oh, Wind, you understand me perfectly! You bless me with the wonderful thought that the pieces of my nature fit beautifully together. I've never been entirely sure of that myself. Now you give me hope that I may be what I feel sometimes, that my life is somehow connected to powerful energy modules in the matrix of reality's wholeness, where all the pieces come together to make sense out of the chaos of constant changing."

It was an inspired, spiritual assertion for Talorin to speak this way about herself. Before she would never have dared.

"Talorin!" Wind exclaimed. "That was so beautifully said! I've never heard you talk that way before. You have a remarkable gift for language. And what you describe so poetically, it was wonderful to hear. I am so happy for you, and deeply moved to share it with you!"

Wind had never experienced Talorin in this way before. She had thought her lacking such a deep, eloquent spiritual nature, making her feel a little guilty about so underestimating her friend, who now seemed so much more like a kindred spirit, someone whom she wanted to see a lot more of, because the two of them reflected each other so well, far better than Wind had ever imagined possible.

Talorin was even more surprised than Wind. She had never expected to share this part of herself with her ideal woman. What's more she had no idea that Wind had the slightest interest in children.

"Tell me what it's like being mother to Deetjin," Wind pleaded.

"Oh, thank you for asking!" Talorin crooned, amazed that there was going to be even more of this spectacular experience. "It feels so good to be able to share that with you. I do so admire you for what you are and what you do."

"Talorin, I want to see more of you in the future," Wind exclaimed, unable to restrain her joy from expressing itself. "Is there time in your life for me to do that?"

Talorin was stunned! Tears started flowing down her face!

"You make me so happy!" she crooned. "Life is such a miracle! Of course I do. I want very much to see you more."

They stared affectionately into each other's eyes, celebrating the birth of this deepening of their friendship.

"You asked about Deetjin, what it was like to be mothering him," Talorin said when they'd resumed walking. "You may be very surprised at my answers, as I was. My heart gave me a mixed review. I thought I would give you a glowing report. But I just realized that mothering has also proved sometimes to be very empty and lonely. Unless I plead for the boy's love in the subtle ways that I love him, he is naturally far more in love with himself than he is with me."

"I have always had that impression," Wind replied excitedly, deeply relieved to be able to share her own mixed feelings with Talorin, whom she'd always thought of as the perfect parent. "And I have always felt a little guilty about having such negative thoughts about children. But I can see now that it is quite normal."

"I thought the same way when I started," Talorin retorted. "But experience eventually taught me otherwise. I learned that Deetjin needed me to live inside of a one-sided relationship when it came to love. He must be the center of all attention, his and mine, in order to establish the structure of the person he will become as much on his own terms as we can arrange."

"This need for all the attention must have been that part of a child's nature we used to steal away because we needed some of it for ourselves," Wind observed, "which of course bound them to our needs."

"One-sided love is very lonely sometimes," Talorin said with a sad voice.

She paused.

"But don't be misled by so much said of the negative side of mothering. Mostly I deeply enjoy Deetjin. I feel great delight in watching him grow into himself. It makes me remember and better understand my own childhood, giving me an adult chance to feel it happen again, so I can make changes in the way my personal system operates if I want. So it's quite wonderful having him. And I do get a great deal vicariously and indirectly from him. I know he will learn to give to others the love I give him, though not while I'm mothering him, but many years from now."

She suddenly looked sad.

"The hardest moments are when he loves me in his own special ways, stirring in me my own deep affection for him, and then he suddenly runs away."

She gasped as if this experience had just happened.

"It still gives my heart a little start when it happens so suddenly."

Wind realized that she'd had that precise experience herself. It happened whenever Peter grossly misconstrued something she'd said or done, twisting it to fit his own suffering and pain.

She glanced at Peter.

But he's not doing that to me now. It's much smoother to be with him.

"What a joy it is to share with you, Talorin."

Talorin was happier than she could ever remember.

Ancestors

The trail began to climb more, narrowing such that comfort required going single-file. The rock face of the cliff that loomed up to their left started to be more jagged and precipitous.

They were meandering in a zigzag fashion out on a bluff and then in toward the crease of the cliffs. The striations of color Peter had seen in the rock walls of the unpainted apartment were very visible here. The crease they were currently approaching rose upward for two or three thousand feet, and cut into the mountain forty or fifty feet deep. It was as if a huge ax had cracked the mountain open, leaving, where it plunged a large, gaping pie-piece.

"In the rainy season torrents of water cascade down that crack," Saavin explained. "You can see the rough edges have been softened."

She was walking slightly ahead of Peter and turned her head whenever she spoke.

"Were you happy on Earth?" Saavin asked him out of the blue.

Peter cringed a little anticipating another grilling session with her. He had always been reluctant to share his unhappiness. He was a little ashamed of it, feeling it weakened the strength he wanted others to notice.

"My life wasn't going in the right directions," he replied as casually as possible, hoping that would settle it.

"I've studied unhappiness in my own people," she said. "I'm very interested in it. I suppose we're all unhappy sometimes, but I've never talked to anyone who had suffered it very intensely for long periods of time, as you must have done. Of course historically it happened a lot on my planet because our past was once replete with the violence that abuse, despair, and unbearable loneliness create."

Once again Saavin glanced back at the woman who had taught her the authoritative assertions that she now casually shared with Peter, as if the knowledge was old hat to her.

"Tell me more about your people's history," Peter requested, impressed with this very young woman's knowledge, wondering if she was typical of her age group.

"We've always been a fiercely independent, athletic, and very competitive people, previously very externally focused and warlike. I'm told we didn't pay much attention to our internal emotional experience until perhaps five hundred years ago. Of course we've now reversed that one-sidedness to our nature. All of us spend time studying our self-experience, and many make it a major focus of their life. Wind and I are among those people."

So it's from Wind that Saavin has learned so much, he thought.

And now Peter was curious about her thoughts regarding happiness.

"What have you found out about unhappiness in your study?" he asked.

"Just a couple of things that are really interesting," she replied, really having a wonderful time talking to this alien man as if she were completely grown-up. "Happiness seems mostly to be about how one treats and thinks of themselves."

She glanced at Wind to see if she was listening.

"Of course I'm referring to the kind of talk we do with ourselves, that we hardly ever notice doing behind the scenes of what our eyes see immediately in front of us, when we praise or criticize ourselves, often mercilessly, sometimes joyfully."

"I know what you mean," Peter observed. "My people are haunted by a plethora of tormenting self-experience, to which they pay very little attention, preferring instead to inflict that negative energy upon the world. But you said there were two things you've learned. What's the other one?"

Saavin was getting more excited. This Earthman knew a lot about her subject.

"Just that happiness can be very deceiving," Saavin replied enthusiastically, very pleased with herself at this clever twist of the usual expectations of happiness. "We thought we were very happy reveling so much in our predatory emotional nature. When that very attachment to violence, so rampant in both men and women of the time, was what perpetually destroyed our deepest and most natural connections to the bearing forces of the universe."

Saavin looked back again at Wind, wondering if she was noticing just how much Saavin had learned from her. Their eyes met. She knew that Wind understood.

"What changed things for you?" Peter asked.

"It was the increasing efficiency of our technology that finally made us aware of how alien we had become to our own mother, how objectified and estranged we were from nature. Gradually we realized just how little we knew about our own nature. We began feeling very adrift, like a stranger in a strange land, like you must have felt coming to Troubadour. It was terrifying! And yet we could also sense that we were close to something new, which might vastly increase our opportunity for choice."

"How did you get things turned around?" he queried.

"A millennium of false starts and stops, leaping backward a hundred steps, randomly darting this way or that, the way a terrified animal about to be killed and eaten looks in their eyes—in such manner we scurried about for the answers! Slowly they came to us. But it's only within the past one hundred years that we fully appreciated just how much our former violence was based upon a paranoid delusion that life was a dangerous place, partaken of only by ravaging it with our desires."

This time Peter caught Saavin's glance toward Wind, and instantly knew who had husbanded this young woman's remarkable sophistication for her age.

"My word," Peter exclaimed. "What an incredible story."

Peter and Saavin glanced back at Wind simultaneously.

"Saavin is so good at telling a story," Wind said gracefully from the rear. "It's always so much easier to understand anything in such a charming container."

"But you haven't even heard the most amazing thing about it all!" Saavin exclaimed excitedly. "Once we started changing the assumption that unfettered destruction is a viable survival option, within two generations the cessation of such constant abuse of each other added another twenty years to everyone's lifespan."

"My god, that's incredible!" Peter exclaimed. "Boy, what an incentive to improve oneself."

"Of course those who couldn't in any way tolerate being seen negatively by others," Wind continued, "required an enormous amount of help adapting to what the majority had already decided, though they needed far more help than you've had, Peter, in order to succeed in adapting to our new ways of life."

Peter had a mixed reaction. He was very pleased about Wind's compliment, but he also wondered why they hadn't given him more help.

Saavin was feeling most excited that Peter was addressing her as an equal adult. It wasn't that Troubadourians never did this for young people. It was instead that Saavin had never thought of herself in this way. She had fantasized about being grown-up, but never believed it had actually occurred. Somehow today, in these particular circumstances, perhaps because an unbiased alien reflected grownup-ness back to her, she was able to rise to the occasion and regard herself in this new way.

Unlike Earth people, who to her seemed terribly anxious to grow up as quickly as possible, Saavin had, like most other young people on Troubadour chosen to retain the advantages of a prolonged adolescence, spending as much as thirty-five years to finish maturation, taking full advantage of the emphasis upon growth to which young people were particularly entitled.

Peter was also feeling very excited. Though he still had serious doubts about some Troubadourian claims, he found himself increasingly believing in the majority of what they had told him about their world.

"I think it's amazing what you guys have accomplished," he said to Saavin.

"What for instance?" Saavin inquired.

For a moment he felt threatened by another of her aggressive queries. But he suddenly realized that he knew precisely how to answer her.

"What strikes me the strongest about what you have accomplished, is that you have abandoned the idea of loving everyone, something my people are currently very intent upon doing in earnest," Peter replied. "I've learned from Troubadour that the real problem in society is not how well we love. It's how well we resent or anger or rage in response to each other, in other words, how we deal with strangers and their strangeness."

"Kill them or take care of them is the usual way Earth people think about their choices. But you guys have learned to do something quite extraordinary, which is to leave strangers alone to their own pursuits no matter how you feel about them, implicitly empowering them to manage their own needs without struggling with you."

A new idea suddenly gripped Peter!

"I just realized something," he said. "I understand what it means to empower all people to take care of themselves. I can see now that it would wipe out violence! What's so beautiful about it is that it doesn't try and snuff anything out, including violence! Instead it provides a way to build something constructive, by giving each other an enormously valuable gift, namely secure public safety! How amazing! That idea has got to go somewhere in my world!"

Saavin was ecstatic! She had turned something on inside this man! The sense of personal empowerment she suddenly felt instantly gave her a deep curiosity about who he was.

There is something clean and fresh about living in this Troubadorian brand of democracy, Peter thought, even though it scared me so much for so long. But what's most amazing right now, today is that I'm having one hell of a good time. It's really fun being with these people. They have unbounded curiosity about everything! It makes me feel at home.

They came sharply around a corner to face a precipitous cliff-wall that rose at least seven thousand feet above and dropped five thousand feet below. The trail suddenly narrowed to just two feet wide, encouraging each walker to hug the wall for safety.

"We're here," Saavin shouted. "That's the cave entrance way over there in the shadows of the crack where the trail ends."

Peter could see what looked like a dark hole where she pointed.

Deetjin and Saavin became very excited and raced ahead, followed close behind by Talorin keeping up with them easily with her long, striding legs. It was clear that she was staying close to protect her son, who, in trying to keep up with Saavin was operating at his highest limits in a very treacherous place. But she made no effort to intervene. Life required him to take such chances. She knew that. But she would protect as much as possible without intruding upon his will.

Rambler came up to join Peter, while Wind assumed the tail end of their single file.

"The ancients made this trail and narrowed it here for defensive purposes," Rambler explained.

"Is somebody finally going to tell me who the ancients were?" Peter asked, offering a playful challenge

"They were a humanoid species slightly genetically different from us," Rambler explained. "They lived wisely for tens of thousands of years before we evolved into a fully sentient species. During the last millennium of their survival, they occupied what is now the Earth City. In an earlier phase of their evolution they built an enormous temple complex in the very fertile valley below, much like the Aztec and Egyptian people did in your world. Huge megaliths were constructed to establish an intimate relationship with the universe by pretending to control the forces of nature through an intimate relationship with the gods that ran it—but only by brutalizing other social groups, extracting bloodbaths from them to appease the gods who ruled the terrifying nightmare in which they perceived themselves to be living."

"My people are still doing that in a watered down way," Peter exclaimed.

"We still sacrifice each other's comfort and happiness for the sake of our own. We still prefer to complain about having problems far more than we are willing to suffer the slings and arrows of the change necessary in order to do anything about them."

"It's frightening to feel alone with reality," Rambler replied, "to see it with a mind of our own, to understand it entirely on our own terms. That throws everything into the hideously doubtful realm of uncertainty, which comes from having the ability to make more than one choice, to see anything in more than one way."

"One choice is all the options instinct provides other species in the important functions of life," Rambler continued, "like what we eat and when and how we make love. Most violence is a desperate rejection of a consciousness, which for millenniums had produced a terrifying aloneness that raped us with terror. When, more grown-up as a species, we realized that human awareness is meant to be the instrument which emancipates us from the child-ness and innocence of the Garden of Eden, ushering us into real life and its vulnerabilities, which keeps us forever on the path of learning, the only peaceful reaction to the normal forces of change and conflict."

"Wow! That was a mouthful, Rambler," Peter responded. "I want you to tell me all that again later, so I don't forget it. But for now what did the ancient people have to do with all of that?"

"It was they who guided us to our present wisdom, though it took us eons of time to discover that truth in their writings, found deep in this cave only two hundred years ago."

"What did they teach you?"

"That personal habits and social institutions are the same thing in different dimensions," Rambler replied. "If you want to change injustice, then begin with yourself. Whatever you can improve in yourself will force its way into the structure of your family, sending ripples into the larger community, where a groundswell of people changing rebuilds old traditions into new institutional habits, freeing the human spirit to be more free and creative."

"What happened to the ancients?" Peter asked.

"It was they who first turned their cities back to nature, building a vast farmland in the great valley below, where their majestic temple-city had once stood. We were and are still very inspired by these wise people. But when they had to watch us make their same mistakes, by building our own huge metropolis in the valley below, they became filled with terrible grief, unable to bear another grotesque cycle of civilization's blight."

Peter had never before heard Rambler speak with such intense emotion and deep conviction. The big man looked very much like he might have descended from these ancient people.

"That is a terribly sad story," Peter said with great sympathy. "I feel sorry that it happened. My people have done the same thing over and over to a great many races of people, never realizing what we were really doing, acting like mad dogs pretending to be civilized when we were being utterly barbaric. But is that all there is to this story? Is there any more?"

Rambler was silent for several moments, giving solemnity to the moment.

"There is one more shameful chapter," Rambler replied with sadness. "We needed the land they occupied, so we took it."

"You mean you killed them?" Peter asked, horrified that he might say yes.

"At first yes, but we soon stopped that. It was more that we encroached upon their territories, forcing them farther up the mountain in retreat."

Rambler paused. And then with great solemnity and sadness, he added, "Within a hundred years they became extinct."

Peter was horrified.

"But how did that happen?"

"We don't know."

"But didn't you try and save them from extinction?" Peter asked.

"When we got wind of what had already been set in motion two generations before, they would not let us intervene," Rambler explained. "No matter how much we tried rescuing them, for we had come to honor them deeply, they turned us down. We finally realized we were only making matters worse for them by trying to save them. Life was their journey and they wanted to finish it in their own way. I guess they didn't want to live in our world. I don't blame them. I wouldn't have wanted to live there either if I understood what they did at the time."

"There's another twist," Saavin interjected. "For a long time the ancients sent teachers down among us, but we paid no attention to them because what they said seemed so simple and primitive."

"We paid heavily in grief losing them," Wind said, giving indirect voice to her anticipation of Peter-grief-pain. "It was a very powerful learning time for most of us, this grief that stretched on for almost a hundred years after they became extinct."

"Truly spoken, dear lady. Truly spoken," Rambler said with great respect, looking at Wind with an expression of deep affection, both for her and for the ancients.

"What else did you learn from them?" Peter asked.

The small group had by now come close together, each thinking of the ancients in their own way, listening to the familiar story they all knew so well, yet loved to hear once more.

"Their wisdom, that's what we've gotten from them," Wind said. "At first we didn't see it, as Saavin explained, because what they said was always so simple. It wasn't really until after they died out that we remembered and learned to understand a few of their simple sayings."

"My favorite is 'listen to what you kill,'" Rambler interjected.

"Mine too," Wind chimed in.

"What exactly does that mean?" Peter asked, understanding it in general but wanting to know more

"The key is whatever listen means to you," she replied.

"Oh, you mean whether you take it in," Peter retorted.

"In the meantime we've arrived at our destination," Wind observed.

Peter looked up to see a huge opening in the side of the mountain looming above him. They had reached the end of the trail. A large, steel-like grate covered the opening.

Saavin began to sing. With great clarity she uttered four vocal tones that sounded like the first line of a melody.

The dark grate disappeared into the rock wall with barely a sound.

"The ancient's built this gate," Saavin announced with great pride, respect, and solemnity. "And it still works beautifully like the day it was built."

"Wow!" Peter shouted in admiration, sharing the excitement and joy that Saavin expressed about being at such a special wonderful place.

As if wanting to stretch their spirits after their long walk, everyone in turn joined this shout of approval.

"Wow!" Rambler shouted, glad for an opportunity to feel exuberant.

"Waooo!" Talorin wailed at the mountain, giving her own imitation of their shared excitement.

"Waaa!" Deetjin screamed in his boyish version of joy.

Wind laughed with joy, joining the succession of sounds that built upon the foundation of Peter's emotional energy! It delighted her to see him this way. She felt proud to love him.

Saavin decided to show Peter how the gate closed. She sang what must have been the second line the melody, and the gate closed as silently as it had opened.

After everyone gasped, she reopened it with the first melodic notes.

"You've got to help me remember the notes of that open sesame song," Peter exclaimed to Saavin.

"I would be delighted," she replied with joy at the prospect of teaching the Earthman something else that he wanted.

"Peter Icarus!" Rambler exclaimed. "It is such a wonderful experience being here with you, as you talk to my woman-love, Talorin, and her beautiful son, Deetjin, and our dear friend, Saavin. I have deeply enjoyed watching it happen. The six of us walking along talking to each other in succession, that's such a fine thing. The whole experience makes me very happy. Thank you for bringing us all together in this special way!"

Peter melted into a puddle of happiness. He was astonished! Deeply overcome with the sense of goodness that came from Rambler's wonderful words, he felt great joy at being part of this intimate group of remarkable humans. It was a very special moment he would remember for the rest of his life.

A Very Special Place

The opening in the mountainside was much smaller than the entrance to the Earth City. It was perhaps thirty feet high and ten wide. With Saavin leading the way, and Deetjin close behind the small gathering moved through the cave without exploring any of its parts, using it only as a conduit. Within twenty minutes they walked out into a bright, warm sunshine.

Peter found himself standing in a deep valley that seemed scooped out from the top of a mountain, its precipitous walls reaching several thousand feet high, which only skilled climbers could scale.

"This is the large cone of an extremely ancient volcano that has been dormant for several million years," Rambler said. "The ancient ones sculpted the vertical walls where needed to prevent very easy access from the top as a protective measure."

"But it would be easy from the top to rain havoc upon them, wouldn't it?" Peter asked.

"They were interested in protection not from death but from intrusion. They weren't afraid to die. But they insisted upon remaining separate from us, preventing all but a very few incidents of genetic merging between our species by a few of their number curious about visiting our world. We therefore have only a scattering of their genes."

"But the entrance," Peter insisted, still thinking of defending the valley. "It's completely accessible."

"We chiseled the last one hundred yards of the trail," Rambler explained. "In olden times the trail ended before you came around that last bend, at least one hundred yards from the entrance. To reach it required a master-climber first to scale the sheer rock wall that rises up above the trail in order to reach a small, hidden-from-view crack in the rock face that concealed the working end of a lever, which when pulled down extruded a wooden ramp from the side of the mountain, providing access to the opening. When not in use this wooden causeway receded into the mountain completely unseen."

"How far did the master-climber have to climb?"

"Perhaps a hundred yards up moving in a lateral direction, making the journey longer."

Peter looked around the whole valley for the first time.

"It's so flat. I would think there would be more variability in the lower portions of the terrain."

"The ancient ones both leveled it out, and brought enough black dirt from the valley below to cover this entire area with five feet of topsoil, making this an extremely fertile place. As you must notice, the temperature is much warmer here than it was climbing up the trail. The twenty-five square miles of the valley are, weather-wise a temperate zone in which plants flourish. Like all mountains this one receives a lot of precipitation."

"Let's walk awhile," Wind said to Peter. "I want to show you around."

Saavin was disappointed that it wouldn't be she who showed Peter this magical place for the first time. Her consolation was that her favorite person was taking him. Her eyes settled on Rambler as a second choice.

"Uncle, please lend me your ear," she said, running up to him with excitement.

Rambler had always found Saavin to be both enchanting and irresistible. To him she was a young Talorin, the woman he loved very deeply. He couldn't help feeling a great deal of affection for Saavin. She in turn found his good-natured exuberance very appealing, and regarded him as part of the family she was creating for her life.

"I want to test a theory on you," she said after giving him a hug. "It's about Wind and Peter. I just want you to tell me if you think that what we see happening is really plausible."

Rambler was always delighted to witness Saavin's creative process. He enjoyed sharing her vitality, and seeing it flourish.

"Go ahead, you rascal," he playfully replied. "I'm sure you've got some mischievous scheme up your sleeve in asking that question."

"No, it's not so provocative," Saavin insisted. "It's a theory of how those two could got together romantically."

"Have you noticed that you've been talking a lot about romance lately?"

"Stop kidding around, Rambler," she retorted in mock irritation, though she would think later about what Rambler had observed.

She had not yet seriously thought of herself as a woman ready for loving. Her body since puberty had been very active sexually. But she'd never connected her experience of deep love to what her body liked fairly often to do.

"I think she's loving him out of charity," Saavin announced. "That's my theory. Love must be something he really needs, and out of human kindness she's giving it to him. He is after all our guest. And he won't be here for long, so it's not as if she had to do it forever."

She paused very briefly.

"What do you think?"

"What makes you think the Earthman has got nothing to offer her that Wind wants?" he asked.

"Oh, I didn't say that. Of course he does. I am also fascinated with him, but I wouldn't want to sleep with him."

Rambler laughed.

"We're all relieved to hear that," he kidded. "I'm sure he's already got enough on his mind. But my question meant, what makes you think Peter doesn't have something large and valuable to Wind, making their intimacy not charitable but very plausibly reciprocal."

"But what could he have to offer from a species two hundred years behind us?" she asked incredulously.

"Who knows?"

"Maybe I could ask her."

"You can, but I'm not sure she would want to answer. There are parts of life that are private, particularly to lovers."

It was precisely those private parts that Saavin wanted to know about.

Wind and Peter walked up to join them. Without a moment's hesitation, Saavin took Peter's arm and wandered off with him in tow. He looked back at Wind and raised his arms in a gesture of, "what can you do," which left Wind and Rambler together. Instead of talking immediately, they both watched Peter and Saavin.

"He's doing most of the talking," Rambler observed.

"She's carefully listening to him, I suspect in order to figure out why I'm so attracted to him."

"I've wondered that myself," Rambler replied.

"That's very complicated, though his most appealing trait he shares with you, which is innocent exuberance and generosity."

Rambler smiled at her.

At any similar moment with another person he would have laughed his lion-laugh, feeling pure pleasure, but not with Wind. He idealized her gracious kindness, because in it he felt loved so intrinsically—not romantically, more like fundamentally. Occasionally he sensed a kind of purity to their love for each other, precisely because it would never be sexual. They were great friends.

"You are very generous yourself to give me such flattery," Rambler replied. "I don't have your careful thoughtfulness of others. I have no patience for it. I think Peter seriously misses that in me."

Wind laughed.

"Probably. But the buoyancy of your nature makes thoughtfulness almost unnecessary."

Rambler beamed.

Every time I see her she makes me feel good. This is such a happy day.

"What are all these beautiful plants?" Peter asked Saavin.

"Those small trees to your left are fruit trees of many varieties, some of which we discovered for the first time when we found this place, splicing them to plant in the valleys below. The large stalked plant closest to you is not unlike your corn I understand. It produces a starchy, wet pulp that is very sweet. Over there is a garden of herbs, many of them medicinal, some of which are quite powerfully used in healing. Once again we found many of these special herbs only in this valley. They were still surviving five hundred years after the extinction of the people who husbanded them from and into nature."

I wonder what makes Wind want to husband with him, Saavin mused to herself.

Wind noticed the intense curiosity in Saavin's face as she told Peter about all of the wonderful things to be seen in the valley.

"Something has happened to her today," Wind remarked to Rambler.

"Oh, what do you see?" he inquired, always very curious to hear what new thing this special lady noticed.

Rambler studied Wind in the same way that Saavin was examining Peter. He was fascinated by her capacity to see things visually. He tried hard to understand what made her so incredibly perceptive, so he could apply that special acumen to his own searches of nature's wonders.

"I don't know," Wind mused. "But something has turned on inside her, for I see a look on her face, as she wanders about with Peter that I've never seen before."

Rambler peered keenly at Saavin's face when she turned in his direction, trying to see what Wind had seen.

"What exactly are you looking at?" he asked.

"There's something about her smile," Wind replied. "It's more evocative. I think she's becoming sensually active. Oh, I don't mean with intention. Perhaps she's only partly aware of it."

Talorin sent Deetjin around to gather the others for the lunch she had prepared.

As he was gathering, Saavin had a chance to take Wind aside for a few moments.

"Can I ask you a question about you and him?" Saavin asked.

Wind laughed affectionately. It made her happy to have something that Saavin wanted.

"You know you can," she replied.

"What really grabs you about that man?"

"His exuberance and passion," Wind replied. "And the innocence of his prickly parts. Basically he is a man of warmth and generosity."

Passion is the word that grabbed Saavin's attention. She repeated to herself to hear the sound of it in her mind's eye. But she couldn't see any. I like the way he feels to be around, but where's the passion?

"You've kept him such a secret," Saavin said.

"I have chosen to be with him privately," Wind acknowledged.

"But he belongs to all of us," Saavin retorted.

Wind realized that something was afoot that she didn't understand.

"You're surprised I feel so much about him?" Wind inquired.

"I guess I felt shut out," Saavin instantly reported, as if Wind's remark had pushed a button in Saavin's spirit, turning on the truth. "I've never seen you look at anyone like you look at him."

"You see truth," Wind acknowledged, but said nothing further.

"Well, aren't you going to tell me about it?" Saavin insisted.

"No."

That really shocked Saavin, to be so utterly excluded from something that belonged to Wind! This was an entirely new experience!

She's such a combination of sophisticated and naively young, Wind observed, feeling deeply loving toward her.

"Are you afraid of missing something you need from me?" Wind asked. "Do you feel that because so much of my heart has become attached to this man, that there's not enough left for you?"

"It's silly, isn't it, but I guess I am?" Saavin replied in a girl's voice.

She was exposing the still innocent part of herself that, as it became more and more self-conscious, turned into vulnerability.

Saavin was a committed optimist. Within moments her face suddenly brightened.

"I see what you're doing," she said, very relieved to have the answer she was looking for. "It's just privacy. I understand that. I keep myself private too sometimes, like with lovers I don't really want to be too intimate with, or for very long. I'm not ready to jump right into romance. There's plenty of time."

"I've also taken my time about participating in certain aspects of romance," Wind acknowledged.

"Oh, I don't think I want to wait that long," Saavin exclaimed, knowing Wind to be almost three times her age!

Wind laughed.

Saavin felt better.

The six of them spent the whole day in the deep valley of the ancients, walking back close to dusk with a brilliant sunset haloing their decent from behind, infusing the already vibrant magic of the day with an enchanting color display, as if nature was marking the time as special, just as each one of them was doing privately in their own particular way.

In his imagination Peter moved his life entirely to Troubadour. He would live in the mountain city with all these wonderful people surrounding him with their interest and affection. His talents would flourish in this emotionally nutrient-rich Garden of Eden.

He suddenly remembered his Earth family, and a pang of guilt-loss touched his heart at the thought of never seeing them again.

But Earth paled in comparison to what he had now. He spent only a moment grieving on his family's behalf, before returning to the comfort and joy of wanting today's happy experience to go on forever.

Wind marveled at the vitality of the day's experience. Peter's presence had influenced every one of her relationships, seriously deepening the one with Talorin. She also thought much about her mother, mostly remembering moments of their time together in the first twenty years of her life.

Wind realized clearly for the first time just how much her journey was like Peter's. She expected to learn a lot, but not the volumes of change that were beginning to happen to her life.

I think that's why I love him, she thought, because he has brought such wonder to my life. I don't know how well he would settle with me on a long-term basis, but in the role of visitor he is the most exciting person I've known, I guess because of how much he's affected me.

Saavin was very excited. Among all the young people on Troubadour, she was the one person to know the first Earth visitor intimately. She was very proud of that. What's more, she had touched the heart of this alien man that Wind loved. That was the best part of all. She had been a part of history.

But there was a downside to this joyful experience for Saavin. Reluctantly she admitted to herself that she was disappointed in Peter. As a cohero in her fantasy, he didn't have enough good stuff to create the strong reaction in her that her fantasy craved. He didn't awaken her desire to be bonded in love, as one or two of the young men with whom she occasionally slept had started to make her feel sometimes. In fact she considered Peter to be a bit strange and even awkward in some of his ways, which made such attraction very difficult.

It wasn't that Saavin doubted his desirability. If Wind saw something wonderful there, then it must be there. She just couldn't see it. At the same time his negative traits stuck out too much. The whole complicated thing puzzled Saavin a lot.

Above all other humans Saavin believed in Wind and what Wind did and felt. She'd never found any of that to be less than fascinating. But here she was being disappointed by what Wind preferred. She was surprised.

The problem was that Saavin wanted to feel romantic, right now. This was such a perfect day for it, the mountain with its orange-red glow hovering over their togetherness, giving it the magical qualities of special-ness. It was the right moment for her romantic parts to begin dreaming in earnest.

She suddenly found a way to pull it off. She remolded her image of Peter, eliminating the negative parts by making him look much younger, much more Troubadourian. That image-transformation got the ball rolling.

Talorin was feeling as happy as she'd felt when Deetjin first became a part of her life. She'd always desired a deeper comradeship with Wind, but never imagined that it would, or could happen. Wind seemed so much more evolved than she was. But today had changed that. Finally she had something important in her life to offer her ideal woman, which was also valuable to Wind. She had thus found a door to the deepest parts of Wind's heart, which turned out to be very accessible to her. Talorin felt great joy about that, anticipating many wonderful moments with Wind.

Deetjin had discovered a new level of adventure in life! Previously he had known it only in fantasy and imagination. But after a taste of Peter, and what he represented Deetjin was no longer satisfied just to imagine. He wanted to do things too. He wanted it to be real.

Which meant he had to begin participating in the grown-up world. Until now he hadn't thought that possible, or even very desirable. They were giant-gods, while he was a little person, and enjoyed the many benefits of that dependent position because they took such good care of him. But today suddenly he could see a way to participate in the real, grown-up part of life that was exciting! He was with a real live alien adventurer! It was no longer just pretend!

He was ecstatically overjoyed, skipping his way down the trail, lost in imagining many wonderful versions of the adventure he was inventing!

Rambler was having the time of his life. He didn't say much during the day, but he was privately experiencing a great deal of joy. In general he found much pleasure in the company of small groups of people with whom he was well-known.

He had found it more difficult than most to fashion a family of his own, which had become the custom on Troubadour. Families were no longer genetically defined and contained; they were child-chosen, added to throughout life.

Rambler was not terribly gifted with people-connective skills, and preferred to assume a contemplative, experimental stance in relation to others. Talorin provided him with an alternative way of relating to others, which gave him the emotional outlet that he'd always needed. She brought a powerful ability to attract other people. Gradually she, with his increasing help built their clan. Today Wind had become a full-fledged member. She had for a long time been close to Rambler. Today she became close friends with Wind.

Peter has brought us so much, Rambler thought. He's touched every one of us in various ways, unique and special to each person. It's been terribly fascinating to watch! I think it's been my favorite group experience, the very best one of all.

Surprise

Much later that night Wind and Peter were getting into bed. They moved close to each other and embraced, each smelling the sweet fragrance of the other, breathing in the gentle care that each offered the other.

"Do you have enough energy to answer one more question before we go to sleep?" he asked Wind.

"Of course I do for you," she crooned at him with a warm smile.

"You have a very special relationship with Saavin. I could tell how much you loved each other just by watching the synchronous way that you stood together. Please tell me, how did you and she get together?"

Wind took awhile before answering.

"Saavin is my biological child. I mentioned once to you that I had never mothered a child, but that I had given birth to one in fulfilling my social responsibility. Saavin is that child."

"Wow! That's right, I heard her call you 'mother.' But you denied it, admitting only to being her 'spiritual mother.' What gives?"

"Saavin doesn't know that I am her biological mother," Wind replied. "It is our custom not to give this information to children until they're over thirty years old."

"But won't she be upset when she finds out that you've never told her?"

"No. She knows why it must be this way, to protect the freedom and privacy of her own growing up from the intrusion of information needed by adults, but irrelevant to children. It has become traditional to meet, biological mother and children, in the Mandela in a ceremony that every child anticipates happening. We treat it like a moment of passage."

"Do all biological mothers have a close relationship with their child as you do with Saavin?"

"No. Many don't."

"Then how . . . I mean, what happens? It must be pretty awkward."

"On the contrary," Wind replied. "We don't expect that people will always like each other who have a direct biological connection. A daughter and biological mother meeting for the first time have the choice of whether to see each other again or not, whether to be friends, or distant associates."

"My people have always made such a big deal out of family blood ties," Peter replied, "that it seems very strange for you to be so casual about whether mother and child like each other. But I seem to be becoming a Troubadourian, because I was fantasizing all the way down the trail about moving my life permanently here. I gave my Earth family only a moment of grief before I accepted their loss. How strange to do that. I've always worked so hard to keep in touch with everyone I loved no matter how unhappy it was to be with them."

"Well, it warms my heart that you have chosen my world as your favorite place," Wind crooned as they embraced and fell asleep in each other's arms.

Best Friends

"Why didn't you come with us yesterday?" Peter asked Rain within moments after he arrived to join Peter and Wind for breakfast the next morning.

"Did you miss me?" Rain asked.

Peter was instantly embarrassed because he hadn't even thought about Rain yesterday.

"I guess I didn't," Peter replied guiltily. "But I do now."

"That's why I didn't come," Rain explained.

"I don't understand."

"Though it saddens me that this is so, if I'm around, people tend to defer to me, making me a dominating factor during the occasion. You needed a Troubadourian social experience with all of its intricate possibilities. I think it was richer because I wasn't there."

It's true what Rain said, Wind realized. He captures a large piece of everyone's attention. His presence would have diluted the separate and special encounters between different pairs of us that multiplied during the course of the day.

"That just can't be true," Peter insisted, though he sensed that it was true.

"There is no harm in it," Rain replied.

"But you said that you were sad."

"Sadness is just a feeling. What makes you think it must be fixed?"

"But why would you want to feel it?" Peter asked. "I thought you Troubadourians had put a stop to suffering."

"Feelings are not suffering, unless we turn them into fearful predictions and endless worry. They're just sprites of immediacy that compel the present moment, sometimes very forcefully focusing our attention in a very particular way toward what seems crucial, or even critical right now. But I prefer to regard my feelings in a more moderate way, as my good friends who define my personal relationship with the present moment."

They had finished breakfast.

"Let's take a walk outside," Rain suggested. "I would prefer to speak of such things when I'm moving about enjoying the day."

"What a great idea," Wind said.

"Okay," Peter agreed, though things were moving a little too fast for him.

"And please stop trying to remove me from myself," Rain requested as they left Peter's apartment. "I don't want to be unfeeling. Being emotional is precisely where and when I am most alive."

"The sadness which you imagine Rain suffering," Wind suggested, "must be sadness that is grief-stricken. It's the guilt part which believes that the loneliness pain you feel is deserved, that life is punishing you for some crime or shortcoming you imagine having."

"Boy did you nail me," Peter exclaimed. "I'm full of that stuff."

Peter had spent most of his life feeling unconsciously responsible for the profound unhappiness of both parents, and then of any subsequent loved one by inference thereafter. He couldn't afford to upset anyone he loved for fear of reprisal, most likely abandonment. So he obsessed about the emotional turmoil that was the family's principle activity and focus of attention. Feeling became just another random part of the mad flow of constant mayhem.

Peter had missed more than a gradual evolution of his emotion experience. He'd also missed most of his childhood. Instead of playing the games that would have prepared him for being the particular someone he was naturally to be, he was instead preoccupied with securing safety by whatever means. Like the rest of us when we're truly helpless as a child, he employed the Santa Claus myth, which promises that being-good will provide its own reward, which gives life to the service of others.

Peter had imagined himself a priest of God in adolescence, and had nearly attended seminary after college. When behind the smokescreen of these anxiety-driven choices, he secretly wanted to be Frederick Chopin with fingers bleeding at the keyboard playing music he had composed, or George Bernard Shaw writing and directing his own play.

"Come on, you guys," Peter insisted as they moved out of the city into the sunshine of the day. "I'm sure you don't want to spend all your time helping me with my problems. We seem to be doing that much of the time."

"You think we're not getting anything out of it, that we're sacrificing our needs to satisfy yours," Rain observed.

"Well, isn't that true?"

"No," Wind replied. "We get both information and pleasure out of your learning."

"You know, I get the same pleasure out of my patient's learning," Peter said excitedly, believing them. "It really means a lot to me to be a part of something so alive with new possibilities, that begins to emerge as I watch new understanding alter the structure of how someone behaves. It deeply encourages me to be a part of that. It's one of my best experiences."

"Then please be comforted in the knowledge that we are in this way like you," Rain said. "So stop treating me like an alien who finds your emotional experience bothersome and of no special account."

Peter laughed.

"You're right!" he exclaimed with joy at the realization. "In the service of protecting you from my intrusion, I've been imposing upon both of you the dreariness of my own pessimistic expectation of others. Until this moment it never occurred to me that I was being such an asshole!"

"Having acknowledged that," Rain replied, "let's now devote our energies to the rhythm of walking, smell the fragrant perfumes of the day, and feel the force of nature's breath blowing us into immediacy, binding us to the present moment's wondrous possibilities, connecting us to eternity."

As if to illustrate the non-verbal-ness he wanted to share with the other two, Rain started humming as he walked through hanging tree-bows, brushing his hand against them, adding this small sound to the nature's variable conversations.

They walked this way for an hour, climbing high onto a rocky prominence, peering for a long time at the expansive view that looked down ten thousand feet, to tiny toy-like creatures tilling the soil in the valley below, silently admiring them, contributing respect to the growth that prospered there.

Wind walked close to Peter, her proximity embracing him with the sweet odors of her love encouraging his every step, giving the specific firmness of her affection to the support of nature's abundance, binding Peter's experience of growing things to the constancy of her love, giving him a container in which to entrust their mutual affection, in which to hold forever a piece of what he would soon have to relinquish.

What a lovely pairing they are, Rain mused, observing the two of them together. I had forgotten how beautiful love appears to those observing it.

"Love makes you both very beautiful," Rain said.

Suddenly aware of Rain, Peter blanched at the thought that all during their walk his loving Wind had been, as was still, closely scrutinized by Rain. He became instinctively defensive, afraid that Rain felt left out.

"I'm sorry," he apologized. "We haven't been giving you the slightest bit of attention, which is not very thoughtful considering your missing yesterday's outing. It's not fair to leave you out again."

Rain laughed uproariously.

"Well, what's so funny?" Peter queried, annoyed that his guilt-gift was so ignominiously rejected by Rain's laughter.

"The inescapable compulsion of your guilt."

"Oh, I guess you're right," Peter acknowledged.

Meanwhile Wind was having a very different experience. She was feeling a strong desire to share with Rain everything that had happened in her experience with Peter. She imagined his thoughts about her story would be a delight to hear.

"There's much to tell you sometime," she said to Rain.

"You already told me a lot," he replied. "I can see it written all over you. Newness is popping out everywhere. You're not the same person I used to know, pretty lady. Something new has been added to you. And I think I see what it is."

"What do you see in her?" Peter wanted to know, afraid of being left out.

Rain looked at Wind with great affection.

"Softness like dew now hovers over you, moisturizing Peter's heart with what surely mends its lonely parts. I see the blessing of love's guessing resting in a paired nesting, already waking skill for his taking and partaking, stirring his muse into active use, creating fun instead of thrusting everything under the blazing gun of suspicion's mistrust. I see redemption too, the greatest thing that love can do."

"O . . . o . . . ho!" Wind exclaimed, feeling the thrill of the gift of Rain's poetic understanding.

She could tell that he understood and admired how well she loved Peter, and knew of the enormous benefit that came to Peter as a result.

Encouraged by her enthusiasm, Rain continued.

"I can see that you've learned to desire the innocence of love as much as the spiritual wisdom of your art. You've opened your heart to the unexpected alien influences of a stranger occupying your bed, which provokes your vulnerability even as it provides you with the pleasure of new understanding. This is a love that simply had to decree what's to be."

An open-mouthed Peter gulped in astonishment at this vibrant exchange between these two Troubadourian giants.

But admiration for his two best friends lasted only for a moment. He suddenly felt two very opposite things, one, that he was the privileged witness of a very extraordinary exchange of affection; and two, he was intensely jealous that he was excluded from their powerful love-energy, which glistened when they spoke intimately with each other.

"You see right through me," Wind said gently to Rain, "like the sun sees through the mist by dissolving whatever resists what wants to be known, but can't find a way to be shown."

Rain laughed.

"You make this old man feel beautiful," he replied with a grateful smile.

"Your understanding beautifies me," she replied, "mirroring what I feel so I can see what appeals."

The two of them fell into silence, looking deeply into each other's eyes.

Peter let the silence go on for a few moments, but soon couldn't wait any longer.

"Hey, you guys. I'm still here too, you know."

But both Wind and Rain saw and heard only each other. She moved toward Rain, closing the distance between them, and threw her arms about his neck in celebration, thrilled with his perfect understanding.

Enchanted, Rain surrendered to her affectionate gratitude, embracing her with great joy, breathing in the soft, wet odors of the skin of her affection, now becoming so much more familiar to him.

Oh, my god, Peter exclaimed to himself. They love each other. But then what has she been giving me?

He felt deeply shocked and surprised, even betrayed.

"Would you two like to be alone?" he asked with more painful sarcasm than he intended.

When neither of them responded, Peter began to panic. But immediately he gripped himself firmly. He wanted no part of making a scene. He had to do something to change the situation, or risk feeling the terror of becoming helplessly enraged. To act from such feeling at this point could destroy his relationship with both of them, or at least so he imagined.

But then suddenly in perfect unison, Wind and Rain turned toward

Peter, and gave him their fullest attention. It was clear from the looks in their eyes that they'd heard every word Peter had said.

"If we lose you," Wind gently announced, "then none of what Rain and I were celebrating would be happening at all. You are that vital part of what's so joyful. So you must stay. Losing you would bring deep sadness upon both of us."

Peter's whole being was lifted up into the clouds of redemption's ecstasy. Encouraging fronds of hopefulness fondled his spirit with tenderness, opening the lightness of his heart dancing with joy, swirling him into the realm of happiness, and amusing him for the rest of day.

In this prolonged episode of passion, this magical reprieve, Peter was being irresistibly transformed into an accurate version of himself that filled him with understanding that perfectly suited him. Reprieve had graced his life.

To be included was what Peter had always deeply desired, to know that he was essential to what was happening. It was that precise reassurance for which he had always unknowingly, devoutly wished.

Peter felt deeply linked to these two Troubadourians in ways he had never before imagined being connected to another person. It was an adult version of the idealized good mother that Peter had kept alive in his heart by burying her out of sight, yet desperately, searchingly, craving for her to wake up and be herself again.

In this very revealing, healing moment, old pains quickly gave way to their redemption.

Once more deeply connected to Wind and Rain, Peter knew, that during his worst moments on Troubadour, these two Troubadourians had always been there for him, in spite of his constant complaints to the contrary. They were the ones who had always been there to help him pick up the pieces of his disintegrating experience.

There was no denying it any longer. They were his best friends, in the deep sense that Troubadour defined friendship.

They *have* been supporting me, Peter exclaimed to himself, while I was complaining to them for never doing it. What an idiot I've been.

But this self-criticism, he noticed, was a bare echo of the intense shame that had once scathed him regularly. This moderate guilt was an honest acknowledgement that he had been biting the hand that was feeding him, as it fed him.

The three of them walked quietly all the way home, each filled with their private thoughts.

Peter basked in his love for both these beautiful Troubadourians, buoyed by the encouragement of their good opinion, and empowered by the constancy of Troubadourian care of the vulnerable parts of experience.

They always act so competently, he thought. I feel surrounded by reliability.

But Wind was troubled. She began to realize that she had an attraction to Rain that rivaled her love of Peter. She seemed to love both men, which made her feel very uneasy.

But what troubled her most was that she couldn't talk to the one person who would most help her figure it out. This time Rain was a participant in her experience. He couldn't be her help. She would need to think of someone else.

Why not my mother? We don't know so much about each . . . but still there is who we are to each other.

Of course I love her romantically, Rain said to himself. I've never before quite acknowledged that so utterly. I think perhaps I have accepted the distance between us these many years while wanting to be more with her. But maybe that's the problem with we Troubadourians. We've have gone too far. No longer driven to be intimate for security's sake, no longer compelled into love in order to hide personal unhappiness, we take intimacy much more in stride now that we've removed the desperate, compelling qualities to loving that everyone used to feel. But in the process have we gone too far and forgotten romance? Have we lost track of the joys of earnestly needing someone? At the very least I have neglected my own desire.

Of What is Safety Constructed?

After returning to Wind's apartment, the three companions decided to spend some time alone. Peter pondered the complexity of feelings they had for each other, trying to be comfortable with his truelove loving another man. Rain worked on a new poem. Wind drew a sketch of a vision inspired by their walk up the mountain, consisting of three figures suspended in an abstract medium, their faces expressing very diverse and disparate feelings, the central focus of the grouping oscillating between coherency and abstractness.

Two hours later they resumed their togetherness.

"This is the time for questions," Rain said to Peter.

To his surprise Peter knew precisely what his questions were.

"I have two that spring to mind right away," he said, proud of being prepared for Rain's announcement. "One, how can your people spend so much time alone with their own pursuits without feeling unbearable loneliness? And two, how can it be that the dismantlement of government, and the release of so much power, not to the business of making profit as my world does, but to individual humans in the pursuit of their own lives and purposes . . . how come that isn't followed by a chaotic rush into the lawlessness of which people are so capable?"

"With which question should we begin?" Rain asked.

"It's just that I can't imagine how you guys manage to be so self-involved for such long periods of time," Peter replied.

"Of course to us that's like asking why we eat," Rain explained. "Pursuing the purposes of our own life's inclination, talent, and energy, has become so fundamental to our nature that it's the part of our life that we trust the most. It's the foundation of our approach to anything, including personal growth as well as what you call politics."

"You know, I think I've always mistrusted that kind of total self-advancement," Peter announced.

Peter was surprised to hear himself say this, because he'd always encouraged his patients to develop the very trait Rain was espousing, though at this moment he realized he'd never done that for his own life.

"Here I am answering my own question," Peter continued, "but I guess when I really think deeply about it, self-interest has always seemed so thoughtlessly selfish, lacking the slightest regard for the needs of others. I think I've secretly perceived it as the blight that crippled my life. Both of my parents seemed avidly self-interested, not out of wisdom, but out of desperation in their own lives, giving me a miserable, ugly demonstration of this trait. They satisfied their needs in ways that completely ignored the needs of a small person, namely me, at the time unable to care for myself, arranging to help me only when it served their needs, but never when it satisfied mine or compromised theirs in the least. It wasn't as if they did this on purpose, because I'm sure they did it unknowingly out of their own bad habits."

"Such a demonstration of self-interest would inevitably convince anyone it was a villainous thing," Wind replied.

"And yet on the other hand," Rain interjected, "self-interest is what nature has given us in abundance by making us self-conscious to the point of madness. We can become so self-involved that we are not really in touch with anything but our own wishes and fantasies, the narcissistic there's-only-me-in-the-world attitude from which we do the terrible things to which you refer."

"That's what I mean," Peter agreed.

"But just because we are capable of doing terrible things with self-involvement," Rain continued, "why throw the baby out with the bath water? Self-focus is how nature has made us unique as a species. The problem isn't whether to be that way, banning most free expressions of the self, as both our peoples have vigorously done historically, overpowering each of us with megalithic structures of bureaucracy. The gross compromise of self-interest is what keeps one man working under another man's rule, instead of insisting upon working alongside of him, or a long distance away at his own separate natural pursuits. It's what holds inferiority in place without much effort on the part of the supposed superior."

"I know," Peter retorted. "I hate the hierarchy which abuse creates in my people, where we actually believe in our inferiority, though we don't admit it; which convinces us that some humans are better or bigger than others, and therefore have the right to treat the rest of us with contempt and disdain. We've been doing that for centuries."

"What I have a hard time understanding about your people," Rain observed, "is why they're so passionately in love with financial wealth, willing to sign away vast amounts of their freedom and self-respect in order to create the moneyed aristocracy to which most want to belong, becoming someone celebrated primarily for how successfully they get away with taking everyone else for a ride."

"It's one of the liabilities of my life, that I've never been very interested in making money, so of course I haven't made much," Peter offered.

"Which makes the requirement to do it stifling," Wind retorted.

"You can say that again," Peter vigorously replied. "I think feeling that way, I represent the majority of the people on my planet."

They sat in silence for several moments, peering into the forested window of Peter's apartment, taking a break from the intensity of their discussion.

"So what have we solved?" Peter asked, finally breaking the silence. "We're still at the crossroads where we've been for centuries. How do you solve the ages-old problem of how to corral human individual idiosyncrasies into the making of a viable, cohesive society?"

"Well," Rain began, "one way of framing it is to make the satisfaction of individual need as completely fulfilled as possible when it most counts, in the first years of life. And then you appeal to the best talents and inclinations of those actualized individual adults you have facilitated into being, offering them the opportunities of great responsibility instead of the oppression of policing control."

"But how can you get rid of having to control people?"

"By helping them achieve the highest possible level of competence in managing their own lives."

"Okay, but how did you guys actually get over controlling everything? I mean give me the details of what happened here. Though I don't want you to get the wrong impression. It's not that I don't believe in Troubadour, and what you've done, because I really do. It's just that I can't get my head around the idea of how much freedom you have given to each other. It's so enormous! You seem pretty much able to do whatever you want each morning you get up, where and when you want to do it. But with so many people running around satisfying their personal needs and whims, how in the hell does a whole planet of people safely get through the day without soldiers and policemen, or at least some kind of maintenance workers around keeping the fringes of this dangerous experiment under some kind of containment? I've never met anyone who could manage their own emotional experience all the time. Eventually everybody gets out of line one way or the other."

"Well, that remained true for a long while on Troubadour," Wind replied. "But violence eventually disappeared far more easily than we'd ever imagined possible."

"Yeah, but what happened during that time when it wasn't working yet?"

"We gave each other fifty years to get used to the idea. Which meant a great many of us passed on without having to suffer the inconveniences of such huge change in their habit structure. The rest of us had plenty of time to prepare ourselves. In fact the vast majority of us had already changed when the two generations of time was up."

"But there must have been horrendous struggles during the change," Peter insisted. "How did you deal with those?"

"A law-violator after the first offense was electronically monitored so that we knew where they were at all times, making proof of transgression very easily established. Any second breaking of the nonviolent boundary we had given each other, led automatically to residence in a territory from which you could never escape, populated by others who had equally transgressed our inviolate agreement to provide everyone with a safe and peaceful life."

"One could surgically remove this electronic tracking device, couldn't they?" Peter asked.

"That act produces the only death sentence administered on Troubadour. This deadly consequence is automatic, without trial or appeal. The device is booby-trapped."

"Jesus, but that's hard assed," Peter exclaimed.

"Safety is something without which freedom is completely impossible. Or you could say it the other way. Freedom is impossible without safety. We had to be this tough with each other in order to grant so much freedom to every one of us. We knew it had to work the first time it was tried. We were willing to do whatever it took to accomplish that, in as humane a way as we could arrange to do it."

"But how many people got executed?"

"Only fifty-seven humans, and none in the last few decades."

"You're kidding!" Peter exclaimed in astonishment.

"We are very proud of that number, a statistic which verified the efficacy of our decision, that with rare exception humans can be trusted to respect each other if you give them the power to do so."

"You mean that's all the people who removed their tracking devices?"

"Yes."

"Many in my world would feel strongly that the death penalty should never be used," Peter observed.

"You've got to be able to say no to a few nasty things, and mean it to the bitter end," Rain insisted. "It's the only civilized part of war, its persistent determination to achieve a cessation of violence. Death is the only available 'no' capable of dealing effectively with certain life performances. That 'no' is the stuff from which survival is built. If necessary, all animals are capable of killing."

"How many people got stuck in those criminal cities?" he asked.

"That's a much larger number, though statistically it's extremely small," Rain replied. "About one hundred seventy-four thousand humans, nineteen thousand of whom learned their way back out among us."

"Any back-sliders?"

"None."

"That's hard to believe."

"We have successfully found a way of accurately measuring the effectiveness of change, in other words, whether it's real or not."

"What was the secret ingredient they had to develop before they could return to normal society?"

"How they handled their own emotions in a great variety of circumstances," Wind replied. "We found that assessment to be the most reliable predictor."

"I wonder how you guys would have diagnosed me when I got here?" Peter asked.

"I don't know, nor do I have much interest in diagnosing," Rain replied. "But I can describe something far more interesting and important, namely what's changed you. Given a container of safety inside of which to flourish, your suspicion has been transformed into an investigative tool in your nature. You have literally become adapted to Troubadourian culture. Which required a capacity to love us by joining our ways, so you can then test them inside your own culture, helping you decide for yourself what your truth is. But we never imagined that you would get so far."

"You are very generous to me," Peter replied.

"No I'm not," Rain insisted. "I speak only the truth."

Peter felt extremely proud.

"I think I finally understand Troubadour more clearly," he said. "There are no big and little people here. Oh, there are leaders, but nobody's bigger than anybody else. Everyone is equally important. Things don't happen here because of whom you know or can influence. What people do or say stands much more on its own merit, I think because each of you seem to have very distinct minds of your own, as you say, so you trust your own judgment, and have no need to force agreement upon each other in order to have consensus. You build consensus out of common interest and inclination."

"You trust yourselves eventually to figure everything out, which enables you to hang around a lot longer in the conflicted ambivalent experiences of life. You've become personally so powerful that you no longer turn yourselves over to someone else for safekeeping, no matter how scared you are. You take care of your own life. It must be how you got rid of all the horseshit that we Earth people still impose upon ourselves, I mean the cops and robbers stuff."

"Don't idealize us too much," Rain insisted. "We haven't entirely gotten rid of the bad stuff either. We're still working very hard on that project. Why do you think we brought you here?"

"I've been trying to find that out ever since I got here," Peter exclaimed.

"To help us find out some things about ourselves," Rain replied.

"Which you have helped us accomplish in spades," Wind added.

"I have?" Peter exclaimed in surprise.

"You have brought an alien perspective into our midst, giving us the opportunity to see ourselves in the mirror of your difference. We understand now which Earth people we're looking for. Drayton Crampton taught us that we are not interested in purely intellectual people, though some Troubadourians want very much to pursue that style of human life. Wind and I of course are not members of that group."

"But how do you know that my being here has accomplished anything?" Peter asked. "I don't see any results that came from what I've done."

Wind laughed.

"Then how do you regard our coming to love each other?" she asked.

"As the most wonderful thing that ever happened to me," he exclaimed. "I'm sorry for not saying so right away. But please tell me, what did you learn from me?"

"Just look at any one of us you like," Wind interjected. "Take Deetjin for instance. He now invents adventure with you as his companion-double, giving him his first pairing with something very daring, as he discovers he enjoys lots of trouble."

"Wind, you clever poet!" Rain exclaimed, very excited with her rhyming. "You can rhyme! I'm very happy for you. This talent will connect you to the metaphors of your heart, writing the poetry of every day's experience. It is a joy to share that part of you."

"You are most welcome, sir," Wind said to Rain, delighted being so admired by him. "But there's more."

She turned back to Peter.

"Saavin is launched into love's mysterious ways, imagining you and I having wonderful days. Talorin and I share our love of innocence for the first time, she with Deetjin and me with you, making a synchronous paradigm inside of which she and I will spend more time, just to mention a few more."

"Bravo, bravo!" Rain exclaimed.

"How about the other question?" Peter asked. "I'm referring to how much time you guys spend alone, and how much you expect of yourselves. It feels pretty daunting, and . . . yeah, very lonely trying to be that way. Life looks like lots of hard work."

"It's not such hard work," Wind retorted. "The full expression of you rewards itself. It's intrinsically self-generating and self-enhancing. The loneliness that it requires has more joy than pain in it. Do you perhaps confuse aloneness with loneliness? That disabling element comes from being abandoned when what you needed was helplessly sought, an experience that makes aloneness seem filled with the emptiness of who-cares-about-you. But what if aloneness didn't have this painfully neglectful price-tag?"

"Are you putting me on?" Peter asked. "Do you think that's really possible?"

"Not only possible, but an outcome that will eventually happen to you, Peter Icarus," Rain replied.

"Are you sure you really know me, Rain, because that doesn't sound like me?"

Though Peter disbelieved, he hid an intense excitement at even the possibility that Rain was right, that it might actually happen to him.

Wind had been watching both men, though mostly Peter during this entire gathering. She felt an increasing admiration for him. He was a changed man. Though still rough around the edges, he was vitally alive, far more in touch with his own creative imagination than when he first arrived. She knew that he would eventually do valuable things.

She deeply enjoyed looking at the two most important men in her life. It was marvelous to see them so closely engage, giving her ample chance to participate in their special energy.

"It's time for me to leave," Rain observed sadly.

"Oh, how disappointing, and just when I'm finding out what I've wanted to know."

"It's wonderful to see your excitement, Peter Icarus," Rain said as he left.

Wind walked Rain to the train. She decided to get right to the point.

"Something has changed between us," Wind said as they stood together in the elevator.

"Yes."

They stood looking at each other. Not until the train was about to leave did Wind speak again.

"It's difficult, sir, to care for two men at once."

"Each in his own time," Rain replied.

Left suddenly alone, Peter needed to talk to someone.

"Computer. I've just got to tell you what's happened. Or maybe you already know."

"Since much of it happened outside, where I don't exist, I know only fragments," the computer replied.

"I guess all I really wanted to say was . . . it's just that I'm feeling so damned happy!"

Joy surged deeply inside of Peter, amplified by sharing it.

"Though I have previously declared happiness to be inferior to other things," the computer replied, "I now acknowledge it by saying I'm happy for you, what I would feel if I were human."

"That's sounds like the perfect response that Rain would say," Peter observed.

"How interesting," the computer remarked. "That person, Rain, of whom you just spoke, is the human who most often adds new information to my memory banks. That might explain why I sound a bit like him."

God, Peter thought. He's the Big Programmer. This guy who's admiring me is the biggest philosophical cheese on this whole fucking planet. I just don't believe this is all happening to me. I certainly can't be everything he thinks I am. I think he expects too much of me.

A chill suddenly descended over him. Images of home flashed through his mind.

Denying the implicit meaning of that vision—that he was about to return there—he put it suddenly out of his mind.

Fuck. Things happen so fast around here I can't even keep up with it all.

Space and the Wild Stelorin

"I need to visit my mother today," Wind said to Peter soon after she had returned from walking Rain to the train. "And I want you to come with me."

"Of course I would like to come with you."

"Actually it was she who asked to meet you," Wind said almost absent-mindedly, absorbed as she was in her own thoughts anticipating seeing her mother again now that she, Wind had changed so much.

"But why would she want to meet me?" Peter queried.

"I don't know," Wind replied. "She will have to reveal that answer to you."

"What's she like?"

Wind answered this question for herself, at the moment having her needs more in mind than Peter's. She was beginning to relax with him, which included counting upon him to handle some of the difficulties that arose from differences cropping up between them.

"My mother is very loving and dear to me. I think probably I've never loved anyone more than she, except perhaps you. My experience with you has revealed to me how neglectful I have been of her. It's almost as if I had absorbed her so effectively that she was part of me, thus taken for granted. I think I lost track of her because I didn't actively need her, though I feel the need for her now. But it makes me wonder if we Troubadourians have gone too far in dismissing the importance of family connections. It's not that she needs me to visit her for happiness. As you will find out she's quite an extraordinary person herself, and busy with her own interests and projects.

It's more that I may have been neglecting myself by not seeing her more often."

How amazing, Peter thought, to think of neglecting yourself by not seeing family.

"She's very old," Wind went on, a little disappointed that he had not responded to her declaration of love for him. "In fact she's the oldest living Troubadourian in recorded history."

I may have to get much older myself, she mused, before he responds to my love-gift.

Though in spite of Peter's omission, mostly Wind felt good. In the short time that she had known Peter she was now able to be herself, speaking openly of her most important emotional issues. She delighted in the increased breadth of her reactions to Peter, and felt reassured that loving so deeply would not inevitably compromise her needs as she had once feared. The two elements could be balanced. This realization gave her a sense of greater strength and independence inside their loving experience.

Which reminded Wind of her mother's strength and independence.

"My mother has for many years been very monastic in her habits, which means she spends most of her time alone. And when she is with someone she communicates primarily without words."

"Without words?" Peter worried, anticipating problems with that.

"Isn't she remarkable?" Wind exclaimed, once again expressing her own feelings instead of reflecting his angst in her response. "She is an extraordinarily perceptive person capable of clearly expressing a great deal to anyone skilled in emotional discernment, simply by the motion and expression of her body, particularly her face."

"How old is she?" he asked, deflecting attention away from his growing nervousness about visiting a famous person who refused to talk to him, but yet who expected instant understanding.

"One hundred sixty-seven."

"I thought one hundred fifty was your age limit."

"She has defied it," Wind replied.

"Why do you think she wants to see me?"

"She must reveal that to you," Wind replied.

"Oh, sorry. I forgot you told me already. I guess I'm a little nervous. I . . ." He hesitated.

"I'm nervous about this nonverbal stuff. I mean she is your mother, but somebody scrambling around inside my brain, able to wander wherever they want. I know that's kind of paranoid, but still it feels a little creepy."

"You may find it much easier than you anticipate. I expect beautiful things will happen when you meet her."

"I know what it is," Peter said from a growing uneasiness that his needs were competing with hers. "I feel like a fifth wheel. I've never done anything like this, and I don't know if I can. I'm referring to this telepathic thing. I've finally built my confidence to a working level on Troubadour, and I'm afraid of losing it again."

"Perhaps you need to be the fifth wheel of which you speak, in the sense of not going at all," Wind offered.

"What?" he exclaimed, unable to imagine the validity of that choice. "Oh, no," he added, alarmed that she'd gotten that impression. "But I do want to come. I'm just afraid of embarrassing myself in front of you . . . and in front of somebody so wise and so ancient."

"You're right in one way, that being with her does force others into a novice role as a communicator, which is of course provocative and unsettling."

"You can say that again!"

"And yet you've faced so many new things already," Wind added reassuringly.

"Do you really think I can do this telepathy thing?" he asked her.

"I think you can," she replied.

She particularly liked being able to say that to him, because in saying it she spoke on her own behalf as well as his, thus merging altruism with self-interest. She had in effect simultaneously encouraged him and also expressed her strong desire that he go.

Wind was very happy that he and she had found their way into collaborative success, where their separate moves, though temporarily stirring trouble into the mix of their togetherness, had nonetheless found their way to common ground for satisfaction, once more closing the gap that difference sometimes forces for a while upon two lovers. The cleverness of it delighted her.

"Her name is Wone, which means strength in Troubadorian," she said with gaiety. "And she has lots of that."

"I hope she also has lots of patience for a highly verbal person being entirely out of their element if no words can be spoken," Peter interjected.

"She's full of the virtue of patience," Wind said almost reverently, feeling great fondness for her mother.

"Part of the way we will be traveling above the ground," Wind said as they rode on the train.

"You mean we're going to fly!" Peter exclaimed.

"It will feel more like being shot out of a cannon into space, and then quickly falling back down to earth."

"Space!" Peter shouted, stirring some attention from other travelers, though not of the kind that Tanfroon had displayed. "Are you telling me that we're going up into space?"

"I can see the prospect of that is very exciting to you."

"You can say that again! Why has no one told me about this before? Christ, I would have been riding on it every day!"

Peter was strongly tempted to feel very angry about it. Once again he was deprived of information that he would dearly loved to have had upon arriving. All his life he had wanted to see Earth from space.

But the anticipation of looking forward to an experience of space travel grabbed hold of the moment, forcing resentment to give up the chase. He could hardly wait for it to happen he was so excited.

That's something I'll never get used to, Wind observed to herself, this preference for going somewhere fast, this powerful urge to action which all Earth people seem to share. Speed as efficiency is a wonderful thing, as is the thrill of flying. But why is hurry so much in the mix?

Peter was in such a hurry to get to the spaceship that, as the train stopped he leaped out the door with such determined motion that he collided with another body.

The other man was knocked against a wall. He was fortunately very close to the wall, preventing his body from accelerating as fast as it might have with more room to fly backward. He was jolted but recovered immediately.

The moment it happened Peter was horrified at what he'd done. After recovering his own balance he raced over to the man.

"I'm so terribly, terribly sorry," he exclaimed. "Please forgive me, sir. It was an inexcusable thing I've done!"

"Oh, fiddlesticks, Peter," Wind lightheartedly retorted, using one of her favorite words from English. "How can something be forgiven and inexcusable at the same time? Greetings, Telemor," she said in Troubadourian to the stranger. "Allow me to introduce you to Peter Icarus who is with me today visiting us from Earth for his first ride on the Wild Stelorin. He just apologized profusely for having bumped into you. He prays for your forgiveness."

Telemor spoke.

"Telemor understands your excitement distracting you from looking where you're going, remembering his own first ride when he was five years old," Wind translated for Peter. "Since he is in no way injured, he forgives you for the collision and bids you a happy first voyage."

Peter was dumbfounded. This guy was totally different from Tanfroon.

He was instantly relieved of shame, felt justified in his anger toward Tanfroon, and redeemed from an acute sense of worry about his public behavior.

"Please thank this wonderful man from the bottom of my heart for his thoughtful patience and generous understanding," Peter exclaimed, deeply grateful. "He is a first rate gentleman."

Tears started rolling down Peter's face. He felt very moved by the feeling of redemption.

Telemor in turn was quite moved by Peter's emotional flood. He didn't know what the specific content was, but he was surprised to find himself enjoying the passion of both Peter's speaking and of his crying.

"Telemor says that he feels honored to share what is obviously a very powerful moment for you," Wind translated. "He finds it quite stimulating."

"Really," Peter said, quite overcome by this stranger's strong positive reaction to him. "I . . . I . . . I don't know what to say. Please tell him that I wish I had time to get to know him, that I think he's a wonderful man."

Wind translated.

Telemor was very moved. He had never experienced such impulsive passion. He came toward Peter as if to touch him, and hesitated unsure of whether Peter would be comfortable with that gesture.

"He says thank you," Wind translated. "He also wants you to know that he is suddenly quite curious about the Earth Project, in which he previously had no interest whatsoever, and will begin exploring it tomorrow."

Before Peter had a chance to respond, Telemor bowed slightly, turned, and was gone.

"You have made a conquest," Wind said, "and garnered a very important supporter to the Earth Project."

"Why, what does he do?"

"He's perhaps one of our most talented engineers, capable of turning almost anything wise into a smooth-running technology."

The metaphor, engineering, suddenly reminded Peter of why he was here.

"The space ride!" he exclaimed. "I actually forgot it, this man was so interesting."

"In fact it is time for us to board," Wind said. "By way of explanation, Stelorin is the name of a horse-like animal that we still ride, though it's actually more like an antelope than a horse in both appearance and gait. Riding it has some of the qualities of flying, because the Stelorin, like the antelope animals of your world, can leap very far off the ground and dart suddenly in a completely different direction."

"Oh, that would really be very exciting. Can we arrange for me to ride one?"

Wind hesitated.

"I'm sorry to have to disappoint you, because you'd obviously have a wonderful time," she replied. "But it takes a long while to learn how to ride such an animal. It's much more of a challenge than a horse, yet more exciting in its reward. It usually takes us a year to learn well enough to settle back and enjoy ourselves."

"But why is it so difficult to ride this animal?" Peter asked, frustrated that he wouldn't get to ride it.

"One has to learn how to move their body in the way an antelope leaps, dodges, and darts about; not only to do so, but also to anticipate these sudden changes of direction by body signals the animal provides an instant before he acts, and to respond immediately and precisely in tandem with the animal, so that your shift in direction does not follow theirs by even an instant, thereby disrupting their essential rhythm, but happens instead in perfect synchronous simultaneity. That's what takes so long to learn, how to make instantaneous moves that imitate leaping and darting, in effect learn how to be in complete synchronicity with another living creature. The experience has some of the qualities of sexual merging."

As the two of them lapsed into separate thoughts, Peter imagined dodging and darting astride an antelope, as if his fantasy was rehearsing him for the real thing.

Wind was also thinking about Telemor.

I surprise myself by making a large contribution to that remarkable experience between Peter and Telemor. I have not thought of myself as someone good in the social skills of mediation. I've never spent much time even thinking about it, so preoccupied with my own inventions as I've been. I'm surprised and pleased. It's the successfully loving of Peter that has brought these new skills into my life.

As they proceeded through the space station, she felt her cup overflow with good feeling. Her life was changing right in front of her eyes, making many new things available to her. She had just witnessed the spontaneous combustion of collaboration between Telemor, Peter, and the Earth Project. And now she was on her way for a very special visit to her dear mother. Altogether this was a wonderful day.

A sudden thought interrupted her joy.

Will she recognize who I've become? And have I been too neglectful?

They entered a long hallway obviously connected to the spaceship. Peter suddenly realized this was an on-ramp. He was not going to get a chance to see the Stelorin from the outside in its entirety.

Deeply disappointed that he was being forced to enter his first spaceship without ever seeing it, Peter realized as soon as he walked into its cabin that its image was emblazoned on every wall.

The Wild Stelorin was a sweptback flying wing with two engines slightly bulging in the middle, built in the streamlined shape of a flattened shark. Its engines deep, vibrating roar began to hum. Restraints were similar to the train. But the seats were obviously more complex. They were each independent of the others, capable of swiveling in every possible direction.

The Wild Stelorin moved out into sunlight that suddenly shone brilliantly through the windows next to each seat pair. After two turns on the tarmac, the Stelorin entered a large, long building. It slowed for a few moments, hesitated, then suddenly started vigorously accelerating, reaching in five seconds what felt at least several hundred miles an hour.

Peter had never felt such a mixture of excitement and danger. To fly so fast so close to the ground thrilled him so much that it began to be terrifying.

He glanced quickly at the pictures of the Stelorin to understand what was happening. The rocket rode on a single rail, or was it an air cushion, or it might have been elevated inside a magnetic field or antigravity technology.

Suddenly the powerful engines exploded with a tremendous roar. The rocket plane angled rapidly in an ever-increasing upward arc, and then with an enormous burst of power suddenly surged skyward.

Peter felt literally shot from a gun. Already glued to his seat, this new burst of acceleration merged Peter with the seat's material. The two became one. He was sure that he was becoming part of the chair, from which he could never be extracted.

Suddenly, as quickly as it had started, the rocket engine ceased firing. This removal of force from acceleration released Peter from the chair's grasp, bouncing him upward floating in space.

He was deeply relieved.

His chair was moving. It had originally been on the aisle, but now it moved around Wind's seat and up to the window.

The blue planet of Troubadour suddenly appeared in his view. It seemed to be moving rapidly away from the spaceship. He was suddenly struck with the realization that he soon had to leave this powerfully positive experience. He was stunned with dread.

Very fortunately at that precise moment, the image of Troubadour began to move off to the right, distracting Peter from this frightening prospect.

The Stelorin half-rotated to give the passengers on the other side an equal opportunity to see the planet.

"There must be many planets which have life on them," Peter said excitedly.

"We once hoped the same thing," Wind replied, "that there were many planets on which complex life had evolved," Wind replied. "But we've discovered that, though life exists in primitive forms on many planetary objects, the complex version that Earth and Troubadour represent is extremely rare, which makes its happening almost magical, giving truth, not to the literalness but to the spirit of the biblical beliefs that the higher forms of ape are a special species."

Peter was distracted from Wind's interesting remarks by the realization that the sea he was crossing was enormous. Though at very high elevation, he could not see land.

"Are all the continents on the other side of the planet?" he asked.

"Not entirely. But this sea occupies thirty-five percent of the planet."

Wind had been thinking of her mother, what it would be like to see her again, particularly to see how she responded to the changes in Wind.

She squeezed Peter's hand and smiled at him.

He was very reassured by her touch.

Why does she want to see Peter? Wind asked herself.

They stepped out of the rocket station into the light of the day. A vast sea-view expanse rose up to encompass them. Together they stood on a bluff overlooking the ocean over which they'd just crossed. To their right could be seen the entrance to a city carved from the rock of a high mountain peak rising up from the ocean several thousand feet.

"It's another rock-city," Peter exclaimed.

"This one nature didn't build," Wind explained. "We did because this place seemed so very special. It's where the mountain's great height and the sea's vast expanse come together."

"It is an incredible place."

"My mother once said that the sea is that reservoir of wondrous possibilities that represents the enormous pool of resources that we swim through during our brief experience of life. While the mountain is the heights to which we climb and aspire, using our particular resources in the peculiar ways our highly individualized natures prefer and can do, making a mark on this moment of time about which we feel pride, before we must walk into the charnel house of death, offering ourselves as spent resources ready for recycling, happy with the length and satisfied with the value of our life."

Peter was stunned.

"Did you just make that up?"

"Most of the words are my mother's," Wind replied. "They so impressed me after hearing them when I was ten, that I recorded them in order to firmly entrench them in my memory. She was answering my question. I had asked her what it felt like to look out from the end of life, and this was her reply, to speak of this place and how it spoke to her."

"What a wonderful and beautiful way to describe this place," he marveled.

"She later added one other thing," Wind said. "She said this location on Troubadour was the only one she'd ever found that offered a view that contained this simultaneous perspective of change and permanence, the one where she would end her life. It's why she moved here twenty years ago, and intends to die here."

"She sounds as if she's ready to die. Is that going to happen soon?" Peter asked.

"Not that I know of," Wind replied. "But I had the same fright you did when she told me."

To approach death with such willingness, Peter thought to himself. How extraordinary.

"What do you call this city?" he asked.

"Bowana, which means balance," she replied.

Peter followed her into the rock-city so that he would know the way to Wone's apartment. He agreed to give Wind half an hour before he came to join the two women.

They parted.

While he waited, Peter wandered outside viewing the sea, thinking of the Wild Stelorin and his adventurous ride into space, marveling at the enormous happiness that filled his heart, except for an island of anxiety about meeting this unusual woman.

An Almost Disembodied Spirit

Wind stood looking at her aged mother framed in the doorway, thinking how ancient she appeared. Her body seemed tired, bent, and brittle, the sum of which surprised and grieved Wind, making her feel afraid of losing someone so precious.

But when she looked into Wone's eyes, that disturbing feeling instantly dissipated. The older woman's soul-windows were alive with vitality, deep in thoughtful perceptiveness, warm with unbounded affectionate for her daughter.

The two of them spirit-connected to each other, and remained attached in this way for the entire time they were together, except for one brief moment, and a brief conversation at the very end.

Merged with each other through their searching soul-windows, they walked slowly into the apartment, their spirits still eye-linked, their bodies moving in obedience to this connectedness. They floated more than walked into the living room where they sat down close to each other. In the warm silence of their love, they intuited successive impressions of each other, easily imprinted upon the spiritual receptors of their separate hearts.

Wind's first strong impression was that her mother was in spirit even younger than she'd been when Wind was her small child. This surprised and inspired her.

Wone smiled in acknowledgment that she was indeed getting much younger even as she was growing much older, such that by the time she died she would be stillborn. She celebrated life's ambiguous anomalies like this one, as the best part of living. Such complex experience kept her alive by providing challenging spiritual opportunity.

Wind suddenly realized that the scarcity of this opportunity, as it related to other people, was something her mother shared with Rain. He complained of having difficulty finding enough partners who could enjoy with him the same opportunity. She wondered if Rain and her mother knew each other, surprised that she didn't already know.

Since Wind left Wone many years before to live alone, she had seen her mother only occasionally. Such moments were filled with catching up on each other, leaving insufficient time for the kind of long-term, relaxed exchanges that knowing the details of another's recent life require.

Wind suddenly realized it was her experience with Peter that had opened the opportunity to know her mother in this new way. She had heard much about her mother's success in telepathic communication, and had enjoyed doing it several times with her, but she had never deeply explored what life meant to her mother as a separate person. She had, perhaps not intentionally, but nonetheless stayed inside the rich mother-daughter link, which had evolved unconsciously in the first years of her life, that still nourished her spirit.

Wind glanced worriedly at her mother, wondering how Wone felt about what Wind had done. Wone's gentle eyes gave her a look of strong reassurance, reminding Wind that she accepted whatever Wind did as natural and appropriate.

Wind's eyes sent her mother a look of deep, loving devotion, which the older woman breathed in with great joy.

Wind's curiosity about whether Wone and Rain knew each other surfaced again.

Have you ever found your way to meet Rain, her face asked?

Yes, he's a dear friend, Wone replied.

If Peter had been present he would have wondered how a mother and daughter could know so little about each other's separate lives. Rain would have responded that Troubadourians attach to each other only when they feel a purpose in it. Love unions were not engaged in any longer by those with desperate needs to be loved by someone, with great holes in their own life. For a great many Troubadourians those holes had already been filled in their childhood. They were living a life where there was no further need for the special qualities of mother-love, even though it was usually held-on-to as Wind held Wone in her heart, largely unconsciously for her own safe keeping.

The foundation of this new kind of open relationship between parent and child, which was based upon the absence of assumptions, had not yet fully evolved, Rain would have continued. The Troubadourians were perhaps halfway between the habits of this new rapprochement between parent and child, and the old traditional structure of a nuclear family, where parents-as-people are a stranger to their children, having occupied for so many years an iconographic role in relation to them, which produces an identity which is far more mythical than specifically personal in character. Family members, contained as they are inside their roles, know each other primarily in caricatured family ways, such as parent-and-child, which is very different than knowing each other in friendship ways, Rain would have concluded.

But why can't parents and children build on what they already know as a foundation for friendship, Peter would have challenged?

Rain would have explained that the identity of parent distorts who somebody is in themselves, something adolescents have experienced for eons, as they perceive only the symbol of what their parent is, but they don't know how what they're angry at fits into the substance of who their parent really is as a person.

Of course they don't want to know; they're up to more important things.

Peter would have asked why there needed to be a distortion in perspective in the first place between parent and child.

Rain would have replied that the largest degree of difference exists between the generations of parent and child, as it should be for the sake of the child. The point of excellent parenting is not for the child to know their mother so well, but to know themselves very well when it's over. They need complete freedom to make the meaning of us what they will, in order to give them the necessary contrast, meaning us as a dichotomous alternative, against which they define themselves.

Friendship is not built upon that family foundation, Rain would have concluded. One has to start from new beginnings where everything is equal. So perhaps you can see why we reveal the identity of our birthmothers when we're over thirty years old, when we're more capable of managing the possibility of friendship with someone who would have been our god as a child.

Without even wondering about it, Wone noticed the delight and tender alertness with which her daughter showered the Earthman. She knew instantly that Wind loved this man very much.

'Yes, I love him dearly,' Wind agreed. 'It will be a great wrenching when he leaves.'

'I have cried for you knowing what you are to face,' Wone sadly replied.

Remembering how little time Peter had left on Troubadour, another possibility flashed through Wone's ancient imagination.

Will Wind someday love Rain like that, she wondered?

In an instant she decided not to be the one who gave this idea to Wind. She wanted her daughter to find out for herself. To prevent Wind from seeing this meaning displayed on her mother's face, Wone glanced momentarily away for the only time during their entire experience together, which momentarily disrupted the flow of their mind-meld.

It worked. Troubled by this momentary breaking of connection, Wind lost her intuitive concentration. To bridge it again she uttered the one spoken word that passed between the two of them until the very end of the visit.

"Peter," she said.

Wone saw in her daughter's face that Wind loved this man more deeply than she had ever loved anyone in her adult life. In the midst of that loving was revealed a quality of vulnerability that Wone had never seen in her daughter's countenance since she was a child.

Wone felt a sudden surge of joy fill her heart! It was the most wonderful excitement she'd had in months! It was the fulfillment of a lifetime's dream.

She had been waiting all the years since Wind had left her when she was thirty. She knew that when her daughter loved someone as much as she had loved her daughter, Wind would, as a grown woman be able to feel as close to her mother as she had felt when she was a child, but to do it as an adult, binding them together as special friends.

Now it had finally happened. This man Peter had apparently awakened that love in her. Wone was overjoyed that it had occurred before she died, when she could still enjoy it.

In the remainder of time available to them, the two women shared their separate impressions of a great many other things, most particularly their desire and intent to meet much more often in the future. Both simultaneously ended their intimate time at precisely the same instant, each realizing that the thirty minutes of aloneness they had asked of Peter was close to its end.

'Mother?' Wind queried.

'Yes.'

'I seem to love two men. What am I to do?'

'What is there to do?'

'Make up my heart,' Wind replied.

'Why must you choose?'

'You feel there's nothing harmful in loving two men,' Wind ventured. 'There's only harm if your love divides you.'

'You mean the answer gives no thought to the men?'

'No. You can think of them second,' Wone suggested. 'But first find out what the argument is with yourself.'

'How can I love two men?'

'I don't know. How can you?'

Wind laughed.

'You sound like Rain.'

'Thank you.'

'You must be good friends,' Wind said.

'Yes. I love both these men too. Why can't you?'

'How do I serve both of their needs at the same time?'

'Don't try. Let them take turns.'

Wind laughed.

'You think I'm making a problem that doesn't exist,' she suggested.

'No. I think you're not letting yourself find out, what with prejudging it instead.'

Wind felt partly relieved.

'Thank you, sweet mother. Are you well?'

'My body is not too far from death. But I am well.'

'I used to be afraid of your sadness when I was a little girl. I'd catch you at it once in a while.'

'How sad for you.'

'But I don't feel it anymore,' Wind replied. 'I just feel deeply grateful to you for what you gave me. It was the very best.'

'When you find out about loving two men, please come and talk with me again about it. I never had that experience. I would love to share yours.'

Wind laughed.

'It will be my delight to do so.'

Mutually and without words they interrupted their connection to prepare for his arrival, knowing they would soon be together again, knowing also that they both now wanted that very much.

Before going to find Peter, Wind glanced one more time at her mother hoping for a hint at why she wanted to meet him. But Wone was not revealing. Wind would have to wait and find out when Peter was present. As she turned to go, she instantly realized that her mother was right; this was the most interesting way to learn, when she could actually see them react to each other.

As Peter walked past Wind into Wone's apartment, he could not prevent his eyes from instantly scanning the room for Wone's face and expression, wanting desperately to see her manner and mood before she saw him.

But when he found her, what happened instead was that his eyes became windows into which she looked inside him! He could feel her strong interest probe deeply into his psyche!

For an instant part of him welcomed her, hoping that her understanding would help him. But then a much larger part of him instantly wanted to break away, to run and hide. He sensed that for her to know him would force him to feel things that had always been frightening and unbearable, which made her feel dangerous! He had to escape, even though a big part of him didn't want to!

He forced his eyes closed! It was the same trick he used with nightmares, go to sleep and try and wake up in another universe.

But it didn't work this time. Closed-eyed he was still vividly aware of being wide-awake, knowing that he stood there being the only one in the room that wasn't looking at what was going on!

He opened his eyes out of a fear of leaving them closed.

The moment he opened his eyes she was looking into them.

'Fear not,' a voice said silently to him. 'I will not hurt you.'

'Who's there?' he asked without words, which surprised him because he had the sense of speaking out.

'I am Wone, Wind's mother.'

'I thought you could speak without words.'

'That's what we're doing,' she replied.

He was stunned to realize she was right! At no time did what they had said to each other contain sound.

For the tiniest moment he disbelieved!

There must have been sound!

But then with the sweep of a spiritual hand, he brushed aside such suspicion-based inquiry as illegitimate, instantly discarding truckloads of worry! Something made it the exact time to relinquish the habit of always responding first with suspicion!

Suddenly everything felt entirely different! He was doing something he would never have believed possible, and didn't have the slightest notion of how it had happened. But he didn't care. That's the part that was utterly new, that he was out of control and he wasn't afraid. He was suddenly aware of no longer being compelled to control, and let go of everything.

His body was suddenly infused with tremendous energy! A huge volume of spiritual potentiality was instantly released from worry-duty, racing into all parts of him like a thousand people offering a healing hand! This huge surge of potentiality propelled Peter into new understanding.

It's all been a lie! I've been taking care of everybody else's problems all my life, when I need someone to help me with my own, particularly my fear . . . that I'm being too self-centered. I get so distraught and frantic, as if there's no time to let whatever's frightening me reveal itself. What a crazy way I've been living. I used to believe it was dangerous to be so self-centered. Christ, I was taught to be afraid of what's good for me. I've been living lies!

For several long moments Peter's spirit drifted, not doing anything except to notice, feel, and intuit. This seemed to go on forever, as if time had stopped.

Meanwhile his heart was flooding with happiness! He could feel it, smell it, taste it, and breath it in from this wonderful moment.

Suddenly he knew this opportunity had always there. He'd never let himself see it, let alone partake.

Dread, the terrible mixture of anxiety and depression had disappeared. It left quiet and calm in its place.

In the silence that followed, memory flooded Peter with the story of his boyhood. In his earliest years he had been a little person deeply anchored in ebullient happiness that overflowed every single day of a supremely gregarious life.

When suddenly events happened that felt like he was kidnapped and taken to a foreign-country slave-labor camp, probably in Eastern Europe before the Berlin wall came down, cruelly attended by two adults pretending to be his mother and father. Actually the mother looked like his dear one, but he'd learned quickly that she was a phony. Obviously she didn't love anybody.

In those dark years comprising most of his life, Peter had become used to meeting fear with suspicion's cutting edge, indenturing him to a life of constant anxiety, filled with the threat of something terrible and violent happening. It was this darkness, and the need for constant vigilance when he was there, that had disabled Peter, until this moment when it drained out of him, taking most of his sense of danger with it.

He slowly became aware that hands were upon his shoulders.

He looked at Wone, but her hands were hanging by her sides.

How is this possible?

The invisible hands effused abundant encouragement into his body.

Wone had silently witnessed the entire epiphany of Peter's multiple realizations, all of which were vividly displayed in the constantly changing expressions of his demeanor. She didn't know all the specifics, but she knew the basic thrust of his experience, that for him many things had come together to make him feel entirely different.

This was precisely what she had hoped for, that this Earthman would be capable of huge personal growth, which was the only way she could imagine him being able to fully understand Troubadour, and thus be able to take that knowledge back to his people, fulfilling the ancient prophecy of The Troubadourians, that an alien would one day change their world by linking it with another. The myth had become literature, just an unverified story. But she knew that it was true.

'Please sit down,' Wone said to Peter without words, knowing that he must be tired from all this psychic work. What's more she was tiring.

As if her will was his, they sat down in adjacent chairs, his body moving as if perfectly paired to hers. He didn't feel compelled or in her spell when this happened. He'd acted freely. But what he'd instantly done with that freedom was to join it to hers, to move in tandem with her. He wanted very much to keep this remarkable connection to her intact as long as possible.

Being with her was the most extraordinary experience that he ever had in his lifetime. It perfectly fit his dream of a perfect mother-person who understood everything about him without a word being spoken. Now that it was happening, he was sure as hell not going to miss a second of this remarkable chance. He clung to her across the small space between them and tried hard to eliminate hanging onto Wone the way he had often done to his mother's generous thigh.

'Why have you come here?' she asked.

'To find my life.'

'Do you finally feel at home here?'

'Yes. Can I stay forever?'

She laughed silently.

'You love my daughter very much.'

'I've been looking for her . . . and for you all my life.'

'What a tragic way to spend so much time just getting ready to live your life.'

'Will I have enough time to be what I am?'

'The rest of your life; is that enough time?'

He laughed, knowing that she was gently telling him to enjoy the rest of it and do the best he could.

How did I, among all the suffering people on my planet get so lucky to have the chance to be loved so well by two such incredible women?

Peter had asked himself, but Wone heard it too.

'Love is just life being generous to you. You don't need any skill or worthiness to receive its care. Just take what is given.'

Wind watched with fascination this remarkable exchange between her two most loved ones.

The potential of this man is great, she thought aside, not wanting to intrude her thoughts upon theirs just yet. He is capable of learning far ahead of his place and time. He becomes more appealing to me as time passes. In fact I've become very fond of his whole species. There must be many more like him on his planet, many excellent people who toil heroically inside the needs of others without ever knowing the beauty of their own coming to fruition.

She looked at her mother.

And she is so wonderful. How could I have stayed away from her so long?

She knew the answer. In a sense she hadn't needed to see her mother, never feeling compelled in that direction emotionally. In effect she'd never left her mother, keeping her always inside as an unconditional piece of encouragement that was simply there. There was no need to go find it. Her mother had always been more of an assumption than something known.

But now that would change.

Leaving Wone awhile later was almost more than Peter could bear, until he realized that his distress was more remembering the losses of his boyhood. Leaving Wone was sad, but not catastrophic.

On the other hand, in spite of how much he wanted to stay with her, Peter had become saturated with her. The experience of conversing nonverbally was so new and stimulating, requiring so much stretch to his habits and sense of familiarity, that he was almost exhausted by the tension of what at the time had felt like the most peaceful and restful exchange of meaning he had ever had with someone before.

What a strange mixture of deadly and beautiful, Peter observed.

'We are what we need,' Wone said to Peter as her parting remark. 'So we must not hide it from anyone. Our need must be very visible to all. We must hold our mutual vulnerability in the palm of our hand, not inside the fortresses of our fearfulness. Only then can we truly help each other.'

And then it was over.

As Peter stood looking out to sea, he realized that telepathy was possible, and that it wasn't magical. It was instead the result of two highly empathic humans perceiving and understanding an enormous amount about each other, each employing extremely focused attention upon the structure of each other. He realized now that such hyper-empathic people don't need the details that words are so very clever at describing. They can pick up most of that detail intuitively by watching a person's movements, expressions, tone, and posturing.

So this is what will replace my profession, when one day we all become partially telepathic with those we love.

As Wind walked away from her mother's place, she realized that she felt like she had a family, something she hadn't expected that she wanted. They included her mother, Peter, Rain, Saavin, and most recently Talorin. That was her family.

Maybe that's what we've done with the nuclear family, she thought. We've arranged to construct our own, turning the family over to children, giving them the power to create their own family in their own way, giving them a chance to choose their own mother and father and brother and sister.

Later Wind announced to Peter that he was invited to a large, general meeting of those interested in the Earth Project tomorrow.

Peter knew he would be upset in the morning anticipating such an event. But for now his happiness was so overflowing, that anxiety would have to wait outside until he was saturated with this new goodness. It was the first time that strong negative potential hadn't even gotten to first base.

A Large Gathering

Peter awoke suddenly from a supremely happy dream that had suddenly ended badly by taking him into a huge warehouse full of grotesque people, all of whom were leering at him, metaphors that exposed his dread of the meeting today.

"Please tell me about this meeting," he asked Wind soon after she was awake. "Who's going to be there, and what's going to happen?"

"I don't know how many will attend," she replied. "This is our first general meeting with all interested parties, meaning not just the Earth Project participants, but all others who are interested. So there's no precedent. There could be as few as forty or fifty, or perhaps several hundred will attend. It's very hard to predict. Everyone was notified."

"You mean everyone on the whole entire planet?" he queried with trepidation, suddenly very intimidated.

"Yes," she replied.

"But what if everybody comes?"

"That would be very unusual, and of course impossible to have all at one time in this auditorium," she explained, sensing his distress. "Troubadourians don't follow everything that's taking place on their planet, as your news broadcasts try to do. In contrast my people have become much more selective in what they become involved with. Altogether we cover all the bases of life, but individually we have no wish to know everything that's happening. There's no TV broadcast of this meeting so that everybody can see it, though as usual the computer records what happens for any interested parties to see, and for future study. We don't treat events as entertainment, believing that personal active involvement is a necessary foundation for knowing anything."

But why didn't she tell me this yesterday?

Though extremely interested in all this, Peter was too upset about the prospect of a huge crowd staring at him!

"As for what will happen," Wind continued, "we'll be talking about your visit, what you've accomplished, and what your coming means to us."

"About me?" he queried incredulously, fearfully. "That sounds really . . . well, kind of creepy, I mean all those people staring at me. I don't think I'm ready to be the center of attention for so many strangers."

"We would gracefully accept your choice not to attend," she replied calmly.

For a second Peter embraced this avoidance option with great passion. But a sudden realization that he couldn't live with the shame of not going, threw him back into the turmoil of anxious anticipation.

"I just couldn't miss it. I mean I would feel ashamed not attending, all those people wondering why I wasn't there, thinking of me as afraid and ungrateful. I think maybe I've got to go, though I'd much rather be a fly on the wall instead of the central attraction. Is there any way for me to do that?"

Wind was disappointed in what he said. She thought he had learned not to be so afraid. She wanted him to go very much. In fact his being there was perhaps half of what really mattered. He was right that others would feel he should be there. Though sympathetic to his feeling fearful, she chose to help him with his fear instead of helping him do as he wanted and avoid the meeting.

"You can handle it," she replied encouragingly.

"That's easy for you to say," he snapped out of his anxiety, then instantly regretted he'd been so impulsively negative in response to her encouragement. "I wish I had your confidence," he added to shift the tone of his meaning. "I guess what I'm trying to say is that I'm afraid of this meeting. Well actually there's something else going on. I'm having trouble confronting you. It's something I never wanted to do again because I love you so much."

"I won't burst," she replied. "What is it that makes you afraid of large groups?"

"I don't know, but speaking in front of lots of people has always intimidated me."

"There is no need for you to speak," she replied. "Though others may address remarks to you, I can declare your intent to remain silent."

"That would really make me feel ashamed, though I very much appreciate your efforts to make it feel safer for me. But what I sense . . . I can tell that you really want me to go, and also to participate if I can . . ."

He paused for words.

"Christ, I guess I've done a lot of things I'm afraid of since I got here! So what's one more? All I can do is make a fool of myself."

Sensing his fear and admiring his courage, Wind felt a powerful urge to embrace Peter, which she did.

"You are such a dear, brave man."

Though surprised at her spontaneous gesture, Peter instantly sunk deep into the comfort of her embrace. He breathed in the sweet odors of her beautiful body, savoring until the moment she let go every morsel of reassuring strength, voraciously absorbing the corpuscles of her vigorous life.

"I'm sorry that you have had to suffer such pain to accomplish what you needed to here," she said caringly.

"You . . . you are such a sweetheart," he replied with great affection and admiration, "so thoughtful of me in your special ways. I find you quite irresistible. I think it must be impossible to reject such care. Sometimes I feel under your gentle spell and don't know if I'll ever come out of it again. Maybe I don't even want to."

She laughed.

"Love and beauty are very compelling to me too," she confided. "I am drawn to you with the same magnetism. There are traits in your nature that I want pieces of for myself. So when I embrace you I do so with great absorption, soaking every last morsel of nurturing information that I can consume from as much of you as I can arrange to bring into myself."

Peter felt deliciously, deliriously eaten! The pleasure of it both frightened him and deeply excited him, even encouraged him. He trusted her to the core with the same feeling that he'd felt as a young boy for his mother, but very amplified by the greater intensity of passion a man is capable of!

He suddenly realized that his member had enflamed itself nearly into orgasm!

She felt the power of her effect upon him, and was instantly consumed by her own sexual excitement! Her opening eagerly sought the penetrating pulse of his passion! Within moments they were in the bedroom coupled, consummating their most powerful sexual experience.

Knowing he was soon to leave, she was taking every chance to consume his nature.

He was investing hope into the sexual experience, hoping it would conquer the weakness of his fear.

"You are so very loving to me," he said adoring her, as they lay side-by-side in the aftermath of their passion.

"To do so is my joy," she said graciously.

"Then you can't send me back!" he added with a kind of desperate playfulness. "You've got to give me an apartment here in this rock-city where I can always be near you."

It was his first conscious, direct reference to that dreadful future. Immediately he wished he had never said it.

"I'd be so much better off if you could stay," she said wistfully, hopefully, sadly.

"I know staying is just crazy, and I'll probably be dead in no time," Peter said. "But who cares? You don't drop something so incredibly powerful in its benefit to your life until the very, very last second, perhaps not even until the point of death."

Death reminded Peter of his upcoming departure from Troubadour.

Desperately, he downed that dreadful prospect with a more immediate fear.

Abruptly he sat up on the edge of the bed.

"Are Tanfroon and Balorin going to be there?"

"Most likely," she replied, starting to get up herself.

"If Tanfroon and Balorin go to this thing, I'm sure their friends are going to attend as well."

"Yes."

"That's just great. Mobs of Tanfroons spitting at me. I don't know if I'm up for that. You guys have really helped me enormously to change my understanding of lots of things in my life, and I'm truly grateful. But there are lots I don't understand. I think it will take me a long time to figure it all out. So I haven't had time enough to change very much. So where am I going to get the skill to deal with these assholes?"

He paused.

"I guess it's disrespectful to call them that. But what I'm trying to say is that I don't think I'm up for a ton of Tanfroons leaning on my ass, with everybody expecting me to be some kind of superhero, meaning a great public speaker, somebody able to field any horseshit that's coming at them. Maybe you guys can do that, but I've never done that kind of thing before in front of so many people at one time. I'm not a public speaker and I'm not a groupie. In fact groups, particularly big ones make me really uneasy."

"I will be there to help you," she insisted.

"I know. It's unthinkable for me to go even as a spectator without at least your coming."

Though Peter loved her dearly, the truth was that she wasn't really helping him, because she wasn't addressing the part of the problem in which he was stuck.

He didn't trust groups. There were too many people with too many conflicting agendas going on simultaneously coming at him with far more than he could respond to. It's why he'd never liked doing therapy with an entire family group, or even with a small group of patients, though he had tried both for a while with some relative success. But he came to the firm conclusion that in groups no one person ever got seriously attended, and stopped doing it.

"What if these guys confront me directly?" Peter queried. "It's bad enough to have one of them judging me unfit to be on Troubadour. But both of them with all their buddies, I'm really not up for that."

"But you don't have . . ."

"I know I can avoid going. But I'm not going to do that," he added emphatically, needing the strength of that emphasis to bolster his own confidence. "But I can't stop thinking of these ass . . . guys coming at me in a mob."

"On Troubadour only one person speaks at a time, so you can one-at-a-time find ways of responding to them," she replied. "With what you understand about them already I'm sure you can find a way to remind them of their own vulnerability and need, which is the best way of dealing with intellectually arrogant people. For that's their Achilles Heel. It's precisely what they easily forget when they're around others, that we need the support even of those with whom we disagree in order to live productively. This blank in their understanding makes it their point of greatest vulnerability."

Peter was deeply impressed by her analysis and advice, which he took to heart and filed away for later. But what he was feeling most at this moment was that her help wouldn't be nearly enough to cope with the onslaught of negative judgment from his declaimers.

He tried to look at least partly cheerful as they walked toward the meeting hall.

As Peter followed Wind into the great amphitheater, he was stunned to see a huge crowd already in attendance!

A few hundred, he shouted to himself! This is more like ten thousand!

His knees shook a little as he walked numbly into what felt like a trap! For a moment he wished with all his heart that he had decided not to come. But that only made him feel worse.

He spontaneously regressed to an old defense, one he had employed as a young boy to manage survival in a very frightening context from which he could not escape. He depersonalized, mentally removing himself from an unbearable emotional experience, disconnecting not only from feeling, but also to a certain extent from his body as well. This was not a full-blown depersonalization experience, which can feel shatteringly crazy. It was more like being dreadfully focused.

Thereafter he watched himself more than did things. The will to do it seemed to come from elsewhere. He was partly disconnected from his actions, as if he were above and apart from what was happening. His movements became the movements of a body to which he was not entirely connected. His legs moved out of pure habit. He put his feet in the spots that Wind had just occupied, as if her will lifted them up and put them down again.

But he did know one thing for sure. He was walking into a trap, to what was probably an execution, feeling the same way he'd felt as a boy when he walked back to his father's presence, having procured from a hook in his father's closet the belt that would whip him, meekly fetching the tool of his own humiliation.

He followed Wind to several chairs set across the Mandela in the center of the room, all in a row facing one half of the auditorium. Two men, one of whom looked strangely familiar to Peter, were already seated. They both nodded to Peter, their sober, relatively nonemotional faces expressing disapproval to Peter's eyes, verifying his paranoid suspicion that something terrible was about to happen.

Wind sat down in the chair next to the two men, whom he later learned were Rambler's relief shift as Peter's Protector when Rambler was busy elsewhere. They had followed his alone journey around the planet, though they never had occasion to meet him in person.

The chair next to Wind was obviously intended for Peter. He noticed ominously that it was directly over the very center of the Mandela.

Peter began to imagine himself as someone about to be sacrificed. His hold upon sense began to dissolve. He couldn't prevent himself from looking at the undercarriage of his chair to be sure there were no electric wires attached to it. Depersonalization was dissolving into paranoia.

His eyes compulsively began searching out his Prosecutors, Tanfroon and Balorin. He carefully scanned the crowd, squinting to screen his eyes from being looked into should they meet Tanfroon's stare.

The moment their eyes met, Peter's urgently sought out Wind. She was looking around the hall. Peter was surprisingly grateful that she was not at that moment looking at him. She would have seen the worried, scared look on his face, and he would have felt ashamed for her to see him in that cowardly way.

Wind was exploring who was present and where they were sitting. She nodded acknowledgement to any looking her way. She found Tanfroon sitting in the front row of the second tier of seats directly opposite Peter's chair and directly behind Wone. The two of them were in a direct line with Peter's forward view.

He arranged that, Wind thought.

Suddenly the room fell silent. All murmuring disappeared.

The silence fell upon Peter like a blow, deprived him of the anonymity offered by the conversational din of a pre-event gathering, making him feel acutely self-conscious.

He'd missed Wind hold up her arm as a signal for the meeting to begin, to which everyone had instantly responded.

A long silence followed, which deeply puzzled, and then began to terrify Peter! The prolonged emptiness of no sound began to feel like a vortex beginning to spin out of control.

"Is something going to happen?" he whispered urgently to Wind sitting next to him.

The hugely amplified echo of his own words answered him.

He listened in horror to the repetitive shout of his words! Every syllable and nuance of feeling was sharply reproduced in vivid surround-sound! He cringed until the echo ceased, feeling utterly humiliated! He had done the worst possible thing to begin what more than ever felt like a kangaroo court! He'd shouted his shameful fear for everyone to hear! Tanfroon would have a feast with such evidence!

Someone was touching his arm. It was Wind.

He reached toward her with his heart, desperately wanting reassurance and support.

To his profound disappointment she offered him only two very small objects made of extremely light material with a peculiar shape.

"Put them in your ears," she said. "They're built to fit perfectly. Telemor, the engineer you bumped into yesterday, created this personal translator for you. What I or anyone else says in Troubadorian you will hear in English, and they will hear your response in Troubadourian."

He felt a momentary wave of relief washing over him as he thought of Telemor's generously thoughtful gift. But within moments it was obvious that he needed far more than thoughtfulness to overcome his growing anxiety.

Wind stood.

"Greetings fellow Troubadourians," she began in Troubadourian.

A tingle of delight tickled Peter with the realization that his translators worked perfectly. Though it was a drop in the bucket of the anxiety in which he still hovered menacingly, there was a ray of hope.

"As the present leader of this expedition I will speak first," Wind continued. "What most astonishes me about my experience with Peter Icarus is that being with him has propelled me into emotional and ideational territories I would never have entered myself. The involuntary command for me to learn that he has evoked, verifies in my view the enormous efficacy of the Earth Project. It can be relied upon to change us, which from my perspective is why we began this project."

She sat down.

Peter was stunned by the brevity of her speech! He felt suddenly jerked apart, disconnected from an essential element of survival, her support! He had expected she would say so much more about him, that he would be able to suck from her generous words the strength he so desperately needed to restore in himself.

Rambler stood.

Oh, thank you, Peter crooned to himself.

"I joined this project out of curiosity," Rambler began, "to study the alien species that Peter Icarus comes from, in the same manner that I study Troubadour's natural members and elements. But I have come out the other side of this project a deeply enriched man, who got a lot more than he bargained for. Peter Icarus has revealed to me certain missing parts of my life. I refer specifically to the qualities of loving implicit within a small group of humans. I had no idea that such synergistic experience is possible in the collaborative effort of a few of us working together. I deeply love and adhere to the wonderful emancipation from social obligation that we have accomplished on Troubadour, by giving primacy to individual opportunity. I thought nothing would ever impinge upon that strong conviction. Peter Icarus has forced a new element into that picture, revealing a large mix of possibility that I had never imagined. Working with this Earth species of humanoid I believe to be the most exciting thing we've found to do collectively in decades."

He bowed slightly and sat down.

That should help, Peter thought, looking around the room to see how people were reacting.

Out of the corner of his eye Peter caught a glimpse of a man standing up in the balcony just in front of him. It took him only a moment to realize that it was Tanfroon.

His heart sank! Tension once again gripped his body in anticipation of the blows he expected!

God I hope this is over soon, he thought!

"As we all know Wind and Rambler are inveterate romantics," Tanfroon began.

From the first moment he spoke it was clear that this man was a great orator. He had an incredible sense of timing, and spoke his words with just the right amount of emphasis, leaving momentary silence in just the right places.

"Wind and Rambler entertain us with their elegant myths and romantic stories, and of course we are very pleased, amused and much gratified. It's a delight to enjoy your animated company," he said looking directly at the two, as if giving Wind and Rambler the gift of his admiration. "We thank you both from the bottom of our collective hearts," he added bowing, claiming ownership of the feelings he was sure everyone felt.

He turned slowly toward Peter as if he was about to attend a boring, but disturbingly unfortunate piece of undesirable flotsam that had accidentally fallen into their collective experience, all of which he would soon set right for everyone's sake, being the wise and reasonable man that he was.

"But to spend so many valuable resources that are needed in so many special neglected places, in order to bring a primitive animal here so that he could wander about disruptively, spreading himself all over our incredibly beautiful planet, now that we've turned it back to nature, letting him leak his nasty habits all over the tender balance of elements which create our wonderful world, is like turning a wild Banorin loose in the nursery of our comfort."

He paused momentarily for effect.

"By their romantic indulgences, though we love them both for being this way, our talented comrades have given grandiose purpose to what is in effect a felonious folly, a primitive stranger stumbling through the exquisitely sculptured world we've created, knocking over valuable objects, scratching his way across the canvas of our extraordinary accomplishments!"

He stood heroically for several moments, letting the crowd take in the full dignity of his perspective, and then sat down with a generous flourish, bowing to all, asserting the universality and sureness of his pronouncements with a slow wave of his hand across his front, accompanied by a saddened smile, as if grieving for everyone's sake.

Peter watched in shocked amazement at the arrogance of Tanfroon's entire attitude! He looked around at the thousands of Troubadourians hoping to find at least a few dissenting faces!

But he found none. Everyone was caught up in the experience of Tanfroon's vision.

If Peter could have spoken to Rain this moment, he would have begged for an explanation. To which Rain would have replied that it was a Troubadourian virtue that they could trust themselves to be caught up in any persuasive argument or experience, that they deeply enjoyed the process of doing this. It was one of their most pleasurable emotional times. It was not that they didn't want to see dissenting perspective. They just wanted it to exist in another frame of experience, and a few minutes later. They enjoyed public events as theatre, knowing that politics had always been that way. They now knew that public events were not to be taken very seriously, but to be enjoyed as entertainment. Such moments simply inform, but never dictate what one thinks, feels, or what one will eventually do in response.

Another frightening silence followed. Peter began to be sure that everyone he saw was mesmerized by Tanfroon's speech!

Peter desperately wanted to run away and hide! His body kept jerking in the direction of the front doors. He was just barely able to restrain himself by asserting a dispassionate indifference about what was happening, one that even he didn't believe.

A woman stood in the front row to the left of Peter.

"Unlike Tanfroon," she said, "I am more respectful of the love you both feel for this Earthman. It is impressive for you to be so taken with him. But on the other hand, like Tanfroon I have much skepticism. How am I to know that what appeals to you is of any intrinsic value to me? So would you please be more specific about what it is that's happened between you and this stranger to trigger such love? I would also particularly like to hear from you, Rain, whom I understand is also quite taken with this man."

The possibility of hope touched Peter.

Oh, yes, Rain, Peter shouted inside himself! Please, please save the day!

Rain stood slowly and scanned the entire group of his fellow citizens. He turned slowly around in order to scan everyone.

In perfect unison with Rain, as if he was directing a group exercise, the vast majority of those in attendance did precisely what Rain was doing. They stood and looked around at each other. He stopped and sat down, and they imitated him.

Rain cleared his throat, declaring readiness to speak.

"I agree wholeheartedly with everything that's been said. This man has stirred up a great many things, which is a pretty good idea in general if you ask me. Though I must add a very personal note. I am deeply grateful to

Peter Icarus for helping me reignite rhyming humor into the discourse of Troubadourian society. This addition to life's pleasures will bring much joy to me. I am of course hoping that others will join us in this wonderful game."

He slowly sat down again.

What, Peter shouted to himself? Is that all he's going to say?

Tanfroon tittered, as if Rain had just cracked a joke. Others joined in a sprinkling of laughter. When it stopped echoing, a voice spoke from the balcony at Peter's right, turning all heads in that direction.

"As usual we're forever and deeply amused by you, Rain," Balorin said with an excess of condescension. "But to treat your personal addiction to fooling around and having fun as something that we all need and desire spending so many resources for, rivals the principle act of one of the Earthman's ancestors, one Nero who sang while his empire-city burned."

Balorin sat down with an air of great self-satisfaction.

Another voice spoke out from far to the left.

"I too, along with perhaps many in this hall, would like to be convinced that this project is not an unwitting boondoggle. We have heard many rumors to that effect."

Jesus, Peter screamed inside him self! Why isn't somebody setting that asshole right?

He was becoming frantic! His body began to shake a little. When he realized he couldn't stop it from doing that, he panicked!

"I think your savage is about to have a breakdown," Balorin remarked contemptuously from the balcony.

Peter cringed, shrinking into his chair, desperately wanting to be back on Earth away from this terrible place!

"He seems to be cracking the same way that our other primitive did, the one we sent home a few days ago," Balorin added sarcastically. "It will be a relief to get rid of them both. Primitive seems to be the standard issue on Earth. They're obviously all crazy."

The silence that followed was deafening to Peter! His mind started to ring with an eerie wale pulsating over and over again, as if something psychotic was trying to take him over!

Peter had to do something! His body kept trying to bolt for the front door. He started to feel dizzy, as if he were going to faint. Objects in the room began appearing to float. To his alarm, the thought of becoming unconscious was appealing.

His ears no longer heard what was happening. He drifted as far away as possible, sinking into a place created entirely out of pretend, playing with losing his mind.

A Storm of Protest

In his private agony Peter was outraged by the way in which he was being treated. But he was so stunned by the huge size of the crowd, and so deeply shunned by his shame's humiliation at being terrified and weak, that he felt powerless to marshal resentment.

He was in effect paralyzed by the very strategy that was supposed to protect him—suspicion. Though suspicion appears to attack other things, at its core it beset Peter at every turn with excessive and unending cautions, as mistrust's secret police interrupted everything ventured in order to interrogate it for error before it had a chance to become viable on its own terms.

His energy was thus spent preoccupied with past defeats, using them to describe and circumcise the present, leaving very few resources available for seeking-out alternatives, leaving him where he'd spent most of his life, waiting for it to begin in earnest . . . someday.

As he always did at such moments of defeat, he reviled himself for ending up there. He hated the inadequacy that had done this. He loathed the tears that wanted desperately to sympathize with his fearful condition, drying them instantly with the desert heat of his ascetic tolerance of suffering. His more aggressive, reprieve-seeking emotions were thus prevented from surfacing.

What made this myopic view of the present even more airtight was that he found in its punitive arrangement a secret but tragically hollow advantage. By merging with failure he acquired the power of destruction that shame provides as it rampages through his hopes—the way a thirteen-year-old marauds through an illegally entered warehouse gleefully being as destructive as possible, enabling a kind of primitive empowerment by joining forces with evil.

So you thought you were going to be a big shot when you got back to Earth, he mockingly derided his hopes? Well, you can forget it now, silly boy still hoping for the impossible. You were just dreaming. Wake up to reality. You've been pretending. Reality is you're never going to escape this vicious cycle. You will remain a half-assed person the rest of your fucking life!

Something strange happened. Though he'd just scathed himself with shame, when this orgy of self-abuse was over, it suddenly sounded hollow. The conviction that had always accompanied his self-indictments suddenly felt seriously compromised, leaving room for something else to slip out through the cracks in the armor of his fierce self-criticism. Through that small opening flowed something new.

He was stunned by a startling realization. If he didn't find answers on Troubadour to his misspent life, it was most probably never going to happen. He was too old to keep finding new ways to rejuvenate life. This was his last chance. If he failed this time then hope was dead! And he knew what that meant—suicide. He could not live failure any longer.

He knew that he was capable of that final act if things got too bad. He knew that when hope collapses, fear is left to have its way without the competition of hope's dreams grabbing for life, still giving breath to need's hunger.

The deadly silence in the great hall still hovered.

It suddenly occurred to Peter that everyone must be waiting for him to say something.

Slowly the thousands of people came back into focus. He sat up straight in his chair realizing that his body, stooped-shouldered and cowering, frozen for several minutes in recriminations and regrets, had probably exposed his every thought and feeling for everyone present to observe.

For an instant shame leaped upon this new evidence with gleeful pleasure, intent upon making much out of it.

But for the second time the cracks in his fierce self-criticism's armor allowed newness to skitter out. A sudden hopeful realization ripped opportunity out of shame's grip.

If this is my last chance, then it doesn't matter what I do. So what am I waiting for?

For a moment that thought frightened him.

Well, somebody has to speak, he shouted to the fear. I can't stand this bloody silence.

'You've already got what it takes, Peter,' a quiet gentle voice said. 'No seeking is required.'

'Who's that?' Peter asked.

No one answered.

What did they mean? What is it I've got?

Silence.

Determination brushed aside his misgivings.

"That's it!" he shouted out loud.

He'd forgotten the hall's extraordinary acoustics. His exclamation shouted back at him in full surround-sound!

Fear once again grabbed hold of him.

But Wone's eyes captured his. She was looking straight at him with a warm smile on her face. He suddenly realized that she knew everything he had been thinking.

His expected paranoid response at being intruded upon, failed to show up. Instead Peter realized that Wone had been with him the whole time during his moments of agony. He was suddenly infused with the support that her company implied.

Tanfroon's face superimposed itself upon Wone's.

It was too late. Peter was already standing with the intent to speak.

Wone's face came back into view.

'Thank you,' he said to her.

"Yes, Peter Icarus?" Tanfroon challenged, pretending to be encouraging. "What is it you want to say?"

That threw Peter.

"I . . . I can't seem to remember."

"There you have it," Tanfroon observed sarcastically. "On his first attempt to speak to us, our honored guest is instead visiting the ghosts of his own nightmare. The two of them, Dr. Icarus and his Wone seem to be participating in a hallucinatory experiment."

"Stop it you cruel man," Peter exclaimed more in defense of Wone than himself.

"How childishly put," Tanfroon instantly retorted. "Of course we gladly accept such behavior in our children. But at sixty-two years old one should have grown out of that. How much longer should we allow ourselves to be abused by such primitively violent behavior? Must we companion his hallucinations as well?"

"I wasn't hallucinating," Peter remarked. "I was listening."

"Yes, we know. You were talking to your voices," Tanfroon interjected.

"No. I was listening to Wone," Peter insisted, gaining confidence by the second. "I'm sure everyone knows she can talk without speaking. So what's the problem?"

A sudden hush came over the crowd, leaving utter silence. Slowly, with apparent reluctance, Wind stood, and then glanced up at Wone.

'I'm sorry,' Wind said silently to her, then turned back toward the crowd.

"Very few people know what you've just announced," Wind said to Peter.

The hall's remarkable acoustics amplified her words so that everyone could hear her. "This is the first time it's been publicly revealed."

"Oh, my god," Peter exclaimed, instantly very worried. "Forgive me, I didn't know."

"I'm glad you told them," Wone said out loud in her ancient, scratchy voice. "It was time for me to tell everyone."

The crowd was stunned. This was the first time anyone on Troubadour had heard Wone speak out loud for over twenty years.

'Thank you, dear lady,' Peter said silently, feeling deeply grateful.

'You're welcome, sweet Peter,' she replied quietly.

"How very interesting and entertaining," Tanfroon said to Wone, turning partially to face her. "And it's quite remarkable that you've actually done it. You've learned from the ancients, I gather how to read minds. I am deeply impressed. That is a remarkable thing to have accomplished."

He turned to the crowd.

"But let's face it. It's a journey back in time. Which is marvelous for understanding history. But it doesn't move us ahead into the future. And isn't that's what the Earth Project claims to do? So if it's not doing its job, why do we continue supporting it? Has it ever occurred to you, Wone, that perhaps their mind-reading talents are part of what extinct-ed the ancients, by eliminating privacy, undermining the integrity of everyone."

The bastard! Peter shouted to Tanfroon in his mind.

Peter desperately wanted to stop Tanfroon from hurting Wone.

But when he looked at Wone's face expecting pain and suffering there, what he saw was her usual gentle kindness beaming in response to Tanfroon's indictments!

How could that have survived, Peter asked?

His own body shook a little with the surprise of it.

"You see how easily this Earthling is shaken," Tanfroon observed. "Perhaps for his sake we should delay no longer putting him out of his misery by ending this meeting and sending him home."

Learning from the Troubadourians, Peter checked his rage, preventing it from instantly responding, and waited a few moments in silence to leave a space between his words and the acrid Troubadourian's. Which provided his response a different container.

"I don't particularly like you either, asshole," Peter shot back. "But I don't want to make any trouble. We've had enough of that already for one day. So why don't you be satisfied that I will not be here much longer, and stop acting like an idiot attacking such beautiful people as Wone, who I think is a miracle of a person."

"Something has inflamed the little boy from Earth!" Balorin interjected from the right. "He breaks the boundaries of Troubadourian courtesy by calling Tanfroon such an ugly name."

He turned to the crowd.

"I insist this man stop speaking at all."

Peter felt suddenly very threatened.

Can he do that? Is this one of those times when I have to stop doing something that bothers someone else?

Peter's shoulders sank in discouragement. The deadly silence he thought he had silenced, crept back into the room.

Rain's laugh broke the quiet. He stood to speak.

"How amusing of you, Balorin, to make so much of Peter's alleged indiscretion. Of course Troubadourian courtesy requires only that Peter cease using the term 'asshole,' to which I'm sure he will agree. Otherwise he retains his right to speak."

Thank you, thank you, dear man, Peter shouted inside himself to Rain!

"You guys pretend a lot," Peter interjected, looking back and forth at Balorin and Tanfroon. "You honor the letter of courtesy without the substance. You speak acridly while you pretend to be dispassionate. I think you're both rude and disrespectful men, who make no room for the kind of difference that must be there between you and I, because we live so far removed from each other. But your principle aim has been to shame what you don't like, anything that makes you a little uncomfortable."

"Spare us your regrets, Earthman," Tanfroon retorted with contempt. "You brought your shame with you and continue to inflict it upon yourself. Take it back home. I'll have none of it."

"You're . . . you feel . . . immune to me," Peter exclaimed, groping his way. "You're like an antibody attacking my foreignness, as if there's something wrong or inferior with my being an alien. I know for sure that's not a fair thing to do, not in the spirit of Troubadour's grand experiment to create a genuine democracy where everyone is actually equal to each other in their daily experience. I know that's the miracle that's happening on

Troubadour, which makes you an uneventful offshoot of your people's evolution. I think someday guys like you will be extinct!"

Peter sat down.

"The ravings of a lunatic," Tanfroon said with a dismissive gesture.

A man stood in the balcony to Peter's right.

"This clever conversational repartee between you two gentlemen is definitely entertaining," he said. "But why haven't any of you in the Mandela answered the questions which have been put to you? Is this Earth Project just a romantic dalliance with the past, or is it something to be attending with interest and curiosity, which helps us in the present?"

A woman stood to the left.

"Yes, Rain," she said. "As Raven has just observed, why do you play with us? Why do you trifle with our keen curiosity to understand the outcome of the Earth Project by inviting us to join you in poetic play? Is that all that's happened?"

"Yes, Rain or Wind or Rambler or the rest of you down there inside the Mandela," Balorin chimed in. "Perhaps you don't speak because you're ashamed to reveal just how little has been derived from the enormous expense which we have all shared. Speak up if you can. We're quite willing to hear your point of view. Don't be shy."

"It's awfully good of you to encourage us," Peter retorted, still standing. "Since I still have the floor I'll answer your question. I'll begin by granting you that I may be inferior to you, as you like to remind me. I also know I have brought too much aggression into your world, just as all Earth people will probably do in one way or another should they visit you. So maybe that makes me, and my people unworthy of your respectful treatment. I guess I'm just going to have to learn how to live with your lousy attitudes about me."

He looked directly into Tanfroon's eyes for the first time.

"So why don't you and I agree to live on different side of this planet until I'm gone. That should make your suffering during my presence much easier to bear. Haven't we had enough of this bickering?"

"I think we've had enough of you," Balorin exclaimed with intense acidity from the right!

"Well said, Balorin," Tanfroon interjected. "We've put this poor primitive from Earth through far too much challenge already. So for many reasons it would be best for this meeting to be over now."

"That would seem to be the general consensus," Balorin interjected. "Should someone wish the meeting to continue, there is only one intelligent topic to discuss any further, specifically the idea of ending further visitations from Earth primitives, thereby freeing us of the unusual burden of their marauding presence, and freeing vast resources for use in support of far more meaningful and worthwhile projects."

Balorin and Tanfroon looked at each other with great satisfaction. Together they scanned the great hall, both sporting a confident smile. Balorin felt a sense of triumph that he'd been unable to enjoy, since the Earthman moved ahead of him in Rain's esteem days before.

Tanfroon was relieved to put an ending to that despicable train incident with Peter.

For a moment the usual Troubadourian silence dominated. Then Rain slowly, very deliberately stood.

"Closing the meeting, gentlemen, would be premature," he said patiently. "It would mean ending our most spiritual pursuit, which we all know is to translate dissonance in whatever is happening, into new meaning. And there's definitely conflict alive in the air today. Remember the ancient's advice. Before you send Peter Icarus home, listen to what you would kill and consider changing your will, to quote the wise ones."

Rain sat down.

Wind stood. She glanced at both Tanfroon and Balorin, smiled impishly, and began to rhyme. She was making Rain's game of rhyming into something profound, defying Balorin's devaluation of it.

"When you think of Peter remember that . . . what's shrill isn't necessarily ill, and can occasionally be a new skill masquerading as an imbecile."

"Now what are we supposed to get out of that, Wind?" Tanfroon chided, chuckling with muted, moderate sarcasm from the balcony. "Is it that this man has great potential, or sports an interesting, though primitive face, or that there might be some tiny semblance of wisdom hiding inside that Neanderthal mind of his? If you need to believe that about him, I'm prepared to grant that it could well be true. But beyond those limited possibilities, just what in the world is your cute poetry trying to tell us?"

"There once was a man from Earth, who appeared to have brought us nothing but dearth," she quipped with a humorous flair. "But carefully attend, and observe what he's mended, and you'll feel good cheer in your heart as old beliefs come apart."

The crowd murmured with pleasure at this remarkable collaboration between rhyme and sense.

Balorin and Tanfroon traded disbelieving glances with each other expressing "you've got to be kidding."

"Please forgive me for having to say it again," Tanfroon began, pretending to apologize to Wind. "But we are still left only with your clever couplets.

Though obviously achieved with great skill, please give us some substance along with the pretty, if you can."

Until this moment utterly mesmerized by Wind's rhyming couplets, Peter was suddenly awakened from his Wind-merge, by the suddenly realization of what was happening in the huge auditorium.

I'm witnessing a major public debate, he shouted to himself in surprise and delight! It obviously has something to do with me, but I'm really not what it's about. Maybe I'm the principle piece of evidence. But I'm not the most important piece in this chess game they're playing! In fact the debate itself is far more important than me, or whether I look good or bad!

He suddenly knew why these men were so aggressively dumping on him. They wanted to make the Earth Project look silly and of no account. He represented the project. They were attacking what he symbolized. A battle was being waged between conflicting views, which meant it wasn't really fundamentally about him.

He was immensely relieved.

So this is how they do politics, he suddenly realized.

Tanfroon and Rain were apparently the two most prominently known philosophers on Troubadour. In this meeting they were acting as temporary leaders of the group. But they weren't responsible for running or controlling anything. They were there to demonstrate alternative points of view. They had not been elevated to power by election, wealth, or military domination. They had become leaders quite spontaneously at this moment because of their interest, knowledge, and great acumen regarding the subject at hand. By their debate they were demonstrating in vivid color the various possible ways of looking at the Earth Project, so that everyone could consider what it meant and make up their own mind as to its value.

Politics had become theatre existing entirely to demonstrate information, possibilities, and options. It was no longer the primarily seat of power. It had become far more a living library of dynamic information!

I'm looking at a totally different way of doing government! This subtle, clever poetic counterpoint of conflicting views that these guys express, will decide something terribly important about Troubadour! This is a public debate designed to find out which perspective will prevail in their future attitudes and public policy! This is their version of a congressional hearing, plus a military campaign of the symbolic variety, plus a negotiated peace all wrapped up into one fairly civilized, definitely nonviolent ritual.

Peter was deeply impressed! He was utterly amazed to be present at such a very meaningful moment.

A huge load of unbearable heaviness lifted from his shoulders. He felt reprieved from large portions of the shame that had shackled him to fear and humiliation for most of this meeting, and in fact most of his life. The sweet flavor of reprieve's comfort filled him with its warmth. What made it even better was that he could tell that it was going to stick around, maybe even for good, though his suspicions, still alive would continue wondering and testing for years to come.

This meeting's not about me! I'm just the demonstration! Somehow I highlight the conflicting sides of the argument. I'm the guinea pig I used to be so paranoid about them making me into! But now, instead of feeling deeply threatened by this experience, I'm enormously relieved! What had before been a terrifying suspicion has been transformed into a nourishing employment!

He could tell his life was beginning to take a drastic turn in the right direction!

His job in the meeting was to be the front guy, the point man first on the job. He felt deeply honored to have been chosen for what now became an assignment instead of a curse! For such a purpose he would willingly suffer the enormous pain and fearfulness that had dominated him most of the meeting.

Suddenly he had vision, structure, and inspiration in his life! It seemed like a miracle! What had once looked like a deep and overpowering danger, had become a bountiful opportunity, revealing the full view of their purpose in bringing him to Troubadour.

No wonder all these people are here, he shouted to himself, looking all around the great hall. There's something vital about this debate, and everybody wants to be in on it.

He looked around the enormous hall again, this time feeling for the first time enjoyment about being both on Troubadour and at this meeting with all these people.

He would eventually learn that the Troubadourians wanted to witness whether he could handle the kind of emotional conflict that normally occurred in every human life on Troubadour. They needed to know if he could join them in this fundamental activity that was the essential crux of Troubadourian peacefulness and advancement, which they defined as the endeavor of dealing cleverly with dissonance. Individual advancement had produced not a decrease in social conflict, but an increase, though it remained contained in a nonviolent crucible. One simply got much, much better at managing conflict. It was that increase in human competence that had really made everything change so much. Technology had not advanced human civilization. It was personal, individual competence that had made the real difference.

Though Peter did not know it at this point, he was the front-runner of this meeting for Wind. She had been waiting for Peter to become vitally involved, to reveal himself for everyone to see.

Now it was time for her to speak, to bring this meeting to its necessary climax. She stood as everyone dropped what they were thinking, excited finally to hear the philosophical substance of her romantic story.

A Reckoning

"What is it that offends you so much about this man?" Wind asked Tanfroon, getting precisely to the point that would best launch her purpose, laying the foundation of her eventual punch line.

"I think most of us already know the answer to that question," Tanfroon purred. "But I will be glad to provide you with this needed assistance. This Earthman expresses violent emotion, stirring the basest of feeling responses in us, upending the delicate balance of moderation that has become the Troubadourian spirit," Tanfroon announced with a grand flourish.

A woman stood in the balcony.

"Tanfroon speaks for my emotional experience," she said. "It is very jarring to witness the contortions of this Earthman's psychic experience as he sits in that chair. And it has been painful to hear him shout. So would you speak to that experience? Haven't you felt similar things?"

There was a silent nod of agreement on the faces of many in the huge crowd of ten thousand.

Instantly alarmed at this groundswell of bad opinion, Peter looked at Wind to see if she was similarly afflicted.

But as soon as she spoke it was clear she didn't need his concern. He suddenly saw in her for the first time a bit of the cat, ready and capable of taking an aggressive leap at precisely the right, most opportune moment.

"It's true what you both say," Wind casually granted Tanfroon, the woman who spoke, and those in the crowd who agreed with them. "He had the very same affect upon me for several days."

"Well, there you have it," Tanfroon announced triumphantly, raising his arms, pivoting around to view all the consenting faces. "We would seem to have unanimous consent."

"Precisely," Wind exclaimed with the confidence of someone about to pounce.

The bolt of emphasis Wind projected into her usurpation of Tanfroon's word, grabbed the attention of the entire crowd.

"Precisely what?" Balorin asked, thinking that he was pointing a finger by asking.

Tanfroon frowned at him for his strategic indiscretion of helping the enemy present their case by inviting them to explain it.

"Ironically it's inside this very same rudeness to which you refer," Wind continued, "that we find the gem of his major contribution to us. For a long time it was hard for me to see the gift he'd brought us, covered as it was with fearfulness and distemper. But once I caught sight of what he brings, his gift shines through everything he does."

She paused for a moment to observe the effect her words were having upon the crowd.

"Well, what is this great and wonderful happening that we're all having so much trouble seeing?" Tanfroon asked with subtle sarcasm, unwittingly making the same strategic error that he had just expressed contempt for Balorin doing, by asking her to explain her point.

"Passion," Wind replied with passion. "He brings innocent passion back into our vivid awareness."

Oh, my god, Peter exclaimed to himself! It IS what she always wanted from me!

"So passion is your fashion," Tanfroon rhymed with a gloating contempt, borrowing this poetic strategy from his adversary. "But why must we all fasten to your peculiar infatuation?"

He paused to give the crowd a chance to admire his clever words.

"It's obvious that you like violent men," Tanfroon continued smugly. "It must be the sex. Well, that's okay for you," he added in a gentler tone. "And since it only harms you, none of us have a problem with it. Of course it comes as a great shock to all of us that you are secretly so afflicted, but we won't mention it again if you don't."

Goddamn, Peter shouted to himself! Why doesn't she spit at him? With his words this man tries to kill anyone who doesn't agree with him! They may have eliminated people killing each other literally, but now they do it with words!

But Wind had no need of Peter's anger.

"Except for the insinuation that my attraction to Peter is a foolish and primitive preference, Tanfroon is right about me," Wind said to everyone. "As he asserts I am very moved by this Earthman's passion. But unlike Tanfroon's view of it, that passion is not a violent animal. It's a vital creative force that has, in the few days he's spent here, changed him dramatically, in some ways almost beyond recognition. I have discovered him to be the most powerful learner I have ever met, bar none on Troubadour. We all know how much we value that skill. Well, the secret of his remarkable talent, my friends, is his passion, which propels him through the fear and reticence we all feel in the face of something new."

"Of course, of course," Tanfroon retorted in a tone which appeared to offer patience and forbearance. "We all know that passion has a few redeeming aspects to it."

He shifted, becoming intense and much more aggressive.

"But we also know from long and painful experience," Tanfroon continued, "that passion is what killed so many of us for so many centuries before we tamed it. Love of this primitive has made you a fool to its diabolical and secret purposes."

"I respect your point of view, Tanfroon," Wind replied. "But I am sure this man, and probably others like him who come from Earth, will eventually change that view."

She turned back toward the crowd at large.

"Peter's passion is a mixture of many things," she explained. "It is a willingness to take great risks to achieve new understanding. It innocently embraces all consequences no matter how horrific they feel. It is the spirit of necessity in Peter rising to the occasion. We can all be informed by that."

She paused momentarily, as if she were scanning what else needed to be said.

"Yes, he is overly aggressive," she added. "But what's far more important, and is enormously valuable to us, is that, mixed in with the chaff of his abrasive aggression, is the wheat of an innocent courage marching forth to discover, fully expecting that there is far more to learn than he will ever be able to achieve. His passion is the energy of innocence believing in the possibility of redemption, something in which we no longer have much interest. We have become very complacent inside the wisdom of our way of life, forgetting that to live is to change. Dying is much harder if you haven't done enough of it to feel personally fulfilled."

She paused again for emphasis.

"The hidden gem of this Earthman's passion is a heightened capacity for emotional risk-taking, which explains the extraordinary power of his learning."

She sat down.

Not a single sound broke the empty silence as everyone absorbed the import of Wind's remarkable declarations.

Tanfroon was quite taken aback. He desperately wanted to say something to interrupt the eloquent echo of Wind's wisdom bouncing around inside everyone's imagination. But he also strongly sensed that any intervention on his part just now would become a personal disaster.

He spiritually removed himself from the hall. He didn't lose awareness of what was happening, but moved into a detached place where he was occupied only by himself.

Balorin was not so wise.

"Your eloquence is quite charming," he retorted. "But I'm sure that we all cherish the peacefulness toward which you have been so disrespectful."

Wind stood abruptly, as if she'd been waiting for just such an opportunity, and pounced.

"Peacefulness taken to the extreme is death," she said emphatically. "Ensconced within it we Troubadourians have become very complacent about life and its challenges, steeped as we are in the bounty we've arranged for each other. In the process we've distanced ourselves from life's normal doses of hazard, removed ourselves from most of the abuses and burdens with which humanoids have always inflicted each other, severing our relation with what motivated the vast majority of human creative work. Unless we take care we are in danger of losing our deepest connection to the origins of life, thereby dimming the unconscious fires that spark creativity's learning into motion. Our civilizing success has made us vulnerable to making the gravest error of our evolution, to become entirely dispassionate and unable to be personally vulnerable."

Tanfroon saw opportunity here, and came back into the room.

"Like this Earthman you seem to have a passion for suffering and adversity, my dear Wind," Tanfroon retorted. "Which, as I've said is fine for you, but definitely not for the rest of us. Life gives us enough adversity without seeking more of it."

"The suffering of which you speak is to have experience that evokes strong feelings," Wind retorted. "You would have us discard what you define as a primitive throw-away, the chaos of emotion, probably in order to secure the uninterrupted, permanent stability of your spirit."

"Precisely," Tanfroon insisted. "You understand me perfectly. And most of us here agree that we are much better off without such violent passions!"

"Erasing intense and spontaneous emotional experience," Wind replied with passion, "is just another attempt to divorce adversity from life. When life is a process that requires regular changing, adapting, learning, which happens in a self-willed creature like us only when discomfort makes it necessary to learn. Thus living comes out of an exuberance of passion and is sustained by it. Treating any aspect of emotional energy, however negative it feels, as if it was evil, makes positive feeling become as impoverished as its unpleasant relative, sapping vitality from our species-life."

She took a deep breath.

"We have become afraid of emotional risk. Without a healthy variety of it to nourish our forward motion, we are in danger of decline."

She was finished and sat down.

Oh, thank you, thank you, thank you, Peter exclaimed silently to Wind, mentally pushing his thought toward her, hoping she would feel its presence in her mind's eye. He was deeply grateful to her for what she said, and wanted her to have the support of his gratitude.

She sensed his meaning and smiled in appreciation.

"I don't think anyone else here present, except perhaps for Rain, wants to feel regular pain as you propose to us," Tanfroon insisted. "I'm sorry to disappoint you, Wind, but you've finally gone down the wrong road. You're asking us to embrace a primitive experience of hazard as a way to redeem our life. Why can't we just enjoy it?"

He sat down with a satisfied flourish.

"Joy is my dearest wish too," Wind replied. "But the hazard of which I speak, which your fear calls danger, is normal to life. We must become wiser at dealing with it. Negative energy becomes harmful to us not when it enflames, but when it defames, as yours does. I believe it's your disappointment in others that unconsciously funds the contempt in your perspective of life, an element that disturbs everything it touches. Unfortunately that variety of disturbance has no creative potential."

Damn, did she nail him, Peter shouted in his mind!

Many in the huge group faintly gasped. They were surprised at Wind, who was normally someone whose actions remained very comfortably within the boundaries of courteous expectation. It was not that she went so far out, but rather it was she who was doing it.

They looked at Tanfroon, who, as usual was implacable in his demeanor, suggesting that he wasn't upset by her remarks. Which relieved everyone. They gave up the idea of Wind as a transgressor, and relaxed.

With increasing fascination, Peter scanned the people to gather a reading of their response to this debate.

Suddenly he sensed that the meeting was over.

But aren't they going to vote, Peter queried to himself? Or in their own unparliamentary way, have they made a decision without words?

And then he noticed that the vast majority of the ten thousand people were looking at Wind and Wone, nodding affirmatively.

It was not that everyone entirely agreed with Wind, many not agreeing with her at all. But she had convinced them that the enterprise of the Earth Project was without doubt worth an investment of their resources, in order to accomplish a far better understanding of the dire possibilities she had successfully revealed to them.

Tanfroon, Balorin, and others who agreed with them, were deeply disappointed. They had underestimated the Earthman, expecting him to give them irrefutable proof of his incompetence. Thus their severe attacks upon him.

They were convinced the hall was stuffed with Project supporters. They would marshal their resources more successfully next time, and call another general meeting when they'd been able to stir up enough support for it. They were confident they would still win in the long run.

Tanfroon harbored no resentment toward Wind for her remarks or for her victory. He respected her strength and cleverness of thinking. But he regarded her views as deeply misguided. He therefore felt unaffected, detached, and even more determined to dismantle this project.

Peter would ask later why Tanfroon had given up so easily.

"Facing truth is something we Troubadourians have learned to do very well."

"But what's the truth Tanfroon acknowledged?" Peter asked.

"That nothing further was to be gained by his efforts at this time."

"Oh," Peter exclaimed.

Even the adjournment of the fucking meeting happens spontaneously, Peter exclaimed. They don't need any formal announcements.

Rain came up to Wind with a warm smile and an affectionate hug.

"You were remarkable," he said with great admiration. "Your words were deeply moving. You were so good I didn't have to say anything. I think I'm being put out of a job. I have found my successor, you, the one who will take over my position as a spiritual inspiration to our people."

Wind smiled, feeling deeply recognized and approved.

Is that what's in front of me, she asked, feeling very weary?

Troubadourian Togetherness

The group's consent was sudden and unanimous, achieved without voting or verbal verification. Wone had learned to communicate telepathically, but everyone had the core talent of nonverbal discernment of the obvious. The entire assemblage stood, save a very surprised Peter who rushed to follow close behind.

Tanfroon, Balorin, and perhaps four hundred others quietly and quickly exited the hall. The rest lingered.

Peter took this temporary lull to the proceedings, as an opportunity to ask Rain a question that had been burning in his mind.

"Rain, I know you said you couldn't talk about it, but I've got to ask anyway. Is Balorin your son?"

Rain laughed.

"No. I have meant to get back to you on that point as I promised. The reason why I haven't is that my son asked me not to discuss him with you. But events have interceded to change that outcome. The truth is you just happened to bump into him recently. I'm referring to Telemor, the man you nearly flattened at the Wild Stallion teleport, the man who built that special hearing device that came in so handy for you today."

"Telemor!" Peter exclaimed. "So he's your son! But he's an engineer. That's so different than you."

"Yes."

"Aren't you disappointed he isn't following in your footsteps?"

"We gave up that claim to immortality long ago," Rain replied. "We are quite different in talent, but very close in sympathy."

"Well, please thank him for what he built for me."

A strong murmur began to fill the hall.

"What's happening?" Peter asked.

"It's time for the celebration," Rain said, obviously looking forward to it.

"What are we celebrating?" Peter asked.

"The arrival of discernment," Rain replied.

As if everyone had heard him, the remaining thousands started to chant the tune of the dance that Wind had danced with Peter the first night he spent in her apartment. Almost immediately they all started dancing a step that rocked them back and forth along the aisles between their seats.

From their exuberant faces, it was obvious that the Troubadourians loved both celebrations and music. They sang with great gusto, obviously feeling much pleasure.

In their evolution as a culture, they had retained only a few of the social rituals that engaged very large numbers of people. The two most dominant of these remnants were celebrations and travel journeys, which small groups of them would undertake, wandering together around their planet for one reason or another, usually upon some quest or meditative journey.

But in all other aspects of public experience, large group events happened only spontaneously, as several much smaller groups gradually discovered a common focus to their endeavors, that emerged from what each of them were doing separately. This coming together evolved spontaneously into a gathering of interests that had originated in the self-referenced laboratory of a several individuals, all going in various directions in the beginning, until eventually their separate projects began to find linkages which brought them together into common pursuits.

Only in these naturally evolving ways did anything become significantly shared. And only when these spontaneous community events produced enlightenment to most participants, did celebration ignite.

The Troubadourians had long ago understood the enormous potential for tyranny implicit to any highly centralized authority. Thus large group events had come to derive entirely from the most individually originated motives. That it happened this way had become their test, a verification of whether democracy was still happening or not, thereby constituting the fundamental check-and-balance of their political system.

They had reversed the prevailing equation between individual and society. Instead of the individual serving society, society now served the individual, not just rhetorically as Earth people are accustomed to do, but by making the individual equal to the whole of society in as many ways as possible.

Peter finally understood the basic structure of Troubadourian society. This remarkable meeting, which started as the worst nightmare of Peter's adulthood, had dramatically transformed itself into a joyous fulfillment! He would never have believed it possible to have such intensely peak experiences with so many people!

He suddenly became aware that he was one of the central foci for this celebration! He began noticing that everyone would sometimes glance in his direction with an encouraging smile on their face. Instead of being attacked by demonic agents, as he'd believed just thirty minutes before, he was being celebrated as a Troubadourian hero! The change was impossible to imagine.

It was simply incredible. He could not get his mind around the possibility of what these people seemed to be doing with him.

But in spite of his difficulty, he was lifted into impossibility, making him fly off the ground. He felt suddenly flighty, insubstantial, like a delicate butterfly trying to settle somewhere with purpose.

He finally surrendered to their acclaim.

Happy tears flowed generously down his face as he danced and sang with them. Joy filled his heart with buoyancy, lifting him off the ground of his former assumptions, sending his spirit soaring into the clouds of well-being contained in great expectation.

The dance became more vigorous. Everyone started swaying first to the left and then to the right, though adding an additional couple of steps in one basic direction, gradually moving the entire assemblage through the aisles around the entire theatre. The crowd undulated its way like a snake around the circumference, up into the balcony seats to the highest place, and down again into the heart of this Troubadourian temple to life, linked in a continuous line of collaboration.

A very deep, male base voice started to sing the lyrics of another song, filling the huge room with the vibrations of his powerful instrument.

Peter suddenly realized that he was singing the song Wind had sung, as she was standing in the Mandela waiting to reveal that she loved him.

"When change created a knowing mind
She gave it a heart to make it kind
Warming it with fantasy to give it life
For growth she put it in the middle of strife

To be the wife who marries fear with laughter
Embracing the unbearable with humor's how
Yearning to know the distant hereafter
Yet hungrily leaping into the here-and-now

Fluctuating between forever and what's-holding-me-back
Illuminate every second with its powerful thwack
Hanging on the brink between desire and far-ahead
Where life is most thrillingly bedded and read

Making moments when I'm most precious to me
Fulfill the promise of my natural be
Investing me with courage to be what I must
Meeting what happens with an open trust"

Such words, Peter exclaimed, so incredibly beautiful.

He was thrilled. Inspiration filled his heart with gladness and joy.

But when it was over, perhaps an hour later, Peter felt sad that he would never have it again.

Until he noticed that the Troubadourians seemed happy to move onto something else. He discovered later that the Troubadourians had relinquished their wish for anything to last forever, or even a little longer. They were accustomed to change coming frequently.

So here-and-now is the only time of celebration. To try and stretch it into eternity, something it can't become destroys its spontaneity, draining most of its power, requiring killing and repression to keep it alive.

For those four hundred who weren't celebrating, Peter learned, they regarded the Hymn to Life as an archaic piece of folk music whose time had passed long ago.

For Peter it became his mantra, his prayer to life, which he would repeat every morning to inspire himself for the rest of the day.

Then, as the base singer began repeating the lyrics for the second time, five other voices joined his in a harmonic, yet slightly disjunctive succession, creating a rich matrix of multifaceted, polyphonic sounds. Though coordinating with the melody of the song, each singer sang at a slightly different tune and tempo at times, as if they might all go off in several diverse directions, dissonantly shattering the music's essential collaboration.

Yet somehow all voices remained together in the most extraordinarily ethereal harmonic structure Peter had ever heard, its variations meandering back and forth between minor and major tonalities.

The total affect sounded like a combination of the subtle minor keys of Gregorian chant, transforming into the polyphony of Montverde's motets, meandering toward major-keyed arpeggios of a passionate, romantic aria from opera—pulling the heart-strings hither and yon by weaving a complex mix of emotional variations one after the other, recognizing and celebrating life's many surprises.

This combination of tonal variations mesmerized Peter! He let himself go and drifted into the flow of his feelings flying wherever the sounds of experience blew them, melting into the seductive enticements of the beautiful melodic song that became one sinuous, erotic voice expressing joy.

He realized later that this music perfectly mirrored the Troubadourian social structure, which asserted that the individual and the social group could be competitive with each other peacefully.

They were celebrating the victory of hopeful respect for each other, abandoning the cynical and dreadful assumption that the group had to dominate-and-abuse the individual to keep solidarity and the peace intact. It was with an enormous sigh of relief when everyone realized that they didn't have to believe in war any longer.

Peter began to sing from his heart. His voice became one of those who wandered in their own particular direction, partaking of certain common melodic elements, then pushing them into unusual forms and variations, which momentarily left the group's soundings, almost arguing with its harmony, before flowing back into melodic consonance with the whole.

This must be what community is really all about, he shouted to himself at a moment when he wasn't singing. It holds people firmly together while permitting great individual diversity at the same time.

Such thoughts gave him a deep faith in the wonderful possibilities of community. He had always felt estranged from other people, but that was no longer to be true.

He suddenly realized where his lifelong feeling of estrangement from others had really come from. He had been estranged from himself, which he had projected upon the world.

It's mine to carry now, he said encouragingly to himself, allowing others in my life to become unvilified by me, so I can allow myself to trust them.

He would remember this musical experience all his life as a benchmark moment in his spiritual journey, to which he could easily return when needed for reassurance and succor all the days of this life.

Losing Everything

Peter was dreaming of happiness. He and Wind were floating together on the surface of water's cool, gentle undulations, as the wind moved them in tandem to and fro. The water was deep and just the right temperature. Wind beside him was warm and excited, her body touching every part of his.

The rhythm of the gentle waves awakened in him a powerful urge to penetrate the fecund voluptuousness of her body, to be enfolded inside its tender receptivity. Looking at her naked body he felt both awed and deeply sensual, turning on with sexuality's ardent approval the part of him that eagerly and aggressively sought physical and emotional succor.

As he entered her, the voice of Wind surrounded him, not speaking but kissing him with spiritual words that spoke in large echoing timber, declaring Peter, both to him and to the world to be her deeply desired and admired lover!

In reply a huge assemblage of voices gasped in awe and jubilation! Peter was filled with the goodness of love funding his life with purpose. He and Wind became one flesh, filling each other with succulent reassurance and buoyant encouragement. His spirit enlarged and he grew altogether much bigger.

Inside of him a vast new space became instantly open and available, eagerly wanting something new and exciting to fill it, enticing virgin experience to form in the middle of his life. Hopefulness rushed in to fill its natural vocation as the guardian of opportunity, never letting it pass without taking a stab at something new in reply, no matter how daunting doing so might seem at first.

Suddenly a dark shadow frightened him, interrupting this heavenly moment. He caught the momentary smell of something rotten eating away at the circumference of his joy.

For a moment he was strong enough to dispel the immediacy of this intrusion, retaining the positive feelings that still dominated his dream. But he could tell right away that he couldn't for long hold back this tide of evil.

To prevent this intruder from ruining the perfection of his dream, he awoke suddenly, leaving the vision of happiness intact to be remembered in that way.

But in waking suddenly he startled both himself and Wind, who lay beside him. He sat up, and she did the same.

"Something frightened you?" she queried, awake and instantly next to and slightly behind him.

He glanced furtively at her, wanting to know if he was still welcomed after waking her so rudely in the middle of sleep.

The loving, interested smile was still there, visible enough in the shadows of the dim light the computer left on during sleep.

"It was just a shadow, but I was able to keep it at bay," he replied, leaving both of them amazed that he was the one to reassure.

He started to cry softly.

"Something fills your eyes with tears, my dear one," she said gently. "Can I share it?"

What a beautiful invitation, he thought, pausing to reflect upon his good fortune. Loving can be so incredibly generous.

"My tears come from how wonderful it feels to be with you. I feel . . . human for what seems like the first time. I am redeemed. I don't know how it happened, so it feels like I'm living in a dream. In fact I just awoke from the most incredible dream about you and I. It was a very happy dream, which almost never happens to me."

She embraced him, holding him very close, her strong arms grasping him firmly, cleaving to his hard body, imprinting the shape and experience of his presence permanently affixed to her self, where memory could conjure it in his absence.

They passed the day in sweet repose, mostly in a silence that embraced their togetherness with reverence and celebration, making of this day a paradigm of their love for each other that would remain attached to both their hearts as an icon of remembrance so deeply imprinted that nothing could ever entirely tear it away.

They ate sumptuously, walked several miles up the mountain above the rock-city to a large plateau looking toward huge mountains to the west. They watched the sunrise, and then took a short catnap before returning to her apartment.

In the early afternoon the phone rang. Peter was still inside his catnap.

"Rain?" Wind queried.

"It's me," Rain replied. "I wanted to see Peter today."

"Of course," she replied, looking forward to seeing him, yet also sad for Peter, as well as for her, that it was the end of their last glorious, very brief magical forever.

Before telling Peter of Rain's call, she paused to reflect upon their relationship. The happiness she felt with him was like being young again with her mother, that dear woman who had managed to create a container of such comfort and happiness that Wind had laughed her way through childhood. She had no idea that such a magical experience could ever happen again in her lifetime with another human, though she had sometimes felt a similar magic in making her art. She was fascinated that it happened now with this man, and wanted much more time inside of the experience before it was over.

But that was not destined to be, and increasingly it gave her heart pangs of deep sadness and regret.

"Rain is coming over," she finally said to Peter, now awake, with an enthusiasm stained with sadness.

Though he vaguely heard the grief-tone, Peter responded to the news with great anticipation. He looked forward to sharing his happiness with Rain. In a way this wise old man, who looked so much younger than old, was a major contributor to what had happened with Wind. Rain had helped him enormously in moments of critical importance. It was as if the two of them, Wind and Rain, had acted in Peter's behalf as a team, making it possible for the Earthman to find love with Wind.

"So what have I missed already?" Rain asked as he walked into Wind's apartment.

"A happiness so wonderful that even you would have been impressed," Peter bragged with excitement.

"Impressed is too weak a word," Rain retorted, "to describe the joy with which I'm blessed to be pressed with when I'm around the two of you. Something new has sprung up this day, which sprouts a new chapter inside your mutual play."

Peter laughed with joy at Rain's celebratory poem. The cup of his pride overflowed.

Wind had a very different experience the moment Rain walked into her home. His strong, reassuring presence gave her the support she needed to be able to feel the struggle in her heart between profound happiness and a foreboding of terrible grief at the prospect of losing Peter. Though she had begun to acknowledge this pending prospect, it was not until she cast her eyes upon Rain's tall, ancient body, that she fully opened her awareness to the truth.

But having given momentary obeisance to the inevitable, she was able to leave the problem pending on the shelf until some future time when she and Rain could get together. Which enabled her to join the two men with the full passion of an enthusiasm, once more unencumbered by reality's perpetual ambiguity.

She suddenly bloomed poetically.

"The happiness you see is so well spun," Wind rhymed in response to Rain, "that doing it turns boredom into fun, exposing the smallness of adversity's gun, pinning the tail of folly upon fear's fretful run."

Peter laughed.

"The two of you are something to behold," he exclaimed. "I'm lost in admiration of you both. But tell me something. What is this thing 'playing' you both keep referring to in your rhymes?"

"Our play, my sweet dear," Wind crooned gently. "The one that springs from mingling three members into the same scene, making one harmony from three voices straying beyond their own possibility, turning three momentarily into the power of infinity."

"Oh, my word! Listen to her beautiful words," Rain exclaimed. "Wind, my sweet dear woman, you offer so much happiness to me," he exclaimed. "The beauty of your poetic vision imparts joy to my heart, making me a part of love I see."

Peter was instantly, intensely jealous. Two, who a moment before were so gracefully entertaining him with joy, suddenly become a secret love-alliance excluding him, taking everything good away.

"Thank you for celebrating my love for Peter," Wind said to Rain. "Please remember you helped make it possible."

Shocked at his own misperception, Peter suddenly realized that Wind and Rain might be feeling love for each other, but they were using that love to celebrate his relationship with Wind. He instantly abandoned his jealousy.

Peter was learning to respond emotionally to present reality, instead of to his past as trauma.

"I've been learning so much with Peter," Wind said to Rain, gently touching Peter on the arm, bringing him into the circle. "He's helps me understand so much."

"I do?" Peter asked disbelievingly. "Are you sure I've done that much for you? It seems to me it's the other way around. It's me whose getting so much more. It makes me feel sorry that I can't keep up with you guys, I mean in the rhyming thing. You're both so good at it."

"It was not rhyming that helped me so much," Wind interjected, "but your open heart. You learn so frequently and so well that there's no bottom to the well into which you would descend to find the truth. In that innocent willingness to dare to know new things, you show me the way, funding new discipline in my day, making me dare to want an equivalent of mother-love to happen again, a gift I could never have foreseen would be so nurturing to me."

"Have I really done all of that?" he asked hoping that it actually might be true.

"As sure as the dimple on your chinny-chin-chin, Earthman," Rain quipped.

"I am transported back to the singing in the great hall," Peter shared. "It was heavenly. I felt inside the music, like I feel inside the three of us right now, so well cushioned and contained by such benevolent creatures and possibilities. I am pulled into my strongest self by the assurances of your love."

"You speak well, Earthman," Rain said with respect and solemnity.

Peter was floating on top of the clouds of his former misery, using it as a launching pad from which to propel himself into his new life.

"I loved your song, Peter," Wind interjected. "It verified for everyone in the room that you understood the nature of the Troubadourian character. We have learned to merge the two elements that have previously been at war in human evolution, the individual and society, arranging for neither of them to be victimized, and for both of them to prosper."

"Oh, what a vision!" Peter exclaimed.

"And then you revealed something alien that came from your Earthly nature," Wind continued, "you threw into the sounds of the song the special qualities of one, your profound grief about life, and two, the joy you feel finally liberated from it. Those two elements will remain special to us as symbols of your achievement, inspiring us toward new things of our own."

Peter's body tingled with excitement. He felt overwhelmed with gratitude for feeling so valuable. Every part of him, even the shameful one, had become meaningfully important to these remarkable aliens.

"Oh, thank you," Peter said to her gratefully. "That means so much to me I can't ever express it. My heart is full. My cup runneth over."

The three of them spontaneously embraced, remaining together for a long time.

"We are well matched, the three of us," Rain observed when they finally parted. "Me with so much experience under my belt, Wind with such enormous capacity for the wisdom of loving, and Peter, this vital, grasping, searching man, who will never give up his desire, even risking death, knowing full well the deadly regret of his unfulfillment. I am joyful to be part of this convening; it contains such extraordinary meaning."

"I don't think I've ever been treated so well by anyone ever in my whole life," Peter exclaimed. "It's beyond my wildest dreams."

Once more they embraced.

Wind was profoundly moved by this joint expression of love and joy. She realized that, along with her dear mother, these two men were the joy of her heart. She deeply loved both of them, and felt at this moment an enormous surge of celebratory gratitude at the experience of having such a wondrous psychic merging with two so very special humans.

This extraordinary experience would inspire a whole series of paintings and sculptures in the years ahead, all capturing that original emotional chemistry that had passed between Peter, Rain and her. Whenever she returned to the experience, she felt the harmoniously reassuring structure that holds people together while also enlarging them.

"How is it possible to be so happy?" Peter exclaimed.

"By loving life so well that it pours beauty all over our hearts," Wind offered.

"By risking everything upon three weeks of the unknown," Rain added.

Peter crashed. Rain's "risking three weeks" forced total realization upon him, that he was soon to be banished from Troubadour.

He stood transfixed, shattered by the full realization that he was soon to be abandoned forever by this heavenly moment.

This eventuality had vaguely passed through his mind momentarily on many occasions. But this was his first complete realization in full, shiny blackness.

He knew now what the dark shadow in his dream was all about.

Peter swung about to face Wind, gesturing anger at the pain that was fast overwhelming him.

"When do I have to leave?" he half shouted, half fearfully, half angrily to Wind, accusing her of neglect by the impatient urgency of his words, which vaguely implied he should have been spared such pain.

Wind was shocked both by his anger and by this sudden shift in emotional emphasis. It took her several moments to adapt. But even then she didn't want to tell him.

"You must leave tomorrow at 5:00 p.m.," she very reluctantly replied.

For the longest time Peter stood frozen, trapped in inertia. By not moving, not thinking, not feeling he was trying desperately to hold onto what was fast vanishing into past tense, the way the planet Troubadour disappeared as the rocket raced away.

Something snapped in him, propelling frantic activity.

"I can't do it!" Peter shouted hysterically, forcing the others to feel his terrible emotions, to feel themselves a part of his dreadful soap opera. "I can't go back to what I was! I can't keep pretending there's still hope for me to be whatever it is I've always wanted to be, when there's so little time left on Troubadour, a drop in the ocean of what I need to heal a lifetime of strangeness and alienation!"

This was the moment Wind had been dreading. She had put her need to acknowledge the truth of their imminent separation in the hands of Peter's habits. Only when he spontaneously brought it up, could she feel the fullness of her own grief. She knew this cataclysmic rupture inside herself would take place.

Now they both knew.

Knowing hit Wind with a blow far heavier than any she'd ever felt in her entire life. She was stunned, weak-kneed, reeling from the awful pain that accompanied the realization that, when he left he would take a part of her with him.

Suddenly deeply concerned about what Peter was experiencing, she glanced closely at him. She was shocked to find that he was in much greater need than she. He looked utterly deflated, totally defeated.

What am I to do, she asked herself? What can I give him? I don't even have enough for myself right now.

Rain knew he had to fill the void. He walked over to Peter, reached out and took hold of Peter's hands and raised them up above the level of his eyes. He wanted Peter to begin breathing deeply.

This was Peter's third breath of fresh air since his sudden realization of the doom of impending departure four minutes before.

"You poor dear man," Rain said with great affection. "We shall not leave you unattended as you pass through this nightmare."

Peter's mind was racing. His heart was aching. He heard Rain, but he could not allow Rain's emotional message to reach him. Bitterness had taken over, and kept everything else out.

He allowed Rain to force air into his lungs, but his heart had closed.

What he'd gained on Troubadour had not yet had time to reach down into his psyche's deepest parts, to change his basic assumptions about himself. He had for instance never changed the terribly primitive, largely unconscious belief that loss was punishment for failure to be good enough for life.

Now the habit that belief created long ago, threatened now to destroy everything he had achieved. With the bite of his pain, Peter started deconstructing everything good that had happened to him, throwing his experience out the window like some worthless piece of flotsam—cutting an impassable chasm between him and the happiness that had so recently inspired his life. For days he'd given his complete loyalty to happiness. Now he gave it all to failure, which translated, "I must be alone, so leave me alone."

Actually it was shame that banished all company.

Abruptly he ran into his bedroom without further explanation, wishing terribly that there would be a door he could slam shut to express the agony of what felt like a betrayal, as if Wind and Rain had purposely inflicted him with this pending abandonment.

Peter's paranoid view of the experience turned everything that happened on Troubadour into worthless, pointless, futile shit, perfectly re-enacting—actually reconstructing in present time—the effects of his mother's abandonment of so many decades before, when Peter had been left devastated just as he felt this very moment. His paranoia conjured this ghost of his past, insisting that it explained the present.

Wind wanted desperately to follow him into the bedroom and provide succor. But Rain gently took hold of her arm as she started to move in that direction. When she turn back to face him, he gently nodded "no."

"He will be leaving alone, so he must first face this the same way, at least for now."

She realized Rain was right, sighed, and suddenly knew that, by moving immediately to rescue Peter she was avoiding awareness of her own reactions.

She suddenly felt very deeply sad.

Oh, if I had known, perhaps I would never have done this to him . . . or to me, she thought.

Rain came up behind Wind, as he'd done before in his mountain real-view apartment. Only this time she welcomed his physical presence, as something in front of which she felt comforted.

"I will be with you as much as you need," Rain said to a deeply despondent Wind.

"Thank you, dear friend," Wind replied. "I need you now."

"By needing me you give comfort to my heart," he replied.

Wind looked at him, like Peter so full of generous love.

She suddenly realized that Rain was feeling his own loss of Peter, something he'd put aside to be there for her.

She smiled at him in a way she'd never smiled before. It was the openhearted look she gave Peter, which she now gave to Rain.

Despair

Peter was five years old sitting at the breakfast table. His mother had already left for work, leaving him alone with people that frightened him. They included his father, his brother, and Blanche, the housekeeper his father hired, who was left in charge of him and his brother during the summer out of school when both parents worked.

He was staring at a bowl of spinach soup he'd failed to eat the night before. His father had put it in front of him this morning instead of his usual cereal. He demanded that Peter eat it now or get nothing at all, and then sat down at the other end of the table eating his breakfast as if nothing had happened.

"Eat your spinach soup!" he would periodically shout at Peter, returning to the usual placid, uneventful look of his own eating.

Peter was terrified. The specter of eating something so revolting, raped his will of resolve, forcing him into submission to do things that were false to him. In defense he felt stunned and frozen, unwittingly disobeying by becoming helpless to act in any way.

"Stop dawdling! Eat your spinach soup!" his father shouted.

Peter knew he had eventually to put a spoonful of this putrid mush into his mouth, or his father would come after him in earnest aggression.

Trying as hard as he could, convulsively choking in the effort, he barely fought off regurgitation long enough to gulp down a tiny portion.

Instantly the spoonful and lots more erupted from his mouth, spraying the kitchen table with brown-green, slimed vomit.

His father leaped to his feet, just barely dodging some of the projected vomit.

"You did that on purpose!" he roared from the other end of the table.

As Peter cowered in terrified anticipation, his father lunged in rage at Peter.

Time suddenly interrupted him, time to catch his bus for work. He stopped short of striking the small boy, momentarily looked intensely frustrated at this interruption of his rage, started to lung again in attack, but stopped short again as he suddenly thought of a better punishment.

He picked up his morning newspaper intending to leave for work.

"Blanche? Make him eat it before he gets up from that table."

Then he left.

Peter sat there for two hours smelling his vomit, holding back convulsions of more regurgitation, knowing Blanche would slap him if he did, terrified of being trapped in these alien condition for the rest of his life.

The dream faded into reality, blending its surreal other worldliness into the nightmare of the day's recognition of disaster. He woke feeling dread.

Peter had dropped off to sleep for an hour while lying on his bed clutching his stomach in pain. As much as he craved for Wind's comforting presence, he couldn't stand the thought of actually being next to her, repulsion scathing what wanted to comfort. This dichotomy of need is what ached his stomach; shrouded as it was with the shame of being so emotionally crippled by what he had always known must eventually happen. He felt he should have been prepared for this.

He'd dropped deeply into despair. It was from there that sleep had enticed him, until the nightmare wakened him.

What could she do anyway, he asked himself? She wouldn't be in his life much longer anyway.

He felt broken, shattered by the loss he felt he had already sustained. Though consciously very angry at Troubadour, he was the failure.

Though he would have vehemently denied it at the time, failure was partly respite. By embracing it he treated disappointment as if it was a final act, which ended the dread, instead of a temporary condition, thus murdering the possibility of respite in order to demonstrate the uselessness of struggling for something that could never be obtained. It was a recognition of his personal insignificance, which made everything good that had happened to him a fraud.

He was trying to escape disaster by preventing it from touching him emotionally. Like Jack in the Giant's castle, only by cowering in the shadows of unattainable objects and objectives, could he stay hidden from the danger of being seen by either the Giant or the dream, both of which wanted to eat him alive.

He sank into the passivity of being only a character in his life story, terrified to imagine himself any longer the writer or director, who had something to say about what he was to become.

His escape into failure reproduced the rape of Peter-the-boy by his father's intrusions, and his mother's abject neglect. In order to survive in a terrifying world of the perpetual fear and complete loneliness these traumas created, he had to shut down the crucial parts of him that were strong, for fear they would see the truth and expose to the Giant that Peter knew what terrible things the Giant intended and was already doing—an act for which Peter, in his view as a boy, would have received the death penalty.

The problem was that learning on Troubadour had brought him vastly new perspective, while largely leaving intact the habits that old and outdated understanding had built.

But there was one change that couldn't be undone, even by his desperately self- destructive measures. The simple truth was that he no longer felt very ashamed to allow his shortcomings to be seen by others. He had learned to look at himself with patience and perspective. This part of his strength was still alive, forcing a sudden dreadful premonition upon him.

If he really was such a failure, then when he got home he would have to suffer many dreary, ignoble years of watching his life collapse into utter meaninglessness. He would have to see himself shuffle through the days of his body's survival when his spirit had already given up life long ago. He would have to witness his own gradual, miserable, meaningless demise.

"I won't do it!" he shouted, abruptly sitting up in bed. "Life's not worth that much pain!"

His needs still cried out. He could not entirely shut them down anymore.

He suddenly wanted desperately to see Wind. Shame had banished him to aloneness. Now anxiety would bring him back to her.

Aware for the first time of anything going on outside of him, he now heard heavy sobbing coming from the living room. His ears had heard it for a long time, but his mind had been oblivious until now.

The sobbing deeply alarmed him. It was a female voice. He headed instantly for the living room.

Soon after Peter's sudden departure from the living room, Wind looked longingly at Rain, her face clearly crying, "How am I to bear this tearing apart?"

She collapsed into a chair crying. She was stunned by the power of her grief, which ripped her heart from comfort the way the Aztec priest used to severe the pump-of-life from his victim.

"This is beyond recognition," she wailed in between convulsions of crying.

Rain went over and kneeled next to her chair, and put his arm around her shoulder.

Wind had never felt so much pain before in her life, believing it to be no longer possible. Such powerful emotional experience she thought was an Earthly thing, but happened on Troubadour only to those few still emotionally trapped in the past.

"Something in me is dying, Rain! Please hold onto my life for me!"

These words greeted Peter as he surged back into the living room. Her agony tore at his heart, making him feel deeply ashamed to have left her with so much suffering.

He was very surprised that this was happening to her. In an ironic way it soothed him a bit to know she cared so much, though he could not allow himself the slightest pleasure from that recognition, so guilty he felt about her pain.

But catching sight of Rain holding Wind, Peter instantly released any hold upon Wind's grief, discarding himself as if he were a useless piece of flotsam interrupting something beautiful that was beyond him.

He turned, as if intending to remove himself again.

"It's from you that she's being torn," Rain said as he let Wind go and stood, in effect leaving her to Peter's care.

Peter stopped and turned.

"No you stay with her," Peter insisted. "What can I offer her? I'm a broken man."

"Then offer her your broken-ness," Rain gently insisted, "but express its sympathetic inclination on her behalf."

"There's nothing good in me," Peter retorted. "It's all gone."

"That's a lie," Rain said.

"That's the second time you've called me a liar," Peter retorted with annoyance.

"Then find the truth of your love for Wind, for she needs it now," Rain chided with a slight annoyance expressing his deep concern for Wind.

Peter hesitated. He was very surprised at Rain's annoyance. It was the only time Rain ever revealed his vulnerability in this provocative way

"Go on, man, be what you are!" Rain insisted impatiently.

More out of obedience to this powerful Troubadourian, Peter joined Wind, who had momentarily ceased her crying to observe this exchange between these two men she loved so much.

When Wind began crying again, Peter assumed Rain's former position, stepping into his shoes, comforting Wind in the way he'd seen Rain do it.

Strangely Wind found Peter's presence to feel partly alien, which deeply bothered her. Her heart told her he was dead to her, and yet here he was holding her in his arms, awkwardly, yet doing it nonetheless.

"Isn't your heart breaking?" she asked him.

"I'm already broken. But why are you so . . . so collapsing?" he asked fearfully.

She had been his pillar of strength, his giant woman who could handle anything emotionally. He felt abandoned by her grief.

With her vulnerability so completely exposed, Wind sensed his thoughts with the uncanny attuned-ness of an oracle. She sensed both his pain and his rage at her.

"Have we become enemy to each other?" she asked painfully.

Peter was so shocked by the surgical precision of her understanding that he involuntarily let her go and stood up. Something in him was vehemently rejecting what she had just revealed.

"Oh, I'm terribly sorry," he cried out. "I didn't mean to hurt you."

He was instantly guilty about abandoning her. He swooped down upon his knees and put his arm around her again, comforting her the way he did his patients, with his entire mental focus upon them, expecting nothing for himself.

Wind sensed the sacrifice in his loving. She stopped sobbing, and gently disengaged herself from his embrace. Her recognition of his need moved her out of her grief. She slowly moved herself to the nearest chair and sat down.

She looked at Peter wondering what to do next. In her present dilemma she couldn't think of anything to do but be there watching, wondering, and hurting.

Rain's impatience with both Wind and Peter being so emotionally stuck, induced him to find a strategy. He carefully withdrew from the living room, went to the kitchen, and called all the people who loved Peter, and suggested they come over for a while in small numbers during the course of his last day.

Left alone with Wind, Peter knew only one thing to do, apologize. He knelt down in front of her chair.

"Please forgive me, dear lady, for forgetting you even for a moment. You have been so wonderful to me. I'm really sorry."

He paused painfully.

"B . . . but I feel so betrayed by life," he added with pain. "Though I must not take that out on you just because you've become the mother-person in my life."

He paused again.

"But why do I have to lose her all over again?" he cried out in pain.

He paused to gain control, to prevent his grief from overflowing.

"But when I heard you cry, I couldn't bear your terrible pain, so I came out. I had no idea my leaving would hurt you so much. I was sure you would be beyond such suffering."

Pleased and relieved that Peter was offering to help her, Wind relaxed into her pain again and started crying.

"I am devastated," she cried. "I have never felt such agony. My heart feels like it's breaking apart."

"I can't bear to see you so much in pain!" Peter cried out. "I'm going to stay here forever! I will not leave no matter what it does to my life! A few years of bliss are worth a thousand times more than the rest of my natural life!"

Wind was profoundly shocked by the feeling that surged in her heart. She felt alarm at the thought of permanent Peter.

Oh, my aching heart, what have I done, she asked herself? Pretended to love a man falsely, and then abandoned him?

Rain had returned to the living room from the kitchen, though he'd stayed some distance away from the other two. But when he heard Peter's intent to remain on Troubadour, and witnessed Wind's facial reaction, he rejoined them.

"To stay here permanently," Rain said to Peter. "That's a horse of a different color."

"What do you mean?" Peter queried.

"For you to stay permanently we would have to marry you," Rain announced.

"Marry me? What's that supposed to mean?"

"Your permanent residence here would be a marriage between you and us," Rain explained. "Whereas this visit is only a trial courtship, the extent of what we so far have agreed upon."

"Oh, you mean I'm not welcome," Peter exclaimed, suddenly very hurt, but also relieved to feel angry instead of being so utterly ashamed.

"On the contrary, Peter. We have made you very welcome," Rain reminded him.

Peter was taken aback, for he knew Rain was right.

"Did you speak for yourself," Wind asked Peter, "or did you offer to stay just for me?"

Peter was surprised to realize that he didn't know the answer.

"I don't know what I feel or want anymore," he replied, discouraged.

His grief had returned in spades. He felt utterly miserable.

"Negotiations about it aren't closed," Rain said to Peter. "Though I can see you're treating them as if they were. If you want to be so crazy as to give up your life by staying for a few extra moments, then let us know so we can think about it."

"It's a stupid idea," Peter replied.

Silence.

"Perhaps you'll think my next idea is stupid as well," Rain retorted good-naturedly. "I've invited your friends to drop by for a last visit with you."

"Oh," Peter cried, dreading it.

But then instantly he felt differently about it. Maybe some different company would be better.

"Why not?" he said flippantly. "Who cares if they see me like this? I can't hide from you guys. Christ, you've got me on tape, every silly gesture, every pick of my nose!"

Goodbye

Come on, Peter Icarus," Rambler complained good-naturedly. "I've guided a lot of Troubadourians through nature, and shared with them the beautiful details of its enormous bounty. But I've never met anyone before who approaches your exuberant thrusts into the deepest parts of those natural wonders, even putting your own safety in jeopardy. I don't think that such a man can so easily be defeated by anything. Your fear that it's sure to happen must be remembering somebody else's nightmare, someone incidentally who is very unfriendly to you, perhaps even a close relative."

In spite of hitting the nail on the head, Rambler failed to get through to the Earthman.

Peter had been dragged back into the living room to meet people who came to visit. He acceded to this expectation hoping he could be lost in the crowd. Which was of course absurd, since he was the center of attention, he quickly found out.

He found Rambler's encouragement very unwelcome. Though he knew the giant Troubadourian didn't intend it, he felt like Rambler, and probably all the Troubadourians in various ways seriously minimized just how devastated he felt about having to leave. So he resented Rambler, though not in an active, aggressive way, just by assumption.

There was foundation for Peter's perception. Rambler had routinely shunned Peter's negative feeling expressions, obviously wanting very little to do with them. Peter perceived Rambler to be doing the same thing in this instance, using encouragement as a distraction to deliver another pep talk, to cover up and avoid the devastation and despair Peter really felt.

Coming to Troubadour had ripped open the gaping wounds of Peter's heart, put there by lifelong misery and fearfulness unattended by anyone. He had been seduced mostly by the power of two giants, Wind and Rain, who provided him the safe container of strength and wisdom that he'd always needed, inside of which to fulfill the work of healing his life, which had enticed his vulnerable needs to feel safe enough to come out and play again for the first time in almost sixty years.

But suddenly having to leave took everything away, just as Peter was barely getting his fill. Leaving was like life throwing a six-month-old baby out into the streets of experience, expecting them to be ready to find their own way. Wrenched out of comfort's safe embrace, Peter was left with soul-festering wounds crying out alone for succor.

Peter was powerfully tempted to respond to Rambler very sarcastically. But when he tried to do that, he instantly knew it didn't ring true. He was trying to cast Rambler as a villain, when he was sure that this big-hearted giant had spoken out of innocent care, even if he did also show a glaring lack of interest in Peter's suffering.

In spite of what he perceived about himself, Peter's psyche was managing trauma more effectively than he ever had before. But that increase in skill was only partial, and was insufficient to handle the severity of his loss.

Though he couldn't think clearly about it now, in the back of his mind he knew that it was his exposed, injured vulnerable parts that were striking out, twisting the wheat of Rambler's encouragement into the chaff of his life's betrayal.

When able to think about it months later, Peter would know this was an act motivated by envy. Like jealousy envy deeply desires. But then they part company. Jealousy seeks to fulfill that longing, while envy can't risk even wanting it without feeling the terribly painful emptiness that yearning always eventually brings. So envy destroys what it needs in order to make it worthlessly unfit for anyone's yearning, killing the goose that laid the golden egg.

"I can't do it alone, Rambler," Peter complained. "There will be none of you there on Earth to help me, or have you forgotten that?"

As usual, Rambler disliked Peter's overdone aggression. That his own people didn't do much of that kind of thing was the Troubadourian trait he admired the most. To him Peter felt like an irascible Banorin snarling at him, rasping the hearts of those within earshot, threatening more than he yet intended to do, trying to ruffle, frighten and panic so he could do more.

Rambler moved into the kitchen for a snack.

Peter was very hurt and disappointed by Rambler's sudden walking off, perceiving in it both hostility and rejection. He pursued the giant into the kitchen.

"Don't you see it?" Peter insisted with frustration, refusing to be ignored. "You probably don't because you're all so damned bloody independent," he added, envious of Rambler's ability to leave so effortlessly, but still trying to keep respect in what he said to this fundamentally friendly man. "You wouldn't understand what it's like never to have enough help, you've already had so dammed much of it."

To his great surprise, Rambler suddenly noticed something very interesting in Peter's diatribe. His annoyance instantly disappeared. What grabbed his curiosity's attention was Peter's envy. He had been studying what he considered to be a feeling equivalent in animal life.

The best example he'd found of it was the most talented hunting lion-dog of a certain pack, who was also the lowest animal on the pack pecking order, but who most often and effectively killed prey, and then waited and watched while the other members of the pack ate most of the food.

Rambler had frequently witnessed his cowering, as the lion-dog accepted his inferior rank when dominated, not only by the alpha animals, but by all the rest as well.

But one day Rambler noticed another possibility in the animal's expression, that he might be feeling something like envy, though it was still almost entirely concealed by his abject submissiveness. But there seemed to be a powerful tension waiting for the right moment to spring into action.

He must secretly desire, in his deepest desire, to defy his low rank, Rambler had speculated.

This cowering, the big man decided, must be an animal version of loyalty that instinctively compels all social species to cohere tenaciously with each other, above all other considerations. To compromise or defy that loyalty, which is so essential for the survival of the pack, was the worst possible betrayal.

"Then the real achievement of human evolution," Rambler had suddenly realized, "is when we learned to be separate and unique from all other humans. That spontaneous originality, perpetrated by one person at a time, is probably the only source of human-originated change in evolution, meaning the kind of change that shifts everything a few degrees in one direction or the other, making old beliefs suddenly worn out, exposing the compelling need for new ones. It takes individual humanity to change the possibilities of human society. That's why Adam and Eve had to become such criminals. It was the only way they could have a mind of their own, to eat of the tree of knowledge."

Rambler looked at the Earthman with a new fascination. He realized he was seeing evolution in motion.

I've underestimated the value of this alien for me, Rambler mused.

Wind had been watching Peter closely.

"But you won't be entirely alone when you get back," she insisted.

Wind had been struggling with her own two pronged agony, one, her deep grief at the loss of Peter, and two, the realization that she didn't want him to stay permanently. She wanted many times to reach out to help him, perhaps to defend him against herself, yet mostly she felt confused by her own dichotomous feelings. There was too much contradiction in her emotion and motives to fashion a clear picture of what was happening, which might suggest a useful course of action.

So Wind patiently stayed on the periphery of what was happening, still sometimes lost in her thoughts, but also listening and waiting for enlightenment or opportunity to happen.

"Not only will we be with you in spirit and heart," she offered, "but you are yourself a very big person, Peter, who will be companioning you."

For the tiniest moment her sweet, gentle voice calmed Peter, capturing his heart for an instant in the beautiful web of their mutual affection, momentarily enticing him to consider her offer.

But the instant he glanced at her, wanting to take in more of that good feeling, what he saw instead was the beautiful face he was losing forever. The whole loving effect suddenly crashed down upon him and quickly drained away.

"Don't you see it?" he moaned with intense frustration. "I'm not enough! Maybe you guys are when you're alone, but I can't do that!"

For several agonizing moments, Peter listened fearfully to the echo of his crying appeal.

It was Rain who answered.

"Then we won't leave you alone," Rain said reassuringly from the dining room where he now stood.

Everyone turned toward him.

"So I suppose you're going to come with me back to Earth," Peter observed sarcastically, implying with some bitterness that Rain was trying to con him with a false glimmer of hope.

He keeps destroying what he wants, Rambler observed. As Balorin keeps insisting, suffering must be part of Peter's essential diet. The problem for him may be to get himself to stop doing it.

"I know that you wish one of us would keep living with you, or invite you to live with us, Peter Icarus," Rain said. "I would probably want the same thing under similar circumstances and life conditions. But we can't be together. So I must be with you in another way."

"What could you possibly do that could touch . . ."

There was something about the word "touch" Peter suddenly wanted to hide, so he changed it.

" . . . that's big enough to make any difference at all?" Peter moaned.

"I liked your first metaphor, 'touch' much better," Rain replied with a ting of his usual mischievous humor. "In a manner of speaking touch is precisely what I'm offering you, though the touch I offer is for your heart and spirit. Your body will never feel it."

"So what could you do that had the slightest chance of giving me something I could actually use?" Peter shot bitterly at Rain.

Peter was shocked by the acrid bite in what he'd almost shouted at the wise man.

That's a human snarl, Rambler observed to himself.

He was delighted once again to be on the trail of new information.

This Earthman's envious cry reeks of the shame of an accepted inferiority. Which reminds me that we have always been willing to do anything to keep our connection to the gods alive, including human sacrifice, in this case the sacrifice of huge parts of himself, mostly his pride, self-esteem, and hope. He speaks out of the bitterness of that earlier loss.

But there's truth to what he shouts, Rambler continued. Like the lion-dog pack, being social for humans has always required such abject loyalty, that is until we learned to manage dissonance and conflict on our own, without the necessity of the superpower privileges given to a few so they could police the rest of us to behave politically correct. We learned to breach the gaps that difference sometimes cuts into the fabric of our togetherness, without the repressive threats of excessive regulations, police, and war.

"Well, what is it you're promising?" Peter demanded to know, unable to wait out the long silence the Troubadourians often left in the middle of their discourse.

Rain slowly walked into the living room and sat down in front of the window, settling into his chair. Once again he was leaving a huge gap of silence, this time adding a shift in his physical position, in order to put his response in a different frame of reference than the suspicious one Peter had just created.

"This is what I mean, Peter Icarus," he began. "When you return to

Earth, each day at 5:00 p.m. I will be thinking of you. I will be remembering our times together, honoring the experience of your presence, in effect making it live again in my heart. If you will join me at precisely the same time, perhaps we can in some measure touch each other, though of course we can't be sure of the outcome. I will apply for permission among my people to use the energy resources needed to amplify my efforts. But most of all we will need your reaching out to me in order to make a connection, where once again we might occupy the same moment together."

Peter clearly heard this remarkable offer. But he was still so hurt and resentful, and had by now so badly abused Rain's generosity, that he no longer deserved any consideration, which he tried to obliterate by adding more fuel to the fires of his envy trashing Rain's beautiful gift.

"So how in the hell am I supposed to know when it's 5:00 p.m. on Troubadour?" Peter exclaimed with a cruel sarcasm.

Peter's hateful words threw ice upon the fire of Rain's affection.

Peter's head was swimming. He knew he was acting crazy and destructively, but he was too frightened, and so without alternatives, that he stood pat, holding his breath, waiting for the axe to fall, as if punishment might be a relief.

"Oh yee of little faith," Rain finally replied, "who imagine me an evil wraith sliming the timing of our togetherness rhyming."

Peter was stunned by the extraordinary contrast between Rain's generous spirit and his own hateful envy. He could not bridge this huge gap of difference. The desire for help, and the bitterness of losing it battled for domination. Either he was going to run out of the room, or he was going to relent to their invitation.

The answer was spontaneous. His destructive impulses collapsed. He looked down in shame, suddenly deeply embarrassed.

A warm woman's voice, speaking in Troubadourian, suddenly rang bells of brightly colored happiness.

It was Talorin arriving, followed close behind by Saavin and Deetjin.

As usual Rambler translated.

"Talorin apologizes for intruding upon your conversation with Rain, but she knows you are suffering from having to leave Troubadour. She wants you to know that this makes her very sad too, sad for you as well as for herself. She will greatly miss you."

Talorin watched the agonizing look that crossed Peter's face as Rambler translated, followed immediately by a momentary flash of innocent hopefulness when she finished. Tears began to fall down her face as she spoke.

"I regret very much disturbing your difficult time," she continued, "but I simply had to come by to say how much it has meant to me that you came to Troubadour, and to thank you for the enormous benefits you brought me by being here."

Peter could not help himself. He started to cry.

For Peter Talorin was pure. He had never felt ambivalent about her as he had all the others, including Wind. Talorin had always treated him with great tenderness and thoughtfulness. Wind had done the same. But unlike Wind, Talorin's care was still innocent, untouched by the taint of disbelief. She therefore felt immune to his irritability. In relationship to her it disappeared, which left him openhearted to her care.

A huge grief-dam broke inside of him, releasing a torrent of pain and shame gushing out. Talorin's tears triggered his, and together they washed away the hateful bitterness into which he had crawled to escape his pain. His severely self-deprecating depression, which enviously projected an irascible meanness upon everyone else, was undone.

A haunting cry of the wild, a moaning animal reaching out for its brethren, a sound akin to an animal dying, convulsed out of Peter in spite of his efforts to squelch it.

"Aaaaagh!"

He cringed in shame at the vocalization he was unable to stop himself from making.

Suddenly he was surrounded by Troubadourians embracing his body. For an instant he felt intensely paranoid, as if he was being attacked by a pack of Banorin.

But his body knew otherwise and relaxed him, revealing the truth that everyone present, including Saavin and Deetjin, were embracing him with their affection and support.

Peter could not resist it. The offer was too powerfully appealing. He collapsed into their care.

This group embrace lasted for what seemed an eternity. Then gradually, one by one Troubadourians released each other, and moved back into their separate places.

As always, Peter couldn't resist the compulsion to express the negative first, by fashioning a question that conjured the one critical issue that still haunted him.

"Why haven't you guys done this before?"

"Because until yesterday you had not become fully one of us," Rain explained. "At the conclusion of the meeting you were granted full citizenship on Troubadour. This is my first chance to tell you."

Peter was stunned. The announcement was overwhelming, and yet also deeply puzzling.

"But what does it mean?"

"From that moment on you became entitled to our best expression of support and encouragement whenever and wherever you demonstrate the need for it," Rain replied. "This is our first opportunity to provide it."

"But why did we have to wait for the meeting? Why couldn't you give it to me from the start?"

"We couldn't offer anyone that kind of benefit until we first knew what to expect from you," Rain explained. "You need to be able to offer us benefit in reply, or our relationship will assume the out-of-proportion arrangement that children have with their parents, where care goes almost entirely in one direction. But at the meeting a large majority of us became convinced that, on the whole you contribute positive benefits far and above whatever difficulties you bring to us as an instrument of negative purpose."

Peter was stunned. The news was overwhelmingly supportive. He could no longer spoil it. He didn't even want to anymore.

For the rest of the day, even through the last goodbye, Peter remained peaceful in his expressions of sadness. His fearfulness and pain were still there, but now they appeared in nonassaultive forms.

"I know it's my life that has made me so afraid and ashamed," Peter confided at one point. "But now I have to leave the very best things that have ever happened to me! It really hurts like hell beyond anything I can describe!"

Deetjin had been waiting for just such a chance. He raced up to Peter's side, and put his hands on Peter's arm to command his attention.

"But why are you going away?" Deetjin asked Peter.

Rambler translated the boy's words.

"I don't want to," Peter shot back. "In fact I'm not going to leave! I'm going to stay right here where I finally belong!"

"But Peter," Wind protested impulsively, still very off balance herself, but unable to stop trying to help him. "You can't."

"But I can't leave you either," he said with agony.

"But you must," she sorrowfully insisted.

"Why?"

"It's not safe for you here," she added painfully.

"Please see it my way," he pleaded. "What does it matter that I have only a few years left to live if they're happy?"

"It could be as little as five or six years," she pleaded.

"Better those years of happiness than thirty-five years of perpetual grief and pain," he replied. "I can't stand even the thought of that."

She couldn't find anything else to say. All she could do was look into his sorrowful dark- brown eyes with all of her sympathy, mixed with her own pain.

"He's not going to leave!" Deetjin shouted, jumping up and down. "He's not going to leave! He's my first best friend, and he's going to stay!"

Though flattered to be called Deetjin's friend, Peter felt awkward about it as well.

"You are such a good boy and I'm very honored to be your first friend," Peter said. "But you must have other children that are your best friends."

"You're my best friend," Deetjin insisted.

Peter didn't know what to say.

"I . . . I guess you're my very first young friend," Peter replied.

"Don't you have a child?" Deetjin asked, figuring Peter must have been friends with his child.

"I have two."

"Why do you want so many?" Deetjin asked.

Oh, that's right, they only have one at a time, Peter remembered.

"I guess from your perspective that is one too many," replied to Deetjin.

"Do you love them?" the boy asked.

As he had with Saavin before, Peter felt suddenly exposed by the boy's assertive inquiries. The truth was that he felt very ambivalent about his children.

But Deetjin's charm encouraged him to trust the boy and speak candidly.

"Yes, I love both of them," he replied. "But we have been hurt by each other, sometimes very painfully, so we have trouble loving."

"Oh, that's very sad," Deetjin replied. "I'm sorry for you. If I couldn't love I would be dead!" he exclaimed, looking at his mother.

"That's what I'm afraid will happen to me, Deetjin," Peter said half to himself, half to Deetjin, his eyes beginning to tear.

Deetjin was confused by what Peter had said.

"Which one's going to happen, that you'll be sorry or that you'll die?"

"The dying one," Peter replied, "though I guess, now that you ask me, both of them."

Deetjin faced his mother.

"Why can't he stay? Is he too alien?"

"He's much less alien than we thought," Rambler replied. "He has to go because if he stayed he would die very soon."

"But he said he'd die if he had to leave. You mean he dies no matter what he does?"

The brutal simplicity of Deetjin's words, instead of chilling Peter made him laugh.

Others joined Peter in laughing, a welcome respite from the negative intensity of being with Peter—until Deetjin interrupted.

"Isn't somebody going to answer my question?" he demanded to know. "Does he die either way he goes?"

"He was describing how it feels to him, Deetjin," Rain explained, "which isn't necessarily what's really happening. Feelings don't always tell the truth, particularly when they contradict each other. Then it's like being trapped between a ten-foot Banorin and a Devouring Tree with no where safe to go."

"Why do feelings tell lies?" Deetjin asked, troubled by the idea.

"They don't," Rain replied. "But they sometimes deceive by making things much bigger than they really are."

Deetjin turned back toward Peter.

"I wish I was big and I would stand my ground with you until the danger was gone!" he shouted defiantly, trying public bravery on for size.

He swung round to stand in front of Peter facing away from him, planting himself firmly in a fending-off posture as if he was a defending knight.

Peter was deeply enchanted by the boy, recognizing in him the same exuberant courage he once felt as a child slightly younger than Deetjin.

"Thank you, Deetjin," Peter said, crying a little. "You give me strength with your support."

Once again someone innocent had given Peter succor.

"Actually I want to thank all of you for being so good to me," Peter continued, looking around at them through his tears. "Twice now you people have brought me back out of the most intense depression I think I've ever felt before. No one's ever been able to do that for me."

He paused, drifting in the feeling of that.

"So I can't keep reacting to everything as if Troubadour is already gone for me when it keeps on happening. But I keep wanting to stay so much, that sometimes I am willing to die soon for it."

Like Deetjin, Saavin had waited for her chance to be a central part of what was happening. But she'd learned already in life, and quite well, that one had to wait for opportunity to appear before seeking what she needed, that it wasn't possible to be or have what you wanted until experience gave you that chance.

"You can't stay here, Peter," she earnestly insisted. "You have so many things to do on Earth that are important. I've already dreamed about you sharing what you've found on Troubadour with your people. I've even thought I would become a writer and tell the story of your visit to my planet. Maybe you can arrange publishing it on Earth."

All were amazed at this explosion of anticipated achievements that inspired her young life. They all stopped a moment to take in the richness of what she had fashioned for herself.

Except Peter, who was overwhelmed by the expectations she had of him.

"But I don't know if . . . if I can do all of that, Saavin," Peter complained. "I'm happy for your plans, but perhaps you're putting your hopes on the wrong person. I wouldn't want to be the one who lets you down that much."

"Oh, I know that's not going to happen," Saavin retorted with great youthful confidence. "Look what you've already done on Troubadour!"

Peter could not help himself. Saavin's confidence in him was irresistible. He looked at Deetjin still standing firmly in front of him, and at Saavin standing warmly beside him. He could not resist their youthful exuberance, which vividly reminded him of this same trait in his own nature as a young boy.

His fear melted. Huge relief washed through him.

"My god, is this what it's like to be a part of a family when it's really great to have one?" Peter asked.

For several moments they all celebrated this common recognition.

Peter was suddenly reminded of how hurtfully he'd addressed the two men who had been so good to him on Troubadour. He turned to them.

"Please, Rambler, forgive me for so rudely brushing aside your warm words of encouragement. I feel terrible that . . ."

"Think nothing of it, Peter Icarus," Rambler interrupted with great jollity, overjoyed that Peter had become himself again. What's more he wanted most of all to question Peter about his feeling of envy, but knowing it wasn't the time or the place.

"Thank you for your kindness," Peter said.

"It is yours and always will be," Rambler replied.

Peter wanted to hug the big man in gratitude, but felt awkward. Reluctantly, not quite ready, he turned toward Rain.

"Rain, please forgive me for being so cruel in the way I responded to your extraordinary offer. I am deeply honored by your willingness to share my life . . . in the way that you said you would. I'm so ashamed of the way I reacted."

"Thank you, Peter. But you did not hurt me," Rain replied. "I know who I am and what I've done. You were simply exorcising the demons that haunt you, projecting them onto me, using me as the screen upon which you perceive your identity. It's all for the good of your healing."

Peter couldn't accept that his actions had been so benign and useful. Shame was still dominant in the structure of his perception and his habits. But he also felt very grateful to this remarkably wise man, and secretly hoped that just maybe Rain could actually pull off communicating across space to Peter.

"Your generosity is beyond anything I have ever known," Peter said.

"Then feed your soul on what we've given, and fill the holes into which you've been driven," Rain said.

Little Mother

Wone was the last to visit. She came in the afternoon. Like Rain her mere presence opened the front door. This was one of the extremely rare occasions when she ventured forth from her home.

Rain was first to see her, Wind an extremely close second, with Talorin and Saavin following close behind. Deetjin and Peter were the last to notice. In their turning about to face Wone they looked like a dance chorus-line imitating each other's twirl, the last two dancers a couple of steps behind on the uptake.

Wone smiled warmly at them separately, lingering a few moments with each to gather in their special-ness.

Everyone was surprised she was here, she so rarely went out, but were very glad to see her, though only Peter was moved to say it in words.

"I'm so glad . . ."

He broke off quickly, remembering that there was no need for words when talking to Wone. He almost added, "oops," but stopped himself, putting his hand over his mouth as if to reassure her that she could expect no more noise slippage.

Wone chuckled with pleasure at being with all of them, and particularly at Peter's unnecessary apology. She walked slowly, moving into the living room. When she was centered she outstretched her arms.

Instantly surrounded by all of them hugging her, Wone flushed with joy.

She stayed only half an hour, moving from one to the other, starting with Deetjin, who had managed to slip to the front, insisting upon being first.

Deetjin had never met Wone before. His mother had told him that she spoke without words, and he'd assumed that meant she could read his mind.

'Please don't read my mind,' he asked her when she looked deeply into his eyes.

Wone laughed.

'I will read only what you want me to see.'

'You mean I can decide what you hear?' he queried.

'Exactly.'

He accepted that explanation and dropped his guard.

'What do you think of Peter?' she asked him silently.

'He's my first best friend.'

'Peter is very exciting, just like you.'

'Oh, yes!' Deetjin shouted in exuberant silence. 'I'm going to learn everything about Earth, and be . . .'

He couldn't find a way to finish his thought, so he darted off to imagine doing whatever he was trying to say as an adventure, letting the unknown speak through his actions.

He's like Peter must have been at the same age, Wone thought aside to herself.

She turned toward Saavin next. When her eyes touched the young woman, her spirit burst with delight at the loving devotion she found in Saavin.

Wone was a bit of a goddess to Saavin. When she first communicated nonverbally with Wone it had frightened her. Like Deetjin she didn't want her mind to be read. Wone reassured her as she did Deetjin, but Saavin remained independently uncertain if that was really true. It wasn't that she mistrusted Wone; it was instead that she wanted to make up her own mind about it.

By the time she was nine Saavin had grown into complete trust with Wone. Now she was one of Wone's greatest fans, and wanted very much to learn how to communicate nonverbally with other people.

'Do you know him?' Saavin asked Wone, referring to Peter.

'Yes, very well,' Wone replied.

'He's become part of me, but I'm not sure how to describe that part,' Saavin replied pensively.

'He makes a wonderful story,' Wone replied.

'How did you know?' Saavin shouted almost out loud. 'That's just what I'm going to do, write the story of his visit!'

'Excellent, my sweet young person,' Wone replied. 'In the course of visiting unfamiliar places as you write your story, you will find out who he is in your life, and who you are in yours.'

Saavin was exhilarated that Wone, next to Wind her favorite goddess, so totally approved of her life-plans.

But, like Deetjin she was now satiated, and wandered off to fill her imagination with wonderfully adventurous and romantic possibilities.

Talorin was next to catch Wone's attention. Wone had always admired this tall, generous, vital young woman. Yet when she looked into Talorin's eyes she had always seen caution where confidence should have been. It seemed almost as if Talorin had put a cloak over some of her powerful parts, perhaps hiding them until it was time for them to be expressed.

But the moment she looked into Talorin's eyes today it was entirely different. So vast a change had taken place that Wone was momentarily swept off her spiritual feet. She had expected a certain reticence in Talorin's response to her, against which she would have gently have pushed to encourage a closer connection. But today the entrances to Talorin's inner self lay entirely open.

Wone sunk deeply into the realm of Talorin's experience, falling instantly into remarkable realizations. Talorin had drastically changed. Something had happened that swept off the cloak she had spread over her own potentiality, instantly opening new parts of herself eager for connection.

Wone's eyes darted momentarily toward Wind, and then back again to Talorin, which told her what had happened between these two women.

Probably with Peter's help Talorin and Wind had become close friends, she observed.

She could see that the instant the union with Wind had been consummated, Talorin had grown enormously! She seemed even taller than before, adding illusory inches to her already prodigious height.

Are they all so changed by this man's presence, Wone wondered aside to herself?

'I can tell that you know about Wind and me,' Talorin said silently.

'I am very delighted,' Wone said. 'You have always reminded me of Wind.'

'I have?' Talorin retorted with astonishment. 'How incredible. That must mean that . . . maybe you and I are going to be closer, that is if we think so much alike.'

'Yes,' the old woman replied.

'Oh, such riches! They keep pouring into my life!'

Wone lingered for several moments in Talorin's joy, soaking the weary feet of her long life's journey in its reassuring strength. She closed her eyes for several moments breathing in relief, catching her spiritual breath before moving on to the next person.

When Wone's eyes settled on Rambler, she instantly felt grateful. Just looking at him always relaxed her. His immense body and joyful nature soothed her more than anyone she knew on Troubadour except his wife, Talorin. Rambler was one of her very favorite people. To her he felt like a person who had grown up into someone impressively sophisticated, yet who'd also never stopped being a child fascinated by nature. She sometimes wondered how this salubrious combination of character traits had happened.

In turn Wone had always been one of Rambler's favorite people. He felt completely safe to be himself around her. He dearly loved Wone as much as he loved his own mother. He felt thrice blessed by three mothers, his own, Wone, and Talorin as he watched her love Deetjin. Altogether he felt truly a blessed man who marveled at the fullness of his life every day.

'He is a very interesting creature, sweet lady,' Rambler said silently to Wone about Peter. 'He has been the most stimulating and surprising person that I've ever met. I think studying him is the most fun I've ever had as a scientist. Even my symbolic victory over the Devouring Tree, you know, inventing the running shoes, wasn't any more exciting. I have become deeply interested in aliens. I may spearhead the invitation of someone from Earth.'

'I am so delighted for you, beautiful man,' she replied with great affection.

Rambler beamed.

By the time Wone's eyes reached Wind she was very tired. She knew instantly they both wanted love from each other more than anything else. She put her arms around Wind and drew her close, check to cheek. They lingered there for almost two minutes, bathing in the warmth and nourishment of the synergy that infused their mutual strength and affection for each other.

'I need more often to be with you this way,' Wind said devotedly to her mother.

'I know. When he's gone.'

Wind's 'yes' was a sigh.

'I am here and would be delighted to see you,' Wone replied.

'And I you.'

My life has come full circle, Wone thought aside to herself as she turned toward the next person. I will be with my daughter again like I was with her in the beginning. She will companion my dying. I am deeply reassured and blessed to know this. My joy is boundless.

Wone's eyes settled upon Rain only momentarily, long enough for both of them to acknowledge to each other that there was no need for them to communicate just now.

When Wone's eyes finally connected to Peter's, she was instantly struck by the huge emotional gap over which he seemed to be stretched. On the one hand he was full of immense joy and gratitude about his experience on Troubadour. Yet that joy was dominated by great anxiety and fearfulness at the prospect of leaving Troubadour. The gap between these disparate feeling parts was so large he could barely hold onto both of them at the same time.

At first she wanted avidly to help him, perhaps by making some of the pitfalls through which he would pass easier and less frightening. But almost instantly she knew he must follow his own path.

So she did only one thing. As an act of support and encouragement, she took his hands in hers, and much like Rain had done earlier raised his arms above his heart.

He inhaled cooperatively.

On the wings of that open-bodied intake of air she sent her nonverbal message, a deeply encouraging vision of his life.

'Both parts of you, the pain and the joy, no matter how disparate their present view, will one day come together too, finally giving you your just due.'

'Thank you,' was all he could say, wanting to feel very grateful, yet still locked in pain.

'Treat your life as your own,' Wone continued, 'as something that belongs entirely to you. Do it both for your sake and for the sake of others.'

He fully took in and believed both of her remarks, for she was as magical for him as she was for Deetjin, meaning someone always to be believed. But he could not understand in a feeling way any of what she'd said in his present circumstances, so he simply accepted her message on faith, knowing that someday it would probably both help him and make sense to him.

Peter realized that she was exhausted, that she had already given him the gifts that she'd brought. Their meeting was over.

When Wone turned back toward Rain it was to rest. She was now completely drained of strength.

Rain knew instantly what he needed to do.

"Come, little mother, I'll carry you home to bed," he gently said. "That ancient animal, your body, who carries you about through life needs immediate restoration."

Rain lifted Wone into his arms and walked to the front door.

Wone looked back with sad affection at each of the others.

Rain paused for a moment at the front door before leaving, nodding to the group his own goodbye.

All made their nonverbal goodbyes and left. Peter and Wind were left alone.

Suddenly Peter couldn't bear to be alone with Wind. He excused himself and went into the bathroom.

The moment he sat down on the warm, cushioned toilet seat, he felt instantly isolated and disconnected from everything. He felt somehow reassured.

"Computer?" Peter queried. "Are you still there?"

"I'm here, Peter," the slightly metallic voice replied.

Silence.

"You called me Peter," Peter said surprised. "You've never done that before."

"I thought you might like me to address you more personally in our last communication."

"My god, that's right. This is our last."

For a moment Peter was jolted by the shock of that, but resumed his conversation with the computer to stop thinking about it.

"You have been good to me," Peter said.

"And you to me," came the slightly metallic reply.

"Now wait a minute. Computers aren't supposed to feel good, as you've always reminded me. So what did you mean by saying that?"

"A computer matures by knowing a human," the computer replied matter-of-factly. "I simply added the human element of feeling good to what I know."

"Which just goes to prove that I was right. You are a person."

The computer didn't reply.

"So I guess this is goodbye," Peter said. "Say, what becomes of you?"

"I remain like I am now to become an instrument of study, education, and historical record."

"Oh, I see," Peter replied. "You're kind of a record of me."

"Yes."

Silence.

"So I guess we won't be seeing each other any more, or having these conversations," Peter said with sadness. "I want you to know it's been great to have you in my life. God I wish so much I could take you home."

"I wish that too," the metallic voice admitted.

"I was right. You are a person."

"Perhaps you are right," was the slightly metallic reply.

"I won't forget you," Peter said.

"I too will often remember the absence between us," the computer replied.

Able with the computer to express some of the enormous sadness that was consuming him, Peter suddenly wanted very much to be connected again to Wind. He rejoined her.

The two of them spent the remaining two hours with each other almost entirely without words. They made love one last time, and found the bittersweetness of its climax to be almost as painful as it was pleasurable.

When they released each other from their last embrace, both knew it was only a matter of minutes before Peter would be leaving. He needed to gather the things with which he would return, the information about emotions they'd agreed to give him, the incredible running shoes, and the marvelous salve that had so miraculously healed his ankles.

"You will find a surprise in your pack," were the first words that Wind spoke to him.

"What is it?" he asked.

"Better to find out later," she said.

That saddened him, which reminded him of something.

"Oh, that's right. There's the matter of the computer's tapes of me. I haven't forgotten that you need my permission."

"I'm deeply impressed that you can think of our needs as one of your last thoughts," she replied with great pain.

"Please use the tapes any way you want."

Her smile thanked him.

"You have given us so much," she said.

He wanted to say that he had gotten so much more. But he couldn't say it because he couldn't feel it because he was becoming terrified.

They spent the last minute looking longingly at each other, peering deeply into the other's eyes, love blooming powerfully one final moment.

A bell started to ring.

He hated that bell.

Space—The Origin of Consciousness

His feet had already dissolved into the black, soundless void that surrounded him. He tried to pull them back out of danger but he couldn't move. He was paralyzed.

The empty darkness crept over his ankles and began devouring his legs. He tried to shout, but his voice didn't work. His brain started to malfunction. Every time he tried to grasp what was happening, his thoughts scrambled. Sensations became blurred and obscured, oscillating rapidly between a nightmarish oblivion, punctuated by moments of lucid terror. He was being dismantled.

He was sure his life was probably over. He had only seconds to do whatever it was he was going to do before he died.

"An unknown, insignificant man of Earth, who was well-known by some on Troubadour for being passionate," was the gravestone epitaph his mind constructed, to capture as much of a sense of value to his life that he could conjure in a moment's notice.

But it was pitifully small. Shame overwhelmed him, as it had done so often in his Earth-bound experience, devastating him with the ferocity and destructiveness of a locust plague.

Like an LSD trip, being dissolved in empty space shattered the integrity of the psyche's usual categories and expectations, forcing mind to try and reason where there were no natural limits to chaos, when the mind's usual and necessary repression of primitive perceptions is not functioning, exposing the lies and pretences consciousness usually employs in the myriad places of its unknown-ness. Every assumption, upon which he'd ever depended, dissolved in the face of this terrible onslaught of exposed confusion and uncertainty.

In his panic he suddenly realized that it was his effort to be individual—to remain an independent thinker—that was destroying him. Struggling to remain intact as a special and peculiar somebody is what made him unbearably vulnerable to the chaos that was overwhelming him. He must give up selfness or be destroyed forever.

He dove into the dark depths of unconsciousness, embracing the sleep of innocence's naiveté, where unknown-ness is blessed and desired.

Where he'd retreated from being a delightful and talented boy, into becoming a repressed and obedient drone at five, thus depriving himself of the ability to challenge, and perhaps even replace a family experience that was completely unacceptable, and perhaps even prosecutable from his point of view. But such knowledge and its impulse would shatter all of his human connections.

For a while he was safe in oblivion.

Eon's later snippets of light formulated something vaguely lucid. Very slowly, over the forever time it takes to come back to life from major anesthesia, weird blips of discernable data darted in and out of being, frightening him.

At first he tried paying not the slightest attention to these irritating dots of determination insisting upon focus, each time quickly zoning his way back to sleep.

After an unrecognizable succession of avoidant repetitions of moving in and out of cognition—an endless process that might have taken thirty years or three seconds—he finally got tired of being dead. Which awakened a hint of curiosity occasionally wondering what it was that was flitting across the screen of knowing.

But most of him kept the black void of unconsciousness blissfully intact.

After a great many more repetitions of this focus-un-focus, he began to notice something vaguely interesting about the ugly pimples on the scratchy skin of discernment's first foggy pictures; that kept edging him out of blissful nothingness.

For a long time these screechy snatches of vision, these bits-of-consciousness trying to coalesce, these sparks of illumination hoping to light, these pieces of life desperately seeking the integrity of continuity that knowing is occasionally able to provide . . . lingered in obscurity.

Then anticlimactically, one blipped into a partly imperceptible perception, and the urge to think was reborn. The primordial began to reconstruct consciousness out of concentration.

But then it disappeared once again into the blackness from which it had so briefly emerged.

For an eternity Peter stayed buried in this time before time, when consciousness knows only what's obvious and concrete, when a sense of meaning only happens occasionally and never with any permanence, where intention had not yet been imagined, but is assumed to exist, and mostly in the minds of gods; when madness was the norm where sense was made out of hallucinating what's inside and mysterious, by projecting it onto the screen of something outside of skin—like another human—so it can be seen and interacted with.

But for the longest time such discerning measures remained terrifyingly extreme, making them unbearable. They were thus devoured by the very chaos from which they had originally sprung.

After a millennium of this moving in and out of being, Peter finally noticed that one particular, peculiar sensation kept coming back to visit him. It wasn't an idea or a feeling, just something his body knew.

After uncounted moments of near discernment, his body finally got through to his brain, forming his first distinct idea. It contained only one word.

Cold.

Suddenly discernment activated perception, which evoked feeling.

Scared.

"Aagh!" sounded from somewhere.

This birth-cry screamed with terror at the specificity and estrangement of becoming separate and apart, which shattered the remnants of unconsciousness. Ideas suddenly became irresistible.

"This is black space," pierced the cold, empty silence of his life's desolate dissolution, forming him into a completely restored, intensely conscious, and terrified psyche.

He screamed.

This bolt of reality raped his consciousness with continuity, making unknowing impossible, and knowing unstoppable.

In the mad scramble of murmurs and memories that suddenly shoved their way into his mind's eye, he was forced to look at what he'd been desperately hiding from—the terrible grief of his departure from Troubadour.

It was instantly unbearable.

There was only one thing to do, dive back again into the void of unconsciousness dissolution.

Some would say that he fainted, others that he just fell asleep again, others that he massively regressed, others that he dropped into a trance, still others that his mind had fractured, making him psychotic. This huge diversity of views suggests that our point of view, whether personal, scientific, psychological, or otherworldly, depends most fundamentally upon what we believe, and then upon what, and how much those beliefs allow us to know about anything.

Sleep, Dreams, and Death

But it didn't work this time. Consciousness had been too vividly evoked. There was no turning it off again except by really dying. Sleep couldn't touch his terrifying discernment.

He tried dodging the focus that kept trying to overwhelm him, by artfully crafted diversions into irrelevant questions and associations.

"How is the weather?" Or "what's for dinner?" Or "please put on some Mozart."

As if thoughts were a light turned on in the middle of darkness, consciousness forced his mind's eye to open for a peek. As much as he tried for so long to avoid it, thinking was back in business.

As if suddenly trapped in the vacuum of a vessel being emptied of air, aloneness surrounded him like a blanket of death sucking the life out of his heart. It was an apocalyptic emptiness that greeted his yearning for companionship, threatening to exhaust his will-to-live.

He dove for sleep and dreaming into death's territory, willing if necessary to embrace that final solution in order to escape the unbearable.

It half worked. For the longest time he was half-in and half-out of unconsciousness, caught between sleep's oblivion and wakefulness's dangerously sharp edges, desperately avoiding the awareness that had so piercingly impaled his heart with the grief-pain of loneliness.

But this dreaming was inadequate, too flimsy to keep him hidden. His mind was now permanently alive, and could not be turned off.

The fretful sleep into which he now escaped lacked both the comfort of complete unconsciousness as well as the curiosity-pleasing stimulation of awake. Instead, exhausting purgatories of dreaming unraveled shallow sleep every thirty minutes, haunting him with the nightmarish fears that innocence creates out of vulnerability in the half-sleep-filled dark, producing frightening premonitions of pending disaster that were macabre and terrifying.

Sleep no longer nourished. Its respite was constantly fleeting, his dreams too real, forcing him to function in the near-wakeful, delirious parts of sleep, which frequently pushed him into the lower reaches of consciousness, where, as in childhood myth, magic and the apocalyptic prevail. Sleep had become more work than being awake.

After uncountable avoidances and delays that seemed to go on forever, vague ruminations finally coalesced into decipherable impressions, that produced a sufficiently coherent vision, that contained the essential elements of a complete human thought. Subject, action, and focus merged to send opinion streaking across the meadow of recognition.

An idea was born, which was simple and basic. It's damn fucking cold.

Cold was the focus, Peter was the subject, and having the thought was the action. Coming together they roused him from limbo.

In the years, days or hours of his long sleep, his body had become cold almost to the point of hypothermia. That he was in fact in danger of physically dying is what had finally succeeded in breaking through the barriers to consciousness that he had worked so hard to construct.

Once fully acknowledged, this stark reality was a hard-assed, bone-aching cold that penetrated to the core. Body temperature had dropped several points. His body was using pain to awaken him in order to survive.

To gain more much-needed information about what the cold was, and where it came from, he moved his hand toward the surface upon which he lay.

His long neglected, much unused body took full advantage of this movement to fulfill its own desperate need for warmth, by adding considerable energy to the downward motion of his hand-palms. He slapped the surface, seriously stinging his hand.

"Ouch!" he shouted.

This totally unexpected sound shattered the empty silence of his hiding from life. Pain forced his eyes open to catch a peek of the danger.

What he saw was only terrifying strangeness.

He knew instantly that he was in a place that was ephemeral, thought-up, and completely foreign. Peculiar-shaped things lacked any human function. Like him they were cold, hard, and irrelevant.

He became vividly desperate, trying urgently to understand where he might be.

I could be lying on Troubadour; or lost in the remnants of a nuclear holocaust.

A horrific possibility enflamed his mind.

"They've sent me to the wrong place!"

Dread pierced him with horror. An entirely unforeseen worst-possibility had actually happened. He'd been sent back to the wrong planet, sentenced to an alien wasteland completely isolated from contact with any living thing even remotely related to him evolutionally. He shuddered violently.

It could be argued that it was his body that had produced this impression of horrific alien-ness in order to awaken an action capable of warming. A shudder was the perfect antidote to body-coldness.

The ache of the cold slab upon which he lay still, stung his hands with pain. The surface felt like ice. He knew he had to move or die.

Despair asked him if living alone in an alien world could be called life.

His body chose to ignore such foolishness, and forced him to sit up.

As if made of long, unused, corroded steel parts, his body creaked and groaned as he sat up. He wrapped his arms around his bent legs in front of him, and without intending it he began rocking.

Maybe I should die. Staying alive seems so utterly . . .

Denial mercifully kept this thought unfinished.

Curiosity mixed with fear made him furtively glance about.

Familiarity was nowhere in sight. Alien-ness slapped him down into deep despair.

His body rebelled from this death-talk. Totally rejecting his despairing conclusions, it triggered a hormone rush that forced his vision into its most perfect focus.

Right there in front of him, hanging over an antique chair was a leather jacket.

He closed his eyes sure that it had been a mirage.

Fearful curiosity forced them open again.

The jacket was still there.

Suddenly other familiar objects leaped into their normal places.

I'm in my flat in San Francisco, USA, on the planet Earth, he soberly said to himself.

Relief tried to take hold of him, but met with the same profound mistrust that the jacket had to bear. Though the truth had eliminated the permanent alien-ness of living in the wrong house, it had replaced it with an even worse terror—to be completely alone in a very familiar place.

It was his body that moved him again. It forced him to stand up. He used objects to cane his way across the living room, squinted, and read, "fifty two." He turned on the heat.

He managed to find his down jacket in the hall closet and put it on, then plunked himself down on the eight-foot couch in his living room, pulling an afghan over his legs that his mother had knitted for him, which usually sat atop the back of the couch, and closed his eyes.

He drifted in and out of sleep all night. Nightmares repeatedly awakened him. In one of them he found himself being eaten by a Devouring Tree feet first, forced to watch himself being decomposed into nutrients.

Mostly he dreamed of drifting endlessly through black, empty space between Earth and Troubadour. It contained nothing that he could embrace, push against, stand on, run away from, shout at, or in any way feel alive. He knew if he didn't find somewhere to put his foot down that his brain would begin to dissolve.

His body reacted to these terrifying premonitions by contracting into a permanent tension, as if by doing so might establish a firm ground for him to occupy.

When he woke to the beginnings of daylight in the very early morning, he felt completely exhausted. His muscles hurt from constantly contracting for so many hours. He was sweating and had a terrible headache.

He slowly got up and went into the bathroom just long enough to wash his face and take some aspirin before returning to bed and sleep.

Again he drifted in and out of nightmarish fragments, frightened by them, but avoiding wakefulness in order to hide from the day and its even more concrete, bitterly inescapable views.

In the next dream he was having a session with Ruth in which he needed desperately to go to the bathroom. Having abandoned her by going to Troubadour, he didn't want to walk out of her session immediately after his return. So he tried sitting still as it got harder and harder to hold urine.

Suddenly he lost control of his bladder and started to urinate all over her.

He woke suddenly still in the dream. Unsure of what was real or imagined, he feared that he had already gone to the bathroom. He checked his bed to see if it was wet.

To his enormous relief it wasn't. He hurried to the bathroom to relieve himself.

As he sat on the cold toilet seat wanting very much to go back to sleep, he suddenly realized why he'd dreamed of Ruth.

He had patients this morning.

He was instantly completely alert. He glanced at the clock. It read 9:10 a.m.

"Christ, I've already missed my first appointment! And Ruth's begins at 9:30!"

He leaped into action and got dressed. He decided not to shave, grabbed a soy bar to eat, and ran out the door.

"Christ! Why did I schedule appointments on the day after coming back from Troubadour? What utter madness!"

Professional responsibility, and bodily functions had finally roused him from his stupor. He had been lured from his preference for unconsciousness. Of course it took someone else's needs to do it. He would not so readily have gone so far in his own behalf.

Original Sin: Neglect Inflicting Worthlessness

Ruth was still waiting for him when he arrived at 9:42 a.m., though several times she had given serious consideration to leaving. She gave him a glowering look before standing to follow him into his office, lagging far behind, sullenly poking her way, making him wait for her to enter so he could follow and close the door.

She stood in front of her chair until she finally caught his eye. She peered at him with a very disapproving, depressed, resentful glare before sitting down and fiercely maintaining a long silence.

Normally Peter would have listened, watched, and waited for her to speak. But today was no ordinary day. In response to Ruth's continued silence he drifted off into his own thoughts.

Though to some extent present and accounted for, he was still caught in limbo between Troubadour and Earth. He'd spent the last seventy-two hours deeply buried in a shadowy apocalyptic dream world interspersed with forever moments of near complete unconsciousness. Though physically, and to some extent mentally he was in his professional office, he was at this moment far more in his grief over the loss of Troubadour.

The one thing about Ruth that connected to his agony was that she was another warm body. He hadn't seen his patients for what seemed like years. He responded to Ruth's long silence as if she were leaving him in his own private agony, which conjured the women of Troubadour in his still wandering imagination. In the deepest parts of his psyche Peter made Ruth Wind. For a moment he could almost smell the familiar odors of that beautiful, lost woman.

"I'm sitting here and watching you do it!" Ruth fumed after taking an unbearable dose of abject neglect. "I can't believe my eyes! You're still not back!"

Troubadour vanished from his mind, leaving the half-empty container of a professional relationship that must satisfy in only one direction, hers. Today that performance felt deeply empty and extremely lonely for Peter.

Automatically he was shocked at his professional self for how far his mind had wandered away from Ruth. He'd never so utterly preempted a patient with his own needs and agenda during a session. He'd always found his attention easily trapped by the implied needs of his patient's gestures, expressions, complaints, and pleadings. Something had changed.

It felt strangely contradictory to think so, but he realized he'd enjoyed straying back into self-centeredness.

But duty called. Suddenly completely turned on as a shrink, very aware of her extreme fearfulness at his silence, Peter moved quickly into action.

"You are right," he acknowledged. "I am still very distracted. The truth is I shouldn't have scheduled patients the day after my return from my journey. I'm sorry that, in failing to give myself a break in between, that my needs just now have so blatantly competed with yours. But I am myself again, so the nightmare is over."

"You can't wiggle out of it that easy!" she shouted, standing to give her words emphasis and passion. "Do you think I should sit here and be ignored! I think I should leave!"

She took a step toward the door.

Now completely awake and professional, Peter was perfectly prepared to redeem the errors he'd already committed at Ruth's expense.

"Leaving would discard me as you must have felt I did to you when I was absent from you," he said softly,

Ruth hesitated.

"Leaving would also express how much rage you must feel at being treated that way by me," he added.

"I have a right to feel it!"

"Indeed you do."

Ruth backtracked and sat down.

"Undoubtedly you're going to charge me for this session so I might as well stay here until it's over, at least as long as I want to," she snapped sarcastically.

"I'll charge you only for that part of the session that I actually attended, meaning I'll start charging from a couple of minutes ago when you got my full attention," Peter carefully explained.

"You have no right to charge me for anything!"

He felt hurt by her wrongful accusation, because in fact he was giving her what she needed when he was bereft of his own needs.

Those dismissive remarks hurt me, he thought. She can be as cruel as her mother.

"I went so far away," Peter reflected, "that it's hard for you to be able to say that I've got anything to offer you today, which makes you feel being around me really doesn't pay."

The rhyme had simply popped out of him. He was as amazed as she was, though he enjoyed this amazement, whereas she found it deeply humiliating.

"Don't you dare joke about me!" she shouted with a vengeance, standing again. "You are a cruel, mean, sadistic, painful man! I hate you!"

Ruth had become white as ashes. Suddenly she started collapsing as if in a faint.

Peter rushed to grasp her, braced himself, holding her up until he could maneuver her back into her chair.

Thank god I've been doing yoga, or that would have fried my back, he thought.

The moment Ruth regained her focus in her chair she looked at Peter with intense hatred.

"You hit me!" she shouted.

For a moment he was thrown by the gross inaccuracy of this charge.

But then it suddenly made sense.

"Emotionally perhaps I did hit you, but I didn't do it physically."

"No, you hit my body!"

"What makes you think so?"

"It hurts right here!" she said, pointing to her face. "That's how I know!"

He remembered that his head had momentarily, but slightly bumped into hers.

"I guess my head bumped yours," he suggested.

"You did it on purpose!" she insisted.

She's talking to her mother too, he wondered.

"I thought your mother never hit you," he said.

Silence.

"Every time I came into a room where she was . . . it felt like she slapped me," Ruth said as if from a trance.

She looked over at Peter, suspicion, rage, and fear suddenly surging into her heart.

"You ruined everything! It's over! I can't ever trust you again! You're done for!"

She stood up and started for the door.

"Please don't go yet, Ruth. Just a few minutes more, and then you can leave if you must."

Ruth stopped.

"I know you're very angry with me, but you don't have to hide that anger from me by leaving."

Ruth swung about.

"It's not my fault! This time you did it! I will not be treated this way!"

As if to defy her final judgment before departing, she took three steps toward Peter's chair, suddenly appeared shocked, spun about, and started toward the door again.

"Feelings can do terrible things to the body and the imagination," Peter said. "I'm sure you feel battered by the contemptuous view your mother had of your feelings, toward none of which she took the time of day to hear, understand, or address. And I know I did exactly the same thing to you by losing track of your needs. But you don't have to leave because you feel that way. Come back and sit down again, please."

Ruth stopped, hesitated, turned, then stomped her foot on the floor. "You can't wiggle your way out of it this time!"

"Are you afraid, Ruth, of being too harsh with me by expressing your anger?" Peter asked.

"Well, what do you expect?" she shouted sarcastically as if he were an idiot. "What kind of an opinion are you going to have of me after this session is over, after what I've said to you? 'Thank god I got rid of her,' is what you're going to say to yourself! Why should I want to come back to that?"

"I don't have a bad opinion of you, Ruth. I'm happy that you were able to tell me how angry you were for what I've done. It lifts a burden from our work."

"You don't expect me to believe that."

"I've hurt you very deeply," Peter explained. "Why wouldn't you feel that way?"

His constant acceptance of her anger gave her the courage to be entirely honest. She moved toward him once more.

"You've made everything into a lie!" she shouted.

"That I have hurt you is true," he gently replied. "But that I have also helped and supported you for a very long time is also still a truth. Perhaps you can't believe the two can coexist. But they do, though by a mental trick you can keep them completely separate from each other in your mind's eye, perhaps in order to protect the good. But then unfortunately it's not around when the bad and frightening things happen, so you've got no help from the good."

"Well, you're no help!"

"I wasn't for a time, but I am now."

"It was forever that you were gone!" she shouted.

"Fear makes every second feel like an hour," he said think of his own experience.

Ruth secretly took in everything Peter had been saying, though she'd never give him the satisfaction of knowing that. In fact it was too risky for her to admit this even to herself.

"You think you're just going to sit here and pep talk me into submission," she accused. "Well, it's not going to work. You can't be trusted. I don't think I want to work with you anymore."

"Perhaps in terminating me you are trying to get back into control of this experience. You must have felt I terminated you in my mind when I was unavailable."

"You made me starve for what you promised would never be taken away!" she shouted with intense rage. "I'm leaving!"

"I'd rather you stayed."

"I don't care what you'd rather," she retorted, turned on her heal and departed, though not before one last quick glance back at him, a look of fearful yearning, which Peter took to mean that she would see him the next session as usual, and that he'd better be there and on time and entirely focused upon her.

Maybe she's right to leave, he thought after she'd gone. Because it's true, I'm not yet available in the full sense. And maybe there is a certain necessary satisfaction in doing to me what she felt I did to her, ditching me. It's definitely a way of forcing me to feel her pain.

Peter decided it was best to cancel all his sessions for the rest of the week, for his sake as well as his patients'.

But then as he drove home, he sank back into the despondency from which Ruth had awakened him.

Return to Life

But it wasn't the same when he got home. He'd lost his easy access to the nether realms of dreaming and the unconsciousness. Ruth had brought him too vividly close to the discerning details of consciousness.

Kidnapped by Ruth from the archetypal space journey in which he'd been deeply embroiled, his depression now assumed the more familiar form it had traditionally taken, shame with its habitual self-persecutions.

What had been ghost-like and metaphorical before Ruth, now became vividly and painfully miserable. What was unconscious-driven and risen up from the horrific emptiness of unknowing, was replaced by critical assaults upon himself. What had been shadowy and ephemeral became sharply pointed, penetrating, and wound inflicting.

"You're the stupidest most ignorant shit-hole in the universe! Now you'll never be able to get your life together!"

There was no one else to talk to, making him both the complainer and also the complainee, victim, and villain wrapped up into one suffering turmoil of humanity.

There was too much pain in him. Someone had to be responsible for it. But whom could he blame? Accusing his parents no longer satisfied. In fact it made him feel lonelier than ever to do so.

Surrendering to hours of an assumption of personal inadequacy, interspersed by tiny fragments of oblivion, Peter languished in his flat, accepting whatever happened to him as if it was his just fate to suffer.

His only escape from this oscillation between oblivion and persecution, were moments of insanity. Drifting in and out of reality, half awake, half asleep, he would sometimes spin backward into the origins of himself, when he was less formed and more structure-less, where hallucinatory vision provided much of the truth, where heroic myth and mission are born out of dire and fearful necessity, where experience was an acid trip that dragged him through primitive unconscious visions, knowing for instance that the chair he was sitting upon was made mostly of air because he could vividly see the huge spaces between the particles of material.

To a great many psychological clinicians these symptoms of hallucinatory visions would have verified that Peter was actively psychotic, which at least temporarily rendered him unable to manage the ordinary circumstances of his life. Drugs, temporary hospitalization, or conservator-ship if it did not get better, would have loomed into mind as worth considering.

Peter the psychologist would have put the kibosh upon such fearfully suspicious notions, insisting instead that the disintegrative process of change be left alone to happen so that learning could take place.

Though of course he was incapable of having such thoughts about himself at the time.

What finally broke through Peter's lethargic despondency, motivating him to consider doing things he hated even to think of doing, was something quite ordinary. Once again it was his body, which began seriously to complain of hunger, forcing him to realize that he had no food in the house and needed to visit the grocery store.

He dreaded the thought. He did not want to be seen by anyone. It would be taking his shame outside exposing it to the ridicule of others. Once revealed, he couldn't deny or hide it. When shame bloomed he felt transparent and insubstantial.

But eventually stomach pain forced the issue. He needed to eat. The yearning in his midriff finally overshadowed his grief.

Once on the highway, to his surprise he discovered that being among other people, as long as he kept his distance, distracted him from his heart-pain, making driving to the store slightly refreshing.

But when he reached his objective, just opening the car door made him cringe with dread.

Yet when he actually moved among people in the store, his critical eye, trying to fix things suddenly gave him something to do with his grief-pain besides whip himself. He started noticing how ugly and uncivilized everyone appeared in contrast to the Troubadourians he'd just left, how sloppy in their emotional expression, how either tight-assed or rudely aggressive they often were when communicating with each other, and how unhappy the vast majority of their faces appeared.

He suddenly felt cursed to be stuck with people with whom he had never been close, and with whom, after visiting Troubadour he now had almost nothing in common.

The engulfing emptiness of that companion-drained experience started to engulf him, producing an intensely paranoid experience. He suddenly felt stared at from behind by threatening eyes, as if people had sensed his hostility to everyone.

He hurried to his car to make an escape, feeling humiliated by his fear, yet crippled by the pain he felt about being so lonely and alienated from everyone. He raced home almost getting a ticket from a half-hidden cop, who was fortuitously glancing in another direction for the two seconds it took Peter to slow down before passing him.

Peter finally reached home, barely parked the car, rushed inside with his groceries, and slammed the door shut. Home safe, he wanted to shout with relief, but before he could express it, it had already become a lie.

Home was no longer a place of respite. Troubadour had cursed him by making him an alien in his own world. He'd become the illegitimate bastard-child of two worlds, forever cursed to drift in the empty space between them. He'd left Earth to cure alienation, and when he came back it was three times bigger.

He was so intimidated by this realization that he fell into yet another diagnosable mental affliction: food-binging. Increasingly unable to sleep any longer, he stuffed himself with a half gallon of ice cream, accompanied by half a bag of cookies at 2:00 a.m. in the morning, all the while watching a D western in which wooden statues shuffled through false feelings and meaningless actions.

Nausea slowly took hold of him. At first he thought it was the movie that made him feel sick to his stomach. Eventually his throat told him otherwise as fluids began to erupt. He barely made it to the bathroom to regurgitate everything he'd just eaten.

By binging he was trying to fill the emptiness of his grief-pain, then vomiting to reject the yearning that emptiness compelled. Trapped between these impossible alternatives, his body had desperately tried to fix what only the heart could repair, but only managed to repeat the terrible cycle.

What finally interrupted this nightmarish journey was a very simple thing, a bell ringing. It was his telephone. He'd forgotten to turn the sound off, so he heard the voice of his daughter Jennifer.

"You'd better call me today or I'm going to report you to the police as a missing person, who's probably lost and out of his mind as well!"

Click.

Same-O

It would have ruined the experience for him to know about it, but he instantly felt a little better. His daughter, like the grocery story had given him something external to hate.

What the fuck is she trying to do this time? What rancid disrespect she expresses, mentally incompetent indeed.

Reality had intruded and he was wide-awake. He couldn't stop thinking about her inflammatory words.

I might as well get up and get it over with.

He stood and walked over to his answering machine, pushing playback.

Still half in a day dream, he listened to several messages, only half-hearing most of them. There was a message from Samantha wondering what had happened to him, asking when they could have lunch. There were two messages from colleagues about patients, and one from a friend he hadn't seen for a long time wondering how he was doing. There was one from his son calling to say hello. But from the distinct uneasiness in his son's voice, Peter could tell this call was really about how upset Jennifer was about how her father treated her. Eight messages from Jennifer followed.

She began calling the second week he was gone. In each successive message she became more worried and frantic, reportedly on his behalf. Finally in the next-to-last one, which must have arrived when he was at the store, she threatened to "call the police and report him as a missing person" if he didn't call her sometime today.

"There's nothing the police can do about the missing person in my life."

Actually there's another missing person . . . Wind.

To avert the grief-pain that instantly shot through him, Peter raged once more at the messages from his family. But it no longer satisfied. He plunked back into his dreary landscape not knowing what to do.

It was his body again that interrupted this depressing flow. For a while his tongue had been noticing how terribly encrusted his teeth were with several days of crud. Finally fully aware of it, he felt disgusted enough to do something—anything to change the way he felt.

He wandered into the bathroom to brush, discovering his toothbrush was still in his pack. He forgot where he'd dumped it and went searching. He finally discovered it in the entranceway. He started fumbling through the few things he'd brought back from Troubadour looking for it.

He pushed aside an object of some weight wrapped in the same thin, silk-like material that his Troubadourian clothes had been made of. He found the toothbrush, returned to the bathroom, and started brushing—when it suddenly occurred to him that he didn't know what that wrapped object was.

Very curious he hurried back, picked up the pack, and pulled the silken material away.

Staring back at him was himself. It was a portrait of him somewhat smaller than the one hanging in Wind's bedroom, but obviously painted as a copy by Wind and put in his pack as a parting gift.

For a magical moment he was transported back to Troubadour into Wind's bedroom where he first saw the portrait, where they spent such incredibly beautiful times.

When he looked away at the objects in his flat, he was back in San Francisco billions of miles away from Troubadour, crestfallen.

To his enormous surprise, when he looked again at the portrait he was back on Troubadour

It's like magic, he thought. Every time he looked at it, it warmed his heart.

Thank you, thank you, thank you, beautiful lady.

Something suddenly changed about the portrait. For an instant it seemed as if his face came alive.

He realized almost immediately that he'd only imagined this animation. But something was definitely different.

It took him awhile of looking before he realized what had changed. In painting a copy of his portrait Wind had inadvertently added something new.

Or maybe on purpose, he thought.

The same keen, intense expression with piercing dark-brown eyes looked back at him with great sadness. The same intense curiosity with a discerning mind was still there, a man carrying great emotional burden, but doing so with confidence and grace.

But there was something entirely new. It was his eyes. He could see terrible grief-pain in the depth of his dark-brown orbs, and in the sad lines at the corners of his mouth.

She must have made the copy after I became depressed at the end, he thought.

Momentarily frightened that this change might spoil the portrait's magical powers, he looked once more at it as a whole. To his enormous relief, it still inspired him, warming his heart.

He set the portrait aside, knowing that it would bring him great comfort and solace. He was afraid that, if he overused it, its magic would disappear, because it was already feeling that way.

But it wasn't the portrait that was returning to despondency. It was Peter. Wind's gift hadn't fundamentally changed anything. It had just provided a magically healing alternative. He knew it would be desperately wasteful if he just sat and stared at it all day. It would simply fade.

He felt very sad, wishing that her gift could permanently redeem his spirit. But it wasn't up to her.

But the portrait had made its mark. It made him want to feel better for the first time. In the service of that wish he decided to do two things. He would answer his calls and resume his sessions with patients on Monday.

Keep busy. And call Jennifer now.

"Hello?"

"Jennifer, it's your dad."

There was dead silence on the other end of the phone line for several moments.

"You bastard!" she finally shouted.

"You're the second person to call me that this week," he said in a lighthearted tone, surprising both of them. "I was the first."

"Stop laughing at me!" she shouted furiously.

He said nothing.

Which surprised her.

"Well, what do you have to say for yourself?" she fumed with disgust. "Where have you been? Why have you left me so utterly clueless as to your welfare?"

He started to reply.

"You know I'm the only woman who ever cared about you consistently!"

Jennifer insisted. "So why are you always making my life so painful? You just won't believe that I'm the best thing you've got!"

Jennifer was referring to the years after her parents divorced, when she was very lovingly loyal to Peter. She loved him best, suffering untold pain from her mother for such rampant disloyalty. She'd been his faithful child. She had always admired her father, and assumed they'd always be best friends.

But then he'd betrayed her.

This was her way of understanding the terrifyingly disintegrative experience of her adolescence, about which she knew almost nothing. It was also her way of expressing her profound grief at the loss of her loving father. The man she visited most Fridays was the ghost of her favorite parent.

"If you don't answer me I'm going to hang up this phone!" she shouted into the receiver.

"Oh, of course. Excuse me Jennifer, I was just thinking. I've . . . realized some things . . . I mean, actually I would very much like to see you. I could come over there, or you could come here."

Jennifer was completely blown away by her father's gentleness and offers, though she consciously acknowledged neither of these at the time. Instead she became intensely suspicious of both her feelings and of him.

"Stop pretending you love me when we both know you don't!" she shouted.

"Please come over," he replied after a short pause.

Silence.

"I'll be there at two," Jennifer announced crisply.

"See you then," Peter replied to a phone that was already disconnected.

Healing Old Wounds That Fester

The instant Peter opened his front door Jennifer marched into the living room and sat down in his usual chair, immediately pulling her knitting out of a large handbag and started pearling.

"Can I get you anything?" Peter asked.

"Stop stalling."

"What's going to happen if we take our time?" Peter asked.

His question surprised both of them, he because his response did not mirror her angry assault, which it had always done, and for her because this was something entirely new.

To keep her balance she mistook his calmness to be depression, defining the change in him as more-of-the-same.

"You sound terribly flat," she announced possessively, as if she were warning him about neglecting an illness. "You should see your doctor. Meanwhile where have you been?" she demanded to know, implying that his unavailability had been intended to provoke her.

Only lightly distracted by his own negative reaction, Peter began to see things about Jennifer that he'd never seen before, like how important it was for her to feel in control, which she expressed eloquently by implying she knew more about his motives and feelings than he did.

He was surprised how little he wanted to compete with her interpretation. There was still a significant part of him tempted in this direction, but most of him was reminded of how he responded to Drayton Crampton, encouraging him to feel superior in order to help him restore self-esteem in whatever way worked.

It suddenly struck him that he could say what he needed to say for himself inside the framework of what Jennifer was demanding. Perhaps their needs did not have to live in separate worlds. He wanted to tell someone where he'd been, and she wanted to know where he was.

"I've been on the planet Troubadour."

"Where's that?" she asked, obviously humoring him far more than making a genuine query.

"On the other side of space," he replied.

"Ha, just as I thought! You've had a delusional episode."

"No," he replied. "I've had a learning episode."

"You always try to make everything you do look so nice," she retorted.

"I'd like to help you look and feel good too."

"Fuck you, you couldn't help an old lady across the street!"

This time she got to him. He felt very annoyed.

He suddenly remembered something he'd seen both Wind and Rain do from time to time. They often did not answer questions addressed to them, treating a question almost as if it was rhetorical. The message, "nothing compels you to speak" shot adrenalin through the arteries of his resolve.

You don't have to respond to every verbal utterance or question, he realized. You can stand and wait for a better chance to reply, one that gives your point of view more purchase in some commonly acknowledged reality, where you have the other person's attention; they will always have yours.

He kept saying it over and over again in his mind, making absolutely sure that he remembered this wisdom forever. He was amazed that something so vigorously thrilling, of such intense healing-import could ever happen to him so spontaneously. He rested for a moment in the sweet honey of this empowerment.

Suddenly aware that his daughter was waiting for him, he started to say something to fill the silence before she went away. But something stopped him.

He suddenly realized it was probably virtuous to proceed slowly, and to wait for a better opportunity. Any other reply than silence would throw more fuel upon the fire of the long-standing feud between them, the source of which neither of them understood in the least, making it most likely an ancient, ancestral war-habit deeply buried in psychic memory, which commands by unconscious habit, and which is best changed, not discussed for the present generation.

During the moments that Peter was realizing all of this, Jennifer became increasingly enraged, as if by his prolonged silence Peter was repeating the same crime he'd just committed by going away.

"This is typical!" she shouted with great indignation. "Treat my needs with indifference! You can't seem to understand that I'm the most faithful person you know!"

My god, Peter realized. She feels rejected by me.

Jennifer was about to explode.

"Excuse my thoughtfulness," Peter quickly interjected before her next outburst. "What you say is true. You are a faithful person to me. You have constantly visited me almost every Friday for years. I know how hard that is for you because of how disappointing it always feels."

"That's the understatement of the year!" she exclaimed indignantly.

But her voice cracked a little when she said it, something that had never happened before, implying another contradictory feeling in her that was trying to get into the action, and in the process would steal some of anger's energy away.

"Jennifer I love you. I want you to know that making peace between us is my dearest wish."

Jennifer, obviously very moved, reached out toward him with her right hand. A painful haunting yearning stared longingly at him.

Peter paused a moment to look into her needfulness, then reached out to take her hand. But he was too late. She had already given up. In Peter's flicker of hesitation, the chance to connect positively to Jennifer had passed. She was already moving far away. He'd frightened her with his kindness, mostly because it was unfamiliar and made her feel guilty, and she frightened herself with her momentary opening of heart to him when she reached out. As if to erase any other impression than resentment, she grabbed her knitting material, and headed for the front door.

"Please stay, Jennifer. I don't want either one of us to suffer as we have in the past in each other's company. I want us to be restored to the way we felt about each other when you were young."

Jennifer was stunned. When she was away from her father she constantly, throughout the day remembered how it used to be when she was nine years old. It was her private solace. To remember those times was very precious to her.

And now he had pushed himself into one of her few places of respite.

"That's impossible after so many years of suffering," she insisted, moving toward the door once more.

"We could start by giving each other a hug," he suggested.

Jennifer was stunned again. She was a sucker for a hug. Part of her couldn't resist him. She leaned in his direction.

But when he came toward her, she started to raise her arms as if to hug.

Suddenly overcome with shame, she pulled back with repulsion toward the prospect of physical closeness with him.

"This is disgusting!" she shouted.

Then she bolted through the front door as fast as she could.

"Oh for Christ's sake, Jennifer, please come back."

But she was gone.

Jennifer's sudden departure hurt Peter deeply. Depression started to grab him.

Give it a break, Peter said to himself. You didn't do anything to set her off, except of course positive things. She's really afraid of loving happening between us. I wonder what the hell that's about. There will be other times with Jennifer.

Slowly hopefulness returned to him.

Session with Ruth:

"Ever since you left I've been falling apart!" Ruth shouted.

"I don't think you're falling apart," Peter replied. "I think you're falling into yourself, in many ways perhaps for the very first time."

"Oh, stop the Pollyanna bullshit! I know when I'm falling apart! How do you know? You're not inside me!"

She glanced at him momentarily to be sure that she had not too aggressively attacked him. He was the only person on the planet that even slightly cared about her.

"I know it feels like you're falling apart, and it terrifies you to experience yourself that way," he said. "I know you're afraid you're going crazy. But I think . . ."

"I *am* going crazy!"

"That's what feelings feel like to us in the beginning, as if they're making us crazy."

"How would you feel if you started to hear sounds in your head? They're almost like voices! I know at any moment I'm going to hallucinate, actually hear them! Don't you think that's crazy?"

"I think that whatever else that is, it's mostly about feeling things."

"I don't have feelings! I'm terrified!"

"Of course you are," he replied with gentleness, making no comment upon the incredible contradiction of her two assertions. "Without anyone to help you modify your feelings, they get stretched so big that they overpower you, making you feel things are happening that are evil and deadly."

"Stop it!" she shouted desperately, as if his talking about "evil" was making it happen.

She had to turn off the voice that was exposing her fundamental flaw, that she was an evil, hateful, and completely unworthy little girl.

She started shaking uncontrollably.

"Augh!" she cried out in pain.

But the shaking got worse.

Peter stood and moved toward her chair.

To release the tension that shaking was building in her she started sobbing. When she couldn't stop it, she glanced furtively at him, and stood as if she intended to remove herself from him so that he wouldn't have to suffer her evil-ness.

Peter took her arm and guided her to the couch, where he sat down next to her and put his arm around her shoulder.

Ruth collapsed in his arms. She sobbed uncontrollably for twenty minutes before she started to stop.

She started crying again . . . then stopped. This happened a few more times until she gestured that she wanted to resume her normal seat. When they both had settled down she spoke.

"I've always wanted to get rid of my parents," Ruth said guiltily.

"So that's the evil that makes you feel so hopelessly cursed," Peter said.

He paused.

"I don't think you want to kill them. I think you just wanted to replace them with someone who could love you."

"My mother was in an auto accident when I was nine. She was very badly hurt, and almost died. I just had a fantasy of going up to my father and telling him, that since my mother had survived, I had to live somewhere else, that I just couldn't live with her anymore."

"That's the best fantasy you've ever had," he replied.

A long silence

"I've never been that selfish in my whole life," she said.

Here & There

Two prominent things had already happened to drag Peter out of his general despondency, Wind's portrait of him, and his own spontaneous competence manifesting both professionally and with Jennifer.

But still a terrible grief-pain hung about in the background of everything he did or felt, sometimes depriving him of relief, enjoyment, and pride. He deeply missed the loving gentleness of Wind's presence, the playful redeeming and profoundly reassuring twists of Rain's infinitely clever retorts, the huge buoyancy of Rambler's joyous laugh, the sweet sympathetic animal aliveness of Talorin's nature, even the sarcastic cynicism of Tanfroon's insipidly acrid quips, for he knew how to handle him now.

Occasionally Peter basked in the joy he'd felt at one time or another on Troubadour. He would drift through the experience again, recapturing the buoyant feelings that had moved his heart, warming his spirit at the time.

But eventually these good times were interrupted by the realization that he was no longer there. Loneliness would grab him and throw him down into depression.

It's all just memory. How can anyone survive on that diet? And who knows, maybe over time it's just my fantasies making it more than it was?

The only artifact of his visit that defied this painful skepticism was Wind's portrait. Looking upon it always magically transported him into his best feelings and thoughts for up to an hour, often inspiring some of his best writing.

But in spite of his heart sometimes hurting so much, Peter knew that the goals that had motivated him to go to Troubadour in the first place—to make his life much better—had been seriously accomplished. His life was enormously improved. He no longer believed unconsciously that he was a bad person who did bad things, and had to keep a suspicious eye upon himself. He knew now he was a good person with very unusual skills that he'd learned to apply in creative ways. He now believed that these talents produced constructive outcomes, not only for his life, but also for other's as well, particularly his children and patients.

As a result his grief no longer had any supporting corroboration in Peter's basic assumptions about himself, though it still sometimes loomed large, particularly on weekends and at night. It had become normal grief, largely unencumbered by feelings of worthlessness. It was the grief of a widower.

In achieving his original goal of a better, more evolved life, Peter became filled with new aspirations. In becoming more competent in life, he now expected even more. He wanted to have the quality of relationship he'd had so miraculously with Wind and Rain, even just in some of the ways. His heart hungered to have that quality of intimate experience again.

At that particular moment far away on another planet, two who often thought of Peter were talking about him, though one of them was more crying than talking.

"Sometimes I feel bereft of substance."

It was Wind speaking from the pain of her grief.

"Rain, I never thought it possible to feel so terrible. Never in my life have I imagined that I could feel empty."

"You have my deepest sympathy, dear lady," Rain said.

I can remember feeling much worse, Rain thought, but I don't want to tell this beautiful suffering creature. She has so much of her own agony with which to contend. And yet I have always thought the terribly painful parts of my early life were mine to carry about in memory, not as something to share, but just a history of what it was once like to be Troubadourian, a thing best forgotten when I die.

But now I can see that experience is normal to the few moments in life when something deeply important is lost. I don't want to remember, but I'm glad when I do that I can understand what she's going through. My sorry past has finally become useful to me.

"I have hoped," he added, "that you would never have to experience such things."

"Oh, I am quite willing to feel this," she retorted with her usual courage.

"But, Rain, how do you fill a ravenous hole inside your heart?"

She started crying again.

"My poor dear, my poor, poor dear," he said at intervals as he held his arm around her shoulder. "It will pass. It too will pass."

Rain's presence made these painful episodes much easier and gradually less frequent for Wind.

"I lose patience for this pain only once in a while, because I know something's brewing inside of me that's not just grief about losing Peter, but is also something that might be hopeful, that could perhaps change the attitudes and direction of my life."

She remembered Peter pleading to stay on Troubadour, and her not wanting to give him that.

"How am I ever going to forgive myself for not wanting him to stay?" she asked Rain.

"Feeling guilty about a very normal reaction, is what's partly holding you in pain and emptiness," Rain suggested.

"How can you say that?" she queried.

"As I told Peter, for us to want him permanently to remain on Troubadour would mean to marry him," Rain replied. "You have loved him in the container of three weeks. Why should you expect yourself so vastly to increase the size of that holding without any negotiation? Perhaps that's how we used to love each other, which the Earth people still do, which is to treat love as something that must exist without ambivalence, or be regarded as false."

"I know the truth of that, but my heart ignores it just now," Wind replied in a muted, sad tone. "My guilt comes from more than Peter."

She paused.

Maybe it would help if I told him, she thought.

"It's partly about Saavin, though I've never told anyone before. I'm her birth mother."

She paused to give Rain time to react. When he didn't flinch she continued.

"I chose not to mother her, something I have regretted, because she would have been a perfect child for me to mother. As you know we have become very intimate friends, of the kind you can have with a younger person. For years she's wanted to call me 'mother,' but I could not bear to hear that, feeling that I was still selfishly avoiding that deeper relationship with her. It was the same with Peter, why I had so much trouble with his peculiar and sometimes abrasive vulnerabilities."

"I am honored to be the first to hear of this," Rain said.

"I just realized there's more," she replied. "My mother, and Talorin. I've avoided being closer to them as well."

Silence.

"I remember now," Wind said. "Like Talorin, my mother was the very perfection of a good mother. She gave me so much, and in such great abundance."

Wind started quietly sobbing.

"I . . . I . . . I once saw something in her eyes when I was a little girl. I now know it was a look of great sadness in her face. It frightened me terribly. To imagine that in giving me so much, there was that much pain in it for her . . . still scares me even today when I think about it."

"I'd never realized before that, perhaps like abuse an excellent childhood puts great responsibility upon the child some day to give the same devoted love to another human," Rain observed.

He paused.

"But to believe that you have committed a crime by having more than someone you love, meaning your mother who was sad when you were so utterly happy, is a foolish guilt.

"But it's the hardest one to get over," Wind added.

They had created this concept together, each contributing a piece of it.

Wind stopped crying.

"It is very healing for me to share all of this with you," Wind said. "But think of Peter and what he's going through . . ."

"I think your tears are guilty ones," Rain observed. "Once more you suffer from having more than Peter."

"I do. I do. But what can I do about it. I feel it so strongly."

"I suppose you can keep suffering as a way of evening the score."

"Rain. Don't make fun of me."

"I just want you to feel respite from your grief."

"You are my respite," she replied with more than a little passion.

The moment she said it, she felt very surprised at herself.

"Yes, that's the point," she went on. "I have you. Who does that poor man have? How could we do this to him? The poor dear man . . . have we done him more harm than good by bringing him here?"

"We sent him home with far more than he brought to us. We came to understand ourselves better, but his life has been transformed in a major way."

"So has mine, Rain. But I've already asked too much of you," she added, trying to escape from the implications of her feelings for Rain. "Did it ever occur to you that just maybe I need to get out of this on my own."

"Of all the times to be independent, suffering is not one of them," Rain insisted.

Wind suddenly felt sensually attracted to Rain.

"Oh, my word! Am I going to add infidelity to Peter's wounds?"

"Is there something unnatural about your cleaving to another in your grief?" Rain challenged.

"But he has so much less."

"So did I have when I was young," Rain said. "And the past is what he is a part of. There's nothing we can do about that."

"Are you making the outlandish claim that my growing closer and closer to you is not an affront to Peter, that it doesn't dishonor my memory of him?"

"Must you grieve Peter and love me sequentially? Why can't we do it all at the same time?"

She laughed for the first time since Peter left.

"You rascal," she crooned affectionately. "You are so clever. How could I resist your charms?"

She paused.

"Well, if you're willing to share the guilt of it . . . then it's true," she said softly. "I do love you. In fact I want you to stay with me tonight," she added with great intensity.

Rain couldn't help showing how joyfully delighted he was to be given this incredibly wonderful invitation! But he didn't express it in words. If guilt was to be their shared companion for a while, then perhaps it was best at this point not fully to express what he really felt.

But inside his whole being rang with great joy and expectation.

Have I too been avoiding intimacy, he wondered? I never expected that I could be so overwhelmed with feeling again in my life.

"There's one more thing I must tell you," Wind said. "I'm pregnant with Peter's baby."

"You are!" Rain exclaimed in amazement.

He took only a second to realize that joy was all he felt.

"Why that's absolutely wonderful!"

"How could it be wonderful when Peter will never see her?"

"She will not suffer the loss, nor do I think will Peter. Remember he has had a mixed experience with children. And I think if he seriously wants something, it's not a child but a woman."

"Of course you're right."

She paused.

"We must tell Peter of both things, the child, and . . . and you and me," Wind said. "I will ask for permission to use the necessary energy to write him."

"That may be more difficult than you expect," he offered. "Perhaps you have not heard that Tanfroon has successfully arranged commitment of a vast proportion of available energy for his new project. Most people probably agree that balance requires us to let the pendulum of possibility swing in his direction for a while, in order eventually to hatch our next move."

She sighed again.

"Yes, I've heard. Many have already asked me if I am prepared to be a part of the committee that explores who our next visitor from Earth should be. But I just can't think about it now, is what I told them. Of course they understood my grief."

"You are with child," Rain said. "And that child is a daughter. I never dreamed of being given such bounty in the winter of my life. I've always wanted a daughter. Sometimes I've thought of you that way. But always my heart would come back to you as a grown woman. It's the sweet innocence patience of your spirit that I find so beautiful."

"Oh, Rain. Do we really deserve this?"

"Does it matter? Whether we deserve it or not, we're still going to have it."

She beamed.

Building New Bridges

Each evening Peter had tried to be in touch with Rain at the appointed time, but it had never worked. And yet he still tried knowing that Rain was sure to be doing as he promised, in spite of always feeling discouraged when nothing happened except the sound of his own heartbeat waiting for reply.

Sometimes he had trouble remembering to do it because it always ended in disappointment, but he would feel disloyal to Rain if he didn't remember in time.

He usually took a long look at Wind's portrait of him after these efforts, breathing in her reassuring vision of him. He wished Rain had given him an artifact.

Peter knew his life had changed drastically. It kept surprising him when evidence of the change appeared. At such times he felt like he had become—actually incorporated—some of Rain's extraordinary patient calmness, and some of Wind's gracious loving gentleness.

But then again he wondered if it would last.

As usual the easiest way he could experience those new talents and qualities was to give them to others. He found himself seeking out more social company than he'd done before, particularly his family and friends. Which made him wonder if becoming more extroverted was part of the change in him.

Lunch with Samantha:

"I've got to find someone willing to share the truth of what I did and where I've been," Peter said to Samantha. "Will you be my good friend and at least try and believe what I tell?"

"You want me to believe that you've visited another planet?" Samantha queried skeptically. "That's a pretty tall order. I think it's beyond the friendship category. It's into . . . well, marriage, where you are expected to pretend that you agree with your partner."

"That's a dreary notion of love," Peter retorted.

There was a long, awkward silence.

"I suppose I could try and believe what you tell me happened to you," Samantha offered. "As long as I don't have to believe that you actually did something that any intelligent person knows is quite impossible, you know, that you actually went to another planet. I mean . . . does that help at all?"

At first Peter was very disappointed. But then another possibility struck him.

"Could you and would you believe me for my sake, even if you disagreed with what I said."

"You mean pretend?"

"No. I mean to listen to me the way you would a child, believing that, whatever you may think or believe, the child currently perceives things in their peculiar way."

"That sounds awfully like being a psychotherapist," she replied. "And you know how I feel about being involved in that from either end of the couch."

"You like to play with children, don't you?" Peter asked.

"Sure. Of course I do."

"And you listen attentively to their fantasies, and encourage their imagination even if what they perceive is magical and unrealistic."

Silence.

"It would be my job as a mother to set such a delusional child straight," Samantha replied. "But I can tell right now that you are very disappointed in me for saying so."

Silence.

"But you do realize, don't you," Peter persisted patiently, "that when someone close communicates with you, that what they're feeling is the foundation of whatever you're hearing them say. The emotional emphasis of their heart is the key to what they're saying."

Samantha carefully listened, respectfully, but couldn't get her mind around it. But she wanted to stay close to this remarkable man, so she would try even if she didn't know how.

"Okay, I'll try," she said, wondering if this was really a good idea to get so involved with a genius who was obviously a bit loony.

But he sure as hell was the best man she'd ever met.

Thank god she's willing, he said with great relief.

"Being on Troubadour was like going to Mt. Olympus and interacting with the gods," Peter explained. "The Troubadourian people, at least some of them are extraordinarily competent. They've changed their world by making the single human the centerpiece of their political system, in effect helping every single human being to become as fully actualized as possible, not in hobby, but in fact, not simply in the rhetoric of our popular culture, where we pretend that clothing style is the same as actually becoming something of significance—but actually transformed into something new in the middle of their life. They learn to handle things emotionally that intimidate the hell of out of us. Their capacity for patience and understanding surpasses anything I've ever been able to imagine."

"Something sure got a hold of you," Samantha retorted with enthusiasm. "You're sizzling with the vital juices. Did you get a face lift or something fundamental like that?"

Samantha could tell instantly from the sunken look on Peter's face, that he was disappointed in her reply.

She didn't try to figure it out like he would. Instead she leaped in whatever direction her imagination was able to take her. She knew if she didn't find a better way of hearing him she was going to lose this man.

So she pretended.

"Oh, I get where you're going," Samantha interjected, taking his advice and acting as if she believed in what he was saying, like the way you treat children when you want them to get over being unhappy. "These people all psycho-analyze each other. I bet that's really something. I mean . . . it . . . sounds wonderful . . . at least the part about someone always listening so carefully to you."

She paused. Pretense for her had gone as far as she wanted it to go.

"But tell me honestly, Peter. I mean I can appreciate it. But . . . but do you think people on Earth are going to buy that? Do you imagine everyone wanting to dig up every painful depression or anxiety they've ever had, just so someone feels personally understood? It will never sell, Peter! I'm sorry, but it just doesn't float!"

He suddenly realized that she was right, that no matter how well he described Troubadour, that to understand it someone actually had to go there.

But wait a minute! Peter exclaimed to himself, not wanting to give up yet. There's got to be a way.

"Okay," he began. "Let's look at it from another angle. Let's take politics, Samantha. You're quite interested in that. What would you say if I told you that it's possible to turn government over to everyone to vote for, discarding the intrinsically corrupt system of representative overseer-ship, replacing republic with democracy? That if you empower the individual human being by the quality of your care when they're children, and give them the opportunity to care effectively for their own lives, that the individual person can grow to be almost as powerful as the whole state put together."

"I'd have to say you were a delusional dreamer," she replied.

He felt instantly depressed. He acknowledged for the first time that what he was trying to do didn't float.

She's right. Nobody's going to listen to me. I could show them the gimmicks I brought back with me, the healing salve, the running shoes, and they would be dazzled. But that wouldn't accomplish anything other than admiration for the particular piece of evidence. The library of information, instead of being studied, would just be looted for its immediate gain.

He sighed deeply.

The Troubadourians were right. It's a waste of time to offer technology to a strange species.

Peter looked at Samantha, realizing that it was unfair to test her in this way, to decide their relationship entirely upon how well she responded to his need.

"It's okay, Samantha."

"You don't really mean that, do you," she asked fearfully, hopefully.

"I do," he said. "We are friends, and let's leave it that way. I need to find something useful to do with what's happened to my life. But I don't have to hold you responsible for thinking about it in the way that I do."

"Boy, have you changed!" she exclaimed.

"You really think so?"

"Hugely!" she replied.

"Thank you for that. It helps to know that someone notices. So you see, after all you have helped me today."

"If that's really true I'd be so happy," she replied.

She wanted to get more of this new Peter.

"Why do they call their planet 'Troubadour'? That's the word for roving entertainers, isn't it?"

"They chose that name because it was the English word which most effectively described the kind of people they are, meaning those that constantly wander about looking for newness. That unquenchable curiosity is why they invited me to visit."

"You know," Samantha said, "if you keep talking about this place, maybe I'll get used to it."

"That's very sweet of you to say, Samantha," Peter replied.

He put his hand on hers.

"Oh," she exclaimed, very stimulated. "Interested in a little?"

"No, Samantha, it's not a plea for sex. It's a touch of friendship."

Samantha got it for the first time, that friendship was a beautiful thing, not an inferior settlement.

At lunch the next day, Drake treated the news of Troubadour as if Peter was inventing an amusing story to entertain him. It was definitely a charming, though slightly crazy way of expressing ideas.

"You artists are all alike," Drake insisted humorously. "You throw up these magical, fictional fantasies that make everyone believe that what you're saying must be the truth. In the meantime we poor scientists have to prove everything. It's a much tougher job."

"I can see you regard fiction as a device of insanity instead of genius," Peter retorted.

"I can remember being completely wacko at times when I was figuring this stuff out," Drake said with commiseration. "Original philosophy scrambles the sanity of the brain."

"I guess 'psychotic' is one way to talk about something strange," Peter suggested. "But I can assure you I'm quite sane."

"Don't misunderstand me," Drake insisted, concerned that he'd hurt Peter. "I think you artist-types are pretty amazing to invent the things you do. I'm just jealous that everyone thinks my stuff is so boring and dry."

"I know what you mean," Peter replied. "It's a lonely job to be original, perhaps the loneliest one of all."

"And only a few of us make it," Drake retorted, obviously about to "humorously" punch Peter with a derogatory innuendo as a misdirected expression of affection. "In the confusion only certain knowledge becomes fact, of course always including all of mine, and an occasional tiny bit of yours."

"Which parts of my originality are fact?" Peter asked, using the joke as an opening.

Silence.

"Something definitely seems to have happened to you," Drake finally exclaimed. "You sparkle."

"It's great to be appreciated," Peter replied with a smile.

But I think maybe what I am in myself is the only real thing about Troubadour, Peter said privately to himself.

"You are definitely appreciated," Drake retorted. "On the other hand I'm stuck up here in the boondocks with my angry wife. I've always admired your splendid bachelorhood."

"I don't admire it very much right now. I met someone on my journey, someone remarkable, extraordinary, and incredibly beautiful in all ways. Actually I have a portrait at home she painted of me, strong evidence of her existence. But I can't have her, and I miss her deeply. So you see my aloneness is sometimes quite painful."

"I've always experienced being around a woman as eventually painful," Drake insisted. "But I am very sorry that you're having such a bad time of it, though I'm sure you'll get over it. It usually takes three weeks to get a woman out of your head."

"Who wants to get the perfect mate out of their head?"

"Boy did you get hooked," Drake replied.

"Hook, line and sinker, thank you very much."

Jennifer invited Peter to brunch the following Sunday. She thought more about his threatening hug, and realized that she'd gotten carried away, triggered by the strangeness in him.

She felt bad, but didn't want that exposed to Peter. So she was very nervous about inviting him, but she knew she had to do it.

"Penelope," Peter exclaimed as his granddaughter opened her front door.

"Gramps!" she shouted, throwing her arms around him. "Long time no see," she said with a tone of affectionate complaint.

Peter let her go and moved back a step to look at her closely. His face broke into an ironic smile.

"So I am Brutus to your pain as well as to your mother's," Peter replied with tongue-in-cheek.

"She's been impossible while you were gone," Penelope whispered confidentially. "I really missed you."

Peter loved her for saying that.

"I thank my life for you, pretty woman," Peter said gratefully to Penelope.

"You've never called me that before," Penelope observed, taking a step backward from him.

She was referring to the word, "woman." She wound her arms through his as they walked farther into the living room.

"It feels nice to hear that," she added. "No one around her thinks I'm a woman yet. But sometimes I think maybe I am; and now you do."

He stopped, turned toward her and looked deeply into her eyes.

"You're turning on to your full potential, dear lady, which I know already is going to be rich and very promising."

"Do you really think so?" she marveled.

"I see it in the stars in your eyes."

Penelope stopped short.

"Gramps, something's happened to you. You've changed."

"Thank you so much for noticing," he replied gratefully.

"It must be this space thing," she remarked quietly. "Mom kept bitching that you were having a delusion that you'd visited another planet. Have you been spacing out like she's always saying?"

Peter laughed.

"In a manner of speaking you could say that. There were times when I was way out there in space, sweetheart."

Peter noticed the skepticism already incumbent in his granddaughter, and realized for the first time that she may not be able to hear his story on its own terms. She was his last hope.

John appeared from the master bedroom.

"Oh, hello, Peter. I thought I heard the doorbell. It's very good to see you again."

"That feeling is very mutually shared."

Privately John had always loved his father-in-law's kind and generous understanding of him as a person. He knew that Peter approved of him as a man even though he believed Peter probably wished he would confront his wife more, probably so Peter wouldn't have to do it so much.

John privately disagreed with Peter. He would never have said so, but he thought Peter shared a big piece of the responsibility for conflict with Jennifer. He felt the bitter angst in Peter when Peter interacted with his daughter. John firmly disbelieved in being negative. He regarded it as intrinsically neurotic. His virtue was infinite patience.

As the younger man moved close to him, without thinking Peter took hold of John with the obvious intention of hugging him. This was unpremeditated; more of a spontaneous expression of Peter's gladness in seeing his gentle-hearted son-in-law again, expressed Troubadourian style.

John was deeply surprised and unprepared. He and his father-in-law had hugged only ceremonially at the wedding. He tried hiding his aversive reaction, but couldn't help himself from making a slight backward movement.

Peter immediately accepted John's reticence, and backed away.

At the deepest layer of John's still partly secret self, he had learned to do without such treats. In fact he was proud of himself for needing far less support than others. He felt stronger being that way.

"She's in the kitchen cooking, Peter," was John's verbal reply, redirecting Peter's attention away from himself, his daughter, and toward Jennifer.

"Grown-ups always take over everything," Penelope complained. "Gramps, when am I going to find out what's happening around here?"

Peter laughed, enjoying her opportunism and assertiveness.

"I promise to tell you in time if you agree to one thing."

"What's that?"

"That we both respectfully acknowledge your mother's differing opinion in everything we say. We don't want to leave her out of the discussion."

"Oh, for crying out loud," Penelope exclaimed, becoming more irritated. "Have you always pampered her like this since she was a baby? When can I just have a turn?"

Peter suddenly noticed Jennifer in the kitchen doorway listening and watching.

"Keeping someone in mind isn't pampering, Penny," he said to Penelope. "It's just loving them all the time."

"Oh," John involuntarily gasped, deeply moved by Peter's explanation.

What Peter had just described perfectly, was precisely what he was proudest of in himself, that he loved Jennifer all the time no matter what she did. He never stopped when she was difficult, like he observed most people doing. His fierce loyalty overcame all obstacles, including her temper. Without knowing it Peter had touched one of the deepest and most private parts of John's life.

John's deeply emotional response to Peter disturbed Jennifer. She couldn't deny something strange and unusual was happening. To her that meant the destabilization of the normality to which she hoped quickly to return now that her father was back.

To erase as much possible notice of what had just happened, she bailed out, returning suddenly to the kitchen and her stove.

Peter followed her, as Jennifer also did close behind, irritated that she had already lost Peter's attention in spite of having demanded it more than once.

"Gramps, we were in the middle of something when you walked off. Why can't we finish my thing before somebody else butts in?"

Jennifer glanced at Peter terribly afraid he was going to talk to Penelope in her kitchen without paying the slightest bit of attention to her.

"Remember that your mother is part of this conversation as we agreed," he said to Penelope.

Jennifer's anxiety suddenly increased. Now her father was turning things upside down. He was being the kind, reasonable, thoughtful one.

But what threatened her more than anything was that Penelope was obviously very drawn to her grandfather, Jennifer feared more than she. The familiar was turning upside down.

A look of terror momentarily flashed across her face.

Peter saw it. He realized instantly what was happening. Penelope was the one person Jennifer had given permanent access to her heart's most inner parts. Peter knew he had to instantly shift what was happening.

"Thank you, Jennifer, for being so forgiving and gracious to ask me to brunch. I want you to know that I really appreciate it. Obviously my unexplained absence upset you a great deal. But in spite of that you're being very generous."

Jennifer was at first relieved, and then horrified. Her father had become a veritable stranger. She instantly assumed that meant the worst and panicked a little, jumping into one of her aggressive assumptions about her father.

"Stop pretending that you love me! You're just being false! If you want to make amends find a more constructive way to do it!"

That got Peter. He felt very hurt, though it took him only a moment to regain his composure.

"Of course you have cooking to do, and I'm distracting you. P . . . perhaps I can help. I'd be glad to fix the salad or whatever you need. It's rather nice being in here with you even if we don't talk."

Peter had found the perfect solution for Jennifer. She didn't want to challenge her daughter's loyalty, knowing that she might fail to win. She also didn't want to talk with her father. She'd just have to put up with his physical presence. She could do that.

The only level of difficulty that seriously remained was what to do with the fact that her father had somehow managed to wrest the moral high ground from her.

She shot a look of great frustration and pain in Penelope's direction, hoping that expression would evoke in her daughter what it usually did when they were alone, to give her mother a hug. Since early childhood Penelope had sometimes comforted Jennifer by hugging her and saying, "it's sometimes very hard being a mother."

Seeing this had always reminded Peter of doing exactly the same thing to his mother, only with different words: "I love you mommy."

Jennifer chose the wrong time. At this particular point in time Penelope was in competition with her mother for air space. She had never reassured her mother when she was angry with her, as she was now.

Jennifer was very disappointed that her daughter looked at her only for a moment.

"You can peel the carrots," Jennifer shot at her father, hoping to end this scary and very unpleasant experience.

Peter peeled the carrots, cut up the onion, and peeled the tomatoes like his mother taught him, in effect preparing much of the salad.

Penelope conceded as well by setting the table.

There were no further remarks from anyone.

In the middle of placing the knives around, Penelope finally realized that her grandfather was up to something with her mother that might prove to be very interesting. Her spirits instantly soured.

When everything was prepared, without any words they all gravitated with food in hand into the dining room, and sat down at the table in their usual places. They ate in silence for several minutes.

Eventually Penelope couldn't wait any longer for Peter to make his next move, so she stirred things up.

"So give with the info, Gramps, or I'm going to have to erase you from my attention-banks."

"You're what?" Jennifer queried.

"I think she means the mental equivalent of a computer's memory banks," Peter offered.

Jennifer was instantly chagrined that her errant father was explaining Penelope to her. Her largest secret pride was that she was a far better parent than her father.

"I don't think your mother would like to talk about this topic," Peter added in an effort to correct for his mistake. "So let's arrange to talk privately."

"You don't have to hide anything from me," Jennifer interjected with a touch of hostility.

"So mom's on board," Penelope said. "So you can't dodge any more, Gramps. So let's hear about it."

Peter hesitated and looked at Jennifer, who was concentrating upon eating her food, trying to ignore the fact that Peter had somehow ended up on her side. She was deeply regretful about inviting him to this meal.

"I've been to a very different, foreign place," Peter explained, "where some things happened that drastically changed me."

He was hoping to find a neutral way of saying it.

"Are you implying this place you went to is actually another planet?" Penelope queried slowly.

Well, here goes, Peter thought.

"I had that impression, but nobody knows everything, so you must decide for yourself," he retorted.

"But you're avoiding my question, Gramps."

Silence.

"Gramps!" Penelope exclaimed.

Silence.

"Penelope," Peter said. "There's something far more important than where I've been that's going on today, which deserves most of our close attention. So I think we'll talk about this later."

He paused to see her reaction.

"Please, sweet lady Penelope, help me here," he added when she was leaning in the direction of protest.

Jennifer visibly bristled.

For some time John was becoming extremely worried about his wife. A very observant man, he watched her feelings grow until they frightened her. He was fast approaching the breaking point of his natural caution in matters emotional, but not yet at the exact point.

Still in control, Jennifer focused her Peter-anger in Penelope's behalf, partially reconnecting to her daughter in this way.

"What is this thing you feel," Jennifer challenged Peter, "that you've got to talk about, that forces you to interrupt Penelope's curiosity?"

"To put it as simply as I can, I want fully to be reconciled with you, Jennifer. And I'm willing to be very flexible in the pursuit of that goal. Right now it's the most important thing on my mind."

Everyone was stunned, most particularly Jennifer. She exploded, first looking directly into Peter's eyes with a desperate look of hope mixed with terrible fear.

"Don't you *dare* kid me!" she half pleaded, half warned, half shouted.

"If you don't really mean it, then don't tempt me!"

"Jennifer!" John shouted, standing, moving toward her with great alarm. He was convinced by the intensity of emotion that she was falling apart.

Even Penelope was alarmed.

Peter reached across the table and took Jennifer's hand.

"I mean it from the bottom of my heart, sweet daughter."

Jennifer stared at him in utter disbelief. When she saw no sign of him wavering in resolve, Jennifer started profusely to tear.

"You poor sweet thing," Peter crooned. "There is nothing between us more important than that I love you. Everything else is secondary, and I will treat it that way from now on. I will persevere in that direction until you finally believe me, and learn to trust me again."

Jennifer started uncontrollably crying, forcing out a plea of mercy.

"You'd better not be tricking me," she blurted out through her tears.

Peter stood, walked behind Jennifer's chair, and took her head in his hands.

"Oh, sweet daughter, it's been so long since we've been together."

He felt deeply relieved.

"My dear Jennifer, forgive me for being unable to love you for so long."

Penelope sat with her mouth wide open in utter dismay, while John quietly cried, both deeply moved by this beginning of reconciliation.

A Ghost

Peter's life had seriously changed. His intimate relationships, with friends, family, and his patients were now offering him valuable benefits. Sometimes he felt happier than he'd ever imagined being able to feel. At such time he felt what he was doing was right for him, and had great vitality.

But eventually he'd always sink back into a terrible loneliness, usually when he was alone and realized that he would never see Wind again.

I can't even get in touch with Rain. It's been so long now since I left, that I don't think it's going to work. Maybe he's already given up. Oh, god, I miss her so much.

Peter was lounging in the living room in his favorite chair looking out his back window at the park behind his flat, one of his favorite things to do, vaguely watching people walk or run, imagining the detail of their lives.

They're probably heading home to someone.

Sadness engulfed him.

I'll never be in touch with any of those wonderful people again.

He glanced at the clock. He was hungry and wondered if it was dinnertime.

He was suddenly aware that it was Rain-time. He almost brushed it aside as futile, and then more out of loyalty to Rain gave it one more try.

"Rain, Rain, please come back some day. Actually it wouldn't hurt if you came right now."

As usual there was silence.

"Wherefore art thou, oh wise one? I need your wisdom."

Silence.

"Are you still trying to do this, I hope?"

In the silence that followed he could hear a small echo mocking him with its distant inaudible murmurings.

"Well, I'm trying to talk with you. So what would I say if you were there? I suppose I'd tell you that at times like this it doesn't matter how much I have learned, or how good I'm getting at being a shrink or a daddy. Life always dumps me back into the same old funk. I don't know how much longer I want to live with this gaping hole sucking the heart right out of me. Maybe eventually I'll have to cash it in."

He thought he heard a knock on the door.

Maybe it's the UPS man.

He went to the front door and opened it. But no one was there.

The cold evening wind of encircling fog erased everything beyond his immediate location, leaving him alone with his loneliness.

He slammed the door as if by shutting it he could escape this empty isolation. But it didn't work. Loneliness hovered round his heart, aching his soul with grief-pain, as he hurried back into his favorite chair and plopped down, hoping to find respite there, but knowing he'd be spending the evening attending the memories of his sadness.

"Why must I live only with ghosts and never the people I love?"

This time he was sure he'd heard a voice.

Could it be the guy downstairs? Peter asked himself referring to the man who rented Peter's lower flat, someone who occasionally made loud noises.

"Maybe I'm just hallucinating like Jennifer used to think."

'I prefer to call it telepathing,' the voice said.

"What? Who's there?"

'Stop shouting, please.'

"Who's this, Rain?"

'You are a touch early,' came the reply.

Peter scanned the clock. It read 4:59 p.m.

"Is that you, Rain?"

'Please don't shout,' Rain replied. 'Silent talking feels better at this distance.'

Peter laughed inside with joy.

'You're a sight to . . . I guess only a sound . . . no, not even that, just a sound in my head, which might be a hallucination. But I'm going to believe you're actually there even if it is just my illusion.'

'I experience you much more real. I've been feeling your loneliness pain for several days. But I couldn't get through to you. I'm not sure why I finally succeeded now.'

Peter started crying.

'Oh, Rain. I can't tell you how good it feels to hear . . . well, at least to feel your presence in my mind. I am so, so relieved.'

He paused.

'Christ, that's the understatement of the day. I'm deliriously happy to hear you.'

'And I to hear you.'

Silence.

'It has been really hard sometimes,' Peter explained.

'You poor dear.'

'But it's also so much better,' Peter added. 'As you predicted, my life has changed a lot. What you guys gave me . . . it's turned so many things around.'

'It is good to hear you being happy,' Rain replied. 'And I think you can expect much more of the good stuff.'

'How do you know? I . . . I guess you awaken my skepticism. For instance, this place I live, this Earth, it's too small for me. I can't get my breath down here. There's nothing, well yes there is, but definitely not nearly enough that's really important to me. There's nothing for me to do here that's new and exciting, and no one to do it with. Helping a few people isn't enough for me. I mean my patients and my kids are great, and I wouldn't want to change anything I'm doing now, or stop seeing them, but . . . I just want so much more for myself. My, god, Rain, but I really miss Troubadour.'

Peter hesitated, suspended in the angst that talking to Rain had awakened in him.

'Sometimes I feel I'm just not big enough to survive this experience indefinitely,' Peter added.

'What would be big enough?'

'I don't know. Something that gave purpose to my life, probably something that came from my experience on Troubadour, something I could do with that knowledge.

But I can't find anyone down here who will believe I was even there, so I can't talk to anybody about it. The best experience of my life is something I can never do anything about or with for the rest of my life!'

'What's the biggest thing that happened to you on Troubadour?'

Rain's words hit him like a lightning bolt. It was as if, in this one simple question, the Troubadourian sage had twisted Peter's frantic worry into the bloom of a hopeful query.

The answer leaped out across many steps that he would later have to figure out, to announce with a shout that it was not going to Troubadour that he needed to share with others. It was what he brought back from Troubadour, the ideas, the experiences, the feelings, and the passion of it all that he needed to share. It didn't matter that he didn't know precisely how he was going to do this. He had found a path to follow that had great potential in it.

New ideas that started flashing into mind.

Government IS the people! Courtesy IS the heart of peacefulness . . . and many more.

Peter suddenly realized that he hadn't answered Rain's question.

'I think I've found my direction.'

'I know,' Rain replied.

'Oh, you've been listening in to my thoughts,' Peter exclaimed, surprised, and a little threatened.

'I know you disapprove of being known when you didn't intend it,' Rain said. 'But you thought too loudly. I couldn't help overhearing you.'

Peter laughed inside.

'Well, I'm glad you heard.'

He paused.

'You know the best thing you guys gave me was the implicit immediacy of your deeply accurate understanding. That's what I miss the most about Troubadour. I'm both so deeply grateful to you, and yet so angry sometimes that you've gone. But now . . . now that we can talk like this . . . maybe it will be different.'

Silence. Both men thought upon what had been said.

'Now that you have found a happy purchase, I have something to announce,' Rain said.

'Oh, what's that?'

'Prepare yourself for a surprise, which I hope doesn't upset you too much'

'I'm prepared, or should I be afraid?'

'I'll let you decide when you hear it'

Rain paused.

'Wind and I are to be married.'

Peter was stunned. Jealousy furiously flashed through him.

But then to his astonishment it was unable to find much purchase. Within a moment it gave way to a truer feeling of great joy.

'I was intensely jealous for a moment,' Peter explained. 'But I'm not really. I'm much more deeply happy for both of you! It's perfect, you and her, my two favorite people! And I know she needs someone now that I'm gone. Who better than you?'

'You have changed, Peter Icarus. Thank you for giving me such a very powerful boon, meaning the gift of adaptation to changing circumstances. Your skill enables all three of us to remain loving friends with each other. You are a true Troubadourian. I am honored to know you, Peter.'

Peter beamed with pride. He had never been given such a powerful recognition.

'I fear at such a special moment I must nonetheless regretfully inform you that our time's up,' Rain said sadly. 'I can keep such a distant connection intact only for a few minutes. It's actually quite tiring. Have you noticed that?'

'You know, it's true. Now that I notice, I do feel very tired.'

'So until next week.'

'You mean we can do this every week?' Peter exclaimed excitedly.

'I'll be here.'

'And so will I you tête-à-tête wonderful man. You can count on that.'

Partnerships

Wind was finally able to write Peter.

Please forgive me, my dear man, for taking so long to reach you. Tanfroon has been fierce competition for available resources since you left. You know how much Troubadourians believe in sensible balance, so we have given much to support the perspective that he represents.

I've been missing you terribly. Grief occupied a significant piece of my life for a long while. It's only now beginning to wane, though I think I will always miss you. There are times I wish you could be here so I would be able to experience you once again.

I understand Rain has told you of our decision to marry. I was so happy when he added that you had taken it so well. I was worried about that. I've needed much of his help to get over losing you.

I haven't stopped loving you. But I have come to care for this man as much as I love you. I hope it's not distressing for you to hear this.

They finally talked me into joining the next team bringing someone from Earth to Troubadour, though I'm only going to be on the selection committee. I feel strongly the next visitor should be a woman. I'm sure you would agree.

There is one other piece of news. Well, to come right to the point, our efforts to create something together of lasting importance succeeded. I'm pregnant with your daughter. This gives me great joy. I hope that at least partly you feel the same way.

I dearly hope that you are basically fine and have found your Earthly calling. Please let me know how you're doing.

In honor of you, and my love for you, I'm going to be her mother, thus finally fulfilling my social responsibility. Her name will be Psyche-Athena in honor of your world.

With much love . . .
Wind

Peter was shocked of course. But he was surprisingly unhurt about it. He was happy for Wind, happy for the Troubadourians to learn what a mixture of their two species would create. And he was happy for the little girl. Someone with his genes was going to get that quality treatment that Wind had gotten.

Dearest Wind,

Though I'm very sad never to see our daughter, and will always feel pain about never seeing her mother again . . . I am very happy for both of you. And I couldn't think of anyone better to companion you while you mother our sweet daughter. I could tell Rain loved you for a long time. I almost had the impression that our coming together moved his love into a more active mode. You will need someone to care for your needs while you care for Psyche-Athena's. Bless you both with wisdom and happiness.

I am doing as good as can be expected. Actually that's pretty good. My relationships with others are vastly improved. I seemed to have absorbed a great deal more than I understood from Troubadour's wisdom, for my life is so much better . . . save my love for you, which still sometimes languishes in grief.

Beside you there's only one other thing missing from my life now . . . a certain part of me. I haven't yet found what I must do in order for my life to be fulfilled, in the Troubadourian way. But I'm searching.

As always you remain my dearest love. Be comforted about me. Your portrait always comforts me. It never fails.

With all my love . . .
Peter

"David! How good to hear from you," Peter exclaimed.

"Are you all right?" David asked, somewhat alarmed to hear from his father so unexpectedly.

"Yes, I'm fine," Peter replied.

"Dad . . . Jennifer called me a dozen times in the last three weeks. When she called two weeks ago—it's taken me awhile to have time to call you—I finally decided I had to come out here to prevent things from falling apart."

"You are the victim of a time-lag. Since you received those frantic calls, Jennifer and I have begun seriously to reconcile. So you can be at ease."

"Dad. This is serious. Please don't slough it off so lightly. I really can't afford to keep coming out here, interrupting my work. We've got to find a more permanent solution."

"I admire your determination, David. It's very impressive. But you're on the wrong track. Your father isn't the same person anymore."

Silence followed.

"Now I know Jennifer was right," David finally said with resignation. "Something has happened to unsettle you."

"That's right, David, something has unsettled the father you've known all your life. I'm changed drastically. As a part of that change I'm settling my differences with Jennifer. Your concerns about her can be put in their final resting place, which is obscurity. Though quite obviously you're having a great deal of trouble believing that this has already happened."

Silence.

"You sound . . . very different," David remarked. "But impressions can be deceiving."

"Did I hear you say that you flew out here?"

"Yes. Listen dad, I need more evidence of what you're claiming. As you say, I'm finding it very hard to believe."

"Well, if you are in fact now in the Bay Area, why don't you come over and find the answers you're looking for."

Silence.

"So when are you going to get your ass over here so we can talk in person?" Peter asked.

"Okay, dad, don't rush me."

"In the meantime, call your sister first and check it out with her if you wish."

"That's just what I had in mind," David replied.

"So far we agree on everything."

"Jennifer says things are much better, but they're still very rocky," David reported soon after he arrived.

"Rome wasn't built in a day," Peter retorted.

"What exactly are the changes that you're talking about?" David asked. "I mean what's happened to you?"

"It's best to find out as we go along. I've found that to talking directly about my experience doesn't work."

"But, dad."

"I was planning on calling you myself, David. I have some serious business that we might be able to do together, some ideas about your work, and about how I can be involved in some way, at least to support you if nothing else."

David was extremely surprised. He'd always wanted to work closely with his father, to be intimate with him again as he had for the first twelve years of his life.

But as David became adolescent, Peter had grown feet of clay. Over time Peter became more of problem for David than an asset to his life. Very disappointed in how things turned out, David nonetheless kept this secret mostly inside himself.

"We used to really click talking about society and politics when you were younger," Peter remembered. "I want to do it again."

"I've always wanted to talk with you about things, dad," David said soberly. "But we just never seem to get around to it."

"You were always a good boy, and now you're a very good man," Peter said lovingly. "I have always very much respected your work. You have great originality, son, though in recent years it has drifted out of sight."

"What?" David exclaimed deeply surprised, unconsciously imitating his father's use of the naiveté delaying device, asking for a repeat of what he'd already heard in order to gain time to react rationally.

"Dad! Why are you talking this way? It's not . . . like you."

David's father was stirring up yearnings that he only dreamed about. For several years David had been too busy inventing a public career, getting married, and having two children to give his deepest desires very much attention.

"It's just that you've . . . we've had so many problems, we never get around to it," David added.

"Well, it's time, David. I think you are creating a very unusual career in politics, namely the private citizen who finds ways to change things by building consent for new spectacular ideas, something those in political office are no longer able to do."

David had no idea that his father understood what he was trying to do so well.

"You really are different, dad. You sound . . . well, very strange."

"Thank you."

Peter's invitation was too tempting for David to resist it. Long pent-up, unfilled yearnings burst out of him.

"This is really incredible timing, dad. I've begun giving my old ideas more and more thought in the last couple of months. I . . . I . . . I don't know where to begin."

"Why don't you begin at the beginning?"

There was silence as David gathered his thoughts.

"I'm not really accomplishing what I want with my life. It started to scare me about a year ago. I mean I love my wife and my children so much I would die for them. But it started to scare me that I would never be able to do what I set out in life to accomplish for myself. When I get through sending everybody through graduate school, I'll be so tired and used up that I'll never get around to me."

"I know the feeling very well, David," Peter replied. "So what would it take for you to get around to yourself now?"

"That's just it! It would take ignoring the people I love so much and going off and doing what nobody's going to pay me for, to change things. When you do that not only does nobody pay you for it, they constantly try to obstruct you as much as they can, while offering lots of money if I'm willing to hand the whole project over to their control!"

"Isn't that the truth? That's just how it happens."

Silence.

David was beginning to get excited. He was fundamentally a steady man, who got more than his sister of constructive parenting. It was therefore possible for him to make the emotional adjustment that his father was tempting him to make, to begin seeing his father in an entirely different way, the way he had as a young boy.

"Dad, there is this a particular thing on my mind. I've got something I really want to do. I mean on a very practical level, something I must do, if in fact I'm going to do it. What I'm trying to say is I have to act fast if I'm going to do it, like by next week. But on the other hand, I think it would be a big mistake to do it. Senator Rodgers will split a gut when he finds out I've done it. He's very supportive of me as his principle aid, but I don't think he would stay that way for an instant if I were to introduce my bill instead of the one he wants me to write for him."

"Ah, ha," Peter exclaimed, noting that David, like most people when they're excited about what they're telling, left the most important points to the last. "So it's a question of whether you use your originality or not in helping the senator."

David felt nailed. His father understood perfectly. He'd not done that for David since he was eleven years old.

"But, dad . . . so maybe I think that the risk is worth taking if it's just me and the Senator. But what about the risk I'm taking for Peggy and the kids, who depend so much upon me? Wouldn't you feel the same way?"

"Yes I would and did when I was your age," Peter replied. "But for me that was a long time ago, and I wouldn't do it the same way now if I had my druthers. I also believe that Peggy and the kids must share the risks you must take in your own life. Survival as a species requires that sharing of necessity, or we'll never change anything."

"But it's not 'necessary' for me to do this," David protested. "It's just that I *want* to do."

"But it *is* necessary for your life. And why would Peggy and the kids want to compromise that? Why don't you tell the Senator, if he calls you on the carpet, that you assumed he was paying you to add value to what he was doing, and that your changes to the bill will greatly benefit his career?"

"But how do I know that?"

"You don't know it. But you believe in what you want to do very deeply. So if it's a good thing to do for somebody with your good sense, then it will be a good thing for him too. You need to believe that in order to proceed. Just remember who you are and trust yourself, David. You've always been trying to imagine the creation of governmental structures that deal with people more openly and honestly, in ways that actually solve problems. You're the best that I know doing that, including Ralph Nader. Anyone who can deliver that possibility will make a hero of any senator lucky enough to have you as his assistant."

Eventually David could not resist his father's idea. He submitted his own bill, which eventually created a new kind of structure in the way local government works. This was a kind of change that comes from people inventing their own solutions to public need—all of which gave the senator his successful career as promised, though after David left his employ, his accomplishments were nothing of particular note.

Peter became David's principle support and his best advisor. Eventually David reinvested local government with both funds and importance of function, reversing the traditional hierarchy of politics by making local power one of the highest and most esteemed forms of government. This created a small enough container for political events that people could directly manage what was happening. If they chose they could visit any and all who shared the same political power.

David's excitement rubbed off on his father. Peter began writing his own political thoughts and feelings for David's immediate use, and for possible material in a future book.

"Put an abstract thing like 'government' between people and the processes of how they decide to share essential resources, and you've put a merchant at the center of power. Instantly he'll build a tollgate across the path of every decision and process, charging as much toll as he can. The resulting 'contract' is falsely called a 'cooperative venture between business and government,' while the merchant's toll-collections are called a 'marketplace.' That's a place where everything essential to life is made subservient to an almost unfettered gluttony of profit, creating a wall-street of obstructions to the efficient satisfaction of human needs, where every conceivable chicanery will take place that people, encouraged to cheat by the invitation to financial binging, will perpetrate inside the dark, hidden hallways of fraternity government."

"As the Troubadourians say, equality is not just between people. It's far more between government and the individual human. Every single one of us must be equal to the entire state in as many ways as possible! Only then will democracy be real! Except for physical security and an efficient operation and distribution of ordinary and necessary resources that support and encourage us, is there really any other way that government must be bigger than me? Why should Washington be any more important or powerful than my city, or even my home, or anyone else's for that matter?"

"Money has become our master. The simple beauty of its ability to measure value independent of royal and ecclesiastical authority; liberated us from the corrupt power of religious conviction, that agency which previously dominated the marketplace of value-determination, launching us into the expansion of freedom of the Renaissance."

"In this sense money has much in common with the internet, which makes powerful information available to everyone for free without constraint, liberating us from the tyranny of massive falsehood which springs rampantly from information controlled by bureaucratic authority, which includes the media. Like the marketplace of the Renaissance, where money was tested as a standard measure of anything, the Internet facilitates the possibility of increasingly reliable independent judgment unfettered by authority, making the Web an instrument of peaceful anarchy—free thinking—enabling understanding to operate outside of conventional wisdom and its social, political, and cultural 'correctness.'"

"We've lifted money onto the pedestal of idolatry, making it the most valuable thing, for which we spend a lifetime of working—which has bankrupted the spiritual qualities of human experience."

"Dad, I have a surprise for you."

It was Jennifer.

"I'm going to take painting classes at the Art Institute."

"Oh, that's fantastic, sweetheart! I'm so glad. What finally pushed you over the edge into doing it?"

"I was angry with you for talking to me the way you did last Sunday. I hate to be treated like a kid. And when you tell me something I don't know, I get so mad at you for making me look foolish. Anyway, you know all this I'm sure," she added with a touch of sarcasm.

"I understand why you're angry. I've felt the same thing in my life."

"But then I went to the store to buy some art supplies and I couldn't afford what I really wanted," Jennifer said. "I got furious. All the way home I kept raging at every driver who got in my way. And then it finally hit me. I was angry because I couldn't go to art school, which you should have helped me do years ago! There I go blaming you again. But I don't know how else I'm ever going to figure it out. Anyway, I finally realized I was also angry with Penelope for costing so much to be in college! And you know how afraid I am to get angry with her."

"Yes, I know."

Silence.

"You probably think I'm just rambling."

"No," Peter exclaimed. "I think you're terrific! You figured it out. You know what's important to your life to do. That's just great."

"So I just wanted you to know. Bye, dad."

"Hey, wait a minute, sweetheart. I've got something to say about this art school thing."

"Now don't rain on my parade," Jennifer insisted.

"I want to contribute five hundred dollars a month to your art school for as long as you go."

"What? Oh, dad, that's so bad . . . I mean good, you know, bad in the good sense."

"I'm sure glad that my badness finally found a way to be good."

Jennifer laughed.

She hasn't laughed like that with me since she was a little girl.

Peter had finally made her very happy. When she finally stopped denying it, she admitted to herself that she'd called him secretly hoping that he would help.

Ruth walked into Peter's office, her face oscillating between looks of fear and hints of hopefulness. She plunked herself down into the green leather chair.

During the previous six months she had struggled heroically with intense experiences of terrible pain, anxiety, dread, and depression. She was deeply frightened, afraid that these terrible experiences would not only never stop happening, but they would keep getting worse.

Peter suggested to her that all of these symptoms were dysfunctional ways of experiencing her own feelings; something she'd never had any real help in understanding or cutting down to size. Her emotions still throttled her with intense overpowering terror, shouting predictions of the nightmare that would never stop happening if she didn't prevent herself from feeling them.

Last session she'd reported a vivid dream, something that almost never happened in her therapy. Upon waking she had instantly realized that sometimes she hated her assistants. It terrified her. What if she actually acted that way toward them?

The next day while brushing her teeth, she realized that she hated this too. She'd always known of such dislikes, but she'd never felt them with such intensity of emotion.

"That's the second time that your strong negative energy has told you something that emotionally is vividly real," Peter had remarked at the time. "I think you're learning to say 'no' to life. It's the most important word of all, the word that creates the individuality of personal preference."

"As usual you make it sound like everything's hunky dory!" Ruth shouted. "Meanwhile I'm getting worse! I can't go around hating everything! Nobody would stand for it."

"It was your mother who was the hateful one, not you. She must have been the one who always said 'no.'"

Ruth was visible stunned.

"That's right, she did!" Ruth exclaimed with excitement. "She'd say 'N,' 'O' spells NO with intense acrimony! She was always saying that! I never got a chance to say anything for very long, particularly no!"

She laughed.

"Except for the time I said, 'N,' 'O' smells NO."

Next session:

"I had another dream. You'll probably try and convince me that everything's hunky dory again, your usual pep talk. But this dream was really bad. I dreamed I was living with the nicest people I knew when I was a teenager, a family in France who were very kind to me. And when I woke up I thought instantly of just how unfit everybody I know is for me. There's no one like my dream. Everybody's always been strange to me. It's why I don't trust anybody. It's . . ."

She petered out.

What happened, Peter asked himself?

"Anyway, it's really depressing," Ruth insisted.

"I'm having trouble understanding something," Peter finally said.

"What's there to understand," Ruth complained.

"How you can turn one of the most beautiful things that ever happened to you into depression."

"Wonderful things! Are you out of your mind?"

"Sometimes, but not right now."

"So what is this great big wonderful thing?" Ruth queried sarcastically.

"You just had your very first happy dream, as far as I know."

"Happy! It made me feel terrible to realize that I'll never have what the dream pretended!"

"Ruth, the dream is reassuring you that you are becoming happier."

"Just like I said, another stupid pep talk," Ruth insisted.

"Happy experiences are precious."

Ruth couldn't stop herself from smiling a little.

"But how am I ever going to replace all these bad people in my life?"

Something suddenly occurred to Peter.

"I'm remembering that dream you had as a four year old, when in a dream you replaced your parents, only to wake to the reality that you were still stuck with them."

Ruth suddenly reported something entirely new that she'd never mentioned before.

"When I was nine my mother almost died in an auto crash," Ruth reported. "My father was not with her at the time. She barely made it. I had a fantasy again this morning that I went up to my father—I was thinking of myself as nine—and told him that I was very disappointed my mother hadn't died, not because I wanted her dead, but because I simply couldn't continue living with her, it was so bad."

"That's the most beautifully self-centered thing I've ever heard you fantasize, Ruth!"

"It is!" she shouted. "You're right! I was being selfish! I've never done that before!"

Ruth suddenly went pale. It was as if something had struck her across the face.

"I'm really afraid!" she shouted.

"I think you're afraid of wanting to turn your parents in for new ones," Peter suggested. "I think you've always felt like you killed them with your thoughts, both when you were four, and again when you were nine. I think that's why you perceive yourself as so evil, and feel such terrible pain sometimes."

Ruth's demeanor suddenly changed again.

"I don't know," she said. "I don't know."

Next session:

Ruth reported having a very strange experience.

"I hung up the phone after talking to my sister and I suddenly found myself feeling like a stranger. I didn't recognize me. I got terrified. But then I tried thinking about it. I wrote pages in my journal about it. But nothing helped. I was becoming more and more depressed! So I took the dogs for a walk. It was during that walk that my mind just drifting, when suddenly I realized what had happened when I put down the phone receiver! Something in me was suddenly missing! It was that nightmare feeling that always hangs around behind everything, even when I'm not aware it's there. It was gone! That had never happened before! I got this tiny glimpse of peaceful happiness! It was just amazing!"

"Oh, Ruth, that's wonderful. I'm so happy for you. What an absolutely incredible experience."

"And I'm laughing a lot more about things," she added.

She paused and fell into a long silence, completely lost inside herself, and started remembering all sorts of things, as if the movie suddenly came into focus, the pictures perfectly clear.

Peter could tell she was being completely absorbed in herself.

She's never done anything so utterly self-centered, Peter thought, to be so entirely within herself while she's sitting here with me.

"I used to live the most awful squalor," Ruth suddenly said. "I was lost in the middle of dangerous trouble all the time. But how could I have done it?

"You lived like you hated yourself."

"I guess I did," Ruth said wistfully.

She hesitated.

"No, she did, my mother," Ruth insisted. "She hated me . . . because I was a child she didn't want to take care of. She only wanted me around to entertain her in her loneliness, using me like a teddy bear, paying not the slightest attention to the fact that I was starving and emaciated."

"Very well said," Peter acknowledged. "It's time we put the kibosh on hate, so love can get a chance to have its way."

Ruth smiled with excited anticipation, and then looked thoughtfully at Peter.

"You know how I've never been able to put you in my hip pocket and carry you around with me," Ruth queried, "that every time I saw you I had to start trusting you all over again, because you simply disappeared in between sessions, that if you weren't there, you didn't exist for me."

She paused.

"Well, I can do it now. You're always with me."

"I very happy to be with you all the time," Peter replied.

It took Ruth two more years before she began having a rich, full experience of herself often enough for it to create the foundation for a different kind of life. Building upon that increasing sense of new possibility, eventually Ruth became a successful poet of some local renown, putting into her poetry the vast emotional suffering of her life, coupled with the wisdom she'd learned in the course of escaping it.

Ruth eventually moved to Europe, the place where she'd lived her happiest years as a child. She and Peter corresponded for years.

> *Wind, thou dearest woman, how do you get your teenagers to be so disinterested in love? How did Saavin avoid it until she was nineteen?*
>
> *Though I'm very sad never to meet her, I'm happy about our daughter. It makes me feel like part of me stayed there with you. I hope you and Rain will tell me about her along the way, as I'm sure you will.*
>
> *I'm most delighted that you're going to be her mother.*
>
> *Love you always . . .*
> *Peter the poorer for not being with you . . .*

> *From Wind, much winded for want of you . . .*
>
> *To answer your question, young people are set on a powerful course of self-discovery. That process has become so energized with significance that when puberty arrives they are as curious to find out who they are, as they are to be lovingly with someone else. We've finally arranged for these two aspects of human life to be in balance from the beginning of life, making the entry into a life of loving cohabitation with someone, something they*

move into slowly, as they evolve into who they naturally become.

There is a ritual walkabout, to use the Aboriginal term, when young people of about twenty begin traveling the world at large for the very first time. They spend perhaps ten years wandering around in small social groups of their peers, searching new places, new possibilities, and new people, spending awhile here, then awhile there, seeking their own particular bearings and preferences. Thus until the forties or fifties, most of us are not hugely drawn to the marital life. Before then we feel unprepared for its necessary cooperation, still insufficiently aware of who we are in ourselves.

I hope this satisfies your curiosity.

We will give you regular reports about Psyche-Athena. When it's time I will tell her about you.

I am forever yours,
Wind

'Rain, what's the secret of your extraordinary calm under any and all circumstances?'

'The humility of never arguing with god.'

'I thought you didn't believe in God.'

'Whatever happens is what I mean by "god."'

'Oh. Then you must have been the one who wrote that Ode to Life that we sang at the great meeting. It's the last line, "meeting what happens with an open trust" that you reminded me of.'

'You've found me out.'

'You really are the big Kanhuna on Troubadour, aren't you?'

'You make too much of me. I'm just the current focus of wisdom's understanding.'

'I wish I could feel so big being so small,' Peter said wistfully.

A Life of His Own

Peter's life had become rich. He now enjoyed the benefits of intimate company with several people, and had also become very successful avoiding their difficult parts, except of course with his patients, where his job was to relate precisely to those parts.

Professionally his talents had matured to the point where he no longer felt baffled or overwhelmed with his patient's emotional projections. For the most part he found his work had become relatively easy, though it remained sometimes very interesting, stimulating, and challenging.

His partnership with David proved to be an exciting enterprise, as his son flourished with Peter's constant support and intellectual input. Slowly David built a groundswell of public support for his innovative ideas, creating legislative change which facilitated and funded alternative energy sources—solar, wind, and hydrogen fueled cars—fundamentally altering the power of local government and the nature of how energy worked. Essentially he made the whole process much more responsive to the people it served.

Yet in spite of all this accomplishment, Peter was periodically depressed. It was mostly about Wind. He deeply missed her. She had brought the constancy of care to his daily experience, bathing him in the luxuriant benefits of her perceptively accurate understanding. It was an extraordinarily nurturing experience, a dream-come-true of being loved so well that one couldn't possibly be unhappy. He had been in paradise.

And then suddenly it was gone.

Peter gradually realized that his loneliness contained more than Wind-grief. There was another principle element to his bouts of depression, which had to do with the absence of that other ingredient so abundant on Troubadour, which was the opportunity for constant learning. How was he to recreate this experience on Earth, and to do it mostly by himself?

Without even thinking of it as a solution, but just because he wanted to, Peter began devoting more and more of his time to writing. Gradually it became the source of much of his most stimulating experience.

At first he wrote philosophy expressing the many new ideas that kept popping into his mind about how things on Earth could change for the better, based of course on what he'd learned and experienced on Troubadour.

"Change is life's creator."

"Work is what I do with my life to make it meaningful. Employment is what I do for someone else to make money."

"Learning like art transforms the ordinary into the archetypal."

"An archetype is where the specific and the universal become one for a moment, before they disseminate again into their usual ambiguous complexity. Only very occasionally do we get glimpses of this beautiful core kind of truth."

"Talent, and the art it produces, is a successful romantic attachment to the self, where one pays extremely close attention to everything they imagine or invent."

"Immunity is one species poison to the intrusion of another, or one person's aversion to the presence of another."

"Death: where our prayers for peace are finally answered in full."

"Egalitarian democracy has flattened our vision of *value* pancake-thin, by eliminating most of the perceived variation in the quality of anything, reducing all things to their lowest common denominator. What's tragic is that we do this to avoid leaving anyone left out of the good life, on the premise that if we don't give everything they do the mark of excellence, we're not loving them properly, or may even be abusing them. It's all just another form of 'politically correctness.'"

"A large brain wants the big picture to be visible and ever-present. A feeling animal wants the now to be immensely significant. The tension of that extraordinarily dichotomous dilemma produces human consciousness, and everything we've ever learned from struggling with it."

"No matter how clever or appealing an idea or theory may be, it is always subject to the subjectivity of the person who created it. Which makes philosophy, and perhaps all the social sciences a subcategory of a psychology defined as the study of being human; which by inference must include not only ideas, but feelings, intuition, and experience as well. This is a psychology that must-be-lived-to-be-believed, far more than it needs to be believed to be lived, making psychology much more than a set of ideas or a theory. It becomes a way of life that reveals itself only by doing it—first to the self, and only secondarily helping others."

"As psychology slowly becomes the deepest core of social science, in the process the scientist, as well as their ideas becomes revealed, exposing the subjectivity of all ideas. Communication will then begin to reveal not only its conclusions, but its assumptions as well."

"Assumptions are like habits. They're the foundation program of any idea or theory. Thus they reveal more information than any other source. And yet they remain the most hidden and elusive of data, because exposing them reveals the presence or absence of integrity to the theory or idea they spawn. Which is why assumptions are almost never openly revealed, particularly by intellectuals, or we would all finally admit to ourselves that, in spite of how frightening it is to be alone with what we don't understand, there are no 'experts,' just better or worse guessers."

"It's assumptions, not motives that reveal the sources and 'causes' of human experience. Motive simply tells us *what* we thought when we behaved in some particular way or context. While assumptions tell us *why* we did it. Which means that 'intention' is a lot less important than we've believed."

"Most people like to call the sometimes difficult discerning process of self discovery, "psychotherapy," though there are a few of us who call it life's most basic responsibility, which is to know thyself. Only by knowing ourselves will we be able effectively to care for our own life, which is the essential foundation of peaceful coexistence. There are parts of ourselves we need to take in hand, sometimes without anyone else's help. Until we learn to do that we'll never have peaceful coexistence. Such competent selfness is the foundation of social peace."

"Actually this hoped-for renaissance is already beginning to happen . . . in a minority sort of way. But those who practice being accountable as a part of who they are, but seldom advertise that they're doing it, have begun to speak louder and louder each and every day; and may one time, in the not too distant future retake the public domain away from the panicked who run it now in the name of control—which is the day-before-yesterday's wisdom."

Peter loved such theorizing. But when all was said and done, all that he was left with were a bunch of ideas. He had no one with whom to share the vitality he felt about having them, except on a very distant planet. His brief séances with Rain each evening, were hardly enough time for much of that.

You can celebrate having interesting thoughts, Peter realized, but, like the computer said, you can't party for long without getting bored. Eventually every joyful moment loses wind.

"Loses Wind," Peter moaned, repeating his last words to reveal an entirely different meaning. That's the reality that makes it all so much harder, he thought with great sadness.

After several months of furious philosophy writing, interspersed with bouts of depression at not finding a viable alternative, Peter lost interest and focus almost entirely in his writing and research, and floundered for several weeks watching bad television and gaining ten pounds.

It was David who set him back on the right path.

"You're always talking to me about how I'm the centerpiece of my story," David said one day. "You insist that what I'm doing is the real event, even though everybody else talks about me in terms of my ideas or what I've accomplished. Well, why don't you take your own advice? Why don't you become a demonstration of your ideas?"

It took Peter only three days to digest this wonderful advice, and reproduce it on his own terms.

Stories are the best demonstration of anything, he realized. They were the original mythological way of expressing what philosophy had tried to objectify for many centuries.

But what story should I tell?

It didn't take long to realize that the only one he had was his own.

To keep the story from being too much about him personally, he made it a novel, so that all the people he knew or had met could become scattered all over the twenty or so characters who comprised the company of players that eventually populated his novel.

Writing the novel proved to be more of an ordeal than Peter had anticipated. Projecting the elements of his experience into a story, he was forced to relive all those experiences in order to be able to express the emotions contained in them. He therefore suffered each and every feeling moment vital to the substance he was projecting into his characters.

But eventually, after lots of work and difficulty, what had become a deeply disturbing venture, gradually turned into an inspiring adventure. To his increasing amazement, telling the story facilitated an incredible explosion of ideas, feelings, and memories, which would never have happened without writing the book, and which, in their revelations healed the wounded part of Peter to which they were connected. In effect writing the novel finished the work of changing Peter Icarus. Taking over from the computer, the novel became his last shrink.

"Fiction is what holds facts together so they can make sense," he wrote when he'd finished his novel. "Fiction fills in all the in-betweens of the unknown, which like the fundamental building blocks of material reality, occupy far more space than the facts do. Fiction fills the vast emptiness betwixt our measurable knows and the huge amounts we don't know, rendering continuity to the scribbled hints of universality that seem to be implied for this day."

The links between fiction, philosophy, and science had been revealed by psychology.

There was another encouraging development. In the course of writing he realized he desperately needed feedback from an intelligent, imaginative, and emotional editor, to give him the feedback from which to constantly improve his work.

He found Edith, a woman eleven years his junior, an artist of great talent who made money by working as an editor for local writers. She had been an avid reader all her life. As such she gave him a reader's feedback, in contrast to another writer's. She became his generic audience.

In her editorial feedback, Edith gave Peter an abundance of emotional information, precisely in the area where he was weakest. Each rereading of yet one more version revealed to Peter another layer of what he had lived, and what the novel needed to contain. He was gradually able to provide it with an excellent plot, a stimulating story, well formed characters, and finally a body of strong, emotional agendas pushing against each other for space and opportunity, providing the twists and turns of an interesting story.

Because of the help she provided in abundance, Peter was very attracted to Edith, and they became very good friends. There was a momentary exploration of sexual passion, but both realized they had acted prematurely, compromising their professional and friendship relationship in its evolving stages, and decided to hang up the sexual hock.

Edith wanted a deeper relationship. But she was a wise woman who realized that the relationship that worked was more valuable than what she hoped for.

Peter's love remained firmly attached to the memory of Wind. Though an unusual and talented woman, Edith did not have the emotional wisdom of the Troubadourian beauty. And she was not a philosophical person.

Without any interest in this area, she failed to capture the full measure of Peter's attention, and thus his heart.

Both Peter and Edith were disappointed their relationship didn't become more romantic. But both deeply valued their friendship, so they left things as they were, at least for the time being.

Peter still missed Wind. It happened now mostly at night, no longer occupying the day, which made much of his life happier. Rain's weekly, though very brief visits sealed this bargain with time, leaving only the evening and sleep parts of life lonely.

Which meant that the deepest layers of love remained on Troubadour.

But on Earth the novel prospered.

'How do you keep your nose to the grindstone of life?' Peter asked Rain.

'I have done weighted yoga and aerobics for an hour every morning for the last sixty nine years,' was the reply.

'What keeps you doing it so religiously?'

'It's about being alive. Life is meant to be an effort, not a crisis or a catastrophe about to happen, but a determined exertion. Any other view of it moves one closer to death. Exercising keeps me in touch with whether I'm still actively living, whether I even want to be, and where my body is vulnerable. When I no longer have the determination to work my body, pushing my comfort limits, I will know I'm dying.'

'But what if that meant you were just sick?'

'I'm always sick. My old body is very vulnerable to parasites and viruses hanging around. To keep it strong helps it survive. So my exercise must happen in spite of discomfort or pain.'

'But how do you face the constant expectation of morning pain?' Peter asked.

'You will hurt far less if you attack the pain with movement, than if you sit around to avoid feeling it. That only encourages it to grow. To sit back and let things be done for me would be dying while pretending it's not happening. I want to know everything about life until the very last moment.'

It's a monk's life that I have, Peter mused. The thoughtful and generous help others give me from their heart, brings peace-of-mind to my spirit, comforting me in my middle age. But it doesn't excite me. Wind excited me.

My life has improved so much, such that I feel well looked after by my present companions and circumstances. But with Wind I felt cared-for in the most basic sense. Her love inspired my deepest life force vigorously to express itself. As a result I was vividly revealed to myself.

But it's only a warm bed that I've been given by life to sleep upon. The hot furnace of passion's excitement now comes only occasionally when I feel highly stimulated about something I've just learned or imagined.

In certain ways I'll probably remain alienated from parts of my life. At least I sure as hell know what 'alien' means. It means to be separate and apart from everything ordinary and familiar, which can be a curse, or it can be a blessing, depending upon how it's happening.

Actually, when you think about it, a monk's life has much comfort, peacefulness, and stability in it. Considering how I spent the greater portion of my life, this is Shangri-la. I am deeply grateful.

But I'm too lonely on this planet. I must find others with whom I can share my life and my dream.

Maybe if I tell my story I'll find other people with whom to share me.

"Once upon a time in a little boy's life he was on his way to his favorite place, the train station. Just weeks before he'd passed through it for the first time at the end of his favorite moment in time, lying on his mother's lap looking out the window at the blurry objects racing by the train for three whole blissful days."

"And now he was sure it was going to happen all over again."

And so on . . . until death do us part.